Praise fo

'Boyle is a genius at capturing social microcosms and excavating emotions simmering beneath the surface of contemporary America ... A gripping and revelatory tale' BBC *Between the Lines*

'Boyle is concerned with humankind's relationship with the rest of the natural world, as well as with idealism – where is comes from, and the often hopeless places it leads ... A fluent, often exuberant writer' *Financial Times*

'Boyle has an acute ear for the tics and tropes of the disingenuous ... T. C. Boyle's sardonic and rueful novel suggests that even when we seek to preserve natural diversity, even when we build an ark, it's all about us' *Times Literary Supplement*

'His engagement with the headlines, with the world beyond his head, is welcome at a time of literary introspection ... Boyle has become one of our finest chroniclers of the American west' *Independent*

'Boyle is a subtle manager of narrative ... One moment you're watching the antics of a particularly narcissistic cast, each member driven by greed, entitlement and constant infantile outrage at the unfairness of not being perpetually at the centre of attention; the next you're finding it all rather heartbreakingly human' *Guardian*

'Boyle is offering an honest picture of humanity here, particularly the sort of humanity that gets involved in such a plainly romantic enterprise ... A writer of palpable intelligence' *LA Times*

'Captures brilliantly (and painfully at times) the nature of trapping the human spirit inside a sterile environment ... A darkly comic insight into how sustaining our world is more than growing crops and minimising climate change. With jealousy, love and animal instinct under a microscope, it makes for an all-consuming read' *Stylist*

'Imagine an earthbound *Interstellar* with a touch of *I'm a Celebrity*' *GQ*

'A sprawling tale of achievement, yearning, pride, and human weakness ... A multilayered work that recalls the tragicomic realism of Saul Bellow and John Updike' *Publishers Weekly*

ALSO BY T. CORAGHESSAN BOYLE

A NOTE ON THE AUTHOR

T. C. BOYLE is the *New York Times* bestselling author of fifteen novels including *The Tortilla Curtain, Drop City, The Harder They Come* and *San Miguel*, and ten collections of stories, most recently *T. C. Boyle Stories II*. His work has been translated into twenty-five languages and has won a PEN/Faulkner Award for Fiction. He is a member of the Academy of Arts and Letters and lives in California.

tcboyle.com

THE
TERRANAUTS

T. Coraghessan Boyle

BLOOMSBURY
LONDON · OXFORD · NEW YORK · NEW DELHI · SYDNEY

Bloomsbury Paperbacks

An imprint of Bloomsbury Publishing Plc

50 Bedford Square　　　　1385 Broadway
London　　　　　　　　　New York
WC1B 3DP　　　　　　　　NY 10018
UK　　　　　　　　　　　USA

www.bloomsbury.com

BLOOMSBURY and the Diana logo are trademarks of
Bloomsbury Publishing Plc

First published in Great Britain 2016
This paperback edition first published in 2017

British Library Cataloguing-in-Publication Data
A catalogue record for this book is available from the British Library.

ISBN:　　HB:　978-1-4088-8175-0
　　　　　PB:　978-1-4088-8176-7
　　　　OME:　978-1-4088-8604-5
　　　　ePub:　978-1-4088-8173-6

2 4 6 8 10 9 7 5 3 1

Designed by Shannon Nicole Plunkett
Printed and bound in Great Britain by
CPI Group (UK) Ltd, Croydon CR0 4YY

To find out more about our authors and books visit
www.bloomsbury.com. Here you will find extracts, author
interviews, details of forthcoming events and the option to
sign up for our newsletters.

For Neal and Shray Friedman and
Roy and Edicta Corsell

Never doubt that a small group of committed, thoughtful people can change the world. Indeed, it is the only thing that ever has.

—MARGARET MEAD

L'enfer, c'est les autres.

—JEAN-PAUL SARTRE, *HUIS CLOS*

Part I

PRE-CLOSURE

Dawn Chapman

We were discouraged from having pets—or, for that matter, husbands or even boyfriends, and the same went for the men, none of whom were married as far as anybody knew. I think Mission Control would have been happier if we didn't have parents or siblings either, but all of us did, with the exception of Ramsay, an only child whose parents had been killed in a head-on collision when he was in the fourth grade. I often wondered if that had been a factor in the selection process—in his favor, I mean—because it was apparent he was lacking in certain key areas and to my mind, at least on paper, he was the weakest link of the crew. But that wasn't for me to say—Mission Control had their own agenda and for all our second-guessing, we could only put our heads down and hope for the best. As you can imagine, we all sweated out the selection process—during the final months it seemed like we did nothing else—and though we were a team, though we pulled together and had been doing so through the past two years of training, the fact remained that of the sixteen candidates only eight would make the final cut. So here was the irony: while we exuded team spirit, we were competing to exude it, our every thought and move duly noted by Mission Control. What did Richard, our resident cynic, call it? A Miss America pageant without the Miss and without the America.

I don't recall the specific date now, and I should, I know I should, just to keep the record straight, but it was about a month before closure when we were called in for our final interviews. A month seems about right, time enough to spread the word and generate as much press as possible over the unveiling of the final eight—any earlier and we ran the risk of overkill, and of course Mission Control was sensitive about that because of what fell out with the first mission. So it would have been February. A February morning in the high desert, everything in bloom with the winter rains and the light spread like a soft film over the spine of the mountains. There would have been a faint sweetness to the air, a kind of dry rub of sage and burnt sugar, something to savor as I made my way over to the cafeteria for an early breakfast. I might have stopped to kick off my flip-flops and feel the cool granular earth between my toes or watch the leaf-cutter ants in their regimented march to and from the nest, both inside my body and out of it at the same time, a female hominid of breeding age bent over in the naturalist's trance and wondering if this earth, the old one, the original one, would still be her home in a month's time.

The fact was, I'd been up since four, unable to sleep, and I just wanted to be alone to get my thoughts together. Though I wasn't really hungry—my stomach gets fluttery when I'm keyed up—I forced myself to eat, pancakes, blueberry muffins, sourdough toast, as if I were carbo-loading for a marathon. I don't think I tasted any of it. And the coffee. I probably went through a whole cup, sip by sip, without even being conscious of it, and that was a habit I was trying to curtail because if I was selected—and I would be, I was sure of it, or that was what I told myself anyway—I'd have to train my system to do without. I hadn't brought a book, as I usually did, and though the morning's paper was there on the counter I never even glanced at it. I just focused on eating, fork to mouth, chew, swallow, repeat, pausing only to cut the pancakes into bite-sized squares and lift the coffee cup to my lips. The place was deserted but for a couple of people from the support staff gazing vacantly out the windows as if they weren't ready to face the day. Or maybe they were night shift, maybe that was it.

Somewhere in there, mercifully, my mind went blank and for maybe a split second I'd forgotten about what was hanging over us, but then I glanced up and there was Linda Ryu coming across the room to me, a cup of tea in one hand and a glazed donut in the other. You probably don't know this—most people don't— but Linda was my best friend on the extended crew and I can't really explain why, other than that we just happened to hit it off, right from day one. We were close in age—her thirty-two to my twenty-nine—but that didn't really explain anything since all the female candidates were more or less coevals, ranging from the youngest at twenty-six (Sally McNally, who didn't stand a chance) to forty (Gretchen Frost, who did, because she knew how to suck up to Mission Control and held a Ph.D. in rain forest ecology).

Anyway, before I could react, Linda was sliding into the seat across the table from me, gesturing with her donut and giving me a smile that was caught midway between commiseration and embarrassment. "Nervous?" she said, and let out a little laugh even as she squared her teeth and flaunted the donut. "I see you're carbo-loading. Me too," she said, and took a bite.

I tried to look noncommittal, as if I didn't know what she was talking about, but of course she could see right through me. We'd become as close as sisters these past two years, working side by side on the research vessel in the Caribbean, the ranch in the Australian outback and the test plots here on the E2 campus, but the only thing that mattered now was this: my interview was at eight, hers at eight-thirty. I gave her a tight smile. "I don't know what we've got to be nervous about—I mean, they've been testing us for over a year now. What's another interview?"

She nodded, not wanting to pursue the point. The buzz had gone round and we'd all absorbed it: this was *the* interview, the one that would say yea or nay, thumbs-up or thumbs-down. There was no disguising it. This was the moment we'd been waiting for through all the stacked-up days, weeks and months that seemed like they'd never end, and now that it was here it was nothing short of terrifying. I wanted to reach out to her and reassure her, hug her, but we'd already said everything there was to be said, teasing out the permutations of who was in and who was out a thousand times over, and all we'd done these past weeks was hug. I don't know how to explain it, but it was like a coldness came over me, the first stage of withdrawal. What I wanted, more than anything, was to get up and leave, and yet there she was, my best friend, and I saw in that moment how selfless she was, how much she was rooting for me—for us both, but for me above all, for my triumph if she should fail to make the grade, and I felt something give way inside me.

I knew better than anyone how devastated Linda would be if she didn't get in. On the surface, she had the sort of personality they were looking for—ebullient, energetic, calm in a crisis, the optimist who always managed to see her way through no matter how hopeless the situation might have looked—but she had a darker side no one suspected. She'd confided things to me, things that would have sent the wheels spinning at Mission Control if they ever got wind of them. It would be especially hard on her if she didn't make it, harder than on any of the others, but then I wondered if I wasn't projecting my own fears here—we all wanted this so desperately we couldn't begin to conceive of anything else. To make matters worse, Linda and I were essentially competing for the same position, the least technical aside from Communications Officer, which we both agreed Ramsay had just about locked up for himself because he was a politician and knew how to work not just both sides but the top, bottom and middle too.

I watched her face, the steady slow catch and release of her jaw muscles as she chewed. "Stevie's a shoo-in, isn't she?" she said, her voice thickening in her throat.

I nodded. "I guess." Linda had tried to make herself indispensable, the generalist of the group, looking to fit into one of the four slots that would most likely go to women. She put everything she had into it, not only with extra course work in closed-systems horticulture and ecosystems management, but especially in marine biology. She'd logged more hours underwater than anybody else during our dive sessions off Belize and she was a champion recruiter of invertebrates, and yet to my mind Stevie van Donk had the inside track on the marine ecosystems. For one thing, she had an advanced degree in the field, and for another, she looked great in a two-piece.

"She's such a bitch."

I had nothing to say to this, though I privately agreed. Still, bitch or no, Stevie was in.

It got worse yet: Diane Kesselring looked like a lock for

Supervisor of Field Crops, and Gretchen was first in line to over-see the wilderness biomes. What was left, when you conceded the Medical Officer, Director of Analytic Systems and Techno-sphere Supervisor—all male-oriented at this point—was really a caretaker position: MDA, Manager of Domestic Animals, the pygmy goats, Ossabaw Island pigs, Muscovy ducks and chickens that would provide the crew with essential fats and animal protein.

"Dawn, what's the matter?" Linda leaned across the table and took hold of my hand, but I didn't respond. I couldn't. I was a mess. "You're not going to break down on me, are you? After all we've been through together? You're going to make it. I know it. If one person's going to make it, you are."

"But what about you? I mean, if I'm in—"

Her smile was the saddest thing, just a quiver of her lips. "We'll see." She looked away. The room was empty now, the people at the far table either gone off to work or home to bed, depending on their shift. My stomach felt bloated. I could feel the blue vein at my hairline pulsing the way it did when I was overwrought. Linda's parents had kept horses, as well as chickens and Vietnamese pot-bellied pigs on their property outside Sacramento, and she knew barnyard animals like a veterinarian—but she wasn't a veterinar-ian, only a B.S. in animal sciences, and forgive me for saying this, she was maybe a bit chunkier than the ideal and not really all that pretty, looking at it objectively, that is. Not that it should matter, but it did, of course it did. Mission Control was looking for the same thing NASA was, people who fit the "adventurer profile," with high motivation, high sociability and low susceptibility to depression, but all of us fit that description, at least the ones who'd made it this far (to what Richard called the "Sweet Sixteen," a sports reference I didn't get till someone explained it to me). Beyond that, beyond the factors they ticked off on the barrage of tests they'd subjected us to, from the Minnesota Multiphasic Per-sonality Inventory Questionnaire to what they'd observed when we worked as a team under stress, I'd have been lying to myself if I didn't think they wanted a candidate who looked good, someone pretty, prettier than Linda anyway.

Am I out of line here? I don't know, but sometimes you do have to be objective, and when I looked at myself in the mirror—even without makeup—I saw someone who'd represent the Mission to the public better than Linda. I'm sorry. I've said it. But it's a fact.

"Yes," I said. "Yes. Yes. I'm praying you get in, I really am—as much as I'm praying for myself. More, even. Imagine the two of us in there, the two Musketeers, right?" I tried to smile, but I couldn't. I felt my eyes fill with tears. The thing was—and I'm ashamed to admit it—they weren't just for her.

Linda set down the donut and licked her fingertips one by one. It took an eternity. Then she lifted her face and I saw that her eyes were swimming too. "Hey," she said, sweeping the hair off her shoulder with a flip of her chin, "no worries. Whatever happens, there's always Mission Three."

* * *

We all essentially wore the same outfit to work, male and female alike—jeans, T-shirt and hiking boots, with a hooded sweatshirt for the cool of morning or the winter days when it could get surprisingly brisk—but on this particular morning I'd opted for a dress. Nothing too showy, just a pale-green tank dress I'd worn once or twice when a couple of us had gone out barhopping in Tucson, and I'd put on makeup and swept my hair back in a ponytail. My hair is one of my best features, actually, so thick you can't see a trace of scalp even when it's dripping wet from the shower—and it's got body to spare, despite the low humidity. Stevie's a blonde, part in the middle, no bangs, as if she's trying out for a part in a surf movie, but her hair's a lot thinner than mine and it just hangs limp most of the time, unless she puts it up in rollers, and who'll have time for that after closure? But, as I said, she was in and Linda was out, or that was my best guess anyway, and it had nothing to do with the fact that Linda was Asian, but only how she looked in a two-piece. And the degree, of course. It might have hurt to admit it, but Stevie had her on both counts, and if I was going to get in, it would have to be over Linda's back and not Stevie's or Gretchen's or Diane's because I couldn't begin to match their qualifications. My own degree was in environmental studies, which pretty well matched Linda's B.S. in animal sciences, so that was a wash. As for the other three women on the extended crew, they weren't really in the running, or not that Linda or I could see.

Eight, that was the number. Eight slots. Four men, four women. And if we've been criticized for lack of diversity, just think about it. In the history of the planet, only twelve astronauts have walked on the moon, and all of them were men. Counting the second mission, we would number sixteen, and fully half that number would be women. Including, I hoped, me.

By the time I'd finished up in the cafeteria, hugged Linda goodbye and whispered luck in her ear, I was running late and that just ramped up my anxiety one extra degree I didn't need at all. I hurried across the courtyard, dodging the odd tourist, slammed into my room and stripped down for a quick two-minute shower (of which I was a past master, training myself for the mission, when we'd be limited to just seventy-five gallons of water apiece each day—for all purposes). I'd washed my hair the night before and laid out the dress, a pair of Mary Janes and the coral necklace I was going to wear, so it didn't take me long. Lipstick, eye shadow, a dab of highlighter, and I was out the door.

The air held the same faint sweetness I'd noticed earlier, though now it carried a taint of diesel from the pair of bulldozers scooping out the foundation for a new dormitory that would house visiting dignitaries, scientists and any friends of the project willing to contribute at one of three levels—brass, silver, gold—to its success. I didn't run into anybody I knew on my way over to Mission Control, which was just as well given the way I was feeling. The tourists were gathered round in clusters, sprouting cameras, binoculars and daypacks, but none of them gave me a second glance—and really, why would they bother? I was nobody. But tomorrow—if things worked out the way I envisioned—they'd be lining up for my autograph.

I took the stairs up to the third floor of Mission Control and if I broke out in a light sweat, so be it: the exercise calmed me. A simple thing: foot, ankle, knee, hip joint, breathe in, breathe out.

I was in reasonably good shape from working the test plots and the Intensive Agriculture Biome and taking extended walks in the desert when I got the chance, but I wasn't a runner and didn't train with weights like so many of the others. No need, that was my thinking. The Mission One crew experienced rapid weight loss, the men averaging an eighteen percent drop in body weight, the women ten percent, and it was probably healthier to put on a few pounds before closure—Linda and I had gone over this time and again. The trick was, you had to distribute those extra pounds in the right places, because Mission Control was watching and Mission Control definitely did not want to present fat Terranauts to the public.

Josie Muller, the secretary, waved me in with a smile, which I tried to return as if everything was normal, as if what was going to transpire in the next few minutes in the control room with its dull white plasterboard walls, oatmeal carpeting and panoptic views of E2 itself was the most ordinary thing in the world. "Just take a seat," she said, "—it'll be a minute." We both looked to the polished oak door that gave onto the inner sanctum.

I hadn't expected this—a wait. I'd assumed my eight o'clock must have been the first interview of the day and I'd timed it to the minute, thinking to walk right in and let the tension flow out of me like water down a drain. "Is there somebody in there?"

She nodded.

"A seven-thirty? I didn't know they'd scheduled that early?"

"Well, there *are* sixteen of you and they want to give everybody a full half hour at least—you know, for . . . well, final things. To wrap things up."

"Who is it, just out of curiosity?"

Early on, in the first or maybe second week after I'd been selected to join the project, Josie and I had shared a pitcher of mango margaritas at El Caballero in downtown Tillman and after that I'd always thought she was on my side. Or at least sympathetic. More sympathetic to me, I mean, than to some of the others. She was in her late forties, her hair already gone gray and her face composed around a pair of tortoiseshell frames that pinched her temples and marginalized her eyes—and she leaned now across the desk to mouth the name: "Stevie."

Stevie. Well, that was all right. Stevie was in and I'd already accepted that. At least it wasn't Tricia Berner, one of the three women both Linda and I had agreed didn't stand a chance, even though, when I lay awake nights staring at the ceiling till the darkness pooled and dissolved into something darker still, I could see that she did. She was attractive in her own way, if you discounted her style, which was right off the street, short skirts, too much makeup, jewelry that might as well have been encrusted on her, and she was the best actress, hands-down, among the crew. And that meant more than you might think—from the start, right from the building phase to Mission One closure and on through the course of our training, the project was as much about theater as it was science, and even more so now, with Mission Two, and the pledge we'd all taken. But more on that later. Suffice it to say that that closed door, no matter who was behind it, made my stomach clench till I could taste the pancakes all over again.

It was ten past eight and I'd already been in and out of the easy chair in the corner half a dozen times and studied the framed photos of the Mission One crew that lined the walls till I could have reproduced them from memory, when the door swung open and there was Stevie, in heels no less, giving me a blank stare as if she didn't recognize me, as if we hadn't hauled lines together and shoveled cow dung in hundred-ten-degree heat and crouched elbow to elbow over one table or another through too many meals to count. I saw that she'd highlighted her hair and layered on enough makeup to be clearly visible from the cheap seats, but I couldn't tell yet whether she was playing comedy or tragedy. They had to have taken *her,* hadn't they? For a fraction of a second I let myself soar, seeing Linda in her place and both of us in, a gang of two, bulwark against the autocracy of Mission Control on the one hand and the tyranny of the majority on the other, but then Stevie's eyes came into focus—hard blue, cold blue, blue so dark it was almost black—and I saw the triumph there. Her lips curled in a smile that showed off her flawless dentition and firm pink gums and then she was giving me the thumbs-up sign and it all came clear. We might have embraced—we should have, sisters in solidarity, the mission above all else—but I stiffened and the moment passed and she was by me, cranking her smile to the limit and gushing over Josie and Josie gushing right back.

The door stood open before me. I didn't even have to knock.

There were four people inside, seated casually, two on the couch and two in a pair of Posturepedic office chairs, three of whom I'd expected and one whose presence came as a total surprise. And, to be honest, something of a shock. *They're not leaving anything to chance here,* that was my first thought. And then I was thinking, *Good sign or bad?*

But let me explain. The two seated on the couch were a given: Jeremiah Reed and Judy Forester, the visionary who'd dreamed up the project and saw it through its creation and his chief aide and confidante. Privately we called Jeremiah G.C., short for God the Creator, and Judy, in keeping with the religious theme, Judas, because she was a betrayer, or at least that was her potential. We all felt that. It was just the way she was wound, a hair's breadth from turning on you, the kind of person who would have gone straight to the top in the Stasi, but by 1994 the Stasi was no more, so here she was, among us. Lately, Linda and I had been calling her Jude the Obscure, given some of her counterintuitive pronouncements from on high. She wasn't much older than I, but she was Jeremiah's right hand—the right hand of God—and that gave her a power over us that was out of all proportion to who she was. Or would have been, if it weren't for the fact that she was sleeping with the deity himself. Did I toady up to her though I hated myself for it? You can bet I did. And I wasn't the only one.

The third person in this trinity was newly anointed, brought in from outside to oversee day-to-day operations by way of cost-cutting and efficiency. His name was Dennis Roper and he affected a ducktail haircut and slash sideburns, à la 1982. We called him Little Jesus. About a month after they installed him at Mission Control, he hit on Linda, which to my mind was not only unprofessional but sleazy too, given the power he wielded. Linda slept with him a couple of times, though it was wrong and we both knew it whether there was a quid pro quo involved or not—*especially* if there was a quid pro quo—and when he was done with her he came on to me, but I wasn't having it. I wouldn't sink that low even if he was halfway good-looking, which he wasn't. I never liked short men—and beyond that, short or tall, I liked them to have personalities.

Anyway, there I was, hovering in the middle of the room, the door standing open behind me because I'd been too agitated to think to shut it, and the four of them (I'll get to the fourth in a minute) gazing up patiently at me, as if they had all day to do whatever they were going to do, though by my accounting they were already running ten minutes late. "Hi," I said, nodding at each of them in turn, then motioned to the straight-backed chair set there facing them and murmured, "you want me to sit here?"

"Hi, Dawn," Judy said, giving me a big smile that could have meant anything, and the others smiled in succession, everything as routine and amenable as could be, no pressure here, all for one and one for all.

No one had answered my question so I took it on my own initiative to ease into the chair—was this part of the test?—gazing straight into their eyes as if to say *I'm not at all intimidated because I'm one hundred percent certain I'm as vital to this crew as anybody out there walking the planet today.*

"Don't worry, we won't keep you long," Dennis said, getting up to tiptoe across the room and ease the door shut before sitting back down. He drew in a deep breath and let it out again, then bent forward in the office chair so that his elbows rested on his knees and he could screw his eyes into mine. "I know it's a big day for all the candidates and we're all looking forward to finalizing things and moving toward closure, so all we want really is to ask you a few things, little details, minor things, that's all, just to set the record straight—you on board with that?"

The fourth person in the room, and he didn't say a word or unfreeze his face or even shift in his seat to relieve the tension in his buttocks and hip flexors, was Darren Iverson, the millionaire—billionaire—who'd financed the project from its inception to the tune of something like a hundred fifty million dollars and picked up the operating costs too, which were in the neighborhood of ten million a year, a million of that for power alone. He was a few years younger than Jeremiah, which would have put him in his mid-fifties, and he didn't really look like a billionaire—or what I suppose anybody would have expected a billionaire to look like. He wore matching shirt and pants combinations he might have picked up at Sears, in desert brown, with waffle-tread workboots, also in brown. His eyes were brown too and so was his hair, or what was left of it. We called him Mr. Iverson to his face. Otherwise he was G.F., short for God the Financier.

I looked to G.F., then to G.C. and Judy and finally came back to Dennis. "I feel like I'm on *Star Trek* or something," I said, but nobody laughed. *Star Trek* was one of our touchstones, as was *Silent Running,* for obvious reasons. "You know, 'Where No Man Has Gone Before'?" Still no reaction. I was feeling giddy, maybe a bit light-headed from the tension and all the energy my gastrointestinal system was putting into digesting breakfast, and whether it was ill-advised or not, I couldn't help adding, "Or no woman."

Dennis pushed himself back up to a sitting position. "Great, but we just want to ask you a few things that really haven't come up, to this point, that is"—and here he made it a question—"about your personal life?"

If this caught me by surprise, I didn't let it show. I'd assumed they'd be asking me about food values, estimated crop yields, milk production and minimum protein requirements, that sort of thing, the technical aspects of the job I'd be expected to fill, but this came out of nowhere. I just nodded.

"Are you currently seeing anyone?"

"No," I said, too quickly, and that was because I was lying. Despite myself, I'd been drawn into a relationship—or no, I'd fallen, full-on, no parachute—with Johnny Boudreau, who'd been second boss of the construction crew when E2 was in the building stages, and who played guitar and sang in a bar band on weekends.

Dennis—Little Jesus!—flipped a note card in his hand and made a show of squinting at the name written on the back of it. "What about John Boudreau?"

I wanted to say, *Are you spying on me now?,* but I kept my composure. I couldn't summon Johnny just then, couldn't picture him or take a snapshot in the lens of my mind, and I realized that if he really did mean anything lasting to me we'd have this month to make our peace with wherever that was going to go, and then there'd be closure, 730 days of it. I shrugged.

Into the incriminatory silence Judy said, "You are using birth control, right?"

I nodded.

"And—forgive me, but you do understand how vital this is, don't you?—have you had multiple partners in recent months, anything that might endanger . . . or, what do I mean?" She looked to Dennis.

"E.," he said, using my crew sobriquet, E. being short for Eos, rosy-limbed goddess of dawn, which I took to be a compliment even if it came by way of left field, "what we mean is we can't risk any sort of infection arising after closure—"

"You mean STDs, right?" I wasn't angry, or not yet—they were just doing what was best for the mission and what was best for the mission was best for me. "You don't have to worry," I said, and I gave Dennis a meaningful look. "It's been only Johnny, Johnny and nobody else."

Judy: "And he's, uh—?"

"Clean? Yes, as far as I know."

Dennis: "He does play in a band, doesn't he?"

"Listen," and here I shot a look past the two of them to where G.C. sat there on the couch like a sphinx and then to the brown hole of G.F., "I don't really see the point of all this. The medical officer, which I assume is going to be Richard, right?" Nothing. Not a glimmer from any of them. "The medical officer's going to do a thorough exam, and even if I had gonorrhea, syphilis and chlamydia—or if any of the men had it—it'd just be treated, right?"

There was a silence. Distantly, as if it were being piped in over a faulty sound system, there came the muffled clank of the bulldozers going about their business across campus. G.C.—lean, pale as a cloud with his fluffed-up hair and full white beard—uncrossed his legs and spoke for the first time. His voice was a fine tenor instrument, capable of every shading and nuance—when he was younger, long before the project, he'd performed on Broadway in things like *Hair* and *Man of La Mancha.* "But the issue is birth control," he said. "You do understand, don't you, that we can't risk having any of our female crew getting, well, knocked up. To put it bluntly."

It wasn't a question and I didn't answer it. "I'll take a pregnancy test, if it'll make you rest easier. Believe me, it won't be a problem."

"Yes," he said, tenting his fingers to make a cradle for his chin so he could stare directly into me, "but what about post-closure?"

And now—I couldn't help myself—I gave each of them a smile in turn and said, as sweetly as I could, "You'll have to ask the men about that."

* * *

I don't remember much beyond that though I'm sure my face must have been flushed and the vein on my forehead pulsing like heat lightning. I felt so grateful—and relieved—I could have kissed them all, but I didn't. Or at least I don't think I did. Dennis later told me I'd practically bowed my way across the floor before pausing at the door to give them all a broad valedictory wave, as if I were ducking into the wings after an ovation, but I don't remember that either. It was heady, at any rate, even if I can't say for sure what was true and what wasn't. And it didn't really matter. Not anymore.

Unfortunately—and here you had to appreciate the subtlety of their scheduling—the first person I saw on coming through the door was Linda. She was seated in the chair I'd vacated, head down, studying her notes on closed systems, group dynamics, technics, Vernadsky and Brion and Mumford, boning up, though there was no point in it now. I saw that she'd put on a dress—a bronze rayon shift that only managed to look dowdy on her—and pinned up her hair, which was usually such a mess. What did I feel? Honestly? Sad, of course, but in that moment it was no more than a fluctuation in the flight I was on, the first stage of the rocket falling away while the payload hurtles higher and ever higher.

She didn't notice me. Didn't lift her head. I could see her lips moving over the phrases we'd chanted together like incantations— *Thought isn't a form of energy. So how on Earth can it change material processes?*—as if the people inside that room would care. They'd asked about my sex life. Asked things like, "How do you feel about Ramsay? Gretchen? Stevie? You think you can work with them inside?" And what did I say? *Of course,* I said. *Of course. They're the best people in the world. I look forward to the challenge. We'll make it work, make it click,* everything. *It's going to be awesome!*

I could feel Josie's eyes on me, but I didn't turn to her, not yet. I glided across the room as if I were riding a conveyor belt and then I was right there in front of Linda and I said her name, once, very softly, and she looked up. That was all it took. I didn't have to say a word. I watched the new calculus flicker like a current across her face and saw her put it all behind her and with an effort raise up her arms for a hug. "Dawn," she murmured, "Dawn, oh, Dawn, I'm so glad, I am—"

It was an awkward embrace. I was standing and she was sitting, the notebook spread open in her lap, her feet planted on the carpet, and I could feel the strain in the muscles of my lower back. Her grip was fierce, almost as if we were wrestling and she was trying to pull me down. I couldn't say anything because there was nothing to say that wouldn't sound like I was congratulating myself—and I couldn't do that, not at her expense.

"Dawn," she said, "Dawn," and drew it out till it was a bleat even as Josie moved forward to get into the act and Judy appeared at the door of the control room. I let go then and Linda sank back into the chair.

"Congrats," Josie mouthed for me alone, an expert at conveying meaning without sound, and then Judy was saying, "Linda? Linda, come on in. We're all ready for you."

* * *

I waited there the full half hour, settling myself into the chair and chattering away at Josie as one thought after another came cascading into my head, already wondering about the closure ceremony and measurements for our uniforms and whether we'd have our choice of living quarters or if they'd been pre-assigned (if Josie knew, she wasn't letting on). At nine, on the stroke, Ramsay appeared, in T-shirt and jeans, a baseball cap reversed on his head and the fingers of his right hand rooting at the beginnings of a shadowy growth of beard. I hadn't seen him the last couple of days, our schedules at odds, and the beard surprised me. If I'd assumed he was in, Dennis' question had pretty well confirmed it—pointedly, he hadn't asked how I felt about any of the men or women Linda and I had relegated to the second tier but only the ones we'd handicapped as the front-runners—and if that was the case he'd have to shave before we were presented to the press or Mission Control would have something to say about it. Beyond that, the way he was dressed—his whole attitude, from the minute he slouched in the door, flashed a grin at Josie and me and perched himself on the corner of the desk as if it belonged to him—bespoke a level of confidence that verged on arrogance. Or inside knowledge. Maybe that was it. He'd been chummy with G.C. and Judy from the beginning, all in the name of public relations, of course, and I realized how naïve I'd have to have been not to understand that there was a pecking order here.

"Hi, girls," he said, "what's happening? Everybody feeling just unconquerable this morning? But wait, wait, wait—E., let me be the first, or maybe"—here he snatched a look at Josie—"the second to congratulate you. Well done! All for one and one for all, right?"

I just stared at him in astonishment. "But how did you know?"

"How did I know? Just look at your face. Quick, Josie, you got your compact? Here, come on, take a look at yourself." Going along with him, Josie fished her compact out of her purse and handed it to him so he could snap it open and bound across the room to hold the little rectangular mirror up in front of my face. "See? See there?" He swung his head round comically to where Josie sat at her desk. "Look at the way the zygomaticus muscles are stretching that smile, and wait a minute, the risorius too, which, in laymen's terms is called the look-how-proud-I-am muscle."

I couldn't help myself: I felt dazzled. And all his cutting-up, which I might have found sophomoric and more than a little annoying in another place or time, seemed witty and genuine, touching even. "What about you?" I asked. "You hear anything yet?"

"I'm the nine o'clock," he said, giving nothing away. He snapped the compact shut and gestured toward the door with it. "Who's in there now?"

"Linda."

"Oh," he said. "Oh, Linda, yeah. Of course. *Linda*." He was watching me closely—he knew as well as I did that if I was in, Linda was out, or that was how it looked, unless Mission Control relented and decided to send all sixteen of us inside.

I didn't have a chance to say anything more, either in her defense or my own, because the door swung open then and Linda was coming through it and you didn't have to be clairvoyant to see the way things were. She was trying to control her face—there was no love lost between her and Ramsay and he was probably the last person she wanted to break down in front of, especially if he was in and she was out. Behind her, at the door, an expressionless Judy was beckoning to Ramsay, who flipped the compact back to Josie and exclaimed, to no one in particular, "What, am I up already?," and walked right by Linda without even glancing at her.

I might have hesitated for just an instant before I rose from the chair to go to her, ready to wrap her in my arms and murmur whatever needed to be said by way of consolation, though there could be no consolation and we both knew it. I'd be lying if I said I hadn't anticipated this moment, rehearsing it in my head over and over, but in every scenario I'd come up with I saw her giving in to the inevitable the way I would have if I were in her position and then the two of us regrouping and fighting through the storm together. She surprised me, though. She made straight for the door without raising her eyes, her shoulders slumped and her feet digging at the carpet as if the room had somehow tilted on her and she was climbing the side of a mountain. By the time I caught up with her she was already out in the hallway, heading for the stairs. "Linda!" I called sharply, more stunned than anything else. "Linda!"

She didn't turn to acknowledge me, just started down the stairs, her pinned-up hair shining like cellophane under the overhead lights. She was short—five-two to my five-eight—and looking down on her from that angle she seemed so reduced she might have been a child clacking down the stairs after a bad day at school. And it had been a bad day, the worst, and I needed to talk it out with her—for my own sake as well as hers.

"Linda!"

Still she didn't turn and I think she would have made it all the way down to the first floor and out the door and into the heat if it weren't for the fact that she was wearing heels (and that was another thing: we'd discussed how inappropriate it would be to wear heels, tacky even, because this wasn't a beauty contest, and here she was in a pair of pumps in the same shade as her dress). I hurried down the steps and actually took hold of her arm in mid-stride so she had no choice but to stop and turn her face to me. "I'm sorry," I said. "It's horrible. It's shit. I mean, how *could* they?"

"*You're* sorry? What have you got to be sorry about? You're in." She shot me a furious look and snatched her arm away.

"I know, I know. It's wrong. Way wrong. They're idiots, G.C., Judy, all of them—we knew it all along. I mean, how many times did we say how out of touch they were, how they wouldn't recognize true merit, if, if—"

"They picked *you*, though, didn't they?"

I ducked my head as if to acknowledge the blow. Two people we both knew, support staff, made their way past us, heading up to the second floor. They knew what the score was as soon as they caught a glimpse of Linda's face and they went on by without a word. I waited till they reached the next landing, struggling with myself. What I said next was false and we both knew it the minute it was out of my mouth: "They should have taken you instead."

"Don't make me laugh. You know what this is all about, and so what if I have the qualifications—better than yours, if you want to know the truth. I'm Asian, that's the fact. And I'm fat."

"You're not fat," I said automatically.

"Fat and short and not half as pretty as you. Or Stevie. Or even Gretchen."

I didn't know what to say.

"Blondes, that's what they want. Or what?" She gestured angrily in my face. "Redheads. Or is it strawberry blonde? Isn't that what you're always calling it?"

I couldn't believe what I was hearing. Did she really think hair color had anything to do with it? When I'd put all that time into food production while she was flapping around in her flippers and wet suit trying to go head-to-head with Stevie? "Come on, Linda," I said, "this is me you're talking to. I know you're hurting right now, but we'll get through this just like we got through everything else they tossed at us—"

"Screw you," she said, and then she was clattering down the stairs, unsteady on the heels, which I realized she must have bought just for the interview since I'd never seen them before. It made me sad. I didn't want this. I wanted to go someplace, anyplace, shout out the news, phone my mother, phone Johnny, but Linda was dragging me down. I called her name again and she swung round abruptly. "What?" she demanded.

I was still poised there on the third step from the bottom. "Don't you want to go someplace and talk things over? I mean, for coffee. Or maybe a drink?"

"A drink? At five past nine in the morning? Are you out of your mind?"

"Why not? They gave us the day off, right? Why not do something crazy, like go shoot pool and get plastered?"

"No," she said. "No way."

"Coffee then?"

She made a face, but she was standing there motionless now,

the heels thrusting her up and away from the gleaming surface of the floor and the shift bunched across her midsection, half a size too small. (The whole outfit was wrong, too blocky on her, which was typical of Linda, whose style sense was always a bit off, and why she hadn't shown it to me beforehand I couldn't imagine. Or maybe I could.) I came down the steps and crossed the lobby to her and she let me loop my arm through hers and lead her toward the door. "Tell you what," I said, "let's go into town to that place with the napoleons. Your fave? Okay?"

She didn't answer but I felt some of the rigidity go out of her and we kept on walking.

This was better, much better, and I suppose I never should have said what came next, but I was trying to be positive, you can appreciate that. "Listen," I said as we stepped through the door and into the glare of the sun, "I know how you feel, I do, but like you said, there's always Mission Three."

* * *

We drove the forty miles to Tucson with the radio cranked and the windows down, our hair beating round our heads in the old way of freedom and the open road, the way it had been before I'd met Johnny and we'd go off on day trips whenever we could just to get away from E2 and all the focus and pressure surrounding it. The car was a hand-me-down from my mother, a Camry in need of tires and paint, with a hundred thousand miles on it, but good still, solid, and it came to me then that I didn't know what I was going to do with it. Put it up on blocks? Isn't that what people did with cars? But where? There was no way I'd have time to drive across country and leave it at my parents' house. Mission Control would give us a stipend to store our personal things, furniture, clothes and whatever, but they hadn't said anything about cars—would they let us leave them on campus? The more I thought about it the more I realized they wouldn't—the cars would just deteriorate and become an eyesore and nobody wanted the press or the tourists to see that. And it wasn't as if I could just park the car someplace and expect it to be there when I got back. But then maybe I was worrying over nothing. Who knew, by the time the mission was over, cars might be obsolete—or mine would be, anyway.

I turned to Linda, who understandably hadn't had much to say since we'd got in the car, which, I suppose, was part of my strategy though I hadn't been aware of it till now—let the wind and the music stand as an excuse while we both privately took the opportunity to sort out our feelings—and had an inspiration. "Linda, I was just thinking," I said, and I had to shout to be heard over the noise of the wind and the radio, "do you want a car? I mean for like when it's too hot to bicycle? Or when you need groceries?"

She was staring straight ahead, her hair down now and floating round her face as if we'd been plunged underwater. "What, you mean this one?"

I nodded, though she wouldn't have seen it since she still wouldn't look at me. The radio was playing a tune by a singer who would kill himself a month after closure, not that the two were related in any way, just that it helps put the time in perspective for me. *Here we are now, entertain us.* That was the lyric. And it droned through the speakers as I stole a glance at Linda, then flicked my eyes to the rearview—trucks, eternal trucks—and back to the road ahead of us.

"You want me to car-sit, is that what you're saying?"

"Yeah," I said. "I guess. If you think you can get some use out of it, I mean. Otherwise, it'll just sit there and rust. Or not rust—dry up, right?"

"And when Mission Three comes around and it's my turn—if it's ever going to be my turn—then what? You're going to want it back?"

I shrugged. The singer droned, soon to be dead, though he didn't know it yet—or maybe he did. There was hair in my mouth. A truck swung out to pass and I winced at the intrusion. I was feeling generous—feeling ecstatic, actually, and what I was doing here and would do for the next four hours on the road and in the pastry shop and the handbag store we both liked was feeling more and more like a duty—and I said, "You can keep it. I'll sign it over and everything. For nothing, gratis, free, it's yours. And when you go in, I'll watch it for you—change the oil, keep it washed and waxed, everything. Deal?"

She shook her head in denial. She didn't want a car. And she didn't want to be here pretending any more than I did. What she wanted, she wasn't going to get. Not now—and I think I knew it even then—and not two years from now either.

* * *

When I got back it was past two, the message light was blinking on the phone and I needed to call Johnny and my mother, in that order. I'd already tried Johnny twice, once from the phone in the hallway of the pastry shop and once from a gas station on the way back while Linda was getting us Diet Cokes, and both times, as I'd expected, I got his answering machine. He was at work, obviously, and he'd get the message when he got it. The thing was, how would he react? He'd be happy for me, or make a show of being happy, but then he'd drop the pose and let his sarcasm take over and that could be harsh. Lately he'd been calling me his girlfriend in a bottle and introducing me around as the woman going into stir. And my mother. She'd go gaga because now she could tell people her daughter wasn't just breaking her back doing menial labor in a greenhouse in the Arizona desert for less than minimum wage, but getting somewhere, getting famous, making use of her degree and participating in a project *Time* magazine had proclaimed to be as significant for the future of humanity as the Apollo missions to the moon. Of course, that was back then, before Mission One soured, and yet it wouldn't make an iota of difference to my mother: *Time* had proclaimed and that was enough for her. And if you want to know the truth, it was enough for me too.

Anyway, there I was, standing in the middle of the room, sweating rivulets, my hair a tangle, the endorphin high of the morning still lifting me right up off the ground and the sugar rush (we'd shared a napoleon and a cream puff) running like rocket fuel through my veins, staring at the pulsing yellow button on the phone console as if I didn't know what it was for. Add to that the fact that I was feeling light-headed from caffeine overload because I'd wound up having two cafés au lait at the pastry shop while Linda and I tried to talk things through. Not to mention the Diet Coke. I was rattled, flying high, but in the best possible way. The message would have been from my mother, I was sure of it, because she was as keyed up about the interview as I was—*Just be yourself,* that was her advice—and I was about to press "play" when the phone rang.

All that caffeine, all that sugar—the sound startled me and it wasn't till the third ring that I picked up.

It was Johnny. "Hey, you hear anything yet?"

"Yes," I said, "I'm in." I'd anticipated this for a long while, weighing the pros and cons, thinking of what I'd say, but now that the moment had come, now that I'd said it, I was surprised at how neutral my tone was. This was dancing-around-the-room news, shouting-it-out-the-windows, but I just dropped it there like a stone.

There was a pause. I could hear sounds in the background, an engine straining against the gear, the clank of metal on metal. When he finally spoke, if anything his voice was even less inflected than mine. "That's great," he said. "I'm happy for you, I really am."

"But not so much for yourself, right?"

"What am I supposed to do while you're in there, get an inflatable sex doll?"

"Dream about me."

"If only. Girlfriend in a bottle. Bottled girlfriend. Girlfriend under glass."

"Sealed-in sweetness," I said.

"What about the four guys—you know who's in?"

"Ramsay for sure. And Richard Lack. The other two I haven't heard yet—the interviews are still going on. Linda's out. But you probably guessed that. She's taking it hard."

Another pause. "So you expect me to wait for you? And what about you—you're going to be locked up in there with four guys and you tell me nothing's going to happen?"

"I never said that. You knew from the beginning—"

He cut me off: "I don't want to bicker. This is a day for celebration, right? When we going to get together—five okay?"

"Five's perfect."

"Dinner at the Italian place, maybe. Or if you want a steak—you won't be getting many of those, will you? Then drinks and dancing, and after we'll go back to my place and talk this over like sensible adults—with our clothes off."

"Sounds like a plan," I said.

"Five," he said, and hung up.

The minute I set the phone down it rang again, the very instant, as if it had been timed to go off like a bomb fabricated of dynamite and a ticking clock. The voice that came at me, high-pitched and demanding, was Judy's: "Jesus, Dawn, where have you been? I've been ringing the phone off the hook for the past three hours now. Don't you realize how short the time is? We need you over here right now for your fitting—*now*, do you hear me?"

I don't know if I'd call myself overly apologetic, but when I'm in the wrong I'll admit it, and here I was in the wrong already (though if they wanted me on call, they should have said so, or that was how I felt anyway). "Sorry," I said.

"What were you thinking? From now on we're going to need you available twenty-four/seven. We're counting down to closure, don't you realize that?"

"Sorry," I repeated. And then, before she could go on I said, "Who's in? Who made it? Who am I going to be living with?"

"You'll find out when you get here—"

"Stevie I know—and Ramsay, right? Richard, I presume, because—"

"One other thing, and we'll fill you in when you get here, there'll be a dinner tonight, five o'clock, at Alfano's, just Mission Control and the final eight, and I've asked two or three journalists—and a photographer—to join us, nothing official, that'll come tomorrow at the press conference—"

From where I was standing, if I tugged at the phone cord and canted my head to the right, I could see out the window to where E2 caught the sun in its glass panels and showered light over the campus, the white interlocking struts of the spaceframe like the superstructure of a vast beehive—honeycomb, that was the term that came into my head just then in all its sweetness, a sweetness so intense it cloyed.

I blocked out Judy for just a moment there, adrift on the future and what it meant and what was happening to me in the here and now. "Yes," I said, "yes, okay," though I didn't know what I was agreeing to.

"So we'll brief you on all this, of course—this is just the beginning, believe me. But for now, for tonight, just remember you're representing the mission from here on out and that means you're going to want to look your best . . ."

"What about the dress I was wearing this morning, would that be okay?"

"What dress?"

"For the interview? You know, it's like a light green, almost a mint?"

"I'm drawing a blank here."

"You know, the tank dress?"

I watched a sparrow clip its wings tight and plummet from the balcony to the lawn below. And what was that? A cloud in the cloudless sky, dragging a moving shadow across the courtyard. Dark, then light, then dark again. "Oh, yeah, yeah, of course," Judy said. "A tank dress, right?"

I didn't say anything.

"I don't know." She let out a sigh. "Haven't you got something with maybe a little more style?"

Ramsay Roothoorp

They can call me a corporation man all they want, yet what's a corporation really but a group of people getting together to advance mankind, and no, we are not and never have been a cult and G.C. is no guru, or not anymore, or he won't be once we're inside because once we're inside nothing's going to shake us and nothing's going to make us break open that airlock short of murder and cannibalism, and even that wouldn't sway me—that would just amount to one more observable phenomenon in the ecology of closed systems. Plus, you'd have to seriously not be paying attention if you didn't understand that the failure of the first mission and the reason the press turned against it, against us, was exactly that: the breach of the airlock. The whole notion of the Ecosphere, of eight people confining themselves willingly in a man-made world for twenty-four months, caught the public's imagination precisely *because* of that hook, the conceit of voluntary imprisonment— not to mention the Mars connection. If E2 was supposed to be an experiment in world-building, it was also about business, the kind of potentially remunerative enterprise that enticed a man like Darren Iverson to put up his money in the first place. The earth was running out of resources, global warming was beginning to be recognized as science fact and not science fiction, and if man was to evolve to play a part in things instead of being just another doomed organism on a doomed planet, if the *technosphere* was going to replace pure biological processes, then sooner or later we'd have to seed life elsewhere—on Mars, to begin with.

All right. The public understood that. The press ate it up, feasted on it. E2 was everywhere, from national TV to the *New York Times* and *Time* and *Newsweek* and every talk radio show in existence. And what happened? Within twelve days after closure one of the crew—Roberta Brownlow—had a medical emergency, the seals were broken, and the deal was off. She was out in the world, your world (what we like to call E1, the original ecosphere) for less than five hours, but even if it had been five minutes, five *seconds,* the whole thing would have collapsed. Because it was the conceit that counted, and couldn't anybody see that?

If they *were* on Mars, she would have died. They all would have died. If not from O_2 depletion, then starvation. The fact was, the Mission One crew was to go on to break closure in a panoply of ways during the course of the mission—once the precedent had been set, they all figured why not?—and the public saw through that and labeled the whole thing a sham. Goodbye. Adios. Forget the lessons learned. Forget ecology. Forget modeling and the Intensive Agriculture Biome and the elegant interaction of the wilderness biomes and all the rest. All that mattered was that the crew had broken closure, reneged on a promise, on the *deal,* and that was laughable, it really was. What did E.O. Wilson say? *If those committed to the quest fail, they will be forgiven. The moral imperative of humanism is the endeavor alone, whether successful or not, provided the effort is honorable and the failure memorable.*

Well, he was wrong. There is no forgiveness and there won't be the next time or the time after that and we weren't about to make the same mistake. Tell me: what does closure mean? It means closure. Period. The good news was that Mission Control was on board with that, one hundred percent. Of course they were—learn from your mistakes, right? They did a whole lot of fast backpedaling and settled into prophylactic mode, as in let's anticipate the problems before they arise. They'd made Gretchen Frost have her wisdom teeth removed, and T.T. (Troy Turner) took a course in emergency dentistry, just in case, and we all lauded that. They didn't go as far maybe as Louis Leakey when he refused to send his ape ladies (or his Trimates, as he called them, Goodall, Galdikas and Fossey) into the jungle if they didn't agree beforehand to have their appendixes removed by way of foreseeing the unforeseen. Because Leakey, like Wilson, a humanist as well as a scientist, didn't want to run even the infinitesimal risk of having one of them turn septicemic and drop dead on him hundreds of miles from any kind of even semi-acceptable medical intervention. Or the blood supply. Imagine the blood supply back in the sixties and seventies in West Africa and Borneo? Or even now. Now it was worse, far worse, with HIV, AIDS and maybe even Ebola pulsing through the circulatory pathways of our criminally expanding species, pandemic, everything a pandemic, apocalypse festering in the blood. But don't get me started.

Mission Control would have liked it if we'd gone under the knife too, I'm sure, but the medical detection these days is far more sophisticated than what it was and they were able to fairly well rule out any signs of incipient appendicitis among the final eight. And, as I said, even if one of us had something catastrophic occur once we were inside—ruptured appendix, gangrene, heart failure—it wouldn't have made an iota of difference. That would be it. Death was as much a part of natural processes as life, and in strictly Darwinian terms, practical terms, that is, it would be a boon for the other seven. As it was, we'd be hard-pressed to feed ourselves, if the Mission One crew was any indication, and to have one less digestive tract up and working would go a long way toward taking some of the pressure off.

I'm talking theoretically here, of course, and strictly in terms of caloric intake—the loss of any of us would be a public relations disaster and an emotional one too, because we *were* a team and we were dedicated to one another no matter what anybody tells you. There are going to be strains in any enterprise that truly breaks new ground, that's only to be expected—witness the Russian Bios experiment in which one of the men wound up sexually assaulting one of the women just three months after closure. Actually, since I've started down this path, I suppose you can never underestimate people's appetite for the sensational—if somebody *were* to die inside, there's no doubt our public awareness factor would shoot up. Simple as that. Not that it was going to happen, but we were prepared for anything. If the eight of us had stopped short of lacerating our palms and taking a blood oath, we'd made our pact nonetheless. Nothing in, nothing out. That was our mantra.

Was Roberta Brownlow's situation unfortunate? Yes, of course it was. And I'm sure you remember the flap over it—furor, really—and how the press came howling after her like hyenas on a scent. Or jackals, I suppose, since hyenas don't howl, do they? She was Mission One's MDA, very good-looking, stunning actually, an exemplar of what our species has come to consider prime breeding stock, with a robust figure, abundant hair and teeth like piano keys—the white ones, that is—and she had a way with the press that was just short of flirtatious on the one hand and all business on the other. She was a perfect choice, not simply by way of looks but because she was first-rate at what she did, which, though it involved the least scientific knowledge or discipline, was on some level the most essential function of the crew: to provide food. She wasn't "Supervisor of Field Crops," the title that would go to Diane Kesselring on our mission, but the lion's share of her work went into food production, more than anyone else's. So she was a fit, Roberta Brownlow, and we were all proud of her. (Yes, *we*: I came aboard, as most people will know, two months before Mission One closure, putting my head down and working support staff till training started for Mission Two.) But accidents happen. And if you're timid—afraid, that is, cowardly, trembling like preschoolers scared of their own shadows—you lose your head, and then everything, if you'll excuse me, goes to shit.

Twelve days in. She was in the basement where all our internal support systems are located—the big air handler units, the water treatment tanks, machine shop—feeding rice stalks into the threshing machine with the crew's medical officer, Winston Barr, whose turn it was to pitch in with the ag work that morning (a lucky break at an unlucky time), when she lost track of what she was doing. The thresher, the same one that's in place now, has a lower cylinder attached where the hulls are separated from the stems, and she was attempting to clear a blockage there when the roller took hold of her right hand. By the time her scream alerted him and he shut down the machine, the damage had been done. Without thinking, in that instant of shock before the pain hit, Roberta snatched her hand back and when she did a geyser of blood erupted from her middle finger, spattering the thresher, the wall behind it, the shirt Winston Barr had just washed and dried the day before. (How do I know that? The shirt detail, that is? He told me. Personally. And I relate it to you because it's one of those maybe overlooked minor details that underpin the meaning of everything that happens in our lives, from the prosaic to the tragic. And this was tragic. Beyond tragic: it was fatal to the mission.)

Two of the other crewmembers, summoned by walkie-talkie while Winston applied pressure and Roberta went from pale to parchment and had to sit heavily on the floor with her head down between her legs, picked through the hulls until they found her severed fingertip so that Winston could sew it back in place. He knew what he was doing. He was dexterous, good with sutures and good with the patient too, but he wasn't a hand surgeon and the medical lab wasn't a hospital. Three days later, when the fingertip, which Roberta held up to the visitors' window for Mission Control and the best hand man in Pima County to examine, turned the color of blood sausage, Mission Control made the call and summoned an ambulance. Which meant breaking closure. Which meant the shitstorm was about to commence.

All right. I wouldn't want to get too critical here, but you can see my point, I'm sure: what's a fingertip compared to the sanctity of the mission and the vow the crew had made to the world? Nothing. If it were me, I'd have given up all my fingertips, all ten digits—hell, if it came to it, I'd have snipped off my toes too. You think Shackleton worried about appendages? Or Sir Edmund Hillary? But you're not martyrs, people would say. You're not really on Mars. It isn't life and death. People would say that—maybe you're saying it now—but they'd be wrong. A pledge is a pledge: *nothing in, nothing out.*

And that's just where things spiraled out of control. Roberta Brownlow was outside for just five hours and during that time, while she went to and fro in the ambulance and they cleaned and re-stitched and re-bandaged the wound at the hospital, she'd breathed in no more than something like five thousand lungsful of E1 air and consumed exactly one granola bar and a Coke Classic—no lobster Newburg, no caviar, no steak tartare or pigs in a blanket—and yet it didn't matter. Every instant of it was photographed and splashed across the front pages of newspapers around the world—and that was just the beginning. When she went back in, when she breached the airlock for the second time, she was carrying two bags with her. *Two bags!* What was she thinking? What was *Mission Control* thinking? This was the moon, this was Mars, this was material closure, not some greenhouse you could just stroll in and out of whenever you had the urge, and why not order up a pizza while you're at it? Pepperoni, anybody? Extra cheese? No. The whole thing was a travesty. And what was in those bags—medicine, machine parts, bourbon, a book of crossword puzzles and the latest CD from the King of Pop? Nobody knew. And nobody ever found out, not even me.

* * *

But enough negativity. I've been called everything from cold and calculating to the face of the mission and its beating heart too. My own assessment? Frankly? Somewhere in between. As for heart, excuse me, but I'm as soft at the core as the next person. I'm not some sort of machine or corporate stooge or whatever, no matter what you may have heard from people like Gretchen Frost or Troy Turner or who?—*Linda Ryu,* whose every comment and so-called insight is nothing but sour grapes, believe me. I get emotional. I get choked up. And you know what? That first official dinner, the one that capped off Selection Day? I'd had a pretty good idea who was in and who was out, but Mission Control could be fickle, and though I had little to no anxiety about my own position, still, after all the shared sweat and second-guessing and bonding, de-bonding and re-bonding with the other fifteen candidates, I have to admit I was fighting back tears when G.C. announced my name at the reception at Alfano's and I stepped forward as the others applauded and Judy and Dennis beamed and the ex officio mission photographer clicked away. I don't know how to explain it, but that night, the night before the press conference, we seemed to rise to an emotional height we never quite reached again. I'm talking brother- and sisterhood here, the solidarity of common purpose, wills united—and, I suppose, in no small measure, simple relief at having made it this far.

But let me set the scene. No one would confuse Alfano's with a quality restaurant, but it held pride of place in the little town of Tillman, Arizona, forty miles northeast of Tucson and gateway to a major tourist attraction that was pumping real dollars into the local economy—us, that is. Most nights, it was packed, and it was no different on this occasion. The space was typical of mall design, low-ceilinged but otherwise barn-like, with booths along both walls and tables that could be pieced together in just about any arrangement to accommodate a crowd. The lighting was subdued enough to hide the frayed industrial carpeting and marinara stains on the walls, and I had no complaints on that score: give me a couple of candles and I'm happy. As for the food, it was about what you'd expect from a generic Italian place no Italian chef had ever set foot in—heavy on pasta, light on substance. But, as I say, it was the best the town had to offer and it was the occasion rather than the cuisine that held us in its sway.

We had drinks at the bar, one round only as G.C. didn't want the celebration to get out of hand with two privileged members of the fourth estate looking on, and I'd ordered a double vodka on the rocks, which partially explained the rush of sentiment I was feeling. We all embraced three or four times, hovering over the bar, our voices garbled and giddy, and I liked the way E. was looking in a long black dress set off with a red belt and matching shoes, and I kissed her twice—on the lips—whereas I kissed the other three women, Gretchen, Diane and Stevie, only once each, and in what you'd call a more glancing manner, I suppose. "Jesus," she said, "you *are* excited," and her eyes were pinballs caroming off one baffle after another.

"I'm excited?" I was rocking back and forth on my feet, grinning like a fool. "Look at yourself—you're practically in orbit."

"Yeah," she said, her voice soft and sugared and coming from someplace deep inside her, a voice of pure satisfaction and *joie d'ac-complissement*. "I've never been so excited in my life. You too?"

I nodded and even as I did I noticed Judy swing her head round at the end of the bar and give me a look. This was awkward. The fact was that while G.C. was planning on returning to Mission Control with Dennis after dinner to fine-tune things for tomorrow's press conference, I was going to take Judy, very quietly and unobtrusively, back to my room, because as risky as it might have been neither of us seemed capable of putting a stop to what had begun as a not-so-innocent flirtation nearly a year ago—and now we had just a month left to get our fill of each other before closure dropped the curtain on it. That was the situation. That was the mise-en-scène. And if Judy had been watching me embrace at least one of my fellow Terranauts with maybe an excess of enthu-siasm, what could I say? I flashed her a quick smile, then turned back to my crewmate.

"But you knew in advance, didn't you?" Dawn said, a teasing note in her voice, but something else too, something accusatory that should have set off warning bells in my brain, but my brain, as I've indicated, was riding high on the moment. And the vodka.

"Not really."

"What do you mean, 'not really'? Nobody dropped any hints? Since you're so, I don't know, *tight* with G.C. and Dennis. And *Judy*."

My smile was like the sun coming up over a big broad-backed river, dawn, that is, on the Mississippi or maybe the Amazon. How much she knew, I couldn't say. "Not telling."

And her smile? Every bit as pleased—and flirtatious. I felt a stir-ring between my legs (strictly autonomous and of course I didn't know then what I know now). Two years, I was thinking. Four men, four women. "Come on," she said, putting her hand on my forearm, five shapely fingers that had grown tough as talons as a result of all that hard labor in the test plots and the IAB. She held her smile. "You're not fooling anybody."

One more glance for Judy. She had her head turned, deep in

conversation with Dennis and Troy Turner. "Maybe just a little," I admitted, and here we were, locked in a grinning contest.

Whatever might have happened beyond that, beyond your essential crewmate chumminess and gum-blistering expression of mutual admiration, never revealed itself because G.C., enthroned on a faux-leather-bound stool at the prow of the L-shaped bar, began rapping a spoon against the rim of his glass. Conversation died. Even the outsiders pounding away at their pitchers and shots at the Formica-topped tables in the bar stopped what they were doing and looked up.

"Before we head in to dinner and start our countdown to closure," G.C. intoned in his rolling melodic voice, "I just want to recognize the eight crewmembers who will soon be going where no man has gone before"—and here, incredibly, he nodded at E., and if my eyes weren't deceiving me even seemed to wink at her— "or *woman*. Except, of course, the Mission One Terranauts, whose legacy Mission Two will seek to deepen and refine." He went on in that vein for a sentence or two more but I wasn't listening, baffled over the meaning of that gesture—why was he singling *her* out? A powerful aroma of deep-fried calamari and parmigiana penetrated the scene and we all shifted our eyes for a quick glancing moment to the waiter gliding beneath his tray to a table of outsiders in the far corner of the bar, and then G.C., without the fanfare he would make fulsome use of the following day at the official press conference, announced each of us—in alphabetical order—so that we could step apart from the group, beaming or blushing as the case may be, for our moment of preliminary glory. Of course, you're all familiar with the names, no suspense there, but since this is an official record—or my personal official record, if that manages to avoid being an oxymoron—I'll list them and their crew titles, just as G.C. announced them that day:

Dawn Chapman, Manager of Domestic Animals
Tom Cook, Technosphere Supervisor
Gretchen Frost, Manager of Wilderness Biomes
Diane Kesselring, Supervisor of Field Crops and Crew Captain

Richard Lack, Medical Officer

Ramsay Roothoorp, Communications Officer/Water Systems
    Manager

Troy Turner, Director of Analytic Systems

Stevie van Donk, Marine Systems Specialist

We were photographed from the neck up, since we wouldn't don our crimson jumpsuits until the following day for the press conference, and then we went in to dinner and sat down to a mediocre-to-fairly-decent meal that provided more calories from fat than we'd get in a week inside. I was seated between Stevie and Gretchen, Stevie on my right, Gretchen to my left. Judy, who saw to every detail with the fanatical devotion of a top-flight manager and anal-retentive A-type personality who can never delegate or let go, had drawn up the seating plan and inscribed the place cards herself in a delicate tracery so flawless you would have thought she was a Japanese *shodō* master, and we were arranged round the table in a male/female pattern as if at a conventional dinner party. Which only made sense, not simply in terms of etiquette but physicality too.

E. was across the table from me, seated between Richard and Troy, and I tried not to stare, or even look at her for that matter, and what this sudden fascination with her was all about—excess of the moment, excess of testosterone, boredom with Judy or deep character flaw—I didn't have a clue. Call it pre-closure jitters. Of course I'd noticed her before, fantasized about her—I'd have to have been blind or impotent not to—but there was something about the moment and how alive she was with this new rapture singing in her veins that just took hold of me and wouldn't let go.

Think about it. If you were suddenly told you were going to be locked up for an extended period with four women, wouldn't you be attuned to their physical presence in a whole new way? (I'm speaking from the male perspective, though I'm sure the women were privately making their own assessments of the four of us men.) The fact was, I wouldn't have Judy anymore—or Rhonda Ronson, whom I'd met at this very bar a month ago—and I'd have to have somebody, wouldn't I? I wasn't signing on to enter a monastery. And E., her face aglow with the light of the candles in their golden globes and her hair shining and her breasts pushing at the fabric of her dress till you could see the outline of her nipples, became the foundation of a whole new way of thinking. But I couldn't look at her. I turned to Stevie, who was flying just as high as E., and we laughed over something, and then I turned to Diane, who'd gone deep inside herself and couldn't seem to rise above shop talk, and all the while I studiously avoided eye contact with Judy, who sat in pride of place at G.C.'s side at the head of the table, with Dennis, Little Jesus, right beside her.

* * *

I went home alone, parked in my usual space and climbed the stairs to my second-floor efficiency in the Residence 1 building on campus. It wasn't till I came through the door and glanced at the clock radio on the nightstand that I realized how early it was: just ten past eight. Mission Control—Judy and Dennis, that is— had orchestrated things so that the evening would be celebratory in a strictly controlled way in order to insure that we'd all be well rested for the public unveiling of the final roster, or The Eight, as Richard had begun calling us. I wanted a drink. The double vodka had long since dissolved in the stew of garlic bread, veal parmigiana and tossed salad in my gut and the red wine accompanying dinner had been so stingily poured it barely had an effect, plus, like all of us except maybe E. and Gretchen, I was working hard to surfeit my vices before closure shut them down (hence Judy, whose knock I was expecting any minute now). I kept a bottle of Stoli in the freezer and I poured myself a good healthy dose, marveling in a purely scientific way at how the viscid liquid silvered the sides of the glass—a beautiful sight, really, as exquisite as anything unfolding in nature—before easing it to my lips.

I held it in my mouth a moment, savoring the cold chemical caress of it against my tongue and palate, and then I crossed the room and lit a cigarette, though smoking was discouraged on campus and about as stupid and self-destructive an activity as anything our species has devised. I knew that. And I wasn't suicidal, or not particularly—no more than the next person. I'd smoked in college for the cool of it, the cigarette as prop and phallic symbol both, but I'd given it up junior year when I first began to think seriously about the environment and the future. My future, that is. I was going out with a girl then who didn't smoke and didn't like the taste of it on my lips and it didn't take much convincing to make me crumple up my pack of Larks, toss it in the nearest trash can and go cold turkey (that's the sort of thing I can do, believe me, because I've got an iron will when I want to bring it into play). But now, as of a month ago, I'd begun smoking again. Why? Because it was a vice and a vice that would be denied me inside where every molecule of the environment was reprocessed in a matter of weeks if not days and you were, quite literally, what you ate. And drank. And smoked. At first, the smoke had tasted bitter and harsh and I went around nursing a sore throat, but by the night of the annunciatory dinner I was up to a pack a day and that was beginning to seem insufficient.

Anyway, I had the drink in one hand and the cigarette in the other when Judy's knock came and I opened the door to let her in. Her face, usually so vulpine and sexy, didn't show much as she swept into the room, glancing first at the drink, then the cigarette, and finally at me. "What was that business with Dawn tonight?" She took the drink from my hand and knocked it back in a gulp, her eyes gone greedy suddenly. "If I didn't know better I'd think you were hot on her or something—"

I shrugged.

"And you're smoking now? You think that's a good idea?"

"No," I admitted, "it's never a good idea."

"Then why do it? Just because you won't be able to inside?" Instead of handing the glass back to me, she went to the freezer, extracted the bottle and poured herself a drink atop the dregs of mine. "And Dawn—she has a boyfriend, you know. Johnny Boudreau? Does that ring a bell? Not that it matters. Once you're inside—the two of you—I suppose you can do anything you want, or are you doing it already? Is that it?"

I didn't like her tone. This was a moment for celebration, con-gratulation, booze and smokes and sex. I didn't need this. "Right," I said, "we can do anything we want—just like the inmates at the penitentiary."

She shot me a look, then turned away to cap the bottle, jerk open the freezer door, and thrust it back inside. I had her shoul-ders to look at—shoulders bared in a spaghetti-strap cocktail dress in Terranaut red—and from the rigidity of the muscles there I could see how angry she was. "You," she said, pronouncing the pronoun so carefully it sounded like an accusation, "are one of the luckiest men on earth, one of the *four* luckiest"—and now she turned to me so I could assess the way the anger sat in her features, heavy there, gravid, anger that was all about two lingering kisses on Dawn Chapman's soft yielding lips and the fact that what we were about to do, the sex we were about to have, was complicated by betrayal and, even worse, the knowledge that it was going to have to end and end soon. "We could have picked Malcolm, you know." (Malcolm Burts was, realistically speaking, my only rival on the extended crew, a former PR man and weasel of the emo-tions who wasn't half what I am, but there you have it.)

"Yeah, I'm *sure*," I said, putting a little weight into it and watch-ing her face the whole time.

She looked less certain of herself all of a sudden, as if she'd been caught out, but that wasn't going to stop her. "You might not want to hear this but Jeremiah actually preferred him—and so did Dennis."

"Bullshit."

She took a sip of the drink and nodded her head like one of those souvenir dolls they give out at baseball games on promo night. "You owe me," she said. "I'm the one who stood up for you. I was like a canary in there, singing your praises—I mean chirping all day and all night, so don't you tell me—"

What this last bit signified, I couldn't say. I wasn't trying to tell her anything—she was the one trying to put something over here, laying down ground rules, boundaries defined in bright yel-low adhesive strips like no-parking zones, acting as if I'd already thrown her over when we both knew we weren't in love and never had been. Sex with Judy was all about getting closer to God—to G.C., anyway—and the delicious danger inherent in that. Whereas she might have been described uncharitably as uptight in her managerial capacity and especially the way she related to people she perceived as being subservient to her (i.e., the members of the crew), in bed she brought a good clean no-nonsense approach and she always got exactly what she wanted out of the transaction. And what she wanted was control. And she had it. Or *had* had it. Which was just what this little contretemps was all about. Okay. Fine. I went to her, took the glass out of her hand and pressed my lips to hers.

It was nice. It was always nice, as all vices are. But what I was thinking was that from here on there would be no stopping me. I was going inside. And once I was inside I could fuck Dawn Chapman, Diane Kesselring, Gretchen Frost and Stevie van Donk in succession—in the same bed on the same night and do it all over again in the morning—and there was nothing Judy or anybody else could do about it.

* * *

The press conference the next day was all business, the New Age trappings that had defined the first mission shunted into the background now, though not entirely. What we were projecting was scientific rigor, emphasizing the array of environmental and atmospheric studies we would undertake—living science—while at the same time reaffirming the ruling principle of closure absolute and unbreakable, i.e., the hook. *Four men, four women, locked up together!* And no, it wasn't a stunt. And it wasn't theater. But certainly those elements were present, because while we were trying to avoid the missteps of the first mission, we were at the same time actively seeking to recapture some of the public attention that had fallen away so catastrophically during the course of it. I don't know. Call it science-theater. Call it a dramatization of ecological principles under the guiding cosmology of Gaia, in which E1, the original world where we were all born and nurtured, could be viewed as a living organism negotiating the heavy cosmic seas—"Spaceship Earth," as Buckminster Fuller, one of our foundational thinkers, dubbed it. Everything connected, everything one. And E2, the new world, the first and only world apart from the original one, was to be our laboratory and our home, Gaia in miniature.

Of course, it was largely up to me, as Communications Officer, to present all this to the press, TV cameras whirring, flashbulbs flashing, my fellow Terranauts at my side with their gleaming faces, far-seeing eyes and the rigid posture of Marine Corps recruits, all of us squeezed into designer jumpsuits the color of tomato juice that had been created for us by the Hollywood costumer who'd come up with Marilyn Monroe's celebrated levitating dress, among other miracles. We stood behind our chairs at a long table set up twenty feet from E2's entrance chamber and the airlock it framed—a visible symbol of what we were committed to.

G.C., as our God and Creator and chairman of the board, kicked things off with a hortatory speech and a florid introduction of each of us. Once he'd had his say—*orotund*, that was the word that came to mind as he compared us to the gods of the Greek pantheon on the one hand and ecological grunts on the other—the baton passed to me. I looked out into the faces of the spectators—some three hundred or so, which was a decent crowd, really, since we still had just under a month to go till the main event and the elaborate closure ceremony Mission Control was planning—and felt emotional all over again. In that moment I was practically dripping the milk of human kindness, lactating like a nursing mother, and here were all my babies arrayed before me, and I loved—deeply, truly and sincerely loved—everybody seated beside me and everybody in the audience too, especially the TV cameramen. The way they crouched, hovered and shifted like some new form of terrestrial life, half-flesh, half-machine. This was my moment— *our* moment—and I made the most of it.

"Greetings, earthlings," I said, aping the robotic diction of Michael Rennie in *The Day the Earth Stood Still,* and was rewarded by an appreciative chuckle. I paused a beat, grinning widely, before continuing. "I want to say that while my fellow Terranauts and I are most appreciative of the self-generating ecosphere you've got here, a beautiful place, really, none finer, we are all of us eager to step through that airlock behind me and become the second set of human beings, the second *team,* to inhabit an ecosphere other than this one. We're all looking forward to setting forth on our journey into the unknown as surely as the Apollo astronauts who first set foot on the moon looked forward to theirs. The moon, however, if I might remind you, is two hundred forty thousand miles away, but the Ecosphere—E2—stands right here before you!"

I'd expected applause at this juncture, but none came except for a faint rasp of dry palms brought limply together under the long low gaze of the sun poised on the horizon (we'd chosen sunset as the appointed hour because of the way the engorged light played magically off the Ecosphere with its struts and pinnacles and the high flaming tower of the library cum observation deck a full ninety-five feet up off the desert floor). Yet this wasn't about applause, I reminded myself, and it wasn't about me. It was about getting information out, about piquing interest *(Four men, four women!),* and I shifted now to pedagogical mode, highlighting some of the numbers that could be found in the press release people had clipped to their notebooks or rolled up in a tube for convenient stowage.

The first number I gave them, perhaps the most significant of all, was 3.15. Three point one-five acres was the total extent of our new world, though the space extended to the stainless-steel tub of the basement underlying the entire structure and its eight-story height. The next number, by necessity an approximate one, was 3,800, the number of species, both plant and animal, seeded in the Ecosphere at its inception, two years and five months previous. Next? Twenty percent. That was the figure, again approximate, of species that had gone extinct during the Mission One closure. And yes, those species would be replaced or substituted for as we experimented with the introduction of new species altogether, one of the investigations in closed-systems ecology we were undertaking here involving what is called "species packing," in which more species than necessary are put in place in order to leave room for extinctions and study the mechanism by which one species replaces another or, more accurately, inhabits its niche. There were more statistics, of course, as you might expect, and I could have stood there at the lectern till midnight running through them all, but I kept it short by design—the intent here was to intrigue and inspire, not put people to sleep. (How did Judy put it when she was grilling me earlier in the day on the parameters of my speech? *We want to tantalize, not tranquilize.*) Mindful of her admonition, and in the way of moving things along too, because I was no amateur at this, I gave them two final figures: five and two. Five biomes (rain forest, savanna, desert, ocean and marsh) and two areas devoted to the crew, the Human Habitat (our apartments) and the Intensive Agriculture Biome (our food source).

"Before opening things up for your questions," I said, grinning vastly, "I'd like to refine the notion of Ecotechnics for you. That is, Total Systems Management as a way of preserving the ecosystem, not only of E2 but by extension of E1 as well. What we are after, what underlies all our experiments here at E2, is synergy, synergy between the ecology of technics and the technics of ecology!" I delivered this last in the way of summing up, but I could see from the flat look of puzzlement on the upturned faces before me that no one was quite getting it (*Read the brochure!* I wanted to scream at them, but didn't). The moment hung there. Finally, realizing I needed something more by way of an outro, I leaned into the microphone, brought my voice down to an electric whisper, and repeated our mantras: "Nothing in, nothing out. Four men, four women. Going where few have gone before."

* * *

There was the inevitable dinner afterward, but Mission Control had arranged this one (to be held at El Caballero, the only other decent, i.e., non-chain, restaurant in town) for the crew alone. No jumpsuits, no photographs. Tacos, burritos, margaritas. They wanted us to let our hair down and have this one evening, the last free evening till the days counted down to zero, for us to escape the pressure of public scrutiny and revel in our great good fortune.

That is, to get shit-faced drunk, dance to the canned mariachi music and either vomit or not, as the case might be. I was feeling pretty good, I must admit, more than a little high on the vibe of the audience and the questions, mostly positive and engaged, that kept coming at us till finally G.C. had to rise magnificently from his seat to thank everyone and call an end to the proceedings (*Read the brochure!*).

Music rattled through the speakers like a bus you can't get off of and I had one cigarette to my lips and another in the ashtray, though three of my fellow Terranauts had already sidled up to me to comment negatively on the habit, which, I assured them, I was well on the way to kicking. We'd eaten hugely, starting with quesadillas and taquitos for the table, then ranging through just about everything else on the menu, enchiladas, carnitas, tacos al carbón, biftec and chicken in mole sauce, the whole washed down with pitchers of watery margaritas and bottles of Dos Equis. Judy wasn't present—as I said, this was crew only—but still I stayed away from E. as much as possible, though of course with all my crewmates I was just as equable and sweet-faced and enraptured with every last detail of our lives and the mission as I could manage to be, and yet still, I didn't see any percentage in pressing things at this juncture. As it turned out, the eight of us seemed to have separated unconsciously into two groups by the end of the evening, the men fixed in place at the table and squinting blearily over the remains of the meal (flan for dessert, which, to my mind, existed only as a medium in which to snub out cigarette butts) while the women swept from the bar to the table to the ladies' room and back, their voices alternately rising in sudden explosions of laughter and falling to the breathy rasp of gossip.

Richard and Troy, across the table from me, conferred in low voices—talking sports, I think it was. They were both fairly well gone, Richard especially, both his palms coming into play as props for his chin, which must have weighed three or four times normal. Tom Cook, our resident geek, whose job it was to repair whatever might break down once we were inside, was waving an empty shot glass and boring me upright with a seminar on the working parts of the air handler units, and I was feeling a little pressure on my bladder because I'd drained one too many beers on top of a glass or two of the punchless margaritas that might as well have been lemonade for all the effect they had on me. I made some noises to qualify my response and was just about to rise from my seat and take a restorative trip to the men's, when I sensed a change come over the room, as if we'd all sent out feelers and they'd suddenly interconnected.

But let me back up here a minute. A word about Tom Cook. His crew nickname was Gyro, after the Disney character, he was my age—thirty-six—and he wore his hair in a military cut. What he was interested in was technics, and that was fine, that was just what we needed, but there were times—like this one—when he could be maybe just a wee bit of a howling *bore* and make you wonder how in god's name (or G.C.'s) you were going to survive two inspilling years under glass with him. His was the sort of personality they would have loved over at NASA, and there were times, not only on this night but on a whole host of others during the long months to come when I wished he *was* an astronaut rather than one of us and that they'd shot him way up there beyond the stratosphere and into the dimmest, coldest and eternally silent reaches of space.

In any case, despite my present circumstances and the urgency I was experiencing with regard to one of the most essential of somatic functions, I felt the change in the room before I was able to locate the source of it. *Click, click, click,* my congested mind ran through a series of visual processes, filtering out the locals, tourists and snowbirds, sectioning the room and then sectioning it again, until finally I saw what it was: Linda Ryu, standing rigidly at the bar in a dress the color of a saxophone, and trying, with a grim, hopeless look, to flag down the bartender. This was wrong, plain wrong, on a number of counts. First and foremost because it was out of bounds—this was a celebration for *Crew Only*—and secondly, and this was inextricably tied up with the first, because it made us feel bad. Thirdly, making us feel bad just added to the pressure that was being put on us not just in the present but far into the foreseeable future, which is precisely why the eight ersatz crewmembers had been excluded—and not just for our sake but for theirs as well, giving them an opportunity to go off and lick their wounds in private. But here she was, at the bar, looking not only grim but maybe even combative.

It was hard for me to say. I knew her least of all the members of the extended crew despite the countless hours we'd spent together in one bonding activity or another and I never could read her expression. She had one of those faces that seems clenched all the time, even when she's smiling, as if to relax for an instant would let all the demons of the universe flock into her soul. She believed in the rights of the mineral kingdom ("'We should be ethical, not merely economic, in our treatment of rocks,'" she once told me, quoting Roderick Nash), and she was a closet vegetarian. I say "closet" because on the ranch we were all expected to learn to slaughter and dress out our sheep, swine and poultry as a means of self-sufficiency and preparation for life inside, and while she participated along with the rest of us I always felt it was under duress. I never saw her actually insert a piece of meat in her mouth, whether it was served up roasted and sliced or buried in one of the predominantly vegetarian stews that had served as our communal meals at the ranch or on board The *Imago,* our research vessel. That was all right. I respected that. But there was a kind of kiss-ass deception in it too. As far as looks were concerned, she wasn't unattractive, but maybe a bit on the short side and a pound or two heavier than she might have been—squat, that is, at least to my taste, though I know Dennis had had a thing with her for a while there.

What do I want to say? There are winners and losers in this life, from the crack babies and Calcutta street urchins to the millionaire sons of millionaires and the movie star daughters of movie stars, and while it's not right and it's not fair, the fact is that everybody, from bottom to top, is competing for space and resources through every O_2-laden breath they draw. Go ask Darwin. Or Spencer. Or Stephen Jay Gould, for that matter. Linda Ryu—and I'm sorry to have to make this judgment, though Mission Control had already made it for me—was one of the losers. What kept me there watching her as the bartender finally connected with her and brought her what looked to be a Manhattan in a stemmed glass, was hard to explain, though Schadenfreude might have had something to do with it. I didn't have anything against her, or not particularly, but her presence amongst us was a kind of violation of the rules we'd lived by as a team and some part of me wanted to see her get her comeuppance. I'd heard that the excluded eight were having their own (consolatory) dinner up the street at Alfano's and I'd been looking forward to wandering up there and laying a little false sincerity on people like Malcolm Burts after we were done here. Had they packed it in early? Was that what this meant? Or was she a loose cannon?

"What are you looking at?" Gyro had broken off in the middle of a surprisingly bitter critique of the condition of the vibration isolators in Unit Two and turned to glance over his shoulder in the direction of the bar.

"You see who's here?"

"No, who?"

"Komodo." (This was Linda's crew nickname, a morph of the original, "Dragon," which was short for "Dragon Lady," a designation we all came to feel was faintly racist, since Linda wasn't of Chinese descent but Korean, and besides, she was anything but a femme fatale; somehow, we settled on Komodo, as in Komodo dragon, the big deadly lizard of the Indonesian archipelago. She seemed to accept it, even to like it, and if she was in the mood, she'd bare her teeth for you and let out with a low reptilian hiss. My own moniker, in case you're wondering, is Vodge, short for Vajra, the thunderbolt that Indra, Indian god of rain and thunderstorms, hurls down at the earth. I won't hazard a guess as to whether it fits or not because that's the province of my crewmates, but it does speak to power and I like that.)

Gyro's face hardened. "What's she doing here? This is crew only, doesn't she know that?" Then he answered his own question: "Of course she does. What does she think, Mission Control's going to change their mind?"

In that moment Linda lifted the glass and drained her Manhattan or Rob Roy or whatever it was in a long single swallow, set the glass down on the bar and looked straight at me. Instinctively, I tried for a smile, but when she pushed herself back from the bar and started across the room for me, the smile died before it was born. We both watched her, Gyro and I, as she made her unsteady way through the crowd on a pair of high heels the same color as her dress, everybody aware of her now, the music rising up to lift her under the elbows and deposit her right there in front of us. Where she stood a minute, unsteady still, though she was no longer in motion. "Hi, Linda," I said, and now I was smiling, despite the hardness of the moment and the pressure on my bladder. "Come to join the party?"

Her eyes were flecked with red, the lids swollen as if she'd been crying, and she had been, of course she had. "Don't give me that shit," she said, and then she shot a glance at Gyro, "—and you either."

"Shit?" I said. "What shit?"

"You knew all along, didn't you? Admit it. You're the snake on this crew. You're the one that reported directly to who, to Little Jesus, to *Judy*—"

I wasn't taking all that much pleasure in the moment, that's what I decided, what I told myself, and it wasn't my job to console sore losers or even, if you want to know the truth, be nice to them. *Get over it,* that was what I was thinking. *Move on. Get a life.* I shrugged.

"You wanted Stevie in there, you wanted *Dawn.* And you, you—"

I didn't get to hear the rest of the accusation or attack or whatever you'd like to call it, because I rose up out of my seat, turned my back on her and headed for the men's, which I should have done five minutes earlier and avoided this whole confrontation. She shouted something at my back, something I didn't quite catch, and I didn't turn to look back till I reached the hallway that led to the restrooms. I was in the shadows now, out of the picture, but Linda wasn't. She was still there, standing over our table in the cone of yellowish light spilling from one of the recessed fixtures overhead, nailed to the cross of her own sorrow and frustration. Troy and Richard stared dumbfounded at her from the opposite side of the table even as Gyro rose to produce a series of comforting gestures that never managed to quite connect with her, and E., her face pale and eyes wild, rushed to her, to embrace her and rock with her in place and then finally lead her away.

* * *

At the risk of trying your patience, there's one more dinner I have to get through here in order to set things up properly—the fact is, when I look back on that pre-closure period, all I see is dinners, dinners I was to reconstruct dish by dish, bite by bite, when I was inside. At night especially. Lying there exhausted in my bed, unable to sleep, the earth musk of E2 wrapped around me like a blanket, I'd stare at the ceiling while my stomach contracted over a bolus of nothing, feeling like a prisoner of war subjected to the slow starvation that eats away your body fat till there's nothing left but muscle and organ meat, then starts in on that. Our diet was high-fiber, high-nutrition, but low on sugar, fat and protein, i.e., the things that make life worth living. Did I dream of the Big Mac, with its two beef patties, slabs of American cheese, special sauce, lettuce, pickles, onions and its three-tier sesame bun? Absolutely. Every night and every day. And I didn't simply visualize it but mentally touched it and smelled it and tasted it too, reliving the times I'd stood in line at the hard plastic counter under the aegis of the yellow arches, popped open the paperboard box and bit in. This was what we came to call food porn and it was more elemental than any erotic fantasy. I dreamed of éclairs, vanilla fudge ice cream, lobster in drawn butter, peanut M&M's, filet mignon, heavy cream, raspberries, bouillabaisse. Potato chips. Doritos. Hot dogs on spongy buns with heaps of sweet pickle relish, mustard, catsup and chopped onion. Coconut macaroons. Good god. Just saying it—*coconut macaroons*—is enough to make me mist over even now.

But the dinner. This was the pre-closure dinner, a catered

affair staged at Mission Control itself, what Richard began calling "The Last Supper" as soon as it was announced and which we all immediately adopted as a suitably ironic reference point (though for my part, and E.'s too, I think, the irony was a cover for something else altogether, something more genuine and sentimental). The dinner was at eight, exactly twelve hours before we would enter the Ecosphere for good, and we were instructed, both by Judy and G.C., to restrict our caloric intake so as to avoid giving the impression that we were anxious about our ability to sustain ourselves come tomorrow. Behind the scenes, once the party was over and the servers were clearing up, we had the green light to heap up our plates and gorge till our cells were replete and food lost its meaning. All I remember of the gustatory part of it, really, was the superabundance, the endless trays of every sort of delicacy imaginable, the Niagara of champagne and the canapés circulating on trays held aloft by female servers wearing armbands of Terranaut red.

Celebrities were there to see us off. Perhaps not the full slate that had turned up for Mission One closure—no Timothy Leary or Woody Harrelson this time, but James Lovelock was busily making the rounds in his shining spectacles and fussily knotted red tie, and Dan Old Elk, who was preparing to publicly hang himself by hooks inserted in his pectoral muscles the following morning by way of propitiating the spirits of the ancients, circulated in full regalia. Beyond that, beyond the press and various hard scientists G.F.'s money had attracted to the project to prop up its bona fides, there was a smattering of Buddhist monks drifting about in their tangerine robes, a couple of recognizable movie stars of the second tier putting on a glow for the cameras and another of our foundational thinkers, William Burroughs, leaning darkly into one of the potted plants and raspily lecturing a pair of acolytes in hipster black.

By the way, if Burroughs' presence surprises you, it shouldn't. As I've said, we were trying to emphasize the way our new technics melded art and ecology in a synergistic flow, and Burroughs' books—especially *Naked Lunch* and the cut-up texts like *The Soft*

Machine and *Nova Express*—helped push our thinking in new directions. He was always making pronouncements about space and the future and how humans should evolve to leave the planet in "astral dream bodies," which might have had just a bit too much of the taint of New Age woo-wooism about them but spoke to what we were doing nonetheless. Burroughs was an amigo of G.C. from the bad old days before G.C. found his true calling as our leader and chief visionary and it was Burroughs' insistence on the Ecospherians' need for a companion primate that prompted Mission Control to include a troop of galagos in the original ark's list of species included in E2. And they were still there, awaiting us, their hoots and mating calls echoing off the spaceframe of the glassed-in structure that lay just across the courtyard, lit from within on this night and awash in the beams of the klieg lights the maintenance crew had set up earlier in the day.

We stood around in our red jumpsuits, daintily nibbling at canapés and taking measured sips of Mumm's Cordon Rouge, each of us the focal point of his or her own circle of admirers, famous now, famous in the moment, and soon to be more famous still. I liked the attention. I'm as susceptible to adulation as anyone, I'll admit it, but as the evening wore on I began to experience a sinking feeling, the sort of thing anybody goes through on the night before a trip. I might have been chatting up one well-wisher or another about our hopes and expectations or fending off a reporter's sly insinuations about the prospect of sexual hanky-panky inside, but my mind was elsewhere. Had I packed everything I'd need? Was I forgetting anything? Toothpaste, floss, my electric shaver? Would three toothbrushes be enough? Five pairs of shoes? A dozen T-shirts? And books. Yes, there was a library inside, but the titles tended to reinforce our training and needs (Bion's *Experiences in Groups;* Mumford's *Technics and Civilization*), and I was afraid of downtime, of being bored, and so I'd packed the inside flap of one suitcase entirely with fiction—short stories, fantasies, domestic dramas, scenarios that would take me out of the new world and back into the old.

I must have looked uncomfortable, because at some point toward the two-hour mark, Judy came to rescue me (after covering herself by making the rounds of each group in succession, doling out smiles and handclasps along the way). "Hi," she beamed, taking hold of my arm to pull me away from the pair of female reporters I was still capable of holding the party line with, excusing herself by claiming some last-minute (minor) emergency. She was looking good, incidentally, in a pink-and-black off-the-shoulder dress, her hair up in a French braid and her heels elevating her till her eyes were fixed in the same orbit as mine. Sexy eyes. Eyes that told me just exactly what she wanted—what she expected, demanded—even before she said a word.

"What?" I whispered. "Not here?"

We were at the far end of the room now, poised in front of the big semicircular window that presented an illuminated view of E2 for the gratification of partygoers, crew and support staff alike. Her eyes jumped round the room to see if anyone was watching us, then came back to mine. "I can't get away later—Jeremiah's hosting an after-party at the house. For Burroughs and"—she named an actor—"and I don't know who-all."

Surfeit your vices. Wasn't that what I'd been telling myself for the past month? "I'm listening," I said.

She unhooked her arm from mine, let her eyes rove the room, then flashed a smile and threw her head back to deliver a fake laugh by way of diversion. Then she pulled away, as if to hustle off and join another group—the hostess, circulating—but hesitated long enough to whisper, "The restroom at the end of the hall, not the public ones—the executive one?"

I couldn't help myself. My blood was up. And now I was the one scoping out the room—was anyone watching? No. Or not that I could see anyway.

"Five minutes," she said, and then she was gone.

I remember talking with somebody about something—and seeing E., with three or four men gathered round her as she lectured on the fine points of our coming confinement, a single earnest groove of righteousness caught between her eyebrows—but I was aflame now and nothing in that room held any meaning for me. The only thing that mattered at that point was Judy, the last act with Judy, and it wasn't going to play out in the familiar precincts of my apartment or the Saguaro Motel out on Route 77, but here at Mission Control, right under the nose of G.C. himself. Was that exciting? Did it add spice, make the prospect of what we were about to do in the executive restroom sizzle in my bloodstream like the Triple X Atomic Bomb hot sauce at El Caballero? Let's just say that I've always been quick to arousal and that while I was making small talk with that somebody, whoever it was, I was practically splitting the seams of my jumpsuit.

The party was still in full swing, though a few of the guests, sated on the exotic fare served up that night, had begun to drift toward the hallway and the elevator. Which made it difficult for me. The public restrooms were out the door and to the left, and I made a feint in that direction because Dennis, his hair freshly greased, was just making his way back from the men's, and though we didn't exchange words, we gave each other a nod of commiseration—all that champagne—and once he'd passed I waited there as if debating whether to proceed or not while a pair of inebriated strangers ambled by and the elevator doors slid open and closed on a clutch of chattering women and their trunk-like purses, then I made an about-face and hurried down the hall in the opposite direction.

I found the door unlocked and the lights dimmed. There was a vase of fresh flowers on the counter, a Persian carpet on the floor. A urinal. Two stalls. Mirror over the twin sinks. The flowers— red roses, what else?—seemed to have no scent at all, not unless you were to bend to them and take a good hard sniff, which I was tempted to do, but resisted. There was no sign of Judy. A wave of desolation crashed over me: had I heard her right? Five minutes, wasn't that what she'd said? I looked at my watch. It had been ten minutes, ten at least. Had she come and gone? Given up on me?

All at once I saw the next two years play out before me, one heel-dragging day giving way to the next, no theater, no concerts, no dining out, no sex, or at least not with Judy or Rhonda, and who knew how E. would respond, if at all? Or Stevie? The other two, Diane and Gretchen—forgive me—were pretty much out of the picture, desperation time only. I caught a glimpse of myself then in the extreme view, a cartoon figure whose commitment was more to himself than the project, shackled by the grasping need for public acclaim, for fame and glory and all the deserts that came with them, and that made the prospect of what was coming in less than ten short hours so terrifying all I could think of was running, getting in the car and vanishing into the vast biomes of E1, the real and singular world, the one that mattered. I was a prisoner in the dock, caught in the moment when the jury pronounces its verdict: guilty as charged.

But then there was a sound, the softest click of the lock of the near stall, and Judy was standing there before me, naked. "Jesus," I said, "I thought—" and all the blood rushed back into me again.

"Did you lock the door?" she whispered.

I hadn't. And I knew I should, knew I was risking everything, but the swing in me from deflation to elation, from existential despair to hot hard animal lust, made me take hold of her, rough and needy and beyond caring—until she shoved me away. "No," she said, and she took a step back. "The door."

We've all been in this situation before—or not exactly and precisely *this* situation, maybe, but you know what I mean. Precoital. In the heat of the moment. Demands made, demands met. I lurched away from her, already working the zipper of my jumpsuit, and snapped the lock shut. In the next moment we were down on the carpet, she naked beneath me, the jumpsuit shucked like a snakeskin, my thinking mind gone into hiding while the amygdala took over. Judy. This wasn't about love, it never had been, but I loved her in that moment. Twenty past ten, March 5, 1994, nine hours and forty minutes before closure. Believe that, if you believe nothing else.

She was on top, her preferred position, riding the springs of her calves and the thrust of my hips, when we first heard a noise outside the door. We were slow to hear it. The scientists of sex have described the vascular and hormonal changes that come over the body in the act of coition, the most surprising of which is the way in which the sense of touch overrides the other senses to the extent that a mating couple loses auditory and sometimes even visual awareness. We were distracted, slow to hear, slow to react, but that sound was the scrape of soles on the natural wood flooring of the hallway and it was followed by the rattling chime of keys removed from a pocket and picked through selectively. The final sound in the sequence was the sharp grating of a key, *the* key, inserted in the lock.

By the time the door pushed open and the lights went up full, we were both in the far stall, Judy perched on the seat with her naked legs pulled up to her chest and I standing on one leg beside her, working the lightweight merino twill of the jumpsuit back up over my foot. What we heard next were the muted sounds of a human being interacting with the features of a washroom, private sounds: a sigh, the release of intestinal gas, the undoing of a zipper and then the stream itself, thunderous against the back wall of the porcelain receptacle. Judy's eyes fell away into their sockets. We both held our breath. And we both knew without doubt just who it was standing there ten feet away and relieving himself in a mighty hydraulic rush: Jeremiah, G.C. himself. What else could we have expected?

Judy was naked still, still perched on the toilet seat, her—how shall I put it?—her functional parts exposed, but there was nothing there to excite me now. I was calculating. If we'd been caught in flagrante delicto—if we were going to be caught—it would almost certainly mean my expulsion from the team, though Mission Control would be hard-pressed to explain that, given how short the time was. They'd say I'd suddenly become ill, seriously ill, but to spare my feelings—the feelings of the team member concerned—they would withhold details. And who'd replace me? Malcolm Burts, no doubt. I had a vision of him, of his self-satisfied smirk and his strut that was like a parody of masculinity, and then I was pushing open the stall door and causally closing it behind me, saying, "Oh, Jeremiah—you gave me a start."

"Who's that?" G.C. peering over one shoulder, Vonnegut-tall, sixty and looking ten years younger. "Oh, Ramsay, it's you." And then: "What do you think of the send-off? You see the way the press is eating it up? And Bill, isn't he a hoot?"

I kept my cool, nodding in agreement, and then I was at the sink, washing up, washing my hands of the whole business—I was going inside and he wasn't, nor was Judy, and that was what I wanted now, I was never more sure of it. "Yeah, Bill was great. And you were great too. That welcoming speech—what did you call E2, 'the cyclotron of life sciences'? That's good. Real good. Mind if I borrow it?"

No, he didn't mind, not at all. We were on the same team. And if God evicted Adam from the Garden of Eden for the sin of disobedience—or, as some people maintain, for getting down and dirty with Eve—my own deity, G.C., put an arm round my shoulder and walked me out the door and down the hallway to where my admirers awaited me against a cornucopian display of earthly riches. And in the morning, the glorious morning I'd been awaiting for nearly three years now, he would lead me right on up to the airlock of the New Eden, the one that had sprung from the forefront of his mind, and appoint me my rightful place inside.

Linda Ryu

I don't know what to say. But everything stinks, that's for sure. I want to tell you I used to live in a world of hope and now I live in a world of hate, but I don't mean to come off as a whiner, so I won't. And I won't play the race card because I really don't think that had anything to do with it, though look at the hair color of the women they chose and you tell me. Mission Control might as well have been curating an exhibit called "Blondes of the Biomes," and was it any accident that the four of us rejects had hair that was either ethnic black or a shade of brown so dark it might as well have been? Dawn was right on the mark when she said Mission Control was more concerned with appearance than accomplishment, even though we both knew she was only trying to make me feel better. Which wasn't happening. Not the day they dropped the bomb on me or the night of The Last Supper or all the days in between either.

But let me tell you something about Dawn and what she owes me, and this is just one of a hundred things I could bring up. The incident I'm thinking about took place in Belize, maybe two or three months after Mission One closure. Mission Control—G.C. and Judy, I mean—had us crewing the research vessel, taking diving lessons, recruiting specimens and doing basic underwater maintenance, like barnacle removal. We ate communally, slept where we dropped, bonded. I want to say the days were idyllic, sun, surf, the clarity of the water that was like looking through a department store window even at thirty feet down, and they were, I can't deny it, though Mission Control worked us hard and got what they wanted out of us, the way any cult will. And we were a cult, no different from any hippie-dippy commune except that we had science on our side, or thought we did. The way it worked was simple, because this was no democracy: G.C. ruled, G.C. saw and created and set us in motion, and Judas—and later Dennis, Little Jesus—cracked the whip. Not that we needed it all that much—the carrot they dangled in front of us, the dream of inhabiting a new world, no less, and the fame that came with it, was enough to keep us on the straight and narrow till we were so exhausted we were all unconscious by nine o'clock at night.

One afternoon, after a bunch of us had spent six hours or so with an orbital sander and a bucket of marine varnish, Diane, who was crew chief, decided we'd take the rest of the day off and hunt up some lobster and reef fish for a feast. We only had one dinghy, and so it was decided that the larger group, which included Stevie, Vodge and two of the other men, would drop Dawn and me off on a very promising tidal island while they moved on to a spot Stevie had located earlier that week, thus doubling our chances of success, or so the reasoning went. That was all right with me. Dawn and I had gotten close and we worked well together, we were a pair, while I still had problems with some of the others. Stevie for one. Vodge for two. And I won't bother with three, four, five and six at this point. Just let me say I was thinking it would be a relief to be away from everybody for an hour or two.

The island was a pale hump of surf-pounded coral that rose out of the sea like the back of a whale. It was no more than a foot or so above water when they dropped us off with our snorkels, flippers, slings and an inner tube fitted out with a rubber lining to hold our catch and keep it out of the water so we didn't attract any undue attention from reef sharks. Troy Turner worked the tiller, cruising in on a silent spreading V, and we jumped out of the boat, the water lapping at our shins, so warm it was like stepping into a Jacuzzi. It must have been around four-thirty or so. Winter. I remember commenting on the sun, a big pink ball sitting just over the water and framing the dinghy and its single white sail as it caught the breeze and ran off toward the horizon. Dawn smiled at me. She was brown all over, all of us used to sunbathing topless and sometimes bottomless too.

"Well, what are we waiting for?" she said, spitting in her mask and rinsing it in the water before fitting it over her head. "Isn't this the hour the lobsters start crawling out of their holes?"

"Bet I get more than you," I said, smiling back.

"Bet you don't."

It became a kind of contest, a friendly one, and though we didn't say it aloud I think beyond that we were both unconsciously working to top whatever total the crew in the dinghy might bring back. We had sixteen people to feed aboard ship and here was the sea, ready to give us what we needed if we were skillful enough to go get it. (If this sounds like play, I guess on some level it was—the kind of thing kids do when they build a clubhouse on a vacant lot, then raid their parents' kitchens to whip up a catch-as-catch-can meal before tumbling into their sleeping bags, an ad hoc gang, secret society, members only. And I was a member. And so was Dawn. And that meant the world to us.)

I don't have to tell you that no matter how warm the water it's not enough to sustain your body temperature if you stay in it long enough. We lobstered for maybe an hour, and I managed to spear a pair of dogtooth snappers with my sling too, and then we were back on the island, which at this point was no longer an island. The water was waist-deep now, and though we weren't chilled, not yet, we both looked to the horizon where the sun was sinking low, ready to put an end to the adventure. I looked at Dawn. She held the tether of the inner tube loosely in one hand, the lobsters—twenty or so, a nice haul—lying there placidly while the fish quietly bled into them. "That was amazing, huh?" I said.

"We hit the jackpot, didn't we?" She was smiling, exhilarated by the hunt and the way nature had provided for us, the moment—and I'm being sincere here—as full of enchantment as probably anything we'd ever experienced. But a breeze came up, something we noticed only gradually, and the tide kept rising till it was at breast level and we both looked off in the direction the dinghy had taken, but there was nothing there. Dusk thickened. The water rose till it was lapping at our shoulders, all the worse for me, since Dawn was half a foot taller.

"What do you think," she said after a while, "they forget about us or what?"

She was trying to sound amused, as if the idea was so preposterous it could only be a joke, but I couldn't help hearing a hint of panic in her voice. She was afraid of sharks. Not that I'm not, or wasn't, but her fear was out of proportion. We all went skinny-dipping off the rail of the boat at night, the whole crew, but she wouldn't join us. Bull sharks were the reason. And she was right—bull sharks, which could grow to eleven and a half feet long and five hundred pounds, swept in on the shallows at dusk and were responsible for most attacks in these waters—but she was wrong too, more wrong than right. The chances of an attack were something like one in eleven point five million and we all quoted the statistics to her—teased her, ragged her, and this was part of the bonding process too—but she just shook her head and ignored us. Now we were in the water, just the two of us, it was getting dark and if the body fluids of those dead snappers were going to leach through the bleached-out rubber tubing and into the water, that was something neither of us wanted to think about.

I won't criticize Dawn. She's a good person and a good teammate. And we were in a tight situation where her irrational fear became more and more rational until it began to affect me too—and if I hadn't put a stop to it neither of us might have survived. She panicked. I mean, she lost it in a major way—so much so I've never seen anything like it, before or since. She was like somebody drowning and trying to take her rescuer down with her. It got worse. At some point we could no longer touch bottom and then we were dog-paddling and clinging to the inner tube, trying to stay over the island so they could find us, and she was babbling and sobbing and thrashing till she could have attracted every shark in the ocean. "Dawn," I kept saying, "Dawn, it's going to be okay," but all she did was whimper. And thrash.

It was a long hour and fully dark before that sail appeared like a ghost in the night and we heard Ramsay calling out to us, and Dawn embarrassed herself. She lost control of her bowels, overturned the inner tube and cost us our whole catch, and when it came in range she clawed at the keel of that boat till her fingernails were torn and she just couldn't stop sobbing, not even with everybody watching, with a pair of flashlights like hot eyes on her and everybody safe, safe and secure, teammates all.

I have strength. I'm a rock. I'm the one that has the ability to remain calm in the face of danger—anything that happens, any shit that comes down the line—and yet I'm on the outside, and Dawn, weepy Dawn, is on the inside. You tell me: does that make sense?

* * *

Ramsay's another issue. He struts around like he's the original man himself when in reality he's the serpent, the seducer, the liar and cheat and rotten core of the whole crew. I have it on good authority (Diane's) that he's Dennis and Judy's spy, feeding his poisonous little assessments—and every shred of gossip, true or not—back to them. He has it in for me, I know it. And while I can't say for sure, my guess is he was the one behind the whole Dragon Lady thing. Yes, G.C. decreed that we should all have crew nicknames, as a way of binding us together, and of course you couldn't pick your own but had to rely on the higher consciousness of the group to give you what you wanted—and what you wanted, at the very least, was dignity. He was Vajra, the lightning bolt. Dawn was Eos. Diane was Meadowlark. And me? Dragon Lady. How annihilating. How shitty. Truly. If they'd wanted to alienate me they couldn't have done a better job of it. And I'll call out Dawn here too because she was so airheaded she didn't even get it—*I think it's kind of cool,* she told me, *don't you?*—until I clued her in and she in turn clued the rest of them and they all got together and abbreviated it to Dragon (and then, getting cuter still, to Komodo), as if that would make me feel any better. And yes, I was a good sport about it—what choice did I have?—and bared my teeth and showed my claws and hissed on command. Talk about team spirit, huh?

And then there's Dennis. He got to me when I was down over the Dragon Lady business and took advantage of my weakness and my naïveté because I thought I was the one in charge, using him to get close to G.C. and Judas when all he was doing was going for a random fuck or two. Or three. We lasted—were an item—for maybe two weeks, if that. I didn't even like him, but when he came on to me one night after some of the crew got together at El Caballero, I was flattered. He was my height, or close enough, and I liked it that when we danced that first time (slow-danced, and who was it? Sade, I think) his body seemed a perfect fit, unlike when I danced with some of the other crew, like Gyro, whose breastbone dug into the top of my head and whose lean horsey body was a total mismatch, though truth be told, I actually liked him and thought he was one of the people, along with Dawn, who was sincerely sorry I'd been thrown under the bus. "Linda," Dennis had breathed, right in my ear, right at the level of his lips and my external auditory organ, "you are just so hot."

"Really?" I said, swaying with him as the tune slid through its slinky arrangement and we pressed our groins more tightly together. "I didn't think you even noticed me."

"Oh, yeah," he said. "You above all the others. You've got"—and here I was listening with every fiber of my attention, wanting him to pour a whole gallon of syrup right into me—"I don't know. But you're hot. You've got such a great, I don't know *shape,* figure, whatever, and your lips—"

This was a signal to kiss and I turned my face to his and the moment clung to me, clung to us both, or so I thought, and though it wasn't what I wanted I have to admit I was calculating too, working him, and I let him take me home. I could leave it at that, but since the whole shitty crew and Mission Control and everybody else has so amply demonstrated just what they think of me, what's to hold me back? Fear of being left out of Mission Three? What a joke. Mission Three seems like it's a hundred centuries away and here I'm left to drudge along on the support staff, picking up everybody's leftovers like what, one of the untouchables in India or something. So know this: Dennis was pretty much a zero in bed. He took forever to get hard and kept apologizing over how much he'd had to drink and he wasn't tender or sexy or even remotely a turn-on so that when he finally did get inside me I didn't feel a thing. Really, I would have been better off masturbating.

But I fucked him again. And again after that. To my shame. Because I thought I was helping my cause, when in fact he was just using me and the true snake on the crew—Mr. Vodge Ramsay Roothoorp—was feeding him nothing but poison about me and Sally McNally and everybody else he wanted to eliminate. And yes, I crashed that tacky haute Mexican dinner reserved *For Crew Only* and made a spectacle of myself, and could anybody blame me?

Our own dinner, spaghetti and meatballs, tossed salad, spumoni, *separate checks,* was a kind of insult, a slap in the face with a wet bar rag that had LOSER written all over it. (And if anybody thought Mission Control was going to pick up the tab for the also-rans' dinner, they were out of their minds, but please stay on and break your back ten hours a day for five hundred bucks a month so you can support the project and the *Final Eight,* who'll go where only eight others have ever gone in the history of humankind and you too, if you play your cards right and show enough dedication and a smarmy ability to suck up to Mission Control in an appropriately reverential way, can be a Terranaut!) Do I sound bitter? Again, who could blame me? To be relegated to *that*? When I had it all over everybody else, a prime candidate, if not *the* prime candidate?

My fellow deportees tried to make the best of it, Malcolm Burts rising from the table to give an extempore speech so laughable it was sick about how we could all hold our heads up and be proud to be part of E2 and essential cogs—he actually said that, *essential cogs*—in the greater marriage of the technospere and ecosphere. "We're all disappointed," he said, pausing to look stupidly round the table. "We'd be lesser people if we weren't. But I'll see you all inside in two short years! Are you with me?" He held up his glass and a few people—Sally McNally, Tricia Berner, *the actress*—actually shouted "Hear! Hear!" and brought their hands together in some kind of deluded effort at convincing themselves. Me? I was humiliated. Worse than humiliated, I was furious. And no, I don't want to get into auto-psychoanalysis here, but maybe I was a touch more sensitive and uncertain of myself than some people who might not have had to live with overachieving immigrant parents and weren't saddled with kinky black hair that frizzed up after every dive or even on a rainy day for shit's sake and who didn't look like a balloon sculpture in a two-piece. So I'm sorry. I went to their shitty dinner.

I'm drunk when I get there. The place is packed, some sort of sporting event flowing across the oversized TVs propped up behind the bar, and at first I don't see them, wondering if they've already finished up their big exclusive celebration and gone off someplace else, someplace cozier, to throw down shots and stroke each other over how amazing they all are. I'm wearing my new dress—my newest dress, worried and vacillated over and finally purchased on my father's credit card by way of making a statement at my interview, a statement, I sadly reflect, that wound up being made only to myself in the full-length mirror on the door of the closet in my apartment. The bartender, neo-Mexican, with a little pencil mustache and eyes that jump to his hands and the blender and the money on the bar, ignores me. If I was hurting when I came in and feeding that hurt with a kind of rage I didn't even know I was capable of, this is the final straw. What am I, invisible? I'm not especially assertive, and maybe that was something Mission Control held against me, but now, without thinking twice, I slam the flat of my hand down on the bar between the elbows of two jerks staring at the TV screen as if it's the Book of Revelation, and the sound of it, the violence of it, seems to wake everybody up. Next thing I know I have a Manhattan in my hand. Next thing after that, it's gone.

That's when I see them, just the men, the four of them, easing back in their chairs over the remains of their self-congratulatory feast, and I lock eyes with Ramsay. The room seems to shrink down till it contains only the two of us, the walls closing in, the ceiling dropping—it's like looking through a periscope. I have no plan in mind. I'm not being the cautious eager-to-please daughter of an M.D. mother and an M.D. father. I'm just reacting. Like when you see the yellow jacket that's just stung you buzzing around on the pavement and you bring your foot down on it.

"Hi, Linda," he says, giving me a big phony oh-so-bemused smile, as if I've come to get his autograph or something, just another tourist, another *fan*. "Come to join the party?"

I say, "Don't give me that shit," and he says, "What shit?," and I level on Gyro too, though as I say, I have nothing against him really except that he's in and I'm out.

I want to be strong. But it's Ramsay, Ramsay as ringleader and smirking symbol of all that soul-crushing business, just getting up from the table and turning his back on me as if I'm beneath even acknowledging or taking two minutes out of his precious celebration to try to make things better or even defend himself, that defeats me. Everybody's watching me, everybody in the restaurant, locals and tourists and the rest of the crew too, and I can't help myself. I break down the way Dawn did that day in the Caribbean, just sobbing till my ribs feel like they're going to cave in and I don't know what I would have done if Dawn hadn't come hurrying out of the shadows to wrap her arms around me and put a stop to it all.

* * *

I'd been angry at Dawn, really upset with her, but I see now that it was all my own doing. I was jealous, that was all. Jealous and hurt. I wasn't happy for her and couldn't be unless I was happy for both of us, and that was no longer in the cards. And I turned on her, lashed out at her in all sorts of inappropriate ways, but she was my true friend and she showed it that night. She took me straight through the restaurant and out the back door, stopping only to snatch up her purse and sweater from where she'd left them at the end of the table that was strewn still with bitten-off taquitos, bottles, glasses, cigarette butts. There was a moon, I remember that. Because I gazed up at it in the parking lot, swaying under the influence of too much alcohol—and we Koreans can drink, believe me, so it must have been plenty—and I say, "Look, Dawn. Look at the moon, full moon, let's howl. You want to howl?"

She's all practical, though. And if she's had too much to drink, which I suspect is the case, she doesn't show it. She's mothering me, befriending me, showing me that no matter what, she's going to be there for me, inside or out. "Did you bring your bicycle?" she asks. "Because we can put it in the backseat of my car—"

"You mean *my* car." She signed over the papers that afternoon and the plan was she'd leave it in the lot out front of the apartments the night before closure and hand over the keys then. She wished it could be sooner. But with all the thousand details coming down on her she was going to need it right till the last minute.

A moment creaks by, narrow as the crack under a door that just won't stay shut. "Did you?" she repeats.

I'm drunk. My face is a mess. I'd brought my bike, of course I'd brought it—how else would I have gotten there?—but I don't want to tell her that because I'm being obstinate. I want her to wheedle, want her to prove how much she cares and then prove it again. On some level, and it's crazy, I know, I'm waiting for her to say she's thought it through and decided to step aside so I can take her place—for the good of the mission—because we both know in our hearts that's the way it's meant to be.

Somebody goes farting up the street on a dirtbike all *wheeee!* and *blat blat blat!* There's the light of the moon, her face swaying above mine. A tight face. Tight cheekbones, strong jaw. Her hair catches the light from the restaurant behind us, drinking up the neon blue of the El Caballero sign till it looks like she's wearing a helmet. "No matter," she says, slurring the *t*'s, "I'll give you a ride home, okay? And tomorrow we can take the car and come back for your bike"—she hesitates, looking beyond me to the alley out back of the restaurant as if she'd spot it in the shadows there. "If you want, I mean."

I don't remember getting in the car, but I must have, because next thing I know we're at her place, which is already awash with cardboard boxes, as if she's known all along. Time shifts on me a bit, and then we're sitting elbow-to-elbow at the counter of the kitchenette, blowing into cups of hot liquid. Mine's coffee, hers chicken broth out of the can, with a squeeze of lemon. She's giving up coffee. Or trying to. There are exactly two coffee bushes inside, and the Mission One crew was only able to grow enough beans to provide a single cup for each crewmember every other week.

"Don't worry," I say, and I'm slurring my words too, "I'll drink an extra cup a day for you."

"What," she says, turning her face to me, grinning now, "you mean coffee?"

I nod. "And I'll have steak for you too, three times a week. And sex. I'll pick up guys and then tell you all the dirty details over the phone—"

She rolls her eyes as if to say *Spare me* and we both have a good laugh. I'm feeling better, or not as bad, the humiliation of the scene in the restaurant gone to sleep somewhere deep inside me. We're quiet a moment, the ticking of the clock the only sound in the apartment, in the whole building, and it's as if we *are* inside, as if the space we inhabit in that moment is the only space there ever was. I think of the Mir astronauts hurtling around the earth in their little monkey cage of a ship, everything sterile and artificial and silent, and then Dawn breaks into my thoughts and says, "Keep an eye on Johnny for me, will you?"

"Johnny? But you don't expect—?"

"No," she says, shaking her head very slowly, exaggeratedly, "I don't. But he's broken up about it, though he's too macho to let it show. If he let it show he'd be weak or sentimental or whatever. 'Girlfriend in a bottle,' that's what he calls me."

I don't have anything to say to this. To my mind he's a jerk. And worse, a distraction. He'd come between Dawn and the mission—between Dawn and me—and now he was fading into the background, now he was irrelevant, and she really expected me to care whether he picked up a renewable slut every night or cried in his beer or went out and drank himself to death? Just to hear my own voice, I say, "Ramsay, Troy, Gyro, Richard."

She laughs again. "Pretty slim pickings, huh?"

"If it was me," I say, and of course it isn't me and that's the whole point, that's what had me making a spectacle of myself in the restaurant and has me sitting here at quarter past twelve sipping black coffee that tastes like machine oil when I should be home in bed, "I'd just order a chastity belt."

She gives me a long look, then drops her voice. "No, really," she says. "Who would you choose?"

"I don't get to choose."

"No, really."

"I don't know. The only one that's like half-genuine is Gyro—"

"Gyro? You've got to be kidding. Really? You're hot on *Gyro*?"

"I didn't say that. This is theoretical, right? I'm just saying—"

"What about Ramsay?"

"He's dirt. And to tell you the truth I don't know how he got picked except for sucking up." She's watching me closely, one hand shoving the hair back from her face. The clock ticks. Ticks again. "Don't tell me you're serious?"

"April Fool's," she says, and bursts out laughing, though it isn't April, not even close.

I laugh along with her, but the coffee sours on my stomach and the hurt comes up in me all over again like a weed you keep on uprooting only to have it grow right back. "He's got a thing for Judy," I say, and I don't really know why I say it except that it comes to me in a flash of intuition, his face, hers, the way they put their heads together.

"Judy? But that's crazy." Her expression doesn't change, but I can see the germ of the idea working inside her. "You don't really believe that, do you? I mean, why? Have you—I don't know, like *seen* anything?"

I shrug.

"That's crazy," she repeats.

* * *

I was there for the closure ceremony on the morning of March 6, 1994, some five months and ten days after Mission One reentry. In the interval between missions we'd all been inside during the weekdays, doing the kind of maintenance chores you'd expect of zookeepers, but then zookeepers made a whole lot more than we ever got. Trim the vegetation, dig the dirt, feed the pigs, milk the goats, weed the garden plots, plant and harvest and store as much grain, sweet potatoes and taro as possible to give the new Terranauts a head start, and all the while, every time you glance up, just remember, the tourists are watching. And they were too. They were everywhere, flitting around the outer skin of the space-frame like outsized moths, their faces pressed to the glass, cameras flashing—paying customers, though their number was something like a quarter of what it'd been at first closure. And don't think Mission Control wasn't sensitive to that—G.C., Judy and Dennis kept harping on the fact that we had to double and redouble that number till we had as many visitors or more than the original mission because this was our chance to start over and get it right.

Judy called it a new beginning. I called it damage control. And though all workers—final crew, extended crew and maintenance geeks alike—were limited to 192 population hours a day so as not to alter the atmosphere of E2 beyond what eight Terranauts would have breathed in and out during a twenty-four-hour period, it amounted to five months–plus of tinkering. The idea was to make sure that when the Mission Two crew completed their two-year closure they could exchange places with Mission Three without a single minute of downtime. Open the hatch, high-five the depart-ing crew, climb in and pull the door shut behind you, that was the idea. Beyond that, of course, Mission Three would give way seamlessly to Mission Four and on and on for an uninterrupted series of two-year closures for the full hundred years G.C. had ordained in the press release for Mission One.

Anyway, I was there because that was what was expected of us, because we had to show our commitment to the project through every minute of every day, whether we'd won the popularity con-test and got to don the red jumpsuits or not. Only one of us—Sally McNally—wound up defecting. She took it for a week or so after the announcement and the losers' dinner and then just packed up her things and slipped off one night. Rumor was she was living under a false name somewhere in the Pacific Northwest, but nobody could trace her, and believe me, Mission Control tried. They had spies everywhere, and not just in the scientific community but

among the teepee dwellers and God's-eye merchants of the New
Age tribe too, and what Sally might have revealed about the inner
workings of the project could have been devastating if it got out
to the press. But it didn't, as far as anyone knew. Meanwhile, the
rest of us hung on, putting the best face on things and doing what
we were told because that was our identity, that was our hope,
each of us secretly believing we'd be chosen next time around. I
was a fool. I knew it. And I hated myself for it. But there I was
in the chill of early morning, seated in the front row of folding
chairs with my fellow rejects and the new woman—girl—who'd
replaced Sally (Rita Nordquist, twenty-four years old and blonder
than Stevie), each of us dressed in a non-Terranaut-brown jumpsuit with a tiny Mission 3 patch sewn over the breast pocket.

I'm surprised at the size of the crowd. It isn't as big as the one
that gathered for Mission One closure, but still there must be a
thousand or more here, a few hundred seated, the rest clumped
around the lawn out front of E2. What it amounts to is that the
world's willing to give the project a second chance, a chance to
bring the science to the forefront and embrace the lessons learned
from the first mission. Voices murmur around me. TV cameras
hump through the crowd. Every once in a while an "aaah!" goes
up as somebody thinks they've spotted the crew and the crowd
turns as one. I'm sitting between Malcolm Burts and Jeff Weston,
both of them rapt or pretending to be. It's seven-fifteen in the
morning, the sun riding in on a plane like a laser beam to play off
the superstructure of E2 till it glows. I should feel proud, but the
truth is I feel nothing but hurt and disappointment, which is made
all the worse as I begin to appreciate the magnitude of what's
happening here, a snare drum in my head beating out the phrase
It could have been me over and over. If there was any justice in the
world, I would have been the one in red with my face plastered
over every TV screen in America—and abroad too—and my parents could have swelled their chests and pointed to the monitor in
their clinic and crowed, "That's our daughter!"

There are speeches, but Mission Control knows enough to keep
them short. Rusty Schweickart, one of the Apollo 9 astronauts,

shouts words of encouragement into the microphone, and Winston Barr, the Mission One medical officer and sole representative of the original crew (if that tells you anything), is there to pass the baton. G.C., dressed in a white linen suit set off by a tie and pocket handkerchief of Terranaut red, gives out with one of his patented speeches about crossing the boundary from the primitive age of living in thrall to the environment to the new one of applying technology to control, direct and harmonize with it. A band plays. Monks chant blessings. And Dan Old Elk sways in the background, suspended like an oversized insect by the hooks penetrating his pectoral muscles. The crowd surges forward. A shout goes up. And here come the Terranauts, chests thrust forward and marching in crimson lockstep through the crowd and on up to the dais, where they stand, trembling with emotion, behind their God and Creator.

I'm miserable. I can't even manage to applaud, afraid of what the percussion might do to me. I feel sick deep in the pit of my stomach, as if I haven't eaten in a week. My hair's an unholy mess, kinked out like a tumbleweed grafted to my head though I saturated it with conditioner and brushed it over and over till my scalp ached, and why, I wonder, couldn't I have inherited the straight black kinkless hair that's standard issue on ninety-seven percent of all Asian women in this world? It's a birthright, practically a birthright. My feet hurt. My nails are bitten down to the quick and I'm biting them now. I feel like I'm going to puke. And then each of the crewmembers takes the microphone in turn to say a few words about the mission, none of which I can even begin to grasp let alone process because I'm so wrought up, until Ramsay, who's last, just stands there waving both his arms as if he's signaling to some entity beyond our range of perception, and brings the microphone to his lips with a grin.

"There's a brave new world not fifty feet away," he says, and he shifts toward his fellow Terranauts and lets the grin spread through three full beats of silence. "What are we waiting for?" And then, in perfect sync, they all do an about-face and line up behind Diane.

Who looks good, never better, erect as a crusader. She's put her hair up—all four of the women have, at Judy's behest, to make them look more serious, more formidable, more like scientists and less like cheerleaders, though you can believe they've all done their faces for the cameras. Diane stands there through another full beat, then lifts one arm over her head, fist clenched in a power salute, before bringing it down with a flourish, palm up, to present the true star of the production, E2. A thousand heads turn, their eyes on the entry chamber and the gleaming white door of the airlock. Where G.C. magically appears now, ready to lift the handle and pull open the hatch as the band blares out the pep-rally version of Fleetwood Mac's "Tusk"—*Just tell me that you want me!*—and the crowd shouts as one.

Part of my problem is that I've been awake since three, too worked up to sleep. It had been one of those nights where you lie there in bed willing yourself into unconsciousness but every time you drift off the twisted sick catastrophe of what's happening to you in the here and now surges up like a rogue wave and snaps you back to attention. That's me. That's my problem. I'm beat. Exhausted. Not to mention sick at heart. At five, as prearranged, I'd walked over to Dawn's apartment in Residence 1 from my own place in Residence 2, and I'd been irritated to see shapes drifting and melding in the pre-dawn shadows of the campus, people already gathering on the grounds as if this was the Fourth of July and they were staking out places along the parade route.

Let me tell you, Dawn was in a state. She hadn't slept either, I could see that the minute she jerked open the door. She was in her robe and slippers, fresh from the shower, hair dryer in one hand, a bundle of wet towels balled up in the other. "Jesus," she said, and just turned her back on me to trot across the room and dump the towels on the floor beside the sheets and pillowcases she'd stripped from her bed. I stepped into the room and closed the door behind me.

"How you feeling?" I asked.

"I'm so nervous I could scream. What time is it anyway?"

"Five. Like we arranged."

"Jesus," she said again, and then, trailing the cord of the hair dryer, she was at the counter, fussing over two overstuffed paper bags. "Help me out here, will you?"

I crossed the room and she set down the hair dryer to lift both bags from the counter and hand them to me. "What's all this?" I asked.

"Odds and ends. For you. Like some perfume, shampoo, conditioner, anything with a scent to it—" This was a reference to the fact that nothing artificially scented was allowed inside for the simple reason that any chemical whatever would constitute a recycling poison in a closed system. The Mission One crew had kept getting skewed readings for trace gases until somebody discovered an open tube of silicone sealant in the machine shop which another somebody had been using, pre-closure, to seal tiny pinprick holes in the seams of the spaceframe—that's how sensitive it was inside. You breathe poison on the outside and maybe it disperses when you breathe out or maybe it accumulates in your body tissues and when you're seventy you get cancer or not, but on the inside poison is poison and its effects are immediate—one day you're wearing Dune or Angel and the next day you're eating it.

I looked in the bag. There was nothing I wanted. I was particular about my shampoo and conditioner and I didn't use perfume. Before I could say anything—and why bother when I could just toss it all in the trash as soon as the ceremony was over?—she thrust another bag at me, this one stuffed to the rigid top with the leftovers from her refrigerator. I saw half a two-quart plastic container of full-fat milk, a stick of butter, jars of pickles, jam, mustard. Three cucumbers in a produce bag, and what was that— zucchini?

Her face was pained. "I just thought you could use it, and, I don't know, if not you can just dump it. But what were you supposed to remind me?"

I didn't have a clue. It was five-oh-five in the morning and I hadn't slept or eaten and the actualization of my worst nightmare was just two hours and fifty-five minutes away. "I don't know. What?"

"The rim."

"What rim?"

"Shit," she said, and she had the hair dryer in her hand again, though she hadn't plugged it in or switched it on yet, "I can't believe you. Remember, you're supposed to remind me not to trip over the rim of the airlock? So I don't go head over heels while CBS broadcasts it to the nation?"

The airlock had come from a decommissioned submarine and it consisted of two doors sealing off an entry chamber. They were made of steel, with rounded corners for an airtight fit. Each featured a circular window at eye level and a threshold that was a good twelve inches off the ground so that you had to step up and over it. I'd tripped on both of them a dozen times myself till finally I developed some sort of autonomous muscular response. Same with Dawn. All of us. I didn't know what she was so worried about, but then I did. "Okay," I said, "I'm reminding you. Don't trip."

"*Thanks,*" she said, her tone caustic, but she gave me a weak smile. "I'm sorry," she said, "but I'm just so worked up. Look, look at my hand." She held out her left hand, the free one, and she couldn't manage to keep it steady.

This was my cue to say something reassuring, like *It'll go great, you'll be great, no worries,* but I couldn't. She was giving me her scraps, her leftovers, turning the key in the lock. "Okay," I said, "look, let me just set these bags down by the door, okay? I won't forget them, I promise. And what do you want with the laundry? You want me to wash the stuff and save it for you, for when you— you're going to need sheets when you come back."

She nodded, her eyes frantic, turned away, plugged in the hair dryer, flipped it on and flipped it off again. "Here," she said, darting into the bedroom and back out, something in her hand—a scarf, a silk scarf flowing on the breeze she was generating. "For you. My parents got it for me in Vienna last year—Klimt, it's a Klimt design." She held it up to the light so that the pattern—circles within circles, a cluster of interlocking blocks, in black, white and gold—stood out. "I want you to have it. I only wore it once—"

"I don't want this," I said.

"No," she said, "no, really—take it."

We stood there a moment, all the rush, all the unfinished business between us stuck in gear. She saw me then, I think, for the first time since I'd stepped through the door, saw what was in my eyes, and it wasn't pretty. "You're not hearing me," I said in the coldest voice I could manage. "I don't want it—or any of this other shit either. Your what, your *leavings*! Your *trash*?"

She wasn't going to go there. It was too late for that. "But it's nice," she insisted. "It'll look great on you, it'll go with that velour jacket you always wear, the black one—?"

"No," I said. "No."

Angry now, her mouth clamped shut and her eyes like two glass balls, she just brushed by me and stuffed the scarf in the bag of cosmetics as if that put an end to it. "Don't do this to me," she said, swinging round and holding her palms out in extenuation.

"Do what?"

"Don't make this hard on me."

"Hard on *you*? What about me?"

"Jesus, Linda," she said, already starting across the room to shut herself in the bathroom with her hair dryer and her lipstick and scent-free foundation, "I can't believe you, I really can't."

So we didn't make up, not really, but that was on me, as I've said. The minutes ticked down. Dawn went her way and I went mine, and while I did take the three overstuffed paper bags with me, I went straight to the dumpster with them, because that was how I felt. Samuel Beckett, another of G.C.'s favorites, said it best: "I can't go on, I'll go on." I dressed in peasant brown. My hair kinked out. I sat there in a folding chair and listened to the shouts and whistles and the full-throated ecstasy of the horns as my former crewmates filed into the airlock, one by one, and if it all came to a head and I cried out "Dawn!" just as she went to lift her right foot—not tripping, not this time—nobody really heard it in all that tumult of the crowd and the steady heart-seizing thump of the big bass drum.

Part II

CLOSURE, YEAR ONE

Dawn Chapman

I don't think I've ever felt anything like it. One minute I was outside in the world and the next I was a living part of E2, waving mindlessly through the glass at a sea of faces while Gyro pulled the hatch shut. It's hard to describe. I'd been through that portal countless times over the course of the past five months—it was our worksite, after all—and I knew the smells, sounds and configuration of E2 as well as I knew the suburban house I'd grown up in, but this was different. I suppose I'd be lying to myself if I said the ceremony didn't have something to do with it, the band playing, cameras flashing, people cheering, and yet it wasn't that so much as the hatch clanking shut and the lever locking in place that made the emotion overwhelm me till the tears started up in my eyes— tears of joy, yes, tears of relief, but of something else too. Anxiety, I guess you'd have to call it. Or maybe uncertainty, maybe that would be more accurate. This really was a new world. And now I was in it and there was no going back.

I think we all felt it, felt it as a team, the atmosphere literally shifting around us. There was a dense green living aura to the air inside that was utterly unlike the thin stingy air of the desert surrounding us. The minute you were inside, there it was, in your nostrils. You smelled mold, spores, damp earth, process, the ants and termites and microbes in the soil breaking things down even as the fronds of the banana trees loomed overhead and the palms reached to the sun-shot lattice of our sky. It was air you could taste. Air that went in and out of your pores as if your whole body was a pair of lungs. And over it all, the great roar of the fans and blowers of the technosphere that kept it all going, our life support kicking in and running as steadily as a heartbeat day and night. That was what it was like inside, that was what hit you—hit me—in those first few moments of closure. And not just that but the wildness of it too, the unpredictability of a self-generating ecosphere, the coqui frogs rattling away at their two-note song and the galagos hooting from the trees as if evolution were running in high gear and there was no end to what could happen here.

"Wow, can you believe it?" It was Stevie, standing right beside me, her face so close to mine I could make out the shallow pit of a childhood scar at the corner of her mouth, an indentation there I'd never noticed before. It was a flaw, the only flaw in that perfect face, and it humanized her, gave her character, Stevie, the real-world person who was capable of suffering and hurt just like anybody else. She'd turned to me, still waving to the glassed-out crowd, her eyes in soft focus. "Can you?"

"No, it's incredible, isn't it?"

We were all jammed there at the window just inside the entrance, where on one side a staircase led up to our living quarters and on the other a mud-spattered plank led to the animal pens and the IAB, and we were all keyed up and flapping our arms so hard it must have looked as if we were trying to sprout wings and fly up into the rafters. One of the men started hooting in imitation of the galagos that were just about to go to sleep for the day and in the next moment we all took it up, filling the place with the ecstatic full-throated cries of another kind of primate, the apex predator of E2, its nurturer and winnower, its gods under glass, going ape. We hooted our lungs raw, then dissolved in laughter, team laughter, and though we didn't know it at the time, this was about as united as we'd ever be, our eight spirits wedded in one. I don't want to get too mystical here, but there was something very special about the moment, and I won't compare it to the first moonwalk, or even the second, but we all felt the pride of accomplishment and the deepening of our bond in this place that was familiar and alien all at once. Of course, the exhilaration didn't last long—Mission Control was big on proportion, as in all things have their time and place, and in our final briefing earlier that morning G.C. had emphasized how important it was that we should disperse and go about our duties as soon as the ceremony was over. This wasn't an amusement park. It was a going concern. And while it was fine—necessary—to put on a show for the press and the friends of the mission, the bottom line was that we were there to work.

So the glow of the moment faded and with a last look over our shoulders we went off to our rooms in the Human Habitat to change into our work clothes and get down to it. For my part, I had to milk and feed the goats, then feed the ducks, chickens and pigs and muck out their stalls before putting in a full day in the IAB, weeding and tending and trying to keep the various known and unknown plant pests from decimating the crops. Diane (Meadowlark or just Lark for short, though for her, as crew captain, this was anything but a lark) would work beside me, and starting tomorrow all the others but Gyro, who was on call all day every day, would be expected to do two hours of ag work after breakfast, five days a week. The truth was, when you boiled away the layers of our scientific accomplishments and our mission goals and all the rest, we were essentially subsistence farmers, albeit high-tech, well-funded and sealed-in representatives of the bony tribe that crouched over cookfires and scratched at the dirt of the wider world. That portion of humanity got its energy and weather gratis via the sun and atmosphere of E1, while it was the technosphere—the three-acre basement whirring with machinery and the external heating plant and cooling towers that circulated water through a series of closed-circuit pipes for temperature control—that gave us ours, plus what we got from the sun, of course. More than once Richard had referred to E2 as the Garden of Eden set down on the deck of an aircraft carrier.

My room (Mission Control had chosen for us, and how could I ever have imagined anything different?) was second in line along the mezzanine overlooking the ag sector and the animal pens, which were tucked underneath. Richard was on one side of me, Gyro on the other, followed by Diane, Troy, Gretchen, Ramsay and Stevie, everyone in a boy/girl arrangement that had us wondering over Mission Control's intentions. Was this a kind of Ecospherian spin the bottle or were they just trying to keep us from falling into male/female comfort zones? We couldn't help second-guessing—why put me between Richard and Gyro, as opposed to say, Ramsay and Troy? Or Troy between Diane and Gretchen and Stevie at the far end? Had Mission Control drawn lots? Not likely. G.C. had his hands in everything, and so did Judy. And, for that matter, Dennis. Wheels within wheels.

As for the rooms themselves, they were identical, except that the first four looked out into the enclosure while the others had outside views of the desert and mountains beyond. We called them rooms, though they were actually mini-apartments, on two levels, sitting room below, mezzanine bedroom above, 350 square feet in all. Each was equipped with an oak bookcase, couch, armchair, coffee table and combination radio/CD player, in addition to a queen-sized bed, dresser and nightstand upstairs, and each had access to the balcony that ran the length of the floor, as well as to the inner hallway, where our front doors were. There were four bathrooms, one for each pair of rooms, and they featured a shower, sink and toilet, the toilet making use of a bidet-style hose so as to eliminate the need for toilet paper. Food preparation and meals were communal and we all had 24/7 access to the big state-of-the-art kitchen, with its gleaming black-and-white tiled floor, industrial-sized refrigerator/freezer and Viking range.

We'd been allowed to move our things in the previous day—books, CDs, clothes, cosmetics, a clarinet in the case of Gyro, a guitar for Vodge, sketchbooks and paints for some of the rest of us—but everything had to be confined, strictly, to two standard-sized suitcases. And everything, no exceptions, had been laid out for inspection by Mission Control and a few select representatives of the press. Was this an invasion of privacy? Did we all resent it? Of course it was and of course we did. But Mission Control wasn't going to make the mistakes it had with the first mission and they wanted to demonstrate to the world that the Mission Two crew was going in with the basics only and that nothing beyond that would be allowed, though there were skeptics who pointed out that we could have smuggled just about anything in during the previous five-plus months when we were in and out practically every day. No matter: this was theater. And it was designed to show the world that we were dead serious about absolute closure and living with the basics—Mars, we were going to Mars, and we wouldn't need a whole lot of baggage along the way.

Like the others, I'd unpacked the day before, adding a few personal touches to the space the Mission One medical officer had inhabited for the duration of his two-year closure, the sole traces of which were a couple of thumbtack holes in the wall over the sofa and a faint discoloration between them where he'd hung a picture—of what I couldn't say. Though I speculated. When you're inside, self-contained, you hunger for some reminder of the outside world, a photo of a waterfall or the moon emerging from the black rim of the ocean (though we had our own waterfall and our own ocean too) or maybe of family members, whom you'd get to see only through the three-by-five-foot visitors' window located just to the left of the airlock. If they bothered to make the journey, that is. My parents, who lived all the way across the country in Yorktown Heights, New York, would manage it only once during my closure—midway through the second year, when things got difficult for me. As for Johnny, he did what he could, but that wasn't much, especially as time wore on.

We were isolated, that was the long and short of it, and Mission Control, having learned their lesson the first time around vis-à-vis press leaks, unflattering characterizations and even diatribes delivered to family and friends that somehow wound up becoming press leaks themselves, had denied us phones as well as connections to the fledgling internet of the time. For communication within the structure, which could seem surprisingly vast given the tangle of hallways, stairways, tunnels and paths not only through the biomes but in the technosphere and the two big football field–sized lungs that kept the dome from either exploding or imploding depending on the outside temperature, we were given walkie-talkies. Outside communication was limited to the Picture-Tel video system with which Mission Control relayed questions, strategies and commands to us and a single telephone line, which might or might not have been monitored by someone on the support staff. Beyond that, there was the visitors' window, where we could meet with anyone we liked and speak to them via in-house phone, just as if we were in prison—and don't think we didn't joke about it, good-naturedly at first, and then, increasingly and inevitably, with a kind of bitterness none of us could have imagined at the outset.

But I don't want to dwell on the negative. I want to talk about the good things. About how I felt that first day, my spirit soaring as I ascended the staircase to the apartments, shut the door behind me, stripped off my red jumpsuit and hung it in the closet until I would don it again for reentry at mission's end. I sat there a long moment on my bed, dressed only in bra, panties and socks, gazing out the window on the luxurious deep-green growth of the farm plot below, reveling in my good fortune. *Every spirit builds itself a house; and beyond its house, a world,* that's what Emerson said, and I never really got it, I think, until that moment. I was queen of the realm, or at least one of four queens, and I looked down on the neatly laid out plots of grain and vegetables below and the potted sweet potatoes lining the rail of the balcony with a pride of possession I'd never known. I kept envisioning our first harvest and then the one that would succeed it and the one beyond that, all our riches brought home to store and consume and nourish us through the seasons, eight seasons all our own. We'd eat healthy, be healthy, live close to the earth. Everything that went on outside, the shootings, regime shifts, political maneuverings, the disasters and plagues and hopeless ongoing suffering of the mass of humankind, was part of another reality. I was inside now—and not just for an eight-hour shift, but permanently—and the security of it, the serenity, was worth everything I'd ever done and been and hoped for. Johnny wouldn't have understood it. Or my parents either. It was their loss.

I drew in a deep breath of E2's air, really filled my lungs, then got up to pull on my jeans and T-shirt and go to work.

* * *

Lunch was at twelve-thirty, our first lunch inside. The day's chef was Ramsay and though he'd been busy all morning tinkering with the wastewater systems and typing out hourly dispatches on the computer in our command center for release by Mission Control (Judy and Dennis were milking the first day's activities for all they were worth), he'd put some thought into the preparation. Which was nice. A nice touch. No one would have blamed him for just throwing something together, but he'd understood the symbolic value of the occasion—let's start on a high note—and he'd made chiles rellenos with a tossed salad on the side and banana puffs for dessert, though none of us expected dessert at lunch. Dinner, yes. We would all but come to demand it as the days went by, but this was special, and I appreciated that.

I was last to the table—the big granite-topped table on the mezzanine where we would take our communal meals within sight, smell and sound of the life ticking around us—because I'd cleaned out the animal pens and taken an extra few minutes scrubbing the odor off me, a courtesy to the others I'd eventually get fairly lax about. To stink was honorable, wasn't it? Especially in a world without artificial scents? But this was the first day and I was determined to make things work. In my own sphere in particular—the Mission One crew had left the animal pens in a sorry state and I wasn't about to repeat that sort of thing. I was something of a neat freak, I suppose, and I'd really gone after the mess there, particularly in the corners and along the walls of the pens where nobody ever thought to clean, filling bucket after bucket and hauling them across the IAB to the compost bin, then repeating the process all over again. I changed the bedding too—we used cuttings of the savanna grass, laid down in a crosshatch of layers, which in its turn was composted too. So I was late. But there was my plate of food, set out on the counter, and there were my fellow Terranauts, in high good spirits, chowing down.

I slipped between Richard and Gretchen (Snowflake, that is) to take the last unoccupied seat, beaming over Ramsay's chef d'oeuvre and feeling a real sense of accomplishment in what I'd managed to get through already—in just the first four and a half hours. There was a buzz of animated conversation, voices blending and separating again, everybody still riding the high of the morning's ceremony. Stevie was across the table from me, waving her fork like a conductor's baton. "Did you see Charles Osgood there—from CBS News?"

"No, don't tell me!" Richard made a face of mock enthusiasm. "Not *Charles Osgood!*"

"Don't make fun of me, Richard. It's exciting. Admit it. Come on, I saw you practically prancing out there—"

"Yeah, Richard, come on now, loosen up." This was Gretchen, at my elbow, her soft pale heavy features held in suspension. Her hair was up still, though two long silver-gold loops of it had come loose to dangle at one shoulder, and she was still wearing her lipstick and eye shadow. She was pretty enough, for an older woman, especially when she smiled, and she was smiling now. "You know the drill: what's good for the mission . . ."

"Is good for us," we all chimed in, as if this were theater rehearsal. And then we were laughing, all of us, team laughter, and I felt so in the moment I was almost giddy.

"What about you, E.? Are you as star-stuck as the rest of us?" Diane asked, setting down her fork and taking up a cup of the mint tea that was to become our chief recreational drink—until Troy produced his first vintage of banana wine and Richard set up his still, but that was in the future yet.

"Oh, yeah, absolutely," I said, grinning down the length of the table. "I've got the hots for Dan Old Elk."

"Right, if anybody ever remembers to cut him down." Stevie gave me a wink that could have meant anything but which I chose to interpret as sisterly. She'd propped her elbows up on the table on either side of her plate, which was already scraped clean (we'd all scrape our plates, not only on this occasion but on into the future; eventually we'd wind up licking them too). Her hair was wet, testimony to her aquatic activities that morning, gliding along the face of the coral reef in her bikini for the benefit of the tourists peering in through the underwater window set in the outside wall. She was looking blonder than ever and I wondered about that. There'd be no Lady Clairol inside, that goes without saying. But she was a natural blonde, wasn't she?

"Too kinky for me," Troy put in. "I didn't know you were into bondage, E."

Richard: "Let's call sadomasochism by its true name."

Troy: "What's that?"

Richard: "You mean medically?"

Troy: "Yeah."

Richard: "Sadomasochism."

More laughter. The aroma rose from my plate and I dipped my fork in while the conversation took off and swirled around me— suddenly I was ravenous. Physical labor will do that to you. Physical labor hones you and reduces everything to the basics: calories in, calories out. I bent to my plate, cut, forked, chewed. "Mmm," I said, gazing up to where Ramsay sat looking smug at the far end of the table, "Vodge, you've really outdone yourself. This is awesome. What do you say, everybody?"

There was a smattering of applause and Troy and Gyro put their heads together for a riff on the ape hoot that was to become our team anthem as the weeks drifted by. Ramsay looked pleased. "Glad to be of service," he said to the table at large, but staring at me all the while.

* * *

I should say something here about the meals and cleanup and how we'd arranged all that in an orderly way, a regimented way, regimentation being the root and foundation of any successful mission, in which each crewmember knows his or her place and what's expected of them to make things run smoothly. Ultimately, no matter the experiments we performed, the physiological analyses Richard routinely ran on all of us or our struggles with balancing the O_2/CO_2 ratios, food—its cultivation, preservation, preparation and assimilation—was the sine qua non of closure. Without it we'd be unable to function. Without it, we'd starve. And if we starved, the mission would be an even more colossal and humiliating failure than Mission One, because the outside world, with its reporters and pundits and scientific opinion makers, not to mention moralists and religious nuts, would be sure to gather at the airlock and insist on breaking closure. So: regimentation. Efficiency. All our eggs in one basket. This was what we'd signed on for.

The way food prep worked was simple: Diane, as Supervisor of Field Crops and Crew Captain, portioned out the raw ingredients for the chef of the day just after lunch, and you never knew what those ingredients would feature and in what proportions, though you could be pretty certain our staples—beets, sweet potatoes and bananas—would figure prominently. Though, of course, we'd have salad greens seasonally, tomatoes, peppers, squash, beans—whatever we could coax out of the ground—supplemented by animal protein, chicken maybe once a week, pork on special occasions, a slab of tilapia from the rice/fish/azolla ponds every other week or so. The chef—we rotated on a regular and unvarying schedule, seven days a week, Gyro, as Mr. Fixit, the only one excused from culinary duties—could be as creative as he or she wanted, given the restrictions of our larder. We had few spices, aside from the basil, rosemary and mint we were able to grow, no bouillon cubes or wine to stir into our sauces, no sherry, no Worcestershire or soy or Tabasco. No butter. And very little cream. (Our four she-goats were of a dwarf African variety, in keeping with the scale of E2, and we got less than a pint a day out of each of them.) At any rate, we wound up competing with one another in a spirited *top-that* sort of way, each chef trying to outdo the next, at least at first, before things settled into routine and meal prep became just another form of the usual.

So Diane, after checking the larder, including our primary source of fructose (bananas, which eventually we had to keep locked up in a separate storeroom, and more on that later), would measure out the ingredients and hand over culinary responsibilities after lunch. The day's chef would then be accountable for that night's dinner, the next morning's breakfast, which was invariably porridge that might or might not be enlivened by papaya, banana or goat's milk, and then lunch, after which the cycle repeated itself with the next chef taking center stage. Ramsay was the best cook, I have to give him credit there, followed by Gretchen, and if I'm not tooting my own horn too loudly here but just being *objective,* by yours truly. The worst, and I think most of us would have agreed on this, were the two other men, Troy Turner taking honors—or dishonors—for Chef the Least, with Richard as runner-up. Troy's porridge was like concrete just before it sets and his dinner menu ran from thin soup one week to thinner soup the next, and Richard, so fastidious as our physician, tended to burn practically everything.

Anyway, we had our first lunch inside and then our first dinner—tilapia and mussel cioppino in a tomato/crookneck squash sauce—and we lingered that evening over cups of mint tea and an astonishing lemon-meringue pie Ramsay had managed to concoct with flour made from the winter wheat we'd grown, harvested and threshed during the months running up to closure, along with our own eggs, lemons, banana sweetener and the yellowish cream he'd managed to separate from the goat's milk. I sat limp in my chair, exhausted, wondering where Ramsay could possibly have found the energy to go all out like this. But then he hadn't had to deal with Johnny and Linda—as far as I knew he didn't have any attachments at all. That had taken a lot out of me, more than I'd care to admit. Plus, I'd been up half the night seeing to all the little details of vacating the apartment I'd been living in off and on for the past two years, cleaning the last items out of the refrigerator and medicine cabinet, scrubbing the sinks, mopping the floor, vacuuming. And it wasn't as if I'd put things off—that wasn't my way. I'd been wrapping up my affairs for better than a month, even before the final interview, but still there are going to be last-minute issues. Like Johnny. Like Linda.

Ramsay, as chef du jour, had agreed to do our first lunch, as well as dinner, breakfast and tomorrow's lunch, as a way of kicking things off, and he'd painstakingly divided the pie into eight equal portions and laid out the slices on the counter, each gracing its own dessert plate in a neat glistening wedge. We praised him. We'd expected maybe a banana mash with a splash of milk or papaya cookies or something of the like, and here he'd really gone out of his way to make our first day special. "Bravo!" Diane said, to the sound of spoons scraping plates while the blowers blew and the galagos awoke to make their nightly rounds, calling softly as they leapt from one tree to another and burst into our field of vision swinging from the white laminated struts of the spaceframe overhead. "Yeah, Vodge, wow," somebody said.

Beyond the glass the world had gone dark. I swiveled my chair around and put my feet up on the rail between two earthenware pots of sweet potatoes trailing their tangle of vines over the edge and down into the arena below. A beetle winged by. One of the goats bleated. I felt a deep contentment.

"Our first night," Gretchen said. She was behind me some-where, still at the table.

"Yeah," somebody said, a male voice, richly affirmative. It might have been Gyro. I didn't turn my head. I just stared out into the dark vacancy that opened up before me, E2 drawn deep into its shadows.

"Beautiful, isn't it?" someone else said, addressed to no one in particular.

"Yeah," I agreed, finding my voice, which at this point wasn't much more than a flutter in my throat. "Most beautiful place on earth."

A moment drifted by, each of us lost in our thoughts, and then somebody—Ramsay—said, "But we're not on earth, E."

Still I didn't turn my head. I was molded to my chair, and my feet, in their workboots, had never been anyplace but propped up on that rail. Very softly, just at the range of hearing, I said, "Not anymore."

* * *

The day before, out there in the other world, Johnny had showed up at the door of my apartment at five in the afternoon, choosing his moment. He knew I'd be tied up later at the party and once the party was over I'd be so harried with final details I wouldn't be much use to him. And if that's putting it coldly, I'm sorry, I'm just being realistic. We'd spent the night together three days earlier and I hadn't seen or heard from him since. Which hurt.

I might have put on a front for him and Linda, as if all this was business as usual, nothing to get emotional over, but I was in love, really and truly, or at least I thought I was, and what I wanted more than anything was for him to be there for me when I came out. If I tried to affect a kind of nonchalance about the whole thing, it was only to protect myself, and I'm sure Linda must have seen through that—she never called me out on it but I'd be fooling myself to think I was fooling her. I wanted Johnny to support me. Wanted him to care and be around for my weekly phone calls and come to the visitors' window to show me who he really was beyond the talk and assurances and the way his body fit itself to mine in the narrow bed in the apartment somebody else would be occupying now, some stranger, some technician or Terranaut-in-waiting.

He didn't knock. The door was propped open with the red plastic bucket I'd been using for the mop, I was barefoot, in a pair of shorts and a tee, and my hair was a mess. There was some music on, I don't remember what, most likely the easy-listening channel though I hated easy-listening and so did he but it was one of the few things you could tune in clearly out there in the sticks. "Hey," he said, pushing through the door, "what's up?"

At the moment I was down on my knees in front of the refrigerator, working a sponge into the crevices of the vegetable compartment. His voice—a baritone he blended in on harmonies with the lead singer's country tenor—always managed to give me chills. There was something primitive about it, about the way women—this woman anyway—responded reflexively to a deep male voice, as if it were a rutting call, even if it was just drifting down a crowded bar announcing, *Johnnie Walker Black, no ice.* That was the way it was in the world of the elk and the elephant seal and in every barroom and nightclub from here to New York and back. The nature of things. Part of the breeding ritual. His voice.

"Oh, hi," I said, flustered to be caught out like that—on my knees, dirty knees, in a pair of dirty shorts, scrubbing—though he'd seen me without any clothes at all and in every position and every light. I got to my feet, wiped my wet hands on the shorts.

"I was hoping you'd stop by—I mean, where've you been? I must have called a hundred times—"

He was just inside the door now, looking sheepish, a tall slightly stoop-shouldered man of twenty-eight with the face of a teenage boy and eyes that never missed a thing. He was alert. He was alive. And he had an excuse because he needed an excuse to get what he wanted, which wasn't going to be so hard since it was what I wanted too. "Didn't I tell you? I was down in Tucson, at my mother's? Remember that guy she found in the paper that was going to put in new cabinets in the kitchen for her? Yeah, well he screwed up. Big time. And I needed to have a little talk with him."

"Oooh, tough guy," I said, reaching out to snatch a paper towel from the holder over the sink and wring it in my hands. "You didn't have to shatter his kneecaps, did you?"

He shrugged, gave me a little half smile as if to acknowledge the dig—and the fact that he was lying, or I was pretty sure he was, not that it made any difference now. "Nothing like that," he said. "I wound up helping him."

"And you couldn't find time to call?"

"You were busy." He crossed the room to me, the heels of his snakeskin boots tapping as he went from carpet to tile. "With all this, right?" He was two feet from me and we were sixty seconds from doing what he'd come here to do, but we both took a moment to glance round the apartment laid bare between its stripped walls and empty cabinets. "I don't even recognize the place—for a minute there I thought I had the wrong apartment." He was right—it was just a stage set now, and here came the climax.

I don't know how much I want to disclose here, but I'll say this: he'd always been a careful, considerate lover, taking his time, watching out for me, for my pleasure, and it was as much about the preliminaries, the kissing and teasing and the slow sweet caresses as about the consummation, which set him apart from the other men I'd known. Not that there were all that many or that I'm any sort of expert or even the kind of woman who likes to get together with her girlfriends and parse the details. He was romantic, all right? And I trusted him. He made me feel good.

That was why this last time felt so different. It was as much me as him, my insecurity, my anger at his having ignored me for three full days and then (most likely) lied about it, but we came together there in the kitchen in a way that was anything but tender and slow and sweet. Just the opposite: it was hard, almost desperate, as if we were wrestlers going for the takedown. He tore the T-shirt off of me and I returned the favor, popping half the buttons on his shirt, and we never did make it to the bedroom.

In the aftermath, he leaned over me for a long lingering kiss, my backside and shoulders gone cold where they were pressed to the tiles, then he pushed himself up and pulled on his pants and what was left of his shirt, all the while looking down at me with a puzzled expression as if he didn't know who I was or what we'd just done or why we'd done it. "What?" I said, propping myself on my elbows to look up at him.

"Nothing."

"I just thought, I don't know, maybe we could get a sandwich or something? You want a sandwich? A drink?"

"Uh-uh," he said, shaking his head slowly, "I don't think so. You've got a big night ahead of you—I wouldn't want to get in your way."

I sat up, reaching round me for my shorts and bra. I wanted to say *You're not in the way,* wanted to say, *Stay, stay until the last minute,* but instead I said, "So that's it then? Is that all there is? Like in the song?"

He didn't say anything, just stood there gazing down at me till finally he reached out a hand and helped me to my feet. He didn't hold me. Didn't seem to be able to look me in the eye. "No," he said finally, working the toe of one boot against the narrow metal band that separated the carpet from the tile. "It's just better this way, that's all." And then he turned and drifted toward the door, which was still propped halfway open, an invitation to the show for anyone who might have passed by in the last ten minutes, though the kitchen counter would have hidden us, or that was what I told myself.

"Well," he said, pulling the door open wide, "I guess I'll be seeing you."

"When?" I said, and I couldn't keep from letting out a laugh. "In two years?"

His face hung there a beat, hangdog, as if he'd just peed on the furniture, and he gave a laugh too. "No," he said, "I'll call you."

"Right," I said, "right," trying to put some enthusiasm into it so that my voice rose airily even though I felt as if all the air had gone out of me. "And I'll call you. Every week. I promise."

I was thinking about that now as I went down the hallway to my room, pushed open the door—we didn't have locks or keys, no reason for them here—and sank into the armchair. It was early yet, not quite nine—too early to turn in, though once I was down I could barely lift my arms. I had a paperback copy of *The Skin of Our Teeth* with me, which was the first play we'd be rehearsing inside—G.C.'s choice—and I thought I'd take a look at it before turning in. The roles hadn't been cast yet, though I was thinking I'd rather play Mrs. Antrobus than Sabina—leave her and her bustier to Stevie. I also had a handful of new CDs Johnny had thrust on me as a going-away present, though of course we both had to smile over the notion since where I was going away to couldn't have been more than three hundred yards from my apartment as the crow flies, even if it would be a long while before I laid eyes on a crow again. There was the radio too, as well as a shelf of books I'd always wanted to read but never seemed to find time for, the Russians mostly—Dostoevsky, Tolstoy, Solzhenitsyn.

So I had my entertainment choices that first night, plenty enough to fill the two hours till bedtime, and beyond that I thought of maybe taking a walk through the biomes, the rain forest especially, just to absorb the atmosphere, watch E2 at work in the way of a trained observer—or no, even better, like a child, in full wonderment. Ultimately, though, I just lay there, dozing on and off, my door open wide to the space beyond, letting the dense air and the drift of night sounds lull me till all the excitement and frantic activity of the past days melted away in darkness.

What woke me, and it might have been ten minutes or half an hour later, I couldn't say, was the whine of a mosquito. At first I didn't know where I was, the layers of unconsciousness peeling away to leave me staring at the ceiling and the soft cone of light cast there by the lamp. I sat up, alert suddenly, searching for the insect. There would be no peace unless I got it, that was for sure, and how many nights had I lain awake in a tent or in my berth on The *Imago,* hands poised to strike, listening for that maddening buzz? Doze off, and there it was; awaken and it was gone. The room stood solid around me. I heard the crickets and frogs calling tirelessly and something else too, something I couldn't identify— remember, this was my first night inside and there was a whole new cast of creatures on the night shift you didn't see or hear during the day, so it would take me a while to acclimate. A current of moist warm air drifted through the open door and I thought about getting up and closing it, though it seemed wrong somehow to shut out the life I'd come here to be part of, mosquitoes or no.

But where was it? My eyes jumped to the wall over the bookcase—something was moving there, but it was too big for a mosquito. I rose to investigate and when I did it vanished behind the bookcase, but not before I saw what it was: a cockroach. I wasn't a big fan of cockroaches, whether they're ecologically sound or not, and so I removed a few of the books from the upper shelf and then eased the bookcase an inch or two back from the wall, at which point I saw that it wasn't just a single cockroach cohabiting with me, but a dozen or more of them. They were motionless, clinging to the smooth cream-colored wall in formation, only their antennae twitching like hairs in a faint breeze. That was when I felt the sharp pinprick on my left forearm and ended the life of the mosquito in a minuscule flower of blood, thereby effecting the first extinction in round two of closure. Which was fine. I was fine with that. Who needed mosquitoes—or rather one mosquito, this particular individual that had taken it upon itself to filch a droplet of my blood with the intention of nurturing its offspring and perpetuating the species, same as any other living thing? Unfortunately, the sudden movement spooked the cockroaches and they scattered in six different directions so that I found myself reacting before I could think.

More extinctions ensued. The thing was, I had to use my bare hands and socked feet, which wasn't all that pleasant, and still most of them escaped, flowing like water into invisible cracks at the juncture of the wall and floor, where they would live on and breed and venture out again once the coast was clear. That was what they were all about. That was their M.O. That was why they were active participants in the world and had been for some 350 million years and counting. According to Gretchen, who's an expert on the morphology of rain forest insects, the biggest ganglia in the cockroach's nervous system have evolved for one purpose only: to detect motion and propel the animal in the opposite direction. Cockroaches sport a pair of anal cerci covered in wind-sensitive hairs attuned to the slightest variation in air movement, which is what triggers the flight response and makes it so hard to terminate them with a rolled-up newspaper or a flung shoe. Anyway, welcome to E2: I wound up with an itchy red blister on my forearm and a mucousy yellow wad of cockroach innards on my right palm and the heels of both socks.

You may be wondering at this point why, exactly, G.C. in his wisdom (and the synergistic wisdom of the four hundred consulting scientists who contributed to the creation of E2) decided to include pests like mosquitoes and cockroaches in the first place. Or maybe you're even reprising Noah jokes from the Bill Cosby era *(I know what he ain't got aboard—termites!)*. The irony here is that while three species of cockroaches were in fact intentionally included in the original suite of species stocked inside the dome (cockroaches are essential detritivores, helping to break down plant and animal matter, thereby accelerating the process of soil production and enrichment, and in addition, they provide a food source for frogs, lizards and birds), the ones overrunning my room and, as we would soon discover, everyone else's and the kitchen too, were the big brown oriental cockroaches that had apparently come in as volunteers during the building phase. The mosquitoes were a different story, though they were volunteers too. Our best guess is that they arrived in larval or pupal form when the mangrove/marsh biome was lifted wholesale from the Florida Everglades and relocated to E2, where it would function as a transitional zone—ecotone, officially—between the ocean and savanna. Of course, as annoying as they might have been, the mosquitoes were part of the experiment too—you could create any sort of world you wanted but as long as it was alive, it would always hold surprises. As G.C. likes to say, "Nature always subverts your expectations."

I was just standing there in the middle of the room, door open wide, nature breathing all around me, trying to rub the insect remains off my palms by working my hands together—we had no paper towels, of course, though we did have the real article, two terrycloth towels I was reluctant to dirty—when I heard the soft shuffle of footsteps in the hallway. In the next moment, Ramsay was there at the door, making as if to knock on the doorframe. "Oh," I said, "hi," and he said, "I saw your light—"

"Yeah," I said, "I was just, I don't know—the cockroaches. Have you got cockroaches?"

He stood there framed in the door, beardless, capless, in a pair of shorts and nothing else, looking amused. "They're ubiquitous," he said. "But hey, they don't eat much—and they're good little detritivores, right?"

"Not the ones I nailed," I said. "They're the detritus now."

"You mind?" he asked, gesturing toward the easy chair.

"No, not at all—come on in."

I watched him perch lightly on the edge of the chair, his feet long and narrow, his legs dark with hair and his chest too, and I remember thinking how different that was from Johnny, whose body hair was confined to his pubis and under his arms. He sat back then and crossed one leg over the other. "You can't sleep either, huh?"

"No, I was—what time is it anyway?"

"Half-past one, something like that."

"Half-past one? I thought it was like nine-thirty or something.

Jesus. I mean, I did doze off there—till the mosquitoes woke me—but I thought I'd maybe closed my eyes for ten minutes or something, max—"

He was watching me out of hooded eyes, gray eyes, almost black in that light. "I'm too excited to sleep," he said. "I tried. But every time I shut my eyes all I could think was I'm really here, really inside, and everything's right out my door, waiting for me. Like an hour ago? I took a walk through the rain forest, just to see what was stirring, aside from the frogs, that is."

"You see anything?"

"Not much. Things are pretty quiet. I did find an unwelcome guest in the kitchen, along with a whole scrum of cockroaches—"

"What was it?"

"Another volunteer that must have come in with the desert biome—or maybe just found itself a niche when the place was going up—a scorpion. And I'm pretty sure it's the one semi-dangerous species that's native outside here, the bark scorpion?"

"A very pale light brown, almost translucent? Long tail, I mean longer than most?"

He nodded.

"Jesus," I said, shaking my head now, "I can't believe it. We're in here less than twenty-four hours and already we run into all these stowaways—those things can kill you, you know that, right? Did you at least get rid of it?"

"Anaphylactic shock," he said, dropping his foot to the carpet. He flashed a grin, then let it die. "You'd have to have a bad allergic reaction, and so that's not likely. Still, they can give you something to think about—"

"Yeah, but did you kill it?"

He looked away, shrugged. "I tried."

"Great, just great. I suppose it's nesting under the micro-wave—or in the basket with the sweet potatoes."

"No," he said, bringing his grin back into focus, "no, I gave him directions to your room, told him it was the best place in E2 to nestle up."

"Thanks for thinking of me."

"Hey, that's what friends are for, right?"

"Right," I said and I was still standing there, still wiping my hands on my shorts, everything redolent of process and life contained, bed awaiting me and the first tendrils of exhaustion creeping up my legs, through my hips and torso and into my shoulders and worn-out arms that felt so numb suddenly they might have been attached to somebody else. It had been a day. And there he was, Ramsay Roothoorp—Vajra, the blazing thunderbolt, Linda's sworn enemy—sunk deep into the easy chair in the sitting room of my tiny apartment in the Human Habitat of E2, and I was thinking it was the strangest thing, but then, after a while, I didn't think it was so strange at all.

* * *

The first few weeks went by so fast it was as if time were accelerated, as if we actually were in a spaceship hurtling high above the earth while the earth stood still. I think it was the regimen that accounted for it, that and the newness of the experience, everything coming at you so fast you hardly had time to think. There was group meditation two days a week, Tuesdays and Thursdays, which helped, but chores occupied us something like ten to twelve hours a day, and meditation, for me anyway, was more a worry-session over what was growing or failing to grow in the IAB than a way of letting my mind go free. We had theater rehearsal on Saturday afternoons, daily meetings over breakfast during which Troy (T.T.) delivered the weather report (temps consistent, water clear, CO_2 fluctuating depending on available light for photosynthesis, the activity of soil microbes and the status of decomposition in the compost bin) and Diane and I reported on crop yields and handed out daily assignments for the ag work.

Most Saturday nights there was a movie in the command center—a videocassette we chose by a yea or nay vote and transferred via cable from Mission Control—and that gave us a chance to let our hair down, chew peanuts, sip mint tea and bark sarcastically at the screen, no matter if we were watching an action film or a tearjerker (especially if it was a tearjerker). Sunday afternoons were free, though Mission Control encouraged us to keep our doors open and engage in some sort of social activity, whether it was playing cards or chess or a board game with one or more of our fellow crewmembers, after which came our big weekly dinner, the only one that routinely featured our most precious commodity—meat—and which eventually floated along on the fumes of T.T.'s banana wine and what Richard charitably called arak, a urine-colored liquor he distilled in the medical lab from a mash of rice and sweet potato.

What else? We had group swims in our ocean and once a week, at least in the beginning, we organized a picnic dinner on the white sand beach G.C. had insisted on for aesthetic reasons, though the sand was forever washing away with the action of the wave machine. Holidays were important too, as with any tribe, as were crew birthdays, and we extended our list of holidays beyond the usual Christianized ones to include Earth Day, the equinoxes and Bicycle Day, commemorating the first acid trip taken by the inventor of LSD, Albert Hofmann, another of G.C.'s inspirations. And amigos. Word has it that he was present for the celebration surrounding Mission One closure, along with a whole raft of other celebrities, but this was before I came aboard so I can't say whether it's fact or rumor. The point is, though, for us, locked in as we were, we had to make our own fun—as Richard liked to say, "Any excuse for a party!"

In looking over what I've just written here, I realize I should say something about our ocean, since for those who are unfamiliar with the layout of E2, the term may seem a bit grandiose. And it is, I admit it. How could you have an ocean in a facility just over three acres total? Actually, what we called an ocean, what G.C. had christened an ocean, was just a big saltwater pool, albeit one stocked with sea creatures and a coral reef uprooted from the Sea of Cortez. It was limited by its dimensions—25 feet deep, 165 long and 85 wide, not much bigger than an Olympic-size pool but for its depth, which allowed for a much greater volume of water. Of course, as our inexhaustible critics have pointed out, the whole thing wasn't much more than a glorified aquarium entirely dependent on the action of the wave machine, without which the corals would have died in quick order. Again, I—*we*—admit it, guilty as charged. But the idea here was to represent five of the typical biomes that self-generate life on planet earth, to model an ecosystem that would allow for living things, including humans, to thrive in a hostile environment—on a space station or another planet. G.C. was one of the first to recognize that our species, through overpopulation, industrialization and the reckless burning of fossil fuels, was well on its way to destroying or at least depleting the global ecosystem and might just need an escape valve—an E2, an E3, an E4. New worlds. Seeds of life.

Just keep in mind that this was an *experiment,* not a perfected and finished product, and that in any experiment there are limitations and that things can go wrong, things do go wrong—that's the whole idea. That's how you learn, isn't it? We were all proud and privileged to be part of E2 and its ecological and sociological investigations, no matter what you might have heard otherwise. And that was why, especially in the beginning, time seemed so fluid, so accelerated, just like the life processes themselves once everything was glassed-in.

That first week was pretty much nose to the grindstone in any case, all of us going out of our way to make things flow smoothly, work a kind of banner we passed from hand to hand. I wasn't really paying attention to anything that wasn't immediate, so it came as something of a shock when my first visitor turned up at the end of the week. As it happened I was chef of the day, and I was anxious about that, eager to come up with something that would tickle the palates of my fellow Ecospherians and win me some points for effort and creativity both, and the last thing I was thinking about was the outside world. Was I competitive? Yes, sure. I wanted to dazzle them, sit back in my chair and bow my head modestly while everybody smacked their lips and murmured compliments to the chef, their little exclamations of pleasure raining down on me like aural manna. The menu I chose for dinner featured banana crepes, beet salad and chili sin carne over a bed of rice, the chili spiced with dried habanero pepper left over from

Mission One and topped with a sprinkle of goat cheese. I couldn't hope to match Ramsay's pie—I had neither the ingredients nor the time, actually, not to mention the skill—so I hit on the idea of making Popsicles from banana, papaya and a trickle of goat's milk, the whole blended and then frozen around eight individual Popsicle sticks, which were actually wooden tongue depressors borrowed from the medical lab for the occasion. The verdict? It was a hit. People licked their plates (as I said, we would all lick our plates eventually, for every meal, no matter who was the chef or what the meal had tasted like, so that was no great achievement but for the fact that this was the first time) and sucked on the big frozen Popsicles as if they were cigars, as if we were all sitting around puffing away in some gentlemen's (or -women's) club.

"E., you've outdone yourself."

"This is great, really wonderful. Like Baskin-Robbins. Have you got the other thirty flavors lined up for us?"

"And that chili, wow—it had a bite to it. Any of the hot peppers left or is that it?"

This was the sort of thing I was hearing as I bused the table and stacked the dishes on the counter preparatory to loading them into the dishwasher, and I have to admit I was feeding on the praise, murmuring "Thanks" and "It's nothing," and finally just "Aw, shucks" delivered with a sardonic enough-is-enough grin. And then T.T., who'd gone off to do his post-prandial CO_2 analysis, Popsicle swelling his cheek and a spatter of something on his shirt, came humping back up the stairs, looking spooked. Or surprised, I guess, would be more accurate. "E.," he announced, "you've got a visitor."

The room stood still. Everyone looked first to Troy, then to me. "A visitor?" I echoed, completely at a loss. How could I have a visitor when we were sealed in? I had a quick fleeting vision of somebody breaking through the glass, a hyper-inflated fan, a stalker or gang member or one of the legion of yahoos sending us hate mail, and then I understood. "You mean at the window?"

All eyes were on me as I went down the stairs, the crew, as one, rising from the table to lean over the balcony and watch me skirt the ag biome and animal pens until I disappeared from sight beneath them. It was gloomy inside and out, our lighting kept to a minimum after dark, and as I made my way across the floor to the airlock and the window built into the wall beside it, I wasn't sure what I was seeing in the convocation of shadows that engulfed the entryway. There was a figure at the window, too tall to be Linda—or my mother, though why I should imagine her there I couldn't say except that in situations like that you always expect bad news, *It's your father, dear, his heart, lungs, liver,* or some such. Of course, that was another factor Mission Control had taken into account in their endless scrutiny of us—family history. I remember G.C. and Judy, notepads propped up in their laps, trading off during the initial round of interviews: *Any illnesses in the family? Your parents alive still? How's their health?*

But this wasn't my parents or Linda or a stranger either: it was Johnny.

The outside light—it must have been a twenty-five-watt bulb, as if to make a feint at saving on electricity when the technosphere was burning through how many thousands of kilowatt hours a day I couldn't even begin to guess—shone weakly on his face. He was wearing his leather jacket, collar up, and a cowboy shirt he knew I liked, sapphire blue with cream piping around the breast pockets. I could see his breath hanging in the air and that was the strangest thing, to think it was cold out there when it was habitually warm if not hot in here, muggy, dense, tropical, the way an ideal world should be. Nobody wanted to put a temperate climate under glass, let alone a Nordic one, but outside E2 the elevation was four thousand feet, the month was March, and the temperatures could drop below freezing at night. I picked up the phone in the very instant he did, as if our motions were coordinated, hand to receiver, receiver to ear.

"Hey, babe," he said, his voice scraping bottom, "how's it? You getting enough to eat?"

I said, "Hi," but beyond that I couldn't think of what to say, and that was unusual for me. Normally I would have had a snappy comeback, especially because this last implied that we couldn't take care of ourselves inside, that we were weak, that the whole thing was nothing more than an elaborate joke. But no, no—he had a sense of humor, that was all, and this was just a routine, not a criticism. He was trying to cheer me, trying to be light-hearted, and he was here, that was the thing, here to show me he cared. Call it shock, surprise, the intrusion of his world on mine, but I just couldn't respond, the double-paned glass hanging there between us like a picture frame. I watched his breath condense in the frigid air, drift away and dissipate.

"What's the matter," he said, "cat got your tongue? But wait a minute, there are no cats in there, are there? Just, what, galagos? And by the way, what exactly *is* a galago anyway?"

"A primate," I said, and the spell was broken. "Aka bush baby. Big eyes, big ears, furry tail. Like a monkey, only it's not."

"The cuteness factor. Like something out of *Star Wars*—the Ewoks, right? Can't build your own world without tossing a little dollop of cuteness in . . . by the way, you're looking pretty cute yourself. A trifle thin, maybe, but—"

"Come on, Johnny," I said, but it was nice, this little interlude. Nice to banter. Nice to see him. Nice to know he hadn't forgotten about me. "I thought you would have forgotten about me by now," I said. "I mean, it's been a week."

He gave me a smile, though in the dim light and the way it angled in from overhead, it almost looked like a grimace. "Give me some credit," he said. He was lean and tall and graceful. He wore his hair long. Strands of it hung in his eyes, beautiful eyes, sparking green where they caught the light. "You know," he said, "I would have brought you a pizza, but I figured that'd only be like torture, unless you could experience it vicariously—I mean, if you want, I'd be happy to go get a double-cheese pepperoni from Alfano's and eat it slowly, slice by slice, so you can see my tongue and teeth and watch my Adam's apple when I swallow—"

"Come on, Johnny."

We were silent for a moment then and his face changed. "So what are we supposed to do," he said. "Hump the glass?"

There were smears on the surface where one of the crew had

entertained a visitor with what we would come to call the Ecospherian handshake, left hand to right, the touch of the glass, outside and in. I gave him a smile. "If that's what gets you off."

"It's not what gets me off—it's what gets you off. You're the one locked away like Rapunzel, so let down your hair."

My hands instinctively went to my hair. Which was dirty. I was dirty. Dirt was our way of life. I wore no makeup, not even lipstick. My T-shirt could have been cleaner. My shorts too. I raised my arms, fluffed out my hair and let it fall to my shoulders.

"Yeah." He breathed, and his voice went through me in an electric shiver. "That's better. Now how about, I don't know, how about showing some tit?"

I couldn't say *Come on, Johnny* one more time because that admonition wasn't real but only a kind of child's play, and this was different. We were bantering, we were lovers, and he could say that, say *How about showing some tit?* without stepping over the line because it was a joke and at the same time it wasn't. "Is this an obscene phone call?" I said.

He was leaning into the glass now so that his breath fogged the window, the phone pinched to one ear. "You bet it is."

I looked round me, looked over both shoulders and off into the shadows of the darkened biomes. I heard the coquis, the galagos. A moth flitted against the inside of the glass, attracted to the light that shone down on Johnny, who was right there now, inches away. Very slowly, as if I had all the time in the world—and I did—I slipped the T-shirt up over my head, then reached back to unfasten my bra.

Ramsay Roothoorp

It was dark, I couldn't really see all that clearly, and if I had second thoughts about spying on one of my crewmates, I stifled them. The whole thing was almost innocent, if you want to know the truth, because I'd gone down to check on the water flows in the fish ponds maybe ten minutes after Troy announced that E. had a visitor, which I'd forgotten entirely about because the conversation had veered off in some other direction altogether, and I was just strolling along minding my own business when I saw movement off to my right and there she was at the window, her shoulders bare and her back too, bare down to the waist. She seemed to be rotating her hips, gyrating against the glass, and I could make out the shifting form of her boyfriend—Johnny, his name was—looming in and out of the weak sepia light like a big fluttering vampire bat in one of the Dracula movies. It took me a minute to realize what was happening, and it wasn't as if I hadn't seen E. topless before—bottomless, for that matter—through the course of one team skinny-dipping episode or another, but this was different, this was E. like I'd never seen her, doing what? Simulating sex with a man who might or might not have had his penis in his hand while the shadows elongated and fell back again and E.'s hips went in and out and up and down in sync with his. It gave me a jolt. It did. And if I eased off my shoes and slipped in along the side of the animal pens so I could get a better look, I really had no choice in the matter. Call me a voyeur, but anybody in my position would have done the same.

Case in point: I'd had a call from my college roommate a week or so before closure. Jason. Jason Fourier. We'd kept in touch sporadically over the years, but he was calling now to reconnect because he'd seen my face on TV or maybe in the newspaper, and the first thing he said over the line, before even identifying himself, was *You're like a pig in shit.* And I said, *Jason?* And he said, *You're not fooling anybody, you dog. The blonde is hot. And that redhead, wow, scorching, man, just scorching.*

I can't say whether Jason's reaction was in any way representative of the larger response, but I have to give G.C., Judy and Dennis credit because here came the hook again, the irresistible fantasy of sex under glass. That was all the public cared about. Living arrangements. Bedrooms. Terranauts going at it like fauns and satyrs splayed out in the high grass under a mango tree. I was caught up in it too—how could I not be? Yes, we were doing science, yes, we were committed, but the human factor had to be front and center no matter what anybody says. You want a space colony? You can fill it with all the species you can manage to net, trap or dig up and you can balance out the O_2/CO_2 ratio to a nice clean earth-friendly 20.9 percent to .03 percent, but if the humans don't *mate,* don't reproduce, what good is it? The Bible might be sketchy on all this, Adam and Eve hunkering down to generate two sons and then another son to replace the murdered one, two more sons after that and a pair of daughters as well, leaving open the question of where the sons' wives had come from (unless God approved of incest or they found some other bright-eyed scampering hominid to trade genes with), but in the worlds we were projecting, sex and genetic diversity were key, for our species and all the others too. If E2's raft of creatures failed to reproduce, then the whole thing was a bust.

I'm not trying to justify what I did that night. I'm just saying that if you put yourself in an overheated environment with a girl like E. and then witness something like that you'd have to be beyond all hope not to find it at least *interesting.* I don't know how long I stood there watching, hard as a brick, my shorts damp with pre-ejaculate and the breath catching in my throat, but the mosquitoes brought me back to earth, or E2's earth, and I slunk away feeling guilty, feeling tainted, but wasn't that the way it always was when you watched porno?

* * *

There were some two thousand sensors distributed throughout E2, gauging everything from soil respiration to ocean salinity levels and systems functions, and cameras just about everywhere. Beyond that—and this was especially true in those first few months—every time you glanced up you were staring into the face of a family of tourists, Dad, Mom, Junior and Sis, clicking away with their Kodak Fun Savers. Or a journalist riffling through his notebook. Girl Scouts, Trekkies, bird-watchers or one clutch or another of non-specified enthusiasts who fixated on the Terranaut narrative as if it was the sole path in life. That first Halloween a whole mob of people appeared outside the airlock dressed as scientists, galagos, cockroaches and Terranauts, one group of eight tricked out in crimson jumpsuits and featuring a girl with her right hand bandaged in commemoration of the accident that brought down Mission One. But I'm getting ahead of myself. The point is, there was precious little privacy under the glass unless you knew where to look—and you had to be aware not only of your surroundings but also of the eyes fixed on you pretty much all the time.

An example. Just days after I'd happened to observe Dawn in her private moment there at the visitors' window, I was in the pigpen with her performing my morning's ag duty, thinking of nothing beyond going through the motions at hand and getting on with my day, which was to include a PicTel conference with an auditorium full of high-schoolers from Michigan's Upper Peninsula (Yoopers, they call themselves, in case you're interested), maintenance on the fish ponds and settling tanks and a video hookup with G.C., Judy and Dennis to take instruction and reveal, as discreetly as possible, any quirks or deviant tendencies—actual or in potentia—arising among my fellow Terranauts (for which, in time, I would be labeled a spy, a snitch, a traitor and worse). Anyway, there we were, Dawn and I, equipped with shovels, buckets and brooms, our bodies decaffeinated and already on the way to being undernourished, slinging shit. We chatted collegially as we bent to it, our conversation peppered with in-jokes, gossip about the six of us who didn't happen to be present, work-related issues, that sort of thing.

E.'s hair had broken free of the ponytail she'd been wearing earlier and now it was a wild sweat-slicked mass obscuring her face every time she leaned into the shovel. Her arms were bare, flecked with mud. It came to me that she was totally at home here, and for some reason I flashed on Thomas Hardy, though I hadn't given him a thought or glanced at a single line of his since college. What came to me was the pivotal scene in *Jude the Obscure* in which Arabella Donn, the lusty farmer's daughter, attracts Jude Fawley's attention by flinging a pig's genitalia at him. And, if I was remembering rightly, scoring a strike right down the middle of the plate.

"You know what you remind me of?" I glanced up from the bucket I was steadying with both hands as she made a wide slashing deposit in its depths.

"No, what?"

"I mean who, who you remind me of?"

She shrugged, the shovel backing away from the mouth of the bucket to rasp against the concrete floor. Behind her, the pigs—two sows, a boar and a pair of piglets—poked their snouts through the gate separating the back portion of the pen from the front, which we crewmates were in the process of slopping out. "I don't know, who?"

The smell—that perfume pigs create as their highest achievement, a mix of sour milk, putrefying blood, shit, urine, vomit and some other unidentifiable element that binds it all together so it hits you like a club, over and over—had us breathing shallowly and through our mouths only. "Arabella Donn," I said.

She stopped what she was doing, put one hand on her hip. She was amused, I could see that. "Who?"

"From *Jude the Obscure*? She was the farm girl, the pig girl, actually."

"I wouldn't know—you were the lit major, not me. I remember the movie *Tess*, though—"

"Polanski. What did you think?"

"It was all right. I guess I didn't know they wore so much eye shadow then, back on the farm, I mean—"

"Right, me either."

"But that's what I've been reduced to, huh? The pig girl? Or wench. Wouldn't they have called her a wench?"

"You're more than that to me, E., a whole lot more. You're the goat girl too, and what—the eggmonger. The shit-slinger, the—"

"Very funny," she said, and made a playful gesture, as if to snatch up a handful of that very substance and fling it at me, but of course I don't have to tell you how *slippery* this medium is, how quickly it can shift underfoot so that someone clowning around in a pair of pink rubber galoshes while standing ankle-deep in it can lose her balance in a heartbeat. Which was just what happened. Looking surprised—and apologetic, that too—she went down hard on her backside, right in the thick of it, and what did I do? What could I do? I laughed.

The pigs, incidentally, were a semi-domesticated variety shipped in from Ossabaw Island, off the Georgia coast. This was a population bred out of a feral remnant stocked on the island by Spanish explorers in the early sixteenth century and they'd evolved to suit their limited environment through the dwarfism many island species exhibit, as E.O. Wilson, whom I mentioned earlier, theorized in positing some of the principles of island biogeography back in the 1970s. As a dwarf variety, Ossabaw hogs were perfect for our purposes, the boar no taller than maybe twenty inches at the shoulder and weighing in at well under two hundred pounds. The idea here was to provide meat, of course, as on any farm, but the complicating factor, as the Mission One crew discovered the hard way, was in finding enough fodder to keep the animals growing into the promise of their chops, hams and spare ribs. (Initially, G.C. had proposed using Vietnamese potbellied pigs, but word got out to the public and there was a howl of protest from hundreds of people who kept them as pets, because if you recall, it was around then that they were, very briefly, all the rage. I remember one overwrought newspaper editorial comparing us to dog eaters, as in, *Would you slaughter, skin and bake the family dog? No,* I said—privately, of course—*we wouldn't. We'd fricassee it.*)

So I laughed. And E., down there in the muck, caught me unaware, scissoring her legs to knock me off my feet and bring me down with her, which ordinarily I wouldn't have found all that funny—who would? Think about it. You can live as close to the earth as you want, but you've got to draw the line somewhere. The thing was, despite the smell, I couldn't help noticing the way E.'s shirt clung to her, as if this were wet T-shirt night down at the local bar—with the obvious limitation that what her shirt was marinated in wasn't anything so innocuous as water. Or beer. It was a moment. And there I was, on my hands and knees, in the thick of it, and I suppose I reacted instinctively, grabbing at her ankle as she tried to get to her feet so that she pitched forward and went down all over again.

It was childish. It was embarrassing. And it was nothing I'd ever had even an inkling of doing in all my life to this point, but what made it worse was that even as we were staggering to our feet like drunken mud-wrestlers the flashbulbs went off and we looked up to see a dozen visitors pressed to the glass and high-fiving each other. Worse yet, there was Judy, tour guide du jour, standing amongst them with a face of stone.

* * *

"You know, really, Ramsay, I don't care what you do—or who you fuck—but when you descend to this kind of thing—"

"Crap, you mean. Call it crap."

"—it just hurts the mission, that's all. I wanted to say 'reflects badly on it,' but that doesn't even come close, does it?"

I was in our office cum command center, sitting before the video monitor, watching Judy's angry face snap at me like a chameleon's (the roll of the eyes, the recoil of the tongue). It was early afternoon and I was scheduled to entertain, instruct and inform the Yoopers in ten minutes, but Judy had summoned me and here we were. I'd had a shower and changed into a clean

T-shirt and shorts, though I suppose I still carried a whiff of the pigpen about me, which was inevitable when you were forced to shower with scentless soap and shampoo. Not that it would have mattered to Judy—or the Yoopers, for that matter. The technology didn't transfer body odor, or not yet anyway. As far as the rest of it was concerned, my teeth gleamed and the haircut I'd gotten just before closure was holding up fairly well, though I'd had to do a quick trim of the sideburns. What I said was, "I'm not fucking anybody, though I suppose it would be bootless to tell you that—"

"Bootless? What the hell is that supposed to mean?"

"Useless. You know, as in Shakespeare? 'I all alone beweep my outcast state/And trouble deaf heaven with my bootless cries.'"

She clenched her jaw. Her face seemed to expand till it took up the entire screen. "Listen," she said finally, and then she appended my name, her voice lower now, as if she were fighting to keep it under control. "We're not playing games here. Those people today? That was a biology class from the School of Life Sciences at U.A. We need their support—we need all the support we can get. And what do they see? You and Dawn up to your ears in shit. Or what—playing in it? Playing in shit."

I shrugged. Looked into the camera. "You try shoveling that stuff and see how clean you wind up. Or your precious biology class—take them on a field trip to the nearest pig farm. Or better yet, the slaughterhouse. You live in a real world, you get dirty, okay?"

"But that was disgusting, just disgusting. And you know what I told them? I told them it was part of an experiment to see how even the dirtiest wash would affect the wastewater systems, as if it was some commercial for Tide or something—"

I began to feel an edge of remorse. I'd acted like an adolescent, like some hormone-challenged teenager, and in the process I'd made the mission look bad. I wanted to apologize, wanted to say *Sorry, Judy,* and move on, but I didn't like her tone, didn't like her bulging eyes and the tight unforgiving slash of her mouth or the psychic cost of what we'd been doing in the executive washroom before we were interrupted or what she expected from me now. "And they bought that?" I said.

She just shook her head and maybe she clucked her tongue too, though the audio wasn't fine-tuned enough to pick it up. "There's another thing," she said, "and then I'll let you go so you can do your conference with the high school kids. It's the play. Jeremiah's anxious to get it off the ground, meaning you've had a week and a half to adjust and it's time to get down to business. Like in rehearsals, which really haven't amounted to much yet, have they?"

"Yeah, fine," I said, "okay. But why don't you tell Diane—she's team captain."

A pause. I watched the screen waver, a pattern of individual pixels blurring Judy's face before the resolution came back. She was disembodied, what I knew of her from that last night and all the times before invisible to me now, inaccessible, as if I'd never stripped her clothes off or climbed atop her or watched her as she clung to me till she stiffened and went slack again. Her eyes held steady, only her lips moving. "Because I'm telling *you*," she said.

* * *

Our first crisis came within a month of closure, and while it wasn't even in the ballpark with Mission One's dilemma over Roberta Brownlow and her severed fingertip, it affected us all nonetheless, and me in particular. It was in early April, the days lengthening imperceptibly and the vegetation responding nicely with a burst of new growth (and O_2). We were all adjusting to our diet of roughly 1,500 calories a day, our muscles tightening and whatever beginner's paunches we might have come in with all but gone, and we fell into our roles without any strain or undue tension. We'd all just sat down to dinner one night, feeling companionable and looking forward to Troy's first vintage of banana wine, of which we were each promised at least one glass and possibly more, when one of the galagos let out with a high riveting call—a screech, really—we hadn't heard before.

"Jesus, what was *that*?" Stevie said, and we all turned to Gretchen.

"I don't know," she said, setting down her wineglass. She looked stricken. "I've never heard anything like it—have you, any of you?"

We hadn't. To this point the animals had almost exclusively confined themselves to an ascending series of hoots or the sort of soft whining cry you'd expect from a baby in a cradle, hence their popular name, bush babies. For a long moment we all sat there poised over our plates, listening.

Richard said, "Sounds like somebody died," and Gretchen said, "Don't say that."

Dinner that night was Troy's responsibility, and if we hadn't been overworked and underfed none of us would have been particularly enthusiastic about what we found on our plates—mashed yams and rice topped with a runny peanut/banana sauce and a side dish of borscht featuring some sort of unidentifiable greens floating atop it. Hands down, Troy was the worst cook among the crew, the kind of clueless bachelor who'd subsisted on fast food and Velveeta sandwiches before coming to the project. The wine, which he'd fermented in his chem lab from a banana mash, peels and all, was presented as a peace offering.

By this time, incidentally, we'd graduated from helping ourselves from the communal pot to having the day's chef portion out our meals on eight separate plates, assuring that everyone received his fair share, and the first thing we did before digging in was assess the wine. It was young, no question about that, and its color ran from the bright aniline yellow of antifreeze on top to a dark sludgy amber at the bottom of the glass. Its nose, as you might expect, was banana-heavy, and that killed any subtlety the vintner may have been striving for. As for palate, it lingered like mouthwash and gave you the same impression of chemical rigor. Still, and credit the winemaker here, it had tested out at nearly twenty percent ABV, and that, as far as we were concerned, lifted it into the realm of fine wine.

"Eco-cru!" Richard cried, hoisting his glass. "Way to go, T.T.!"

That was when the shriek echoed through the biomes and we all froze, glasses in hand, and Stevie looked to Gretchen and Gretchen set her glass down. This was her province—the rain forest and its creatures—and she spent every waking moment obsessing over it. It was she who'd reported that one species of ant—*Nylanderia fulva,* the crazy ant—was taking over, wiping out the insect fauna not only of the rain forest but the savanna, marsh and desert as well and she'd made the discovery, pre-closure, that the failure of Mission One's bee colonies was due to the cockroaches swarming them at night when the bees were at rest and all but defenseless. Which led us to restock the colonies and attempt measures to keep the cockroaches out of them, with mixed results. As for the ants, one of *Nylanderia*'s survival strategies is to breed multiple queens, so though we eradicated nests wherever we could, it was essentially a losing battle. Chalk it up to experience—you can bet the next generation Ecosphere won't include any species of crazy ant, not *Nylanderia* or *Paratrechina longicornis* either.

The shriek came again. And then again. And in the next moment two of the galagos burst into view, hurtling through the fruit trees below us and scrambling up the steel struts of the space-frame till they were overhead, biting and clawing at each other all the while. Fur flew, literally, and the tiny canines came into play. "What are they doing, fighting?" Gyro asked, his thin beaky face turned upward, and I couldn't help thinking what a stupid question it was.

"It's Lola," Gretchen said, jumping up so precipitously she knocked her chair over. "And"—she was at the rail now, peering out into the darkness—"Luna. That's Luna, I'm sure of it." She turned to us, to me, even as the cat-sized creatures shot across the spaceframe and disappeared into the rain forest beyond, still shrieking. "I was afraid of this. It's the alpha female going after the beta, and that's inevitable, I suppose, but I was hoping—"

"They'd all get along?" Richard gave her a smile, raising his glass again. "Let's toast to prosimian harmony."

"Sip it, sip it," Troy coached. "Don't just throw it down—"

But Richard wasn't listening. He took a good healthy swallow of the swirling amber liquid and made a face. "Holy shit—it's like setting your socks on fire."

In the next moment we all raised our glasses solemnly to our lips, hoping—or no, praying—that Troy's libation was the answer to what was already becoming something of a slog, all work and no play, one month down and twenty-three to go. I liked to drink, one of the vices I'd always indulged, and not just in the rush to closure. We all needed intoxicants, as a crew and as a species too, something to lift us out of the ordinary, and if there ever were to be a space colony, the colonists would need their intoxicants same as anybody or risk going quietly mad. I flashed on half a dozen bar scenes, the vodka I'd kept in my freezer, the Flor de Caña rum I loved on the rocks with a splash of Coke, the taste of pinot noir on Rhonda Ronson's lips when we shared a bottle in bed, then I closed my eyes and took a hopeful swallow of our first vintage under glass.

I didn't spit it out. And I didn't gag either, though I had to fight the reflex. Judging from the faces of my fellow Ecospherians, we were all in agreement. All but Gretchen, who hadn't touched hers—or her meal either. She was at the rail still, listening for further signs of strife, while we sipped and chatted and lifted our forks to our mouths. Troy—he wore his sandy hair long so that it covered his all but perpendicular ears—smacked his lips thoughtfully and looked round the table. "It's almost there," he said, "really. It just needs maybe a bit more aging."

"A bit more than what—a week?" Richard said, and we were all laughing now, or most of us anyway, the alcohol running through our veins and loosening the cords that still bound us to the outside and whatever commitments we'd left behind. We were having a party, our first true and veritable party. Even the food, bland as it was, began to taste better.

"Come on, Gretchen," Richard called out. "Worry about that later—we're having a party here."

Gretchen was leaning over the rail, propped on her elbows and staring off into the distance where the artificial mountain and dominant trees of the rain forest rose against the starry screen of the superstructure. The night pulsed with the calls of the smaller creatures and the intermittent roar of the big vacuum pumps sucking water into the wave machine, a roar that blurred the distinction between artificial and natural so thoroughly I sometimes thought I was hearing whales and walruses blowing in open water (though the biggest thing in our sea was a two-foot parrotfish, if you discount Stevie, who measured five-seven and weighed in at one hundred and twenty-four beautifully proportioned pounds). Gretchen seemed hesitant, but there was her food, getting cold, and her wine—we were all eyeing it—sitting there untouched. In the next moment she was at the table, righting her upended chair and sliding in between E. and Gyro, her face pasty and her glasses catching the light so you couldn't see her eyes. She was looking old, or older, the worry over the galago scuffle and god knew what else—*ants*—sitting heavily in her jowls. She was only four years older than me, but carried herself like someone much older, and maybe that was an effect of her total absorption in her work and the humorlessness that underpinned it. I'm not saying she wasn't fit—she could outwork practically anybody, except maybe E.—it was just that she seemed distracted and didn't much bother about her appearance, beyond the occasions that is when Judy demanded we all clean up and face the cameras. What am I trying to say? She was unstylish, unhip, frumpy. That's the word. *Frumpy*.

"You think it's anything serious?" E. asked, turning to her. "They wouldn't really hurt each other, would they? They don't go to war in nature or anything like that, do they?"

"That's reserved for our species," I said, and Richard, leering from across the table, said, "I second that."

"And ants," Diane put in from the other end of the table. "Don't forget ants."

Gretchen—hardly anyone used her nickname, Snowflake, which we'd shortened to "Snow," though I thought "Flake" would have suited her better—let out a sigh, brought the wineglass to her nose, sniffed, and set it down again. "Who can say? In their native habitat, in equatorial Africa, they've got space and sanctuary, so a beta female can go off and if she's lucky hook up with a beta male cast out of another troop—but here, in an enclosure, anything goes." She lifted the glass again and again put it down.

"That's what we're doing here, right? Finding out. And I really hope they'll respond and adjust to their environment, but there's no telling—"

That was when the shrieks started up again, as if the beta female, Luna, had found a hiding place and now, suddenly and spookily, Lola had found it too. And here they came again, the same pair (Jimbo, the male, and Lana, the other female, nowhere to be seen). Again they went from the branches to the superstructure, rocketing overhead as if they'd been shot from an air gun, and again they closed in a blur of teeth and claws and whirling limbs, only this time, in desperation, Luna made a leap for the railing right in front of us and just barely made it, bunching like a cat and emitting a low hiss of distress, her eyes trembling and huge.

This couldn't have happened during the Mission One closure, by the way, as the original structure of the Human Habitat was glassed in to prevent just such an intrusion, not to mention keeping out the mosquitoes that bred in any errant puddle and the no-see-ums that would rise up out of the marsh come May. We'd voted as a team (seven to one, Troy the lone holdout) to remove the glass during the transition phase from Mission One reentry to Mission Two closure, seeking a more authentic experience. We were here to be one with nature, after all, not separated from it— wasn't it enough that there was glass everywhere we looked? So we took the panels down and left ourselves open to everything, snakes, lizards, beetles, butterflies and birds—and now this, the galago, our "companion primate," crouched on the railing just feet from us while her antagonist chittered curses from above.

"Oh, my god," E. said. "She's bleeding."

And so she was. We all saw it. A gash over the flexor of one hip, the fur there gone a brilliant saturate red, and the left ear torn. (If you don't have any experience of galagos, picture a furball with a fluffed-up tail, oversized ears and big night-seeing eyes, the sort of thing Disney would put front and center if one day the Magic Kingdom should devise its own ecosphere.)

"We've got to treat that," Gretchen said, and Richard, our source of sutures, anesthetic and antibiotic salve, made as if to rise from his chair. "No, no—shhh!" Gretchen hissed. "Nobody move."

I looked to E. Her face was white (not yet orange, as all our faces would eventually be, due to an excess of beta-carotene in our diet) and she sat there rigid, her shoulders clenched and her hands suspended over her plate. I could see she was thinking the same thing I was—that is, how in Christ's name were we ever going to catch the thing before it either bled out or the other one got hold of it and killed it? Not that it would be an insurmountable loss—this was the way of nature—but the well-being of these things, of all the creatures and plants under this roof, was our responsibility, and the loss of Luna would carry a symbolic weight the media would gleefully take up and strap to our backs. So here it was, our first failure—or potential failure—staring us in the face. Only problem was, what to do about it? Any sort of trap would have to be fabricated in the shop and whatever netting we had was in one of the storage rooms in the basement. Making a grab for the thing—and I thought of it, briefly, before dismissing the idea—would be futile. Besides, they did bite, didn't they?

In the event, the decision was taken out of our hands. Suddenly—so suddenly none of us actually saw Lola suspended in mid-air as she made a leap every bit as desperate as her victim's—there were two galagos on the rail and just as suddenly there were none. Why was this? Again—we were moving in human time and they were moving in prosimian time—it took us a moment to understand that they'd now been transposed as if in some magic trick to the space beneath the table, where they snarled and hissed and spat while we sprang up in something approaching collective panic—what would they do to bare legs?—and finally became spectators to the violence that was as elemental as life itself.

* * *

Later, after Gretchen had separated the combatants with a timely thrust of the kitchen broom and they disappeared in opposite directions, we were more or less able to take up where we left off, though the interruption seemed to have put a damper on things.

The wine helped. As it turned out there was enough for a second round for the four of us who wanted it (Troy, Richard, Stevie and me) and we wound up draining the beaker to the last precious alcohol-infused drop. After which I sat down to a game of five-card draw with Troy and Richard while the others went off to their rooms—except for Gretchen, that is, who when last seen was stalking the rain forest with a butterfly net that might or might not have had sufficient tensile strength to contain a wounded and no doubt thoroughly riled galago.

Everything was quiet—no one even had a radio going—and the game so absorbed me I lost all track of time. I was a pretty good poker player (a champion bluffer, certainly), but Richard was good too and he usually wound up winning the biggest pots, no small thing when you consider that we were playing for peanuts, *literal* peanuts, hoarded from the handful Diane doled out each day for our mid-morning snack—and beyond that, that we were so hungry we ate them shells and all. What I'm saying is that to lose in the outside world, while it's always disappointing, hurtful even, isn't so much a matter of survival as a drain on the income, but here, inside, it went much deeper. To see Richard—or Troy— rake in a big pot made you ache in the deepest, hollowest, emptiest crevice of your alimentary canal. Those peanuts, and the essential oils they contained, not to mention protein, were the cornerstone of our diet. Losing was beyond tragic. In the long run—and I don't mean to overdramatize here, but indulge me—it could be fatal.

Happily, on this particular night, I was the one raking in the biggest pot, nailing Richard on the last hand, my three queens beating his two pair, and when I bade them farewell—I who had come to the table with thirty-two peanuts—I went off to my room in possession of a hoard of sixty-seven, and I have to say I was feeling as good as I'd felt since the exhilaration of that first heady day of closure. The night was a fine and welcoming thing, same as it always was, temperature in the seventy-eight-to-eighty-two-degree range, humidity high, O_2 levels dropping fractionally as photosynthesis shut down during the hours of darkness. I closed my door, and not simply to keep beetles, moths and mosquitoes from sailing in to bat variously around the lamp or feast on my exposed flesh, but because I had a hoard to watch over. Sixty-seven peanuts. A fortune by any measure.

For a long while I lay spread-eagled on my bed, one hand in my shorts, idly massaging myself so that I went hard and soft and hard again (if E2 was a cyclotron of the life sciences, it was a hormonal accelerator too, a kind of perpetual steamy night of the adolescent soul, clothes a nuisance, shoes even, every pore open wide), while the other sifted through the comforting mound of my winnings. I was chewing idly—again, shells and all: to this day I can't imagine eating a shelled peanut and wasting even that scant bit of nutrition—and letting my mind drift until everything went still.

It was late when I woke and after I got up to use the bathroom I found I couldn't get back to sleep. I won't say I'm an erratic sleeper—most nights I sleep right through—but every once in a while, whether I'm stressed or not, I wind up tossing and turning, sometimes for hours. I definitely wasn't stressed on this particular night—I'd won at cards, I had a belly full of peanuts, Judy had retracted her claws and in any case couldn't physically get to me, and as far as I knew G.C. was in the dark about what had gone on between us—but I just couldn't seem to drift off. Eventually, I found myself slipping out of bed and padding out into the darkness, thinking maybe I'd sit by the ocean a while or maybe even take a swim.

Snakes—did I mention snakes? Snakes were not a worry. Outside, beyond the glass, the Sonoran Desert hosted something like seven or eight species of venomous reptile, including the Gila monster, the sidewinder and coral snake, but ours was the kind of paradise in which the serpent was represented by two species only—the garter snake and the slug-eating snake, both harmless enough and essential too, the garter snakes dwelling in the stream and ponds and feeding on excess frogs and mosquito fish (*Gambusia affinis*), the slug-eaters doing what their name suggests. Ours was an innoxious paradise, built to serve our needs and sustain itself in perpetuity, a working example of what NASA labeled

CELSS, for Controlled Ecological Life Support Systems. If I came across any of our snakes, so much the better.

By now it was just past three in the morning, moonless, the superstructure admitting a soft washed-out sheen of starlight that glowed like pale fire on every leaf and branch. My toes read the soft trucked-in earth like braille. Life seeped into my lungs. Outside, beyond the grid of interlocking windows, I could just make out the dark gap of the Santa Catalina Mountains to the east and the big wheeling strip of stars rising out of it. I'd never been much of a stargazer—never had the time, frankly—and I didn't recognize a whole lot beyond the Dippers, Orion's Belt and the tiny glowing ember of Mars, but as I made my way down to the beach and stretched out in the sand, I found myself studying the night sky in a whole new way. It might have been humid inside—we had enough condensation from the air handlers alone to provide our supply of drinking water—but outside, in the desert, where the air was thin and light pollution unheard of, you could see right up into the back molars of the universe.

That thought occupied me a while, tranquilized me, actually, until one of the stars separated itself and began to hump across the dome of the sky, vanishing and reappearing as the struts of the spaceframe erased it and brought it back again. It was a satellite, maybe the space shuttle itself, and I thought of how strange that must be—a moving star—to the aboriginal tribes of Australia or New Guinea who'd built their cosmogony on the original stars, the ones that moved only with the progress of the night. What did they think—that a new god had appeared? That the end had come or at least been foretold? Or no, their shamans or medicine men or whatever they called them would have worked it into the received narrative the way any priest or rabbi would. What choice did they have? The whole wobbly construct of gods and hexes and celestial divination would have come crashing down around them if they didn't. Right. And then they'd be out of a job. (Of course, our civilization is different only by degree, so let's not pat ourselves on the back here. We send up our shuttles, satellites and probes, but we have no clearer idea of ultimate purpose than the aborigines.

To say that the universe originated as a single atom or that space is infinite is to indulge in a belief system that doesn't do much more than apply labels to the unknown and unknowable.)

Some time passed, the thump of the vacuum pumps as regular as a giant's heartbeat, and then I got up, shucked my shorts and took a swim in the placid people-friendly aquarium that was our ocean (no stingrays here, no sharks or barracudas or jellyfish, no crosscurrents, no undertow). When I got out, back at the beach, I realized I'd forgotten a towel, and, improvising, I began patting myself down with my shorts. That was when I became aware of a low-threshold sound—a kind of wheezing or rustling—emanating from the wall of bamboo that separated the rain forest from the ocean and the other biomes. And what was it? One of the lizards? A frog? A snake? I moved closer, curious in the way I'd been trained to be—as a naturalist in a state of nature, the sand muffling my footsteps. There was a shadow there, a dense clump of darkness against the deep green cane that had gone black in this light, and the shadow was breathing—or no, snoring. It took me a moment, my eyes homing in on it, to realize that I was staring down at one of the galagos—a very specific one, its shadowy ear torn and a black crescent of dried blood defining its left rear leg.

Again, my first thought was to grab it, pin it to me and take it to Gretchen, but again I resisted—Gretchen had a pair of elbow-length leather gloves to employ in situations like this, and beyond that, she knew what she was doing and I didn't. Very carefully, so as not to awaken it, I backed away, stepped into my shorts and went off to fetch her. I found the Habitat deserted but for the cockroaches, everybody asleep at this hour, and went down the hallway to Gretchen's room, which was right next door to mine. The door was shut and I knocked softly a moment, chary of waking the others—how would I explain being outside Gretchen's door, dead of night, in a pair of wet shorts? There was no answer. I tried again, a touch more forcefully. Still nothing. A mosquito buzzed in for the kill and died in the effort. I pushed open the door and stepped into the room, calling softly, "Gretchen. Gretchen, are you awake?"

There was a stirring above. Gretchen's voice drifted down, hoarse with sleep: "What is it? Who's there?"

"It's me," I said. "Vodge. I found Luna—down by the ocean?"

"What time is it?"

"I don't know—three, three-thirty. She's just lying there, asleep, I think. She snores, did you know that?"

There was a moment of silence, then the bedsprings played a little tune, a light flicked on above and Gretchen, in her nightgown and sans glasses, was staring myopically down at me. "Is she all right? Does she look hurt? I mean, why should she be sleeping now, unless, I don't know. Where'd you say she was?"

So we made an expedition, just the two of us, Gretchen in her nightgown (which was filmy, but not see-through, and long enough to trail behind her like a wafting mist) and me in my shorts. She carried the flashlight and the leather gloves, I the cage we dug out of the storeroom. Things were quiet—or as quiet as they got in E2, what with the racketing of the coquis, the hum of the fans and the belch of the wave machine, but the creatures were as still as if they were locked in suspended animation, and our fellow Terranauts, as far as we knew, were busy negotiating the terra incognita of their dreams. We talked in whispers. When we entered the ocean area we fell silent, communicating by hand gestures only.

I took Gretchen's arm, led her across the strip of sand and pointed to the knot of shadow where the animal lay sleeping. She had her glasses on now—she was all but blind without them, or so she said—and she bent close to make sure this was Luna and not one of the others, but that should have been obvious since the animals are active at night and this one wasn't. Once she was satisfied, she backed off a few paces, worked her hands and forearms into the leather gauntlets and stalked forward again, step by step. My instructions, agreed upon in the hurried moments in her room while she slipped into a pair of flip-flops and extracted the leather gloves from a drawer in her oak entertainment center that was the exact duplicate of my own oak entertainment center, were to flick on the flashlight when she gave the signal and have the cage open and ready to receive the animal. Once she got hold of it, that is—and there was the trick.

"Now!" Gretchen said into the darkness and I switched on the flashlight in the very instant Luna came hissing to life, springing up so fast she might have been hot-wired, but Gretchen was there and Gretchen had her and in the next moment she was in the cage and the latch had been latched. By me. "Now what?" I asked, and I will say that my pulse would have registered above normal right about then.

Gretchen just stared at me, looking, I don't know, un-Gretchen-like, in the diffused light at the margins of the beam, which I was training on the cage now. "What do you *think*? We take her back to my room and treat her wounds before they get infected." And then she added, gratuitously (and, I think, because we'd just watched *The Godfather, Part II,* as our team movie the previous Saturday), *"Capiche?"*

I have to admit she was more than capable, our own veterinarian, though she wasn't a veterinarian in any sense the outside world would have recognized—she was a Ph.D., not a D.V.M., and that was a huge distinction, apples and oranges, out there beyond the glass. I set the cage down on the coffee table in her sitting room, Luna chittering and clawing at the mesh—and shitting, that too, shitting out her disappointment and fury—and in the next moment Gretchen had a syringe in her hand and in the moment after that the animal was lying inert on the floor of the cage.

I stayed there for the whole thing, lending moral support, I suppose, because I was all but useless as far as medical procedures were concerned. Gretchen patiently wiped the animal clean, then tended its wounds—the dilapidated ear, the big gash—first with hydrogen peroxide, then Neosporin, all the while thinking aloud. "Bandage? No. She'd just chew it off. Or it would make her even more of a target. What do you think, Vodge?"

I'd gone into something of a trance, watching her hands roam over the gray-brown fur of the thing in her lap while her hair fell free to soften her face. And what was I thinking? That age is relative. She was four years older than I, but what was four years? Nothing. Nothing at all. When I was younger, just out of college and teaching at a high school in suburban New York, I was callow enough to see everything in terms of age, and a gap of four years seemed insurmountable to me, impossible, a kind of temporal mountain I couldn't imagine scaling. The school was a good one, devotedly academic, and we had a big English department, twenty-eight of us, more or less evenly divided between the older teachers and those of us in our early twenties. In my second year, a new teacher joined the faculty—Mary Watts, a blonde with a sad face and an exciting physique. I was twenty-two, she was twenty-six. Word had it that her sadness derived from what had happened to her in her previous position, a sorry affair—a cliché—in which she fell for one of her colleagues, a man in his fifties who was firmly and immovably married and who strung her along for a couple of years before dumping her and getting her fired into the bargain. Mary Watts. Twenty-six years old. I studied her face and saw the lines etched at the corners of her eyes, crow's-feet, battle scars, and thought how very, very old she was.

So what am I saying? I looked at Gretchen now and Gretchen was totally different from the Gretchen I knew—or had compartmentalized in my mind. She was softer somehow, younger, her arms smooth and muscular in just the right proportion—shapely—and her legs too. Her feet. Her hands. She dipped her head to fasten the latch on the cage, all done with her doctoring now, and her hair fell away to expose one ear and a tiny red jewel pinned in her earlobe and glowing like the one planet I recognized when I looked up into the night sky, like Mars, Mars in miniature and caught right there in the isolated lobe of Gretchen Frost's warm pink ear.

She turned to look up at me. "It's late," she said.

I agreed, but I didn't rise from the chair I'd been sunk into for the past twenty minutes.

"Real late," she said, and her smile, slow and soft and sweet, transformed her face.

"Yeah," I said, and appended a little laugh.

"I don't know how you feel," she said, "but after our little adventure, I'm not tired at all, not a bit. I mean, my heart—here, come here, put your hand here, yeah, here, right on my heart. Feel that? It's still pounding."

* * *

"I hear you helped Gretchen out the other night. With the galago? Which one was it?"

"Luna."

"Right. You think it's going to be okay?"

"I don't know, I guess so. It's in a cage now—in her room— almost like it's a pet or something."

"Any idea when she's going to release it, because I've got a reporter from the *Los Angeles Times*—Albert Cooney?—who wants details. We're trying to talk him into a series on the situation, you know, work the preservation angle and the cuteness thing too, maybe get the school kids involved—"

"Yeah, great, and if he wants to talk to me—"

"He does. I've already set it up. Tomorrow, three p.m., visitors' window."

"I'll have to check my social calendar."

Judy and I were on the phone this time because it was cheaper— and more private—than videoconferencing, so I couldn't gauge how this had gone over until she let out a little laugh and said, "Yeah, right. What's tonight—movie night?"

"We voted six to two for *Alien,* my nomination. Thing is, I'm starting to feel like I'm pregnant with something—something with claws and all these cascading sets of teeth—"

"And spit, don't forget the spit. Hydrofluoric acid, *n'est-ce pas?*"

"Scary proposition, Jude—it could burst right out of me, gobble up E., Stevie and Lark and then drool right on down through the stainless-steel tub that keeps this ship afloat. And then where would we be?"

She was silent a moment. Then, in another voice altogether: "You miss me?"

The question took me by surprise. It had been more than a month and I knew her now mainly as a distant face on the PicTel monitor and a voice on the telephone. "That goes without saying."

"Is that all? Is that as passionate as you can get? I would have thought, locked away like that . . ." She trailed off. "Don't you want to fuck me? Don't you want me to suck you and put you inside me?"

I admitted that I did.

"Well, come on," she said. "Tell me about it. In detail."

I told her, though I wasn't all that good at this sort of thing—I was more a doer than a talker when it came to sex—and then she gave me her version and the whole business, I have to admit, was pretty stimulating. Finally, after two or three minutes of this, I said, "Even the inmates at the penitentiary get conjugal visits."

"And you don't. Pity, huh?"

"You seeing anybody?"

"Are you?"

"What do *you* think?" I said, putting some emphasis into it. "But you haven't answered my question."

"Jeremiah," she said. "Just Jeremiah."

Why I was jealous, why I was even having this conversation, was beyond me. She was going to do what she was going to do and I was going to do what I was going to do. I was picturing G.C.—her and G.C.—going at it, and then a thought came to me, a nightmare of a thought that made the image vanish in a puff of smoke as if in some X-rated cartoon. "This line *is* secure, isn't it? I mean, nobody's listening in, right?"

"It's secure when I want it to be," she said. "And that's how I want it now. Obviously. But you never answered *my* question—"

"What question?"

"When's Gretchen going to let Lola—or is it Luna? Luna, right? When's she going to let Luna back out into the rain forest? It'd be a great photo op, you know what I'm saying?"

"Why don't you ask Gretchen?"

"Believe me, I intend to, but as long as I've got you on the line,

I thought I'd get your take on it. Especially if Lola's going to attack her again or even, god forbid, if she should kill her . . ."

I took a moment, gazing out into the middle distance where a dark mass of bees struggled against one of the glass panels, disoriented by the hard edge they'd come up against. "I don't know," I said finally. "It's a jungle out there."

Linda Ryu

I have a confession to make, something even Dawn doesn't know about. On top of everything else, what with sorting out my feelings about the mission and trying to be productive and keep up the pretense, I wind up becoming a snoop—a spy—no different than Ramsay. It's not something I'm proud of really, but it was more a question of evolution than anything else (and I won't say survival of the fittest because Mission Control makes a joke out of any notion of fair competition). I'm still furious over the way I was passed over—screw them if they think they can look down their noses at me and then turn around and throw me back into the competition for Mission Three with the also-rans and the new candidates, every one of which—or *whom*—I would have rejected on sight. So what I do is I became a cog in Mission Control, as essential to them as the air they breathe in the command center. It's funny really. All at once I'm on the inside of the outside, if that doesn't sound too pathetic, trying to impress G.C., Judy and Dennis with my rigor and focus, which, of course, means doing their bidding whether I like it or not.

When I'm not bent over a hoe in the test plots or cleaning and maintaining and whatever else they want me to do, I'm right there in Mission Control, monitoring the cameras and the phone line and the computer too, reporting back to Judy and Dennis on even the pettiest things like who's wearing the same clothes three days in a row or staring into space during team meetings, looking for what Judy calls anomalies. We're building psychological profiles on each of the crewmembers as a component of the sociological and behavioral experiment going forward here, just as Richard, with his blood-pressure cuff, urine samples and monthly strip-down physicals, is documenting the physiological side of things.

NASA's interested. So are a handful of universities and government agencies doing research in Antarctica and Greenland and looking to us for real-time lessons in group dynamics. And if I happen to extend my role to include snooping into what Mission Control's doing—what *Judy's* doing—then as far as I'm concerned it's only tit for tat.

Judy and Vodge. That's the big secret I turn up, not that I didn't have my suspicions all along, but it's a shock, believe me. It's not so much him—nothing he does would surprise me because he's as slimy and two-faced as anybody I've ever met in my life—but Judy. Yes, she can be gratingly obnoxious one minute and pour on the charm the next—and Dawn and I mistrusted her from the start, her motives and her methods both—but even so I never thought she'd take that kind of risk for someone like Ramsay. If G.C. finds out, she'll be gone in a heartbeat and he'll find a replacement in the beat after that because there's no shortage of women out there just *dying* to be a Terranaut—or even to be mentioned in the same breath with one. *If* he finds out. That's a big if, but the thought of it, of what G.C. might do and the repercussions that would surely rock E2 right on down to its stainless-steel cradle, makes me grin inside. I've been powerless to this point, powerless and cast off, a footnote in the Terranaut narrative, but here's something I can build on, maybe even use to my advantage.

This is how it comes about. One afternoon, late, no more than a month or so after closure, I happen to be passing by in the hallway and see Judy sitting there in her office in the command center, the phone cradled under her chin and her face running through so many changes you'd think she was a contestant on a game show. It's that late-afternoon interval between the end of the day shift and the arrival of the night shift, nobody really settled yet and the offices quiet while people pass each other on the stairs or in the elevator, some going up, some going down. The phone—this is the line into E2, the only line, since for this round of closure Mission Control is strictly limiting the crew's access to the outside world—has four connections in the command center so G.C., Dennis, Judy and one other person, who might or might not be

G.F., can do conference calls with Vodge or Diane when they don't want to videoconference, or even when they do because the hookup only has one microphone and more often than not the audio's fuzzy.

I'm on my way to the restroom before heading home for the day—back to Residence 2, that is—but now, seeing Judy there, seeing her *face,* I pull up short. What makes me slip into the command center and beyond that into G.C.'s office, I can't say. An intuition, I guess. Luckily, G.C. isn't there—he's off in Boulder for the week, doing something at the Naropa Institute—and if I'm concerned about somebody coming in (like Little Jesus, for instance) and catching me where I'm not supposed to be I don't let it stop me. I can always make something up. I needed such-and-such a report from the filing cabinet and since Judy was on the phone and I didn't want to bother her, here I was—there I was—in G.C.'s office, where G.C.'s phones, outside and inside lines both, squat on his desk in molded plastic relief. I shoot a glance out the door (Judy's back, the empty office), then pull it softly shut and pick up the receiver.

Nothing. It's dead. I try the other phone, thinking I've got the wrong one, and I'm rewarded by a dial tone. Which is odd. Beyond odd—it's suspicious. A moment's investigation reveals that G.C.'s inside line, the one that communicates directly with E2, has been disconnected—unplugged, that is. By Judy, no doubt. It's a revelation, a thrill—something's up—and before I can think I plug the phone back in, lift the receiver ever so carefully, take a deep breath and put it to my ear.

What I hear, though I've come in in the middle of the conversation, leaves no doubt in my mind. Her voice is low and throaty, not at all like the voice she uses with us, which is all angles and sharp edges. "Would you like that, huh?" she breathes. "Tell me. Would you?"

He says he would. And then he says, "Even the inmates at the penitentiary get conjugal visits," and she says, "And you don't. Pity, huh?"

Next thing—bingo!—he asks her if she's seeing anybody and

she throws it right back at him. "Are you?" That's when I know I have them, though beyond that they really don't say anything incriminating and it isn't as if I'm taking notes—though I wish I'd had a tape recorder. The rest is business, Lola, Luna, Gretchen, PR and more PR. I wait till they say goodbye ("See you"; "Yeah, see you too—on PicTel") and hang up before easing the receiver back into its cradle, unplugging the phone again and tiptoeing out of the office. Out in the hallway I run into Malcolm Burts, the night spy, and if I pass him by with barely a nod of the head it's because I'm not any part of his world, not anymore. I'm beyond that now. Down the stairs I go, exultant, holding my secret close, as if it's a gift-wrapped package meant for me and me alone. News! I have news!

The campus is quiet, the tourists back in their motel rooms by now or maybe doing a little vicarious eating and drinking for the Terranauts at El Caballero or Alfano's, the day crew gone and the night crew already on the job, so I have the place pretty much to myself. It's my favorite time of day, everything in shadows except for the peaks of the Santa Catalinas, the thermostat turned down and the desert creatures venturing out into the stillness. That's one of the perks of being here—E2 is out in the middle of nowhere, surrounded by wild nature and views to kill for. Before G.F. bought up the 3,500 acres that make up the property, there'd been no development of any kind, which means the flora and fauna have remained undisturbed. There are javelinas here—I see them all the time, brown scurrying little pigs that aren't really pigs at all but an entirely unrelated species. There are deer too, rabbits, roadrunners, bobcats—even, rumor has it, the odd coatimundi or ocelot drifting north out of Mexico.

As I make my way across the plaza out front of Mission Control and start down the gravel road to Residence 2, I spot a Harris's hawk, its wings aflame with the late sun, drawing a tight circle over a cluster of saguaro, as if searching for something. I stop a moment and stand perfectly still, watching it, until suddenly it makes a knifing dive into the scrub and comes up with a kangaroo rat clenched in its talons, right place, right time. I can't help seeing it as a sign. And right then, a new mantra—a little song, actually—begins looping through my brain. *Judy and Vodge,* I sing to myself, *Vodge and Judy, Judy and Vodge, Vodge and Judy,* and it sustains me all the way home.

But then I'm in my apartment, immersed in the familiar, the dirty pans on the stove, books, magazines, the clothes I've been meaning to wash and haven't got around to, and my mood evaporates. What I need is to get out, I realize that right away. It's Saturday, Saturday night, and I haven't been off campus more than two or three times since closure, and only then to run errands. I picture the bar at Alfano's (not El Caballero, because there's no way I'm going to go there again, *ever*), and see myself leaning back on a barstool drinking chianti and dipping a crust of Italian bread into a little cruet of olive oil. But who to go with, now that Dawn's unavailable? The members of the old crew, the losers, aren't even worth considering because I'm not a loser and when we look at one another it's with downcast eyes, with shame, and I've been shamed enough as it is. Really, no joke, I've begun to wonder how I'll ever get through a two-year closure with any of them when our time comes—if it comes. And the newbies, as Malcolm likes to call the eight new candidates Mission Control brought in to fill out the extended crew and keep us all on our toes, aren't much better. At least from what I've seen of them so far, all burning eyes and nose-to-the-grindstone and all of them absolutely one hundred percent certain they'll ace us out and be among the final eight for Mission Three. They're younger too, mostly in their twenties (like Rita Nordquist, Sally's replacement) and they don't show a whole lot of diversity except for one of the men, Francisco Viera, who's from Uruguay, though he speaks English without an accent and has his Ph.D. in oceanography by way of Scripps.

I go to the cupboard where I keep a bottle of the snake wine my grandfather brought back from Seoul on his last trip and which I told everybody is for emergencies only because I don't want them getting the wrong impression, all the while mentally thumbing through the faces of the new crewmembers until I hit on Gavin Helgeland, who's funny and sympathetic and really goes out of his way to be nice to me (but then they all do, sucking up to us veterans in the baldest way, as if that's going to do them any good). I shake up the bottle to get the scales of the pickled mamushi viper inside floating around like those little white flakes in a snowglobe, then pour myself a drink and throw it back neat, still high on the secret I've brought home with me, the Dragon Lady herself. Still, standing there at the counter blinking my eyes against the sting of the drink, I begin to reconsider. We're teammates, yes, and I'm one of the only ones with a car—Dawn's car, now mine to keep and use and chew up into little pieces if I want—but nonetheless it would be awkward to just stroll over to his apartment in Residence 1, knock on the door and say, "Hey."

No matter. A second drink does the trick (and what is *Bem Ju* for anyway, if not strength and resolution?). I change into a dress and strappy sandals, do my face, tame my hair as best I can by pinning it up and spraying detangler right on down to the roots, then go back out the door and up the road to Residence 1 to see if Gavin's in the mood for a drink—and who knows, maybe more? Be bold, that's what I tell myself. And if I'm asserting my prerogative as veteran crew, wielding what little power I have over somebody who has even less, so much the better.

Still, I'm tentative about the whole thing, nervous, actually, nervous as a high-schooler, as I knock at Gavin's door, especially when nothing happens and I have to knock a second time. I stand there listening for movement, then I hear a thump and the shuffle of feet, and there's Gavin, in a set of headphones, bobbing his head to a beat only he can hear. His apartment is just like mine, only messier, and he isn't alone. Two of the other crew—Ellen Shapiro, a newbie, and (this throws me) *Tricia Berner*—are sitting at the kitchen table, sharing a marijuana blunt and a bag of potato chips. "Hi," I say, or more likely, chirp, because I tend to chirp when I get nervous. "Hi, Gavin. Hi, Ellen, Trish—but hey, it's Saturday night!"

I'm still standing there at the open door and all three of them are just gazing up at me with a look of surprise, as if this is the last thing they expected (and am I really all that threatening or stand-offish or whatever? Is it really so out of bounds that I might show up for some R&R with my crewmates? Somebody help me out here, that's what I'm thinking).

"Saturday," I repeat, but with maybe just a tad less enthusiasm this time. What had I expected? Gavin (six-two, one hundred eighty pounds, the exact same eyes and ragged haircut of that singer in The Cure) sitting home alone doing crossword puzzles or playing solitaire?

But it's okay, everything just as cool and stress-free as it can be, the spell broken in the next instant and all three of them glad to see me and as eager to take me up on my offer of a drive into town (maybe nine or ten miles one way and no joke after dark when the cars come at the lone bicyclist like mythical beasts, like *dragons*) and I begin to wonder, despite the exhilaration of the news that crackles deep inside me, if I'm just being paranoid. They like me, they do, smiles all around. Everybody's happy. And everybody's in motion now, Gavin slipping out from under his headphones, the two women getting up from the table with big stoned smiles plastered to their faces, and here's the blunt, freely held out for my inspection—and use, that too. Don't be surprised if I tell you I took a hit or two—we weren't nuns and we weren't saints, but Terranauts-in-waiting who were no less tuned-in than anybody else, or maybe even more so. It was marijuana, that was all, another fruit of the earth. Rumor had it—and Winston Barr confirmed it after the closure ceremony when we were all standing around with drinks in our hands and the band kept on playing—that the Mission One crew had not only clandestinely grown marijuana inside but ayahuasca too. That was all right. And so is this, sharing a blunt with my crewmates while the snake wine slithers through my veins. It's all good. Just as long as Mission Control doesn't find out.

My eyesight, I have to admit, isn't the greatest, and once I get behind the wheel things seem to blur even worse than usual, and the pot isn't helping. Still we somehow manage to make it into town undetected by the guardians of the law and roll on up to a parking spot conveniently located right in front of Alfano's, just as if it's been reserved for us. All this is prelude to what doesn't happen—no accident, no arrest (which would have spelled certain doom in Mission Control's eyes)—but what does happen isn't exactly in the realm of anything that anybody, Dawn especially, would have called good. Or even neutral.

* * *

Have I mentioned Johnny? Or that I don't have much use for him? Well, he's there that night, propped up at the bar on one elbow, a drink in front of him (Johnnie Walker Black, and isn't that just too coolly ironic for words?) when by all rights he should have been down in Tucson playing in some bar with his bar band. The dining room's full, but we haven't come to dine—we couldn't afford it, in any case—but to drink, get loose, listen to whatever the jukebox is giving up and confine ourselves, strictly, to the bar. Which is crowded, with tourists and locals both, locals like Johnny.

At first he doesn't seem to see us. Gavin finds us a table just behind the door, which we soon discover is the worst table in the house, since every time someone comes in, the door swings wide and cracks the edge of it, wood on wood. We get a round of drinks—beer for me, though I'm sensitive about my weight and so's Mission Control—because I'm feeling the effects of what I had back at the apartment and the marijuana too and don't want to get totally out of control. I wonder what my hair looks like. We had the windows down coming into town, a sweet mesquite-smelling breeze and seventy-eight degrees of temperature wafting in to fan our mood. Tricia Berner's going on about the play—*The Skin of Our Teeth,* which G.C. decreed was to be performed both inside and out, the Mission Two crew responsible for an array of roles (in a play I personally find corny, endless and outdated), and we of the extended crew for dividing those roles up in sixteen ways for a performance to be given consecutively with theirs, ours at Mission Control and theirs in the command center on the second tier of E2. She's talking up the role of Sabina, the best role really except maybe Antrobus himself, and you can see she's priming herself for it, when I cut in to say, "Yeah, but why this play when there's like a million other choices out there?," trying not to sound too negative but only interested in the question rhetorically, in the way of a theater lover who's totally on board with it.

"Isn't it obvious?" Tricia (waist-length hair, brunette, with a pretty-enough face if you like freckles, moles and pre-cancerous lesions) waves her drink at me. Gavin and Ellen Shapiro lean into the table with knowing smirks. This is a topic that's been batted around before. "G.C. *is* Mr. Antrobus. He *did* invent the wheel. And fire. And everything else."

"Plus," Gavin puts in, "there's the whole environmental thing—"

"And *Bib*lical," I say.

"What's wrong with that?" Tricia's studying me closely, an ironic look on her spotted face and her eyes blunted with what we smoked at the apartment and in the car too. "E2 has all that going for it, New Eden and all, so it just seems natural—"

"God the Creator," somebody says in a voice rumbling like a garbage truck going down a back alley, and everybody's looking up now, looking behind me, and I turn my head to see Johnny slouched there, drink in one hand, cigarette in the other. "God the Financier," he says, a singsong lilt to his voice. "Little Jesus. Judas."

Johnny's wearing a cowboy shirt and cowboy boots, but he doesn't look like a cowboy. More like a round-shouldered lounge lizard dressed up as somebody's idea of a cowboy. He takes a pull at the cigarette, puts the drink to his lips. Gavin, Ellen and Tricia just gawk, the conversation fallen off a cliff. What they're wondering is how this interloper, this poser in the blue satin shirt with white piping sewed around the breast pockets, has access to these cryptic identifiers—and more, how he can pronounce them aloud. In public. "But I don't know," he says, another puff, another sip, "for my money the play's pretty lame. If I remember rightly. From high school. Isn't that the sort of thing you *only* see in high school?"

"Hi, Johnny," I say.

He squints his eyes against the smoke, smiles. "Hi, Linda."

"Tricia? You know Johnny?"

She shakes her head.

I make the introductions, starting with Tricia, then Ellen and finally Gavin, who can't resist saying, "That's not the point. The point is it's got relevance for us, for E2—Wilder was way ahead of his time there. I mean, global warming. Glaciers. The flood."

"Johnny's Dawn's boyfriend," I say, to clarify things. I give him a sidelong glance, as if we're playing cards and I'm stealing a look at his hand. "Or was. You been to see her?"

He just smiles. "You?"

The same songs repeat on the jukebox, the dining room clears out, the bar gets noisier. No one asks him to join us, but at some point Johnny pulls up a chair and settles in and the conversation drifts away from us and our hermetic worries and obsessions to bands, baseball (Ellen's a huge Padres fan), bow-hunting for javelina, hiking the Santa Catalinas and what bottled beers are recycled horse piss (Johnny's term) and which ones you can actually drink, with taste-testing following hard behind. For my part, maybe I'm a little icy at first, but after the third beer—or is it the fourth?—I feel a warm glow come over me and my secret rises to my lips where I keep it like a dab of raspberry-flavored gloss, tasting it over and over with the tip of my tongue. Everybody at the table's a good person, a very good person, the best, even Johnny—no, especially Johnny—and my apartment and E2 and Dawn and Mr. Vodge Ramsay Roothoorp are far off in the distance like some sort of mirage. Is Johnny hitting on Tricia, right in front of me? Maybe. Maybe he is. But somehow I don't really care, because I just fall right into the deep trough of his voice—and because he's hitting on me too.

That's how it is. And once we've left, once I get my fellow Terranauts-in-waiting back to their apartments without incident and pour myself one final little nightcap of *Bem Ju,* I guess it doesn't come as all that much of a surprise when the knock echoes through the apartment and I open the door to see Johnny standing there, propped up in his grin. "Can I come in?" he says. And what do I say? I say, "Why not?"

* * *

I do see Dawn. Nearly every day. Or at least communicate with her. Sometimes, when the phone's free, we just chat, or gossip really. She'll tell me about what's going on inside—what I don't already know, I mean, and no, I'm not working her or pumping her for information or anything like that, just talking. Call it girl-talk. Or if that sounds dismissive or sexist or whatever, I'm sure boy-talk would be pretty much the same thing, like when Dennis and Ramsay connect, which they seem to do just about every day. Ditto Judy and Ramsay. Though, as I discovered, that was a whole different animal: girl/boy talk. I never caught them at anything beyond that one incident, by the way—I never got the opportunity—but what I'd overheard was enough to pack into a bomb and bring the whole creaking edifice down.

More than the phone, though, Dawn and I wind up talking at the visitors' window, where we can see each other, which makes things more personal. Sometimes, sitting there on opposite sides of the glass, it's almost as if we're out in the world, free of all this artificial maneuvering and the constraints that go with it. She asks me about Johnny, who's visiting her less and less often, and I tell her I hardly ever see him because there's no point in risking our friendship over what happened—once and once only—that night after the celebration of my brand-new shiny secret at Alfano's. And I don't tell her about that either. That's something I'm hold-ing on to in the way the Russians are holding on to their nukes. Pow! Boom! The Dragon Lady strikes!

We're well into May now, the world I live in growing hotter and drier by the day while the world she lives in stays at a fixed temperature with humidity up in the range of a steam bath, the sealed pipes that deliver hot and cold water constantly tweaked by the maintenance staff in the power plant. As for rain, as I'm sure most people know, the crew just turns on the overhead sprinklers whenever it's needed—and that's Diane's call, unless G.C., who's always studying the data and consulting with her and Vodge, decrees a shower over the marsh or the savanna, but don't misunderstand: this is internal water only, what's locked in and re-created hour by hour, day by day. Drinking water comes from condensation on the air handler coils in the technosphere (basement, that is) and the rest is recycled from the kitchen, the animal pens, the bathrooms and the biomes and collected in settling tanks in the basement and in the two lungs that rise out of the ground like big white mushrooms on either side of the main structure.

G.C. and his engineers might have got a lot of things wrong, by the way, but not those lungs. As far as I'm concerned they're the truly groundbreaking innovation in a project that is, as advertised, groundbreaking in every way. I'm sure others can explain the concept and its function better than I can, even if I have made it my business to know as much about every aspect of E2 as I possibly can, good student and every bit her overachieving mother's daughter that I am, but I'll give it to you in short. The lungs are essential as a kind of pressure valve, regulating the internal air pressure so as to keep E2 from exploding when the outside temperature peaks or imploding when it's cold. Two long tunnels—walkways—lead to these two big circular arenas that are roofed in rubber and weighted down by a sixteen-ton aluminum saucer so they can expand and contract along with the air pressure, thereby keeping the thousands of glass panels from popping and allowing E2's atmosphere to spew out and mingle with the earth's. Mingling is what we don't want—not of air or people either. Nothing in, nothing out.

Anyway, I do stick with Dawn and gradually I begin to get over my jealousy—the thing with Johnny helped, both with my self-esteem and in finding common ground with her, or maybe that sounds too blunt. She's locked up, but so am I, and all that one night with Johnny represented was a jailbreak, that's all. It's not as if he cares about her. He proved that in my bed. And the fact is, Dawn needs me more than ever, not only as a confidante but as a buffer between her and Mission Control. I'll give you an example. G.C. and Judy are really pushing for the play, as if we all aren't exhausted enough with the hours we have to put in every day, and I've come to dread rehearsals as much as Dawn. But at least I have a pressure valve that operates in E1 just like those lungs in E2: I can get in the car and take off for anyplace I want. Dawn's stuck. By choice, yes, but stuck all the same.

The part G.C. assigned her (he's directing both productions, inside and out) is Mrs. Antrobus, who's basically just an airhead and performs a thankless role that's so distantly pre-feminist it really is beyond the pale. But this is comedy and firmly tongue-in-cheek absurdist, the way G.C. (and to tell the truth, most of us) likes it and after the earnestness of what we're doing day in, day out, a few laughs are just what the doctor ordered. My own part, or parts— and I'll admit up front that I'm one of the worst actors on the extended crew, far too self-conscious to let go the way somebody more natural would be able to—is really like what you'd expect from an extra in a movie. I put on a papier-mâché helmet and mope around as the Mammoth, and I'm one of the Muses and one of the Conveeners and a Drum Majorette as well. Of course, we're not going overboard by way of stage setting and scenery since we're playing for ourselves only. (Or actually, via live-feed TV, the Terranauts-in-fact are playing for the Terranauts-in-waiting and vice versa—and for our God and Creator, which goes without saying.) Basically, we're doing something that falls between a line reading and a walk-through, but still G.C. insists that we learn our lines and block out the action. So, though we'd both rather be doing something else, Dawn and I wind up spending a whole two weeks of our evening free-time in late May of Year One Closure standing at the visitors' window feeding each other lines.

I remember one night, both of us flat-out exhausted, when the whole thing kind of breaks down. We're doing Act I, Scene 1, and I'm reading Sabina's lines and Dawn's playing from memory, or trying to. Sabina's just stepped out of character to say that she doesn't understand a word of the play and then, back in character, "Yes, I've milked the mammoth," so that Mrs. Antrobus can fret over the fact that they'll have no food or fire till her husband comes home and conclude by saying, "You'd better go over to the neighbors and borrow some fire." But after I say my line, Dawn just stares at me through the glass, looking desolate. "I'm drawing a blank," she says. "Really, I mean you can't imagine the kind of day I've had. It's been shitty, really shitty."

I don't have anything to say to this. *She's* having a shitty day? What about me? What about all the rest of us who aren't famous, who aren't inside, who haven't been plucked up and rewarded for the thousands of sweaty malodorous overworked hours we've put in? Who're getting five hundred bucks a month and a pat on the back? Who're the workers and drones to her queen bee? I watch her face, lines of privilege converging at her hairline, her mouth drawn down in a pout. Shitty day, shitty day.

"Have you lost weight?" I ask finally, going on the offensive because I know this is a worry of hers. She's sensitive about her figure and she's afraid the low-cal diet's going to shrink her breasts down to nothing like with the aboriginal women in the outback who just have two little flaps of skin there even when they're pregnant. "You're looking thin."

"No. Yes. I don't know. I guess so. But it's not that, it's Diane, the way she was riding me today? And then *Judas.* She summoned me to the phone this morning after crew meeting to tell me I wasn't getting enough milk out of the goats, and then she gave me a whole useless holier-than-thou lecture about how forty ounces a day wasn't going to do it when you were splitting it eight ways because that was just five ounces per person per day, as if I couldn't do the math, and how I had to give them better fodder when she knows as well as I do there just isn't any, not till the savanna grasses get cut again, which Diane says isn't going to happen for like three weeks yet. So I'm frustrated. So frustrated I could scream. And you know Judy, on her high horse, and it's like I'm to blame if milk production is down or egg production or whatever, as if I have any control over it—"

"Judy's such a bitch."

She looks down at her lap, clenching her hands as if she's trying to squeeze water out of a sponge. Her head is cocked to one side, pinning the phone to her shoulder. Her T-shirt—E2 MDA, it reads in cardboard-gray letters on a crimson background, a gift from her mother—seems to hang on her. Beyond her, the ag biome, flooded in evening light like the clerestory of a cathedral, shines a brilliant green in defiance of the desert that radiates out for hundreds of miles. I snatch a look at the lines of the script and try again: "'Yes, I've milked the mammoth.'"

Her eyes jump to mine, but she doesn't give me her lines. She says, "Does Judy say anything about me? Like job performance or anything? Or G.C.?"

"How would I know?"

"You're there, aren't you? Like all day?"

"Yeah, so?"

"You haven't gone over to their side, have you? You're not spying on us—you're not reporting back?"

The smile I give her is tentative, cheesy, unconvincing I'm sure. "No," I say. "Never. It's still just you and me, right? I'm just staring into the monitors, that's all. In case there's an emergency. You know that."

Again she's silent. She switches the receiver from one side to the other.

"But you're collecting data, right?"

"Well, yeah, that's what they want. For the project." I'm trying my best not to sound defensive, but I can't help feeling irritated all over again.

"What about Johnny?" she says, and it comes out of nowhere. "You see him lately?"

"Not really," I say, stalling for time. I don't know how much she knows. Gossip runs from Mission Control to E2 and back as freely as the hot and cold water coming from the power plant. There's no closure on gossip.

"I heard you saw him at Alfano's?"

I tell her I did. That I'd been there with Gavin, Ellen and Tricia, that he'd come over to the table and we'd all had a couple of drinks together. And that he told me he was missing her. "He said he was lonely."

"What," she says, "no groupies?"

Groupies. The term—the notion—makes me wince. He'd come on to me, that was the way it was, and I was as far from being a fan of his strutting pathetic regurgitation of other people's hits as I was of intramural politics. On some level I'd slept with him for her, though I couldn't tell her that, because on another level I'd done it *because* of her, to spite her, to get some of my own back in a relationship that was all one-way now. I pretend I don't hear her.

"Linda? You there?" Her eyes go wide. "I was only joking. Because I know him and I know how the girls come on to him. I know it can't last. But still, the more I think about him the more I think I'm in love with him. Is that crazy? Or is it just that I'm in fantasyland here?"

She's looking pleadingly at me, the pressure of the phone at her chin compressing the flesh of her cheek into tight bloodless bands. What she wants is reassurance, the give-and-take that came so naturally to us for the past two-plus years, and I see that and register it, but all I can do is shrug.

* * *

Then it's Gyro's turn, and this has got to be one of the more cringe-worthy incidents of the Mission Two closure, which I wouldn't even mention here except that it wound up being duly noted for the record in any case (Gyro wasn't identified by name, but still it shows just how intrusive Mission Control could be). I was the first to notice him engaging in what Judy called "anomalous behavior," but I wasn't the one to record it in the log because to my mind it was just too personal, nobody's business but Gyro's. Malcolm had no such scruples, though, and so the whole thing came out, a matter of record and of debate too, the first rubbing of our collective noses in what my high school civics teacher quaintly called ethics. We'd reached June by this point, the fourth month of closure, the days stretched to the limit and both inside and outside crews looking forward to our summer solstice celebration (few of us had any religion beyond G.C. and E2 and so we built our feast days around the old calendar, the one that had existed before the current crop of gods came into being). We were going to coordinate our celebration with theirs, preparing the same dishes—and choking down the same rank banana wine—in solidarity. But that was only fair, wasn't it? Or at least that was the question Dennis asked at team meeting, giving us all his best impression of an evil smirk.

As it happens, I'm on night shift that week, alternating nights with Malcolm while Tricia and Jeff Weston go to day shift—and the incident with Gyro's a nighttime thing, definitely a nighttime thing. I have to say I don't really care for the night shift all that much—it plays havoc with my diurnal rhythms—but Mission Control dictates the hours and I'm a dutiful little Terranaut-in-waiting (and also secretly pleased because it's only the four of us who're entrusted with the video monitoring, and that has to be a good sign as to who's favored for Mission Three). So I sit there in the wee hours, most of the lights dimmed so as not to disorient the night creatures, reading sci-fi (Clarke, Bradbury, Salmón and especially Clayton Unger's Bigger Bang series, about terraforming distant planets) and staring blearily into the ten TV monitors at Mission Control like a night watchman in a warehouse.

Every once in a while something of interest snaps me to attention, like a parade of tail-twitching mice (stowaways—that goes without saying) doing their thing in the IAB in defiance of the traps the crew set and baited with precious scraps and whatever cockroach meat they had on hand, or the galagos leaping red-eyed through the biomes, shifting range from one camera to another fifty times in the course of a night, but basically it's just leaves and more leaves. But then Gyro's there, triggering one of the rain forest cameras, his hands empty—no toolbox, so he's not out to make any emergency repairs—and his feet bare, striding gawkily along in a pair of shorts and T-shirt. At first I think he might be going for a shower under the waterfall that cascades down from our artificial mountain, but then he slips out of view of the first camera and doesn't reappear in the waterfall view. We have the ability to reposition the cameras and that's what I do now, trying to keep him in sight not so much out of duty or even nosiness, but boredom, simple boredom, just that. Mostly when the crew goes out at night it's to get away from the sterility of the Human Habitat and into a state of nature, which is what we've signed on for to begin with, ecologists all, people selected for their love of the outdoors. Or, in this case, this very special case, the indoors.

He dodges off-camera briefly, then comes into view again, looking what you could only call furtive, and my first thought is he's going to sneak some bananas or papayas from the trees or even dip into the Purina Monkey Chow Gretchen sets out daily in half a dozen feeding stations to sustain the galagos, who're having a hard time dietarily on what E2's providing in terms of insects and fruit. Next thing, he's off the path—and this is pretty much discouraged because Mission Control wants the wilderness biomes to remain as undisturbed as possible. But what *is* he doing? I shift the camera, refocus. The image is grainy, the colors washed to shadow. He seems to be preparing a place to lie down, as if he's going to take a nap, which doesn't make any sense since his bed is just minutes away. Is he going for the nature experience, is that it? Sleeping with the ants, mosquitoes, cockroaches and frogs? Is he our nature boy, our true nature boy? I don't have a clue.

When he lays himself down, the vegetation screens him so all I can see is his lower legs—his shins, which cast a faint glow—and his feet. He's doing something there, something vigorous which make his legs stiffen and his feet stir, and it isn't till I notice that his shorts are in the picture now, bunched at his knees, that it comes to me like a dirty secret. I flush. Gawk. Smile to myself: now I have something on him too. But I stop right there—the fact is I like him, and honestly, no matter what anybody says, I'm not that kind of person. What he does privately is nobody's business but his and I know in that moment I won't report it. Unfortunately, as I say, Malcolm has no such scruples. He'd seen something on his shift (I never found out what, exactly, but it had to do with Gyro, so I can pretty well guess), then went back and reviewed my tape, which he brought to Judy and Dennis, and Judy and Dennis watched it I don't know how many times before they summoned me.

They're in the command center, sitting before one of the monitors, and they're the only people in the room at the moment. Judy gives me one of her automatic smiles and Dennis, his little spit-curl frozen in place on his forehead, barely glances up. "We just want to know what you saw, when was it, Dennis? Four nights ago? When you were on night shift?"

Dennis looks up now, his face neutral (and you could have tortured him, pulled out his fingernails and toenails and cut off his ears before he'd acknowledge even the faintest glimmer of what had once passed between us), and pulls out a chair for me.

"So what we're wondering about is what looks like an anomaly with one of the crew," Judy goes on, pressing the "play" button on the recorder before her so that the screen springs to life, the picture murky, jumpy, a slice of movement, Gyro, the rain forest, night. Across the top of the screen, the time scrolling in fuzzy white relief, seconds, minutes, hour, and the date—06/14/94—blinking in confirmation. "This is your feed, right? You were on duty that night—?"

"Yes," I say, and I'm not giving up anything.

"Listen, Linda"—Dennis now—"we were wondering why you trained the camera here, on Gyro. Were you, I don't know, suspicious or—?"

"Or what?" I say.

"Bored, maybe," Judy puts in.

I look round the room, the sun bright in the windows so that they seem glazed, chairs and desks untenanted, everybody conveniently on break. "If you're asking if I was tracking him because he was out there in the middle of the night and I didn't know if he was repairing something or what he was doing, then the answer is yes. That's what I'm supposed to do, isn't it?"

Neither of them responds. For a minute, a full sixty seconds that seems ten times longer, the three of us watch my cinematic efforts play across the screen to the climactic moment—the stiffened legs, the intent feet—before Judy punches the "off" button and the image dissolves. Judy turns to me, her mouth tight. "Do you have any idea what this is? What he was doing?"

"I don't know," I say. "I was just recording an, an *anomaly,* that's all."

The fact is, the literature on small group interaction is rife with anomalous behavior, from violence and mental instability to the formation of cliques and factions and the total breakdown of societal norms. One overwintering crew at the Antarctic Research Station split off into two separate factions—gangs— that raided each other's food supplies, though there was more than enough food to go around, and even adopted identifying insignia and colors as if they were Crips and Bloods fighting over turf. By the time the relief crew arrived in the spring, there had been two all-out brawls (the first over whether the movie of the night would be *Ice Station Zebra* or *The Sound of Music*), resulting in a fractured ankle, a broken wrist and two misaligned noses, and one faction went so far as to try to falsify the other's data. Which, of course, defeated the whole purpose of their being there in the first place.

"But you didn't report it," Dennis says.

"I didn't think it was anything."

Judy—*she's* the dragon lady, not me—lets out an exasperated puff of air. "He was masturbating, for Christ's sake. Do you know what would happen if, god forbid, one of the visitors should see anything like this? Or the so-called reporters out there that are just praying for us to fall flat on our faces?"

"It was night," I say. "Who's watching at night? And besides, you can't be sure. Maybe he was, I don't know, getting into his naturalist's trance—"

"Don't be cute. Or naïve. Or whatever you're playing at—he was jerking off and you know it perfectly well."

This is a warning. My job, above all else, is to suck up to Mission Control if I ever hope to get what I want, and what I want is to go inside and spin out my own anomalous behavior. I keep my mouth shut.

"Apes do it, monkeys," Dennis says, leaning in so he's too close, encroaching on my personal space, working me. "In the zoo, especially. You see them whacking off all the time. It's a boredom thing. A cooped-up thing."

Judy stiffens, makes a face. She's uptight. Humorless. The

manager, managing. "We're not apes," she says and gives Dennis a look that's like a warning shot across his bows.

"I'm sorry," I say, "but that's exactly what we are." I know something about Judy that Judy doesn't know I know. A soft smile comes to my lips. "Technically speaking."

Dawn Chapman

People always asked about intimate things, body-function things, like how the toilet worked and whether we took vitamins (we did: vitamin D, because UV rays didn't penetrate the glass panels) and what we women did about birth control and our monthly cycles. I got questions like these from journalists when it was my turn to sit for an interview via PicTel or at the visitors' window and I got them from friends and from my own mother too. It wasn't anything I looked forward to, but I wasn't embarrassed—or tried not to be. Daily life at its most basic—exercise, respiration, caloric intake, personal hygiene—was the gold standard of E2, the way forward for any off-earth colony that was to follow us in the future. How do you do it?—that was what people wanted to know. How do you recycle waste, protect the environment and balance out natural processes in a closed-loop, bio-regenerative, self-sustaining system? Or, actually, how do you live without Safeway, Walmart and the CVS pharmacy?

As for birth control, we all had the pill, which Mission Control insisted on, though as far as I knew only Stevie was taking it. This was something Mission Control wanted to play down, of course, and initially they'd put out a couple of bland press releases couched in the language of a family planning brochure and emphasizing our status as scientists, as if to imply that scientists, interested only in their experiments and observations, were above expressing anything so primitive as sexual needs. Since we were all unmarried, there was endless speculation in the press about which of us might pair up, one rag even going so far as to post odds, while on the other side, the moral watchdogs hissed and blew and the Just-Abstain sect demonstrated out on the main road for the first month or two. Really, I think Mission Control would have been happier if we'd all been sterilized at the outset.

What Diane did, I never knew, but both Gretchen and I felt pretty strongly that we didn't want to put anything artificial in our bodies—again, wouldn't that be a violation of the compact we'd made with the ecosystem of E2? I did get fitted with a diaphragm—to be used as needed. Or not. But I went off the pill the day I stepped inside, and so did Gretchen. For their part, the men were supplied with condoms and Richard had a reserve supply, just in case, but everybody tiptoed around the whole issue, at least at first. Living this intimately was sticky enough as it was, and we all tried to keep a professional outlook, as if E2 wasn't any different from a rooming house. Or a coed dorm, where you could keep your door shut for privacy or leave it open when you wanted company. The condoms, incidentally, were of biodegradable lambskin (lamb's caecum, that is) and not plastic, which was strictly excluded from E2 in any of the myriad forms that study after study had shown to be degrading the earth's ecosystems and working its way up the food chain so that animals as disparate as polar bears and Kemp's ridley's turtles harbored its by-products in their tissues. By the same token, tampons were banned and we had to use a silicon cup instead, reusable, disinfectible and non-polluting, but a pain for all that, and whoever said living under glass was going to be easy?

Every two months Richard gave each of us a thorough physical exam, including body measurements, blood and urine samples, pulse rate (both resting and after five minutes on the exercise bike), blood pressure and lung capacity. He did vaginal exams, checked our breasts for any sign of cysts or tumors and examined the men for hernias and prostate enlargement and/or cancer, concluding with a set of three full-body nude photos of each of us, front, side and rear. Why the thoroughness? Because, as G.C. explained at the outset, our bodies were laboratories in themselves, as invaluable to the project as anything either animate or inanimate in E2, and Mission Control was unwavering about our compliance here. To pick just one example out of many, during our mission it was shown that after six months our blood became flooded with lipophilic compounds (PCB, DDE and DDT) which had been released into our bloodstreams as we burned off the fat where they'd been stored, and there wasn't one of us who wasn't sobered by this evidence—*evidence in the blood*—of what was wrong out there in the world. None of us had been miners or worked in chemical plants or nuclear facilities. We'd lived normal American lives in the wealthiest country ever known and nonetheless wound up accumulating these toxins in our bodies just from having lived and breathed and consumed the food and swallowed the water in E1, and if that doesn't tell you something, I don't know what does. And that's it, that's it exactly—people were always criticizing us, asking *Where's the science?* Well, here it was, right in your average American bloodstream.

I remember one physical in particular, at the end of June of the first year, and I think it stands out because it was the first time I really got a sense of who Richard was, beyond the aura that surrounded him as our physician and healer or the persona he took on as the team member who could always manage to see the dark side of things and make us laugh about it at the same time. Which was an act, a way of lightening his load, because deep down he was a very giving and caring person who was there for us 24/7 and really did try to stay impartial when things got contentious. Or that doesn't sound right. Of course he was there 24/7—where else would he be? What I mean is, no matter what your problem you could always take it to him and he'd make you feel better, and I'm not just talking about medication—he saw me through some rough patches, and I owe him, I do. His crew nickname was Lancet, for the obvious reason, but because of his wit too, the way it cut and sliced and revealed what lay beneath the surface of any issue we might be batting around, and yet for some reason it never stuck and mostly we wound up calling him by his given name (for a while there Ramsay tried calling him "Doc" and then "Bones," after Dr. McCoy on *Star Trek,* but neither stuck). So he was Richard. Plain Richard. The elder amongst us at forty-eight, with hair transitioning from charcoal to gray, a serious nose with a little bump at the bridge of it and eyes that might have been set too close together but could laser right in on you, especially if you said something fatuous or sanctimonious, which some people (think Stevie) seemed capable of doing about fifty percent of the time. If not more.

I was scheduled right after morning break, which happened at ten-forty-five punctually each day, and after I'd sat down with the handful of peanuts and mug of mint tea the chef du jour doled out, I followed Richard around the corner to his office.

He shut the door behind me, lifted his lab coat down from its hook and shrugged into it while I slid myself up onto the examining table and let my legs dangle over the side. The table was covered with a sheet of the standard antiseptic paper you saw in any physician's office, with the difference that this one wouldn't be going to a landfill—it would be packed up with the others Richard would use today, then shredded and fed to the goats, who would process it in their unique goaty way so that at least partially we'd be getting milk from medical waste, which I bet really didn't happen all that much in the outside world.

I watched Richard's back and the movement of his shoulders as he looped his stethoscope around his neck and pulled my chart from his filing cabinet, and if I was thinking about anything it was the uphill slope of the work I had to get through before lunch— weeding, mostly, and turning over the soil in the peanut plot we'd just harvested so we could plant it with a new crop of sweet potatoes—and wondering how much time this little interlude was going to cost me. I should have been relaxed, I know, but our schedules inside were infinitely more demanding than on the outside. We couldn't just punch the clock, nine to five, and go home and forget about things—we had a whole world to prop up.

"So, how are we feeling, E.?" Richard asked, turning round to face me. "No complaints, no pulled muscles or back spasms?" This was a reference to the lower back issues I'd had a month or so ago after a couple of especially strenuous days, going from cutting back vegetation in the rain forest to climbing up with Stevie and Vodge to scrub the windows over the IAB, which had begun to sprout a brownish scrim of mold that was blocking enough of our sunlight to become a problem.

"I don't know," I said, "the usual. A few twinges maybe, right here?" I reached back to indicate the muscles just over my hips. "But nothing, really. Not like that first time." (Which had laid me up in bed and cost two full workdays, much to the irritation of Little Jesus. And Judas.)

"Good," he murmured, "good," and he listened to my heart and lungs and checked my blood pressure, which, at 110 over 68, was in the range of what you'd expect from a long-distance runner, or so he told me. "You haven't been competing in any marathons lately, have you, E.?"

"Not that I can remember." I gave a little laugh. "Maybe in my dreams, does that count? But wait a minute, you're wearing glasses." He'd slipped a pair of standard-issue spectacles over the bump of his nose, black frames, rectangular lenses, the sort of thing you'd find on a rack at the drugstore. They made him look studious. And old. Or *older* anyway. "I didn't know you wore glasses?"

"I don't," he said, ducking his head, and it might have been my imagination but he seemed to be blushing. "These are just for up-close, for reading—I picked up two pairs at Walgreens a week before closure, just in case. They're an aid, that's all. A tool." He laughed. "It's not like I'm getting old or anything."

"No," I said, "none of us are."

"Uh-uh, not in here, no way. E2's the fountain of youth."

I couldn't think of anything to say. Technically, Richard was old enough to be my father, though my actual father was eight years older than him.

He peered over the frames of his glasses like a lecturer looking up from his notes and he was Richard again, the Richard I knew. Or thought I knew. "Seriously, though, with our diet and work schedule and the purity of this place and no communicable diseases it'll probably add ten years to our life span. I mean nobody's going to need a flu shot. And I think I can confidently declare the common cold extinct in Ecosphere II."

"Oh, I like that. That's great. Tell you the truth, I hadn't really thought of it—not in those terms. But it makes sense, doesn't it?"

"Absolutely."

I looked at him and felt a whole new wave of appreciation rising in me. We were safe here, safer even than I'd imagined. Diseases had been driven to extinction in the larger world—smallpox for one and polio not far behind—but they'd never even existed in our world. We had only what we'd brought in with us. I'd say it was a humbling thought, but it was just the opposite—if ever I'd felt privileged, like one of the gods, like the original Eos spreading her rosy fingers across the horizon, it was in that moment. Everybody outside was vulnerable, even G.C., but not us. "Okay," I said, even as another thought came to me, "I'll grant you that—but how can you be sure? I mean, what about all that sneezing Diane was doing at breakfast this morning? That's not a cold?"

"Allergies. Mold spores, pollen—that stuff's going to be concentrated in an environment like this, even what we've got in the soil, what with the aerators. We've got to watch out for that, yes, but any communicable disease that didn't come in with the crew isn't going to show its face. We're clean. We're pure. World, get over it."

Flu had twice stricken the Mission One crew, or so we'd been told—by G.C., as a sort of object lesson. They'd broken closure right at the beginning, as everyone knows, but during the second year they began to pass medical samples through a sleeve to the right of the airlock, and incredible as it might seem, the flu virus came in on the surface of the new test tubes sent in to replace the exported ones and everybody got sick. Another little parable about the corruption of the outside world and the need for an absolute unwavering commitment to material closure.

"All right, E."—he handed me a paper hospital gown, which would also ultimately pass to the goats—"let's get down to business." He flashed a smile. "I'm sure you've got better things to do than sit here jawing with me—like growing us some more people fodder, and what's it today? Beets?"

"Sweet potatoes."

"More beta-carotene."

"Good for the eyes," I said.

I tried not to think about it as he inserted the speculum and examined me, telling myself it was strictly impersonal and necessary in terms of documentation, our bodies laboratories and such, but still it was different with Richard. I was young, in good health, and the few times I had gone in to see a gynecologist it was always a female, which just seemed to make sense. Though we'd had a male G.P. when I was growing up—Dr. Moskowitz—and that was as ordinary as the mumps and whooping cough he'd treated me for, and the doctor at the college health center was male too, which really didn't seem to make a difference, though admittedly, he looked to be close to seventy and so haphazardly put together as to be all but genderless. Did it really matter who inserted the thermometer in your mouth or prescribed an antibiotic as long as they were sympathetic—and competent, of course? There was a compact between patient and physician that made gender considerations irrelevant as far as I was concerned. I was an adult. We were all adults here. Still, Richard was one of us, one of the team, and that made the impersonal shade ever so perceptibly into the intimate.

He kept up a soothing patter, his touch as warm as a compress, and I found myself relaxing, my gaze falling idly on a poster of the human skeletal system he'd tacked to the near wall, across the top of which someone (Ramsay, I later learned) had inked *Dem Bones* in a black Gothic script. If I felt anything it was that I was in good hands and that I was being cared for, pampered even, and that the mission and everybody concerned with it, from G.C. on down—Judy, even Judy—was benevolent and pure of motive. I was a Terranaut and that was a very special thing.

When he was finished, Richard set his instruments aside and went over to wash up at the sink. "You know, I hate to disappoint you, E.," he said, turning round while drying his hands on a spotless white towel, "but I can't find anything wrong with you. Congratulations. You're a perfect physical specimen. A paragon."

I was already up and off the table and reaching for my clothes when he reminded me that we weren't done yet. "Measurements," he intoned, going for the mock-pompous delivery he brought to bear when he assumed the voice of the narrator during rehearsals of the Wilder play, all puff and blow, and I realized this must have been difficult for him too. "And the photos, don't forget the photos."

So I stood there naked—and unembarrassed, or as unembarrassed as I could talk myself into being, considering that we'd been through this twice already and there were nine more sessions to look forward to after this one—while he took a tape measure to my upper arms and thighs, my breasts, waist and hips, then posed me (without reminding me to stand up straight because the slouch I was developing was an indicator of how close to depletion our diet and regimen were bringing me—and this not quite four months in).

"You know, you've lost nearly ten pounds," he said as I perched on the edge of the examining table, reaching back to refasten my bra and pulling the T-shirt down over my head. "Overall, since closure. And half an inch at the waist and something just over that across the chest."

My jeans had been loose, I knew that coming in, and I knew E2 was a natural weight-loss clinic that would have put Jenny Craig right out of business if we opened the airlock to all the women fighting their weight out there in the world, but still the news came as a shock. For just a moment, just as the words passed his lips, I felt something well up in me, a canker of fear and misgiving over the loss of who I was and what I'd been and a bigger fear of what I was becoming.

"I'm going to lose my figure, is that what you're telling me?"

"Your figure's fine, Dawn. You're a beautiful woman. Be happy. It's only adipose tissue—and it'll come back the first two weeks of reentry, just as soon as you get your teeth around a nice filet mignon with a baked potato topped with what, sour cream, chives and bacon bits, with asparagus hollandaise on the side and a salad drenched in Roquefort dressing, with, uh, maybe crème brûlée for dessert—or would you prefer the white chocolate mousse, madame?"

"Richard, stop. That's just mean to talk like that," I said, but I was smiling. He was smiling too. A moment ticked by. "That it?" I said.

He nodded. "That's it. Oh, wait, I almost forgot—one other thing."

I stood there at the door, tugging at the bottom of my T-shirt where it had bunched up in back. "Yes?"

"We're going to be doing a urinalysis to look into stress-hormone levels, so I'm telling everybody that as of tomorrow morning—and every day for the next month—I'm going to need a urine sample. First thing in the morning. Fasting."

"Stress hormones?"

He shrugged. "It's just routine. Are the levels going to be lower or higher than they'd be outside? If they're higher, that tells us something about what the hidden costs of living in close confinement within a small group might be."

"And if they're lower?"

"All to the better."

"Jesus." Another intrusion, another inconvenience, pee in a cup. "I feel like a lab rat."

Peering over the little black glasses, his eyebrows cocked in amusement: "If it's any consolation, E., they don't get paid either."

"Thanks, *doctor*. That's really reassuring."

"No problem."

"And thanks for the exam. I wouldn't exactly call it fun, but you do make it entertaining, got to give you credit there."

"No problem," he said, his hand swinging the door open for me. "If you want to know the truth, it's really not all that hard looking at naked women. For a living, I mean."

* * *

The summer of that first year was one of the hottest on record, and when Linda came to the visitors' window it seemed all she did was complain about the heat. She'd taken to bringing a folding chair with her and we'd improved things on our end by setting a stool by the phone and rigging a curtain behind us for privacy's sake, in case—well, there was that one night with Johnny, which could have been potentially embarrassing if anyone had been around. And then Troy Turner had come up with a girlfriend no one even knew he had, a busty Latina with fire-red lips and stiletto heels who'd done a striptease outside the window for his birthday. After that, by a vote of 6–1, Ramsay opposed and Troy abstaining, we agreed on the curtain, which was actually just a pair of spare blankets drooped over a length of rope.

Linda had been coaching me on my lines and then we'd switch off and I'd coach her or at least rehearse her because I wasn't exactly an expert at this—nobody would have mistaken me for an actress and the best I could hope was to hold my own onstage. You might think the whole thing trivial—certainly Linda did—but G.C. was right about this as he was right about so many things. The play gave us a chance to get outside of ourselves, to have fun and weight our lines with special meaning, making a throwaway line like "Have you milked the mammoth?" a kind of inside joke, especially coming from me, the E2 milkmaid tricked out like a 1940s housewife in the only dress I had (and a pair of hiking boots in place of heels or even flats). So this was funny. Very funny.

Anyway, on this particular evening, the low sun streaming across the lawn behind her, Linda came sweating to the window, unfolded her chair, set it in place, pushed the hair out of her face and picked up the phone. "You are so lucky," she said, first thing.

"What do you mean?"

"To be in there. Obviously. Can you even imagine what it's like out here? It's what, eight o'clock at night and it's still like a hundred."

I hadn't even thought of it, really. You don't feel anybody else's discomfort any more than you can feel their pain, everybody inside a bubble of their own making whether they like to admit it or not. "The heatwave," I said. "Right?"

"*Duh*," she said, making a face. "And the air-conditioning's down in the Residences and nobody for all their technology here can seem to figure out what the problem is—and of course Dennis is reluctant to call in an outside contractor, like what's wrong with the Yellow Pages, because one of the guys from the power plant can fix it just as easily. *Not*." She gave me an exasperated look. "I wake up all sweaty—or no, I go to bed sweaty and wake up sweatier."

I made a noise of sympathy, but what I was thinking was that I'd be happy to trade places with her. So what if she was hot? She could go anywhere she wanted. High up into the Santa Catalinas, where the pines spread their branches and rocked on a cool breeze—or into Tillman to sit at the bar in Alfano's or El Caballero and let the air conditioner fan her hair and chill her bare arms so she had to put a sweater on just to keep her frozen margarita from giving her the shivers. A furlough, that was what I needed. A one-night furlough.

"I'll trade with you," I said.

"Very funny."

"No, really. Come on in. Take my place, why don't you? Tolerable enough in here." I watched her wrinkle up her nose. "I'd just like a night on the town, that's all. Scope out the bars, take a walk in the moonlight—"

"Very funny."

"Come on, Linda, you know I'm only joking. I'm sorry it's so hot. But remember that time in Australia, when we went out looking for that missing calf and the heat was like a sauna, or no, like wearing thermal underwear in a sauna?"

"Not a happy memory," she said, making a face. We'd found the thing, dead of thirst, splayed out on the checkerboard of a dried-up watercourse, the buzzards hopping round it like big black fleas.

"You want hot," I said, feeling oddly self-righteous, "—that was *hot*."

She was silent a moment, then leaned in close so we were no more than a foot apart. "I just wanted to warn you," she said, and threw a look over her shoulder to see if anyone was watching. Or listening. There was someone there—Roy Teggers, one of the security guards who patrolled the grounds to keep the crazies out and watched at the ocean window when Stevie was in the water, an extra set of eyes in case she got in trouble—but he was two hundred yards away and staring off in the opposite direction.

"About what?"

"Or not a warning, really, just a heads-up."

"I'm listening."

"I think they might be planning to give you a call—G.C. and Judas, I mean. Or maybe just G.C."

"Me? For what?" I felt my stomach fall. It wasn't as if Judy didn't communicate her needs and requirements daily and G.C. almost as often, but usually—especially with G.C.—it was during a conference call with all of us, the speakerphone rumbling and squelching as if the connection were three hundred miles away instead of three hundred yards. "The play?" Suddenly I was angry—put upon—and I suppose my voice gave me away. "I'm trying my hardest and I'm not—I'm just exhausted all the time. Don't they realize that?"

"It's not that," she said, "though you know G.C. and his standards. No, it's just that I heard them talking—overheard them, really, when they didn't realize I was in the room?—and it's not about you, or I mean I don't know what they're going to ask. Or maybe I do. Maybe they want you to report to them. Or get your take on things—"

Now I was starting to feel uneasy. What was she talking about? Was it Johnny? He'd been back twice after that first week and we'd given something of a repeat performance at the window, though nobody was around and by then we'd hung the curtain, but Troy had been just as outrageous, as far as I knew, and some of the others had had their assignations at the glass too. Why single me out? Didn't they think we had a right to our own lives? Was everything all about G.C. and Judas and the project?

"What *things*?"

Her eyes dodged away. She fanned her face with one hand. "Gyro," she said.

"Gyro? What about him? What does that have to do with me?"

She shrugged. Behind her, in the distance, a pair of deer had appeared on the twilit lawn to take advantage of our little oasis of green. "I don't know, exactly. But when you find out, let me know."

She hesitated and I called her on it. "You're not holding back on me, are you?"

"He's been doing—I mean it's nothing really and none of their business—but late at night, like last week?" And then she dropped her voice and told me all about it.

* * *

The next day work caught me up and I really didn't have a whole lot of time to worry over what Linda had confided to me, but if I thought about it at all I was in agreement with her: what Gyro did on his own time was nobody's business but his. And it was beyond intrusive that Mission Control should even know about it, let alone try to make it an issue. E2's cameras were in place to record ecological changes over time—and for safety's sake too, in the event anything went amiss with any of our tech systems, and to warn us of fire or a ruptured sprinkler head, but not to spy on us. It was shameful—not what Gyro had done, which really wasn't much more than a matter of speculation anyway, given what the video feed showed (or didn't show), but what the mission was doing in trying to control every aspect of our lives. For me, and I think for some of the others too, it was the beginning of resent-ment—I won't say rebellion, because ultimately I went along with Mission Control's agenda, or at least gave it lip service, but for the first time I said to myself, *I mean really, who do they think they are?*

I have to admit that at the breakfast meeting that morning, while we spooned up our porridge and sipped our mint tea and Diane and Vodge went on about assignments in the desert and marsh biomes and Stevie complained that she was falling behind on cleaning the scrubbers that kept the ocean from being over-run with algae and needed somebody to pitch in and help her, I couldn't help sneaking a look at Gyro. There he was, all elbows and jutting angles, nose, ears, the hair he'd let grow out till it stood straight up on his head like a crown of feathers, bent over his bowl of porridge, looking glassy-eyed, and I wondered about that. But he always looked glassy-eyed, didn't he? At six-five he was the tallest Terranaut, with a good four inches on Vodge and T.T. and maybe seven or eight on Richard. If his voice was a dull drone and he tended to go into just a bit more detail on the workings of the air handlers or one sensor or another than any reasonable person could possibly absorb (or want to), that was what we'd expected of him: he was our geek, our tech obsessive, and he fit the role so perfectly he might have been cast in it. (And if so, what about me? Giving it a cold hard look, I'd have to say I'd been cast as the buxom milkmaid in the larger theatricals G.C. had put together here, though I wasn't so much buxom at this point as whittled down, the role player losing her adipose tissue in all the wrong places.)

At one point Gyro raised his hand to object to something Troy was saying about the rust that was bleeding through the paint on the struts over the ocean biome, but he was ignored because Diane hadn't recognized him. Or, actually, because he didn't have possession of the day's banana (to keep everybody from chiming in at once we'd adopted the rule from *Lord of the Flies* that only the person in possession of the conch had the floor, but since our ocean didn't contain any conch, we substituted a banana. Same principle, different device). I watched him nurse his disappointment a moment, then go glassy-eyed again, off in his own world, and I couldn't help thinking of him out there in the rain forest, dropping his shorts and doing what Linda had said he'd done. He wasn't my type—more Linda's, really. But still, he was male and he was present, sitting right across the table. He had his urges, just like anybody else, why wouldn't he? And here, locked in here, where was his outlet? You'd think Mission Control would give him a medal for taking care of business—or at least ask him to do what he was going to do in the privacy of his room. The thought of it—the picture I summoned, his leanness, the tensing of his muscles, his cock rigid and his hand pumping—made my breath come quick and I had to look away.

When Troy was done, Diane took up the banana and gave out the day's assignments, pairing Gyro with Stevie on the algae scrubbers and putting Ramsay with me for the late-afternoon milking because she herself would be busy teleconferencing with a community college in Woodland Hills, California. Gretchen said a few words about how some of the rain forest trees were going to need bracing up, given that the lack of wind in E2 had weakened development of their trunks, then T.T. gave the weather report (O_2 at 19.1 percent, humidity at 72.3 percent), and that was it. The meeting concluded, and breakfast with it, and we all went out into the biomes to tick off our chores, one after the other. I scratched in the dirt, did my weeding and slopping out and all the rest, there was lunch, siesta, more scratching in the dirt, and then it was five-thirty in the afternoon and I found myself in the goat pen, leaning over the rail and talking softly to my wards, waiting for Ramsay to show up, because milking was a two-person job, definitely a two-person job.

Just to catch you up here, we had five goats at that point, the four does and a buck. The does had to be milked twice a day and they'd learned over time to have things their own way and they could be stubborn about the order of precedence going into the milking pen—or even going in at all. The ringleader—and best milk producer—was Goanna, Goanna Goat, named after the monitor lizards crawling all over the place on the ranch in Australia, but not so much for her looks or appetite but just because we— I—loved the way the name sounded. Especially when you paired it with Goat. Anyway, she was hard to lure into the milking pen unless she liked what you were offering as an inducement, peanut greens being at the top of the list, with beet greens not far behind.

I was lost in my thoughts, idly stroking Gerry the he-goat's bony head, when Ramsay slipped up behind me, put his hands over my eyes like a sixth grader and whispered, "Guess who?"

That was all right. I didn't mind. In fact, I kind of liked the attention he gave me, goofy humor and all. After that first night when neither of us could sleep and we'd sat chatting about nothing and everything till the night deepened around us and even the crickets gave it a rest I'd seen him in a new light. Like Richard, he put on a front, arming himself with a shield of cool because that was what was expected of men in society, or at least the society out there beyond the glass. Was it, as Linda would say, a guy thing? The horseplay, the towel-snapping mentality, boys in the locker room, boys on the field, boys trading round dirty jokes like collectors' cards and never, absolutely never, growing up? I didn't know. For all I knew, this *was* his personality, and, as I said, it could have its charms. Plus, the longer he was away from society and its expectations, the more genuine he became. He was Vodge. He was my teammate. And despite Linda—despite myself—I liked him.

"I don't know," I said, "feels like a thunderbolt to me."

"Sizzling, huh?" he said, and maybe he leaned into me a beat too long before I turned around and we were face-to-face, as close as dance partners. (And no, I didn't kiss him that night or have sex with him or with anybody else during the course of those four long months, and that was a burden I was carrying, or felt I had to carry. For Johnny. In memory of Johnny. For love. Or what felt like love the more I thought about it and the more I didn't see him.)

I couldn't think of anything to say, though I was considering making some sort of onomatopoeic sound, a sort of drawn-out buzz meant to convey lightning or maybe just a loose wire, but I didn't. For an instant, I thought he was going to kiss me, but that didn't happen either. What happened was Goanna. She let out a long jagged bleat of complaint, butted Gerry aside and glared up at us out of her slit amber eyes.

"Good news," I said, dipping to the bucket at my feet, "—we've got peanut greens today, so she's not going to give us any trouble." (The worst that could happen, and it did happen if you weren't attuned, was that she'd fight you and kick over the bucket—and this, of course, was a minor tragedy, because every precious drop counted, and would count even more when fall and winter came on and crop yields fell off from their peak, making calories all the harder to come by and our stomachs all the tighter.)

There was the stink of the goats—and of the pigs too, who looked on from their own pen with indifference. It was nothing to them. They weren't getting milked. They would have liked the greens though, that was for sure. Or practically anything else they could get their teeth around. Ramsay had backed off a step. He was dressed in his usual outfit, shorts and tee, but he bore a three-day growth in defiance of Mission Control, which demanded clean-shaven Terranauts, and had tied a red bandanna round his head so that strands of his hair spilled over it and into his eyes. "Great," he said. "No sense in fighting a goat that has its own agenda."

"I hear you," I said, and turned to give him a smile. "Should we get to it?"

He fed, I milked. We made use of a wooden platform to elevate the goats and make the task easier, an innovation of the Mission One crew, and Goanna sprang right up on it without hesitation, her crosscut jaws already working at the greens Vodge dumped in the manger. I don't know how he felt about it, but for me this was a pleasant interlude, the sun high still, slicing through the glass and lighting everything like a stage, the day's work trailing down to its end. We chattered away, gossiping about everybody who wasn't present, which had almost become official Terranaut policy, but we stayed near the surface, no criticism really, nothing catty, though Ramsay did have a few less-than-complimentary things to say about Diane's attempts at doing charcoal portraits of each of us and Gretchen's taste in music (show tunes, *The Phantom of the Opera,* in particular, which she played on an endless repetitive loop till even the coquis and crickets must have been driven mad by it).

"If I hear 'Think of Me' one more time I'm going to become a phantom myself—look for me in the deepest, darkest, dirtiest nook of the basement," he said. "*The Phantom of the Ecosphere*— why doesn't Lloyd Webber write that one? It could have a goat chorus—and the frogs backing them up, what do you think? But Christ. I mean I've told Gretch she's got to upgrade her taste in music, and I don't necessarily mean she has to listen to that techno T.T.'s always playing, but what about a little Bach or Mozart? Or Philip Glass, what's wrong with Philip Glass—?"

I just laughed. "Glass under glass?" I felt good, felt breezy. I was working but it didn't feel like work. Goanna behaved herself.

Garbo was next and she behaved herself too. We were silent a moment, my hands squeezing, the milk sizzling into the bucket. Then something came to me, an intuition that flared up in my brain like the answer to an equation I'd been puzzling over, and it had to do with the way he'd said Gretchen's name, said "Gretch" instead of "Gretchen" or "Snowflake," and the way he'd softened his voice when he said it. A whole slide show of fragmented scenes began to play before me, of him and Gretchen conferring in low voices two nights before out on the balcony, of his sitting beside her more often than not at meals, of the way I'd caught her stealing glances at him when she thought no one was looking. Could they be—?

I couldn't complete the thought. Gretchen and Vodge? It was bad enough what Linda had told me about him and Judy, which I could believe, but not Gretchen. She was so—what?—*inappropriate.* So matronly, so old before her time. And dumpy, dumpy too. Not that it should matter, because truly there's a mate for everyone out there and no accounting for taste, which was one reason why our species was so successful. That and the fact that for us sex had no season—if it did, if all the women of the world came into heat for a given period, say two months a year, we'd never have evolved a civilization. But here was my hunch, my intimation, buzzing round my brain, and the next thing I said was, "You hear anything more about Lola and Luna?"

He gave me a blank look and I rushed on, "Because of how you helped out that time? I just thought Gretchen would have—?"

This was the moment he chose to bend down, lift the bucket of greens and dump it into the feeding trough, and when he did turn round his face showed nothing. "No," he said, "not really— beyond that one night when they were trying to kill each other, I don't think it's been that drastic, really. Not that I would know." He paused. "Especially."

Garbo was played out. I stood, wiped my hands on my jeans, opened the gate and ushered in the next goat. "So they're all get-ting along just hunky-dory then?" I said, looking him in the eye. (Hunky-dory? Where had that come from?)

"Oh, yeah," he said, and I could see he was making an effort to hold my gaze, if that meant anything. "Everything's fine, the peaceable kingdom, right?"

* * *

"So, Dawn, we just wanted to know how things are going, how you're feeling—everything okay?"

"Sure," I said. "Yeah. Couldn't be better."

It was past ten at night and what I wanted was to be asleep, but G.C. kept odd hours and when G.C. summoned you, you came, no matter the hour. So there I was, alone in the darkened command center, staring into the monitor while the camera captured my image and relayed it up the hill to Mission Control, where G.C. sat before his screen, also alone as far as I could tell (that is, I didn't see Judy in the picture or hear her either; ditto Dennis). From where I was sitting I could gaze out the near window on the black vacancy of the desert and the star-strewn sky that drew down like a curtain to meet it. The room was still, no sound anywhere but the faint crackle of the microphone. The only light was the light of the screen.

"Great, that's just what we want to hear," G.C. said, his voice rolling out across the room, deep and vibrant, maybe not so deep as Johnny's but richer somehow, more sustained and edged with a tremble of vibrato, as if every word he spoke was the most significant you'd ever hear. He was an actor. I knew that. But he inhabited his role fully and I was listening hard, wondering what was coming next—and yes, I was nervous, or tentative I suppose would be a better word, though really, what G.C. said or did once we were inside didn't have anywhere near the weight it might have had before the final selection was made and the airlock clanked shut behind us. We were inside and he wasn't and the chances were about zero that he'd ever break closure to remove any of us, no matter what we did, but still he was our authority and his will was our law and in a very real sense we lived to please him.

"So tell me, how about your teammates—everything okay with them, everybody adjusting?"

Again the affirmative—"Yes"—though my voice was softer, barely audible as it turned out, because he said, "What? I can't hear you. For Christ's sake, E., I know it's late but speak up, will you?"

"Yeah," I said. "Great. Everybody's great."

He was silent a moment and I watched his face, G.C.'s face, the thin compress of his lips, the ascetic's eyes, the skin that was so wrinkle-free I couldn't help wondering if he'd had plastic surgery—and if so, when, since he'd hardly been out of our sight these past two years and more. Or maybe it was just the softening effect of the camera's lighting, maybe that was it. I saw that he'd cut his hair, though it was still longish, or long enough to flow over his ears, but his beard looked as if it hadn't been touched—if anything it was fuller and longer than ever, as if he was trying to live up to Michelangelo's portrait of the Creator giving Adam the spark of life, a reproduction of which he kept on the wall behind his desk at Mission Control. Lest we should ever forget.

"Glad to hear it," he said, "but what I mean is *specifically*. How's Lark working out as crew chief—in your opinion, I mean?"

I shrugged. "Fine."

"E.," he said, his voice dropping an octave till the empty room quavered with it, "you're not getting it. I'm asking you how she's working out. 'Fine' doesn't tell me anything. 'Fine' is like the weather report. Is she doing her job or is she not, that's what I want to know."

It was only later that I realized all this was by way of diversion. Yes, he did want the dirt on everybody, I'm sure, but that was being gathered voluminously and continuously and he hardly needed my take on things. "Well," I said, treading cautiously, because the last thing I needed was to provoke the woman I worked most closely with and who even now was just across the hallway—asleep, most likely, but who knew? "She can be a little grouchy sometimes, abrupt, I mean. Like when I got distracted last week and Goanna let loose with a couple of pellets in the milk bucket? I was in the wrong, I know, but she really blew things out of proportion, yelling and everything. It was humiliating."

"This isn't a confessional. We're not interested in venial sins, E., just the bigger picture. How is she holding up—mentally, I mean. Any cracks in the surface? As far as you can see?"

I have to admit I was puzzled. What was he getting at? Diane was as sane as anybody on the crew, saner, actually. She was a dedicated ecologist with the degrees to back it up and she was as good an on-site manager as we could have hoped for. Did she sometimes throw her weight around? Did she have her moods? Yes, sure, but then who didn't? I felt like a prisoner in an interrogation cell, unwilling to give up any real information but ready to feed her inquisitor whatever tidbits might have even the slimmest chance of satisfying him. "I don't know," I said finally. "I guess she's fine."

He grunted, whipped his hand across the screen in a swift white slash of disgust. "Don't act like a moron!" he shouted, the rumble of his voice reverberating in the speakers. "And don't you try to work me either. I couldn't give a flying fuck what you guess or who's fine and who's not, I want substance here, I want an opinion, I want dirt. Talk to me!"

If ever I'd felt small, it was then. Small and powerless. And, let's face it, abused, verbally abused by a man I probably had more respect for then than anybody else alive. I don't cry easily. That's for weak women. But I'll tell you, I felt a scratch in my throat. I was worn thin. I wanted bed. And here was G.C. thundering at me out of some private agenda I couldn't quite pin down, aside from his trying to provoke me to rat out my teammates. Was this a test? Was he going to call in the others, one by one, and shout *J'accuse*? I didn't have a clue.

So it went on. G.C. queried me about each of my fellow Terranauts in succession and I did what I could to placate him, racking my brain to think up anything I could, no matter how trivial, while at the same time struggling to hide my true feelings (Stevie? She was a princess, so much into herself and her public image her head had swelled till it was bigger than both E2's lungs combined; Ramsay? Her male counterpart; Diane? Bitchy). G.C. counted off the names like beads on a rosary and I fumbled and dropped clichés in his lap and couldn't think of a thing to say to lighten the mood or get me off the hook.

It was ten-thirty. The sky held fast, but for the gradual dip of the constellations beyond the windows. G.C. was still there. I was still here. And then, finally, everything began to come clear.

"Gyro," he said. "And how's he doing? You notice anything about him?"

I shrugged.

"The reason I ask is because, well, Judy says he's feeling lonely. Do you get that? Is he lonely?"

"No more than any of us," I said, but here came Gyro's *anomalous* behavior rising to the surface to illuminate the subtext. "Now that you mention it, though—"

I don't know what I would have said next, how far I would have gone in trying to balance my loyalty to a fellow crewmember and a compulsion to placate the boss, because he cut me off. "What I want to know is, do you like him?"

"Sure."

"Do you *really* like him?"

All at once I could see just where this was going, and as exhausted as I was, as cowed, I couldn't help feeling the revulsion come up in me. It burned like acid in my throat, a waste product I needed to get rid of. Or no, swallow. Swallow right down. "Yes, Jeremiah," I heard myself say, "I really like him," and I didn't bother to add the official tagline *Just like all my crewmates,* because it didn't apply here, not now, not anymore.

"Good, E.," G.C. said, and a smile flickered across the thin flaps of his lips. "That was what we were hoping to hear. We wouldn't want any of our Terranauts to feel alienated from the others—or neglected by them—because that wouldn't look good, would it? It wouldn't show the world the esprit de corps that underlies everything we're dedicated to here, agreed?"

I could just make out the vague image of my own face superimposed on the screen like an ethereal mask. The mask flickered and shifted and then G.C. was wearing it, his mouth right where mine was, his eyes staring out of my own. "Agreed," I said.

Ramsay Roothoorp

Novelty is what makes the world go round, news, gossip, the latest CD, newest band, hippest director, trends, styles, the dernier cri, but novelty wears thin and by the time we reached the fifth month we saw a significant drop-off in public awareness of E2, let alone engagement. Tourism, and along with it gate receipts, dwindled to something like half what it had been at closure (but that could have been attributable to the season because who in their right mind would want to visit Arizona in July?) and we had fewer requests for interviews. G.C. fretted, Judy was in a furor. I did what I could, cooking up weekly press releases on anything that might be considered even remotely interesting to the public, from Ecospherian recipes (Broiled Tilapia Under Glass, Beet Bigarade à la Ecosphère, Sweet Potato and Carrot Velouté) to a sampling of our daily logs and puff pieces about each of us and how our individual responsibilities meshed into the cogs that turned the great wheel that kept E2 humming.

Maybe I was reaching a bit the week I featured my own specialty, wastewater management, which could hardly qualify as breaking news—but at least I was trying. The piece, into which I'd put some time—this was something I believed in, a process as vital to our survival as balancing out the O_2/CO_2 ratios or maximizing yields in the ag biome and it was my baby and I was protective of it and proud of it too—generated exactly three letters, all from sewage plant managers and all hand-pressed to the visitors' window by Judy so that I could fully appreciate the fruit of my efforts. "Dear Mr. Roothoorp," one of the letters began, "while I cannot find fault with your description of your primary (solid waste) and secondary (biological) treatments to remove suspended solids, biodegradable organics and pathogenic bacteria in a closed system, I do think you would be well advised to go the extra mile and set up a tertiary system to remove additional nutrients like phosphorus and nitrogen that are no doubt contributing to the runaway algal growth in your fresh- and salt-water retrieval systems."

Beyond that, there'd been a flurry of interest over the galagos and the altercation they'd had back in April, and that gave us an opportunity to talk about territoriality, alpha and beta females, wildlife management and the pressing need to preserve these animals' native environment in Africa, both with the green media and the six hundred or so elementary schools around the country following the doings of our bush babies, as Judy began to insist we call them. Bush babies? Gretchen objected and so did I. Why dumb things down? Gretchen pushed for using their scientific name, *Otolemur crassicaudatus,* because this was all about education, wasn't it? Judy was immovable. As usual. "These are kids we're talking about," she insisted during one of our group teleconferences, "and to kids, *Otolemur*—is that right?—doesn't mean a thing; you might as well be talking about doorstops or widgets or something. They want babies, babies they can relate to, *bush* babies—and that's what we're going to give them."

As it turned out, the issue was a non-starter after what came down on the Fourth of July. Call it Crisis #2, Galago Division. This was our first holiday since summer solstice two weeks earlier and we were taking the day off, no different from all the other red-blooded Americans out there, and the chef of the day—E.— had arranged for a picnic supper on the beach, which would float along on a group swim and two full liters of the arak Richard had been promising us as he toyed with his still and experimented with one flavoring or another to make the result taste more like vodka and less like disinfectant. The day began like any other day that summer—bright and getting brighter, which was just fine with us, because that meant photosynthesis was cranking to the limit, every frond, leaf and blade pumping out oxygen. We had our usual group breakfast-slash-meeting, but the meeting portion of it consisted of Diane taking up the banana and announcing "The meeting's adjourned. Enjoy the holiday."

There was still the milking and feeding of the livestock, which she and E. took care of, per usual, and T.T. had to check the sensors and do his chemical analyses, the most significant of which was the twice-daily O_2 reading, just to be sure we weren't all going to fall down dead in the garden plot or asphyxiate in our sleep, but beyond that we had the day to ourselves. For my part, there was a brief but intense early afternoon phone conference with Judy, who was planning on going into Tucson for a party G.F. was hosting at a resort there.

"Hi," she breathed, her voice small and soft and moist. "You miss me?"

"I don't know. Is the line secure?"

"What do you think?"

"I think you know everything about us, even our dreams. You got my dreams on record there?"

"Why so edgy, *Vodge*? It's the Fourth. Be happy."

"Yeah," I said. "You too. Have a nice pinot noir for me. And some Swedish meatballs—you think Darren'll serve up Swedish meatballs or is that too declassé?"

"If you want to know, I wish you could be there with us, like the old days. I miss you. But you've got your duty, duty above all else, right?"

"And you've got your duty too, only it's to Jeremiah and what, Swedish meatballs."

"And you, what about you? Is it all that onerous to sit on the beach and eat banana fritters and get looped on Richard's booze? And the swim—is it going to be suits optional? That's what I heard, suits optional, right?"

The conversation had gotten off on the wrong foot, obviously, but I wasn't able to do much about it. I was feeling boxed in, sorry for myself, sorry I'd ever signed up for this whole charade—Judy, E2, Gretchen. It wasn't the first time I'd wanted to break out, no different from any incarceree, but today for some reason, call it desperation, disaffiliation, the need to be alone for once, I felt I'd been pushed beyond endurance. It was my own fault, of course. I should never have started in with Gretchen—I should have had some discipline, should have held out for E. if I was going to fool around with anybody (which probably didn't make a whole lot of sense in any case, considering the way most office romances turn out even in offices where you can go home at night). But there she was, Gretchen, inescapable, her room right next door to mine, Gretchen settling in beside me at the communal table three times a day, Gretchen coming up with one pretense or another to seek me out in the command center or at the fish ponds with a question she could have answered herself.

The ball was in her court, and that's the truth whether you want to believe it or not—she'd pretty well initiated things that first night, not nearly so retiring and non-assertive as we'd all taken her to be, and definitely the sort of woman who looks a lot better with her clothes off and her hair down, but still the whole business had begun to cloy. Or no: it was a full-on disaster. There were the meaningful looks as we passed in the hallway, the way she brushed against me in the kitchen or on the staircase, the nighttime tapping at my door and worst of all the need to hide what we were doing from six pairs of hyper-attuned eyes and the array of cameras people like Linda Ryu and Malcolm Burts were staring into all day long.

So I was in a funk. Out of sorts. Pissed off. And I didn't want to listen to Judy laying her guilt trip on me while she went off and did anything it came into her mind to do, whether that was cheating on G.C. with the next stud who came along or kissing up to the celebrities he gathered round him like saltshakers or cracking the whip over the likes of us.

"What do you care?" I said.

"I don't. I was just thinking it would be a chance for you to gawk at Dawn—that'd be nice, wouldn't it? Or who—Gretchen? But she's pretty hopeless, isn't she?"

"Listen," I said, and though the ambient temperature was something like eighty degrees I felt chilled right down to my bare soles, "I gotta go."

"Yeah," she said. "Me too." She gave it a beat. "Enjoy the swim."

* * *

Then it was evening and we were all gathered on the beach while the waves rolled in and the nine volunteer sparrows that had frustrated our efforts to trap and terminate them sailed out of the bamboo above us, across the rippling surface of the ocean and into the savanna beyond, where they'd peck up the seeds of the next generation's grasses, after which they'd bed down for the night so as to get a good start on the ag plots in the morning. Still, here were the birds, here were the waves, and as we lay back on our towels, we were at peace, the little and not-so-little irritations of working in close proximity forgotten or at least buried for the moment as we sampled E.'s goat-cheese frittata, sweet potato fries and garden salad and rocked our souls with Richard's arak, which was in the range of a hundred twenty proof and so dry it leached the moisture out of your mouth.

I'd brought my guitar and did a couple Nirvana songs as the light began to fade, then some early Dylan, and Gyro joined in tunelessly on his clarinet while the others sang along. E., who'd been plowing through the Russians in her spare time, gave a reading from *One Day in the Life of Ivan Denisovich*, which seemed grimly appropriate (and, god help me, hilarious) under the circumstances. As for the swim, it would certainly be suits optional, but that would wait till the evening deepened into night and any tourists who hadn't already departed for the local watering holes would be hard-pressed to see what us Terranauts looked like au naturel. Not that it would have mattered to us all that much—we were on display, like any other zoological oddity—but Mission Control insisted on the proprieties, as if we didn't have breasts and nipples and genitalia. Wouldn't want to traumatize little Tommy or little Crystal, Tiffany or Serena either.

"God, wouldn't it be great if we had a campfire," somebody said—Stevie, to my right, and here was Gretchen, pale face, pale limbs, stretched out on her towel beside me in her modest one-piece. "I know we can't, but isn't this like the perfect time for it? A bonfire, I mean?"

"Yeah, sure," Richard put in, and here he was, dimly figured, three towels down. "We could all chill. And roast marshmallows."

"And sing camp songs," E. said, ignoring the sarcasm. She was off to my left, on the far side of Diane and Troy, a long smooth run of flesh in her bikini, and yes, I was looking forward to seeing her take it off, the moment poised deliciously on the pointy little cusp of its erotic charge. All of us felt it, I'm sure, our inhibitions unknotted by the arak and the sweet lingering promise of our group moment, though nothing was going to happen, or likely to happen—no orgy, certainly, despite rumors to the contrary—but why not enjoy the good healthy frisson generated by lean and fit men and women frolicking nude together in an artificial ocean under an artificial sky?

"Anybody here ever go to summer camp?" E. again, continuing the thought. I sat up to look in her direction and watched her come to life in the dim glow of the single strand of white LED lights Gyro had rigged up for the occasion and just now, at the very moment, plugged in.

Stevie said, to no one in particular, "I was living with this guy, Jason Bonner? Right on the ocean in Malibu, almost directly across from Big Rock? We were in the water all day, catching waves, and then at night people would collect driftwood and we'd just sit there in the sand, pass around a bottle and let that good feeling of a day well spent sink into us, everybody with a buzz on and the sparks going up like comets—"

"Now that you mention it"—Troy, propped up on his elbows, glass in hand—"any of that arak left? Richard?"

"'There was a farmer who had a dog,'" Gretchen started singing in a piercing soprano that cut into the night like a drill bit, "'and Bingo was his name-o, *B-I-N-G-O*,'" she sang, but no one joined in and she trailed off on the last wide-open vowel. It came to me that she was drunk, and that if she was drunk there was no telling what she might do or how it might impact me, because it came to me at the same time that I was drunk too. And more: that I wanted no part of Gretchen, who might have looked good (or better, or passable anyway) with her clothes off but was appealing only in the way of the gruel Ivan Denisovich had to swallow for lack of anything better and that I wanted E., and only E., and that I was crouched there on my damp towel with the expectation of seeing her rise up in the wavering light, strip gracefully and plunge into the water that was warm as a bath and ready to receive me too. What the other male Terranauts were thinking, I couldn't say, but I suspected that their thoughts would be running very much along the lines of my own, which put a little competitive urgency into the moment on top of all the rest.

Then E. stood and said, "Well, what are we waiting for? Is this a group swim or what?"

Stevie rose from her towel too and in the next instant they'd both shucked their swimsuits and stood there naked, while Gretchen sat up and tugged her suit down over her shoulders to expose her breasts and the pale scallop of her belly and Diane, our crew captain, stood and shrugged out of her suit in a single graceful motion. There was a giggle—a flurry of giggles—and then four explosive splashes, the wave machine belching, the night thickening, the pale flicker of the women's bodies drawn down and away from us in the dark enveloping embrace of the water. The four of us men hadn't yet moved, as if we'd all been paralyzed by this vision, a vision we'd all witnessed before, it's true, but one that was inexpressibly potent in the present circumstances, given our degree of inebriation and the rarefied strains of captivity.

Gyro was the first to break the spell, kicking off his trunks and knifing into the water in one long thrust, then T.T. and Richard stripped down and followed suit. I alone held back. And not because I wasn't eager to join in the fun but because I was aroused and to be aroused under these conditions was to break with group protocol, or at least the pretense of protocol, which dictated that we were all neutral to one another except as crewmates united in purpose. It was like one of those parties where everybody does a quick strip and climbs into the Jacuzzi as an exercise in control and titillation both. You can't tell what the women are feeling just by looking at them, but for a man, his emotions are located between his legs, and where's the control in that? So I gave myself a minute, the beach deserted, the sounds of various frolics and cavortings rising to the glass panels above me, while I concentrated on non-stimulatory thoughts, like wastewater treatment options and skimming the azolla off the surface of the fish ponds. Or maybe I had to give myself more than a minute. Maybe it was more like five minutes, but finally—and yes, I'd been scanning the hazy surface of the ocean for the moving shadow that was E.—I was sufficiently, well, *relaxed* to drop my trunks and make my own shallow dive into those same dark waters.

John Cheever, one of my favorite writers, was eloquent on the redemptive power of the cold plunge, and I'm thinking specifically of "The World of Apples," in which the old poet is purged of his lust in a mountain pool, but there was none of that here. The water was the same temperature as the air, I went into it as if I were tearing silk, and lust was the name of the game, or at least in my mind anyway. And, unfortunately, in Gretchen's. There I was, propelling myself through the pool like an Olympian, with one object only: E. But where was she? Heads were bobbing. People were laughing, chattering, there was the rush of the water and the groan of the wave machine. A sickle moon, perched high, threw down a pale strut-striped light. I kicked and heaved and tasted salt on my lips. And just as I reached E., who was treading water at the far end of the pool, where it was deepest, just as I sluiced up to her with the intention of making accidental body contact, there was Gretchen, popping up between us like a seal, her jowls frosted in the silver light of the moon, her hair hanging like weed in her face. She spat a strand of it out of her mouth, giggled, and took hold of me in a way—and in a place—that was beyond familiar. I said, to both bobbing women, "Wow, can you believe it? Isn't this awesome?"

"Yeah, totally," E. said, her voice rich with satisfaction—and arak too.

Gretchen didn't say anything. Just held on until I kicked away, plunged straight down like a pearl diver, all the way, deeper and deeper into the blackness till I touched bottom—or touched something—and came surging back up again, ten feet away. I treaded water. Watched the bobbing heads. Pretended I was enjoying myself.

It was then that the galagos started in, a single startled shriek echoing through the immensity of the enclosure till it was the only sound there ever was, except that it was repeated and repeated again, and here they came, two shifting dark shapes flowing across the wall of bamboo behind us like archetypes of the unconscious.

This time it was bad. The shrieking and growling, the baring of tooth and claw, the furious scrabbling in the bush and rocketing overhead was a whole factor removed from what had gone down the first time. Gretchen let out a low exclamation and started for shore in an awkward dog-paddle, somebody said, "Oh, shit, what now?" and I took hold of E.'s hand beneath the waves and said, "It's nothing; let Gretchen handle it," and she said, "I better go help her," and that was that. Laugh if you want. The bachelor king's erotic fantasy obliterated by a dramatic display of prosimian territoriality. I know, I know: this isn't about me, it's about the mission, and my deflation that night was nothing compared to the mortality that followed on its heels. This time, Luna wasn't so fortunate. We found her, next morning, her limbs limp and fur matted with the dried blood of her aerial combat, and not in the rain forest where she belonged, but deep in the bowels of the technosphere, amid conduits and concrete and aluminum and steel, dead not of her wounds, but of electrocution. Gretchen was distraught. Mission Control wasn't especially pleased, but took it in stride, and I put out a press release calling the whole thing a regrettable accident while the gift shop quietly removed the "Luna" figures from the phalanx of plush toys they were selling at $14.95 a pop. And while none of us wanted to think of suicide, of a caged animal driven to seek refuge in an alien place amidst transformers and electrical connections and an improperly grounded wire in order to put an end to the brutality, it was hard nonetheless, very hard, to try to put things in perspective.

* * *

I'd say this was the first vertebrate death recorded in the Mission Two closure, but that wouldn't be strictly accurate. Both the piglets had preceded Luna, the first to provide us with our May Day feast, the second for the solstice, and that was natural, that was planned, and we didn't really think twice about it. We'd all learned to slaughter and dress-out animals as part of our training and we tried not to develop an attachment to them, though inevitably some did, two of our number eventually trying to forgo meat altogether, albeit unsuccessfully. As for Luna, we buried her in the rain forest, where her body would rapidly break down and give up its essential nutrients to keep the soil fertile and the vegetation burgeoning. I did the honors, going down three feet in the active soil we'd trucked in during the building phase and which went as deep as twenty feet and more in some places. It was a small, private ceremony, attended only by me, Dawn and Gretchen, though a few flashbulbs flared in the distance and half a dozen tourists and at least one journalist pressed their faces to the glass behind us. Gretchen wept quietly. I said something inane about the cycle of life, the dirt fell, the shovel tamped, and we went our separate ways to our separate tasks.

The next day dawned clear and hot, hot beyond the glass anyway. By ten a.m. the exterior temperature was up to 103°F, which shouldn't have been a concern to us, or wouldn't have been, but for a freakish chain of events transpiring in the outside world. What happened—and we didn't find out about it till Mission Control stepped in and set off the emergency alarm that burned like eight heart attacks right on through us—was that a trucker out on Route 77, who was later found to have both alcohol and methamphetamine in his bloodstream, veered off the road and took down a utility pole, which in turn ignited a wildfire that ultimately fried a series of transformers and shut down power to some six thousand households in the greater Tucson area, including ours. Now, as you may know, G.C. originally planned to provide power for E2 through solar energy, but the technology then was still in its infancy and prohibitively expensive, so we relied on the Tucson Electric Power Company (TEL) for our outsized needs, though it was hardly what you'd call a green solution. Still, Ecosphere II was as well planned a venture as anything out there at the time, including the various ongoing missions of G.C.'s touchstone, NASA, and so such a contingency had been foreseen and we had three backup diesel generators to be brought online in an emergency. And this, as it turned out, was the mother of all emergencies.

The accident, which occurred at nine-thirty that morning in a world that was as foreign to us as if we really were on another planet, was something like twenty miles south of E2 and even if we'd known about it—or any of the other thirty or so fender-benders that occurred daily along the various highways and byways of Tucson and environs—it would have been beyond irrelevant. So we didn't know about it and wouldn't have cared if we did. One hundred three degrees at ten a.m. out there in the Sonoran Desert, eighty-two and holding steady inside. Or so we thought. What we didn't know—another thing we didn't know, that is— was that Mission Control was having trouble bringing the generators online. One of the three was currently under repair and so out of service and another didn't seem to want to start up, which left us with a single generator to cover the enormous wattage necessary to keep E2 afloat, the problem being that an enclosed glass structure would rapidly become a pressure cooker without the action of the air handlers and the pumps that circulated cold water through our network of pipes. Without electricity, the inside temperature would climb beyond the point of no return and everything, except maybe the cockroaches, would succumb. It wasn't a happy prospect. In a real sense, it was our defining moment.

We were going about our business as usual, all of us looking forward to the ten-forty-five break and the handful of peanuts we devoured like trained monkeys, when our walkie-talkies began buzzing. It was T.T., calling each of us to the command center, *urgently*. This was unusual, the first time it had happened, actually, but still I was more curious than alarmed as I made my way up the tunnel from the south lung, where I'd been checking water quality in the holding pond there, and if it seemed hotter than normal I didn't really register that either, except in retrospect. I ran into Stevie on the way (her crew name was Barracuda, shortened to Cuda, but I don't think I used it more than a handful of times, though E.—Dawn—began to insist on applying it as time went on). I'd come up the south stairway from the basement, the one that gave onto the desert biome, then worked my way up to the ridge above the ocean, and there was Stevie, in shorts and bikini top, her hair wet from whatever she'd been doing in the water that morning after ag duty.

"What's going on?" she asked, falling into stride with me, and I couldn't help noticing how her eyes widened and her mouth pursed as she tightened the muscles there for the interrogative and how they relaxed in the next instant. She was congenitally flirtatious, unconsciously so, as if it were a reflex—she had a pretty face, expectedly pretty, model-pretty, and she knew it. I let her loop her arm through my mine even as I said, "Beats me," and we walked on, arm in arm.

When we reached the Habitat the air seemed denser somehow and she stopped me a moment. "Does it feel hot in here to you?" She wrinkled her forehead and sniffed the air. "Hotter than normal, I mean?"

E. was just coming up the stairs below us, and I really don't know why but I disengaged my arm from Stevie's, trying to be casual about it, extending both hands in a gesture of puzzlement, palms up. "Now that you mention it," I said.

"So what's up?" E. asked, at the top of the stairs now and falling into stride with us as we started off through the dining room and down the hall to the command center, where the others were already gathered. If I answered her, it was with a shrug: I didn't have a clue.

Troy was standing there in the middle of the room, looking perplexed. Like Gyro, he was one of those can-do types whose range of talents extended beyond the chem lab—if anything ever happened to Gyro, T.T. would have gone a long way toward filling the gap. Even if he was something of a bore, along the lines of Gyro. But then what would you expect from a chemistry major?

"Okay, good, great," he said, waving us into the room, "everybody's here. We're having a problem, I'm afraid, a glitch with the power, if you haven't noticed. The temperature right now is ninety-one point four and rising—"

There was a clamor of voices, Lark's the loudest among them. She was crew chief. It was her job, her authority, to take charge. "What's going on?" she demanded, first of Troy, then Gyro.

"It's some sort of power outage, something with the electric company." Troy was trying to restrain himself, just the facts, ma'am, but I saw how agitated he was, and that really rearranged the moment for me.

"What about the backup generators?"

"We're not going to fry like wontons, are we?" Richard said, putting on a face, though he knew as well as anybody just how critical this was. Better, actually—he could tell you at what point heatstroke set in and what the complications were likely to be in the worst-case scenario, which would mean eight Terranauts down and nobody to revive them.

"That's the problem," Troy said. "They're having issues getting the generators online, and so, in the meanwhile, and I don't know what else to tell you, we're going to need to start throwing switches here—"

Gyro, rising tall from his seat on the far side of the room: "What he means is we're going to have to shut down all non-essential systems, the Habitat, the stream, the waterfall, any grow lights—the computer too. And the wave machine. How long"—turning to Stevie—"will the corals go before damage sets in?"

Stevie's face was beaded with sweat—all our faces were. It was hot and getting hotter and we were all in the mix now. E. seemed flushed and I had to stifle the impulse to go to her. Gretchen just stared. "Shit," Stevie said, "don't tell me that. We can't shut down the wave action—I mean that's suicide."

"Polypicide, technically," Richard put in.

Troy ignored him. "I'm asking for a number."

"Three hours. Four, max. Then you'll start to see damage, but the real problem is with the temperature. If the water temp rises that high and stays there—what did you say it was in here, ninety-one?—then it's goodbye to everything." Stevie widened her stance, shot a fierce look round the room. "I'm not going to allow that to happen, and I don't care what anybody says—"

A gabble of voices. "Fuck that"—Gretchen, mild Gretchen—"and I don't care either. The rain forest has got to be our number one priority—"

Diane was clapping her hands, sharply, and where was the banana now? Not that it would have mattered. We were in a panic, or the closest thing to it. "All right, all right, everybody just stay calm. We need to get on the horn to Mission Control and get an estimate on how long it's going to be before they can take us back to full power, and in the meanwhile, like Troy says, let's go around hitting every off-switch there is, right, people?"

People? What was she talking about? This wasn't one of those Hollywood disaster flicks with some dyke in sweatpants handing out emergency supplies, this was E2, this was us. We weren't *people,* we were Terranauts. To this point, I'd stayed out of it, absorbing the news in the way I might have listened to the dentist trying to explain the procedure as he swung the drill into position, but now I couldn't hold back. "You mean you haven't got them on the phone yet? Where's Judy? G.C.? Isn't anybody dealing with this?"

"No, no, they're on it," Troy assured us, waving his arms like a referee. "Have been on it. G.C. and Judy are in Tucson still but they've been apprised and Dennis is going to do a conference call in exactly"—he consulted his watch—"five minutes. To update us."

That was when the alarm sounded and every one of us just about jumped out of our skin.

* * *

What Dennis had to tell us was a whole lot of nothing, nothing interspersed with assurances that things were under control. But things weren't under control, not even close. The tech staff fussed, the temperature rose. The tipping point came three hours later.

By then the internal temperature was at one hundred fourteen, two degrees higher than outside, and we were all thinking the same thing: they're going to force open the airlock. Which would mean failure, another failure, worse even than the first mission's—and whether or not we were in any way responsible, as Roberta Brownlow demonstrably was, or the victims of what our insurers would call an act of God (or of one drunken, amped-up trucker), no matter: we would feel the world's opprobrium all the same. Our critics had accused us of hubris and of elitism too, as in let's preserve a handful of privileged white people in a hundred-and-fifty-million-dollar bomb shelter and leave the rest of the world to face the blitz of global warming and the storms, droughts and mass starvation that come along with it, and now they'd fill the airwaves with their derisive laughter and poison every aspect of the mission regardless of what we might have accomplished.

Me? I was grim, scuttling around like a crab in a pot set over a gas burner, running from one hopeless task to the next. I was down to my shorts alone and my shorts were soaked through with sweat. My hair was matted, greased to my head. I felt heavy, oppressed, as if I were wearing a parka lined with lead. Twice I'd plunged into the ocean to cool off but only for the smallest fraction of a moment because adrenaline had me charging from one pool to another with buckets of water to keep them from going dry and then bolting headlong across the IAB to the fish ponds, where I kept churning the surface in the hope of keeping the water oxygenated. Warm water carries less O_2—the warmer the water, the more oxygen-depleted it is—and though tilapia have been selected for their ability to withstand water temperatures as high as a hundred degrees, which would kill off just about anything else, I could see them gulping at the surface and I was wondering just how long it would be before they started turning belly-up.

That was when my walkie-talkie squawked again. I was knee-deep, oblivious to the mosquitoes, churning, churning, and at first I couldn't remember where I'd set the thing down—but there it was, a dull metallic gleam etched into the face of one of the artificial rocks in the wall behind me. There was a hiss as of the air going out of a balloon, then Troy's voice came at me in a terse tense bark. Everyone was to report immediately to the command center, Code Red.

Code Red? I didn't even know what that meant—I'd never been in the military—but I didn't like the sound of it. Given what we were facing, who would? I gave up the fish for dead, tucked the walkie-talkie into my waistband, and made for the Habitat as fast as I could, the words of a half-remembered prayer rising to my lips, the prayer I'd worn thin the day they took me out of school to tell me my parents had been in an accident. I saw my aunt's face, my grandmother's. *They'll get better, won't they?* I was nine years old. *Animals die,* I solemnly informed my grandmother in the hospital waiting room that was like a cold-storage unit, *but people don't. They don't. Do they?*

This time there was no pretense. We were doomed and we knew it. The command center was an oven and we milled around inside it, edgy, everybody trying to talk at once, and what I was thinking was that if anybody tried to break closure I'd go ballistic, whether it was one of the crewmembers or G.C. himself, because there was no way they were getting me out of here, even if I had to croak in the process. Or fry. Like a wonton. But Richard wasn't making any jokes now. He looked haggard, looked depleted, old. The sun swatted at the steel struts and glass plates overhead. The temperature jumped and jumped again. We were on the verge of heatstroke, all of us, and there wasn't a thing we could do about it.

"We're going to give it five minutes more," Diane said, raising her voice to be heard over the clamor, "and then we're going to assemble at the airlock." A look for Stevie, for Gretchen, and then me. "No exceptions."

"I can't believe it!" E., inflamed. She was down to shorts and bra, her limbs greased with sweat, her hair drenched and hanging limp. She turned an outraged face to the room, to all of us, in mute appeal. "Can you believe this?"

"We're not breaking closure," I said, the words out before I knew my lips were moving. "No matter what. That's the pledge we took."

"Pledge? We're going to die, don't you get that? Fluids or no—and keep hydrating, all of you," Richard said. "Listen, I'm sorry, but as medical officer, I'm with Lark on this one—with our *crew chief*. We have no choice."

"A vote," I said. "Show your hands—who's for sticking it out?"

"This isn't a democracy," Diane snapped, shooting me a look that put her on the other side of all I wanted and believed in. "Not when it comes to crew safety, it isn't. Four minutes," she said, clenching her jaw. "And counting."

I looked wildly round the room. Every face was drawn, eyes receding, shoulders slumped, sweat dripping. "Show of hands!" I cried, my right arm jerking up over my head.

Three hands rose: E.'s, Gretchen's, Gyro's.

"It's not a democracy," Diane repeated.

"Come on, guys, it's not worth our lives," Stevie cut in, and I couldn't believe it. Had all that over-my-dead-body business been nothing but a show? Was she that soft? That banal? That uncommitted? "It's just not. We can always—"

"Live to fight another day," Troy said, wagging his head back and forth as if he'd lost control of the muscles there. He looked pained. Looked wilted.

"Always *what*?" I demanded, hating Stevie, hating everything about her, and if I was a heartbeat away from physical violence, so be it. This was wrong. Misguided. Idiotic. What if the power came back on two minutes after we'd broken closure? What then? What would we look like then? "Always quit, is that?" I snarled, throwing it back at her.

"Go to hell," she said.

"No," I roared, "you go to hell!"

That was the low point, the point at which the whole tottering edifice came as close to collapse as it ever had, but then—and we were so wrought up it took us a moment to register it—the PicTel pulsed to life, the screen going light, then dark, then light again, and G.C.'s face appeared before us in a wavering electronic flicker. It was a face nagged with worry, but tanned and confident for all that, the face of the man in charge, come to redeem us. "I just want you all to know that we're doing everything in our power on this end," he said, "so I'm going to ask you to hang in there just a little while longer, right to the point where you think you can't take it anymore, because I know you can, and will. Richard? You there?"

Our medical officer bent forward to peer into the camera, and he didn't look good, I'll admit, didn't look inspiring or even equal to the situation, if you want to know the truth. What he said was, "I'm here."

"How crucial is it? Because we're not prepared to put anybody's life at risk—"

"Fifty-fifty," Richard said, with some effort. He looked as if he were about to pass out. Heatstroke shuts down the body's ability to regulate temperature, resulting in cramps, disorientation, fainting, seizure. Brain damage, that was another medical term to consider. So was death. It was a hundred and eighteen degrees in that room and rising. Richard wanted out. Stevie wanted out. Troy wanted out. Diane wanted out. I wanted in, to stay in, no matter what.

"All right," G.C.'s voice, rolling and deep, a liner cutting a trough through a furious sea, "I'm going to authorize breaking closure on the grounds of crew safety in exactly ten minutes' time, and I'm sorry, I am, because you all know it's the last thing I would ever want to do . . ." His voice trailed off.

We all looked at one another. E.'s eyes were full. Gretchen, her emotions rubbed raw, let out a low moan and pressed both hands to her face. I'd never been in a plane wreck, but what I was thinking was that this must have been what it was like when the oxygen masks dropped and the wings shrieked and you held on to your tray table with a grip that was like death. And what were you supposed to do—cradle your head?

But then the miracle—all at once the fans started up and the water gurgled in the pipes and the lights we'd forgotten snapped back to life like so many flashbulbs and the temperature stabilized and then began to drop. And drop. By evening, we were back to normal, eighty-two degrees, all systems go. So we were saved, the tech staff in the power plant propping us up till the tech staff at the

Tucson Electric Power Company could bring it home, but it was close. That close.

I learned something that day. Learned how to divide. Learned who was committed, truly committed, till death do us part, and who was just along for the ride.

Linda Ryu

So I start putting on weight and I have nobody but myself to blame, but that's no fun so I blame Dawn. It's like I'm eating for two, or that's the joke I try to make anyway, not that it matters to her. She's completely self-absorbed, so much so I'm beginning to question what I'm getting out of the relationship, especially the time I spend at the visitors' window or on the phone with her, time that could be put to better purpose. Like getting laid by someone who might actually care about me—Gavin Helgeland, maybe, though he seems more interested in numbing-out his brain with Tricia Berner and Ellen Shapiro, who, by the way, are with him constantly, one under each arm, as if they've been grafted on. But Dawn has her problems and her problems take precedence over mine because she's a Terranaut and I'm not. Only fair, right?

The fact is I'm trying my hardest not to quibble over things or show my resentment and when it comes down to it I can say without a trace of irony that I'm sticking with her out of loyalty. That's right, loyalty—I'm nothing if not loyal. And if that means sitting there sweating outside the visitors' window while she goes on about the minutiae of every interaction she's had since she rolled out of bed that morning, who said this or that, who's feuding, who she suspects of stealing bananas from the storeroom that doesn't yet have a lock on it because a lock would be an indictment of them all and the ideals they live by and for, then I just have to grin and bear it. She'd do the same for me, I'm sure.

I went to her the day after she'd had her talk with G.C., which, as I understood it at the time, was all about harmony. I knew it had to do with Gyro and his personal brand of disharmony and the way he was expressing it—or relieving it—but I didn't know the extent of what G.C. was driving at, how outrageous it was, really, till I actually got to sit down with her. This would have been late June, as best I remember, before the galago business and the power outage that put a scare into all of us (or more than a scare: I heard Dennis actually pissed himself, though I wasn't there to witness the stains, so don't quote me on that).

The heat had set in with a vengeance. I was sweating. And itching. I'd just showered but any relief I might have felt was gone by the time I toweled off. I was chafed under my arms and between my legs and heat rash was creeping across my abdomen and up under my breasts in a pink prickling band that defied talcum powder and even Tinactin. There was no relief, of course, because the air-conditioning was down in the Residences (which should have been an indication or at least a hint as to what was to come when the tech staff encountered a real emergency, but that wasn't for me to say). Anyway, when I came round the corner of the building for our prearranged chat at eight p.m., I saw that somebody was already there at the window, but what with the hair hanging in my eyes and the heat haze and all the rest, I didn't realize it was Johnny till I was almost on him.

He's wearing a black T-shirt, black jeans and a black denim jacket—in this heat!—as if putting on a pair of shorts, flip-flops and a Tommy Bahama shirt would undermine his image, which is all about cultivating his lounge lizard credentials (he's seen *Stranger Than Paradise* something like twenty times, if that tells you anything). I'm fifteen feet away, thinking I'll walk right on by as if I have business elsewhere, when he shouts something into the phone, jerks at the cord as if he's going to pull it out of the wall and then flings the receiver aside to let it dangle there like a miniature corpse. That's when he swings angrily round to see me walking toward him and for just an instant we're both at a loss as to what to say or do, poised there like antagonists when in fact we were anything but the last time we met up, and now, suddenly, a quick jolt of fear goes through me: has he told her? Is that what this is about? And if so, how am I ever going to face her?

In the end, he chooses to ignore me. There's no greeting, no "hi" or "how you doing?" or even a nod of the head. It's all just squared-up shoulders and an icy glare, as if I'm to blame for whatever just happened between them, and then I'm looking at his back, and then he's gone.

"Dawn?" I say, unfolding my chair and settling heavily into it.

The glass throws back my own image, an effect of the westering sun, but I shift in my seat and there she is, pale to the roots of her hair, and the look she's giving me is hard and unforgiving and I'm thinking, *So that's it, then,* and beyond that, *Where am I ever going to find another friend like her?* And more, much more, along self-accusatory lines like *You idiot* and *Was it worth it?* and *How do you like your one-night stand now? Feeling cheap?*

But I'm wrong—or I've jumped to the wrong conclusion. He didn't tell her about us at all (which, despite my relief, sticks a little knife in me, as if what we've done is so irrelevant to him it's beneath notice).

"He can be such a jerk," she says.

I could say, *Who?* or *Uh-huh,* but I just sit there. Waiting.

"Johnny, I mean. He can be such a"—her voice thickens and for a minute I think she's going to lose it, weepy Dawn—*"pain."*

I just nod.

"So it's really crazy and I don't even know how to explain it, what G.C. said to me? And why I ever told Johnny, I don't know. Because nothing's going to come of it, I swear—"

"What did he say?"

"Johnny?"

"No, G.C."

"G.C. was just unbelievable, the worst. But Johnny's got me so upset, frustrated, angry, whatever, I can't even think—" She runs a hand through her hair, gets up off the stool and paces the breadth of the window, stretching the phone cord to the limit, then rubs at an imaginary spot on the glass, blows on it, and settles back down again.

"He's been fooling around, of course. And of course that's what I expected, but that doesn't make it hurt any the less, especially when he gives me details—like what is he thinking? It's a turn-on? Or is he trying to punish me?"

I don't feel particularly good about any of this—or my part in it—but I make sympathetic noises and hear her out, because that's my job as best friend and confidante (and, though I hate myself for it, Judy and Dennis' spy). "But what about G.C.?"

"Crap, as if I don't have enough problems." She gives me a distracted look, and for a minute I'm afraid she isn't going to elaborate, but then she refocuses her eyes as if to recapture the thought and goes on. "You know what he wants me to do—or what the implication was, a heavy, heavy implication?"

I lean forward. "What?"

"He wants me to be, I don't know, friendly to Gyro—so he doesn't feel so lonely. 'Alienated from the others' was how he put it."

"You mean he's—?"

"Pimping me out?"

"I'm not saying that, I'm just like stunned, is all."

"Well, that's about what it amounts to, doesn't it?" She's staring right into me and I can't shift my eyes, can't even blink, for fear of giving myself away. "*You* like him, though," she says, "don't you?"

"G.C.?"

"No, stupid: Gyro."

"I never said that."

"Yes, you did. Distinctly. Several times. More than once."

"Name one."

She waves her hand in dismissal, case closed, she's right and I'm wrong, but I see Gyro in my mind's eye then, the couple of times we danced together, the way he looked all lean and hard with his skin shining like candle wax when we stripped for group swims in the Caribbean, and I have to admit, at least to myself, that she has a point. "I'm not going to sleep with him or anything," she says, and her voice is drawn down to a whisper, "but I did try to, I don't know, go out of my way to be friendly to him, friendlier, I mean."

"And?"

"That's just the thing. Now I can't get rid of him."

"Wow, you must've really turned on the afterburners—it's only been like a day, not even a day?"

She laughs. "You know me, Dawn Chapman, world-class tease."

"No, really, what did you do?"

Another laugh. "I plunked myself down next to him at breakfast, gave him a big hello-there smile and asked him about the air handler units."

"That's all it took?"

"Guys," she says, and we both have a laugh over that.

* * *

High summer might be a long sweaty nightmare for me and the rest of us relegated to the air-conditioner-less Residences, but it's the high point of the year for the people inside, because things grow like gangbusters and the oxygen flows and the real problems— empty bellies, infighting and claustrophobia, not to mention the buildup of trace gases and CO_2—still lie in the future. But then the power crisis comes along and wakes everybody up to the fact that their whole existence hangs by a thread, a thread that could have been snipped right there if they actually were off-planet, and that's a wake-up call to us all, inside and out. I'm not saying that everybody doesn't still cling to our ideals and the notion of E2 as the ultimate solution to mankind's ecological problems here on earth, but that things just take on a darker cast. They escaped disaster, yes, but there's no way to erase the memory of how close it came, and at least one of them—Dawn, back to self-pitying mode—began to have nightmares over it. *(Linda, really, I mean I wake up covered in sweat and think it's happening all over again. And then it's like I can't breathe, like I'm in a coffin or something.)* My surface reaction? *That's awful.* My true feeling? *Get over it.*

The routine helps. It's a military thing really, though only one of the crew (Troy) was actually in the armed forces (navy), but G.C.'s grand plan apes NASA's, which hums with the language and attitudes of the military and somehow that seems to put things in focus. Maybe the best way to explain it can be encapsulated in what Ramsay said in one of his press releases in the wake of the power outage: "It's like we're a battleship and the enemy lobbed a couple shells over the decks, but now the seas are calm again and all we have to do is keep on swabbing." One day falls into the next in a clutter of details—they're busy, we're busy—and the crisis begins to recede, as does the inevitable hand-wringing over the lack of preparedness and backup plans, with the inevitable rolling of heads among the power plant techies. Two people get fired outright and another—he'd been supervisor—gets demoted to team electrician, whatever that means.

Actually, before we know it, before we can even catch our breath, we're throwing our autumn equinox parties, theirs behind the glass and ours on the lawn right outside the visitors' window. We all wear togas—toga party—because Judy thinks it's a fun idea, and we have a full spread and the same music playing inside and out, which means we can dance right up to the window and the crew can partner with us from the other side. I wind up dancing, if you can call it that, with Troy and Gyro both—and Dawn, of course—and Dawn dances with just about everybody, including, weirdly, G.C. himself, considering what went down between them. G.C.'s a Dionysian dancer, all flailing arms and angular twists, so connected to the moment he's like ouroboros swallowing his own tail over and over again, and Dawn does her best to keep up, though the little anteroom behind the glass is too packed for any of the crew to really let loose. Judy gets into the act too, letting her toga slip to reveal her bra, and Ramsay, shameless, boogies along with her, his head thrown back and his mouth gaping in a kind of parody of abandonment. He's a jerk. But he's a good dancer, I have to give him credit there.

As for food, I remember the inside crew insisting we spare nothing—they want to see us glut ourselves, and it's not cruel or thoughtless at all, as the reporter for the *Sun-Times* kept insinuating in his nasty little article on the day's events, but a group bacchanal, outside and in. They *want* to see us pile up plates of potato salad, bratwurst, cheeseburgers and ribs, they cheer as we raise steins of beer and glasses of California red and drool over the cream puffs and napoleons Judy trots out for dessert. And if I take a little extra satisfaction in tearing into a chocolate éclair while

Stevie and Ramsay look on from behind the glass, it's all in good fun, isn't it?

Next up is the play. The energy crisis and its aftermath pushes it back a bit, but we finally have our first (and last) performance as part of the equinox celebration, G.F. himself showing up to film the Mission Control version with a movie camera the size of a motorcycle sidecar and Gyro doing the honors inside with a pair of fixed cameras, one on either side of the improvised stage in the command center. Our version's a little more elaborate than theirs for obvious reasons—we have limitless access to materials for costumes and set building and they don't—but theirs is better, I think, viewing it dispassionately, not that I care one way or the other. To me, and I'll be frank about it, all these trumped-up bonding activities are so transparently manipulative they make me feel like puking, but if you want in then you'd better do what you're told and smile while you're doing it.

Malcolm takes on the Antrobus role for our performance and Tricia's Sabina, with mixed results. Malcolm, with his blowhard delivery, is way over the top, contorting his face and stomping up and down the stage as if he's channeling George C. Scott in *Patton* instead of a slightly loopy inventor who finds himself in command almost by accident, but Tricia's spot-on, though I hate to admit it. She plays Sabina with a light touch, so effortlessly funny I actually find myself laughing aloud when the next night we all gather to watch the videos back to back. Ramsay takes the Antrobus role inside, and Stevie—again, though I hate to admit it—does a creditable job as Sabina. Ramsay's good though, a whole league removed from Malcolm's walking disaster, but then Ramsay's talents definitely lie in the direction of playacting, which is pretty much all he does day in and day out. The joke about how do you know if he's lying could have been written with him in mind: *if his lips are moving.*

Dawn fumbles her way through, mainly reading her lines off the teleprompter, but she looks good, looks great actually, the camera really flattering her, and I don't know if it's her weight loss or the way she's adjusted to life inside, but she seems serene and above it all, just floating across the set. Her lines get laughs too, but she doesn't have to work for them the way Stevie does, yet to be fair, Stevie's role is broad comedy, all butt-wagging and mugging for the camera, not to mention bending over to show her tits every chance she gets. I don't know. It's all what G.C. likes to call *gemütlich,* and as we gather round to watch the videos I find myself softening toward the whole notion of our amateur theatricals—if nothing else, they give us a release valve.

Do I scoot my chair in between Gavin's and Ellen's and maybe have one too many cups of the sauvignon blanc Judy's offering up? Maybe. But I have Gavin there beside me to trade off quips and running commentary and at the after-party I wind up in a corner with him having a long lubricated conversation about the way the world's nature preserves are nothing more than dying islands and how vital projects like E2 are in the larger context, with digressions into the problems of invasive species and habitat loss, but it doesn't go any further than that, or get any more intimate, I mean. Though I want it to. There's a point there when I'm right on the verge of screwing up my courage to ask him over to my apartment to try a hit or two of *Bem Ju,* but then Tricia, still high on her performance, comes over and plunks herself down in his lap, and I have no choice but to get up and leave. Which is humiliating. I feel like I'm in high school all over again.

What does come out of the theatricals—the inside theatricals—is my relationship with Gretchen, my new relationship, that is. Of all of us, both inside and out, her performance (in a number of subsidiary roles, one-liners and such) was easily the worst. People attributed it to her shyness, but she isn't really all that shy, once you get to know her. She might be a bit naïve, or maybe straight is a better word, but she knows how to assert herself and get what she wants, with the proviso that she's a lot more subtle about it than the flamboyant types like Ramsay and Stevie—or Dawn, for that matter. I like her well enough and I don't resent her the way I do some of the others because her credentials speak for her—who else is anywhere near as qualified to oversee the wilderness biomes? Granted, she's hyper-focused on her work. And she isn't all that attractive. There's her age too. I think that's why people tend to discount her, to label her a nerd and leave it there, which isn't really fair or in the so-called spirit of things, if you think about it. Anyway, she goes through the performance like one of the living dead, her face frozen, eyes unfocused, a million miles away, and that has Mission Control questioning her state of mind in general, which is where I come in.

Two days after the performance, Judy summons me to her office. I don't know what's going on, except that whatever it is it's going to mean more work for me, but when I see Dennis sitting there on one side of Judy, and Rachel Rudd, the team psychologist, on the other, I can't help thinking it's something a whole lot worse than that. Something along the lines of *We've looked over your psychological profile, Linda, and we're sorry but we feel you'd be better off somewhere else.* I stand there looking stupid, just inside the door, skittish as a cat. "Hi," I say. And then: "You wanted me?"

"Have a seat," Judy says (or no: I think she actually said, *Take a load off*).

I sit. Smiles all around. The air conditioner hums its little tune, everything working just fine here.

What follows is a grilling on the subject of Gretchen. They begin by telling me how pleased they are with my work and how they know I'm going the extra mile with Dawn, which really is invaluable, and kudos for that, but—and here Rachel speaks up— they want to know if I've noticed anything out of the ordinary with Gretchen, anything I might have picked up on camera, the way I did with Gyro. "Does she seem depressed to you?" Rachel asks, leaning forward over her notepad and tapping one knee with the sharpened end of her pencil, her eyes maddeningly neutral. *Here we go again,* that's what I'm thinking.

The upshot is they've decided to go with a buddy system, choosing eight of us to pair with the crewmembers inside, as a way of giving them "that extra level of support," as Rachel puts it, because the literature showed that as time went on the pressures of confinement manifested themselves increasingly in mental tics, moods, even instability. Which, it goes without saying, they want to nip in the bud. Gretchen is clearly depressed. They want to know why. So they're putting me on it, and why not? I've proven myself a good little team player to this point, haven't I?

The very next day, during free-time after lunch, I meet with Gretchen at the visitors' window. Judy arranged the meeting, so as to make it official, explaining in an electronic mail memo to the inside crew that they were to be paired up with eight of us on the outside for "mentoring purposes," making it sound as if the Terranauts-in-fact were doing this for the benefit of us Terranauts-in-waiting, when in truth it was the other way around. We were there to dig. To spy. But also, in all fairness, to act as amateur psychologists, actual buddies and true girlfriends, sympathetic ears and whatever else we might care to offer. (Gavin, who's the only one of the newbies chosen for this hallowed task—paired with E., which doesn't make a bit of sense as far as I'm concerned, since it should strictly be woman-to-woman, man-to-man if they ever hope to actually get anything out of it—claims that *Popular Science* ran a recent article predicting the growing role of artificial intelligence in future psychotherapy, which has to make me laugh. Imagine sitting there across the desk from a robot that keeps asking you in a mechanical voice, So how did that make you feel?)

Gretchen's five minutes late and when she does show up, parting the curtains and coming to the glass with her shoulders slumped as if she's ducking in out of a hailstorm, she just stands there, unsmiling, and I have to prompt her to put her hand to the glass and give me the Ecospherian handshake, her right to my left. It's been a while since I've seen her—up close, I mean—and I have to admit to being a little shocked by her appearance. She looks nothing like the Gretchen who went inside back in March. She's visibly aged, her hair more gray than blond, and I realize she must have bleached it before closure and now her natural color's showing through, same as with Stevie, whose dirty-blond roots are inching across her scalp day by day like some sort of scab. She's wearing a droopy blouse, which emphasizes her weight loss, and her face seems more lined and pitted than I remembered. When she picks up the phone, it's almost like an afterthought. "I'm supposed to be mentoring you?" she says, making it a question.

I have nothing against her. As I say, she really does deserve her spot inside, and I always got along fairly well with her in our various adventures in the time leading up to closure, even if I didn't feel the kind of bond with her I did with Dawn or even Diane. She's too stiff. Older, that too. I smile. "That's what they tell me."

She just nods. "So what do you want to know? What we're eating? Or you already know that. You're the one monitoring the cameras, right? And who else, Malcolm?"

"Right," I say, "that's part of what they've got me doing. And Tricia and Jeff."

"How's that working out for you?"

"Fine, I guess. But I'd rather be inside with you guys."

Her eyes search mine a moment, as if she's trying to see through me to Judy and Dennis and G.C., a kind of divination I don't like at all. "Patience," she says finally. "Your time'll come soon enough. But really, what do you want to know? Technical stuff?"

"I think we're just supposed to chat, I mean for now, for today—and if there's anything going on out here in E1 you want to know about? Or newspapers—I could hold a newspaper up to the glass, no problem. Or *Cosmo*—you like *Cosmo*?"

"No," she says, and now she smiles, a slow rueful smile that hangs on her chapped lips like a piece of rope, "I don't think so. I've got everything I need right here."

"Is this a good time for you?"

She looks off beyond me, out into the open field burning bright with the sun, then shrugs. "I guess."

"Twice a week?" Am I pressing her? I don't know whether to back off or not because I'm really not that good at this sort of thing. I look down at my hands, then back up again. "Tuesday and what, Thursday—or is Friday better? Or Saturday? I can do Saturday"—I let out a laugh—"I mean, what with my social life. Or lack of it."

"I don't care, it's all the same to me. I really don't know what I can teach you anyway, unless you want to get the down and dirty on the rain forest and marsh biomes—is that what you want to do for your closure, or is it Stevie's position you're after? Or E.'s?"

I tell her it would be an honor to learn everything I could about the wilderness biomes, particularly the rain forest, and though I'm itching and sweating and I only want to get this over with, I feel myself softening. Here she is selflessly offering me something that might actually give me a leg up over the rest of them when it comes to the next selection, and what am I giving her in return? It isn't loyalty, that's for sure.

"So is it all right if we talk on the phone too? I mean, beyond this—just to chat? Or gossip? We can always gossip, can't we?"

There isn't a trace of animation in her face. She just stands there, oblivious of the stool behind her, her shoulders slumped, arms hanging limp at her sides. There's something wrong here, something that stretches way beyond any kind of grief over the death of an animal, and whether I'm beginning to have second thoughts or not it's my job to find out what it is.

"I guess," she says.

* * *

It doesn't take long. The second time we met we must have talked for an hour about the mission, about our families and hometowns and our likes and dislikes, but not much beyond that, though in retrospect I can see that she was dropping hints I failed to pick up. The third time's the charm. She comes right out with it and it's something I never would have guessed in a million years. If I pictured her getting together with anybody, and I didn't really, it would have been Richard, who was more her age—and style, I suppose. But then that just goes to show how blind I was— and Dawn too, because more times than you could count we'd gone over the sliding scale of who was likely to hook up and who would be more or less celibate for the duration and we never really included Gretchen in the picture. She seemed sexless. Or maybe beyond sex, maybe that was it. But when she tells me, when it finally comes out that Ramsay's the problem, all I can think is, *Wait till I tell Dawn.*

206 - T. CORAGHESSAN BOYLE

I don't know what I was expecting that day, if anything—more talk of the university town in the Midwest where she'd grown up as a professor's daughter and survived the usual adolescent entanglements and heartbreaks—but as soon as I saw her perched on the stool behind the glass, I knew something was up. I could see it in her face. She looked downcast still, jowly, sorrowful, but her eyes were alert and I saw that she'd brushed her hair straight back instead of parting it on the side like she usually did, which gave her more of a no-nonsense look. This was at the end of September, by the way, and the day stands out because it was raining, the first rain of the fall, a storm blowing up out of Mexico to put a damper on the heat wave and break the monotony. If I was thinking of Gretchen as I made my way across campus, it was only in the way of duty, of ticking off one more task on a schedule crowded with them, and I wasn't expecting much. Plus I was late, which wasn't like me, but the rain was a revelation—the fact of it, the scent of it, the transformation of the earth underfoot, and I guess I must have dawdled a bit.

Anyway, she's already there waiting for me when I come up to the glass. "Sorry I'm late," I mouth, trying to unfold the chair with one hand while holding my umbrella steady with the other and wondering why G.C. and his architectural geniuses hadn't thought of erecting an awning here. (Or maybe they had thought of it and rejected it, by way of giving the crew the pleasure of watching their guests soak, shiver or bake as the case may be.) Then I sit down and pick up the phone.

"It's Vodge," she says.

"Excuse me?"

"That's what all this is about"—her voice cracks and she draws in a sharp breath, as if she's been poked with a stick. She glares at me, actually glares. "And I don't care anymore, I really don't."

I'm not getting it, that's how thick I am. "Who?"

She gives me a slow steady look—she's actually proud of it—and repeats his name so there's no mistaking it. "I've been—him and me?" Again she has to stop. "And now he won't even look at me. Or no, he literally pushes me away, can you believe it?"

I get all the sordid details. There was that first night in her room after he'd helped her dress Luna's wounds and then came on to her in a very aggressive way when she was still in her nightgown and he had nothing on but a pair of shorts and she really couldn't refuse him. It wasn't rape or anything like that, but he was—this is how she puts it—*insistent*. As in he wouldn't take no for an answer. And then two nights later he'd slipped in her door with a candle, though candles were verboten, and a marijuana cigarette, equally verboten because of the smoke factor, which he'd convinced her to share and which had made her have a kind of out-of-body experience involving dizziness, colors and sex, more sex. After that, he started pestering her day and night as if she'd opened up a dam inside him and before she could think she found herself falling in love with him and kept wondering why the others didn't catch on because it must have seemed so obvious. She was floating. High on it. Oblivious to everything.

She'd been married before, did I know that? It was an impulsive thing, she tells me, during her senior year at Iowa—he was in her botany class and they began taking field trips together, scouting rare plants at the margins of the corn and soy fields, collecting dandelion greens, morels, fiddleheads and the like and whipping up these enormous salads, until one thing led to another. They were young, too young, and the marriage fell apart when he went off to England to do fieldwork after graduation and never came back. There'd been a couple of other men—an older professor at a conference on epiphytes, a one-night stand on her way back to The *Imago* after visiting her parents for Christmas—but nothing like this. She'd told herself not to fall for Vodge, told herself it was unprofessional, messy, a detriment to the mission, but she just couldn't help it.

And what do I say? What can I say, beyond *Uh-huh* and *How did that make you feel?*

"I feel so stupid," she says.

"Don't," I say. "It happens to us all. Bad choices, I mean."

"All I think about really is work. He woke me up, he did—he's so tender, so virile, nothing at all like Paul, my ex? Sex was like a duty for him. And I never, I mean, I never felt anything, or not really, not the way it's supposed to be . . ."

Virile? Ramsay? A little song starts up in my head: *Vodge and Judy, Judy and Vodge, Vodge and Gretchen, Gretchen and Vodge.* It's too much. Laughable, actually. I can't see it, I don't want to see it. All I feel is revulsion, with myself, and, I'm sorry, with Gretchen too.

"Linda?"

"Yeah?"

"You won't tell anybody, will you?"

"No," I say. "We'll keep it a secret. Just between us."

* * *

Et tu, Linda, right? The fact is I feel more loyalty toward Gretchen, Dawn and the others than I do toward Mission Control, and I don't tell Judy, or not right then anyway—I'm saving up, stockpiling for the right moment—but Dawn has to be in the loop and I plan on paying her a quick visit before I go into work. But then things shift on me a bit and I come maybe a hair's breadth away from doing something stupid. Or incomprehensible anyway. I'm at the supermarket in Tillman, picking up a few things with the notion of cooking at home for a change, when I look up after giving a bunch of cilantro a good quick sniff to see Johnny standing there looking nonplussed, a basket of Top Ramen in one hand and a pink grapefruit in the other. The moment might as well be hammered in stone. Bas relief. The satyr and faun. (Only which one's the satyr and which one's the faun?)

"Hi," he says finally. "Dining in tonight, I take it?"

I nod at his basket. "You too, I say."

"Yeah, keep it simple, you know?"

I don't know what else to say to him, or at least anything that doesn't begin with *About that night,* so I say the first thing that comes into my head: "That an old family recipe? Grapefruit Ramen?"

The slow smile, the tapping of the boot heel, a tug at the strings of his hoodie. Then he reaches into the basket and plucks out a package of noodles. "Dinner," he says, waving it in one hand before holding up the grapefruit in the other: "Dessert."

People go by pushing carts. There's a hiss as the misters come on to invigorate the produce behind us. I start a sentence with "Dawn" and he says, "I don't want to hear about it."

I'm about to say, *Well, nice seeing you,* when I catch a glimpse of myself in the glass panel of the cooler across the aisle. I don't like what I see. Maybe it's the distortion of the glass—it isn't a mirror, after all, just some cheap display case—but I look foreshortened, stumpy, actually, and my hair's up to its usual tricks, flattened on top by the action of the umbrella and snaking out now on both sides. I feel unattractive, ugly, out of my depth, and maybe that's why I say, "She told you, I guess, what G.C. wants her to do?"

He doesn't say anything, but I have the satisfaction of watching his jaw tighten ever so perceptibly, Johnny, coolier than thou, who'd fucked me twice in my own bed because that was what he'd wanted on a random night of his random life.

"It gets worse," I say, and why I'm telling him this I don't know, "because Gretchen—you know Gretchen, right? The rain forest expert? Gretchen's all heartbroken over *Ramsay*."

He's giving me a new look now, caught partway between brain-freeze and interest. "What am I supposed to say? Sorry to hear it? Jesus, you people need to get a life."

"I do have a life," I say. "And so do you. We can go anywhere we want"—and here I'm treading on dangerous ground—"do anything we want." I let that hang a moment. "But they're stuck—I mean, don't you find that fascinating? Or sexy? Or whatever?"

"You might as well be telling me about people in China, or where—Uganda. The dark continent. Tell me about the dark continent."

"Dawn's not on the dark continent," I say, and jerk my head in the direction of E2, which lies out there behind us in the gathering darkness, ten miles off, its glass panels aglow in the rain. "She's just down the road."

"I get that," he says. "You want to know the truth, I really get that."

I catch another glimpse of myself in the cooler and hate what I see there all over again.

He's watching me the way he did that night at Alfano's, distantly amused, as if some higher power has set me down here in the produce aisle for his entertainment. "You know what?" he says. "I feel like a drink. How about you? You want to have a drink?"

I can feel the thick stupid weight of my head as I slowly shake it, asking myself, not for the first time, *What am I doing with my life?*

"Uh-uh," I say finally, already turning to go. "I don't think so."

Dawn Chapman

I'm not claustrophobic, unlike Linda, but as the days grew shorter that first fall, I began to feel the burden of them in a way I don't think I ever would have on the outside. It had to do with the superstructure, with the glass, the way the sun was never really there but always shifting and dim, now you see it, now you don't, as if it was artificial too. I didn't mind so much when I was in the rain forest, where the understory was drenched in shadow anyway, which was fine, just what you expected, but out in the open areas of the IAB or the savanna it started to get to me after a while, especially as the hours of daylight began to fall off. I don't know how to explain it, except to say that there was a real disconnect between what I was experiencing at ground level—nature, life, the biomes teeming with activity and rich with the fullness of the earth—and what I saw when I looked up. The sky wasn't there any more than the sun was, everything divided and faceted like a mosaic. It was as if I was carrying a shell on my back, as if my two legs alone were holding the whole place up. I felt squeezed. Stifled. There were times when it was all I could do to keep from throwing open the airlock, it was that bad.

What Linda would have done in my shoes, I can only imagine. Here she was so hot to get in—and I supported her, I did, and would continue to support her as far as I could—and yet what nobody knew but me was how panicky she could get when she felt boxed in. Not that I blamed her—she'd almost died, actually— just that if I was feeling this way after nine months inside how was she going to feel? She'd sworn me to secrecy on this and if I'm outing her it's only here, on paper, and it's because I care about her on the deepest level and yet at the same time I'm dedicated a hundred and ten percent to the mission too. How would it look if she got in as Mission Three MDA and had an episode? Or worse, had to break closure?

Here's what she told me—and it doesn't go beyond this page. When she was seventeen her mother bought her a ticket to go visit her cousin in Ohio over Thanksgiving break, where she could see ice form in puddles and snow creep over the ground for the first time in her life, a real change from Sacramento. Her cousin was in his freshman year at the University of Cincinnati and her mother thought it would be a good idea for her to pay a visit and get a sense of campus life, since she was actively applying to schools around the country and had her sights set on going east. His name was Wayne Park, he was the only son of her Aunt Gwen, and he was crazy for rock and roll, the original British Invasion bands especially. And especially the Who. It happened that the Who were set to perform in town the day after she arrived and he had two ten-dollar general admission tickets. Did she want to go? She said yes, a resounding yes, though she was actually into more current bands like the B-52s and the Cars, but how could she pass up a show like that?

This was in 1979—Riverfront Coliseum, December 3—if that rings a bell. Anyway, the show was sold out, stadium seating, and by the time Linda and her cousin got there, people were already pressing up against the doors. What complicated matters was the guiding principle of stadium seating, first-come, first-served, and the fact that one of the band members had overslept so that the Who were doing their sound check at six-thirty for a seven p.m. show and the crowd, which numbered close to twenty thousand, hearing the band playing inside the arena, thought the concert had already started—without them. People in back began shoving forward and Linda and Wayne were caught in the crush. Before long, they were wedged in so tightly it was hard to breathe. Literally. In a squeeze like that your lungs become compressed, no different than if you were a rabbit in the coils of a constrictor, each exhalation fractionally deflating your lungs and making the next breath all the harder to take in. People—the smaller, the weaker, women, girls—began going down. Clothes were shredded, shoes torn off.

There were screams, sobs, people pleading, begging, gasping for air, the stronger among them flailing their elbows to make space, violent now, panicked, but the mass of bodies was packed solid. And the doors they were surging toward in a slow tidal flow—two doors, only two—opened outward rather than in so that the press of the crowd kept jamming them shut.

At first, Linda and her cousin hadn't realized what was happening. They were in line, as anxious as anybody to get in and race to the prime spots in the pit beneath the stage, but then there wasn't a line, just a crush, and she began to feel herself heaving forward even as the crowd ahead of her broke against the closed doors and recoiled backward. She grabbed hold of Wayne's hand, held on as fiercely as she could. He was slightly built, five-eight, a hundred twenty pounds, and the force of the crowd was too much for him. Suddenly his hand was gone and there was somebody else there, everybody else, a solid wall of flesh that wouldn't give except when somebody went down and the crowd surged in to close the gap. Linda couldn't breathe. There was a guy her age pressed up against her, the side of his face locked to hers as if they were slow-dancing. She couldn't see past him, couldn't see over the crowd, and she had no idea where she was, whether she was close to the entrance or stalled two hundred feet away.

Guitars shrieked from inside the arena. People screamed. She felt something butting up against her, a hard insistent force like a battering ram, and looked down to see a girl with crushed hair and a bruised face stretched out right there at waist level, floating on the hips of the crowd, her legs and feet buried somewhere behind her. *Help me,* the girl gasped. *Somebody help me.* Linda didn't scream—she didn't have the breath for it. What she did do, inch by inch, was work her back to the guy pressed up against her and the girl too and lock her arms in front of her to gain those few precious centimeters for her lungs to expand.

Others weren't so lucky—or resourceful, I suppose. Eleven died. Hundreds of pairs of shoes were scattered round the entrance, purses, jackets, sweaters, shreds of clothing. Wayne escaped—he was in—and then, after the worst thirty-five minutes of her life, she was in too, the shoulder torn from her parka, her sweater ripped down the sleeve and her bare arm scraped raw where somebody's nails had raked her. She ran down the steps to the arena below the stage, thinking that was what she wanted, and then she knew better—shoulders, heads, another crush—and kept on running, skirting the crowd, the stage and the band thundering above her, until she found the emergency exit and pushed through it and out into the bitter night. When finally she was safe, when she could breathe and feel her heart begin to decelerate, she glanced behind her and was puzzled to see the imprint of her Converse high-tops on the white concrete under the glare of the streetlights, and that was strange, a mystery, till two other people came hurtling through the exit behind her and she saw that they were making tracks too. And what was it? What had they stepped in? Blood. That was what it was. Other people's blood.

That was her trauma and nobody knew about it but me (and maybe her mother, and Wayne, of course, who'd stayed and watched the show while she walked all the way across town and back to his apartment, assuming that she was boogieing away in the mob somewhere and just as transported by "Baba O'Riley" and "Won't Get Fooled Again" as he was). Ever after—and again, who could blame her?—she'd had a morbid fear of confinement. Aboard The *Imago*, she slept outside on the deck whenever she could because the berths were like coffins, or that was what she claimed. She avoided buses, trains, airplanes—any enclosed space—and she never went to another rock concert in her life. "MTV, give me MTV any day," she said, trying for bravado after she'd confessed all this on a night when we'd both had too much to drink. "I don't care what band's playing, I don't care if they send me a telegram and beg me to go up onstage and sing lead for them, I'm just"—and she made an effort to keep her emotions in—"it's just not worth it, okay? I got scared. I'm still scared."

And here I was, feeling sorry for myself. I had a case of the winter blues, my first winter inside, but Linda? What if she'd been picked over me—could she have handled this? Would she even want to try? Seriously? I didn't know. And I didn't know what to do about it either. She was going to have to take care of herself, that was what I was thinking then and what I'd thought all along. If we'd gone in together, it would have been different. I could have looked out for her. But now, as it was, there wasn't much I could do—and it was still a long ways off till she did come in, *if* she made the cut next time around, that is, and truthfully, without trying to sound harsh or discount Linda in any way, I had enough problems of my own.

* * *

For one thing, there was Gyro. At heart he was a good person, kind, sweet even, if you could get past his straight-ahead personality that didn't really allow for much by way of wit or insight—or the fact that all he seemed capable of talking about were specifications and the requirements of one system or another and the type of p.c. he was going to get after reentry, which involved long disquisitions on hard drives and memory. Which was fine. All fine. Except that now I had to somehow fit him into a crowded schedule, trying to do G.C.'s bidding without compromising myself—I wasn't going to sleep with anybody for any reason other than mutual desire and love, no matter if G.C. himself threatened to break closure, storm in and cast me out into the wilderness. So that was where we were. I befriended Gyro in what I thought were the small ways, never quite working up to the larger issue of his anomalous behavior because it was just too embarrassing—and none of my business when you came down to it. I smiled at him. Made small talk. Went out of my way to sit beside him at meals—but that didn't mean I was going to let him come on to me in any meaningful way (or as Linda put it, be there to hand him a Kleenex next time around). The problem was, he misread me. Or read me in the way I'd intended, only to a degree that pumped up the volume to an unacceptable level.

What am I trying to say? He became a nuisance. Every time I turned around, there he was, at my elbow, giving me his weird grin that was all lips and oversized teeth but that just stuck there frozen in the middle of his face so it looked as if he was wearing a mask and why they hadn't steered him toward Gretchen (yes, Linda had confirmed my suspicions there vis-à-vis her and Vodge), I couldn't imagine. It came to a head one night in November when I was feeling pretty low—the winter blues combined with worry over the falloff in beet production and the infestation of broad mites that was withering our precious Idaho potatoes, plus exhaustion, pure and simple. If I remember rightly, that was when several of us, Stevie, Diane, Vodge and I, had decided to tackle the morning glory problem, and I ached all over as a result. (The morning glories, a Mission One mistake, had grown up from the ground to cover the canopies of the trees in petite blue flowers that might have been pleasing to the eye but cut off light to the biomes, especially the rain forest, where it was dark enough already. Mission One thought they'd eliminated the problem, but that wasn't the case. The morning glories had re-seeded themselves—they had their own agenda, just like everything else inside—and while our backs were turned they'd pretty well taken over whole sections of the spaceframe, their thin ropy vines dangling everywhere you looked.)

It was ten at night and I was just sitting there in my chair staring into the pages of a book and trying to summon the willpower to drag myself up to bed, too tired even to shower though I was pretty much a mess from the day's labors, when there was a knock at my door and before I could say "Who is it?" the door cracked open and Gyro's head was floating there in the lee of the frame, his frozen grin locked in place. I felt a flash of annoyance.

"What?" I demanded. "What do you want?"

"I brought you something," he said, edging into the room uninvited. The last time he'd brought me something it was a sculpture in the shape of a human head he'd fashioned from bits of wire and crowned with a bouquet of morning glories, as if he was afraid I might not have enough of them in my life.

"Not tonight," I said. "I'm wiped, okay? I just want some privacy, that's all." I yawned, entwined my hands over my head and stretched, which made his eyes jump to my breasts, another annoyance. "If you want to know, I was just getting ready to go to bed."

It was then I noticed how he was dressed—in jeans that actually had creases down the front of both legs, leather shoes, a long-sleeved button-down shirt. He seemed to have trimmed his hair too, the fluff he'd let grow out reduced to partial fluff and tamed with some sort of hair oil that shone greasily in the light of the lamp. Warning signals went off in my brain: he'd made it a formal occasion, planned this—whatever it was, this moment—while I'd been sitting here in a miasma of my own body odor, too tired to plan anything beyond a ten-step excursion up the stairs and into my bed.

"You look beautiful," he said.

I made as if to get up and usher him back out the door but my legs felt like pillars and the best I could do was wave my hand as if shooing flies. "Not now," I said.

He was fully in the room at this point, tall, taller than the bookcase, watching me intently, and he quietly pulled the door shut behind him. "But you don't understand—I have something for you," he said, and he held out his hand and I saw what it was and all the exhaustion drained out of me in an instant.

"For me?" I exclaimed, coming up out of the chair so fast I think I startled him. "Really?"

What he held out before him was an artifact of the outside world, treasure, pure treasure—a single glittering bright yellow package of peanut M&M's (and please don't laugh at me here unless you've been locked inside yourself, because you can't begin to imagine what I was feeling in that moment—nobody can except maybe Solzhenitsyn's gulag dwellers or the crews of the early Russian Bios experiments who had to get along on water, algae and boiled millet once the potatoes and sausage ran out). M&M's. The crinkled yellow wrapper, the bold brown letters. One hundred forty-four calories per serving. Chocolate. Peanut. Sugar. Hard candy shell. *M&M's!* I couldn't believe it. I was entranced. "For me?" I repeated, and I don't know—I don't really remember—but I was so worked up I might have actually tried to snatch them out of his hand.

"Yes, of course they're for you," he said, his fingers opening and closing again on the shiny flash of the wrapper. "I mean, that's why I'm here. To bring you a present." And now, finally, he handed them over and I had the top edge of the bag between my teeth, tearing the paper to get at the intoxicating smell of the chocolate inside. "Because I love you," he added by way of clarification, but I wasn't listening, the first sweet glistening morsel at my lips, then tucked between my cheek and gum—I was tonguing it and I wasn't going to bite down, not yet . . .

"I thought," he was saying, and here the room came back into focus and I did bite down in a single ecstatic crunch that drowned my mouth in saliva, "we might share them—"

"Oh, yeah. Yeah, of course," I said, and I very nearly spat the sweet bit of it into the palm of my hand, staggered by the thought that we were going to have to be fair, count them out, two equal piles, *weigh* them. "But where did you get them?"

His grin dissolved into a little end-stop of confidentiality. He loomed over me, sky-tall, gangling and big-footed and small-chinned, then leaned in and dropped his voice. "I smuggled them in with a box of air-handler parts, like a month before closure?"

I let this information gestate for just a beat and then I asked the question it made all but compulsory: "Have you got any more?"

If he did, he wouldn't say. He did his best to give me a mysterious look, the two of us moving deeper into the room as if by unspoken accord, and he sat himself down in my sole chair and counted out the M&M's on the shining surface of my oak veneer end table while I plugged in the hotplate and made us each a mug of mint tea. "One extra for yourself," I called over my shoulder, "—remember, I already had one." I put on some music (Corelli's Concerti Grossi, which just about saved my life around then), handed him the tea and settled down cross-legged on the carpet beside him. We listened to the interplay of the strings and made small talk that managed to skirt both of his principal concerns—his love of technics and his love of me—and savored our sweet little nuggets of candy, one by one. It got late and then later.

I was feeling a kind of contentment I hadn't felt in weeks and if it was attributable to so trivial a thing as a chocolate high then so

what? He was thoughtful, Gyro, that was what I was thinking—
and he was a nice guy, genuinely a nice guy. And while I wasn't
about to roll over and go to bed with him (though I wouldn't have
been the first woman seduced by chocolate), I did wind up making
out with him for a while, tasting the sweet burn of his tongue in
my mouth and feeling, through the fabric of his jeans, the pressure
of the long hard deprived organ that had got all this going in the
first place.

* * *

I talked it over with Linda a few days later. We were at the glass,
Linda bundled in a parka, the night drawn down like a shroud
behind her. I could see her breath hanging in the air.

"Like I told you," I said, "he's not my type."

She gave me an impatient nod. "What does it matter, really?
It's either him or somebody else—Ramsay, *Jesus*—and you've got
to have something more than just, what, playing with yourself?
I mean, for your own sanity. Two years, Dawn. You're going to
dry up and blow away, that's what's going to happen—aren't you
afraid of that?"

"Please. People have gone without sex before, and it's not as if
it's going to make my hair fall out or anything. Or my teeth."

"Monks," she said. "Nuns, castaways. The Virgin Mary. That's
about it."

"And convicts, don't forget convicts—"

"Are you kidding me? There's nothing *but* sex in prison."

I would have gone on, would have talked about discipline, self-
control, science, but I knew she was right. What they were asking
of us wasn't natural. But then what G.C. and Gyro were asking of
me wasn't natural either. If I was going to have sex it was going
to be on my own terms—either that or I'd just forget about it and
wait out the fifteen and a half months till I walked through that
airlock and into Johnny's arms. If Johnny was there still. And there
was no guarantee of that. I hadn't told him about the diaphragm
because it was none of his business, and yet I'd made the appoint-
ment and gotten fitted for a reason, so why fool myself? It was a

stopgap, a just-in-case, or that's what I told myself, and yet here I was tongue-kissing a man I wasn't attracted to because I was desperate and he'd had the sense to be there at the right time—and with a bag of M&M's in his hand. What's more, venal or not, I couldn't help thinking that where there was one bag there had to be another.

"You know what else was weird?" I said, looking out beyond her to where the west wing of E2 abridged the night like an ocean liner on a flat sea.

"What?"

"Richard came on to me. The other day—during siesta?"

"Richard? You've got to be kidding. He's old enough to—"

"I know, I know—I'm just saying."

"So what happened? Tell me."

"I don't know, it was weird. I was coming back from the goat pen, barefooted—I've pretty much given up on shoes, did I tell you that? Look"—I held up a foot in evidence, the nails chipped and horny, the sole yellow with calluses. "And my feet were beyond dirty—and I probably hadn't washed my hair in days, I don't even remember. Pretty was the last thing I was feeling like, but Richard, who never came down to the animal pens unless it was his turn for ag duty, was right there, where that board goes over the mud puddles, like where it's always wet? 'E.,' he says, 'you're looking pretty this afternoon,' and he has this strange look on his face like he was holding something in, almost as if he was going to let out with one of those crazy honking sneezes Diane's always lighting the place up with. 'Thanks for the compliment,' I said, 'but I'd feel a lot prettier if I could find the time for a shower—or a swim,' and he said, 'You're gorgeous the way you are, the dirtier the better. In fact, and I'll bet you didn't know this—medically speaking, all this obsession with cleanliness in modern society is giving us a generation of asthmatics and allergy-prone latch-key kids. They go outside, take a breath of real air, and they're prostrate. Give me some good clean dirt any day.'

"'Yeah,' I said, 'great, that's just what I wanted to hear,' and I stepped off the board and into the mud for emphasis, and that was when he reached down for me—for my breasts, I mean he actually took hold of my breasts, before he slipped his hands under my arms and lifted me back up onto the board. 'Napoleon,' he said, going on as if nothing had happened, 'he knew the score. Did you know he wouldn't let Josephine bathe—at all, not once—while he was away on his campaigns because when he got back he wanted to experience the true essence of a woman?'"

Linda wrinkled her nose. "Oh, *please*," she said. "Is that true?"

"That's what he said, which was just Richard being Richard. But what really threw me is it put everything on a different basis. I mean, he's our doctor and he gets to see us all nude every two months, one on one, in his lab—and the measurements, all that. And he was definitely coming on to me. You know what else he said? He gives me this look and says, 'As your physician, E., I'd be remiss if I didn't remind you how important, how vital, an active sex life is to good health.'

"I was standing there on the muddy board, wanting only to get back and shower some of the crud off me, and frankly, I felt kind of awkward. More than awkward—I was embarrassed. I mean, this was Richard, and he didn't just accidentally brush his hands over my breasts while pulling me back up, which I hadn't asked for or expected, and now he was offering me sex advice? And blocking my path? Come on. So what I did was just step right back off the plank and start splashing through the puddles. 'Thanks for the advice,' I threw over my shoulder, and then, just to get him, I added, '*Doc*.'"

"Jesus. Why doesn't somebody hook him up with Gretchen? Like you, for instance. That'd be more age-appropriate anyway. And she could use it, believe me."

Of course, I'd watched Gretchen's sad affair with Ramsay play out across the dining table through three meals a day (and what had *he* been thinking?) as Gretchen's rapture turned to sullenness and finally a depression so crushing we all started to worry about her. She made a point now of sitting as far from Ramsay as she could and she never addressed him directly. During team meetings, no matter what he had to say, whether it was something we all agreed with or not, she took up the banana and opposed him. As time wore on—it had been over for something like three months now—she began to come around, though I have to admit I didn't have all that much sympathy for her. I mean, what did she expect—that they'd get married? Plus, I couldn't believe it was all one-sided, that Ramsay had initiated things, practically forced himself on her the first time if you gave any credence to her version of events. Which I didn't. Ramsay wasn't like that. He was a charmer, a persuader, and he wouldn't have done a thing if she hadn't put out signals.

"I'm sure," I said. "But I didn't sign on to play matchmaker."

"Ramsay's a dog, that's all. And it's obvious he doesn't give a shit whether he screws up the mission or not—I mean that's about the long and short of it."

I saw Gretchen's face then, her sorrowful, hopeless pout, woe-is-me and pity the poor victim, and I just felt how wrong it was. "She's no innocent," I said. "She's forty years old—going to be forty-one next month. She was married before. Come on, we're all adults here."

Linda laughed. "So you keep telling me. But I can't believe you're actually defending him."

"I'm not."

"Listen to yourself. I wish I had a recording."

"He's not what you think—that's all an act. And when you get to know him, I mean day to day, in here where everything's so different, he's all right. More than just all right—he's a good person, he really is."

Linda made a face. "I can't believe what I'm hearing. You're not actually thinking—?" She stopped right there, tried to compose herself. A look over her shoulder, which was just a feint to give her time to cook up some poisonous little assessment, as if it was any of her business anyway. "Don't tell me that, Dawn," she said, turning back round to face me. "Please. Anything but that."

"I'm just saying, he's not what you think."

"Yeah, right. And G.C.'s not God and the sky isn't blue either."

We sat there in silence a moment, at an impasse. Best friend or not, she was sticking her nose in where it didn't belong. I had no intention of doing anything with Ramsay other than what was required of us as crewmates to make the mission run as smoothly as possible. All I had to do was think of him with Judy—or *Gretchen*—and it made my stomach turn. But still, and maybe it was because we *were* crewmates, real Terranauts thrust together in a common purpose and not just support staff poking and prodding us from the outside, I couldn't help defending him. I folded my arms, leaned back on the stool and just stared at her.

Linda must have felt it—she'd gone too far and really, she couldn't begin to know what I was going through—because she abruptly changed the subject. "Gavin," she said. "What about Gavin, what does he have to say these days?"

Gavin Helgeland had been assigned the duty of mentoring me (not the other way round, as Linda most emphatically let me know at the outset). Mission Control was worried about us, about our collective mental state, about things breaking down and people forming cliques or withdrawing from the team or going into a funk like Gretchen, which was where all this was coming from, of course. I liked Gavin. He was good-looking, smart, enthusiastic, and he had what Gyro most definitely lacked—wit. We chatted once a week at the glass and he tried to draw me out in terms of any problems I might be having inside, beyond the winter blues, that is, but I was nimble enough to sidestep divulging anything that might have compromised things with Mission Control and steer the conversation to him and his hopes and desires and the way the world was treating him. I was inside and he wasn't and that gave me the advantage.

He was from upstate New York, in Putnam Valley, not far from where I'd grown up, and that gave us common ground, as if we needed anything to bond us beyond E2. We found we had mutual friends, or at least friends of friends, and we made a game of guessing when we might have been in the same place at the same time, a Talking Heads concert at Bard I'd attended when I was just out of college and living at home for the summer, the Fourth of July fireworks in Cold Spring that year, random nights in a place called Jimmy's by the train station in Peekskill that served a wicked appletini and featured one of the best jukeboxes in the county. We'd shopped at the same market, got sandwiches and cream sodas at a little deli in Roe Park, the best. He was four years younger than I and had played on the Lakeland soccer team, and so we were able to establish that I'd definitely, incontrovertibly and without doubt had to have seen him in the flesh at least once in that period because my mother and I were on the sidelines for a match with Yorktown to cheer on my brother, Randy, who was center fullback for the home team. *Small world,* he'd said, and I laughed and raised my eyes to the ceiling of the big beehive structure that soared above us and said, *Right, and it seems to have gotten a whole lot smaller.*

"Dawn, you there? Earth to Dawn, earth to Dawn?"

"Oh, sorry. What were you saying?"

"Gavin. How's that working? Anything new?"

"Not much," I said, and then it occurred to me that her interest was maybe a bit more than simply collegial. "Why, you like him?"

"I don't know. Maybe. Does he ever say anything about me?"

The question took me by surprise and I spent a brief puzzled moment reviewing the talks we'd had, talks that had focused on me, on him and Mission Control, in that order.

"Not really," I said finally. "I guess your name never really came up."

* * *

If I had the blues in November, they just intensified as the Christmas season came on. Christmas had always been special for me, ever since I was little, and more than anything, more than the gift giving and the Christmas cards and all the rest, it meant family to me, and E2 excluded family. I had a new family now and new rituals, and yet still I couldn't help being sentimental about the holidays, and when I spoke to my parents at Thanksgiving, it just made things worse. They weren't sure if they were going to be able to make the trip out west for Christmas, which they'd been planning since closure. "It's your father," my mother told me. "He doesn't think he can get away." I should have seen it coming, but that didn't make it hurt any less. My father had been scathing on the subject of E2 from the beginning, aping some of the more cynical pronouncements of the press, i.e., that we were a cult, that G.C. was a guru and a manipulator and that the project had little scientific validity and less application. I wanted him to be proud of me, of my dedication and success—and fame too, because that was no small thing and nobody I knew of from my high school or college could begin to match it—but he wouldn't even give me that. "We're still going to try," my mother whispered into the phone before she hung up, "but no promises."

Two years ago I'd spent the holidays with my crewmates on The *Imago*, off the coast of Belize. This was Christmas with palm trees instead of firs, white sand instead of snow, and yet we had our celebration all the same—on the island of Caye Caulker, where we strung lights in the palms, read Dickens aloud round a campfire and arranged for one of the local families to serve up a feast of lobster, land crab, black beans and rice. It was different, not at all maybe what my mother would have envisioned by way of Currier & Ives, but we made do. Last year, when I was working support staff and things weren't (obviously) so rigid as they were now, G.C. had allowed some of us to go home for the holidays. I had a week. I slept in the attic room where I'd grown up, my mother cooked a turkey, we sang carols, baked cookies, watched *It's a Wonderful Life* on TV. We even had an intermittent snowfall on Christmas Eve. That was magical, it was, but by the fourth or fifth day I found myself anxious to get back, not only to be with my crewmates but also to show G.C. and Judy just how dedicated I was and how deserving too. I wasn't a part of that life anymore and that made me sad. And now, locked in here, I felt all the sadder.

I think we all felt it to one degree or another. The year was closing down, oxygen levels were at their lowest—sixteen percent, which was comparable to living at seven thousand feet—and everyone seemed subdued. It was Ramsay, at team meeting one morning, who snapped us all out of it. He took the banana from Diane after she'd given out the day's assignments and leaned back in his chair. I remember he was wearing a cap that day, one I'd never seen before, a bright red cap with the letter A stamped prominently across the front—some baseball team or other. Or maybe football. Not that I would have known the difference—and I don't know why I fixated on the cap, except that none of us wore hats, even in the IAB, since we didn't have to worry about protection from the sun. At any rate, the shadow of the brim hid his eyes and that made us all lean in to try to gauge the expression on his face, expecting him to say something about the fish ponds or his latest press release, but he surprised us by flipping off the cap and sailing it high into the air and over the railing, where it coasted down out of sight and into the vegetation below.

"Have I got your attention?" he asked with a grin. "Because I want to know what we're going to do about Christmas. Are we going to put on a feast to end all feasts or not? I'm down with it, that's for sure. And you can bet the press is going to jump on it, first Christmas inside, peace and harmony and all that? Brotherhood of man. And woman. Or sisterhood, whatever, you get the point." He turned to Richard. "About time for a new batch of arak, right?" And then Troy. "And banana wine, Christmas vintage! What do you say?"

It was amazing how everybody came to life—this was just what we needed to lift the gloom, a project, a break in the routine, something to look forward to, *Christmas*. Everybody started talking at once, but Ramsay, insisting on the protocol of the banana, hushed us. "And what are we going to eat, that's the question." He looked at me now, dead on. "About time for Petunia to go, wouldn't you say, E.? We can barely feed her as it is, right? And, Diane, what do you say?"

Petunia was one of our two sows, brought in from our on-site piggery after Mission One reentry, along with her older companion, Penelope. Penelope had given birth to a litter of piglets, two of which had come in with us to provide meat, which was the function of all their tribe, including, eventually, Peter, the boar. Both piglets had been sacrificed to earlier feasts, and since Petunia had now reached the prime butchering age of ten months, it was logical that she should be the one to go at this point, given that we still had hopes Peter would impregnate Penelope again.

Ramsay had asked my opinion and I gave it even before he handed the banana over. "It makes sense, I guess," I said, and then Diane took up the banana and seconded the motion, giving us a mini-dissertation on how we were coming to the point of diminishing returns in any case—all three of the pigs were losing weight because of the seasonal falloff in ag production, and even finding the fodder for two mouths was going to be touch and go, let alone three, and of course we couldn't cut back on what the goats were getting because the goats were our dairy machines.

She paused, looked round the table. We all wanted meat, that went without saying, and no matter how attached some of us had gotten to Petunia, who was an intelligent, well-adjusted pig, almost a pet on the order of a cat or dog—smarter in fact than a dog, as most pigs were—this was the right thing to do, no doubt about it. "So," she said, "we're all agreed?"

"Goodbye, Petunia," Ramsay said, speaking out of order, and Richard, also out of order, added, "R.I.P.—in ham heaven."

* * *

I won't pretend it wasn't hard. As much as I tried not to get sentimental over the animals, I couldn't help myself. I was the one who spent the lion's share of her time with them, and in the absence of pets, they were there to fill in the gap. There were the galagos, of course, but they weren't really domesticated—you couldn't pet one of them, couldn't even catch one—and while they provided us all with their share of excitement and amusement, it was all distant, a whole other dimension from what the livestock gave us. You could talk to the pigs, stroke their ears, see the interest in their eyes when they recognized you as the tall ape with the bare feet and the bucket of slops in hand, and I won't call it love because their attention went out equally to anyone in possession of food of any kind, but there was recognition there, if not real affection.

And no, I'm not going to deliver a lecture on cruelty to animals and vegetarianism as the only enlightened path to human nutrition—we'd all put in our time on the ranch in the outback and had come to slaughter and dress-out animals we'd known just as intimately as Petunia. Or almost. Again, as with just about everything else, E2 wound up concentrating our emotions and forcing us into a far greater intimacy with all the creatures of our world than would have been the case outside. The pigs and goats lived right beneath us, in the way of the medieval farmhouse, animals on the ground floor, humans upstairs, an arrangement that had served our species well down through the ages. I was opposed to the factory slaughterhouse and its casual cruelty, as any thinking person had to be, but death was the inevitable result of life, and if an animal was humanely raised and humanely slaughtered, I had no issue with that. Or so I thought.

The fact was so much harder than the theory. To this day I can't read E.B. White's "Death of a Pig" without choking up—or even *Charlotte's Web,* for that matter. Petunia—P.P., Petunia Pig—sailed through the last three weeks of her life on double rations, frisky and fattening while her companions grumbled and fought over their own reduced portions, and as the days drew down I found myself dreading what was to come. She was a good pig, a very good pig, whose soft mobile snout fit just perfectly into the cupped oval of my hand and who would actually cut capers around the pen in her excitement over the second bucket of slops reserved for her while Peter and Penelope looked on resignedly from behind the slats of the inner pen. When the time finally came—on the morning of the twenty-first, winter solstice, our pagan feast that night to be meatless by general agreement so as to reserve the place of honor for Petunia on Christmas Day—Diane was conveniently busy elsewhere and so it was left to me to see things through to their conclusion.

We'd set up a worktable and the scalding tub on a fallow plot in the IAB, reasoning that any mess—a spill of blood, the odd scrap—could be hosed off the table and worked into the soil, but also of course we chose the IAB because it was out of sight of the animal pens. The essential thing was to avoid exciting the animal—any release of stress hormones would affect the quality of the meat, and we wanted to sidestep that. Easier said than done. For the past several days I'd trained Petunia to a leash, with mixed results, but by baiting her with the slops bucket I was able to walk her through the livestock area and into the IAB, where the sight and smell of the vegetable gardens were a real stimulant to her. Now I showed her the bucket. Showed her the leash. Without hesitation she allowed me to fasten the leash round her neck and she trotted out of the pen in high spirits, the routine already ingrained in her—she was a clever pig, as I said. We got as far as the IAB, within twenty feet of table and tub, in fact, when she pulled up short, sat on her haunches and refused to move.

It took me a moment, stroking her ears, whispering endearments, before I understood what the problem was: Troy and Ramsay. They were there to do the grunt work—Petunia weighed a hundred sixty-four pounds and muscle was going to be needed to shift the carcass and hoist it into the scalding tub—and Troy and Ramsay had made themselves available, all for one and one for all. Stevie was in her ocean, fighting algae. Richard was in his lab. Gretchen was recording the growth of select trees in the rain forest, measuring tape and clipboard in hand. Everything was still but for the bees and butterflies dancing over the crops. It was quiet. Serene. But Petunia wouldn't budge. She was unsettled by seeing the men there because when I'd brought her to the IAB all those other times—for a reward—no men were present. It was just her and me.

"What's wrong?" Ramsay was barefoot, dressed only in a pair of cutoffs, figuring it would be easier to wash blood from his skin than his clothes. He was standing there, arms folded across his chest, with Troy—also stripped down—beside him. They'd already laid out the tools we were going to need: the sticking knife, the bell scrapers for removing hair and scurf from the hide, a hacksaw and our only axe, the blunt end of which would be used for the stunning.

"I don't know. I think she's just a little, *tentative,* I guess, because she's not used to seeing people here." The pig let out a soft grunt—she was interested in the bucket, that was what she'd come for, but still she didn't move. "Maybe if you two sat down—"

"Where?" Troy demanded, gesturing toward the table, the tub and the buckets reserved for blood and viscera. He was in a temper, his eyes boring into me as if all this was my idea. Which wasn't fair. This was a group decision, a necessity, and he knew as well as anyone that if you wanted meat you had to work for it.

"On the ground. Just till she gets used to things—something new. She hates anything new."

"Oh, Christ," he snarled, but he folded up his legs and sat down in the dirt, and so did Vodge. They didn't want stress hormones released into Petunia's bloodstream any more than I did. Keep her calm at all costs, that's what we were thinking. Even so, I was anything but calm myself. My hands shook. I couldn't seem to swallow. I felt a sorrow so vast it was like a cavern opening up inside me and it was all I could do to keep from breaking down in front of my teammates, which would have been totally unacceptable. Beyond the bounds. Childish, even. Terranauts had to steel themselves, had to be unsentimental, practical, devoted to the mission and its survival above all else. Terranauts didn't cry over the death of a pig—they rejoiced in it. The only relevant equation here was that a dead pig equaled meat and meat equaled calories and protein and essential amino acids. So get a grip.

A long moment descended on us, Petunia in her penultimate act of will forcing us to wait on her as the morning thickened in the glass and a pair of volunteer sparrows shot into the wheat patch to gorge themselves. Then, finally, she rose and followed the pail swaying in my left hand up the plank to the table, where I set it down and she plunged her head into the depths of it to savor the final tender morsels of her life.

* * *

Ramsay was right. Christmas gave us a huge boost of publicity, all eight of us sitting for interviews via PicTel before lining up at the window in our red jumpsuits while the cameras rolled and the flashbulbs sparked. The telephone had been hooked up to a loudspeaker in the courtyard and we took turns counting our blessings in a muted roar, each of us stressing what a joy and honor it was to be part of what G.C. had begun calling "The Human Experiment" and delivering individual paeans to group solidarity and team effort. We praised Mission Control, spoke of how pleased we were with the overall health of our ecosystem and the low rate of extinctions to date, and then we talked up our excitement over the homemade gifts we were looking forward to giving and receiving and the Christmas feast we'd be sitting down to later in the day, which, far from being Spartan, would include pork roast, duck à l'orange, pan-roasted potatoes, mashed turnips, a salad of field greens and not one but two of Vodge's incomparable banana crème pies.

At Mission Control, G.C., with Judy and Dennis flanking him in red windbreakers, gave a brief speech about old traditions and new frontiers, which was broadcast to us inside and picked up by a number of TV stations, not only locally but nationwide, and to close it out the cameras recorded all of us gathered round the glass singing "We Wish You a Merry Christmas" and "Let It Snow." Beyond that—and the cameras lingered on this too—well-wishers had built a mound of gifts ranging from poinsettias to home-baked cookies, tinfoil angels and miniature Christmas trees on the sidewalk outside the airlock, and never mind that we couldn't actually make use of them, it was the gesture that counted. And got us an extra boost of goodwill and free publicity, though I could just hear Linda complaining about how tacky it all was and how G.C. was no better than a carnival barker.

The morning flew by under a pale sun. Linda never showed, or not that I could see. Johnny either. People began to drift off, the press thinned and the cameramen packed up, and just when we thought we were free to retreat to the Habitat and kick off our own celebration, two troops of Girl Scouts, backed up by the chorus from Calvary Chapel in south Tucson, showed up to serenade us with selections from "The Messiah" for the better part of an hour. It was touching, Christmasy in a way that tugged at me and made me think of home all the more, and we applauded and thanked the girls (all forty-two of them) with Ecospherian handshakes at the glass, but ultimately it was just another duty, one more ceremony to sit through with patient smiles while nodding our heads self-consciously to the faltering beat. I don't mean to sound cynical, but as time had gone by I'd got less and less used to being onstage and more integrated into the life of the moment and E2 and what it meant to be inside, truly and unconditionally. I didn't need ceremony, I needed peace.

The girls were adorable, and they'd taken time out of their own holiday festivities to be there for us, and I appreciated that, we all did, but by the time they launched into their third number, "For unto Us a Child Is Born," I was thinking, *Please, enough already.* I watched the choir master exert himself, a stumpy heavyset man of indeterminate age with his arms in constant motion while the wind kept beating his long fringe of reddish hair across the shining dome of his scalp, watched the girls' mouths open wide as their breath trailed away and the sound, muted by the glass despite Gyro's acoustical efforts on this end, came to us in a muddy rhythmic thump. I exchanged a glance with Ramsay and he gave me a look of commiseration—and apology, that too. After all, he was the one, along with Dennis and Judy, who'd cooked all this up.

When finally we were released, waving and throwing kisses over our shoulders, everything changed. All at once I was overcome with emotion, almost as if I were a child again. For the first time in weeks I could feel the vague uneasiness I'd been experiencing slip away from me. It was our first Christmas inside, that was what I kept telling myself, *Our first Christmas!* We were going to indulge ourselves—pig out, as Stevie would say, sans irony—and laze away the hours without worrying over schedules, broad mites or CO_2 values. I was just going to let go—we all were. That was the spirit of things, that was what I was feeling—I was ready to party, more than ready. And if Gyro delayed me at the bottom of the stairs, trying to make a joke about the choir master I didn't get, or wasn't getting, I didn't care—nothing could spoil my mood now.

I watched his lips move, gave out a wild girlish laugh, then turned my back on him and bounded up the stairs to the Habitat, thinking I'd go straight to my room and change out of the

jumpsuit, but there was Diane, already in the kitchen, already dicing onions to braise in pork fat, and I went to the counter instead,
took up a knife, and pitched in. If I thought of Petunia, and I
did, of course I did, I told myself it wasn't so much with sorrow
as gratitude because what most people don't realize is that one of
the hardest things in living without a grocery around the corner
is the little matter of cooking oil. You can't just reach for the corn
or safflower oil in the convenient plastic bottle with the twist-off
cap—you've got to make your own. Or find it. Petunia had died
the way she'd lived, a good pig. When Troy brought the blunt end
of the axe down, three times in rapid succession, she went out of
this world without a peep, and now here she was, providing for us.
Naturally. And if there were tears in my eyes, blame the onions.

At some point, early afternoon still, the buzzer Gyro had hooked
up at the visitors' window sounded and Troy, who was expecting
his girlfriend, ran down to see who was there. A moment later, his
voice came sailing up the stairs: "E., it's for you!"

I thought, *Johnny!* and snatched a quick look at myself in the
dark glass of the microwave before starting down the stairs, which
was when I noticed the palm-sized stain on the left knee of the
jumpsuit—grease, pig grease—and hurried back up to take a damp
rag to it.

"Back already?" Stevie said, looking up from her glass of banana
wine as she sat at the table putting the finishing touches to a platter
of crudités with a goat cheese–yogurt dip set in the center of it.
"Who was it, anyway? False alarm?"

"No," I said, working the rag over the material, which just
made the stain worse. "I must've spilled something, or—you think
I should change?"

Gretchen, who was at the far end of the table, mashing turnips,
said, "Is it Johnny?" and we all looked to Troy, who said, "Not
saying. It's a surprise."

"Just go down," Stevie said. "Who cares about a stain? It's not
as if"—and here she looked first to Gyro, then Vodge—"he hasn't
seen worse, right?"

I was breathless by the time I got down the stairs. I hadn't seen

Johnny, hadn't even heard from him, in a week or more, and I wondered about that, about what he was doing and whether he was losing interest, and though I didn't want to admit it to myself I suppose that just added to the depression I'd been feeling. I had a present for him all set aside, a card I'd made to splay out against the glass. It featured the two of us in an embrace in front of a stone fireplace festooned with holly and candy canes and hung with stockings. We both wore Santa hats and were just about to kiss, him in his leather jacket and snakeskin boots and me in my jumpsuit. I wanted to see his grin, wanted to tell him about Petunia and my parents and the Girl Scouts who'd come all the way up from south Tucson to serenade us, and beyond that I was hoping, fervently, so fervently it made me hot just to think about it, that we might have one of our trysts at the glass come nightfall. If he was up for it.

Unfortunately, I'd never know if he was or not because it wasn't Johnny standing there but Linda. I tried to hide my disappointment but Linda saw it right away—as I said, she could read me better than anybody alive, including my mother. She was leaning into the glass, shielding her eyes with both hands to peer inside, and as soon as I got there she reached down for the phone.

"He's not coming," she said, "if that's what you're waiting for."

There was something about her posture that was off, the way she wasn't so much leaning into the glass as using it to brace herself up, and I realized she was drunk, drunk at two in the afternoon—which wasn't like her. "Are you plastered or what?"

She didn't answer right away. Behind her was the pile of junk people had left behind, useless to anybody now, except maybe the support staff—they could always use a tin of cookies or homemade brownies, though it came to me that you'd have to be crazy to trust anything anybody left out there, no matter how innocuous it might seem. Even if it came from the Girl Scouts. There were still a few people milling around in the middle distance and I couldn't help wishing security would send them on their way and leave us in peace. For once. One day out of the year. Was that too much to ask?

THE TERRANAUTS - 235

"I had a drink, yeah, so sue me. With Gavin and Dennis and who, Malcolm. G.C. too. G.C. was there. He even . . ." She trailed off. "At the party. Isn't that what parties are for?"

Mission Control had kept a skeleton staff on for the holidays—and Linda was part of it, too essential to operations to be allowed a trip up to Sacramento, which was good news on the one hand and bad on the other—and apparently G.C. and Judy had insisted on a not-so-little get-together at Mission Control after the morning's ceremonies. There'd been cold cuts, canapés, a potent rum punch and a deceptive eggnog. Now it was over and Linda was here at the glass to wish me, her best friend, a Merry Christmas.

"We're in the middle of preparing the feast ourselves," I told her, "but all we've got is banana wine—and Richard's arak, which is pretty much like gasoline. No eggnog for us. Or chestnuts roasting over an open fire." I let out a laugh. "No fire either."

She was still staring at me, her pupils so dilated they were like holes dug out of her face. She wasn't wearing her glasses or contacts either, as far as I could see. "He's in Sedona," she said.

"Johnny?"

A nod. "He's got a thing going there—he told me like a week ago when I ran into him at the post office when I was mailing those presents for my parents? His band. They're filling in for two weeks for the regular house band because the regular house band's in Mexico. Or something like that—"

"Did he say anything about me?"

She pushed herself back from the glass so that the whole panel, tempered for strength, bowed inward and settled back again. "I don't know," she said, and her tone shifted. "Did Gavin say anything about me?"

So she was throwing it back at me, drunkenly, right here at the glass. On Christmas. I didn't want to fight, didn't want to deal with her resentments and moods, not now. "I'm sorry," I said. "I'm not trying to cut you out or anything. Or trivialize things, not at all. You like him, don't you?"

She was at the far end of her tether—the phone cord, that is—and still giving me that accusatory look. "What does it matter to you? You know what he talked about today when I was trying to have a private moment with him and maybe see if he wanted to come over for a drink later or whatever? You. He talked about you. About how great Dawn is, Dawn this, Dawn that, and how he hoped we'd have somebody like you on our crew—"

There wasn't much I could say to this, but I tried—for her sake, though god knows she should have been the one consoling me. "You want me to drop some hints? I can talk you up—subtly, I mean. I could do that."

And here came that look of umbrage again, the I-can't-believe-you stare that swelled her eyes and dug two trenches at the corners of her mouth. "Screw you, Dawn," she said.

"Come on, Linda. Don't be like that. It's Christmas."

"Some Christmas." She was rocking back and forth over the fulcrum of her too-small feet, totally hostile now, out of control. "You know something?"

"No," I said, and I was angry too. *"What?"*

"Why don't you just go and find yourself another best friend, okay? Like Stevie. Why don't you pal up with Stevie, or whoever," and then she dropped the phone and turned her back on me. I wanted to call out to her, but she wouldn't have heard me anyway. I watched her stalk off, her shoulders bunched, her gait unsteady, and she never gave me a glance, never even turned around. She went straight to the pile of offerings splayed out on the sidewalk and stood there a moment under the pale rinsed-out sun, swaying ever so slightly. Then she bent to sift through it, looking for something to take home for herself.

Ramsay Roothoorp

To tell you the truth, Christmas is beyond irrelevant as far as I'm concerned, a coercive brainless holdover from primitive times when people saw the sun sink lower every day and it scared the living bejesus out of them. What if it never came back? What if the days kept counting down, getting shorter and shorter, till night was all there was? They shivered in their huts, built up the fire, chanted, cast spells, made sacrifice to appease whatever gods they suspected of having a hand in things, and sure enough, the days began to grow longer and everyone was saved—for another year anyway. Then the historical Jesus came along and his followers just happened to conveniently fudge the date of his birth so they could prop the whole Spiritus Sanctus business up on the shoulders of the ancient solstice rituals, birth of the sun and the son of God too. But really, who can argue with a tradition that goes back two millennia? If people have believed that long, it must be true, right? I like to think about the kind of historical gravitas something as manipulative and patently absurd as Mormonism—or worse yet, Scientology—will be busy accumulating over the next millennium or two. Picture it: in two thousand years you'll have everybody scrambling around the malls and carving up turkeys over the birth of our true savior and redeemer, second-rate sci-fi hack L. Ron Hubbard.

No, I see Christmas in strictly practical terms, the way the Japanese do—as an excuse to indulge and overindulge and move product, with no religious connotation whatever, if you discount Santa Claus, who looms large in Shibuya come December every year. That other figure, the scrawny bearded one nailed to the cross in his loincloth, isn't all that much fun, really, when you come right down to it. He doesn't shake it out like a sumo champion squatting in the *dohyō* or dress himself in red from head to toe and shower gifts on everybody—and if there's any culture built on gift-obsession, it's the Japanese. So what I'm saying is that while I was inside I made use of Christmas strictly for its PR value, doing my best to tie the commercial and religious aspects to us, the new saviors, the Terranauts celebrating Yuletide inside the only man-made ecosphere in creation—suffering, but rejoicing too, and all for the good of mankind and the future of the earth.

Richard called it a dog and pony show, and I guess it was. But it produced results. We enjoyed the widest news coverage since closure and I worked hard with Dennis and Judy to arrange for the choir and the Girl Scouts and the photo opportunity at the window and all the rest. And when things died down and everybody but the hard-core nutballs and eco-crazies had packed up and gone on home to their trees and wreaths and menorahs, we had our own calorie-packed feast that was as rich as anything you could get on the outside, though I would have wished for a splash or two of Sriracha or even a sweet butter pickle or a slice of cranberry sauce still indented from the can. Or mustard. I would have died for mustard. I'm sorry, but pork needs mustard, no matter how much you smother it in caramelized onions and ground sage. At any rate, we did the best we could, which was the whole point.

The centerpiece was the pork roast—the sacrificial flesh—and the mental picture I still hold on to is of E., lit with arak and joining lustily in the singing of Christmas carols round the table, fully vibrant and open and giving herself a hundred percent over to the festivities, and yet all the while steering her fork around the oozing redolent slab of meat laid out on her plate. I made chitchat with Diane on my left and Troy on my right, but what I was really doing was watching E. without letting on. She went at the turnips and potatoes and all the rest of the trimmings as avidly as anyone, but finally, when everybody was distracted by Stevie doing a kind of pole-dance version of "Santa Baby" at the head of the table, she quietly slipped her half-inch-thick slice of pork back onto the platter.

Again, to repeat, I'm not the heartless manipulator some people have made me out to be—I feel, and feel as deeply as the next person, and I have to say that little move on Dawn's part really got to me. She was the one who'd overseen the slaughtering, directing Troy and me through the whole process, because that was her job as our MDA and there was no shirking in her. She never hesitated, though her hand trembled, I saw that much. Troy did the killing, three quick blows with the blunt edge of the axe, but she stuck the pig herself and drew the blade down to slash open its gut and remove the viscera—a team player all the way—but she was hurting inside and here was the proof of it. She loved that pig, and why not? It just showed how compassionate she was, how compassionate we all were, or could be, no matter how practical or dispassionate the task at hand. And the task at hand was to keep E2 afloat. Dawn believed in that a hundred percent, believed in it more than anybody, even Gretchen, even me, as events would prove.

But the gifts—did I mention the gifts?

We'd all drawn names out of a hat a few days earlier to ensure that each of us would receive a modest gift, eight names, eight gifts. I was ready to shout hosannas when Gretchen drew Stevie's name instead of mine—our breakup, and I'll get to that in a minute, was nothing short of catastrophic—and my mood improved even more when I drew E.'s name. What I was thinking, the slip of paper in hand with E.'s neat cursive flowing across it—her whole name, first, middle and last, written out as if it were a school exercise—was that here was my opportunity. Or *an* opportunity. I'd taken baby steps up to this point and I knew she knew about Gretchen, though she never mentioned it, or only, I suppose, in a glancing way, but I was building toward something with her, something genuine, something real. I'm talking love here, or the possibility of it. Stevie left me cold—and Diane was too remote, too focused on the mission to ever let loose. And Gretchen. Gretchen was like a volcano that's been waiting six centuries to erupt. But E. was my girl. E. was just right for me. E. was what I wanted—for herself, for the sound of her voice with its sweet trilling notes and its faintest catch of a lisp, for her body, her legs and breasts and lips, the way her eyes seemed to bring everything inside her to the surface and nothing coy about it. She didn't play games. She was genuine, the real thing. And Johnny, the guitar-strumming clown in the cowboy shirt (and I could play guitar too), was remote now, gone, vanished, glassed-out. It had been gradual, but we'd drawn closer over the months, E. and I, and what I thought was that I'd give her something special that might draw us even closer because, understand me, I couldn't wait forever.

The gifts, homemade of course (or E2-made, I should say), went round the table, giver to receiver. All were decorated with flowers and wrapped in whatever scraps of paper were available or folded up in banana leaves, and all—or nearly all—were gifts of the one and only thing that mattered to us: food. Diane presided, her jumpsuit radically compressed and pinned up on her head to represent the sort of stocking cap Santa wore, though to my mind it looked more like a flame-red *pallu* and she less like the merry old elf than a pale-faced version of Indira Gandhi. "Who's first?" she called out, and I said, "E."

Dawn was sitting beside Diane at the far end of the table from me. She'd washed and combed out her hair and it flared in the late-afternoon light—not in the way of all those Tropicana dye-jobs out there in the world, but more coppery, more gold. Like the rest of us, she'd changed out of her jumpsuit once the day's public activities had been put to rest, and she was dressed now in a clean pair of jeans that had gone ever so slightly loose on her and a low-cut top, light blue or maybe turquoise, I'd never seen before. "Me?" she said, flushing, and covered herself with a laugh. She turned to Diane. "Why don't you go? Or somebody?"

I pushed the gift across the table, where Richard took hold of it and nudged it toward her. "Open it," he said. "Come on, E., you're holding up the proceedings here—"

I'd wrapped E.'s present in a single banana leaf, using the slim elastic runners of our nuisance plant, the morning glory, for twine. Inside was a foot-long section of sugarcane I'd squirreled away from our last harvest—my own portion, which I'd hidden in the drawer of my oak entertainment center while the others had gnawed greedily at theirs till there was nothing left but sticky fingers and sucked-out fiber to feed to the goats. I'd wanted the sugar rush as much as anyone, of course, but I'd seen the value in that length of cane, and whether I was thinking of E. or not—or temptation or seduction or whatever you want to call it—I restrained myself and set it aside. I might have chewed something else that day—azolla, probably, with its earthy taste and rubbery texture—to take my mind off it. (By the way, azolla, if you don't already know, is a tiny nitrogen-fixing aquatic fern that floats on the surface of freshwater ponds like duckweed and doubles its biomass every two to three days. It's packed with protein, amino acids, vitamins and minerals, and Asian rice farmers have made use of it for centuries as a way of discouraging weed growth in the paddies and providing nutrients at the same time, after which it's harvested for animal fodder. We used it as chicken feed for the most part, though toward the end you saw it ending up more and more in our soups and stews.) At any rate, let's just say I chewed a cud of the stuff that day to keep my mind off the sugarcane. Which I was saving for some as yet unspecified purpose, which had now achieved specificity: it was for E.

I watched her face as she undid the twine after shooting a quick glance at me, her benefactor, and then she had the cane in hand and was brandishing it aloft. "Sugar for Christmas!" she sang out, then looked me full in the face and said, "Thanks, Vodge."

"Who's next?" Richard leaned into the table on his elbows, gazing round expectantly. He was excited, and why blame him—who doesn't light up at the prospect of receiving a present? (Better to give than receive, though, that was what I was thinking, especially as it was Diane who'd drawn my name out of the hat and I didn't want to feel beholden to her—or anybody else for that matter.)

"Stevie, what about you?" Gretchen cried, a little too loudly, her second glass of arak already half-drained. She had an interest here, since she was the one who'd drawn Stevie's name, and as everyone boisterously seconded the motion, I tried to catch E.'s attention. "E.," I said, my voice a kind of elevated whisper, "there's a note with that. I mean—see, tucked inside the banana leaf?—so don't throw it away."

A momentary frown and then the smile. "Yes, oh yes, I've got it," and she held up the little three-by-five envelope I'd fashioned from a sheet of lined yellow notepaper. As I'd hoped, nobody was really paying attention because they were all focused on Stevie, pretty Stevie, with her white-blond-going-to-dirty-blond tresses tucked behind her ears, as she unwrapped Gretchen's gift: a selection of rain forest fruits and palm nuts only the galagos would have known where to find.

What my note said was this: *Meet me outside my room after the festivities—there's more to come. Much more. And it's not a jot less than you deserve, E.* What I said now, in a whisper, was: "Later."

* * *

The whole thing with Gretchen was regrettable—I admit that up front. And if I was being honest with myself, I'd say I'd known it all along, say I should have known better, acted like an adult, restrained myself for the good of the mission. But the flesh is weak, and that first night, after the whole crazy business with the galago and the way she'd so patiently and skillfully tended to the thing while I looked on and her breasts gathered and released and her limbs flowed hypnotically beneath the filmy material of her nightgown, I just couldn't help myself. And she initiated it, as hard as that may be to believe—she was the one who put my hand on her breast, and if she wasn't my type exactly, or hadn't been up till that very minute, the problem was that I was her type and that night set something loose in her. All right. I'm venal. A dog, just like my old roommate Jason Fourier said. She was easy, she was needy, and we were both locked up together with no way out.

For the first week or two it was nice, her room right next to mine and no one the wiser. I came to her, late, at her signal—a coded knock at the wall that separated our rooms, three beats, two beats of silence, three beats more—and believe me I might have sat there pretending to read or work or whatever but my every cell and fiber was just burning for the moment when that knock would come. Unfortunately—and isn't this the adverb that inevitably descends on just about any love affair, especially one as lopsided as ours?—she started to turn spooky on me.

Jesus, I look at that line and wonder what it means. Spooky? Let me try for something a little more precise: she was demanding, possessive, moonstruck, never happy unless I was there at her beck and call. She began coming up with projects in the rain forest or the marsh biome that just couldn't do without a man's help—mine—and by the second or third week she'd given up all pretense and kept wanting to hold hands like a teenager or bump hips as we passed in the hall, which made me shrink down to a nugget inside because the last thing I wanted was for anybody to know what was going on between us, least of all E. Or Judy. Christ, I could only imagine what Judy would have to say about it—and how she'd make me pay too.

But Gretchen was hard to shake. More often than not she'd wind up sitting next to me at meals, once even snaking a hand under the table to take hold of me where I was most vulnerable, all the while making a game of joining in the general conversation as if she didn't have my cock in her hand at all and things were just as normal as normal could be. I hated her then. Hated the way her face looked, smug, as if she were getting away with something, which she wasn't, as it turned out, and she had nothing to be smug about. She was childish. Needy. Told me she couldn't live without me. Worse: she began to talk of long-term commitment, every other minute mentioning some couple she knew who'd been together for ten years, twenty, old people in love still after a lifetime. Her parents. Her grandparents. What I mean is, she began talking about marriage, which came as a shock to my system, because marriage was a state of being I'd never really contemplated, not with her or anybody else, but especially not with her. One night, out of nowhere, as we lay there naked in my bed, she said, "Let's get married. Inside, I mean. Wouldn't that be great? I mean, Vodge, think what you could do with *that* in terms of publicity—a Terranaut wedding? We could hold the ceremony at the glass and G.C. and everybody—the press—could be there with the cameras rolling, right? What do you say?"

I tried to back off. The next night, when she rapped at the wall, I didn't respond. She waited fifteen minutes, then tried again, and the sound of her knuckles tapping at the plaster was nothing but an irritant now and I wished I could lock the door and keep her out, but of course, there were no locks on our doors because a lock, by its very nature, connoted a failure of mutuality and trust. I tiptoed up the stairs and got into bed and when I heard the whisper of the hinges and her soft furtive tread first on the carpet and then the stairs I pretended I was asleep. But I wasn't asleep and she knew it. "Vodge? You awake?"

"I'm sleeping."

She was naked. I could just make out her form hovering over me like a succubus, and I'm sorry for that image, but there it is. She put one knee on the bed and the bed sank under her weight. "Don't you want, you know—? It'll help you sleep." I didn't respond. I didn't want anything to do with this and I wished I'd never started it, wished I'd smuggled in a quart of saltpeter or gone Gyro's route, strictly. "Vodge?" She laid a hand on my shoulder and it was like a hot iron, like a claw, and I just snapped. I rolled over, sat up, peeled off her hand and flung it away from me.

"Get out," I said before I even knew what I was saying, and then I tried to soften it by claiming I was exhausted—and sick, feeling sick—and just needed to be alone, that was all.

It was dark, but I could make out her face in the glow of the night-light, her face that was still heavy, jowly, despite her weight loss, her old woman's face that showed what she was going to become in a few years' time, her face that had always looked old, probably even when she was young and none of us had yet to lay eyes on her. She began to cry, very softly, a sound like rain in the gutters on a night when you never suspected a storm was brewing.

I listened to this for a while, both of us silent, her effort to keep from sobbing out loud radiating through the mattress and right into the core of me. "What are you saying? Don't you"—she choked back a sob—"want me anymore?"

I should have been harder, colder, should have broken it off right there and chased her out into the dark night of the biomes, but I didn't. Coward that I was, fool, and let's face it, shit—shit too—I whispered, "I'm just tired, that's all."

* * *

The party wound down by eight or so, all of us moving in slow motion by then, too exhausted by the demands of keeping our world together to really let go. We had to be up and at work first thing in the morning, as usual, no winter break here, no bank holiday—no bank, for that matter—the twelve days of Christmas shrunk down to one, and that was just about over. Mission Control had opened up the phone line so that we could schedule times to call friends and relatives and wish them the best of the season and have those wishes returned, and we'd all taken advantage of that. I called my grandmother, who, along with my grandfather, had raised me after my parents' accident, and she sounded like her old self despite the fact that she was a widow now. She told me she was glad to hear from me and that she was proud of me too. "Everywhere I go, I can't help bragging, you know that, don't you?" she said in her voice that seemed more fractured and reduced with every breath she took (she was a smoker and I couldn't help seizing on the implications—if god forbid she should die over the course of the next fifteen months I wouldn't be at the funeral, that was for sure, and of course I'd had to lie to Mission Control right from the outset about the force of my attachment to her). "Did you see him on *Good Morning America*? I say to people like Evelyn Porter down at the library and Dorie Stachowitz across the street and just about everybody else I can grab hold of—or where, in *Time* magazine? Evelyn's got a big Terranauts poster on the wall over the checkout desk, did I tell you that?"

I thought of calling Judy, for reasons that were complicated, but I didn't because I couldn't. Somebody would be listening in, you could bet on that, and just the fact that I'd placed the call would raise red flags over in Mission Control, even if all I wound up doing was wishing her a Merry Christmas and a Happy New Year.

So I didn't make the call and she didn't call me either, whatever that meant. And frankly, as the day wore on and others were getting called to the phone, I began to realize I wouldn't be hearing from her, and good riddance, that was what I was thinking. I had E. now, or was going to have her, and the whole thing with Judy was just worse than bad, a kind of tiptoeing around disaster neither of us needed.

I'd had maybe two or three glasses of Richard's latest batch of arak, which seemed smoother and less astringent than the batch he'd cooked up for winter solstice, especially if you squeezed half a lemon into it, which I did, and after dessert—my banana crème pie—I ignored the way Gretchen was ignoring me and sat down next to E. "Merry Christmas," I said, and it was the most natural come-on line in history. "You having fun?"

She opened up her megawatt smile, her lips—have I mentioned her lips?—so ripe and wet and full I almost kissed her right there with everybody looking. The thing that got me about her lips was how they always seemed ever so slightly parted, as if she were about to whisper something dirty or at least seductive, and tonight she'd put on lipstick and done her eyes and brushed on a fine layer of makeup to hide the orangeing glow of her skin. The effect was devastating, especially considering what I had in mind for the rest of the evening. "Absolutely," she said. "This is like the best Christmas ever."

"Me too," I said. "I mean, Christmas inside. A year ago—" I didn't finish the thought, but she knew what I meant. We were talking about privilege here, intimacy, the brother and sisterhood of E2 that brought us together in a way nothing else ever could have. If we were on the outside, we might never even have met. Or no, we would have met—we did, of course, as members of the extended crew—but if one of us had been excluded from E2 we would never have had this moment, this feeling I could sense deepening between us. She'd had a bias against me, I knew that, and it stemmed from an incident long before Gretchen—or Johnny—but that was behind us now. I had a present for her, a very special present even rarer than a stick of sugarcane and it was meant to show her how much I cared about her—once I got her to my room, that is, and hopefully without being too obvious about it. "Did you get my note?" I asked, even though I knew she had, but I was asking by way of reinforcement.

"Oh, yeah," she said, "yeah." The smile, the lips. "You have something else for me? I mean, really, the sugarcane was more than enough, and thank you, did I say that?" She leaned in and pecked a kiss to my lips, an official thank-you kiss, one the others could register for what it was. It came to me in that moment that she was drunk, drunker than I was at any rate, and that this was a good thing, a happy let-go-of-it-all sort of moment that was to be prelude to all the rest. *If I could get her to my room.*

The incident I referred to above had come during the first month or so after the extended crew had been chosen. We were on our first cruise on The *Imago,* it was one of those magical Caribbean nights, and everybody was stuffed to the gills with conch fritters, black beans and rice and flying high on local rum mixed liberally with the real Coca-Cola sweetened with real sugarcane in some no doubt unsanitary bottling plant in San Juan or Santo Domingo and all the better for it. We were just feeling each other out at that point, men and women alike, and I'd naturally gravitated toward Stevie because Stevie was like one of those cheap disco balls, all glitter and shining facets, and in my shallow go-straight-for-the-target brand of inveterate male obliviousness I was dazzled by her. I sat with her on deck and we shared a drink. Thinking I had a read on her, I steered the conversation around to what I had in mind, but before I could gain any traction her face tensed up and I saw my mistake. I tried to cover myself with a joke but the joke fell flat and she just gave me a long withering stare. If you quizzed me about it now I'd say that she lacked a sense of humor—still does— but that would only be scratching the surface of the situation: it was my bad, I admit it. I was the one out of bounds.

Anyway, she got up abruptly and went off to throw her golden head back and laugh with a group gathered round the stern railing and I sat there feeling like an idiot. But an idiot who doesn't learn, an idiot who happened to spot E. sitting alone in the bow and went up to her and tried the same approach with the same result. Ever after, E. had been wary of me—she considered me a player, I guess, or that was what I gathered from talking to some of the others, from hints dropped, body language, the way she dealt with me, neither particularly friendly nor unfriendly either. Wary. Just wary.

All that changed, or began to change, once we were inside. There was the elaborate praise she'd given me that first night over my cuisine—and the pie, oh, the pie!—praise that was rightly deserved because I'd put my all into that lunch and that dinner too. And then there'd been the night in her room when we opened up to each other for the first time and really talked—beyond the self-congratulation and the party line and the usual self-replenishing stream of gossip, I mean—and after that, as I say, we'd become closer and closer so that I really did feel things building toward the moment of truth, and never mind the detours with Judy, which she didn't know about, and Gretchen, which she did.

I stood and offered her my hand and she rose lightly from the chair, still with that smile in place, but there were the beginnings of a frown there too now, a quizzical expression working its way into her eyes and brow, as in *What now?*

"Just give me a minute," I said. "I'll go ahead. I'll leave the door open."

"Vodge," she said, holding on to my name as if it were something sweet to lick off her lips, "you really have something for me? Seriously?"

"You just wait," I said.

I'd made some preparations. The lights were down, I'd cleaned up to be sure there was no lingering trace of Gretchen anywhere about the place (though there was the problem—or potential problem—of her being in situ right next door), and I would have lit a joss stick or scented candle except that we couldn't do that in our world and I'd already wasted my only candle on Gretchen. I'd found and evicted a stream of crazy ants that had, in their turn, already evicted the cockroach colony that had persisted in the back corner of my closet. The odd crusted-over dish or for-gotten utensil had been returned to the communal kitchen and I'd made use of some of our scentless dish soap to scrub the fine green scrim of mold from the walls, something I'd been meaning to do for months. Nat King Cole, the reigning regent of corny Christmas ballads, was cued up on the CD player because I knew how susceptible E. was to what the retailers like to call the spirit of the season. But that sounds too cold. I just thought she would enjoy the album, that's all, and when I borrowed it from T.T.'s col-lection it was for that purpose only because to me, no matter how sensitive the interpretation, you couldn't separate the song from its function, viz., to narcotize the shopper while the cash register jingles in the background. Sleigh bells? What about the *ka-ching!* of the cash drawer?

I wasn't nervous, or not particularly. I knew E. in a way I'd never known Judy, at least before our first time together, which wound up being as much a function of her initiative as mine—more so, actually. Judy and I had worked together, of course, but our relations had been strictly formal for the first year or so—she was my boss, after all, or one of them—until she began to sin-gle me out from the others. It was nothing radical, just that she seemed to be a whole lot friendlier all of a sudden, going out of her way to consult me on one thing or another, as if she really valued my opinion. Then came a sun-scorched spring day when the air conditioner was down and she wound up adjourning our regular late-afternoon meeting early because of the heat. As the others filed out, she asked if I might have a minute to spare—she wanted to solicit my take on what might be going wrong with the wastewater systems inside because the crewmember I was ulti-mately to replace, Walt Truscott, was having trouble with clogs in the pipes leading from the solid-waste settling tanks. I didn't have a clue, but of course I spouted whatever nonsense came into my head that sounded like something she might want to hear (not enough circulation over the gravel at the bottom of the tank—or maybe too much) and went on until I realized she wasn't listening to a word I said.

That was about when I realized too that the way she was look-ing into my eyes couldn't be described as the impartial gaze of one team member receiving information from another but something else altogether. And what did that look, and the ruse of holding me back after the meeting, have to do with the fact that G.C. was in Pasadena in the company of G.F. and three of their consulting ecologists, addressing a gathering of JPL engineers on the subject of terraforming? I might have been a bit slow that night, but I got it, I did. "Forget wastewater," I said, breaking off in the middle of the next empty sentence. "How about a little taste of good clean spring water fortified with scotch whiskey?" And she said, "Vod-ka's my drink." And I said, "Really?" And she said, "I hear you keep a bottle of Stoli in your freezer." I was about to ask her how she knew that when I realized I already knew the answer and just moved in to kiss her.

Truthfully? That was just a warm-up, the kind of affair peo-ple have because it's available, and I make no apologies. Or for Gretchen either, though Gretchen could get at me—and did—while Judy couldn't, which put the Judy situation to rest except for the phone snits and PicTel recriminations, which, thankfully, had begun to taper off as the months stretched out and she set her snares elsewhere. Or at least that was what I assumed. Maybe she and G.C. were humping merrily away, as she claimed, or maybe she was fucking the pool boy at her condo or one of the suits G.F. trailed in his wake. It was all the same to me. But Gretchen was something else. That was hard. That was a horror show. The point came when I had to cut her off altogether—I told her, point-blank, *I can't do this anymore*—but there she was, right next door, right there every time I opened the door, or, god forbid *left* it open. "I need my space," I kept saying, but she wasn't listening.

It all came to a climax one night after I'd explicitly said no, after I'd tried to indicate in every way I could that whatever we'd had together was over, that she was annoying me, crowding me, hurting me. For a full hour I ignored her knock, then went up to bed after first taking the precaution of edging my oak enter-tainment center across the floor and blocking the door with it. I hadn't wanted to do that—it was as heavy as if it had been carved of stone, I was exhausted, and I'd just have to move it back again in the morning—but I really felt I had no choice. The knocking continued for a while, fainter now, and the human sounds began to fade all up and down the hallway as my crewmates turned in and the thrum of the biomes gradually took over. I heard the galagos, heard the coquis and crickets, and then I was asleep.

I awoke to the sepia glow of the night-light and a new sound, breath in, breath out, a moist sound, steeped in fluid, discontinuous, disconnected: the sound of Gretchen feeling sorry for herself. She was fully clothed this time and she was sitting cross-legged on the floor at the foot of the bed. My reaction? Outrage. Put yourself in my position and you might begin to imagine what I was feeling because there was no escape from this, no privacy, no *surcease*. "Shit, you scared me," I said.

Out of the shadows, her voice low, shaky, dripping wet: "Good."

"What are you doing here? How'd you even get in?"

"You think you can stop me?"

I didn't want to be having this discussion. Not in my own room, not in the middle of the night. "Get the fuck out of here," I said. "Get out and don't come back. Ever."

"You think you can just toss me aside? What do you think, they put me in here for your pleasure, or what? You owe me."

"Owe you what? I don't owe you a thing—"

"You make me feel cheap. And I'm not cheap. And I'll tell you another thing—I'm not going anywhere. I'm going to sit right here, *right here,* till you give me an explanation—I mean, what were you thinking?"

"I wasn't thinking anything. I just wanted a fuck, that was all."

She was silent a moment, everything held in suspension until the murmur of the biomes began to leak back in to fill the void. "I still do," she whispered, and I could see the outline of her there on the carpet, a hazy lump of shadow, legs tucked under her, arms folded across her chest.

I don't enjoy inflicting pain. I'm a temporizer, a diplomat, a talker—above all, a talker. But she'd crossed a line here and no matter what it cost me I wasn't going to allow it. "Well, I don't," I said, coming down hard on the negative. "Can't you get that through your head? It's over. It's finished. Could I make it any plainer?"

"It's Dawn," she said, "isn't it? It's Dawn you want."

I didn't try to deny it.

"Or who," she said, "—Judy?"

I didn't deny that either. I didn't say a word. Just got up off the bed, slipped into my shorts and made for the stairs, but she wouldn't let me go, snatching at my ankles—raking them with her nails—till I kicked free in the dark and she began to scream, not even cursing me, just screaming. I got as far as the door, where I had to fight to get by the oak entertainment center, and I still don't know how she'd managed to move the thing—that far and no farther, because she was right there now, jerking at my arm, and if I shoved her back into the room, shoved her to keep from balling my hand into a fist and breaking every bone in that white surging face, that was as far as my rage would take me. In the next moment I was out the door, thinking only to get away from her, to hide myself in the deepest darkest hole of the technosphere till things cooled down.

But things didn't cool down. Just the opposite. Everybody was awake suddenly, doors flinging open up and down the length of the hallway, Stevie's face hanging there like a flickering lantern, and Troy behind her asking what was wrong, what was happening, and E. too, E. squinting into the glow of somebody's flashlight, and what could I say? Was I at a loss? No, never. Not me. I said, "It's nothing. It's Gretchen. She had a bad dream, is all."

"Bad dream?" Troy had come up to me, right in my face now. He was barefoot, in a pair of shorts. His hair was mussed. I could smell the funk of his nighttime breath. "Sounded like somebody stabbed her. Gretchen?" he called, pushing past me. "Gretchen, are you all right?"

I kept going, past Stevie, past Richard and Diane and E., slipping down the stairs, through the orchard and out into the cover of the sealed-in night.

* * *

"So I'm embarrassed because I don't really have anything to give you, besides maybe—do you want to share the sugarcane?" It was twenty minutes after we'd shut down the Christmas party, and E., in her turquoise top, blue jeans and a pair of open-toed clogs on her pretty feet, was sitting in the chair in my living room, holding up the (untouched) length of sugarcane I'd given her as the first installment of her Christmas present. Nat King Cole dripped treacle from the speakers, working his patient way through the changes of "Silent Night," and the three-way bulb in the one lamp I had on was turned down low.

"No," I said, "that's for you. What kind of present is it if you have to share it around?"

She was a little drunk. I'd seen that earlier and I saw it again when she had to catch herself on the doorframe to keep from stumbling as she stepped into the room. "Come on, Vodge. I want to share. Really. Come on, help me out here—"

I was a little drunk too. All the better. When you're drunk you're not really thinking—or calculating—but just going with the flow. I let the flow take me to the counter, where I picked up the first thing that came to hand—a plate I'd been meaning to take back to the communal kitchen—and a kitchen knife I kept around for occasions like this. (Or not like this—there hadn't been anything like this, and if somebody had told me E. had been in my room more than once or twice since closure, I would have been surprised. I suppose she had, but it would have been with some of the others, for cards or music or just a change of scene, a feature of the ongoing fiesta that was downtime in E2.) Next thing, I was slicing through the cane's woody outer layer and digging out a section of the sweet fibrous pulp. I handed it to her and she leaned forward to take it from my hand, her cleavage staring right at me in a way that made me re-dedicate my mission here tonight, and then she was chewing—we were both chewing—and she said, "Hmm, good. Great, actually. Isn't it amazing how the simplest things can give you the most pleasure?"

"Oh, yeah," I said, "yeah. Absolutely. And it's nice to have you here to share it with. Really nice."

She was silent a moment, chewing, but her eyes never left mine. "You really have something else for me?" Her smile was hopeful and doubtful at the same time, and what did she think—I'd lured her here under false pretenses?

I gave her a grin, probably what you'd characterize as a loose-lipped grin, given my muscular response at that point, but I wasn't the one observing it. I answered her with a question: "You don't think I'd be satisfied with just the sugarcane as a present, do you? I mean—we're teammates, right? And I really"—I was going to say "respect you" but caught myself. "I really admire what you bring to the table. Of all of us, of all the Terranauts, you're the heart and soul of this mission, you really are—"

She was smiling, full-on, her eyes bright, dimples showing, and she caught a little loop of her hair and twisted it round one finger in a self-conscious gesture. "Go on," she said. "Just keep telling me how wonderful I am—I could listen to this all night long. But what is it? What do you have?"

I didn't know about Gyro's stash of M&M's, or not yet, but even if I had known it wouldn't have fazed me. What I did then—and yes, I'd had it all planned out, from the sugarcane to the formal invitation to this, the moment of truth—was reach into my shirt pocket and produce one of the fat overstuffed spliffs of *Cannabis indica* I'd secreted beneath the flap of the false bottom of the suitcase I'd spread wide for the reporters the morning of closure. I'd rolled it in bright yellow papers so that it looked like the one Bobby "Blue" Bland is offering up to his two bikinied beauties on the inside cover of the *Dreamer* album. (I don't know if you're a Bobby Bland aficionado, but he makes Nat King Cole look sick—and he never recorded any hokey holiday albums either, or not that I know of.) "For you," I said.

"You're kidding! Where did you—?"

"I have my sources."

"You smuggled pot into E2? I don't believe you!"

I just shrugged. I felt good. Better than good. "You want a toke?"

From the look on her face I thought she was going to say something like *Does the pope shit in the woods?* but that wasn't like E. Her friend Linda, maybe, but not E. What she said was, "Is it strong?"

This was a question I hadn't been prepared for and for just a fraction of a second I hesitated, wondering what she wanted to hear. Of course it was strong—what would be the point if it wasn't? Beyond that, beyond the wallop this particular strain of *indica* gave you, it was a potent aphrodisiac. "You bet it's strong," I said. She was leaning in close to me now, staring as if hypnotized at the joint pinched between my thumb and forefinger. "And I've got to warn you, it's sexy too. Sexiest pot I've ever smoked."

Nat King Cole butted in then, if only briefly. *All is calm,* he sang, his voice hushed and hymnal, *all is bright.*

E. leaned in even closer, braced herself with one hand against my chest and gave me a long slow kiss. Then she pulled back so that she was looking into my eyes again, right there, six inches away. "What are we waiting for?" she said.

Linda Ryu

Have I got news! News that makes everything else look sick by comparison. It makes me want to vomit, actually, but it lights me up too, because if Dawn's been cutting me loose, transitioning from best friend to frenemy, then this just goes to reaffirm what I've said all along: it should have been me in there, not her. Talk about judgment, why don't you? Talk about misplaced priorities and sheer, I don't know, *randomness,* or maybe desperation, maybe that's it. Here's the bomb she dropped on me not two days after our fight on Christmas: *she had sex with Ramsay.* Admitted it right to my face. Worse, she just about crowed over it, as if this was what she'd wanted all along. *Ramsay.* Not T.T. or Gyro, who's been mooning after her for months, or even Richard, who at least has character even if he is older, but the one shitheel any woman with any sense would have steered clear of, though I have to admit Johnny isn't a whole lot better. But Johnny isn't glassed-in with her and Ramsay is. Mr. Vodge Ramsay Roothoorp, resident cancer.

It's like this: we're at the glass, late afternoon, my post-Christmas hangover nothing more than a cellular memory at this juncture, and I'm feeling more upbeat than I have in a while. For one thing, I'm looking forward to driving into Tucson later with Gavin and two of the other newbies—for a showing of the live-action remake of *The Jungle Book,* and if they're taking advantage of me because I have a car and they don't, I am totally on board with that. The blessing is that Tricia won't be tagging along. Or Ellen Shapiro either. G.C. granted them both one-week leaves to go home, Tricia to Miami and Ellen to wherever she comes from in Idaho.

The other thing is G.C. He took me aside at the Christmas party, gave me an audience, that is, and if he was staring at my

tits as much as my face, I didn't really mind, though when I told
Dawn she said, "That's creepy," and I had to admit I agreed with
her. Creepy squared, really. But he told me how much he appreciated what I'd been doing for the team, the hours I was putting
in, the sensitive issues I'd handled (Gretchen, Gyro, eyeballing the
video cameras) and how he felt I was all but a lock for Mission
Three. That was music to my ears, I tell you, justification from
the lips of God Himself, and I could have listened to it all night,
but then Judy—*Judas*—saw us together in the corner, where G.C.
had balanced himself on the arm of the chair I'd more or less fallen
into, a flute of champagne in one hand and his beard in full flow,
and she came over to clamp her claws on his bare forearm and
deliver him up to the more noteworthy guests (the same nip-and-
tuck B-list celebrities and minor millionaires and their puffed-up
fur-bearing wives who'd attended the closure ceremony and were
back in attendance now). But I didn't have a chance to lay my news
on Dawn because she was all wrapped up in her own Christmas
party, the most exclusive Christmas party in the world, if you
think about it, and far from giving me an inch on Gavin, she was
just one hundred percent full of herself. And worse, much worse:
warming up to go to bed with Ramsay.

"I can't believe what I'm hearing," is what I say to Dawn after
the ten-megaton blast of the initial shock wears off. "You actually
fucked him?"

A shrug, a smile, her face catching a reflection off the glass so
that it goes watery for an instant. "We slept together, yes," she says
and I hate the way she says it, as if she's chewing taffy or something. "Christmas night, actually. It was—nice. He's nice. I know
you don't agree—"

"*Christ,* Dawn. How could you?"

"—but you don't know him, you really don't."

I'm fuming, and I don't want to admit to myself that I'm jealous, so I turn it back on her. "So that's it, huh? Kiss the mission
goodbye?"

"Hardly," she says, and she laughs, actually laughs. "We just
slept together, that's all."

258 - T. CORAGHESSAN BOYLE

"What about Gretchen? What about *Johnny*?"

Another shrug. She's out there, flying high, and she should know better, she really should. There's no way I'm going to sit here and listen to her talk about love or infatuation or whatever she thinks this is, but I know what he thinks of it, or I can guess, and I know where it's going too—nowhere good. "And Judy," I say. "What about her? You really want to make an enemy out of her?"

"He told me about that. It's over. Case closed."

"That's not even close to being true—"

"And Gretchen, that was just an accident, but you already know that."

My heart's going as if I've just biked all the way to Tucson and back, as if my blood pressure's up, as if I'm having an *argument,* and really, I ask myself, what's it to me? What do I care what she does? But can I let it go? No. I'm outraged. *Ramsay.* It's as if she did it just to get to me. "Don't tell me you're going to let this go on, because believe me the repercussions are going to be a whole lot more than you could even begin to imagine—"

"I don't know," she says, looking right at me, "aren't you the one that said I was going to wither up and blow away? How did you put it? 'You've got to have something more than just playing with yourself'?"

"Yeah, all right. Maybe I did say that. But I didn't mean *Ramsay.*"

After that it's all just hot air and I'm the one that cuts it short. "I've got to go," I tell her, squeezing her off in the middle of a hymn of praise to her new Adonis. "I'm going to the movies. With Gavin."

The movie winds up being a major league stinker, by the way, the movie's a joke, but Gavin's there and the other two—Phil Lockhart, who might make it inside, and Julie Ott, who won't— are more or less a pair, so it's as if Gavin and I are on a date, and that's nice. While it lasts. But then we're in the car on the way back—nobody wanted to go out for drinks—and Phil and Julie are very close and very quiet in the backseat while I flip through the channels on the radio and Gavin and I talk about a whole lot of nothing interspersed with long stretches of road-staring silence, and then we're back at the Residences and the car doors are slamming and I say, "Anybody want to come over to my place for a nightcap?" and Phil and Julie say "No, thanks," and Gavin says he has to be up early, and that's that.

I don't want to be a drunk. I know the dangers. Two of my uncles are what my father calls wobbly walkers and my Aunt Lacey has a hard white arrow of a scar at her temple that disappears into her hairline and reminds everybody in the family that drinking and driving do not mix. Still, when I get home, I go straight for the bottle, and the next morning I wake up in a fog and can't remember if I'm on day shift or night shift. Did I mention vomiting? Oh, I'm a champion vomiter. So that's what I do, kneel over the toilet and feel the burn of my innermost self coming right up my throat and out into the open, where the cool wet flush mercifully takes it all away.

* * *

January creeps by, cold nights, a week of rain. It doesn't matter so much to us on the outside—rain is rain—but things are at their lowest ebb for the people inside. They're suffering from SAD, Seasonal Affective Disorder, though Dawn tells me the rain pounding on the panels is pleasing for the most part, a novelty, something to fight back the tedium. But rain means clouds and clouds mean less available light. Less O_2. Weaker crop yields. The broad mites don't mind it, though—they're thriving. They've pretty well decimated the potato crop despite the pre-closure importation of predatory mites *(Amblyseius swirskii)* to eliminate them. It's anybody's guess what happened to the predators, but they could have died off for lack of prey once they wiped out the initial infestation. The broad mite is a tropical pest, by the way, one that wouldn't survive outside the glass, but then E2, with its high humidity and uniform eighty-odd-degree temperature, is essentially tropical, the desert biome notwithstanding. Beyond that, the pea plants have blackened and fallen away to nothing (root rot, Diane says), and the cloudy days, combined with the effect of the panels and superstructure, have dropped available light inside to something like fifty percent of what it is in E1. Which means the vegetation isn't pumping out enough oxygen or taking in enough carbon dioxide, so the O_2 levels have dropped to their lowest yet, comparable to what you'd find at eight thousand feet, which in turn makes everybody feel sapped all the time. That and cranky. Which tends to amp up the inevitable slights and misunderstandings until they're full-fledged feuds, like the one going on between Gretchen and Dawn, both sides of which I get to hear, ad nauseam, every time I go to the glass. Gretchen: *I hate her.* Dawn: *What's she got against me?*

The fact is, just as Gretchen was beginning to heal over the whole Ramsay episode, the way he'd treated her like some fuck toy and then threw her aside, here comes Dawn, and I don't know whether Gretchen saw her slipping into Ramsay's room that night or heard them going at it, but she knew right from the start. I'm at the glass with her a few days after Dawn drops the bomb on me, and the first thing she says is "I don't care, it's just not right," before I can even get the phone to my ear and since I'm not really a lip-reader I have to ask her to repeat herself and when she does I say, "What's not right?" Which opens me up to the deluge.

From what Gretchen says, it seems they're going at it regularly. I'm trying for a neutral expression but I can't really hide my look of disgust.

"Like I went next door? To consult with him about the flows on the waterfall?"

I nod.

"And she was there. But not just there—she was in his lap, sitting in his lap like they were in the back of the bus in junior high or something, and they must have seen the look on my face, so I say 'Sorry to interrupt' as nastily as I can and back right out the door. Humiliated. Never more humiliated in my life. This was after lunch, free-time, yes, but didn't they have anything better to do? And Dawn, what's with her? She knows how I feel. She knows what Vodge and I had, what we *have,* or will have again, I know it—"

I tell her I'll talk to Dawn, get her side of the story.

"Her side? What's her side? That she's an opportunistic little slut? That she doesn't respect other people's feelings, that she thinks she's some kind of queen? I've had it. Really. I mean it. I've had it with both of them."

"It was him," I say, trying to redirect things here. "He planned it all, invited her over, actually lit up a joint he'd smuggled in, as if there was nothing wrong with that, as if the rules counted for nothing—"

But Gretchen's already on her feet. She looks as if she's been slapped, all the color gone to her jowls till they glow like fresh wounds—"I don't want to hear it!" she says—and then she drops the phone, turns her back on me and disappears behind the screen.

* * *

For the sake of my own sanity, I try to bury myself in work, and if the Human Habitat camera shows T.T. and Stevie sitting together in the kitchen one night at one a.m. looking into each other's eyes before sidling off down the hallway to his room, it's just one more secret in a whole file of them. Let them screw and screw alike, it's nothing to me. That goes for Dawn too. And Gretchen, pathetic Gretchen. All right. Okay. Fine. But as the winter creeps along, January giving way to February with hardly a break in the clouds—this *is* Arizona, isn't it?—I can't help feeling the malaise too. There's still a month to the Year One anniversary celebration and then another dragged-out interminable year till it's my turn (if it really is going to be my turn, no matter what G.C. says because can I really trust him?), and if this is the low point for the people inside it's my low point too. Gavin's unreachable. Dawn's inside. I'm so depressed I want to spit in Judy's face, set my turd-brown jumpsuit on fire and pedal-to-the-metal Dawn's piece-of-shit Camry all the way back to Sacramento. So what I do is start drinking. And not privately, because that's the first sign of a problem, but publicly, at Alfano's. Maybe, in the past, I might have been there once a week or every week and a half, but now I'm there practically every night, sitting at the bar, alone, like the loser I'm beginning to feel I really am.

My drink of choice at this point is vodka and soda, with a twist of lemon, because I'm thinking of calories, of my waistline, even though I'm letting my mind go to pot and I know it's wrong and know it's got to stop but it's like picking a wound. You know you shouldn't do it, you know you're letting yourself in for pain, infection, loss of a digit or a limb, but you can't help yourself, you don't want to help yourself. I am not a drunk. I repeat it because I want to make myself clear. It's just that right now, as the first year winds down and the disillusionment sets in with a vengeance, I need this, and as long as Mission Control doesn't know about it, as long as I don't wreck the car or wind up behind bars with a DUI, I tell myself I'm all right because this is just a phase, and maybe I *am* wearing nothing but low-cut tops and short skirts and my fuck-me heels, maybe I *am*. Maybe I want to feel good about myself and I'm looking for a shortcut. I'm not proud of it. I shouldn't be going there at all. But I am.

So what I'm building up to here is my latest encounter with Johnny, not that anything comes of it, nothing beyond a little liquored-up give-and-take, that is, but it's just that I find it interesting in the context of everything above and the way life on the outside is affecting me right about now. Let's say it's a Saturday night and I'm sitting there at the bar tracing my way through an unsurprising and basically boring conversation with one of the regulars (John, older, with his hair drawn back in a white ponytail, three gold bicuspids and granny glasses with lenses so powerful they make inland seas of his watery blue eyes), when I glance up and see Johnny at the far end of the bar.

He just happens to glance up then too and for the briefest fraction of a second our eyes meet before he turns away, and it's not that he doesn't recognize me, that's not it at all. More that he doesn't *want* to recognize me, for the very good reason that he's all but glued to the girl on the stool beside him. A blonde, another blonde, though this one looks as if she comes by her hair color the same way as Stevie. What she's saying to him must be punishingly fascinating because she has his full attention now and I can only guess at the subject—office politics, previous boyfriends, the trouble she's having finding a brassiere big enough to fit her, *cats*. That's it, cats. She's holding him spellbound with tales of Missy and Missy II and all the naughty little tricks they've been up to, first-date stuff, which is about the only time a guy will actually bother to put up even a pretense of listening. She's dressed like a slut, of course, leather skirt riding up her crotch, boobs hanging out, stiletto heels—not all that much different from me, that is.

I have had—I have consumed, slowly, sip by sip—two vodka and sodas and I am not even close to feeling the effects, and yet still something propels me up off the stool, "Sorry, John, back in a minute," and down the row of drinkers and schmoozers and cowboys and tourists until I'm standing right beside Johnny, staring at the back of his head, in fact. His hair's just long enough to look tousled, but not so long as to misidentify him as one of the good old boys, though of course he isn't that old and he doesn't play in a cowboy band even if he does wear cowboy shirts. As a goof. That's what he says, *I'm just goofing*. Anyway, there I am, there he is, there she is. And I'm getting a good look at her now, up close, and see that she's pretty, as pretty as Dawn, actually, but that her style's all wrong. Cheap, like Tricia Berner's. That's when her eyes jump to mine, and Johnny, alerted, swings his head around. "Oh," he says, "hi. Hi, Linda." And then, "Do you know Rhonda?"

I want to smile but I really can't so I just nod.

"Rhonda Ronson," he says, "Linda Ryu."

"Nice to meet you," I mumble.

"Yeah," she says, looking daggers at me (I wonder what he's told her?), "nice to meet you too."

The jukebox switches from Frank Sinatra (this *is* an Italian restaurant, after all) to something with a beat to it, rock and roll, classic rock and roll, a tune I've heard so many times it might as well have been inserted in my DNA, but I can't for the life of me think of what it's called or even who's singing it. Johnny's watching me. His date's watching me. The music lopes along on a heavy bass line.

"You know something?" Johnny says, looking from Rhonda to me and back again. "You two have something in common."

Neither of us takes the bait, though I can see she wants to say "What?" if only to please him.

"Give up? You've never seen each before, right, and you're wondering what is he talking about, am I right? Well, listen up. You're both mainlined into the Ecosphere. Rhonda"—addressing her now—"did you know Linda's one of the Mission Three crew—and Dawn Chapman's best bud?"

Rhonda gives him a blank look, as if she's never heard of E2, Mission Three or Dawn either, though she'd have to have been living in Tibet if that's the case.

Johnny's grin. The grin that got him everything he ever wanted, from the time his mother started breast-feeding him to this moment right here and now. "So, Linda, guess how Rhonda's related to the big eco-project? Or was, I should say, right, Rhonda?"

"I don't know," she says, and her mouth tightens. "I used to date one of them."

I'm sucked in despite myself, and even if I will wind up going home with John of the silver hair and the three gold teeth, this is where I suddenly feel out of my depth, and why I'm picturing Malcolm Burts I really don't know. "Who? Somebody inside, or—?"

Her mouth is so tight, so drawn down, I can't help thinking she's about to spit at me, though I can't imagine why or what this has to do with anything. "Ramsay?" she says. "Ramsay Roothoorp? You ever hear of him?"

* * *

The play this time around will be Ionesco's *The Bald Soprano,* another of G.C.'s darlings. (We staged a public production of *Rhinoceros* as part of the buildup to the final selection, just to remind everybody of our commitment to theater and its foundational function, which served to generate a certain amount of press, though if you told me we'd played to more than a hundred people I would have been surprised.) The plan is to put on two consecutive performances, inside and out, as with *The Skin of Our Teeth,* and to time them to coincide with the festivities surrounding the Year One anniversary in early March. After G.C. announces it at team meeting one morning, without inviting comment, we all go back to our work stations to mull it over till we can get together at break. Then it's ten-forty-five and we're gathered in the courtyard out back of Mission Control, five or six of us, variously smoking and drinking coffee against the long afternoon ahead, when Malcolm, as if he's letting air out of a tire, says, "*The Bald Soprano.* Can you believe it?" No, nobody can, but then we have to believe it because G.C. has spoken.

"I mean, what's the obsession with the Theater of the Absurd?" he goes on, clearly disgusted by the choice, as I am too—what does this have to do with the mission or the environment or anything, really? It's just stupid, that's all, amateurish, like something you'd see in a TV sitcom if sitcoms allowed for long strings of non sequiturs. I'm drinking black coffee, forgoing creamer because of my weight issue, and it tastes like nothing, like so much hot water. I set the cup down on the granite picnic table that's an exact duplicate of the one inside E2, and wave my hand to take in the scene— the courtyard, Mission Control, the gleaming white-boned sprawl of the Ecosphere itself—and come up with the answer, "Because we're living it, that's why."

Of course, the people inside don't really see the humor in it, dragged down as they are by the O_2 issue and the mid-winter blues. Gearing up for a theatrical production is just one more burden laid on them, and while they're all looking forward to hitting the one-year mark, I don't think any of them are all that enthusiastic about the kind of celebration Mission Control has in mind, even Ramsay, and it's his *job* to be enthusiastic. He's on the phone or PicTel half the day now, consulting with G.C., Judas and Little Jesus over the lineup of musical acts and speakers and invitations to various representatives of the fourth estate, not to mention the participation of the crew, which will involve the donning of the red jumpsuits and interviews at the window, followed by feasts inside and out amid the usual milling herd of scientists, ecologists, NASA types and celebrities like Burroughs and Harrelson and maybe even Albert Hofmann, who G.C. is trying to coax into flying over from Switzerland.

We get some sun finally, rain gone, clouds gone, plenty of sun, Arizona sun, and that helps a bit both with crew attitude and photosynthesis, though they've had to shut down the soil aerators and let the compost bins dry out so as to reduce CO_2 emissions there, and by the last week of February things begin to perk up inside. I'm on day shift currently, watching the cameras, and I can actually see it in their body language, people going about their chores and projects with just a bit more bounce to their step. They're almost over the hump, that's part of it too, but the literature on closed-group psychology flags this period as one of the most dangerous in the way of the glass-half-full-or-half-empty syndrome. The day you reach the halfway mark you butt your head up against the wall of the inexorable fact that you're only fifty percent of the way home, with a whole long turtle-creep of a year to go, and this, typically, is when crew relations begin to break down, factions forming, people withdrawing, feuds boiling over, but of course for this crew it's already happening.

At any rate, I persist with Dawn (her true friend, etcetera, as I've said), and I'm at the window with her two days before the March 6 celebration, rehearsing our lines. If you don't know the play, let me just say it's a whole lot more confined than the Wilder, with only six characters and a single set—and it's shorter too, much shorter. As best I can figure, it's a satiric thrust at middle-class banality and the meaninglessness of polite chitchat, in which the two main couples—the Smiths and the Martins—are interchangeable. The mise-en-scène says it all: *A middle-class English interior, with English armchairs. An English evening. Mr. Smith, an Englishman, seated in his English armchair and wearing English slippers, is smoking his English pipe and reading an English newspaper, near an English fire . . . Beside him, in another English armchair, Mrs. Smith, an Englishwoman, is darning some English socks. A long moment of English silence. The English clock strikes 17 English strokes.* What this has to do with us, with the environment, with closure, I can't imagine. But then that's part of G.C.'s mystique—he's forever laying the unexpected on you, playing with the conventions, and when you think about it, that's liberating, it really is, and no irony intended. Not that I have to like it. I just have to look as if I do.

This time around, Dawn and I have the same part—Mrs. Smith—which makes things a little easier. Though on this particular bird-hung evening Dawn doesn't really want to rehearse. She wants to stare over my shoulder and into the twilight beyond, a dreamy look on her face, and I am not going to go there, absolutely not. In fact, and we've agreed on this, the only way I'm going to keep up these visits is if there's no mention of Ramsay, not a word. So I shift in my chair, flip back the pages of the script, and without preliminaries, announce, "Why don't we start with the Bobby Watson stuff on page twelve? I'll be Mr. Smith and we'll go up to the point where the Martins come in and then we'll switch, okay?"

"Okay, but really, Ramsay's going to play Mr. Smith for our version and he's been rehearsing me, I mean, we've been rehearsing each other—"

"*Who?*"

"Ramsay."

So I'm furious already and I can't help myself, the very mention of him throwing up a wall of flames between us, and I say, "I thought we *agreed* not to—"

"Oh, come on, Linda. Really. Grow up."

I want to say something like, *Me? I'm not the one jeopardizing the whole mission, I'm not the one sleeping with the enemy,* but instead I go on the offensive. "I saw Johnny the other night. At Alfano's? And guess who he was with?"

She flicks one hand at me as if to say it's nothing to her, but I know better.

"Rhonda Ronson, that name ring a bell? Blond, twenty-five, looks like an ad for implants? No? Well, let me clue you, just to give you an idea of the kind of men you get yourself involved with—she was Ramsay's little squeeze. And now she's Johnny's. Nice, huh?"

Her face shows nothing.

"It brings it all around again, doesn't it, like this stupid play we've got to memorize because G.C. says so, the characters just switching places at the end? Or did you even get to the end?"

"I don't care about Johnny," she says.

"Yes you do."

"No, really, I don't. I never laid any restrictions on him, and anyway, that's all in the past. What I really—" Her voice drops and there's a tension in it, a quiver, and I'm startled because I can't help thinking she's going to start crying on me again. And over what? Johnny? But it's not Johnny, that's not it at all. As I'm about to find out. "Linda"—her voice a whisper—"promise me you won't breathe a word of this?"

I'm sitting up straight now, rigid in that hard plastic rack of a folding chair, and I'm all ears. Something's wrong, I can sense it, smell it, see it in her face. "Yeah, of course," I say, too quickly. "What is it?"

Her voice sinks even lower. "It's probably nothing. It's just, I don't know, I think I missed my period—"

"What are you saying?"

"It's probably nothing. Diet, maybe, you know? Sometimes, when you're starved for calories, women are, they don't menstruate, I mean it's *common*—"

"Christ, Dawn. How long?"

"I don't know," she says, dropping her eyes, and she won't look at me, she won't. "Maybe two months?"

Part III

CLOSURE, YEAR TWO

Dawn Chapman

I wasn't really all that worried—or not at first anyway, because I'd been careful and so had Vodge. Despite my better judgment, despite the complications, despite *everything,* I was deep into it with him at this point, deeper than I'd ever been with Johnny. Johnny was just a phase, or that was what I told myself. A crutch. Something to cling to on the emotional roller coaster leading up to closure—if I'd thought I was in love it was love as a kind of quick fix, bandaid love, a distraction from what Mission Control was putting me through and maybe an acting-out too because who were G.C. and Judy to dictate my private life? I understood that now. Johnny had pretty much stopped showing up anyway, and when Linda told me about Rhonda Ronson, I didn't feel a thing. Actually, I felt more jealousy over Vodge's involvement with her than Johnny's. That was how far I'd come. And Vodge was diplomatic about it, giving me what I wanted to hear—she was just a fling, nobody really, a secretary at a doctor's office who just happened to be available, though even then he'd known he was in love with me. He was looking for a quick fix, same as me. There she was one night at the bar at Alfano's and one thing led to another.

We'd been inside a long time—forever, it seemed. To think about the world beyond the glass was like looking down the wrong end of a telescope, everything shrunk to irrelevance. We *were* on another planet and nothing that happened back on the home planet really mattered anymore. Still, I couldn't help myself: I wanted details in the way I would have wanted to know about a car wreck along the highway we couldn't even see from here, and it had nothing to do with Johnny, I swear it—only Vodge, only him. "What does she look like?" I asked. "Is she pretty?"

We were on the couch in his room, books propped in our laps,

just being together, siesta time, the sounds of our world, both natural and manufactured, ticking away in the background. "I guess,
yeah—in a kind of cheap way," he'd said, pushing all the right
buttons. "Nothing like you. Nothing at all."

"What about—in bed?"

He held my gaze. He was good at that, Vodge, good at putting
things over, smooth, very smooth. "The usual," he said.

"And what about me? Am I the usual too?"

"No way," he said and he reached for my hand and pulled me
to him.

As I say, I wasn't worried, but after I missed my period for
the second time I went up to the library and paged through half
a dozen books, including *The Family Medical Guide* and *Basics of
Human Physiology,* until I found what I was looking for in a study
about dietary deficiencies in the Japanese concentration camps
in World War II. The women there, overworked and underfed,
stopped menstruating—for months, years even. The medical
term for it was "hypothalamic amenorrhea." At the bottom of a
page detailing the prisoners' starvation rations of under a thousand calories a day, was this footnote: *Women who regularly perform
overtaxing exercise or lose a significant amount of weight are especially at
risk of developing the condition.* There was more, about how weight
loss can cause elevations in the hormone ghrelin, which inhib-
its the hypothalamic-pituitary-ovarial axis, which in turn alters
the amplitude of GnRH pulses and causes diminished pituitary
release of luteinizing hormone and follicle-stimulating hormone,
and though I didn't have much of an idea of what exactly that
meant, I was satisfied and relieved too. Here was the rationale for
missing my period, laid out for me in the language of authority,
a dense cluster of medicalese that made everything come clear: I
wasn't pregnant, just undernourished. Simple as that. It would all
go away on reentry, and in the meanwhile, looking at the bright
side, I wouldn't have to bother once a month with the silicon cup
we all hated.

As it happened, Diane strolled into the library just as I was slipping the book back into its place on the shelf and though I really

had nothing to hide I couldn't help feeling like I'd been caught out. I picked up another book at random and flipped it open, then glanced up, as if abstracted, and gave her a smile.

"Oh, hi," she said, crossing the room to me. "I didn't know anybody was up here—"

This was pre-dinner (Gretchen's turn, a meatless stir-fry, sure to be heavy on peanuts). I'd already done the evening milking, fed the pigs, chickens and ducks, washed up and shampooed my hair in anticipation of seeing Vodge, though we wouldn't sit next to each other because we were playing it cool (despite the fact that everybody must have known what was going on, thanks to Gretchen and her big vituperative mouth. Not that it was any of their business, but still there were all sorts of invisible sensors here, feelers and tentacles that made the human sphere as mysteriously interconnected as the wild ones, and you had to be careful, very careful—with everyone, all the time). It was past six, the windows darkening behind me, everything still, the chatter of the biomes and the hum of the technosphere muted up here so that when you closed the door this was the quietest place in all of E2. "Only me," I said. Then added, all innocence, "Just looking for something to read."

"Oh, I've got a ton of things, if you're interested—" Her taste, judging from the bookcase in her room, ran from detective stories to romance (anything with *Love* in the title), which you wouldn't have expected of her—Gretchen, maybe, but not her.

"That's okay," I said. "I was actually just doing a little research."

"Really?" She was leaning over me now, inspecting the shelf where I'd just slipped *Starvation in the Shanghai Camps* back in its slot and plucked up—what was it? Swami Vivekananda's *Raja Yoga*. How was I to know? It was a book. And it was in my hands.

Diane—*Lark*—gave me a curious look. "Yoga?" she said. "Good for you." She let out a sigh. She'd just turned thirty-eight two weeks earlier and looked ten years younger, especially with her hair cut short, very short—not quite as severe as Sigourney Weaver's in *Alien,* but close. She'd cut it for her birthday, claiming she didn't have time to bother with styling it anymore—and didn't want to waste the water either, which made the rest of us feel prodigal. "I could only wish," she said. I thought she was going to go on, wondering aloud why I'd looked so distracted lately, pry a bit, indulge in a little exploratory girls' talk vis-à-vis me and Ramsay, but she didn't. "The way you work, E., I can't imagine how you find the time, let alone the energy."

"Me either," I said and she let out a laugh.

So it was all right. Everything was all right. Diane liked and respected me and I liked and respected her in turn. I was suffering from nothing more serious than hypothalamic amenorrhea and maybe a little cramping. I was fine. We were all fine. The human experiment marched on, the O_2 had stabilized, the goat's milk was holding steady and the whole world was watching us as Mission Control beat the drums in the lead-up to our first anniversary inside.

Only problem was, on the day of the celebration I woke up feeling out of sorts. I don't want to say nauseous, actually, but more as if I were off balance, dropping in an elevator or an airplane that suddenly loses altitude. You must know the feeling. It's as if your stomach can't adjust, as if it's falling faster than the rest of you. I didn't vomit, though I walked around all morning feeling I was right on the verge of it, which in some ways is worse than vomiting itself, which at least gives you some relief, and I had to force myself to eat my morning porridge—and still I wound up slipping half of it to Vodge, who lifted his eyebrows because no one ever gave up so much as a molecule of food here no matter what. Again—and call me an idiot—I didn't really put two and two together, thinking the queasiness was a reaction to the previous night's dinner, a rice and beans dish Diane had gone overboard in spiking with our new crop of those deadly little green serranos that look so innocent on the cutting board but can really do a number on you if you're not careful. I wound up picking half of them out of my portion, but still I'd felt the heat—and felt it all over again on the toilet that morning too. So I was nauseous, an inconvenience, nothing more.

It was early yet, just after breakfast (the celebration was to kick off in the afternoon, thank god, rather than at eight, the hour we were afraid Mission Control was going to insist on for the sake of proportion), and I was in bra and panties, ironing my jumpsuit for our two p.m. appearance at the visitors' window. The nausea had already twice propelled me to the bathroom, but nothing came of it and I wound up just sitting there on the toilet seat staring into space. At the moment I was feeling marginally better, and if I was thinking about anything it was whether I would wear my hoop earrings or the pearl studs—or none at all—for our official presentation at the glass. Just then there was a knock at the door and before I could holler *Just a minute!* Gyro, already dressed in his jumpsuit, was pushing his way into the room and pulling the door closed behind him.

I felt a tick of annoyance. A closed door meant *Privacy, please,* and we all knew that and respected it. Again, given the cameras and the tourists and the inescapability of our crewmates, privacy—private space—was our most precious commodity, aside from food, that is. I wanted to be equable, wanted to be nice, but I was at the end of nice right about then. "*What?*" I said, making an accusation of it rather than a question. "Didn't you see I had the door shut?"

His face dropped. "Well, I—it's a special day, right, a whole year now, can you believe it? And I just thought I'd do something special—for you."

The rooms were small, as I've mentioned, almost claustrophobically so, he was right there on the other side of the ironing board, three feet away, and I was in my underwear—ironing, for god's sake, and couldn't I have a minute to myself? Was that too much to ask?

He was fumbling in the deep outer pocket of the jumpsuit, his eyes roaming over me, and then he had the package in his hand, the crinkled yellow paper, bold brown lettering, M&M's, peanut M&M's, and my first thought was, *So he does have a stash,* which was immediately followed by, *No, there's no way I can accept it.* "I'm sorry," I said, "I can't, really, not now—I'm not feeling all that great this morning if you want to know the truth, and really, I have to do this"—gesturing with the iron—"and get ready for the party."

The room was lit by the early sun fingering its way across the IAB and spilling through the window, strands of the wool carpet lit like trees in a miniature forest, a whole ecosystem there, moth larvae, dust mites, flakes of shed skin. I was holding a hot iron in my hand. And despite my resolve—it wouldn't be right to accept anything from him, not under the present circumstances—my mouth was watering. I wanted that candy, wanted it more than ever, but I fought myself.

"I can't believe it," he said. "I'm offering you sugar, chocolate, *M&M's*—like last time. Remember last time?" He rattled the bag suggestively. "And you're saying you don't want them, that you're what, refusing even to accept a present from me?"

I set down the iron, shook my head. "I'm sorry," I said.

"What is it—Vodge? That's it, isn't it?" He dropped his hand, jamming the yellow bag back in his pocket. "I'm a better man than he is, you know that, don't you? He's a cheat. And he's reporting on us to Mission Control—like the spy he is."

I had nothing to say to this because I knew it was true and yet it didn't matter because no one seemed to see Ramsay's authentic self, what he was like beneath the surface, and it was no use arguing over it—or trying to defend him either. My stomach clenched. I felt a weird sensation as if I were itching all over and when I reached up to adjust my bra strap and scratch my shoulder there I saw the look in his eyes, the hungry look, adoring and needy at the same time, and I just nodded and said, "I know."

* * *

The celebration wound up being a bigger deal on the outside than in, the band playing, G.C. speechifying and parading his celebrities past the visitors' window for dutiful Ecospherian handshakes and photo ops, the whole followed by more speeches trumpeting our accomplishments and then the dancing and feasting that went on past dark. Inside, it was different. We were all more than a little weary of these ceremonial occasions, tired of forced cheer and the pretense that everything was going swimmingly when in actuality the cracks had begun to show, Gretchen against Vodge (and now me) and Gyro increasingly embittered while Stevie and T.T. seemed a separate force, as if they knew something nobody else did. Diane was in her own world, our boss and taskmaster. Richard was a cipher. Yes, we'd got through the winter, but there was another one to come, and if the oxygen levels had stabilized with the increased sunfall we all knew what to expect next time around, and it wasn't especially joyful to contemplate. What did we have to look forward to? More hunger, more scrabbling in the dirt, more work. Fifty consecutive two-year closures began to seem an awful lot to expect from an environment as delicately tuned as ours, even if conditions were sure to improve as the vegetation—and soils—matured. More and more, we began to feel it was a trial just getting through our own closure, only the second in a string of forty-eight more to come. Forty-eight more. I'd be long dead by then and god knew what E1 would look like at that point, what with the effects of global warming, species extinction and habitat loss, let alone E2. Would it really be a kind of ark to save humanity? Was humanity even worth saving?

I don't know. Maybe it was just me. Linda had warned me that this was going to be a difficult time and I tried to keep that in mind, to rise above it and join in with my crewmates in our own celebration—to be a good sport—but even after the tourists, reporters and celebrities went home and we were mercifully left alone to enjoy our own feast, I still couldn't get into the spirit of things. I felt dragged down, exhausted. Everybody else acted as if nothing was wrong, Vodge clowning around and heaping up a plate for me, Richard pouring arak, T.T. rigging up a pair of speakers to shake the place with rock and roll and Gretchen at one point raising her glass to propose a late-night group swim to cap off the day. Pork was the centerpiece of the feast (Peter, disposable now that he'd served his function in impregnating Penelope and had become just another mouth to feed) and the meat, sliced thick and oozing juices, seemed to excite everybody. I tried to eat but just didn't seem to have much appetite. Which didn't go unnoticed.

Richard, seated across the table from me and clutching a glass of arak, turned away from Diane, whom he'd been deep in conversation with, and suddenly focused on me. I was pushing the food around my plate and trying to listen to what Stevie was barking in my ear about Albert Hofmann, inventor of LSD, who had shown up after all, though he wasn't much to look at, to say the least, and never seemed to leave G.C.'s side. And, of course, none of us got closer to him than the three-eighths-inch thickness of the reinforced glass at the visitors' window.

"What's the matter, E.," Richard said, "too excited to eat?"

He'd meant it to be funny, an ironic jab at Mission Control and the way they expected us to switch on the esprit de corps on command, but he wasn't smiling. He was giving me his clinical look, doctor and patient. I didn't answer right away. Stevie was in the middle of a reminiscence about a singularly vivid experience she'd had with Hofmann's product—*Like when I was nineteen?*—when she suddenly pushed herself up, announced, "I've got to pee," and hurried off down the hall. We both paused to watch her go—I couldn't help thinking how he'd examined her, measured her, photographed her, how he knew everything there was to know about her, about all of us—and then I turned back to him, my heart fluttering now till I could feel it in my throat. If anybody could see through me, he could.

"I don't know," I said, the racket of T.T.'s music—industrial rock, Ministry or maybe Nine Inch Nails—drowning out all the conversation around us until we might have been alone in his consultation room. "I think I'm coming down with something."

"We know it can't be flu," he said, and he was smiling now, "—or the common or not-so-common cold either, right? You sure you're not just exhausted? I mean, you do look a little pale, or maybe *drained* is a better word. You could just go to bed, you know—our official duties are over for the day. All those people, all that glass. Enough already, right? You feel that? I sure do."

"I guess."

"Of course, as your physician, what I'd recommend at this point is a judicious shot of homemade arak, just to make it all fade away. What do you say?" He lifted the bottle—or beaker, actually—and reached for my glass, but I put my hand over the top of it.

"No," I said, "it's my stomach. Actually, I'm feeling a little queasy."

He took a sip from his own glass, made a face. "Really? And how long's this been going on?"

"I don't know, couple of days."

"Couple as in two—or more?"

I picked up my fork and set it down again. Diane had turned to Gyro and was talking him up now, her hair jagged in the glare of the overhead lights, punkish almost. For a minute there I drifted out of myself, staring at the back of her head, watching her increasingly animated gestures as she semaphored her ideas, and it was as if I'd never seen her before, as if I weren't here in E2 but in the food court at a mall somewhere, people watching.

"Dawn?" Richard was giving me an inquisitive look. The music screeched, buzzed, thumped.

"I don't know." I let my shoulders rise and fall. For some reason, whether it was fear, denial or just plain exhaustion, I felt on the verge of tears. I glanced up to where Vodge and Troy stood at the kitchen counter, waving glasses at one another. "More, I guess. Maybe like three or four?"

"That doesn't sound right. Could be bacterial, I suppose, but then we'd all have it, and"—the smile again—"it'd be on Ramsay, wouldn't it? He's our water man, he's our purifier, and if we can't count on him, who can we count on?"

That was when I had my first glimmer of the truth, but as soon as it flashed across my mind I snuffed it out because it was inadmissible—so wrong, so terrifying, it made me catch my breath. No, the problem was I'd picked up a bug, it had to be, something my immune system could handle or in the worst-case scenario an antibiotic out of Richard's kit. But from where? The water was as pure as anything E1 had to offer, purer—Vodge was a fanatic about it—and there was no way I could be infected with anything we hadn't brought in with us, which would have been long extinct by now. But the animals, what about the animals? I thought of bird flu, swine flu, the stew of bacteria the pigs—pig—lived, ate and defecated in. That had to be it. It had to be.

"I could have picked up something from the ducks—or the pigpen . . ." My voice trailed off. "I mean, that's got to be a possibility, right? Realistically?"

Richard was still watching me closely, still smiling, although the smile had begun to settle around the edges. He wasn't just looking at me now, he was examining me, as if he knew something I didn't, and it made me uneasy. "You want to come in and see me tomorrow? I'm open all day—and I take all the major credit cards, Visa, Master Card, American Express—"

What I was thinking of was that first night with Vodge, Christmas night, in his room. We'd both been drinking, that much I remembered, but he'd used a condom, hadn't he? We'd been careful since, rigorous, to the letter, no matter how carried away we were, because getting pregnant, *knocked up,* would be the end of everything we'd worked for, all of us, as catastrophic as blowing out the airlock with a stick of dynamite. That would be ridiculous, crazy, wrong. There was no way I was pregnant, no way. And yet I was flashing on the second time, the following morning when he'd slipped into my room before anybody was up and he was all over me and I was all over him and still I'd said, *Wait, wait,* and gone into the bathroom for my diaphragm and he'd said, *I thought you were on the pill?*

"I don't think it's anything, really," I said, looking Richard in the eye. And then, to prove it to him, I reached across the table for the beaker, filled my glass and downed it in a single defiant gulp.

* * *

The nausea didn't go away, hitting me the minute I opened my eyes the next morning, waves of it rising inside me like an internal tide, and it didn't fade when I pulled on my clothes and went out to the IAB to put in my hour's work before breakfast. Next thing I knew I was seated at the granite table staring into my bowl of porridge and willing myself to eat while my crewmates compared notes on the party and Gretchen plunked herself down at my end of the table without acknowledging me, let alone wishing me a good morning or even a *Hello, drop dead.* Gyro withdrew into himself, spooning up his porridge as if he were alone in his room, and since Vodge was late for breakfast, the burden of chitchat fell on Richard, Stevie and Troy, all three of whom seemed lit up still in the aftermath of the party. When Vodge did come in he took the only open seat, which was next to mine, even as Diane pushed her empty plate away, brandished the banana and laid out the day's assignments with a speech that started with the phrase "Listen up, people."

When Diane paused to pass the banana on to Stevie, who was going to give us her weekly status report on the ocean and its finicky corals, Vodge tilted his head toward mine till we were almost touching and I felt a shiver go through me: the tickle of his hair, the heat of his breath, the familiar comforting smell of him. "You don't look so hot," he whispered. "Still under the weather?" The night before he'd wanted me to come to his room but I'd begged off on the grounds that I wasn't feeling well, telling myself it was only rest I needed.

Now I just nodded and watched him purse his lips and tighten the groove between his eyes till there was an imprint of flesh clamped there, and was he thinking the same thing I was? I couldn't guess—and, truthfully, I didn't want to. After a minute, when everybody was focused on Stevie, he slipped his hand under the table and took hold of mine.

I began to feel better as the day wore on, which just managed to scare me all the more. The term "morning sickness" came to me, a term I was familiar with in the vague way of things like "coronary bypass" and "radiation treatment," neat two-word descriptors of calamities that happened to other people but never you. Women of my generation had careers instead of babies and I'd never known anybody who'd been pregnant except my mother, but I'd been only three years old at the time and that hardly qualified. I thought of calling her, of confiding in her, of getting some *information,* but

Mission Control strictly limited our outside calls and I was afraid somebody'd be listening in on the other end—*Judas*—and I let things slide, hoping the nausea would go away, hoping it was in fact no more than a temporary infection I'd picked up from the animals. My stomach settled. I worked with Diane and Vodge in the rice paddies cum fish ponds and if I felt more worn down than normal, the hard physical labor helped cleanse my mind. I was fine by lunch. Which I plowed through like a marathon runner, licking not only my plate but the utensils too.

After lunch, at siesta-break, Vodge waited till everybody was otherwise occupied—doors shut up and down the hallway, Troy dozing in a chair on the balcony and Stevie gone to the beach, with a towel—before coming to my room. Everybody might have known what was up, but we were being discreet as a way of sparing people's feelings—Gyro's, Gretchen's, even Richard's, really—and making a show of the way we felt about each other would just be asking for trouble. Inside and out. Judy hadn't weighed in yet, if she even knew about us. Nor had G.C.

What can I say about him, Vodge? He was beautiful, that was all, with a grin that was genetically programmed to trigger the lights in his eyes—if he was wearing a bandanna across his lower face like a bandito you'd still know he was smiling, just from the way his eyes jumped out at you. I loved his hands. Loved the way he looked in the doorway when the light was behind him, defining his shoulders, his arms, the hard knots of his calves. Love. I was in love. Careening through that delirious stage when sensation rules everything, my skin a sheath of nerves firing at his slightest touch, my brain swamped with dopamine, everything flashing and sparking as if I'd taken one of Hofmann's little pills. I'd been deprived of physical intimacy for nearly ten months, even if he hadn't (Gretchen, not that I was jealous of *her*), and we'd come together with the kind of urgency you see in the movies when the lovers, kept apart by one plot point or another through two-thirds of the film, are suddenly pawing at each other while the music swells and the camera goes fuzzy. That was us. That was how it was the first night, revelatory, passionate to the tenth power, and it was as if we couldn't get enough of each other since.

But now, right now, in the slow sweet hour and a half given us for siesta each day, I felt him on top of me like a burden, an excrescence, something I'd given birth to, and if we were making love it didn't feel that way to me. I had something to tell him, something that terrified me whether it was just my imagination or not, and I couldn't stop thinking of it the whole time. When he rolled off me and we were both lying there staring at the ceiling, the condom still clinging to him and my skin burning from the touch of him, I was trying to put the words together in my head—I didn't want to just come out with it because it was probably nothing and I'd only embarrass myself. There was an interval, our shoulders touching, his hand clasped in mine even as my mind raced and a beetle crept upside down across the ceiling as if the rules of gravity had been suspended, and then, incredibly, he began to snore with a soft rattling insuck of breath and the moment went up in flames. "Vodge," I said, rising up on my elbows so I was looking down at him, at the pits of his nostrils and the cavern of his open oblivious mouth, "there's something I want to say, to tell you, I mean—"

I watched his eyes flutter open, the consciousness gradually creeping back into his features. "What? What is it?" He was sprawled there still, still wearing the condom, his limp penis like something that had crawled up out of the sea and died before it could shed its skin. "Is there anything wrong?"

* * *

I didn't go to Richard till the next day. I woke at five, feeling as if I'd had the air punched out of me, as if I'd been strapped down and couldn't breathe, and the next thing I knew I was in the toilet, retching—the toilet I shared with Richard, his door giving onto it from the right side, mine from the left. I'd fastened the latch, but I was afraid he'd hear the noise I was making, though he wouldn't have been awake yet, or he usually wasn't at that hour. I didn't bring anything up. It was just dry heaves, a whole churning cycle that left me feeling light-headed and weak. After a while I rose to my feet, unlatched the door and went back to bed. I wound up being late for the morning milking and I just went through the motions in the IAB, feeling as if I were down at the bottom of the ocean with Stevie, everything happening in slow motion. Though I didn't have any appetite for breakfast, I sat there and dipped a spoon in my porridge as if there was nothing amiss while the others went through the usual morning routine and Vodge, derailed by what I'd told him the afternoon before, made himself scarce.

I shouldn't have said anything, I saw that now, not till I knew one way or the other, but I was scared and I couldn't keep it in any longer. I needed reassurance, that was all. Needed him to hold me and tell me it was all right, there was nothing to worry about, I was just being foolish. But when I told him I'd missed my period he just about exploded, not only jumping to conclusions that were in no way justified but blaming me, though he was just as culpable—more, because we hadn't been in my room that first night but his and if it was on anybody it was on him. "Everything's up in the air yet," I kept telling him, "it could be a thousand things, nothing definite, nothing written in stone." He wouldn't listen. He was infuriating, hurtful, acting like a shit. To say he was a disappointment would be an understatement. But then it was only typical, wasn't it? Men had their needs, and women too, but it was always the woman left holding the bag. Like Tess. The knocked-up milkmaid.

But I wasn't knocked-up and this wasn't the end for us either, not till Richard said so.

I spent the morning in the paddies again, up to my knees in muck, transplanting rice seedlings, Diane lost in the work, Vodge solicitous with me but unusually quiet, and as if I didn't have enough on my plate, here were two families who must have been Mormons—two couples, thirteen children, count 'em, ranging from infants to leering pimply boys—pressed up against the glass just inches from me, watching the clumsy Terranaut splash, stagger and fall flat till her face was a mud pack and her hair hanging limp and dripping a pasty liquid the color of tobacco juice. When our walkie-talkies buzzed with the first call to lunch, Vodge hosed off

Diane and me and then I hosed him off, changed into a clean shirt and shorts and sat down to the table with as fierce an appetite as I think I've ever had and it didn't matter a whit that T.T. was the cook and the food—what he was calling a beet, bean and sorghum casserole—so bland you could barely taste it. I felt fine, though my back ached from bending over all morning and I was so tired all I wanted was to sleep through siesta, but I made myself go to Richard because that was what I had to do, if only to get it over with.

Nobody was around—people tended to scatter after lunch—and so nobody saw me duck into Richard's office, which was the first doorway off the hall from the kitchen before you got to our rooms. At first I didn't think he'd be there because this was his break period too—and maybe I was secretly hoping he wouldn't be—but there he was, his back to me, slumped in the reclining chair, his feet up on his desk. He didn't stir even when I pulled the door shut behind me, and I realized he was asleep, napping, his head lolling to one side. I saw he had a bald patch I'd never noticed before, a single beam of sun through the window picking it out as if it were a spotlight and we were onstage and the drama about to begin. Here he was, Richard, the man who was one of my best friends on earth, who'd photographed me nude, who'd cupped my breasts in his hands and made his intentions clear in the most unprofessional way, Richard, asleep.

I felt powerful suddenly, calm, all my fears shrunk down to nothing, because I could just walk back out that door and never have to listen to him ask if my breasts were tender or put his fingers there and comment on the way the areolas around my nipples had darkened and enlarged. I'd actually taken two steps back when he woke with a snort and swung round in the chair.

"Oh," he said, "it's you, Dawn. I thought—I guess I must have been dreaming. Or maybe I still am. You look—good. Pale, but then we're all pale in here, aren't we?"

"Yes, I guess we are," I said, wondering if he'd forgotten our discussion of the night before last and if so, exactly how I was going to broach the subject. "First thing I'm going to do when we get out of here is go lay out in the sun—"

"I hear you. But be careful with that tender skin, E.—you don't want to age before your time. Redheads, right?" He rubbed his eyes, yawned, then stretched his arms over his head. "Now, tell me again, what was this business with an upset stomach? Still bothering you—or did my special prescription take care of it?"

At first I didn't know what he was talking about, but then I remembered the arak, which, strangely, hadn't seemed to have any effect on me at all. "Yes," I said. "Or no. I mean, it's still bothering me"—and here it was, out in the open—"especially in the mornings?"

What he was doing was staring into me in that way he had, all business now, no cynic, no lover-in-waiting, but the physician who was there to assess and diagnose and cure, our priest of the age that had left priests behind. Richard. "You mean morning sickness?"

Maybe I colored. I don't know. I was still standing there in the middle of the room, feeling guilty, devastated, like a betrayer, the one who was going to bring the whole mission crashing to the ground, worse, far worse even than Roberta Brownlow, because that was an accident. But then this was an accident too, wasn't it?

He got up out of the chair quietly, came across the room, took me by both hands and gazed into my eyes. When he spoke it was with the softest voice, a voice so soft it could have been my own, seeping out of someplace deep inside me. "You remember when you had your last period?"

"I don't know. Like two months ago?"

"Could be dietary," he said. "You're on the pill, right?"

I dropped my eyes. "Diaphragm."

"Well, let's have a look," he said, but he didn't lead me to the examining table, not yet, and he didn't let go of my hands. Just held on till we were both conscious of the moment.

"You're with Vodge now, aren't you?"

I didn't say anything. But I lifted my eyes to his, to show him I wasn't evading the question. What everybody else knew, he knew.

"And you're being careful?"

"As far as I know. Except maybe—"

"Yes? You can tell me."

"That first night?" And now I couldn't hold it back any longer, the truth laid out right there for both of us like some slide in biology class, and I started to cry. "Maybe. I don't know. I just—I don't know anything anymore."

Ramsay Roothoorp

All right, so call me heartless, call me a shit, a poser, a hypocrite and anything else you can think of, but when E. laid the news on me, it struck me as the ultimate act of betrayal, not to mention *stupidity,* and if I was less than sympathetic, I'm sorry. That she wasn't on the pill was beyond comprehension. Every female in this country from the age of menarche to menopause was on the pill—wasn't that what the sexual revolution was all about? I'd never known a woman who wasn't on it, never even imagined it. In college, I'd even had a girlfriend who worked for Planned Parenthood, doing outreach work in the projects and trailer parks, and she was on-message pretty much all the time—female empowerment, population control, no more womb slavery and the like. She pinned a poster of Dr. Pincus up on the wall over our bed, as if I needed a reminder. Well, I didn't. I had no intention of bringing another mouth into this world, not then or now or ever—I was an environmentalist, we all were, and it was clear that the fundamental problem facing our species, the root of all the world's woes, the very reason we needed a place like E2 to begin with, was overpopulation. *Nothing definite,* E. told me that first afternoon, *nothing written in stone,* but even if that was true it put a chill in me—really, what had she been *thinking*?

We were in bed. I'd dozed off. Five minutes earlier I'd made love to her, had been *in* love with her, floating on the ascending beauty and rightness of it as if I were stretched out on a raft in the middle of the big hot tub we called an ocean, and now she was telling me she'd missed her period two months running? And it was just a dietary problem?

"It's probably nothing," she said.

"Then why mention it?"

She was propped up against the headboard, gazing down at me, her mouth clamped tight. She'd pulled her T-shirt back on and pushed the hair up away from her temples, where it flared in the light coming through the blinds. "I just thought you ought to know."

"Ought to know *what*? You just said it's probably nothing, didn't you?"

She was silent a moment. "I'm saying, just in case—"

"In case you're knocked up? In case the mission's fucked? *We're* fucked? I mean, is that what you're trying to tell me, because I can't believe what I'm hearing." I'd pushed myself up to a sitting position, and though we were in bed together, inches apart, we might as well have been shouting across canyons. I wanted a cigarette. I wanted a drink. My hands were shaking. "I can't believe you. Really, I can't. Did you tell anybody?"

She shook her head.

"What about Richard? You see Richard yet?"

"It's probably nothing."

I came up off the bed then, naked, enraged, the wet condom still clinging to me as if in some X-rated cartoon, and before I could think I snatched it off and flung it across the room. "Christ, talk about a circular conversation—I mean, we could be doing Mr. and Mrs. Smith here. Talk to me. What do you mean, it's nothing?"

In a small voice: "I looked it up. In this book about the Japanese camps?"

That was when I learned about hypothalamic amenorrhea, our big hope. "Okay," I said, *"okay,"* but I wasn't mollified, not even close. She'd put a scare into me—everything we'd worked for crashing down around our ears—and I wasn't about to let it go. "And the pill," I said. "Tell me again why you're not on the pill? What kind of sense does that make? In here, of all places?"

I didn't like the look she was giving me—it wasn't a loving look and it wasn't apologetic either. "If you want to know, Gretchen and I felt right from the beginning we didn't want to put anything artificial in our bodies because wouldn't that defeat the whole purpose of E2?"

That made me go cold all over: *Gretchen*. Jesus. What had I gotten myself into? Did I have any dignity in that moment, standing there naked, limp, dripping, trying to summon the proper degree of inquisitorial outrage? Did I have gravitas, did I even have a reason for being part of this ridiculous conversation in which nothing was decided and everything pushing us farther and farther apart? "I don't see your point," I said as savagely as I could, bending now to snatch my shorts from the floor and press them to my groin, as if my privates had become private all over again. "I mean, wouldn't being"—I could barely get it out—"*knocked up* defeat the purpose a thousand times more?"

I avoided her the rest of the day. I was angry, furious, right on the verge of snapping—and as soon as I left her room, slamming the door for emphasis, I went out into the rain forest to try to calm down. At first, I just sat there on a damp rock, blind to everything around me, but before long I got up and began to lose myself in work, cleaning debris out of the deep pool at the bottom of the waterfall and adjusting the flow in the smaller pools at the top of the cliff above it. This was our tepuis, or cloud forest, replete with misters that were timed to come on at five-minute intervals, and since I was there anyway I decided to clear the vegetation away from the nozzle heads, hacking at things with my sickle while the stream gurgled and the mist rose like steam around me, and before I knew it the afternoon was gone. I was a no-show for dinner—Stevie, who was chef of the day, set a plate of food aside for me, which I took down to the beach so I could be alone—and I didn't go back to my room till it was past midnight. I didn't want to see Dawn, not till I had time to think. What she was going through, what she must have been feeling, really didn't cross my mind, or not yet anyway. Understand me: this wasn't like the young wife laying the happy news on her befuddled hubby while the music soars and the robins burst into song, this was like stabbing seven people in the back. Or no, hundreds of people, thousands even, everybody who'd invested in E2, from the four hundred consulting scientists to G.C., G.F. and Judy and every schoolchild who'd written a report and crayoned a galago leaping across the white margin at the top of the page. If she was pregnant, and that was the crux of it, that hovering fateful *if,* then closure would have to be broken, if only for the five seconds it took to push her and what was growing inside her through the airlock. Nothing in, nothing out. What a joke.

I didn't sleep well that night—how could I? Every time I dozed off it felt as if there was a craps game going on in my head, lucky seven (she isn't), snake eyes (she is), lucky seven, snake eyes, snake eyes, snake eyes. I woke exhausted in an envelope of sweat. I'd had three or four hours' sleep, total, and maybe that was part of it, but I felt calmer. She wasn't pregnant, I was sure of it—I mean, really, truly, what were the chances? It was a scare, a false alarm, a warning. The phrase *Led by his dick* came into my head. I was a fool. Worse than a fool. Hadn't I learned anything from the Gretchen fiasco?

The thing was, I still wanted E., wanted her more than ever. I'd acted in the heat of the moment, thinking of myself first, thinking of the mission and Judy and the nightmare of how I was going to spin this if the throw of that infinitesimal chance did turn up snake eyes, and I regretted that now. I'd showed my true colors, that was for sure. I hadn't done a thing for E., hadn't given an inch, and I wondered how that would affect us going forward— she must have been suffering all this time, holding everything in, never breathing a word of it, and of course she was as dedicated to the mission as I was, as anybody was, and the implications must have been even starker for her than for me. I'd been wrong and I vowed to make it up to her. Especially since I couldn't imagine going through the next three hundred sixty-three days without her, without her lips and her laugh and the way she clung to me and caught her breath when she came.

Still, I couldn't bring myself to face her just yet—she was going to see Richard that afternoon to resolve the question one way or the other—and so again I prevailed upon Stevie and asked her to set aside a plate for me at breakfast, which I wound up taking back to my room. I didn't actually lay eyes on E. until we were in the paddies together, setting rice seedlings, and of course we couldn't talk because Diane was there. Watching. And listening. Not to mention a whole mob of straight-arrow tourists and their monkey-faced progeny tapping at the glass till we were all three of us waving and smiling our official Terranaut smiles every thirty seconds. I did ask how she was feeling—everybody knew she'd been under the weather so I was covered there—and I tried to help with the lifting and bending a little more than usual and let her know through my body language that I was sorry about what had passed between us the previous day. Then there was lunch. I sat next to her, though she didn't have much to say and seemed content to let the communal conversation wash round her. After lunch I went out into the savanna, where our resident acacias and thorn bushes were—a prickly place, the only place in E2 where you had to wear shoes—and found a spot to spread a towel, stretch out with a book and try to take my mind off what was happening in Richard's office.

At first I couldn't get into the book at all (the first volume of the Bigger Bang series, which Linda Ryu had insisted E. bring in with her), rereading the same paragraph over and over, but finally I lost myself in a description of how a team of eight—eight!— terraformers went about defrosting the ice of a frozen planet with nuclear heaters inserted beneath the surface and seeding it with blue-green algae, the first step in producing a viable atmosphere. They were six men and two women, but the disparity in numbers didn't matter because the women were heroically built and sexually free, and I was just getting to one of the juicier passages— the ship, the void, the greening planet floating beyond them in a globe of radiant light and astronaut Vita Novgorod stripping down to step into the zero-gravity shower with two of her male teammates—when my walkie-talkie buzzed. It was E. "We need to talk," she said. "Over."

"Sure," I said, "of course, yeah." I could feel my pulse accelerating. "Everything cool?"

"Not now. Not over the air."

Her voice was drawn tight, bad news, I knew it was bad news, but then the walkie-talkies distorted everybody's voices so you could barely recognize them. Or so I told myself. "Just give me a word, one word, that's all." And then I added, superfluously, "Christ!"

Nothing.

"Come on, E. I'm dying here. Over."

The connection crackled and that crackle infuriated me—here we were almost at the end of the twentieth century and they couldn't even make a reliable two-way communications device?

"Meet me in five minutes," she said. "The rain forest. Over."

It was that tranced time of day when everybody was in their rooms, dozing, digesting, writing in their diaries, and there was nothing moving but the animals—lizards, frogs, toads, turtles, snakes, crazy ants running crazy over every surface in their long anfractuous streams, dragonflies maneuvering, bees fumbling over the flowers. The air handlers blew. The wave machine coughed and spat. In my hurry I wound up stumbling into one of the acacias that formed the border of the savanna and felt the sting of a two-inch thorn puncturing the flesh of my upper arm as if I were taking an inoculation, blood there, surface pain as prelude to the deeper trauma ahead of me because the tone of her voice had told me everything I needed to know and all I was doing now was careening blindly through the biomes to pick up the pieces.

What would I say, what *could* I say? She was out. No two ways about it. Dawn Chapman, the Terranaut who brought down Mission Two. Disgraced. Cast out. Number one on the Roll of Dishonor and Roberta Brownlow right behind her. I let out a curse, swatting at the heavy drooping leaf of a plantain that just happened to be in my way, right in my face, as I burst into the rain forest and started down the path. "Dawn!" I called, my voice a hurled whisper. "E.! Where are you?"

Nothing. I stepped over the *várzea* stream that wound its way out from the waterfall pond, conscious of the cameras overhead. Something rattled in the undergrowth. "E.?" I called, louder now, because who would be listening—except maybe Gretchen, and she could be anywhere. I was sweating heavily, the shirt glued to my back, the air barely circulating. "E.?"

Her voice drifted to me then, thin, battered by the roar of the waterfall, a plaintive bleat that threaded its way through the call of the tree frogs and the chatter of the insects: "Here."

"Where? I don't see you."

"Here," she repeated and suddenly she came into focus, her limbs separating themselves from the vegetation around her and her face a pale cameo floating there in the greenery as if it were separate from the rest of her. She was on the ground, in the mud, buried in the dense stand of ginger the Mission One crew had planted around the margins of the rain forest to protect the under-story from the blast of Arizona sun, hugging her knees to her chest. Her face was dirty. She'd been crying.

If I were to stop here to enumerate my strengths, my virtues, I could go on for pages, but one of them, most emphatically, is not empathy. I've never been good in situations of loss, hurt, sorrow, because I just can't summon the standard clichés, not least because they sound false in my own ears. There she was, crying, wrapped in her own arms and rocking back and forth, and what consolation could I offer? We both knew what this meant and it was beyond consolation. Forgive me if I was thinking of Judy and G.C. and how they might tend to view my part in all this and what I could say in my own defense, because if one person was going through that airlock they might as well bring down the cleaver and make it two. I went to her, squatted over my knees. "It's that bad then?" I said.

She lifted her head but she didn't answer, just stared right through me.

"He's sure? I mean, it's not like he has one of those test kits on hand, does he? What would be the point—in here, I mean? It's not as if—" And I stopped myself right there.

"He did an examination, Vodge—he *examined* me."

I wanted to raise objections—there'd been no urine test, no blood test, so how could he be sure, how could the guillotine drop so finally and definitively?—but she just said, "He can tell. He's a *doctor,* don't you get it? I'm pregnant!"

What he'd done—and this made a shiver run through me despite the temperature—was have her climb up on the examining table and spread for him while he inserted his speculum and noted the dark purplish-red blush in the vaginal mucosa due to the increased blood supply there (Chadwick's Sign, after James R. Chadwick, 1844–1905), which appears around the sixth week of pregnancy, before moving to her breasts to probe their tenderness and observe how her nipples had enlarged and darkened in preparation for milk production and delivery. Richard had measured her, measured all of us, and of course he'd examined every inch of her too, but I hadn't been involved then, hadn't even thought about it. Now I was involved. And I didn't like the picture developing in my mind—of him, of her—not one bit.

"How long? Did he say how long?"

"Two months, maybe a little more."

"What about Gyro?"

"Gyro? What has he got to do with it?"

"I don't know, weren't you two—I thought, for a while there?"

"God, you're a shit—you can't be serious?"

"You tell me."

"It was that first night, *Christmas,*" she said, as if she hadn't heard me. "I'm sure of it. It was the only time we—*you*—didn't use protection."

That was when I became aware of the thumping on the glass behind us, some moron there with his camera, and then the flash, and I was beyond caring at that point, all my training, all my slickness, my *cool,* deserting me, and I gave him the finger—and more, and worse. "Fuck you!" I shouted, and in the next instant I was there, pounding on that three-eighths-inch-thick panel of safety glass as if I could burst right through it.

* * *

"So, Richard, you got a minute?"

This was after dinner that night, E. having excused herself because she wasn't feeling well. Diane, with a face set in concrete, had stalked down the hall to bring her a plate of lablab bean burritos and baked squash and suss out the problem (sickly Terranauts just wouldn't do, and whatever was wrong, whether it was a dietary deficiency, monthly cramping or simple exhaustion, it ultimately came down on Diane, as crew chief). I'd lingered in the kitchen, helping Richard, our chef of the day, with the cleanup, and to this point our conversation hadn't risen above the trivial, though we both knew what I was doing there.

He gave me a hooded look, then leaned over the counter to shoot a glance round the dining room—only Gyro was there still, sitting over a book at the end of the table, his elbows splayed and his chin cupped in one palm. "Sure," he said, straightening back up and giving his hands a quick wipe on the apron, which he then removed and hung ceremoniously on its hook beside the refrigerator. "You want to go to my office?"

The office had its own smell, a lingering undertone of medicinal odors, and it hit me the moment we stepped through the door. It was subtle, but the effect was magnified because I was so inured now to an atmosphere free of artificial scents, and I couldn't help commenting on it. "Whew," I said, "what's that smell—or don't you notice it?"

"You've been out in the biomes too long," he said, sinking into the chair behind his desk. "Call it the sweet breath of healing."

"What is it—alcohol? Camphor? Like Vicks VapoRub or something?"

"Actually," he said, gesturing to the seat in front of the desk, which I dutifully slid into just like any other patient with medical issues on his mind, "it's probably the still you're smelling. Got to have our arak, right?"

"Oh, yeah," I said. "Yeah. Couldn't do without that."

We were silent a moment. He was watching me carefully in that way he had, as if he were back in med school laying a corpse out for dissection. I took in the scale, the examining table, the diagram of the human skeleton across the top of which I'd written "Dem Bones" in black Magic Marker the first time I'd been here to submit to my bimonthly probing. Richard was our doctor, our man of healing, and he knew me as minutely as anybody did. What he said now, tenting his fingers and staring right down into the depths of me, was, "So we've got a little problem here—"

I felt like a condemned man at the moment the hood is drawn over his face. A black coil of despair settled in my stomach. I wanted to deny everything. "Are you sure? I mean, could it be anything else? Dietary?" And here I trotted out the term she'd given me: "Hypothalamic amenorrhea?"

"That's 'A-menorrhea,' long *a*, like in *ape*."

"All right, yeah, thanks for the lesson, but what about it?"

"Nothing's a hundred percent—and it won't be till she starts showing. And I'm not an obstetrician, mind you. But—" He paused.

"But what?"

"What's a nice small fraction you can subtract from a hundred percent—without getting into decimal points? Let's say maybe an eighth of one percent, just for the sake of argument. That leaves me ninety-nine and seven-eighths sure. Okay? That good enough for you?"

"Oh, come on, Richard. Shit. You don't have to get sarcastic on me—I feel bad enough as it is—"

"Uh-huh," he said, and I swear he hadn't blinked his eyes since we'd sat down. "And so does Dawn. Believe me." And then he reached down to pull out the bottom drawer, extract a packet of Naturalamb condoms and slide them across the desk, wordlessly.

"Yeah, *thanks*. If you want to know if I feel like an idiot, the answer is yes. If I'd known this was going to happen I would've come in here and had you cut my dick off, but I thought she was on the pill, I mean, wasn't that the understanding, the *requirement,* for shit's sake, that all the women had to be on it?"

"Even the pill's not infallible. Or an IUD or a diaphragm either. The only thing that's infallible is no sex, no intromission of the phallus in the vagina, period."

"Very funny. You got any sex-ed pamphlets back there?" I was glaring at him now, all my wheels spinning. "The question is, what are we going to do about it?"

He took his time, pulling a pair of reading glasses out of his shirt pocket, breathing on the lenses and polishing them on the cuff of his sleeve before putting them back again, unused.

298 - T. CORAGHESSAN BOYLE

He held out his palms, gave an elaborate shrug that could have meant anything from *It's your problem, not mine* to *Go ask G.C.,* pausing long enough for me to recall just what side he'd been on when the electricity went down. "Nothing much," he said finally, looking glum. "Unless she spontaneously aborts—has a miscarriage, that is."

"What are the chances of that?"

"Up to the thirteenth week it's something like fifteen to twenty percent, so you never know. But after that it goes way down—"

I was leaning forward in the chair now, my hands resting on the edge of the desk. The smells, whatever they were, seemed stronger than ever. *Fifteen to twenty percent.* Long odds. I was sweating. My shorts were stuck to my crotch. I felt sick to my stomach, sicker than Dawn, sicker than anybody. "Couldn't you—?" I didn't know quite how to put it. "Do something?"

"What are you saying?"

"I don't know—couldn't you, like, give her an abortion?"

It took him a minute, his face hardening until he was wearing the same inflexible look he'd worn the day he announced we were going to have to break closure or risk dying of heatstroke. "And what, take the fetus and feed it to the pig?" He let that hang between us, then dug out the glasses again and fixed them over the bump of his nose, though we both knew they were just a prop. "You know, *Vodge,*" and he put an emphasis on it I didn't like, not one bit, "we may be crewmates and we may be locked in here together, but you're just beyond the pale. You're not even human. *Untermensch*—you know what that means?"

"Fuck you," I snarled, pushing violently up from the chair. "You talk about me? What about you? You pretend to support the mission but at the first sign of a problem you just what, abandon ship—hey, let's just throw open the airlock, right? This is the end, you know that, don't you? Because they're never going to let her—"

He leaned back in his chair, very carefully lifted one leg, then the other, and crossed his feet on the desk. "Yeah," he said, "and fuck you too. *Vodge.*"

* * *

Rachel Carson said, "In nature nothing exists alone," and what she meant was that every ecosystem is interconnected and interdependent, a community of organisms working inscrutably to sustain its own existence. Ours was no different: what affected the individual affected the whole. Various species might have gone extinct during the first mission and others—nuisance species, like the morning glory—had flourished and crowded out more useful things, but that was by way of natural selection and as minders and keepers we could tweak the process one way or the other to suit our own needs. Tear out the morning glories and increase the sunfall available to the crops and the understory of the rain forest; run the ocean water through a series of algae scrubbers by way of filtering out the excess nutrients that otherwise would make pea soup out of it and spell slow death for our corals. Accident claims a galago? A shame. But if we were lucky the others would reproduce and the cycle would go on. Pigs consuming too much? Slaughter them. Tilapia aren't breeding up fast enough? Tighten your belt. But this—E.'s situation—was something else altogether.

We were a team, each of us an essential cog. We were working ourselves to the point of no return as it was—how could the mission possibly go forward without any one of us? Eight wasn't just ideal, eight was *necessary*. I saw that now. E. was our MDA. Without her, we'd lose the biggest factor in food production, not simply in terms of the animals—milk, cheese, meat—but as a full-time field hand too. Diane could fill in, sure, but she'd need help, a whole lot of help that would cost us all in time, effort and calories and drive a stake into our own projects and specialties. When Mission Control found out (if they didn't know already; news travels fast in a fishbowl like this), they would cut her loose in a heartbeat. G.C. wasn't part of our team—or Judy or Dennis either—and they couldn't begin to imagine what it was like. They weren't inside. They didn't have to starve themselves, didn't have to work till their muscles were tight as wire and their backs aching every minute of every day. If somebody on their team lost it or got cancer or took a maternity leave, they could just hire somebody else. There were millions of replacements out there, billions—but not in here. Here there were only eight of us.

But what if they did decide on a substitution? A new MDA? If they were going to break closure for the five seconds it would take to expel Dawn, then why not shove somebody else in through the airlock since the mission was compromised anyway? And who would it be, who was next in line? Linda Ryu. Linda Fucking Ryu. The thought came to me as I was making my way through the tunnel to the south lung, where I was planning to check on the settling tank, though I'd checked it twice that day already, and it stopped me right there in the passageway as if I'd been hit in the face by a two-by-four. *Linda Ryu.* Linda Ryu in place of E.? No, it wasn't going to happen. We weren't going to break closure, no matter what anybody said, whether it was G.C. or G.F. or the governor himself. I'd kill first.

So where did that leave me? I'd slammed out of Richard's office not twenty minutes ago and still I hadn't gone to E. It was eight-thirty in the evening. There was a wind rushing up through the tunnel as the big aluminum saucer in the lung below descended in the cool of the evening and the pressure began to equalize. I was in this tube, the long narrow underground gut of E2 that might have been lifted wholesale from the set of a sci-fi movie, a place that seemed suddenly alien, eerie, so confined you couldn't even stand up straight without banging your head, and I was contemplating violence—or extreme measures anyway—because I had a world to protect and nothing short of an asteroid strike would make me back down. To hell with Richard. To hell with Judy and G.C. and all the rest of them. There was no putting it off any longer: I had to go to Dawn, get things out in the open, *think*—in concert, as team members, lovers and whatever else we were—because there was no way I was going to let this fall apart. She was the key. She was the one. It was on her, not me. Anything can be negotiated—wasn't that the basis of civilization?

I went to her room first, but she wasn't there. The kitchen

and dining room were deserted, ditto the balcony. I heard music coming from Troy's room, but the door was shut and she wouldn't have been in there anyway, so I went on down the hall, thinking maybe I'd go up and check the library. Gretchen's door was open, and I noted it absently, almost casually, as I passed by, but I had no intention of letting her in on any of this—or even asking if she'd seen Dawn. Fortunately, Gretchen wasn't there, or at least not in her sitting room, where she liked to lurk like a big gray spider, looking for somebody to draw into her web, but that somebody wasn't me, not anymore, not ever again. Dawn wasn't in the library, but Richard was. With Diane. I cracked the door and there they were, sitting side by side in a pair of easy chairs. Did that give me pause? Did that make my heart rate jump? They looked awfully chummy, their faces soft and composed, and what they might have been discussing, what confidences they might have exchanged, what gossip, rumor, *fact,* I could only imagine. I tried to back quietly out the door but in that moment they both glanced up.

"Oh, hi," I said. "Richard. Diane." It was all I could do to keep from screaming *What about patient/physician confidentiality!* but I controlled myself. Nothing had happened. You could see from Diane's face that the poison hadn't entered her system. Yet. And maybe it didn't have to, maybe there was some way out of this still. "Anybody seen E.?"

Richard just stared. Diane murmured, "Hi, Vodge," and set down the book she'd been pretending to read. "She isn't in her room?"

"I already checked."

"What about the animal pens?"

"Oh, yeah, good idea. Though it's late—" I had a picture of E. then, crouched in the pen with her goats, stroking their ears, murmuring to them in her softest whisper of a breath, the goats more comfort to her than I was, and what did that say about me?

"She sometimes goes down there, just to check on the animals before bed," Diane said. "But you know that already, don't you?" And here was the insinuation, the link, the presumption that if we weren't busy screwing in bed we'd be going at it out in the biomes or down there amongst the goats.

"Yeah, thanks," I said. "I'll go have a look."

I was just turning to make my exit when Diane said, "Vodge, what was that business with the tourist today? In the rain forest?"

"I don't know—what tourist?"

"He's some retired science teacher from somewhere in Georgia, or that's what they're saying over at Mission Control. He put in a complaint—said you gave him the finger, is that right? Beat on the glass. Used the *F*-word? Is that right?"

"I don't know what you're talking about." I was already pivoting on my heels, heading for the door.

"Just to let you know," she called, "Judy's on the warpath."

I found E. in the animal pens, the only illumination what little light managed to leach down from the floor above—that and what the stars provided. There were the usual smells, homey smells, the natural funk we'd all gotten used to and which made Richard's office and T.T.'s chem lab seem so alien to our reprogrammed olfactory lobes (or maybe I should say "rewilded," because that was what we were doing here, rewilding ourselves in the way of the circus animals released back into the game parks of India and Africa or the pet wolves let go on the tundra). At this point, after a year inside, this was what I expected the world to smell like. I drew in a deep breath. All was still. A soft drawn-out bleat escaped one of the goats, followed by the matter-of-fact rattle of its pellets hitting the ground. The pig—alone now—snuffled from the dark confines of her pen. "E.," I called softly, and it was like a replay of the scene in the rain forest, only this time I was going to stay calm and see things through, clearly, reasonably. "You there?"

"Vodge?" She rose from where she'd been sitting on one of the rails of the pen, the pallor of her face and bare arms reflecting the light so faintly I had to look away and back again to be sure she was there.

"Yeah, hi," I said.

Very softly: "Hi."

"You look ectoplasmic rising up there out of the pen, you know that?"

"Look *what?*"

"Like a ghost."

She let out a laugh, a good sign, bury the hatchet, get on with it. "No, I can assure you I'm flesh and blood." A beat. "Though I wish I wasn't."

"I'm sorry," I said, and the smell—the stink, the muck and the shit and all the rest of it—flowered till it was like a bouquet. "I acted like a jerk. I *am* a jerk. But come here, let's go sit someplace and talk this out, okay? Sound like a plan?"

A moment of silence. The goat, the pig, a shuffling there in the pen. In the distance, the mewl of the galagos—the bush babies—grieving over something in the night. "What's there to talk out? Unless you've got a time machine and we could go back to that first night and do it all over again, I'm screwed. You know that—" Her voice caught and she couldn't go on, and let me tell you, that was about the saddest moment of my life, because it wasn't on her—I saw it then—it was on me.

"It's not over yet—we'll work it out, you'll see."

"How?" she said, but it wasn't a demand, wasn't harsh and accusatory, just a question.

"Here, take my hand," I murmured, and she reached out and we were touching, skin to skin, for the first time since all this came down. "You want to go to the beach? Let's go to the beach and just sit for a while, okay?"

She didn't say anything, but in the next moment she was climbing out of the pen and I had her by the hand still, bracing her, guiding her forward, up the stairs, through the deserted Habitat and down along the side of the cliff to where the beach sat glistening in the starlight and the miniature waves rolled in to reconfigure G.C.'s trucked-in sand. We walked out to the edge of the beach and sat in the sand with our feet in the water and I told her I was sorry again, that I was there for her now and would be there for her no matter what happened, and if I didn't get to give the speech I'd intended (she was going to have to go to Richard and ask him—beg him—to terminate the pregnancy because of course he wouldn't listen to me when it was her decision and her decision only) it was because she put her arm around me and gave me her lips and leaned into me with all the inescapable weight of her heat and sadness and beauty and I found I could support her, after all.

* * *

"So, look, I know you're under a lot of pressure in there but there's no excuse for this kind of thing. None. Zero. Zilch. We're selling something to the public here, Ramsay, which you, as Communications Officer, should be aware of even more than anybody else, right? And I don't want excuses, there *are* no excuses, so don't start giving me your patented line of crap—"

It had been a while since I'd talked to Judy about anything other than whatever matter was at hand—the First Anniversary Celebration, most recently—and it took me a moment to acclimate myself to her tone, to the whole tenor of what had been to this point a one-sided conversation. What I was getting was a dressing-down, well deserved and a long time coming, at least in her estimation. And I was getting it face-to-face, at the visitors' window, because she wanted me to see her in the flesh, it was that earth-shattering, that huge, and so she could underline her points with her eyes, her mouth, her breasts and her legs. She was wearing her business attire, jacket, blouse, skirt cut at the knee, stockings, heels. Heels. I hadn't seen a woman in heels in a year and I have to admit the sight of them and the way they sculpted her calves and brought out the sweet articulation of the bones of her ankles really moved me in a way anything she had to say couldn't have begun to.

"I'm talking to you—Ramsay? This is no joke. What in Christ's name were you thinking—or were you thinking at all?"

"No, I wasn't thinking, just reacting. Like an animal in a cage." I held her eyes. "Which is just what I am. You know something? Why don't you put up some signs, like DON'T MOLEST THE ANIMALS, NO TAPPING ON THE GLASS, that sort of thing. And what about FUCK OFF, will that work?"

"Everything's a joke, right? We're out here busting our butts and waving the banners, trying anything, giveaways, press junkets, anything to raise awareness. And dollars. That man you gave the finger to? He paid his admission fee, ate at the snack bar, rented a motel room in town—dollars and cents, Ramsay. That's the bottom line here. And you don't—*ever*—let anything like this happen again, you hear me?"

This little interlude was colored, of course, by what had gone on between us and no longer was going on—and wouldn't go on after reentry either. Or at least I didn't think it would. I had E. I'd always have E. But the way Judy was looking, the umbrage in her turquoise eyes, the way she bit her underlip and how full it was, those ankles, those *heels,* made me lose my concentration.

"And what was this I heard about Dawn being there? Was it some kind of argument you two were having? Or what, a *lover's spat*? Was that it? The two of you going at it like rabbits in there?"

I didn't have anything to say to this. I was thankful word hadn't got out yet about just what E. and I had managed to produce while going at it like rabbits and I was hopeful too that the three of us involved—E., Richard and I—would find a satisfactory way to put it all behind us without anybody catching even the slightest intimation of it, and so I just nodded. And grinned.

Judy, inches away, the phone pressed to her ear and her face contorted by a grimace, snapped, "Yeah, that's right—smile, you jerk."

"Come on, Jude," I said, "what else do you want me to do? Nobody can touch me in here, don't you realize that?" I took in a breath, held it, then added, "Not even you," and put the phone back on its hook.

Linda Ryu

So it gets worse. And you know something? It's no less than she deserves, and I tell you, if it was me in there we wouldn't be having this crisis because it never would have happened, and I don't care if they lock Mel Gibson and Brad Pitt inside with me, because I am one hundred percent dedicated to the mission and Dawn is not. Apparently. She's fundamentally unserious—I don't want to say frivolous because that's an unfair characterization, but for her the mission's more about posing for the cameras and being a big celebrity than the kind of life-and-death proposition it would be for me. I respect her for her decision to get off the pill, I'm not saying that, but rolling over for Ramsay, of all people—who's not even wearing a condom?—and she "forgets" her diaphragm because she's swept up in the moment like a sixteen-year-old in the backseat of her boyfriend's car? *Please.*

I don't really find out about it, the extent of it, that is, till a week or two after she told me she missed her period and tried to claim it was nothing more than a dietary deficiency. Which I believed, because I just wasn't thinking, too stunned by the news she was hooking up with Ramsay, I guess, to put two and two together. In any case, I'm at the glass one evening, a cold drink in my hand (Diet Coke, lots of ice), giving her a tired smile, expecting nothing more than a little gossip. The sun's vicious, I'm a sweat factory, drenched, absolutely, and she's got the phone in her hand, saying "So what's new under the troposphere?," trying to be blithe, putting up a front as if I don't notice something's wrong, still wrong and not getting any better, though to this point I haven't guessed or even suspected what the true problem is. The last few times we talked I'd forgotten about what she'd told me, or at least put it out of my mind, and she never mentioned it or alluded to it again so

I thought everything was just fine, plus it would have been awkward in the extreme for me to bring it up beyond asking something innocuous like, *Everything okay?*

"Nothing," I say in answer to her question. "The usual," I give out with a sarcastic laugh. "G.C. should stage *La Ronde* next, because that's what it's been like lately. Phil and Julie broke up, did you hear that? You see them out with the crew tending the test plots and they won't even look at each other. Dennis has been coming on to Tricia, who's always been a suck-up, but you know that already. And that means—good news for me—Gavin won't have anything to do with her. But then"—and here our eyes lock through the glass and I see a flash of what's coming—"he probably already told you. Since you're his special bud, right?"

"Sure," she says, giving me a weak smile, "the best. But he didn't tell me, no. Really, though, good for you."

I can read her—every nuance, every inflection—and I can see she's not in the conversation at all, just making her mouth move like some Prozac-numbed housewife, and my sixth sense makes me say, "What about you—what's new under the glass? Everything okay?"

At first she doesn't answer, and I can see she's working up to something.

"Not so great, if you want to know," she says finally, dropping her head so her hair sweeps across her face. Her hair seems thicker than ever, by the way, nourished on the humidity inside till she looks as if she just stepped out of a shampoo commercial. Her skin isn't looking so good though, pale as an office worker's and with a faint yellowish cast, as if she's suffering from jaundice. But then that's nothing new. Or maybe it is. Maybe it's getting worse.

"What is it," I say, "Ramsay?"

"Yes," she murmurs, lifting her face and sweeping back her hair with a quick flick of her wrist, and I can see the hurt in her eyes now and it's all I can do to keep myself from saying *I told you so.* "Or yes and no. I mean, we're still together, I still love him—"

"Oh, *please,* give me a break—"

"It's not that. It's—promise you won't tell?"

"Promise."

"You remember when I told you I missed my period? And it was nothing, really, just dietary?"

The truth—the sick twisted impossible truth—hits me like a rush of adrenaline. My eyes are wide open, my ears, even my pores. "No," I say, "don't tell me. Dawn, Jesus, you're not *pregnant*—?"

Weepy Dawn. Her eyes tell me everything. Already, instantaneously, I'm spinning out the implications—if she's pregnant, she's gone, and so much for breaking closure. But in the same moment it occurs to me that if they're going to break closure, then they might as well make it a revolving door, one in, one out, quick as an eye blink, the smallest glitch, mere seconds against the twelve and a half months already stacked up. They're going to need an MDA, that's what I'm thinking, and with what I've got going for me and what G.C. all but promised, that's me. I'm next in line, I have the seniority, the experience, the *pull.* Dawn's pregnant, and that's too bad, that's regrettable, a tragedy of the very first magnitude, but all I can think is *I'm going in!*

In the thunderous minutes that follow she gives me the details in a hushed tearful voice—the first night when they were both drunk on Christmas arak and she thought he was using a condom and he thought she was on the pill, the morning sickness, Ramsay's refusal to accept the facts, Richard's diagnosis, how only three people in the world know and how she's never going to leave, never, no matter what, even if they try to drag her out—

"But you're sure?"

Miserable, penitent, sick with it: "Yes."

"And Richard can't—do anything?"

"What, you mean bend a coat hanger?"

"You know what I mean."

"I'm not going to put that on him."

It takes me a moment, recalculating, before I say, "All right, good for you," and if I'm being disingenuous, can you blame me? It's her fetus. It's her problem. And if the problem doesn't go away then I'm heading inside. Or that's the way it looks, that's the probability, and I have to say I'm more than ready. But first, one more question: "What are you going to do now?"

* * *

Things simmer for a while, a hot March ascending into a hotter April, and though she must be three months gone at this point, Dawn doesn't look any different—by this stage a baby's only three inches long and weighs an ounce or so and *her own tiny unique fingerprints are now in place* (I looked it up, suddenly keen on the whole process of human gestation since I have a vested interest here, which makes things a lot more complicated than just being a best friend and wishing the expectant mother all the joy of the event). The only question is when the cat's going to claw its way out of the bag because as far as I can see nobody's the wiser. I'm the eyes of E2 and sometimes the ears too, and if I didn't know, if Dawn hadn't confided in me, I'd never have guessed anything was wrong. And no, I haven't told Judy—or Dennis or G.C. or anybody. That wouldn't be fair to Dawn. Besides, she's not going to be able to hide it forever and when the shit does hit the fan I'll be ready, not only to smooth things over but go inside and do what I've been trained to do, Linda Ryu, Mission Two Terranaut, with a head start on Mission Three.

So nobody knows. And life inside goes on as usual as far as anybody can tell. The big news is Ramsay's arm, which gets infected from a thorn prick and turns an ugly shade of red, causing his temperature to spike and stirring up a hurricane of hand-wringing in Mission Control till Richard drains the wound and scours him with antibiotics, a problem in itself since who knew Ramsay was allergic to penicillin? That billows into a crisis, inside and out, and the result is an explosion of press coverage ("Terranaut Takes Turn for Worse, Refuses Hospital"; "Mission Control Ponders Breaking Closure"; "Jeremiah Reed Insists Crew Safety #1 Concern"), but Ramsay winds up pulling through and three days after Judy leaked the news to the press he's posing for the cameras at the visitors' window, grinning his oily grin and flexing his biceps as if nothing can keep him down. Or daunt him. But what the press doesn't know—or Judy either—is how totally daunted he actually is.

The other thing that happens to distract everybody is a whole lot more positive, unless you consider Ramsay's recovery a plus, which, I have to admit, I don't. Malcolm's almost as bad—he thinks way too much of himself and give him the chance he'll bore you into an ambulatory grave—but he's not in Ramsay's league when it comes to backstabbing and shape-shifting. Still, if they did have to haul Ramsay out of there on a stretcher and Malcolm went in in his place, then that right there establishes the precedent for me once Dawn's belly starts to look like she swallowed a watermelon. Anyway, the good news is on the galago side of things. Gretchen, all animated at the window, gives me the privilege of being the first to know about it: Lola's a mother. Of twins. "It's a total surprise," she tells me, her eyes swelling with excitement. "Truthfully, I didn't even know she was pregnant."

"Sneaky little bastards," I say. "You never saw them going at it?"

She shakes her head. The inside of the glass seems to be misting up for some reason and I wait a moment while she leans forward and smears a palm across it. "Uh-uh," she says, "but of course whatever happened would have happened at night . . . you didn't see anything, did you? On the cameras, I mean? Or you haven't been on night shift lately, right?"

I tell her it would have been Jeff, most likely. "Or Ellen Shapiro. They've got her on it now too."

She's nodding her head in thought, the blurred image of her face receding into the smear across the windowpane, then bobbing up again, watery, gray, and yet with the same orangey saffron cast as Dawn's. It comes to me that they're all poisoning themselves in there, even if it is with beta-carotene, and I wonder what I'd look like after a year inside. Darker? Yellower? More *Asian*? *Is that your favorite color, Linda, yellow?* one of the boys in elementary school— Eddie Bricker—used to taunt, though it baffled me at the time since maybe a third of the class was either Chinese or Korean and all I could think was, *Why me?*

"You know, I'll have to ask her," she says. "I'd be interested to know if she saw anything—or better yet, if it was captured on film. You think it would be on film?"

"Hey, your guess is as good as mine. But they're so secretive, right? And there's so much vegetation—"

"I guess they're not really exhibitionists," she says then, laughing, really lit up by the news, a fact I find both pathetic and touching—pathetic because she really ought to get a life, as Johnny says about us all, and touching because it says so much about her, about her dedication and the kind of teammate she is. She's giving this her all, mentally, physically and spiritually, totally submersed in the universe of E2, maybe the most dedicated Terranaut of them all. What I'm thinking in that moment is just how she's going to react once Dawn's secret is out—it won't be pretty, that's for sure. And if that gives me a kind of anticipatory thrill, I'm sorry—call it Schadenfreude. Call it being fed up with my so-called best friend who goes right ahead and sinks her hooks into Gavin Helgeland even though she knows I'm totally into him and all the while she's screwing my biggest enemy on this planet. And telling me she's in love on top of it, as if I'm supposed to care, or what, cheer her on? Well, let her stew in it, that's what I'm thinking. Let Gretchen have at her. And all the others too.

"But she's being a good mother? Lola, I mean?"

"Oh, the *best*. Since I discovered them? I mean, it was just yesterday night and at first I couldn't be sure—they're so tiny, like mice almost—I've pretty much done nothing but scope her through the binoculars and as far as I can tell she's not rejecting either one of them. Which, as you know, isn't always the case with galagos bred in captivity." She pauses to swipe at the window, leaving another long smear. "Like poor Luna. Did you know her mother at the primate center rejected her and she had to be bottle-fed, which we were afraid would make her too dependent on humans?"

"Isn't that the whole point, though? They're not captive, not anymore, not if E2's working—"

"Right," she says, "you're right, absolutely." Her voice rides up out of a deep well of satisfaction, and she's as different in that moment from the woman who beat herself up over Ramsay as to be another person altogether. "It's working. It's really working."

* * *

All this aside, you have to realize my job is what defines me more than anything during this period, more than the circus going on in E2 or the so-called night life of Tillman, the vodka and soda and the ever rarer one-night stand. I'm no longer anonymous, not the gofer I started out as or just another set of eyeballs and a good strong back in the ag plots—by this point, by dint of fierce dedication and cultivating the right people (read Judy, not Dennis) I've become pretty much indispensable at Mission Control, Judy relying on me increasingly for press duties, correspondence, even conferences. She's come to my desk a dozen times to solicit my opinion on one issue or another, from whether so-and-so's important enough to invite to the solstice celebration to evaluating my fellow Mission Three hopefuls. And to collect the dirt on everybody, of course, which I serve up on a regular basis. That said, I'm still no workaholic/alcoholic, or don't want to admit to being one, and I continue to nourish my hopes as to having a relationship that lasts longer than twenty-four hours, like with Gavin, for instance, a relationship I could see carrying us right through Mission Three closure, whether I go in early or not (which is my highest hope and ambition and what really gets me out of bed in the morning).

At any rate, after spending the afternoon weeding in the greenhouse in the company of Gavin and two of the other newbies (and why is it that what you plant never seems to want to grow and what you don't just seems to thrive no matter how much you hack, abuse and uproot it?), I'm thinking of nothing but a cold shower and a colder drink and maybe a nap, when Gavin says, "You feel like going into town?" and I say, "Yeah, sure, it can't be any hotter than here." The greenhouses were scorching, of course, like the hole they put Paul Newman in in *Cool Hand Luke,* and he's thinking of the air-conditioning at Alfano's, same as me. "Give me ten minutes," I say, and then, thinking of my hair, "—or twenty,

twenty okay?" And if we see Tricia Berner trudging by (fucked and abandoned by Dennis, as per his modus operandi), neither of us even bothers to glance up.

So Alfano's. There's some sort of jazz trio set up in the corner, guitar, saxophone and drums, and the place is packed, which really seems to be taxing the air conditioner, but I'm relieved to see that Johnny's not there and if John (of the white hair and three gold teeth) trots over to our table to dribble out a few pleasantries, it doesn't bother me a bit. Gavin's all smiles and talking nonstop, pouring on the charm, which means he wants something—the same something I want—and after the second vodka soda I switch to wine and once we get beyond the shop talk I'm feeling no pain. Of course, there's a game being played here, the same game that plays out hundreds of thousands of times a day through all the time zones and all the countries of the world, the male plying the female and sweetening the deal with drink and comestibles (I was dying for the veal scallopine but didn't want to get into the whole meat-is-murder business so went with the scampi), but it's the most enjoyable game I've played in a long time. He's good-looking, Gavin, really good-looking, with his ready smile and his filled-out chest and shoulders that have nothing to do with the moronic practice of pumping iron but just genes and good honest E2-consecrated hard work, and if all he can seem to talk about is frogs for the first half hour, that's just fine with me.

"Why frogs?" I say.

He's got a bottle of beer to his lips and pulls it seductively down to where we can both see it propped in his hand as if he's doing a TV spot for Coors. "Because they're essential to the food chain," he says, waving the bottle. "Because they're our canary-in-a-coal-mine and they're going extinct all over the world quicker than you can blink."

Frogs. I am talking frogs with Gavin Helgeland as a prelude to dinner, more drinks and sex, either at his place or mine. Or both. I've never had so much fun in my life. "Go on," I say. "I'm listening."

"They can't figure out what's killing them off—and there's all sorts of theories on this, from loss of habitat to pesticides to some kind of fungus. You hear about this?" He's really working himself up, giving a virtuoso performance, showing me he's got a brain as well as a body, which I already knew, but pour it on, that's what I'm thinking. "There's one theory that it's coming from the African clawed frog, the ones they used to use for pregnancy tests all over the world?"

I don't know what he's driving at, actually, or what he knows (Dawn's best bud), but at this point, because it seems relevant—crucial, really—to what's to come, I just say, "I'm on the pill myself."

"Great," he says, brushing the hair out of his eyes, "great. Of course you are. But before the pill—and, more to the point, those handy little pregnancy test kits, they had the frog. Which has the weirdest property. You know how they did the test?"

I shake my head.

"Take a urine sample, inject it into the frog's dorsal lymph sack in the morning—a female frog, that is, and only the African clawed—and within eight to twelve hours the frog'll be laying eggs. If the woman's pregnant, that is. Otherwise, no reaction."

"What woman?" I say, toying with him.

For a minute he looks lost, as if he just woke up and found himself here, across the table from me, with a scent of garlic and tomato sauce hanging heavy in the air and the drummer in the corner swishing away at his cymbal with the brushes they use instead of sticks when they take the volume down. "The woman who gave in the sample," he says finally, searching my face to see if I'm joking.

"Oh," I say, "so that'd be the woman who peed in the jar."

He laughs. At just the right minute.

I set down my glass, fold my hands and lean in confidentially. "And what about the poor frog," I say. "Doesn't she even get laid?"

At some point, after Gavin excuses himself to go to the men's for the second time, I'm sitting there going with the flow, the bar chatter rising and falling, the cymbals swishing, the saxophone groaning all the way down in the lowest—and sexiest—register, when I feel a tap on my shoulder, and there he is, Johnny, standing there in a retro white-on-black zip-up jacket, giving me a quizzical look. "You here by yourself?" he asks.

I shake my head. "I'm with Gavin," I say, nodding toward the men's.

He's standing there, shifting his weight from one boot to the other, waiting for me to invite him to sit down, but I'm not going to do that and he gets it, or at least seems to. "Which one's he?" he says, at the same time patting down his pockets as if he's looking for a smoke, which he's not.

"The good-looking one," I say, and bring the wineglass to my lips just to have something to do.

He lets a beat go by, still standing there over the table, while the jazz trio lurches from "Night and Day" into "The Girl from Ipanema," as if they're doing a medley for schizophrenics, then he says, "I saw Dawn the other day."

"Good for you," I say. "What do you want me to do, applaud?"

He ignores this. His hands are stuffed deep in his pockets now, and what's he doing, rattling his keys? Is he nervous, is that it? With me? "She's not looking so hot. Kind of skinny in the wrong places. And her skin's this weird shade of orange that makes her look like one of the aliens in that movie, what is it—*Buckaroo Banzai*?"

"I don't want to be rude, Johnny, but really, what's it to you?"

He ignores this too. "I hear she's with Ramsay now."

"Why ask me? Ask her, why don't you?"

"I did."

"And?"

It's hard for him to get this out and I realize it's because it's just too uncool to admit to having lost her not only to science and the glass walls of E2 but to somebody on the level of Ramsay on top of it. The saxophone rises to a kind of syncopated wail. A couple of people are trying to catch hold of the rhythm on the little eight-by-eight strip of dance floor, but not very successfully. "I was just wondering how serious it is—I mean, once she gets out . . . like when she has more options?"

It's been a night. Best night yet—for weeks anyway, months even. I can't emphasize how much I enjoy seeing him standing there squirming. I'm not even looking at him, just letting my gaze wander round the room till it settles on the back of the bleached head of some random woman in her forties, nodding to the beat, and then I do look at him and say, "Don't flatter yourself."

That's when Gavin reappears and the two of them have to take a minute to assess the situation, their faces showing nothing but their minds working overtime to pinpoint just who exactly this other person is and why does he look so familiar?

"It's Johnny, Gavin," I say, my voice riding up over the *shh-shh-shh* of the snare drum and rasping buzz of the saxophone. "You've met before. Dawn's ex? Boyfriend, that is."

The light of recognition. A mutual application of *Oh, yeah, yeah, how's it going?* and then Johnny cocks a finger over one eyebrow in a farewell salute and he's gone, picking his way through the couples on the dance floor and back to his seat at the far end of the bar. Gavin sits heavily, tips back his empty glass. The interlude seems to have deflated us, not least because it's managed to bring Dawn back into the picture, and maybe it's my bad luck or maybe I'm imagining things, but from that point on the whole night just seems to go into a tailspin, from Gavin saying, "You ready to call it a night?" to my saying, "Sure," and the mostly quiet ride on the way back with me driving and my glasses clamped over my face like a torture device, which ends with—not sex—but a long tight full-body embrace with some tongue in it, but no more, because Gavin, well, he has to get up early.

* * *

A week goes by, then another, and from all the day-to-day activity inside you'd never guess anything has changed, which it hasn't really, or not yet, apparently. The secret remains secret—Richard's not talking, Dawn and Ramsay aren't talking, and I'm certainly not, though the tension's killing me. I'm on the monitors now as much as possible, whether I'm assigned to be or not, studying faces—not galagos, not systems, not the African leopard tortoises installed in the savanna to graze on the grasses there or the door to the banana storeroom in the basement, just faces. Ever since Dawn clued me, I've been in a state of high anxiety. It's like being out on the Great Plains when you can see a storm coming from thirty miles off, the wind picking up, the ceiling closing in, and you're just waiting for the first twitchy flash and the thunderclap that breaks the sky open. I've gone to the window three times at our appointed hour and three times she blew me off, twice sending Gyro down to make an excuse for her—late milking, repairs to the goat pen because Goanna's been breaking out and chewing her way through the IAB—but the third time not even bothering. Finally, at the end of the second week, I get her on the phone, but of course I can't really say anything over the line since (and who would know better than I?) it might as well be hooked up to a public address system. Still, I get her to promise to come to the window that night at eight—"Why, what's up?" she wants to know and I say, "Just to catch up, that's all"—and after dinner I head over to the window with my folding chair.

Right away I can see how stressed she is—Johnny was right. She doesn't even look like herself anymore, her eyes so huge and wet they're bleeding out of her head and her cheekbones like some sort of galvanized metal screwed in place, as if I'm talking to the Tin Man—or the Tin Woman. I can't help myself. "Dawn, Jesus," I say, "you look like shit—"

She's perfectly still a moment, the phone clamped to one ear. Her legs are bare, stippled with scratches, moles, the odd purple blotch of a bruise. She's wearing her red MDA T-shirt, the one her mother got her, and it drains all the color right out of her. "Thanks for the compliment."

"I don't mean it that way—I just mean you look like you need a rest. More than a rest. Like a week in bed. What does Richard say? Have you been to him—for a checkup, I mean?"

"Maybe I am a little tired," she admits. "Beat, if you want to know the truth. More than anything? It's the tension." She drops her eyes, studies her nails. "You can't imagine what it's like, knowing that any minute this is all going down the tubes—and even worse, that I'm going to wind up the butt of a joke, the Terranaut who couldn't keep her pants on. Ha-ha-ha."

We're both silent a moment. Above me, the sky is shading into night and the bats are out, jerking themselves back and forth after whatever slim pickings the desert's offering up by way of flies and moths. Plenty to eat inside, if only they could break through the glass—and no competition either, since the original E2 bats died off mysteriously during Mission One and the mosquitoes, from what I hear, have become the most successful species in there, aside maybe from the cockroaches.

"So you still won't put it to Richard? Have you even talked to him about it?"

Her voice goes cold. "I've talked to him, yes. And he feels the same way I do—it's not worth the risk because what if something went wrong?"

"Jesus, listen to yourself! If something went wrong—*hello,* it already has. I mean, what's the choice—either you're going to have to come out or Richard's going to have a whole lot more on his hands than what, a *procedure*?" I give an incredulous laugh. "Can you see him delivering a baby?"

"Yes," she says, very softly.

"Yes, what?"

"Yes, I can see him delivering a baby."

Talk about a defining moment. I'm on my feet now, right there at the glass, no more than a foot from her. Her eyes won't go away. She seems to be clenching her teeth, a hard line of muscle tightening all the way up her jaw and into the hard metallic cast of her cheekbones. "I don't believe you," I say. "Have you lost your mind?"

She just shrugs, as if the question's irrelevant, as if the whole fate of E2, the fate of all of us, isn't hanging in the balance. "What about Ramsay, what about *Vodge*?" I say, looking to use anything I can, even him, as if I could care about his feelings—if he even has feelings, which I doubt. "You're telling me you're going to dump this on him? Does that make any sense?"

"He wants me to get rid of it. Obviously."

"Well?"

Now she looks away, evasive, rocking on her feet. "What choice do I have?"

"Get down on your knees to Richard—you said he was coming on to you, right? That one time? He'll do it. I'm sure he will. For you, but for the mission too. I mean, it's as important to him as it is to any of us, right?"

"I already told you, I'm not going to put that on him."

"What are you telling me—you're not a feminist? You don't own the rights to your own body?"

Another shrug.

"You're going to have to break closure then. G.C. and Judy certainly aren't going to let you go through with this, you know that." (Of course, I have mixed feelings here, talking on the one hand as best friend, while on the other I should be arguing for her to have it, because then she's out and I'm in. Or that's the way the signs are pointing.) "And besides, Richard's no obstetrician, you said it yourself—and there could be complications, you ever think of that? People give birth in *hospitals,* Dawn, for a reason—"

She gives me that little smile of hers and in that moment I hate her, I really hate her. "What about all the thousands of years before hospitals even existed?" she says. "What about the women in the fields who just went off under a tree and came back an hour later with the baby strapped to their chest and went right back to work? What about them?"

"This isn't the fields," I shoot back at her.

"Oh, no?" She drops the phone then and backs up to where she can reach the draped blankets that serve as a screen, giving the nearest one a good yank till it drops at her feet and we can both see clear through to the animal pens and the crops standing tall in the IAB, wheat, sorghum, white-tasseled corn, everything reaching for the sky. The look on her face? It's hateful, stupid, reckless. And nothing short of triumphant.

* * *

I'm not one to betray confidences and I'm not all that happy about what I do next, but it has to be done, if not for my own sake—and yes, why shouldn't I think about myself here, is that such a sin?—then for the sake of the mission. And not only the current mission but all the ones to follow. Dawn doesn't really leave me much choice, does she? And friendship, what I have with her—what I had—can't always be the first consideration, not when the issue's the overall cohesion and well-being of the group. Any sociologist will tell you that, any ethicist, for that matter.

Next day, after work, I linger at my desk, waiting for the right moment to approach Judy. Give her credit, Judy, she puts in long hours, the telephone practically an extension of her right arm—it's as if she's become a new species altogether, *Homo telephonicus.* (I coined that one myself, making a lunchtime joke with Gavin and some of the others, none of whom seemed to find it all that funny, but so what? I do.) Mission Control features a series of big arched windows looking out on E2 from the front and the Santa Catalinas in back and all the wide-open space in between, and it's a beautiful building in its own right. At times it can really hum, what with visiting scientists and scholars, reporters, maintenance people, conferees, the sixteen of us plus Dennis, Judy and, when he's around, G.C., but right now isn't one of them. It's midweek, the schedule vacant, no crises in the air and the next celebration—summer solstice—still over two months off. Judy's on the phone. I'm at my desk. It's just past six and Jeff and Ellen have arrived and settled in, Jeff making the rounds and Ellen sitting at the bank of monitors fed by all those continuously operating cameras inside the Ecosphere.

My plans for the evening, once I get this over with, are to walk back to the Residences, pour myself a cautiously celebratory shot of *Bem Ju,* get into bed and watch a movie on TV, something light, the lighter the better—a chick flick, preferably, because that's what I am, a chick, and sometimes I want nothing more than to just wallow in sentiment, whether it's artificial or not. I'm thinking about the limited options we get here by way of broadcast TV out of Tucson and wondering if maybe I could borrow a videocassette or two from Rita, who's a real movie junkie, when I see Judy stirring around in her office as if she's getting ready to lock up and leave. G.C.'s away this week and I have no idea what she does with her private life (now that Ramsay's no longer available, that is), but I can't picture her getting into bed with a movie because she's not that kind of person, or at least not the way I read her.

I catch her just as she throws open the door of her office, her purse slung over one arm and her jacket—an orange-and-black cotton batik she got in Sedona—over the other. She's wearing all black to set off the jacket and her silver necklace and earrings and she's in a skirt and heels, which is typical for her—let the rest of us wear jeans and tees, but not her, not Judy. Her official title is President and Director of Operations of SEE (Space Ecosphere Enterprises) and she's my age but at the same time she manages to look younger and seem older, if that makes any sense. Let's call her serious. All business. A bitch, classically defined. And if she doesn't exactly radiate warmth, well, neither do I.

"Judy," I say, "got a minute?"

She gives me a blank look, then the official smile snaps into place. "Depends. I'm just on my way out the door." We both take a minute with that, her hand on the door, me blocking her way, and why is my heart pounding? "Literally," she says, and I take this as a signal to smile myself.

"It's about Dawn," I say, lowering my voice.

Dawn Chapman

The thing that always amazed me is how we could have built any world we wanted—or worlds. If there were ten G.F.s, ten billionaires willing to open their wallets, we could have built ten more ecospheres and stocked them with any biota we wanted and let the ecosystems balance themselves. Or not. People always wondered why we didn't just stick to one biome, let's say the rain forest—three point one-five acres of rain forest—and stock it exclusively with the living things that had evolved together over the eons, as a suite, which would have made more sense than attempting the mix-and-match world we inhabited, with galagos from Africa living in a forest from the Amazon amidst coquis from Puerto Rico, anoles from Cuba, blue-tongued skinks from Australia and cockroaches from everywhere. But that misses the point: if we wanted to study the rain forest, we could have just gone there (we did, in fact, or at least G.C., Judy and a team of biologists did, to extract most of the plants and creatures for our sample), yet nowhere could you find an ecosystem like the one under glass in E2. And think about it: purists criticized us for creating an artificial environment stocked with species of plants and animals that normally wouldn't come into contact with one another, but outside the glass we're all living in what scientists have begun calling the Anthropocene Age, dominated by man, which has defined itself by doing just that. To take an example, look at our volunteer house sparrows. They weren't supposed to be in the Arizona desert—or even in America at all. They were introduced from England in 1851 all the way across the country in Brooklyn, New York, and here they were in E2, creating their own niche under the glass.

What people didn't realize was that the special gift of E2 was in presenting a *possible* world with an eye toward tweaking it over the course of a century to create an ideal one. The whole idea behind species packing is to see which ones will find that niche and survive and how they'll contribute to the whole—at the end of a century we'll see genetic variation that makes E2's biota unique from anything else on earth. And, of course, beyond earth—because from the outset, in G.C.'s vision, the big question was could we create an independent self-generating ecosphere to take us into space (or in the worst-case scenario, sustain life on this planet in the face of a systemic worldwide collapse). Better than three years in, we were proving it could be done, and I was as proud of that fact—and as proud to be part of it—as anyone on the Mission Two crew. And what does that mean, what am I trying to say? That means closure absolute and unbreakable, nothing in, nothing out, no matter what happens to me or anybody else.

The more I thought about it—and since Richard had confirmed what I already knew in my heart of hearts I'd thought about little else—I began to realize the human element was as vital to the experiment and as random as any other factor. If it wasn't Ramsay in here it would have been somebody else—Malcolm, Jeff Weston—and if it wasn't me it might have been Linda or Tricia or any of the others, and then this wouldn't have happened, or not exactly in this way, not to me. Not to Vodge. Not to everything we believed in and lived for.

I went through my days. The nausea came and went. Richard didn't say a word. Vodge pressured me to deal with the situation (*Get rid of it,* he said, over and over, and I said *How, how, tell me how?*), while Linda kept urging me to come back out into the real world and get the kind of medical care I was going to need, because why take chances, that was what she felt. She was thinking of me, Linda, thinking of me above herself, and to her mind my safety and well-being took precedence over anything, even the purity of the mission. ("You could *die,*" she'd said, coming down heavily on the verb. "People don't die in childbirth anymore," I countered. "They do if they're not in a hospital." "Don't be ridiculous," I said. "You're the one being ridiculous," she said, as if that was the end of it.)

When Judy called me in for a PicTel conference a day or two after my talk with Linda, I didn't know what to expect. I was sick with anxiety, of course, though I wasn't ready for the full extent of what was coming. More than five weeks had passed since the day I'd gone to Richard, everything in limbo, and as far as I knew my secret was still intact. There were only three of us in on it (plus Linda, who was sworn to secrecy, at least till I could sort things out on my own terms), I had unshakeable confidence in both Richard and Vodge, and certainly I hadn't let anybody else know—and I definitely wasn't showing, not yet. Not unless I stood in front of the mirror, naked—and I did, every morning—and felt the protrusion there, the little bump of a belly we'd all lost within a month of closure and I was now putting back on.

What day was it? A Monday or Tuesday, I think, though it's hard to pinpoint since our days were so much alike as to be interchangeable, but for Sundays, and it definitely wasn't a Sunday. Call it a Tuesday, mid-April, Year Two of Closure. I'd got up earlier than usual, feeling steadier, as if I'd come through a storm at sea and now the decks had leveled out. The first sensation I felt was hunger, and no ordinary hunger, the hunger we all lived with day in and day out, but something more basic yet: a craving. Not for pickles and ice cream or chocolate fudge brownie batter straight from the mixing bowl (though that would have been just fine, all of it), but for meat, lobster, shrimp, the pepperoni pizza Johnny had teased me about so long ago, Chinese takeout hot from the carton, bratwurst buried in sauerkraut, the things I didn't have and couldn't have. I found myself out in the rain forest at first light, and yes, I picked a half-ripe banana and bolted it down, though it wasn't right and wasn't fair to the others, and after that I slipped on my shoes against the thorns and drifted into the savanna where our passion fruit vines had gone crazy, climbing right up over the canopy of the acacias. I devoured three passion fruits in quick succession, split them open and jammed them in my mouth, seeds and all, and still that didn't satisfy me (pulp, sugar, potassium, iron, copper, magnesium and phosphorous, vitamins A and C and yet more beta-carotene), so I went back to the rain forest, barefoot again, and found a hideaway off the path where I could filch a handful of the monkey chow Gretchen put out for the galagos. It was grainy, like dog biscuit, and faintly sweet, and I didn't know its analysis though it must have contained protein, but that hardly mattered—I chewed, I swallowed, it became part of me. Someone would have been on the cameras up in Mission Control, but there were a lot of cameras and if you had twenty people watching they couldn't have picked up everything. Or so I told myself.

Then there was the morning milking (and yes, though I hated myself for it, I took a sip—just one sip—out of each of the four tins, the milk warm in my throat and what was inside me crying out for more). I worked the IAB, sat down to breakfast like a prizefighter—or no, one of those huge-headed football players you see on TV—and was the first one finished and licking her plate. Which didn't go unnoticed by Richard. Or Vodge. Though neither one commented on it, nor anyone else either. And me? What was I looking forward to? Lunch. It was my day to cook and the cook invariably snuck herself a little extra as the veggies gathered on the cutting board and the soup thickened in the pot. Beyond that, there was a void. Everything anybody said, every movement they made, crushed me, because nothing had changed, because there was life inside of me and it wasn't going away and I could see my crewmates spinning out and away from me, growing more unreal by the day. They were ghosts. The living dead. It was all going to come thundering down—and it was my fault, mine and nobody else's.

The first thing Judy said when I sat down before the PicTel screen was, "You're alone in the room, right?"

I looked at her, at the bleached-out mask of her face, her no-nonsense hair swept back behind her ears, the sharp glare of her eerily lit eyes, and knew exactly what was coming. "I'm alone," I whispered, the blood pounding in my ears.

"What's that? I can't hear you! I *said*, 'Are you alone?'"

"Yes."

She paused, as if too worked up to go on. I watched her lick her lips, tug at an earring. Her eyes never left mine. "I hear we have a problem, is that the case? Because if it isn't, you tell me now."

I felt ashamed, guilty, deeply guilty, but something else too: irritated. All the weight had been on me. I was the one who couldn't sleep, who'd vomited through a whole month of mornings and lived in terror of this moment, but appearances to the contrary, I was no lab rat to be prodded, examined and dictated to. It came to me that I didn't like Judy. That I'd never liked Judy. "Ask Richard. Or I guess you already did, right?"

"I'm asking *you*. The rumor I hear is that somehow, despite everything, despite what all this means—to everybody concerned, *Jeremiah* especially—you've managed to go and get yourself knocked up, is that right?"

I didn't say anything, just held her gaze on the monitor, which was unsettling in itself, both of us electronically disembodied and contending over what was happening in the flesh, deep inside of me. Of me. Not her, not Jeremiah, not anybody but me. "That's the way it looks," I said, and felt the burden lift from me.

Another pause. Her face, grainy, overlit, artificial, took on a pained look, as if she'd swallowed something unexpected, vinegar instead of water. "We are not breaking closure," she said with slow deliberate emphasis.

Before I could think, I said, "Agreed."

I watched her strain to process this—she'd clearly expected something else, opposition, entreaty, defiance—and now she had to back up and recalibrate. There were two possibilities only if you followed her logic: either Richard was induced (ordered) to do a second trimester "procedure" or I would come to term and deliver my baby inside. I wasn't fooled, of course—she wasn't offering a choice, just the opposite, but in that moment I began to see how right it was to go ahead with what my body was telling me no matter what anybody said. If Lana could give birth, if Penelope could produce a new litter of piglets and the frogs and lizards and all the rest regenerated their kind, then so could we, so could I—and wasn't that the most natural thing in the world?

"We're not," she repeated. "And no, I haven't talked to Richard about it, but you can bet I will, because we need to come up with a solution here, do you understand me? ASAP. We can't have you going around, what—*showing*—with all the tourists, the scientists, the press? That's not going to happen. And we are *not* breaking closure—so you tell me."

"Tell you what? It seems like you're doing all the telling here."

"Christ, how could you be so stupid! Aren't you on the pill? Isn't that what your contract specifies? And Ramsay!" She had to stop again. "What an idiot, what a fuck-up! Don't you think, don't you ever think? Any of you people?"

At this point, I was no longer listening. All I felt, beyond the relief of finally getting it out in the open, was anger. Anger at Judy, yes, but even more at Linda, because if Judy hadn't found out from Richard, then it had to have been either Linda or Vodge who'd gone behind my back, and I was as sure of Vodge as I was of myself, wasn't I?

* * *

Next morning, at breakfast meeting, Diane took up the banana and announced, "People, we have a problem here," then slid it across the table to me. "E., maybe you want to tell us about it?"

This was the moment I'd dreaded most—having to explain myself to my crewmates and let them know that we were no longer unified as a team, that I'd let them down and the mission too. Despite what Judy had said, her insistence on maintaining closure was just a bluff, a way of pressuring me to undergo the procedure she would pressure Richard to perform, and what she was really saying was that if I didn't comply she and G.C. would have no recourse but to throw open the airlock and fatally compromise the mission. Which put it all on me. Not Vodge (who was sitting right beside me, slumped down in his chair, holding his head in his hands) or the life force or even the conditions under which E2 molded the way we lived. I remember looking round at the expectant faces of my crewmates, counting off the ones who didn't yet know—Gyro, Stevie, T.T. and Gretchen—and wondering just how to frame what I was going to say. I felt choked up. The moment hung there, huge and inflated, all eyes on me, and I didn't think I could go through with it till Vodge sat back up, threw a glance round the table and took hold of my hand right there in front of everybody.

"I'm pregnant," I blurted. "Three and a half months. Or four, closer to four. I'm sorry. It's the last thing I—" I had to stop to compose myself. I was sweating. My heart rate must have been off the charts. No one moved. They just sat there in shocked silence, Gyro hardening his jaw, Gretchen searing me with an incendiary look, Stevie and T.T. very nearly smirking, as if they'd expected nothing less, as if I was dirt, not to be trusted, and they'd known all along it would come to this. Or something like it. Which was absurd. And wrong. And showed me just how tenuous and artificial our relationship had been, which I think hurt me more than anything. "It's Vodge," I went on, "but you all know that. We're in love. And we never in our wildest dreams—or nightmares, because that's what this is—ever imagined anything like this." I was giving a speech, nervous, rattled, the words pouring out of me like I'd lost control, and I would have gone on, would have tried to *explain,* but Gyro cut me off, though I still had possession of the banana.

"So what does that mean?"

"I don't know." My voice shrank down to nothing. I tried to hold myself perfectly still but I was trembling and there was nothing I could do about it. "I really . . . I don't know."

"You're not telling us you're going to *keep* it?" He shot a look to Richard and now so did everybody else.

"I'm sorry, but I don't believe what I'm hearing," Stevie put in, and she had hold of Troy's hand now, as if to make her own statement about who was in love with whom and just what it meant. "You're four months' gone and you wait till now to tell us about it? What did you think, it was just going to go away? Aren't we supposed to be a team here?" Then, to Richard: "Well, what about you—how long have *you* known?"

The seating arrangement that morning had Diane at the head of the table with me at the far end, Vodge, Gyro and Gretchen to my left, T.T., Stevie and Richard to my right. Overhead, the ceiling was canopied to give us shade, but an intense coruscating light streamed in from the orchard beyond, making the dust motes visible in the air. We could hear the technosphere breathing for us and circulating our vital fluids, while the usual sounds of the biomes chirped and honked and croaked in the near distance. I realized that in my distraction I was holding on to the banana and I slid it across the table to Richard, because that was the right thing to do—we had to maintain protocol, now more than ever. I dropped my eyes. Took a deep breath.

Richard picked up the banana and gave it a long look, as if he'd never seen anything like it, then answered Stevie with a shrug.

"Go ahead, Richard," Diane said, though she was out of turn herself. "I'd really like to hear this."

Richard's gaze went to me. His eyes were soft, calm, leached of color in the morning light. "Dawn?" he asked, lifting his eyebrows.

"Yes," I said, giving him permission. There was nothing to hide, not anymore.

He set the banana down on the tabletop before him, gave it an idle twirl so that it spun like a pointer in a child's game—and who did it point to, whether by accident or design? Vodge. "To answer your question, I guess I'd have to say something like four, five weeks now. As her physician," he added.

"But why?" Diane demanded, beyond protocol at this point. "Why didn't you tell us—tell me, your team captain? Did you think nobody would notice?" She leveled a furious look on all of us, as if we were all equally to blame, but no one more than Richard. "You're our *medical officer,* and you never thought to do anything about it? Were you going to just let her, what, get big as a house?"

"Do what?"

"It's obvious, isn't it?"

"That's not my decision."

"Then whose is it?"

"You want to take a vote? Christ, I didn't sign on for this. And I am definitely *not,* let me emphasize, an obstetrician. Or a back-room abortionist either."

"We are not breaking closure," Diane insisted, her voice crack-ing. This was hard for her, for all of us, and her insistence, just like Judy's, rang hollow. "We all agreed to that right from the outset. We're different from the Mission One crew, didn't we say that? Didn't we?"

Gretchen's hand shot up, as if we were in a classroom. "This isn't like a severed finger, it's totally different—that was an infec-tion, that was life and death—"

"That's exactly what this is," Stevie snapped, staring right into me. "Life and death. That's what we're talking about here, isn't it?"

I could feel Vodge beside me, tensing in his seat. He'd thought all this out beforehand—we both had, up past midnight the night before and sorting through all the possibilities over and over—and he couldn't hold it in any longer. He made a sudden lunge for the banana and brandished it like a fetish. "Yes, we said that. Of course we did. And nothing has changed."

"Are you out of your fucking mind? She's *pregnant* for Christ's sake!" Gyro came up out of his chair, as angry as I'd ever seen him, and that anger was all about me—he'd made his declaration, the bag of M&M's in hand, and I'd rejected it. He was all angles in that swelling light, thin, towering, ungainly, and I remembered we'd very nearly nicknamed him "Stork" before settling on "Gyro." By one vote. Mine.

Vodge, the banana in his left hand, his right entwined in mine, not budging an inch: "Christ had nothing to do with it. He came way after."

"What the fuck are you saying? After what?"

A smile for the table. "Adam," Vodge said, and then he gave up the banana.

* * *

Everything was so strange in that period I can barely keep things straight even now. I thought I'd known what to expect, thought everything was on course, and suddenly it wasn't. Take Johnny (and this was among the stranger things because I'd thought that was over for good). One evening, out of the blue, he showed up at the visitors' window. This would have been before my secret was out, but how much before, I can't say. A week? A month? I don't know. I was in my room, I remember that much. I was alone, feeling cored out, angry, afraid of everything and everybody, Vodge acting like a shit and Richard's news pinning me to the bed like a new form of gravity. Maybe I was crying. I probably was. I cried a lot then, though I hid that from everybody too. There would have been a knock at the door. Gyro. "E., there's somebody here for you."

Despite myself, I felt a quick sharp flare of interest. "Who?"

Gyro's face would have hung there, fighting for a neutral expression when he wasn't neutral at all. "That guy you used to go with—Johnny?"

It was siesta time, early afternoon, the world ablaze outside the glass, and there he was, Johnny, without his leather jacket for once, trying to squeeze himself into the narrowing strip of shade cast by the side of the building. He was wearing his jeans and boots—no sandals or running shoes for him—and a black T-shirt featuring the logo of a band I'd never heard of. But then I hadn't heard of much lately—they could have been the newest thing, number one on the charts, and I wouldn't have known the difference. As soon as I picked up the phone, he winked and unfurled a mock bow. "How's it, babe?" he rumbled, receiver to ear, one hand propping himself up against the glass. "You're looking"—he hesitated—"good, real good. Considering."

"Considering what?" I was glad to see him, more than glad: he took me right out of myself. He'd always had that way about him, that insouciance, the ability to change my mood just by walking through the door, and though it was a pose I fell for it all over again.

"Oh, I don't know—the fact that you look like a survivor of something. That and your skin color. Which is just about midway between a peach and an orange. You working on that in there, in lieu of a tan, I mean?"

"I was just saying, the first thing I'm going to do when I get out of here is go lay out in the sun—"

"Careful what you wish for—radio said it was a hundred and eight. You'd fry up like a *chicharrón* out here. All in all? I wouldn't advise it—not till ten minutes before sunset anyway. Or dawn. When you get out of there, let's go do it at dawn, like that time we stayed up all night and went down to the river, remember that?"

I remembered it. We'd stayed up smoking pot and drinking beer, then took a swim and made love on a towel with the sun just grazing the peaks of the mountains. The memory—the picture it gave me, outdoors, freedom, a river that didn't need pumps to keep it flowing—filled me with longing. There was nothing I'd rather do—if I wasn't in here. If I wasn't with Vodge. If I wasn't pregnant.

"Yeah," I said. "I remember."

Neither of us said anything for a moment, then he pushed back from the glass, rearranged himself so that his right shoulder was propping him up and he had to turn his head to look into my eyes. "You're with Ramsay now," he said, a flat statement of fact, not a question, though it had the flavor of hope in it.

I nodded. "Uh-huh. But you knew that, didn't you?"

He would have shrugged, but his shoulder was pinned there against the glass, holding him. up. "No harm in asking, right?"

"What about—what was her name, Rhonda?"

Now he did push himself away from the glass and lift both shoulders in an abbreviated shrug. "She's all right. I guess. Fact is, I haven't seen much of her lately—"

I didn't have anything to say to this. I'd told myself that what he did or didn't do had no bearing on me, not anymore, but you have to understand the state of my emotions just then—suddenly I felt so desolated it took everything I had not to break down right there in front of him.

"She's on hiatus, I guess. On the shelf. The top shelf, way in back?"

"What do you want me to say? I'm sure you'll find somebody else. Knowing you."

He laughed, kicked one boot in the dirt a minute as if to catch his balance, then pressed his right hand to the glass. I matched him, pressing my hand to his, and if I felt the warmth there it was only because the glass was infused with the heat of the desert. "You'll be out before you know it," he said, "you realize that?"

"I wish. It seems like years."

"I'd like to—you know, maybe get together sometime?"

I shook my head, very slowly, three full times.

He looked over my shoulder and let out a sigh. "So that's it, then—no chance for me?"

I started to shake my head again, but then I caught myself. I was all alone—remember, this was before Linda outed me, before Judy, before Vodge grew a backbone—and I didn't know where to turn. What I said was, "You never know."

* * *

A second trimester abortion is called a dilation and evacuation procedure or D&E for short. It most often includes a combination of vacuum aspiration, dilation and curettage, and it's performed in a clinic or hospital on an outpatient basis. The doctor gives the patient a sedative and a dose of antibiotic to guard against infection, positions her on her back on the examining table with her feet up in stirrups, cleans the vagina with an antiseptic solution and inserts the speculum. He then dilates the cervical canal with progressively larger metal probes and passes a thin glass tube (a cannula) into the uterus. The cannula is attached to a pump to remove tissue—fragments of the living fetus—from the uterus. Next, the doctor inserts a forceps to extract the larger pieces before scraping the uterine lining with a curette (a kind of long-handled spoon), finally suctioning out whatever scraps might remain. Potential problems? Heavy bleeding, severe pain, fever, vomiting, abdominal swelling, death. Potential upside? No more worries.

I gleaned all this from the pamphlet Richard gave me after he'd had his own conference with Judy—*and* G.C. *and* Little Jesus. He handed it to me in the hallway at lunch that day, the day it all came out, and I'll tell you lunch wasn't much of a comfort for anybody, the usual gaiety and clowning almost non-existent, conversation kept to a minimum, everybody going around with faces of stone to the point where I felt so hurt and humiliated I had to take my plate and shut myself up in my room. Where was Vodge? I didn't know. He'd been summoned to the command center after breakfast and I hadn't seen him since. I ate alone, on the couch, studying the pamphlet with a kind of numbed fascination, E2 breathing all around me and a spider—a wolf spider, another volunteer—come to join me where it was safe from lizards and chickens. I lifted the fork to my lips, turned the pages, watched the spider pin itself to the wall—it didn't belong here, not officially, but here it was, going about its business, and if it negatively impacted the cockroach population behind the bookcase, nobody was complaining.

I spent the rest of the day in the IAB, tending the plots with Diane, and if she didn't have much to say, that was fine with me. We worked at separate tasks at separate ends of the garden, both of us lost in our thoughts. I made my way up and down the rows of crops, knelt in the dirt, trimmed, weeded, harvested a basket of cherry tomatoes, green peppers, lettuce and scallions, all the while trying to lose myself in the task at hand, but I wasn't very successful. I kept reprising the morning's events, kept seeing the faces of my crewmates twisted in disgust, kept coming back to the fact that not one of them had offered a word of sympathy or consolation or even fellow feeling. What if I'd lost a leg, had a stroke, developed breast cancer? Would they have acted the same way? Or was this different because I'd brought this on myself? Because I'd been weak. Because I'd been stupid.

What I felt worst about was Richard—for having put him in this position. I could only imagine what his meeting with the holy trinity must have been like, the badgering and hectoring and the appeals to loyalty and the higher purpose, Judy's knife edge, G.C.'s thundering, Little Jesus' reedy insinuations, the result of which was evident: he'd handed me the pamphlet, hadn't he? I saw Judy digging it up somewhere and sending it over electronically, where Richard would have had to format it and print it out on six sheets of our precious paper, each sheet neatly quartered and the whole stapled together in its original form—no memo but a *pamphlet,* a how-to, with illustrations. Here was the dilated cervix, here the tube, the curette, everything so neat and simple, simplest thing in the world. Richard could do it. Anybody could. Just take hold of this. And this. Step 1. Step 2. It was a procedure, that was all. And if he was willing, here was my way out—*our* way out.

That was the knowledge I held close as I bent and rose and plied the garden trowel and the clippers while the sun baked my back and the bees hovered over anything in bloom. The logic was clear: if Richard had given me the pamphlet, then that meant that he'd agreed, at least tacitly, to resolve the problem for me, for *us,* and yet why didn't that make me feel any better? Why, actually, did it make me clench inside, as if I were experiencing cramps all over again? I knew why, and it came to me right there in the garden just as it had come to me when Linda first brought it up at the glass, though I wouldn't admit it then—or was just beginning to grope toward it. This was my baby. This was my body. And nobody was going to tell me what to do with it.

Ramsay Roothoorp

When I made that crack about Adam it was only to shut Gyro up, shut them all up, because they were going at E. like hyenas and that just wouldn't stand. I never meant it seriously because the farthest thing from my mind was that she would actually give birth, inside or out—Mission Control would see to that—and all I could think was to help get her past this till we could reason things through. There was no excuse for the way they turned on E., no matter how stupid or careless we'd been—*we,* the two of us, and weren't we equally guilty? I stood up for her, of course I did. Push it any further and I would have gone after them one by one, starting with Gyro—as it was, it took everything I had to keep from planting a fist right in the center of his clenched moronic face. And Gretchen. You'd think after what she'd been through she'd have some sympathy, at least. Or Troy and Stevie, because it could as easily have been them as me and E.

But here was the thing: I was on their side, one hundred percent, the mission *über alles.* Yes, I defended E., but I was determined to keep the pressure on her (and Richard) till the two of them went into that medical lab and shut the door behind them. Or not just the two of them—there'd have to be a nurse, wouldn't there? Diane, maybe. Or, though I hated to think of it, Gretchen. Somebody to hand Richard whatever it was he was going to need, and I have to admit I was fairly hazy on this, my experience of the operating room limited to what I'd seen in the movies and on TV. Was there a danger to E.? I suppose there was, but abortion (or "choice" or "termination" or whatever euphemism you want to use) was one of the commonest medical procedures in the world and the chances of complications were right down around zero.

Two percent, actually. Granted, we had to take into account the fact that Richard had never done anything like this before, but how complicated could it be? Women had been having abortions since the first penis had gone up the first vagina—and imagine what the population of the earth would be without it? We'd have ten billion by now, fifteen, who knew how many?

At the conclusion of the meeting, which settled nothing, of course, and felt like it went on forever, E. and I went directly down the steps and into the orchard, thinking to have a minute to ourselves while the others lingered at the table, their voices a thin buzz of complaint and outrage as everybody tried to sort out the implications of what had just gone down. E. was a mess. I had hold of her hand still, but it was as if I was holding on to an abstraction. She was slouching. Her feet were dirty and there were smudges on both cheeks where she must have been crying at some point, though with the intensity of what we'd just gone through I'm afraid I hadn't noticed. Still, I'd never seen her more beautiful—or pathetic, really, and maybe that had something to do with it. She was like the Madonna of the Sorrows. Or no, I don't want to say that. No Madonna, no mother, just E., Dawn Chapman, the girl—woman—I was in love with and whose trouble was of my own making, trouble I was determined to put an end to. And what did I come up with then, of all the possible things I could have thought to say? A banality. A phrase as meaningless under the circumstances as if I'd been reading from the label of a can of peas. I said, "There, that wasn't so bad, was it?"

She pulled her hand away (I'd say "jerked it away," but that wouldn't be accurate—she just disengaged, that was all, as if she couldn't stand the touch of me). "Are you for real?" she said. "I thought I was going to die."

"But you didn't, did you? And now it's over, at least—"

"*What's* over, what are you talking about? Are you out of your mind?"

The sun, which had apparently (who was paying attention?) been obscured behind one of our rare clouds, came at us in a sudden burst, striping her face with the thin shadows of the struts. "I mean it's off your chest now—off *our* chests, I mean—and we can start to do something about it—"

"You're the one talking in circles now."

"I'm not. I've told you right from the beginning, from the minute you laid this on me—"

"*I* laid it on *you*? We're back to that? Jesus, I thought you were going to stand up for me, I really did—"

"—that there's one solution to this and one solution only. Mission Control's going to come down heavy on Richard, you know that. And if Richard comes aboard, problem solved, right? Right?"

But she wasn't talking—she just gave me a sidelong glance and turned her back on me. I felt a surge of anger and I don't know what I would have done next, though I was a heartbeat away from snatching her elbow to jerk her around and *make* her listen, when Diane entered the picture. She called my name—not my crew name, but the one I bore out there in the real world, if that says anything about the momentousness of the occasion—and I turned to see that she was right there behind me, the chopped-off mess of her hair like some avian display under the assault of the sun, and what she'd heard or hadn't heard I could only guess.

"What is it?" I snapped, and I almost added, *Can't you see we're having a moment here?,* but thought better of it.

"You're wanted up in the command center." She gave us both a long look. "It's G.C. Says he wants to talk to you."

* * *

The receiver was lying there next to the phone on the surface of the desk I used in my day-to-day conferences with Dennis, Judy and sometimes G.C., depending on what events were coming up, what promotions we were pushing or school groups were looking to schedule one-on-one visits at the glass with a real, live, in-the-flesh Terranaut. I picked it up, thinking guiltily of how long it must have been lying there—upwards of five minutes, certainly— and thinking too that Judy would be on the extension, which would make things even more awkward. I steeled myself. Said, "Hello, Vodge here."

It wasn't G.C.'s basso that came back at me or Judy's punishing whine, but Dennis' voice, thin and slippery, Vaseline on a wet branch. "Ramsay, hello. I just want to say we're going to need you to dig deep here and do everything in your power to see that this thing is resolved, and no, we're not going to point fingers or say how incomprehensible this is, how staggeringly stupid—of both you and Dawn—because there's really no point. The only relevant point is, we've got a problem here that has the potential to kill the mission—"

"And not just the mission"—Judy now, her voice like the blade of a stiletto extracted from a block of ice—"but the whole SEE, our credibility, our ability to raise funds, now and into the future."

"Right," I said. "I get it. Believe me, I *really* get it."

The window in front of me, diamond shaped, floor to ceiling, looked out on the buff hills to the west, a view that was less than inspiring but had the advantage of being on the far side of E2 from the building that housed Mission Control. Small mercies. I wouldn't have wanted to have to see them high up behind their own reflective windows, looking down on us. I knew G.C. was listening in on his own line—I couldn't hear him breathing or shuffling papers or anything like that, but could divine his presence from the strained stick-up-the-ass way Dennis and Judy were talking. I took a stab at it: "Jeremiah, you there?"

His voice, percussing in my ear like the thump of a big bass drum: "I'm here. And I want to reiterate what Dennis said—I'm not going to rebuke you because we're beyond that now, way beyond, though you've really fucked up this time, my friend, you who were given the keys to this mission right from day one, the only member of the crew, along with Diane, that is, who had the wherewithal, the fiber, to be given any authority—" He went on in that vein for a while, the other two holding their collective breath while I just took everything he had to throw at me, murmuring, "Yes, uh-huh, you're right," at appropriate junctures, till finally he came down on the point to which we were all four agreed: "This has got to be resolved. Now."

Dennis: "We'll be talking with Richard next."

Judy: "If this got out to the press—"

The last thing that had got out to the press—my infection—had got out because she'd wanted it to and we'd all managed to spin that into gold, though I was the one who had to get up from what felt like my deathbed and parade my bloodless half-delirious self around for the benefit of the cameras. "What do you want me to do?" I asked, cutting her off before she could continue the thought.

"What do we want you to *do*?" G.C. cut in, throwing it back at me with all the trumped-up might of his actor's bluster. "Are you not paying attention here? Are you not getting it? What we want, what *I* want, is for you to make it clear to your—your *girlfriend*—that there's only one way out of this, because"—and here I could have harmonized with him—"we are *not* breaking closure."

Dennis: "We're going to run this by Richard, of course, to be sure he's on board—"

Judy: "And capable, of course."

G.C., in full thunder now: "He wouldn't be in there, wouldn't be the Mission Two medical officer, if he wasn't capable, for Christ's sake. Of course he's capable."

"This isn't open-heart surgery," Dennis put in. "I've looked into it, and pretty much any qualified physician can . . . and we're going to bring in a really top-flight man . . . Doctor—what's his name, Judy?"

"Reston, Wallace Reston, from Johns Hopkins—he heads up the Obstetrics Department there."

Dennis: "For a run-through at the window, so everybody knows what's expected of them."

I was a team player. I was in awe of G.C. And I had, indeed, fucked up in a major way. Still, I was feeling just a bit *abraded* here, and I couldn't help wondering aloud, "Everybody who? Does that include *E.*?"

The silence that greeted this was tomb-deep. I heard nothing over the line, not the slightest crackle of static, not the squeak of a chair, the rustle of a sleeve or even a drawn breath. After a beat, G.C., his voice rolling out over the line, intoned, "We'll be talking with her this afternoon. Just after Richard."

"Right," Judy added, "Richard's the key." And here she paused for effect. "And so are you. *Ramsay.*"

* * *

It happened that one of my tasks that day was to wade into the fish ponds with a net and harvest our bimonthly ration of tilapia, which the chef du jour—Stevie—would gut, scale and marinate in lemon juice before skewering for the evening's kabobs, reserving the heads for the fish stock that would form the basis of a mussel-less bouillabaisse for tomorrow's lunch. Believe it or not, this was one of my favorite tasks, a break from the routine and a chance to be off by myself for an hour or two. The first thing I did was take a dip net and skim off a good portion of the azolla to add to E.'s bucket of chicken feed—the more nutrition the better when you're talking about egg production, and you should have seen the way the hens laid when we figured out how to trap cockroaches en masse and add them to the dietary mix (position a bucket on a stool so it's roughly at counter level and stretch a piece of string across the mouth of it, with a second piece dangling in the center to within a couple inches of a nice redolent layer of culinary scraps; the roaches can't resist making the leap but they're unable to get back out, and the whole mess just gets upended next morning in the chicken yard). Then I lowered myself into the water, which was waist-deep and in the eighty-degree range, ignoring the alarmed squeaks and splashes of our various frogs (and yes, we'd eventually wind up eating them too), while focusing on the way the miniature ruptures and eddies roiled the surface, giving away the movements of my quarry.

Tilapia were virtually unknown in this country—as a food source, anyway—until the last few years, when commercial fish farms began to crop up in California and various southern states, but of course they'd been harvested for generations by farmers in

Southeast Asia in the rice/azolla/tilapia feedback loop I mentioned earlier. They're a tropical fish, from Africa originally, requiring warm conditions, and the species we stocked (*Oreochromis*) is a mouthbrooder, so you don't have to worry about trampling nests and eggs as you would with other species. They're incredibly prolific, maturing at two to three months, and the average life span is eight years. We collect them at five or six inches, the size they'll grow to in the time it takes a single rice crop to go from seedling to maturity—four months—which is a pretty good return on investment.

At any rate, there I was in the water, my feet molded to the muck at the bottom, net at the ready, enjoying myself and trying in the process to rigorously suppress any thought of E. and the grilling to which she was no doubt being subjected at that very moment up in the command center. I was accompanied by a cohort of recently hatched damselflies, electric blue, and a couple of their dragonfly cousins that danced and hovered and shone copper-red under the sun, and, of course, by the mosquitoes they were designed to feast on, the average dragonfly capable of eating its own weight in thirty minutes. For once, there didn't seem to be any tourists in the immediate vicinity, and if I blocked out the struts overhead I could imagine myself out in the real world, in a swamp that looked and smelled and felt just like this one, no different from the creek bottoms I'd plied as a boy who thought he'd grow up to be a biologist (which seemed the apex of the professions to me at the time because the vocation of Terranaut didn't yet exist, and, of course, I hadn't yet discovered the power of the written word, which was to take me in a whole different direction altogether). Before long I wasn't thinking at all, just tracing the ripples on the water and swooping in on my prey, one flapping pink-orange streak of protein at a time.

I don't know how long E. was standing there watching me, but at some point she slapped a mosquito and I turned around. "Oh, hey," I said. I took a moment to study her face, me in my wet shorts, the muddy water lapping at my crotch and the odd dab of mud drying in my chest hair like impasto, she in clean shorts and tee, her hair freshly washed and combed out so that it draped her shoulders and trailed down her back, which was different, very different—she usually wore it pinned up or in a ponytail. I saw then that she was wearing makeup, and that told me something—none of the women wore makeup in here, except on special occasions. "Everything okay?" I asked, and instead of answering, she eased herself down on one of the artificial rocks that lined the pool, pulled off her sandals and dipped her feet in the water.

There was the trickle of the stream circulating from the upper pond to the lower and back again, a distant murmur of conversation, Diane—and who was that, Richard?—at the far end of the IAB, bending to one of the plots. Birdsong. The blowers. "Don't keep me in suspense, E.—how'd it go?"

She studied her feet, paddling there, churning the water, then glanced up at me. "Fish tonight, huh?"

"Right," I said, holding up the bucket in evidence.

"How many you catch?"

"Six."

"Two more to go."

"Yeah," I said, glad to be talking about anything other than what was hanging over our heads, "eight Terranauts, eight tilapia. Wouldn't want to deprive anybody. But I tell you, the fish aren't as stupid as they look—once you catch the first couple, they hide out in the shallows between the plants, which makes it hard because I don't want to cripple any stalks, you know?"

"Actually, it wasn't as bad as I thought it was going to be," she said, paddling still. "Everybody was—nice. Even Judas. And G.C. didn't say a word—of criticism, I mean. I thought he was going to chew me out, big-time."

"So that's why you did your hair and put on makeup?"

A tepid smile. "I was a little nervous going in. I still am."

"But it's all settled, right?" I scooched myself up out of the water and onto the rock beside her, the shorts wrinkled up like very old skin and four leeches along for the ride, dotting my left thigh in a private vermicular code.

"*Vodge,*" she said, jerking her feet from the water. "That is just plain gross—why didn't you tell me there were leeches?"

"You mean you never got any when you were setting out plants?"

"No, no way. What are you talking about? Leeches? How'd they even get in here?"

"Same way as everything else. They must have just had a hatch or something—don't worry, the fish'll take care of most of them. And really"—I was peeling them off now, one by one, carefully grinding them between the pitted surface of the rock and a flat stone—"they don't eat much." There were four bright pinpoints of blood on my inner thigh where the leeches had been at work, letting the blood flow into them as if they were supererogatory veins. Wonderful how evolution works: they secrete a combination anesthetic and anticoagulant and hang on till they can't absorb another drop. Then, just like us after a six-course meal, they go off and mate.

We took a minute with that, with the leech mentality and the way the stowaways just kept popping up, and then, as gently as I could—it was a delicate moment and I didn't want to press her any more than I already had—I repeated the question: "So it's all settled then?"

She didn't answer right away. She was bent over her feet, running a finger between each of her toes in succession before lifting first one foot, then the other, to inspect the undersides. Needlessly. Because a leech isn't going to take hold when you're just dunking your feet—you've got to be still. If you want leeches, that is, like the old leech gatherer in the Wordsworth poem. Who baited them with his own blood.

Finally, she looked up and flicked the hair out of her face with a shake of her head. "No," she said, "nothing's settled. Not even close."

* * *

T.T. was helping Stevie with dinner prep that evening, and he was pouring his latest vintage of banana wine, which normally would have made for a lively pre-prandial gathering on the balcony or down in the orchard, but the only people in the kitchen when I stepped through the door, besides chef and sous-chef, were Gretchen and Diane, and both of them were looking fractious. E. was in her room, doing what, I couldn't say—brooding, I guess, after our little disagreement at the fish ponds, which had quickly escalated into a shouting match when I saw how pigheaded she was going to be about this whole business. Gyro, mercifully, was off somewhere doing whatever he did with his wrenches and ratchets, and Richard was in the med lab—I'd caught a glimpse of him with his feet up and staring into space as I went by. Despite what had gone down between us, I felt a quickening of sympathy for him: he was the one who was going to have to do the dirty work here, and if anything went wrong . . . I stopped myself right there. Nothing was going to go wrong. Still, as I passed the med lab I couldn't stifle the image of E. splayed out there on the table, the paper gown hiked up to her breasts, and everything below as bloody as butchery. So forgive me if I was out of sorts when I came round the corner and saw the four of them arrayed on opposite sides of the counter and caught Gretchen saying, "What else would you expect from Dawn—and *Ramsay,* Christ."

"I don't know," I said, striding into the room and going straight to the counter, where eight scrupulously measured glasses of amber wine stood arrayed on the serving tray, "what *would* you expect from Ramsay?"

No one was going to touch this—no one was even going to open his mouth. Troy and Stevie looked caught out, the way people do when they've been talking about you behind your back, which was pretty much all we did in E2 in any case. Gretchen visibly flinched. Diane gave me an even look, no worries, all is forgiven—as team captain she'd been fully apprised of the status of things, or at least the Mission Control version, i.e., that E. would offer herself up as directed and Richard would preside and the problem would just melt away in the compost like all the rest of the biological waste.

The counter, for convenience's sake, connected with the

cooking area through a four-foot-high portal that ran the length of it, and Gretchen and Diane were seated on the near side, while Troy and Stevie sat across from them, skewering the fish kabobs and dicing beets for the borscht that would serve as first course. I let the silence settle, bending to compare the levels in the wineglasses, looking for the advantage—yes, every precious molecule counted—before lifting one from the tray and downing it in two bitter gulps. Making a show of smacking my lips, I complimented the vintner—"Delicate nose and a nitro kick, towering stuff, hombre"—which seemed to take the tension out of the air, but then tension was exactly what I wanted just about then.

I turned to Gretchen. "You were saying—about E., I mean?"

Her eyes darted at mine and then away again, red-rimmed eyes that were like pink little fishes, tilapia eyes. "I wasn't saying anything."

"No, of course not. It never could have happened to you, could it? Even though I find out you're going primitive too—why take birth control when you can just count on what, chance, fate, luck of the draw?"

"That's none of your business."

"No," I said, gazing round the room, "not anymore. But, Stevie, what about you—you on the pill?"

Stevie, pretty Stevie, gorgeous Stevie, our bikini queen, didn't have a knife in her hand at the moment, just a skewer, but she leveled it at me all the same. "You bet your sweet ass I am." A glance for Troy, as if to reassure herself the reinforcements were on alert. "I, for one, would never compromise the mission, and you ought to know that, all of you."

"Diane?" I said, turning to her now, the wine curdling in my stomach and hissing through my veins. "You on board with that?"

She outranked me, as if that mattered anymore. And, as I say, if it were only the two of us in here I'd have had to go celibate for seven hundred and thirty long days and longer nights (of course, I'd said that about Gretchen too, but you get the idea). I didn't dislike her, though she'd been on the other side of the divide, along with Richard, Stevie and Troy, the first time the shit had hit the fan, and I was angry in that moment, angry at Mission Control, the full roster of my fellow crewmembers and most of all, E.

She held on to the moment long enough to make me uncomfortable. What she said, finally, was no answer at all. She said, "You can be a real pain in the ass, Ramsay, you know that?"

* * *

There's one final scene that stands out here, and that's the one between E. and me later that evening—or night, actually. Dinner—the kebabs, basted in an herb/lemon sauce and grilled to perfection under the broiler in the stove—was a real treat, protein enough to go around for once, and a second pouring of banana wine to top it off. E. didn't want to come to the table—"I can't face them," she said, "I just can't"—but I convinced her she had to make an appearance or the negativity would just keep spiraling down till it took the whole mission with it. We came into the room hand in hand and sat beside each other, so close our shoulders were touching. The wine sent up its fruity reek and a contingent of fruit flies appeared out of nowhere—spontaneous generation—to hover over our glasses, though E. wasn't drinking. She donated her first glass to me, and in a gesture no one missed, her second to Richard. Conversation was muted, which, as I say, was unusual for a wine night, but then the information about E.'s condition was raw and festering yet and everybody went out of their way to avoid any sort of confrontation or even mention of it. All that would come later. For her part, E. hardly said a word to anybody, even me, and it was almost a mercy when Troy put on one of his mix tapes of thrash or industrial or whatever he called it, full volume. Stevie rose from her seat to dance with him, Diane and Gretchen partnered up with Richard, and after a while Gyro joined them, his every movement so spastic and uncoordinated he looked like a pole vaulter coming down hard over and over again. I nudged E., and under cover of the music, we slipped off down the hall to her room.

Anybody can cultivate misery, but that gets old, and after three glasses of banana wine and a full two hours in which nobody so much as mentioned our little problem, I was feeling a surge of optimism, albeit alcohol-forged. E. shut the door and put on a CD of choral music—one of Bach's masses—to mellow things out after the assault of Troy's stuff (I won't call it crap because everyone's welcome to his own taste, but it would be charitable to say I didn't get it. Nor did E). E. ghosted around the room in her bare feet, lighter in her movements now, as if shutting the door had changed everything and made us safe not only from the reach of our sealed-in world but the larger one outside the glass too, the one that included G.C. and Judy and Dr. Wallace Reston of Johns Hopkins University. She produced a pitcher of mint tea clacking with ice cubes and bent over the coffee table to pour us each a glass, then set out two bowls of hoarded peanuts before settling into the couch beside me, one arm round my neck, her head on my shoulder.

Can I say that the touch of her was electric? That I found myself coming awake all over again? It occurred to me that we hadn't had sex in a week, a week at least. I kneaded her hair, stroked her arms, kissed her ear and absorbed the scent of her, all natural, the real scent of a real woman and not something manufactured in a perfumery or chemistry lab. Bach's voices rose and fell, separated themselves and conjoined again. It was a moment of peace, deep peace, after all the unrelenting drama of the past few days, and I held on to it, embraced it, appreciated it, until I had to go and open my big mouth. I said, "So you're not drinking? And thanks, by the way, for giving me your portion—it really hit the spot, though I'm probably going to have to take a wire brush to the roof of my mouth to get the residue out of there."

"No," she said, very softly, "I'm not," and her voice blended so perfectly with the music it was as if she'd joined the heavenly chorus.

Of course, I couldn't leave it there, though I tried, though I knew I was skidding down the slippery path from sex to no sex, from Eros to abnegation, so I said, "Any reason?" and she said, "Isn't it obvious?" and I pushed myself up and said, "I thought we were in agreement here," and she said, "You thought wrong," and I said, with heat, real heat, because I could see where this was going and just where and under what conditions I would be bedding down that night, "I can't believe you. I really can't."

I could drop it and let the whole episode stand in evidence against me in all those accounts that want to paint me as the villain of Mission Two, but the fact is that was the night I had my first inkling of the notion that would redeem the whole mission, though it was going to hurt and I wasn't ready for it and I resisted right to the brink of the point of no return. Earlier, when we'd had our shouting match down at the fish ponds, she'd accused me of being duplicitous, heartless, as cold as the tilapia flapping against the sides of the bucket in my hand, and that was nothing less than I expected. But then she'd said something—tearful, overwrought—that opened things up in a whole new way. She said, "You're the father, aren't you?," and before I could affirm it or deny it or even see where she was trying to go with it, she put her hands on her hips and leveled one more demand on me: "Well, *act* like it."

Linda Ryu

There comes a point when I just can't take the drama anymore and so I go to Judy and tell her I've got to have a couple days off or I'm going to shoot myself and she gives me a soul-stripping look, a kind of visual psychometric test, and then nods her head and says, "I'll need you back on Tuesday." If that sounds generous, it isn't, because the day I ask is a Saturday. So she's giving me a whole two days to go off and party or take care of personal business or whatever else she thinks I might be up to—not that she cares enough to ask—and I have to bow and scrape and gush gratitude, as if asking for two consecutive days off is so radical as to qualify as a labor dispute. Judy. How totally sick I am of her and her demands and her sanctimony, but at this point I'm even sicker of Dawn. No matter what I say to her or how much I emphasize the hopelessness of the trajectory she's on, she keeps insisting she's not coming out. Worse, when I point out to her (on a loop) that Mission Control won't hesitate to break open the airlock and drag her out by her ankles if it comes to it, she says, *Just let them try.* She says, *I'll make a stink in the press like you can't believe.* And where does that leave me and my hopes for taking her place? Right where I've been from the start: sitting on my hands in Residence 2 and waiting for my sentence to tick down to zero.

So I've got two days. Great. Terrific. But where to go? I'm certainly not going home to my parents (for a whole host of reasons, not the least of which is that I'm not one of the lucky few in a red jumpsuit with her face plastered all over the magazines, which means I'm not a Terranaut, and if I'm not a Terranaut then what, exactly, am I?). Sedona's too touristy, Phoenix a nightmare of heat and congestion. And I definitely do not want to spend all my free time behind the wheel. That's when I hit on Mexico. Incredibly, considering it's so close, I've never been there, but that just goes to show what giving yourself up to a cult can do for your travel horizons.

I'm picturing some town just over the border, pottery, silver jewelry spread out on a blanket, discount alcohol to bring back and hoard, a cheap motel with a cheap bar next door where nobody knows me and I can forget all about E2 and the way it's just totally cannibalized my life. For two days. Two whole days. Problem is, once I get to Nogales (sixty miles south of Tucson, straight shot down 19), I lose my nerve and wind up staying in a motel on the American side that night, figuring I can just walk across the border in the morning, do some shopping and come back without having to hassle parking or worry about getting ripped off or winding up with some full-blown bleeding gastrointestinal infection I'll pass on to everybody else in the Residences. Or TB. People tell me Nogales is a hotbed of Multiple Drug-Resistant TB.

The motel is six blocks from the border, a gray cinder block structure called The Hidalgo (that's Ee-dalgo, because you don't pronounce the *H,* though everybody does), and it advertises Magic Finger beds, air-conditioning, color TVs and a swimming pool, which, unfortunately, is out of service and as dry as the back of my throat. The month is April, mid-April, the temperature, even in the evening, when I arrive, is over a hundred, and as soon as I dump my bags on the bed and crank the air conditioner to the max, I ask the woman at the desk (she must be sixty, with a baked-on, multilayered face and a pair of eyes the color of cigarette ash) to point me to the nearest bar and I head back out into the blast. One block north, half a block east, and there it is, the Oasis, windows plastered over with aluminum foil and the thin neon outline of a palm tree glowing green above the door.

Rumor has it that I'm unsure of myself, shy, introverted, the sort of person who needs a couple of drinks to loosen the strings, but that's not true. Or maybe it was at some point, but not any-more. Still, it's never easy being a single woman walking into a strange bar or even a familiar one, no matter how confident you are, but I've had a lot of practice lately, not only at Alfano's but some of the places in Tucson too, and when I pull open the door there's no hesitation at all.

It's cool inside, frigid actually, and blissfully dark. Twin TVs tuned to different baseball games, a pool table, maybe a dozen or more dedicated drinkers lined up at the bar, men mostly, mostly in their thirties and forties, mostly dressed in jeans and boots and sporting earrings, and every one of them looks up when I come in the door and stride right to the bar and order a margarita, rocks, salt, and though I have no intention of getting picked up by anybody, I can't help feeling a little spike of excitement: *I am having an adventure,* I tell myself. And how long has it been since I stepped out from under the wing of Mission Control and the SEE and my Mission Three crewmates? Forever, that's how long.

Anything can happen, but of course, nothing does. At least half the men wind up approaching me at one point or another, taking their shot, asking serially if I'm from out of town or from China or the Philippines or maybe Vietnam, dusting off their repertoire of small talk but too chintzy, to a man, to offer to pick up my tab or even buy me a drink. That's all right. The margaritas are cheap. And cold. And I'm enjoying myself, watching the way they hover over my tits trying to express their needs and desires in a way so backhanded and meandering you'd think they're translating from another language, and after a while, after they've all given up and the other three women in the place (including the bartender, who features tattoo sleeves and a rooster haircut) stop glaring at me, I get down to the business at hand—getting pleasantly, airily looped while Dawn and Ramsay and Tricia and all the rest recede into some dim cavern in the deepest unworked mine shaft of my brain.

In the morning, I wake up feeling more or less normal (but for the weirdness of the plastic room with the cobwebs in the corners and dust bunnies under the dresser, not to mention the neon-orange oil painting of three Mexicans in orange sombreros asleep on their orange burros just to the left of the TV. Which is hung crookedly, so it's not only an outrage of taste but proportion too). I'm not hungover, which is kind of scary, actually, because I had six margaritas before I lost count and unless I'm already as hard-core as my Aunt Lacey I should be feeling like warmed-over shit. But no. I get right up—albeit at half-past noon—and find my way to a Denny's for a Cobb salad, no dressing, and half a gallon of iced tea (and there it is, the thirst that's the consequence of all that alcohol leaching the water out of your system). Then—and I'm still tentative about this and tentative about my high school Spanish too—I make my way for the border. On foot.

Right away, I don't like what I see. Which is a scrum of white-haired white people with swollen jaws from the cut-rate dental clinics that promise nothing but cut rates and then all the discount *farmacias* where you can get any drug known to man for mere pennies on the dollar. And then—I'm only a block in at this point—the stench and the poverty and the trembling distempered dogs and begging children and legless begging adults fill in the scene and I know I'm in alien territory. I'm not a germaphobe, or not particularly, and I don't really see myself as looking down on people or being any more uptight than anybody else, but maybe I'm just oversensitive. I suppose that would be a good way to describe it. Anyway, I'm wandering around aimlessly, little kids tugging at my sleeve, teenage punks leering, barkers trying to interest me in strip shows or live sex or prostitutes or whatever else they've got for sale, and I just feel uncomfortable—in a major way.

Is it too early for a drink? No. But whatever glass you might sip your margarita out of would have been washed in shitwater—and the ice in it would be nothing more than frozen shitwater. Do I really want to go there? For a long minute I find myself contemplating a touristy-looking bar that's open to the street so you can see how non-threatening and ostensibly clean it is, and finally, though I'd rather be back at the Oasis, I make my way in past a bunch of knife-faced guys in loud shirts and plunk myself down on a stool between two supersized gringo couples sunk in their his-and-her fat. The barman gives me an expectant look and I give him the line I've been practicing in my head since I stepped through the door: *"Yo quisiera tener una margarita sin hielo y con sal. Por favor."*

Nothing happens. He just keeps looking at me. So I repeat

myself—and still nothing happens. Finally, the woman on the stool to my left turns to me and says, "You don't have to speak Spanish here, honey. What do you want, a margarita? Double shot, fifty cents more?" And she turns to the bartender, says, "Hey, Eddie, give this lady a two-fer margarita, will you?"

So that's it. I drink the margarita out of the glass washed in shitwater with the shitwater ice slushing around in it while a wave of conversation crests over me, both in Spanish and English, and a blurry TV shows an army of men in shorts running around after a soccer ball *(fútbol)* and I tell myself how much fun I'm having. Nothing happens. Nobody steals my purse, none of the rabid dogs darts in to bite my bare shins, none of the professional hustlers tries to hustle me. Still, I am not happy and I can't really say why. Awkwardly, I pay my bill. And awkwardly, walking the three blocks back to the border in a volcano of heat, I poke through a couple racks of embroidered blouses and consider one glazed pot or another (though I don't have a single houseplant) and actually go into a shop displaying silver earrings in a hundred different designs, but ultimately feel so intimidated by the idea of negotiating in any language that I just turn around and leave without even lifting a single pair from the display rack.

Finally, half a block from the border, I shove through the door of a liquor store and without saying a word either of Spanish or English purchase three bottles of Pedro Domecq brandy, one for Gavin, one for Judy (to ingratiate myself) and one to keep in the apartment for those special occasions when Gavin (or whoever) comes over and we're sitting around making pre-sex chitchat. On impulse I buy a sombrero too. Which is right there at the checkout, one of a whole stack of them, and maybe I'm a bit too frazzled to try it on for more than ten seconds—and maybe I pick a size too big so that it rests on the bridge of my glasses instead of my forehead—but there you have it. Total Mexican purchases: one margarita (double), three bottles of brandy, one too-large sombrero.

By the time I get back to the motel it's late in the afternoon, my hair's kinked out like a toilet brush and I'm sweated through to the skin. It's Sunday. I've got tonight and all day tomorrow, and as I'm showering and then combing out my hair and putting on my makeup, that period of time begins to seem more elastic than fixed, and even before the gas pains start up in my abdomen (so this is what Dawn must feel like), I begin to understand that there is absolutely no reason in the world to be here a minute longer. I fight it. Of course I do: this is my vacation. But the gas pains are only getting worse and though a part of me wants to go back to the Oasis and let the earringed men gather round and whisper hopeful things in my ear, I just throw my clothes in the suitcase, climb back into the sweatbox of the car and head back where I belong.

* * *

Funny how these things work out. In my absence—all of what, twenty-six hours?—everything in E2's been turned on its head and I'm the last one to know about it. It's dusk when I get back, after a trip interrupted by mounting waves of cramps, three pit stops to use the bathroom at fast-food places and the purchase of a bottle of Imodium, which I wind up swigging like a beer all the way home. As I pull into the parking lot, tires squealing, and hustle up the walk with my suitcase in one hand, the tote bag in the other and the sombrero boxing my glasses, the last thing on my mind is seeing anybody because all my focus is on getting to the bathroom ASAP, so when Gavin comes running after me shouting out my name all I can do is wave him off, slam through the door, drop my bags and lock myself in the bathroom. I'm feeling light-headed, feverish, all of Mexico pouring out of me in a foul-smelling fecal rush, and Gavin's in my apartment now, footsteps thumping across the floor. "Linda," he's calling, "where've you been? We've been looking all over for you—Linda?" Knocking at the bathroom door. "Linda, you in there?"

Me, weakly: "Just a minute." I flush, then flush again. Of course, there's no air freshener, just an empty container with a rusted cap the team member before me left on the shelf above the towel rack, so I squirt half a bottle of Jojoba shampoo into the toilet and uncap my only bottle of French perfume and anoint the walls with it before dabbing a splash on my wrists and behind my ears, all the while frantically trying to brush out my hair and apply some lipstick and eye shadow.

"Linda?"

"Just a sec—"

"I've got to talk to you—it can't wait."

"Can you go sit on the couch? For a minute, that's all. I'm coming, I am." My voice booms and echoes in the confines of the bathroom till it sounds like somebody else's voice and I begin to think I'm hallucinating, wondering if it's dysentery I have—or cholera—and a shiver runs through me, then another, and my hand quavers over the lipstick. If anything, the perfume only manages to intensify the smell, some sort of molecular reaction that sweetens and deepens it at the same time, so that when I do finally slip out and pull the door firmly shut behind me I'm practically gagging.

Gavin's right there, bounding up from the couch to cross the room to me before I can even catch my breath. He's looking boyish, wide-eyed, like one of the cutouts from the boy-band fanzines I used to pin up on my bulletin board when I was an uninformed tween in the Nowheresville of Sacramento. "Have you heard? I mean, have you talked to anybody yet?"

I'm confused, cramping, sick, and yet suddenly all my senses are on alert. "Heard what?"

"About Dawn," he says, and I relax, because what could be worse than what's already happened to her and no, I don't want to talk about Dawn because why is everything about her, why can't I go away for a single day without having her thrown in my face the second I get back? From the look of him you'd think the whole mission revolved around her, not to mention the Residences, the power plant and the desert beyond. *Dawn*. Why can't it ever be about Diane or Gretchen or Stevie? Or me? What's wrong with me? I'll give him his brandy, I'm thinking, give him his brandy right now and shift the focus here, show him who counts, who's thinking of him, even if she is sick and cramping and on the verge of passing out, but a little tic of annoyance makes me say, "*What* about Dawn?"

"She's going to have the baby."

"What are you talking about?" And here my heart rate starts a slow acceleration, like a car shifting through the gears. "You mean she's breaking closure?"

"No, that's just it"—and he's excited, practically trembling—"she's having it *inside*."

"No way. That's impossible. You know as well as I do Mission Control would never . . . Who told you that?" And what am I seeing here, Dawn and Gavin, best buds at the glass, she'll tell him anything, thinking aloud, but you can't take that seriously because that's only her point of view and it's just not going to happen. Not with G.C. presiding. And Judy. And Little Jesus.

He's standing there looking down at me, so worked up he can't keep still, toes tapping, fingers jerking at some invisible thread hanging in the air, even his shoulders twitching. And he's smiling, actually smiling, as if he's glad of it, as if nothing could be better or truer or more fitting than Dawn Chapman, Eos, fucking up the mission out of sheer stubbornness. "Who told me?" he says, smiling till his teeth glisten under the rinsed-out light from the flickering fluorescents overhead. "Only G.C. himself, that's who."

* * *

"Thank god you're back. I mean, of all times to take off—"

Judy. On the phone. Waking me from the sleep of the dead after Matt Holst, the Mission Three medical officer, came over and gave me a shot in the butt, a little plastic vial of ciprofloxacin and another of Lomotil. I'm feeling . . . disoriented. What I say is, "Judy?"

"Listen, can you talk?"

"Yeah, I guess," I say, looking simultaneously at the clock radio on the nightstand and the filmy half-glass of water beside it. The time, presented in an icy blur of LED hieroglyphs, is 11:22.

"I mean face-to-face, just between us."

Face-to-face? Is she out of her mind? Or, more to the point, am I out of mine? "I can't, I mean, I just got back and I'm not feeling—"

"Listen, sorry to call at night but this is important—no, crucial. Ten minutes be okay?"

I'm lying there on my back trying desperately to orient myself. Whatever Matt Holst injected me with seems to be working, though there's no sensation in my legs and my stomach feels like it's made of concrete. Who summoned him? Gavin. The memory comes back to me in a mortifying rush, me flopping down on the couch and unable to get up again, Gavin on the phone, the stench from the bathroom, from me, and then Matt showing up with his black bag and the two of them helping me into the bedroom . . . and then what? The phone. Judy. And whatever possessed me to answer it?

"Linda? You there?"

"Uh-huh. I was asleep—"

"I said, can you be here in ten minutes?"

Still in a fog, all the connections slowed down, my voice rattling like a coin disappearing into the gummy slot of a pay phone: "Where?"

"Mission Control, where do you think?"

So I climb out of my sickbed, feeling better, but shaky still, pull on my shorts, a sweatshirt and flip-flops, avoid the mirror, forget about my hair and go out into the night. For Judy. And Dawn. And myself too, because Judy's scheming something and she's picking me to scheme along with her.

The nights here, incidentally, are a small miracle, the air cool and dry-scented with verbena, cow parsnip, chia and sage, the stars so vivid you don't even need a flashlight. Except for the rattlesnakes, that is. They roam at night, using their heat sensors to home in on rodents, and they tend to use the same paths we do, so I always carry a flashlight after dark. Which I do now, making my way through the silence to Mission Control and on up the quiet stairs to where Judy's waiting for me in her office.

"Oh, you're here," she says, not bothering to get up from behind her desk but just nodding to the chair set in front of it. "Thanks for coming. You see anybody on the way over?"

"Uh-uh."

"Okay, good. And I just sent Jeff out on his coffee break—he's on the monitors tonight, but you already know that, don't you?" And here comes the briefest tic of a smile, nothing genuine, just a pre-programmed response from her bank of facial gestures. She's about to say something more, the *D* for Dawn stuck right there behind her front teeth, but she stops herself. "I thought you weren't supposed to be back till Tuesday?"

"I got sick."

"Really? So where did you go?"

"Nogales."

She gives a little laugh, into the moment now, enjoying herself. "I could've told you that—Montezuma's Revenge, huh? Stick to E2, Linda, stick to us and you don't have to worry—I just hope you get rid of it before you go inside. Did you see Matt?"

"I did." I want to say more, tell her how quickly it hit me and how hard, if only to arouse a little sympathy and demonstrate what a trouper I am to be sitting here at her desk when four hours ago I thought I was headed for the morgue, but the phrase *Before you go inside* changes everything.

"Good," she says. "We can't have you—" and she cuts herself off again, impatient with the small talk. "You heard about Dawn? About the unbelievable stupidity of what she talked Jeremiah into?"

"No," I say. "Or yes. A little."

"I mean, it comes out of nowhere. Outrageous enough she gets knocked-up, and then it's like pulling teeth to get Richard to play along and he's a team player, let me tell you—but to be so selfish, so stubborn, I mean, it's just hard to believe." She's got something in her hand, a brass letter opener, a little sword, and she's stabbing the air with it to underscore the vehemence of her emotions. "It's Ramsay, of course. He schemed all this up. And got to Jeremiah without my even knowing about it because I happened to be at a fund-raiser last night and they went behind my back as if I'm not the one from the very beginning who put every ounce of my being into this thing, up nights, unable to sleep even—"

She seems on the verge of tears, Judy, Judas, the ice queen, the manipulator, and I hate to say it but I don't feel a thing for her. In fact, what I'm feeling is, *Let her cry, let her see how it feels to be stepped on for a change.* But what I say is, "I can't believe G.C.—I mean, Jeremiah—would go along with it. That's crazy."

"It's Ramsay," she repeats, her voice tightening. "Mr. PR. Spin it this way, he says, first child born off earth in the history of mankind, E2 the New Eden, make it *biblical,* and Jeremiah buys it—without consulting me. And it's beyond stupid, you know it is—the press'll tear us apart. And the nuts, the hate groups, the *Christians*—as soon as it's announced there's no going back. And they want to announce day after tomorrow."

There's more, a whole lot more, Judy crouching over every sore point in her life, time ticking by, my throat parched, the concrete set so hard now in my stomach you could take a hammer and chisel to it, Jeff back at the monitors and the night holding fast, before she comes to the point. She's going on about Jeremiah, how he has no common sense, not a whit, how she had to fight him over the blueprints every inch of the way, how he wouldn't know a scientist from a used car salesman if it wasn't for her, but suddenly stops herself in the middle of a sentence, as if she's just remembered I'm there. "Linda," she breathes, "I'm counting on you—you realize that, don't you?"

"Sure," I say, nodding vigorously, though my head hurts and I have no idea what I'm agreeing to, and why I think of the brandy in that moment I don't know, but I'm wishing I had it there to hand across the desk and win a smile from her and maybe a thank-you for all I've done and will do, without stint, on into the future. And forestall her too, just to give me time to think—but I can't think. I'm sick. I can barely keep my eyes open. *Get me out of here,* that's what I'm thinking. *Just get me out of here.*

"What you've got to do, Linda, is you've got to talk her out of this. You're her best friend, she'll listen to you—"

I almost want to laugh out loud: talk her out of it? I've done nothing but talk, doesn't she realize that? "I've tried," I say, the ship sinking right before my eyes, all hands lost and the captain going down with her. "Believe me, right from the beginning, I mean, from the day I found out—"

Judy, hair and makeup flawless though it's well past the end of the day, flashes the letter opener, this time aiming it at my heart. She says, "Try harder."

* * *

I wind up missing breakfast the next morning, still groggy and played-out from my little bout with Mexico, and already the phone's ringing—Judy, wondering where I am and when I'm going to get to the glass for my tête-à-tête with Dawn because she really can't overemphasize just what this means to everybody, to the mission, to *her*. And I'm listening, believe me. Do her bidding and I'm in. Fail her and see how I like watching Rita Nordquist or Tricia Berner take my place come Mission Three closure. That much is clear. The problem is, how am I going to do it? The feint I'd made at talking Dawn into going through with the abortion was only a way of leading her around to the inevitability of having the baby—outside, in the hospital, where she'd be safe and I could take her place as MDA and she could come visit me at the glass and wave the little newborn's perfect little fingers at me, his beaming Aunt Linda, the Mission Two Terranaut. I'd be the one milking the goats and thumbs-upping for the cameras, I'd be the one inside and fast-tracked for Mission Three—which would be the first legitimate mission, the first one to count, because it would be the only one to date that wouldn't have to break closure. I'd see to that. Even if I had to personally force the pill down the throats of the other three women—or maybe Mission Control would just go ahead and sterilize us all and make things easier on everybody.

I'm not really up for eating anything, but I down two glasses of orange juice in quick succession and force myself to nibble at an untoasted Pop-Tart on the walk over to Mission Control, where I arrive just under an hour late (but then this is supposed to be the second of my two days off, so who's to complain?). Judy's there—I can see her in her office, mouthing things into the telephone. I'm feeling better, if far from normal, and I've brought my sombrero along so everybody can ask about my Mexican adventure and what I think about the integrity of the water delivery systems down there south of the border. Gavin never did get his bottle of brandy, by the way, but I'm thinking maybe I'll give it to him tonight, after work, depending on how I'm feeling and whether I'll be able to act on any romantic possibilities the gift might suggest, but then I picture the way I must have looked—and smelled—the night before and think better of it. Give it a few days, that's what I'm thinking.

But to the matter at hand. Dawn. I'm hoping to catch her during morning break, in something like an hour and a half, and till then I bend over my desk and do what amounts to some serious doodling on a lined yellow legal pad, all the while marshaling my arguments like a prosecutor going into trial. If I feel helpless, aligning myself with the second in command and against (or at least behind the back of) our God and Creator, I try to put it out of my mind, picturing Dawn, all the great times we had together, how close we were, how she'll do this for me, how she's got to once she understands what's on the line here. For *me,* for once.

Ten-forty-five and I'm at the glass, pressing the buzzer that nobody pays any attention to, hoping to get lucky because this is hardly the time anybody would be expecting visitors. I could have called from Mission Control, but I want to do this at the glass, where Dawn can see me and what I'm going through, and if she hasn't heard about my trip to Mexico, I'm wearing the sombrero as a conversation starter. For a full five minutes there's no response, but then a face emerges from behind the curtains—Gretchen's—and I make urgent gestures to draw her to the phone, which she picks up with a questioning frown.

"I need to see Dawn," I tell her. "It's urgent. Really urgent. Can you go get her?'

Gretchen's face goes through a quick shuffle of emotions, from wonderment to intrigue to irritation. "But it's break—" she says, as if I've interrupted some holy ritual.

"I know, I know. I'm sorry. But can you get her?"

It takes her a moment, assessing me, no doubt reviewing in her mind the catastrophe named Dawn and what her latest mood swing or stance or whatever you want to call it is going to mean to the mission. "Yeah," she says finally, slow as syrup, "sure, I'll get her. But what's with you"—gesturing at the great straw boat slipping down over my glasses—"you been to Mexico?"

I nod.

"How I envy you. Wow. Beautiful country, especially when you get into the rain forests down south along the east coast, down into Belize, I mean. Did I ever tell you I spotted a jaguar there once—in Belize?"

"Great," I say, "you've got to tell me all about it, but right now? I *really* need to see Dawn."

Three minutes later, as if in some magic trick, Gretchen's vanished and Dawn's there, easing onto the stool like a woman already so far gone she has to shift her weight carefully, though you can hardly see she's pregnant, not if you aren't looking for it. "Hi," I say, and she says "Hi" back.

"What's with the hat?" she asks, peering through the glass to get a better look. "I like it. It looks good on you, but maybe it's a little too big? I mean all the way around? Almost makes you look"—and she laughs—"like a toadstool or something."

"Come on, Dawn, there's no call for that."

"Only *kidding*. Can't I even make a joke anymore? Jesus, Linda, you sure are quick to take offense these days."

I want to jump on that, want to give her a riff on it, light her up, let her know just how and why and to what unplumbable depths the offense really reaches, but I don't. I say, "So what is this insanity I hear about you not only having this baby but doing it *inside*? After all we said about it, the dangers, I mean? You really trust Richard? A thousand things could wrong—and then what?"

She just smiles, looking serene—or no, looking spaced-out, as if she's lost all sense of who she is or what she's doing to herself, to the mission, to *me*. "We'll cross that bridge when we come to it."

"What bridge? Death? A what, a deformed baby, because Richard can't get his act together? You've got to listen to me. For us, for our friendship. Aren't we friends? Aren't we best friends?"

"Of course we are. And we always will be. And when you're in here I'll be there for you, I promise. But really, I don't see what you're so upset about—it's all decided. G.C. himself said so. Think about it—it'll be fine, it will. And like I said, women have been giving birth down through the ages—"

"Right. And dying in the process. It's not like we're stuck in a Victorian novel, you know—right out there, right down the road in Tucson, it's state of the art. I already checked it out, the hospital there. It's state of the art, Dawn, I'm telling you—" If an edge of desperation has crept into my voice, Dawn doesn't hear it—or doesn't care. She just sits there, ever so slightly swollen in the abdomen beneath the folds of her oversized T-shirt (which, I realize, she must have appropriated from one of the men, from *Ramsay*).

She's not responding. Not giving me what I want, not budging an inch. What she says next is, "And I forgive you, I really do."

"Forgive me? For what?"

"For outing me. For telling Judy. It *was* you, wasn't it?"

I want to deny it, steer things back on course, but there's no use: she can see right through me. "I had to," I say, pleading now. "For your sake. So you wouldn't have to keep on torturing yourself, so we could address this as a *team,* the way we always have, and—and find a solution that's best for everybody."

"I was so mad at you, furious really—I can't tell you how mad." She sets her mouth to show me just how deep the rift was, or *is,* but then her jaw relaxes and her eyes go vacant again. "But now, I don't know. Maybe it was for the best."

It's hot. My stomach begins to cramp again. I should be in bed. I should be a thousand miles away from here—Hawaii, why didn't I go to Hawaii? Why don't I? Like tomorrow? "Dawn," I say, cry, plead, "can't you just listen—?"

"Oh, Jesus"—and here she slaps her head in a what-am-I-thinking kind of way. "I didn't tell you yet—"

"Tell me what?"

I watch the smile bloom on her face, her eyes focused now, right in the moment, right there with me. "You didn't hear? Really? Nobody told you?"

"No, nobody told me anything—what are you talking about?"

She holds it a beat more, then brings the phone to her lips. "Linda," she says, "Linda—I'm getting married."

Dawn Chapman

We both wanted a simple ceremony, but with G.C. pulling the strings, nothing's ever simple. The whole thing happened so fast I barely had time to think, if you want to know the truth. From the time I dug in and let Vodge know I'd made up my mind to have the baby no matter what anybody said, to the lightbulb going off in his head and our meeting at the glass with G.C. the next night—the night Judy was thankfully off in Phoenix at some fund-raiser and powerless to do anything about it—I felt like I was on a Saturn rocket shooting up into the stratosphere. *Whoosh,* ignition, liftoff, and suddenly we were looking down on everything in creation, two gods, Vajra and Eos, soaring hand in hand. I was trembling, actually trembling, so high on the moment I could have been on drugs. And yes, it was romantic, just like the press release makes it out to be, Vodge taking charge, standing by me, in love with me and ready to prove it to the world. But just for the record, since what came out of it is so deeply ingrained in the mythos of Mission Two and myths do tend to paper over the reality: it wasn't Vodge who proposed to me but G.C. Or, actually, G.C. who proposed that Vodge propose to me.

We really hadn't thought beyond the moment—the term "marriage" wasn't even part of our vocabulary at that point. All I could think was that here was the end of our problems, if only we could sway G.C. and make him see that having the baby inside was the only solution—and Vodge could, I was sure he could, and I'd do my part too, ready to burst into tears on cue, and I didn't care whether that was unprofessional or not. Everything was coming at me in a rush, especially after all those crippling weeks of shame and suspense, and I was in a state. Nobody would talk to me—nobody would even look at me. I went through my chores like a robot. The day seemed to go on forever.

When Vodge left me to go off and arrange the meeting with G.C. I didn't know what to do with myself—I certainly couldn't eat, though he brought a plate to my room. I picked up a book, put it down again. I paced, stared at the walls, kept running my hands over the bump in my abdomen as if I couldn't fathom what it was doing there, which wasn't far from the truth. I wasn't denying the process, only the timing of it. Yes, we're animals, hormonally programmed to reproduce—reproduction is, in a real sense, the only purpose of life—but why did it have to happen to me? And why now? Why not a year from now, two years, never? I watched the clock till Vodge came back for me at eight-thirty, dinner over and everybody else off doing whatever—out of the loop, unconsulted—and as we went down the stairs and through the orchard, we kept looking over our shoulders to make sure nobody was watching. (Even if they were, I told myself, they would have assumed we were headed for the fish ponds or the animal pens, which wouldn't have been out of the ordinary for that time of day.)

When we were in the clear, we made a sharp right for the visitors' window, Vodge steering me with one hand pressed to the small of my back. I was sweating. My stomach was in knots. I was so worked up I was practically hyperventilating—not only because the sudden appearance of Diane or Gretchen or anybody who might be out and about would ruin everything (this most emphatically was not a group moment), but at the prospect of facing G.C. Again. It was bad enough to have him chew you out over the phone or on the PicTel screen, but to have him there in the flesh was all the worse. He *never* came to the glass, not unless he was squiring some celebrity or dignitary around, and now he was coming for us.

The goats had heard us as we passed by and were giving voice to their complaints, filling the void with their raggedy bleats. They'd already been milked and fed, of course, but they wanted more, just like any other creature deprived under the glass, except maybe the slug-eating snakes, but then I didn't know much about them and hardly ever saw one. Maybe they were doing just fine, maybe the slugs were so plentiful they went to bed with full bellies every night, but the rest of us? We were hungry. And, it occurred to me, if G.C. gave his consent we were going to be hungrier still.

It was dark in the little cubicle by the window and Vodge flicked on the lamp there (strictly low-wattage, just enough so the visitor could see inside, but not so bright as to compromise the intimacy we all craved, and of course I was thinking of Johnny then, but the thought—and his image with it—flew right out of my head as quickly as it had appeared). Vodge pulled out the stool for me and slid it in beside the phone and I perched myself on it, one foot propped on the rung, and we both stared out into the darkness of the world, waiting for G.C. to appear around the corner and pronounce our fate. Vodge had already outlined the plan for him over the phone in the command center—i.e., have the baby inside, no breaking of closure, no "procedure," even the rumor of which would have doomed us in America's eyes, and milk the whole thing for its PR value—and G.C. at least listened, though he was still stuck on the direct course of action, the one he'd bullied Richard into and me too, or so he'd assumed. He was a towering figure, and towering figures don't like to be contradicted—I was aware of that, never more aware of it, but we'd made up our minds and for me, at least, there was no going back. As I'd told Linda, if they wanted negative publicity, if they kept *pushing* me, they'd get enough to kill the next six missions dead in the cradle.

But here came G.C., detaching himself from the dense shadow of the superstructure and loping along the path toward us. He was dressed in some sort of safari outfit I'd never seen on him before, khaki shorts and shirt, his kneecaps palely flashing and his beard flaring sporadically under the lamps along the path. Then he was standing at the glass, beneath the dim light fixture there, lifting the phone to his ear and peering in at us.

Vodge picked up the receiver, but G.C. waved him off, and I could hear his voice thinly resonating over the line even as I watched his lips form the words: "No, no, it's E. I want to talk to."

I gave him a nervous smile, took up the receiver and whispered, "Hi." And then, because I couldn't stop myself, because I wanted to be gracious, ingratiate myself, I added, "Thanks for coming out. Thanks for listening to us. At this hour, I mean—"

He was staring through the glass at me, noncommittal, wearing my reflection like a mask, which made me think of the time (an eternity ago, it seemed like now) he'd summoned me to the command center to let me know I should be extra-friendly to Gyro— for the sake of the mission. And now he'd come down out of his office at eight-thirty on a Saturday night to stand there in the heat on the other side of the glass when I'm sure he had better things to do—for the sake of the mission, yes, but for our sake as well. Terranauts were disciplined, duty-bound, given over wholly to the mission's objectives, but they were human too, and he understood that—or had to be made to understand it. "I hear"—a glance for Vodge—"there's no point in trying to talk sense to you, is that right, E.?"

I just nodded. But I didn't drop my eyes.

"You've really thought this out? Because you're not the only two involved here—you're part of a team, don't forget that, and team harmony trumps everything. You're asking six hungry people to tighten their belts another notch and somehow come up with the extra calories it's going to take to sustain you through this? I mean, I don't operate by fiat here, and I could say yes just to have them say no, and then where are we? Right back where we started."

I could say yes. That was all I heard, all I needed to hear. My heart stopped knocking at my ribs. I didn't want to smile, not yet, but I couldn't help myself. I said, "We'll work with them, we'll do everything we can, we'll find a way—"

"Easy to say now, but what about next winter when the light fades and there's not enough to go around, because the surest way to failure here is to present an undernourished baby to the world."

I wanted to protest—and Vodge was trying to grab the phone away from me—but G.C. held up his hand to silence us.

"I'm talking theoreticals," he said. "It's going to be a bitch—and the biggest gamble we've ever taken, because there are so many things that can go catastrophically wrong." He paused to give us a minute to think about that, a premature baby, a dead baby, a baby that never stops shrieking for want of food. "But the upside is beyond belief. The minute we announce, we'll get coverage like you've never seen, like none of us has ever seen, I mean the cameras'll never stop clicking—you ready for that? Both of you?"

Vodge took my hand and leaned into me to share the receiver. "Yes," he said, his breath mingling with mine, a sweetness there, an internal flowering that was all his own. "We're ready for anything."

"Glad to hear it," G.C. said, lifting his free hand and dropping it again, as if he were saluting us. "It's good, it's all good. But there's one more thing—"

"What?" I breathed.

"I mean for you, Ramsay—"

G.C. looked as if he were about to deliver the punchline of a joke, but it was no joke, and what he was about to say went a long way toward providing the liftoff I was talking about earlier. "I was just wondering," he mused, a finger pressed wryly to the corner of his mouth, "when you were going to get down on one knee and ask this girl to marry you. I mean, that's the way we do it out here in E1—"

* * *

My wedding dress was white, at least. (Or as white as we could make it without the phosphates, chlorine, ammonia, petroleum solvents, alcohol, butyl, glycol ether or nonylphenol ethoxylate you found in standard detergents.) Diane and I cut and hand-sewed it from a pair of bedsheets I'd be doing without from that point on and since we didn't have any lace to trim it with, we incorporated bright green arrows of broad-leafed savanna grass around the neckline, twists of morning glories at the wrists and a long braided train of them to trail behind me as I came down the staircase and Gyro leaked his way through "Here Comes the Bride" on his clarinet. For shoes, I had to settle for flip-flops, but

I put on makeup and did my eyes and put my hair up in a French braid with a crown of blue-flowering salvia stems rising out of it. Blue and white, that was the extent of the color palette, and it was enough, believe me, keep it simple, which was the whole point of E2 to begin with, and if we really didn't have much by way of flowers for a bouquet (flowers were a luxury when you needed every square millimeter of soil for crops), we did manage to mix and match a few cactus flowers with the salvia and wrap it all up in a bundle of peanut greens, which the goats would enjoy after the ceremony as their own invitation to the feast.

The groom had come into E2 with a purely practical wardrobe consisting of three pairs of jeans, half a dozen of shorts, six or seven tees and two long-sleeved shirts, with collars, both now so torn and stained as to be all but useless for any formal occasion—and this was a formal occasion, or as formal as Mission Control could make it, given the constraints we were under. Of course, nobody had a tie. Or cuff links. Or, needless to say, a sport coat. Gyro, being Gyro, had imported a more extensive wardrobe, including the leather shoes and baby-blue button-down shirt he'd worn the first evening he came to me with his M&M's, and he'd offered both the shirt and shoes to Vodge, let bygones be bygones, but of course neither came even close to fitting. Troy came up with a chrome-yellow Hawaiian shirt that featured a pair of outsized pink chameleons flicking their glutinous tongues at equally pink bugs that might have been either beetles or cockroaches, you couldn't tell which, but that didn't work either, not when the whole ceremony was going to be telecast nationwide. Finally, Mission Control made an exception in this instance and allowed Vodge to wear his official Terranaut jumpsuit—his uniform—which was fine as long as the cameras didn't focus on his feet. Like most of us, he'd been going around barefoot to save his cracked and blistered shoes, and the best he could come up with for the occasion was a pair of flips-flops repaired with a shiny gray strip of duct tape.

June brides, that was what all the magazines held up as the ideal, as if humans were no different from any other Northern Hemisphere species that have to build their nests and rear their young in the season of abundance. Actually, I'd never given much thought to being a bride, beyond that girlhood phase when you play with dolls and watch Disney movies and imagine yourself the princess awakened by a kiss—marriage, family, all that was something that would unfold in some vague unconstructed future. Or not. But now here I was, a bride-to-be myself, and we couldn't wait till June because of the way we were going to have to present all this to the public—I was no virgin bride, and no one would have expected it of me, but even the thickest reporter could count off nine months on the fingers of two hands and Mission Control felt—insisted—that sooner was better than later. I won't bother going into detail over the contentious team meetings or the things some of my coworkers said to my face, but as it came about, we decided to skip our Bicycle Day (April 19) feast in order to have enough resources for the wedding, which G.C. decreed would coincide with our May Day celebration. (And, of course, when he'd claimed he wasn't ruling by fiat it was only a kind of rhetorical flourish, because that was exactly how he ruled, whether Judas and Little Jesus or my six non-engaged crewmembers liked it or not.)

The strangest thing—beyond my parents, that is, who were flown in on the shortest of notice, along with my brother and Ramsay's grandmother, and more on that later—was Linda. After everything had been decided and G.C. laid down the law for everybody concerned, both inside and out, Linda came to me at the visitors' window and tried to talk me out of it, going on and on about the procedure all over again, and when she saw that wasn't working, she started back in on how the only right thing to do was break closure. For my own good. For my safety and the baby's safety too, not to mention nutrition, basic nutrition. How was I ever going to get enough calories inside E2 to feed a baby? Even now, probably, the fetus was underdeveloped. Hadn't I thought of that? Didn't it worry me? Well, that was all *she* was thinking about day and night—she couldn't even sleep, she was so worried.

She was wearing a sombrero that must have been two sizes too big for her, ridiculous really, like a breadbasket or something, and it shaded her face so I couldn't really read her expression. All I saw was the flash of her glasses and a void where the rest of her face should have been, a trick of the sun—and that was another thing that got me wondering: what was so earth-shatteringly important that she had to come to me in the morning, at break, instead of at the usual hour when we could both relax? So I said, "You shouldn't worry so much."

"But I do." There was something strained in her voice, a tearfulness, as if she was the one who was pregnant and had to endure all this tension and hatefulness.

I reassured her, told her it was all going to work out. "I'm really touched," I said, on the verge of tears myself. "Really, I am. Sisters, right?"

"I want you to come out of there," she said, shifting in her seat so the sun fell full on her face for a moment and I saw the way she was looking at me, all tense and wound up.

"Come out?" I echoed. "You know I can't do that."

"Do it for me."

I was going to say, *For you, what are you talking about?*, but then I began to put two and two together, and who did I see staring back at me but Judy. Judy was behind this. Judy wanted me out, gone, vanished for good, and if the price of that was breaking closure because I wouldn't submit to the procedure she had in mind, then so be it. But Linda. Linda was my best friend. Why would she—? And then it came to me. "You're not just saying this because you want in, are you? To take my place?"

She didn't answer right away, both of us sitting there clinging to the phones waiting for the other shoe to drop. Finally, and now she shifted again so her face was hidden in shadow, she said, "Yes. Yes, I want in. You fucked up, Dawn. You forfeited your place."

"And what, Judy promised you if you talked me into breaking closure you could take my place?"

"Nobody promised me anything."

"But that's the long and short of it, isn't it?"

She shook her head, the sun slashing at her mouth. Her mouth was very small and tight. "She wanted me to talk you into getting rid of it, if you want to know the truth—"

I'm sorry, but I'd had so much thrown at me over the course of the past six weeks it just felt like I was getting slapped in the face over and over again, and I had no patience for this. "Well, I'm not getting rid of it," I said, making my voice as nasty as I could. "And I'm not coming out either." I pushed myself up off the stool, furious now. "You can tell Judy from me to go screw herself. And you know what?"

"What?"

"You can go screw yourself too. And I don't care. I really don't."

* * *

As soon as things had been finalized, I called my mother from the phone in the command center, which Mission Control had linked up to an outside line. "Hi, Mom," I said, already tearing up at the sound of her voice.

She didn't say "hi" back, didn't say my name. "What's the occasion?" she asked, sounding bitter. "You mean they actually let you talk to your own mother?"

I'd planned on easing into things, to just chat a minute before getting to the business at hand, but that wasn't to be. "Mom," I blurted, "I just wanted you to know—I'm getting married."

To say she was surprised would be an understatement (mortuary silence punctuated by the background chatter of talk radio and the intermittent barking of our family dog, Pearly, a silence that went on so long I had to ask if she was still there).

"I'm here. I'm just floored, I guess. Who's the lucky man?"

"Ramsay. Ramsay Roothoorp. You know, my crewmate. Inside?" And I began talking in a rush, filling her in on all the details (except the most salient one, that I was pregnant and this was a shotgun wedding, with G.C. standing in for the outraged paterfamilias). I was telling her how we'd been in love for a long time without knowing it, or expressing it, that is, both of us tentative and not really connecting as anything more than colleagues until things had begun to heat up around Christmastime, when she cut me off.

"Roothoorp? What kind of name is that?"

I told her it was Dutch, mainly Dutch. "I think," I said. "Actually, I never really bothered to ask. I mean, I'm assuming."

"He *is* American, though, right?"

"Yes, Mom," I said. "Born and raised. And as far as I know, nobody in his family has a tail. Or retractable claws."

Just for the record, I should say that I had what could be described as a normal childhood and that I love my mother, even if she doesn't have much of a sense of humor, at least where I'm concerned. A lot of parents are like that, I suppose—they don't expect their children to be funny because being funny lies outside the bounds of the prescribed parent/child relationship, which is built on a platform of mutual support and the dispensing of hard information. Anyway, my attempt at a joke—at deflecting her—fell flat. All she said was, "Which one is he again? Not the tall one?"

She still wasn't clear on it all even after SEE flew her, my father and brother into Tucson and the three of them came to the glass to see me the morning of the wedding, which was planned for seven that evening, both to coincide with the magic hour of dusk and accommodate the scheduling of TV broadcasts across the time zones. It was ten-forty-five, break time, and heating up outside. I'd done the morning's milking, slopped the pig and fed the chickens and ducks, though I'd been excused from ag work because I'd had to do my hair, put on makeup and sit for half a dozen interviews, including one for an Anchorage radio station during which a pair of typically juvenile morning DJs kept asking me if we were planning on going to Vegas for our honeymoon and I kept saying "Not this year," and they kept crowing, "But how can anybody tie the knot without roulette and Wayne Newton?" as a kind of idiotic refrain that got very tired, very quickly.

My mother would have been in her mid-fifties then, old by my standards (and of course, she'd always seemed old to me, even when I was a child and she wasn't much older than I was now on this sun-burnished morning of my wedding day). The thing was, and maybe it was because I hadn't seen her in so long, I was struck by how young she looked, so young I barely recognized her. There she was, standing between my beanpole of a brother and my beanpole-with-a-belly father, in heels, a knee-length skirt and silk blouse (white, as if she were the one getting married), wearing a pair of pearl earrings and a matching necklace I'd never seen before. She'd let her hair grow long and she'd had it lightened so she was nearly as blond as Stevie. "Mom, you look great," I exclaimed, because she came up to the phone first, while my father and brother pantomimed their greetings and congratulations and a scrum of photographers, seeing action at the window, came rushing across the courtyard snapping pictures.

"Thanks, honey," my mother breathed into the phone. "I'd like to say the same about you, but truth be told, you're way too skinny. Aren't they feeding you in there?"

She was smiling when she said this—it was meant as a joke, but I was as unprepared for her attempts at humor as she was for mine. I said, "It's just like the salad bar at Sizzler, all you can eat all the time."

"No, I mean it," she said, the smile fading. "You really think you can hold on for another, what, ten months, isn't it? Because I have to tell you, and this isn't just a mother speaking, you're practically skin and bones—maybe you don't notice it because it might seem gradual, but to me it's really affecting you."

"I'll be fine."

My mother had turned to my father and I could faintly hear her asking, "Isn't she too skinny, Todd?" and I watched my father grimace and nod and give me an I-told-you-so look. Then my mother was pinning the phone to one shoulder so she could free both hands to rummage through her purse until she came up with what she was looking for: a little square of white tissue paper. Which she carefully unwrapped to reveal a ring. A diamond ring. "This was your nana's," she said, pressing it to the glass.

I didn't know what to say. It was simple and elegant—a one-carat brilliant-cut diamond in a plain gold Tiffany setting, a ring my grandmother had worn till she died, and that my mother, thinking of me, must have set aside and kept in the back of her jewelry box through all the years I was growing up—and though I'd trained myself to reject material things, especially in here where the only currency was utility, in that moment I think I would have died to get hold of that ring, to have it for Ramsay to slip on my finger as we were pronounced man and wife in front of the whole world and all the cameras it contained. As if to remind me of that world, a camera flashed suddenly, and then another, and I saw my father turn and say something to one of the paparazzi crowding in to make public what was private and existed between me and my mother and the memory of my grandmother, a woman I'd hardly known, who'd died when I was a child but was present here today in the empty circle of her ring.

"It's beautiful," I said. "Really beautiful. But you know I can't—"

My mother's features sharpened. "Can't what? Connect with your own family on the most important day of your life? This was your *nana's ring.*"

"I know, I know. But we can't break closure, you know that as well as I do."

"Don't give me that, because that's just crazy. What about Mission One—they did it, over and over, sending medicine in, food, what, oxygen even. And you're telling me these people can't send a ring through that thingamajig right there?" She pointed to the sleeve to the left of the window through which Mission One had passed medical samples back and forth. "Or what, they open the outer door there and I just toss it in in a little box and back right out without taking even a single breath of your precious air and then you open your side for like three seconds? Tell me you can't do that—"

Another flash. Another look from my father—and now my brother was getting into the act, making shooing motions as people kept crowding in with their cameras. I smiled, waved, always on display and never more than now, then turned back to my mother. "I can't do it, Mom."

The fact was, Gyro had fashioned a pair of rings from a steel spring he'd dug out of his spare parts drawer, and they would have to make do till reentry, just as my baby would. Which didn't make it any easier.

My mother didn't respond. She just stood there, pressing the hollow of the ring to the glass and staring into me as she'd done so many times when I was a child, trying to unnerve me. After a moment, she said, "What's the hurry? I mean, why couldn't you wait the ten months and have a real ceremony, one your parents could attend?" Without waiting for an answer, she raised her purse to eye level, unsnapped the clasp and carefully tucked the ring back inside, then moved back a step to raise her head and take in the monumentality of the structure rearing over us in all its harsh geometric beauty.

"All this is great," she said, waving a hand at the spaceframe and the visitors' window and everything that lay behind it. She'd already divined the answer to her question, I was pretty sure of that. I watched her eyes gather in the knowledge and hold it close. "I just want to know if it's worth it." She took another step back, glared round her—two more flashes, three—then leaned back in. "I mean, doing this to your own mother—and your father, of all people. Your father too."

* * *

At six-forty-five that evening, Richard led me down the stairs of the Habitat, through the orchard, past the animal pens and up to the visitors' window, where Ramsay was already stationed, his grandmother standing at the glass just beside him. Inside, we had Gyro, as I said, aspirating his way through Mendelssohn's wedding march, while outside Mission Control had arranged for the Tucson Symphony Orchestra to entertain the crowd, which was overwhelmingly composed of reporters and cameramen, with a spattering of the sort of celebrities G.C. could hustle up on short notice, as well as the Mission Three crew and support staff, including the secretaries, techies and anybody who worked in any capacity on campus and could stand upright on two legs.

I suppose all brides are nervous, and not just because of the irrevocable leap they're making but because of all the pomp and circumstance and the very real worries of tripping over your train, dropping the bouquet or screwing up in any number of ways, minor and major both. I was no exception. In fact, and I'm sure you can appreciate this, I was under the kind of spotlight few brides have ever had to endure, if you except people like Pamela Anderson or Princess Diana. What I was dealing with, aside from the press, my disgruntled parents, G.C., a jealous and resentful Judy and an equally jealous and resentful Linda, not to mention the small detail of my being four-plus months pregnant, was the fact that I'd instantaneously become the face of Mission Two while everyone else, even Ramsay, faded into the background. That was the quid pro quo—you can have your baby, but you're going to have to dance to a new tune, a faster one, a tarantella of whirling cameras and talking heads. That was the deal. That was the bargain. And I'd agreed, because what choice did I have?

Richard dropped my arm, as arranged, when we got to the window, where my father touched his elbow to mine through the glass and led me the remaining three steps to where the groom stood, looking radiant—literally—in his Ferrari-red jumpsuit. The music ceased. The crowd out in the courtyard focused their attention on the window while my fellow Terranauts—Richard, Troy, Stevie, Gretchen, Gyro and Diane—arrayed themselves behind us. Vodge fixed his gaze on me, something like merriment in his eyes, as if this was all a big joke, which, in retrospect, I suppose it was. As I say, everything happened so quickly we really didn't have time to talk things out—the good of the mission, that was all that mattered—but if I'd thought about it I would have wondered if any man in all of human history who'd got his girlfriend pregnant didn't feel at least the smallest bit resentful.

Did it show in his face? Maybe. But I was so swept up in the moment I hardly noticed and before I knew what was happening, the presiding authority (Tom Yellowtail, one of Dan Old Elk's Crow tribesmen) was beginning the ceremony with a Native American blessing projected through the phone that had been wired to loudspeakers inside and out. Vodge took my hand. We gazed into each other's faces while the cameras rolled and flash-bulbs detonated and Tom Yellowtail chanted:

From above house of heaven
where star people and ancestors gather
may their blessings come to us now
From below house of earth
may the heartbeat of her crystal core
bless us with harmony and peace to end all war
and from the galactic source
which is everywhere at once
may everything be known as the light of mutual love.

And then Richard presented the rings, G.C. stepped up to the mike to deliver the vows, Vodge said, "I do," and I repeated it, and then we kissed and we were married, in the eyes of the TV cameras, in the eyes of my parents and fellow Terranauts, and most importantly, in the eyes of G.C., God the Creator himself.

Ramsay Roothoorp

So we got married. At G.C.'s insistence. And if it precipitated a whole shitstorm of intramural friction, so be it. We reaped the kind of press coverage we'd never dreamed of, even at closure, and if I felt put upon, cornered, prodded, forced into an arrangement I'd never have contemplated if it didn't make such good sense for the mission, I told myself those were the terms I'd signed on for. I'm not saying I didn't love E. at that point or that I wasn't fully committed to her, because I did and I was, but that somehow our arrangement, our *relationship,* didn't seem to carry the same erotic charge it had before all these complications set in. I didn't go out and take a poll of married men—I hardly knew any, actually—but I suppose there's got to be an inevitable letdown after the knot's been tied, especially if your spouse is already pregnant (or *embarazada,* as the Mexicans so aptly put it), which basically rules out the extended period of stress-free sex play the traditional honeymoon is meant to offer up. We had no honeymoon, in any case. It was pedal-to-the-metal news conferences, photo shoots and TV interviews, the two of us gazing lovingly into the cameras and spouting sticky clichés about love and commitment before going on message about E2 and its salvational function as the very heartbeat of the planet.

As you can imagine, even as the press and the great swelling tide of ecophiles, retirees and schoolchildren around the world hung on our every word, nobody in the inner circle much liked our new status. The rest of the crew was almost hysterically resentful, shoved into the background at a single stroke and with nothing more to look forward to than cutting their already reduced rations in favor of providing for the mother-to-be while E. went on hiding her condition from the public because Mission

Control—rightly—wanted to put a little distance between the nuptials and the official announcement of E2's first successful *Homo sapiens* mating, which was just what this was, as clinical as that may sound.

How did E. look? You've seen the pictures. She was too thin, like some ectomorphic runway model, her arms and legs stripped of any trace of fat, but shapely still, and, of course, her face just seemed to glow on the page and screen both. When she undressed, I saw how the fifth month was settling into the flesh around her waist and I have to admit I found the whole thing maybe just a little bit of a turnoff, a downer, really, because I could see where this was heading and it didn't make me feel loving or proud or protective—just, I don't know, *irritated*. I won't say "disgusted" because that wasn't it, or not till near the end anyway, when the fact of her body, her *swelling,* seemed to dominate everything in our lives and she was like an upright piano made flesh and couldn't seem to stop pissing. I wasn't prepared to be a father—I'd had no interest in the position, zero, and for a while there in my early twenties actually considered a vasectomy because as an ecologist I felt it was nothing short of obscene to contemplate bringing yet another human into the world—and that was part of it, I suppose. The mission needed me to accept responsibility, publicly, and I did, but that didn't mean I wouldn't have given anything to go back to that first night with E. and make absolutely one hundred percent certain she was on the pill and wearing her diaphragm too. I'm just trying to be honest here. I took one for the mission—and for E., of course—but the worst of it was I had to go around wearing a rhapsodic smile no matter how I felt, because that was what Mission Control wanted and what Mission Control wanted was what I wanted, quod erat demonstrandum.

Right. And then there was Judy. Let me give you a sample of Judy's reaction, if you'll bear with me a moment and reserve your judgment.

Throughout the whole business, Judy had been quietly (and not so quietly) seething, but when we talked it was always in crisis mode and always in a group setting, worrying the details of the press releases and the nuptial ceremony and the parties afterward, both inside and out, and a few weeks went by before she managed to pin me down, one on one. It would have been toward the end of the month—May, that is—when E. was dropping terms like "lanugo" and "vernix" into our conversation and expanding to the point where we were going to have no choice but to announce her condition to the world, especially now that she was the subject of pretty much nonstop photographic scrutiny. The time was night, late night, when not a creature was stirring, not even the original rent-a-cops and the two backups Dennis had hired to ensure that no one attempted to breach the glass in an excess of enthusiasm over the newlyweds. Earlier, in the interval between chores' end and dinner, I'd been called to the phone for a message delivered by Josie Muller, the secretary at Mission Control. All she'd said, keeping her voice professionally neutral, was, "Judy wants to arrange a meeting. At the glass. Midnight. Tonight."

And what had I said, thinking of E. in bed beside me, snoring lightly over the bump in her abdomen that was now beginning to move and shift under her skin like a sea creature plowing along just beneath the surface? I said, "I'll be there."

Outside the glass was the deep void of a moonless night in the Sonoran Desert; inside, things were still, or as still as they could manage to be when your existence depended on the regimented working of a concatenation of pumps, conduits and gauges. I thought I'd get there early so I could occupy the power position and watch Judy emerge from the darkness before she'd had a chance to compose her face, and with that in mind I left the room at quarter of twelve to make the two-minute trek down the stairs and past the orchard to the visitors' window (my room, that is; E. and I still maintained our separate rooms, but most nights we slept together, usually in her room), which should have given me the advantage. But didn't. Judy must have been thinking along the same lines as me because when I turned the corner and pushed through the curtains, there she was, seated in a folding chair, her bare legs crossed. She was wearing a scalloped top, a skirt as short as a cheerleader's, and, of course, the heels that had so inflamed my imagination the last time we'd met like this.

We just stared at each other a minute before we reached for the phones and I watched her uncross her legs and then cross them again, her head tilted ever so slightly to pin the phone to one shoulder. She spoke first. She said, "So how's married life treating you?"

"I don't know," I said. "How's it treating you?"

"I'm not married."

"Might as well be."

She let out a sigh. "You ought to know, huh, Romeo? You and your wandering dick?"

"You want to know? You really want to know? Everything's fine."

"Don't make me laugh. You fucked up big-time and now you're paying the price. And so are your crewmates. But what's it like screwing a woman with a tire around her waist, who smells like what, yeast? A brewery? Who's just going to get bigger and bigger? You finding that fun?"

"Come on, Jude, that's just tired and you know it. We did what we did for the good of the mission—and because G.C. wouldn't have it any other way."

"Right. And you fucked her for the good of the mission too."

"Accidents happen."

"Hm-hm, so I'm told"—and here she uncrossed her legs and flipped back her skirt so I could see the point of departure there, the locus, and observe, even in the poor light, that she wasn't wearing any underwear. "But we never had any accidents, did we?"

It was one of those moments. Like showing a starving man a ham-on-rye or an incarcerated sex fiend a porno. But then, I *was* an incarcerated sex fiend, or the closest thing to it. I knew what Judy was doing. Did it matter that I knew, that I saw right through her (or, actually, right into her)? No, because in that moment E. didn't exist, had never existed, and if Judy had left it there she would have made her point ten times over, but she didn't leave it there. She spread her legs even wider, her pale muscular legs arching away from the twin fulcrums of her heels so that they glowed against the creep of the shadows, and began to stroke herself, ever so slowly, just to rub it in.

* * *

When she was through with me I went straight to E. If I'd been thinking about sleeping in my own bed that night, just to get a full night's rest without awakening over and over to the heavy shift of buttocks and the fluty gargling snore of the thickening woman beside me, that wasn't what I was thinking now. I stripped off my shorts and T-shirt as I came up the stairs, switched on the lamp and tried to displace as much volume as I could when I hit the mattress.

"What?" she gasped, starting awake.

I didn't paw at her or tear off her nightgown or anything like that, but I have to admit I was feeling a real sense of urgency as I hovered over her and began stroking her hair and kissing the side of her face.

"My god, Vodge," she said, her voice numbed with sleep. "What have you been *doing*?"

"Listening to the frogs," I murmured, my hands all over her, and if she was a little groggy still and not fully present, that was all right because I had a need and she was my wife and this, I reminded myself, was what was called connubial bliss. It was all right. It was fine. But once I worked the nightgown up around her breasts and saw the way she was lying there all wrapped up in herself, I hesitated. I won't say I was intimidated or turned off—or not quite, or not exactly—but I did reach over her and shut out the light.

* * *

We made our official announcement in mid-June, well into her sixth month. Rumors had been coalescing in the press and I'd been asked two or three times point-blank if she was, indeed, pregnant, as she appeared to be, and I'd only managed to make things worse by saying, "No comment." A series of candid pictures appeared in *People,* showing E. bent over a basket of sweet potatoes, her shirt stretched tight across the middle, above the caption, WHAT'S REALLY GOING ON INSIDE? And there were cartoons, of course, the most recent caricaturing E. and me on our wedding day, with G.C. standing just behind us loading a shotgun on the other side of the glass. So really, the time had come. We talked it over, as a team, in a PicTel conference with Mission Control, and ultimately decided to keep the announcement simple, sans marching bands, TV cameras, caterers, celebrities, gurus and Native Americans dangling from meathooks, not only because we were afraid of a backlash from the PG crowd who were quite capable of doing the math but because we didn't need any of that claptrap—the very notion itself, of the first child born off-earth in the history of humankind, was enough to get us everything we could ever hope for.

Judy arranged the press conference, which took place, like our wedding, in the evening, when the light still held its clarity and the temperature was a little more bearable. She invited ten journalists, all from print outlets—TV would come later, once the news had been quietly digested over America's collective breakfast—and they ranged from the highbrow *(Wall Street Journal, New York Times)* to the middlebrow *(Time, Newsweek)* to the popular rags *(People, Us, USA Today)* that out-circulated them all. We were both wearing our red jumpsuits, which I thought was a bit excessive, but which G.C. and Judy insisted on, as a way of rebranding the team image. Mine sagged on me a bit, but as you can imagine, E. couldn't even get into hers without doing a little alteration (but not too much: the pendulum of her midsection was what this was all about and we wanted the photographers to capture it). For once, G.C. resisted the impulse to preside, and he let us do the talking, though he was there, along with Judy and Dennis and the full complement of the Mission Three hopefuls, seated in folding chairs behind the select group of journalists.

I was feeling . . . neutral, I guess, both keenly aware of my new role as progenitor and chief human animal of E2, male division, and all the possibilities for advancement now and after reentry that came neatly wrapped up with it, and thoroughly sick of it too. I didn't always feel like grinning, all right? Or portraying wholesomeness when I didn't feel wholesome at all—just the opposite, really. More like the subversive that some of my crewmates, inside and out, tried to portray me as after the fact. For her part, E. looked terrific, the Madonna in red, finally able to admit the truth—and show it off too.

We stood together at the phone, holding hands. Gyro had rigged it so our voices were projected to the reporters gathered there against the fading glow of the sun, while the swallows dove for insects in mad loops and plunges and the iced drinks Mission Control had provided sweated in their hands. "Good evening," I said, grinning—or no, not grinning yet, hold that just a beat—"and welcome to Ecosphere II." Now the grin. "Dawn and I have some very good news for you, news that should, I hope, gladden the hearts of all those who've been tracking our progress and giving us their love and support since we stepped through the airlock on March sixth of last year." A pause, a wide-eyed scan of the expectant faces, and then a nod for E. as I handed over the phone. "I think I'll let my wife deliver the news, since she's the one who's going to be doing the heavy lifting here."

She gave me a loving look and raised the phone to her lips. "We're going to have our first child," she announced, "*E2's* first child, and we're absolutely thrilled."

Then I took the phone from her to reiterate how absolutely thrilled we were and opened the floor for questions.

The first question, delivered by a sweating woman from *Us Weekly* who was wearing what looked to be a terrycloth pool robe and turquoise-encrusted sandals, was the obvious one, the one we'd been dreading: "When's the due date?" she asked, tugging at the phone cord and looking first to us and then over her shoulder at the sun-draped forms of the audience behind her. "And is there a chance the baby'll be born inside?"

Dawn took the question and she didn't hesitate: "Dr. Lack says late September. So yes, definitely, our child will be born in E2, the first of what we hope will be many."

One of the photos that appeared in the next day's papers showed me giving her a startled look, though I don't remember acting out in any way. I did take the phone—lovingly—to supply a little clarification: "Among *future* Terranauts," I said, and got a laugh. "Don't forget, the human experiment is as vital to the project as any of the systems functions or the well-being of any of the thirty-eight hundred species of plants and animals making this new world in here with us. There are forty-eight closures to come after this one—and by then, in ninety-seven years' time, I have no doubt we'll be doing this on Mars, in earnest, for real, and all the children of E2, like our son, will be pioneers to the stars."

I'd worked on that line the night before and had expected a little applause here, but none was forthcoming, so I called for the next question and summoned the *Newsweek* reporter, Gordon Saltonstall, to the phone. Gordon wanted to know if we had any concerns about having the baby outside of a modern hospital, and both E. and I assured him that E2's facilities were absolutely top-notch and that we were absolutely (the catchword of the day) confident in Dr. Lack's abilities. Gordon thanked us and as he backed away from the glass to resume his seat in the first row of folding chairs, I began to realize this was going to be softball all the way, nobody expressing outrage or questioning our morals or the timing of our marriage or the fact that we were putting our unborn child at risk by insisting on closure though we weren't really on Mars or Pluto or anywhere else but Tillman, Arizona, with a modern hospital right down the road in Tucson. But if they had asked, if they'd insisted, I was prepared to give them the party line—i.e., that crew safety was the guiding principle of E2 and that we wouldn't hesitate to break closure if the life of any crew-member was in danger. Though that was a lie. Because I would have endangered everybody's life, would have killed, to keep that from happening. *Nothing out,* I told myself, *nothing,* already seething though the question hadn't even come up.

* * *

The real problem, as it turned out, wasn't the press—they soft-pedaled the story, as eager for the kind of feel-good news that sells copies as we were—but the six members of the crew who weren't invited to the press conference, who weren't wearing their red jumpsuits at the glass or sharing in the goodwill and approbation of the wider world, who weren't stars, or not any longer. The celebration after the press conference—muted, boozeless, already strained because it was E.'s night to cook and she'd had to switch off with Troy while taking yet another star turn at the glass—was so testy it was more like a skirmish than a party. (All this exacerbated by the fact that though Mission Control had isolated us from the outside world, people nonetheless pressed one magazine cover or another to the glass day and night, and every one of them featured E. and me, variously smiling, gazing off into the distance or looking self-contained, the Lady Diana and Prince Charlie of E2.)

Stupidly—I wasn't thinking, I admit it, high on the press conference and my own galloping celebrity—I talked E. into going straight up to dinner without stopping to change out of our jumpsuits, so that when we walked into the dining room where everybody was sourly waiting dinner for us, we were immediately set apart. My bad. My very bad. Because if resentment was running high, as it already was, the jumpsuits just inflamed it because we were meant to be eight and to wear them in concert—officially, not casually. Plus, G.C. had specifically banned the others from this particular press conference by way of focusing attention solely on us, because we were no longer selling team solidarity so much as the miracle of generation under glass. (And why not? If the galagos could do it, so could the humans.)

"Well, how'd it go?" Diane asked, everybody in motion now, pouring mint tea from the big pitcher on the counter, selecting their plates (but leaving the biggest share for E., as per Mission Control's directive that everybody, including me, was to donate one pre-measured ounce of each meal to the expectant mother in respect to her burgeoning need for calories, so suck it up and do your duty, everybody). Diane had already eyeballed the plates and selected hers and was all arms and elbows, working her way through her fellow crewmates to her place at the head of the table, her hair bristling and her eyes drawn down and greedy—like all our eyes when food was the issue.

"Good," I said, two plates left now on the counter, the biggest portion and the smallest, and though I was starving—all that energy expended at the glass!—and seriously coveting E.'s ration, wondering for one heart-thumping instant if I could get away with switching plates, I had to follow orders too. And set an example. I didn't want a baby, any baby, but I especially didn't want a deformed or retarded one, crippled in the womb by dietary deficiencies and the avarice of its solipsistic progenitor—i.e., *father*, a term that sat too heavily on my tongue to actually pronounce, even inside my own head. "Great, actually," I went on, sliding in at the far end of the table with my reduced plate in hand. "Nothing but softball questions."

Richard, who was seated directly across from me, dressed in a stained cap and a T-shirt I'd seen about a thousand times (sky blue, with a legend in fading white script across the breast: DON'T MIND ME, I JUST WORK HERE), looked up from his plate of stewed greens, eggplant mush and sweet potato fries innocent of ketchup, mustard, soya or malt vinegar, and said, "No math questions?"

"Nope." I gave him a smile, a true smile—beamed, actually. We'd made up our differences, for the good of the mission and the good of Dawn too. He was the one the whole world would be watching come September.

"Where are all the yahoos when we need them?" This was delivered straight-faced, as with any comedian, and I took it in the spirit in which it was meant: he was trying to lighten up a very heavy room, a room that had sucked in all the gravity of the galaxy in true black hole form.

"Or the Chrustians," Stevie said, working the exaggerated pronunciation like a TV preacher from Tuscaloosa, and Troy laughed in a quick sharp bark so that for a minute there I thought we were going to get through this, reduced rations, red jumpsuits and all, but then Gretchen silenced the table with a sudden star-tled screech. Her face was red, instantly red. She was glaring at E. "You get your dirty hands off my peanuts!"

She was sitting next to Richard, across the table from us, and E., deep into her food now and oblivious to everything, had plucked a peanut out of the pile between them, assuming they'd been set aside for her since we'd missed out on the hors d'oeuvres—a per-fectly reasonable assumption, but unfortunately a mistaken one. Gretchen was a hoarder. Open the refrigerator at any time of the day and there were two or three plates with the odd bite of cheese, bread or fruit she'd squirreled away (bearing a grease-spotted strip of cardboard on which she'd written *Property of Snowflake*). There were various moldering bits of this or that in her room too, as I could attest from my days as her special guest. So they were Gretchen's peanuts. And E., innocent of that fact and starving now for two, had already popped one between her teeth, shell and all, and was reaching for another when Gretchen seized her wrist.

"How dare you!" Gretchen snapped, even as E. dropped the peanut and looked round her confusedly. "Don't you get enough as it is?"

"I'm sorry, I didn't—"

"Just because you and"—dropping E.'s wrist to point an accu-satory finger at me now—"went ahead and screwed without a condom, *recklessly,* and now we all have to suffer, because, what, you're too pure to use the pill? That doesn't mean the whole world owes you a living—"

E.'s face changed. Her eyes hardened and her brow clenched. This was a low blow, dishonest and spiteful at the same time, and she wasn't going to tolerate it. "Don't give me that. You and I both, we agreed—"

"But I'm not the one that got knocked up. And I'm not hog-ging an extra ration—or *stealing* peanuts, right here in front of everybody." A wild look around the table. "Did you all see that? She *stole* from me."

Somebody—Richard, I think—told her to calm down, that nobody was stealing, and hadn't they set aside a handful of peanuts for her because they knew she'd be late, and if she'd assumed this was her portion it was an honest mistake, wasn't it?

Maybe so. But Gretchen wasn't having it. She worked her mouth as if she couldn't imagine what to say next, and she probably couldn't, since group dynamics wasn't exactly her strong suit, then snatched up her plate—and every last peanut and the empty shells too—and stormed off down the stairs till she disappeared in the orchard. Followed, a moment later, by E., who got up heavily from the table, picked up her own plate and shuffled down the hall to her room. Where she could eat in peace.

Me? I shrugged, tried to make a joke that fell flat, glanced round the table—Richard, Stevie, Troy, Diane, Gyro—picked up my fork and dug in.

Linda Ryu

Everybody's pissed at Dawn, but nobody more than me. She's selfish, privileged, all wrapped up in herself, and, I hate to say it, *white*. If she wasn't white I'd be in there instead of her and nobody would have to give up three ounces of their precious dwindling barely adequate rations a day for her and her fetus, which is what's really going to bring the mission down, if anything is. If it was me I wouldn't have fucked Ramsay or anybody else, except maybe Gyro, and if I did you can be sure I would have been on the pill, which I am now and always have been. What do I want to say here: *Duh?* Anyway, the whole best friends issue is all but dead now and when I do see her at the glass I really find it hard to hide my resentment because the option she picked—have the baby and have it inside—is the single option that does me, does all of us, the least good. Harm, actually, in my case, since I'm not going in as her replacement and might even have jeopardized my Mission Three chances because Judy was counting on me to sway her and Judy's a queen bitch. Though I did give Judy her brandy and Judy acknowledged it with one of her automatic smiles, and automatic or not, she has to realize on some level that it wasn't my fault but Dawn's. And Ramsay's. And G.C.'s. I'd done her bidding—or at least tried to—and when the smoke cleared I think she saw that and probably looks at me now in a whole new light. At least I hope so.

The thing is, everywhere you go, whether it's the supermarket, the drugstore or even the bars, you see these big cheesy close-ups of Dawn on the cover of one magazine or another, including in the display case in the hallway to the restrooms at Alfano's, where the owner, a lame little fat man named Joe Oliverio (lame as in clueless, that is), does everything he can to trumpet his association with E2, right down to naming a vodka/passion fruit concoction the "Dawn Chapman." Ramsay's in some of the pictures too, of course, trying on his big dazzling hypocrite's grin in his role as proud father, but he's not the one the reporters want. Dawn's the one. Dawn's going to get bigger and bigger and Dawn's going to give birth, which makes Ramsay an afterthought. Plus, sex sells, and you can be sure the hidden agenda behind all these articles is to make people wonder what that's like, sex with Dawn, just like the average porno features the woman front and center and spread wide while the guy's all but hidden behind her, doing what needs to be done. It's funny. All the men want to screw Dawn and all the women want to be her.

So where does that leave me? Just right exactly where I've always been since the day Dawn walked out of that room in Mission Control as the Mission Two MDA and this whole pathetic *human experiment* started: nowhere. Or no, somewhere I don't really want to be, or in a role I didn't really sign up for: supporting actress. Truly? I didn't see it coming. The press explosion in the wake of the wedding and the big reveal, yes (Judy and Dennis, both on board now that they have no choice, talk it up all day every day), but not the extent that I'd be caught in the blast radius. Who, the reporters began asking themselves, is Dawn Chapman's de facto best friend? The one Terranaut-in-waiting who's privy to all her innermost workings, her thoughts, her beliefs, her likes and dislikes, and what's her favorite color? Her favorite food? Her favorite season? Sports team? Music?

The night it first hits me comes at the end of an otherwise calm, even boring week, nose to the grindstone, sun like a furnace, Gavin uninterested or busy elsewhere, and I'm too lonely, pissed off and miserable to just sit home so I hop in the car and buzz down to Alfano's for a drink, not even bothering to do more than a slapdash job with my hair and makeup and I'm wearing a T-shirt and shorts and a pair of flip-flops because I don't really give a shit who's there or what they might think or even what my possibilities are. I just want to get drunk, that's all (and I'm not a drunk, as I keep stressing, but everybody has to get rocked once in a while just to keep from bursting into flames, and on this particular night I'm even more worked up than usual because Dawn's been all over *CBS Sunday Morning* spouting off about living the simple life in harmony with nature and the trials and tribulations of motherhood under glass and how her pregnancy has really opened her eyes to the abiding miracle of life on earth—and in E2, of course).

So I'm a little off-kilter. Feeling betrayed. Resentful. Angry. And when the reporter from *Us* comes up to me pretending to be just another tourist, it takes me a while to realize what's going on—and what my role is. He's my age, maybe a little older, shorter than I'd like him to be, though I'm on the barstool and he's standing so it's a bit hard to gauge, and I like his smile, tight-lipped but with a gleam of flawless white enamel showing through, and his eyes too, which are hazel, with the minute hand of a tiny golden clock in the iris of the one nearest me as he leans in and says, "You look pretty comfortable there—I bet you're a regular, aren't you?"

I nod, on my third drink and not quite ready yet—not prepared, not *dressed*—for whatever's on tap here. "Why do you say that?"

"I can tell."

Giving him a coy smile, "What if I told you I just got off the bus from Toledo?"

"I'd say you were a liar—"

"Really? How come?"

He flicks his eyes at the bartender and a beer appears on the bar between us, so he takes a moment with the wallet and credit card before answering. "Because there's no bus stop here."

"Okay," I say, feeling better all of a sudden, "you got me."

He offers to buy me a drink, which I accept, and before I know it we're deep in conversation, that kind of special just-me-and-you-and-anything-can-happen kind of intimate conversation that excludes everything else—the screams of the idiots on the far side of the bar, the bump and throb of the jukebox, the TV, the lights dimming to signal the end of happy hour. Which is okay, which is great, until the subject shifts ever so subtly to E2 and it dawns on me—*Dawns*—just what's going on here.

"Why are you so interested?"

"Isn't everybody?"

"I wouldn't know," I say. "I'm just, I mean I just live here, is all."

He gives me a long amused look—his name is Josh, by the way, or was, or that's what he told me—and says, "You're not fooling anybody, *Linda*. You are Linda Ryu, aren't you?"

Let me just step back a minute here to examine my feelings at this juncture. On the one hand, I'm crushed because he's working me and everything to this point's been a sham, but on the other hand, I admit it, I'm flattered. Because whether it's artificial or not, whether it's bullshit, at least finally somebody's recognized me for who I am, even if it is in Dawn's shadow. Does he want to know about her, really know about her? Well, he's come to the right person.

"So what's Dawn Chapman really like?" he asks without waiting for me to affirm or deny my identity or even catch my breath. He's managed to work his way in between me and the tourist on the stool beside me, leaning into the bar on both forearms while his beer sizzles on the bartop and the ice in my vodka soda glints and crackles. "I mean, is she really the holy eco-mother she makes herself out to be? Who says things like"—he's flipping through a palm-sized notepad now—"'To know my baby's going to be born in an unpolluted world is to me one of the crowning achievements of Ecosphere II' and 'Nutrition's a somatic thing, of course it is, but it's holistic too, and I really feel we get well and stay well just by breathing the air in here'?"

I'm about to say something I'll regret, a sentence beginning with the term *Horseshit* that will no doubt wind up as the lead-in to a pictorial featuring me looking hair-challenged and fat and angry, a sentence that will ricochet through the corridors at Mission Control like a terrorist's bomb and earn me a rebuke—or worse—from Judy, when I feel a pressure on my arm, right at the elbow, a significant pressure, a vise of pressure, and I turn around and Johnny's there, saying "Hey, Linda, how you doing?"

Josh's face falls and why that is I can't say, but all I feel is annoyed. "Fine," I say, glaring at Johnny. "What's it to you?"

There he is, the hair, the smirk, the boots, the jacket. "I don't know," he says, straightening up to flick the hair out of his eyes with a snap of his neck. "I just wonder if you really want to talk to this clown—I mean, without thinking about it for a minute?"

"What's it to you?"

The grin goes tighter. Josh—if that's even his name—just hangs there, notebook in hand, and for the first time in our very brief acquaintance he seems to have nothing to say.

"What's it to me?" Johnny repeats, his eyes jumping from mine to Josh's and back. "Nothing, I guess, except that he just hit on me not ten minutes ago, trying to get me to badmouth Dawn—and that's something I don't do." Significant pause. "Something I will never do." The pause, redrawn, a beat longer this time. "You know what I'm saying?"

* * *

That was a close one, and I have Johnny to thank for it, as if he's in any position to lecture me about ethics or what loyalty means—loyalty to Dawn, especially. But he did stop me from venting inappropriately, disastrously, and I'm grateful to him, as far as that goes. Sad to say (and I have to say it with a shiver of disgust with him and myself too), the sex I had with him was the best out of maybe the three or four one-night stands I've had since closure—worse than sad, pathetic. Have I mentioned Gavin? If there's any good news there it's that since Dawn's wedding— and pregnancy—he seems just a tad less enthusiastic about how unbelievably wonderful she is and how every word out of her mouth is pure gold. Which just goes to prove what I've suspected all along—he wanted to get into her pants, just like all the rest of them, from Ramsay to Gyro to Richard and half the camera-toting husbands and fathers and voyeurs out there, though how he expected to do it beats me because he's probably a lock for Mission Three with his good looks, smarts and gung-ho team spirit, which means that when she comes out, he goes in. But you know what I mean. He had a crush on her, big-time. And now that she's doubly unavailable—triply: married, pregnant and

under glass—and June spills into July and Dawn just keeps swelling, he's looking like he's ready to get over all that and maybe
develop a crush on somebody else. Like me, for instance. And
yes, I did give him his Mexican brandy and yes, he did appreciate
it, and that's as far as that went except to say that we're teammates
and teammates naturally tend to draw closer as time goes on. Or
do they?

Anyway, I've been making overtures lately and he seems to
be responding as something more than just a friend and teammate, so that there comes an evening toward the end of July when
he appears at my door and all my hopes rocket right up off the
launching pad all over again. "Hi," I say, patting down my hair
with one hand and pulling the door open wide with the other,
"it's great to see you—it's a nice surprise," and since I can't seem
to stop myself from chattering to cover my nervousness, I go on
about the weather—we're getting an intermittent lashing of rain
from one of the hurricanes working its way up out of the Yucatán
and because it's something different, something new, everybody's
been excited all day long.

He's tall. He always ducks—instinctively, automatically—when
he goes through a doorway, through my doorway, and now he's in
the front room, his hair glued wet to his forehead and I'm saying,
"Isn't this weather wild? Don't you just love it?"

He does, he agrees he does, and he takes a seat on the couch
without asking and accepts the beer I hand him without comment.
There's a flash of lightning, a rumble of thunder, another flash. I
crack a beer for myself and sit down across from him in the easy
chair, putting my legs—bare, in a pair of denim shorts cut off at
the crotch—up on the ottoman where he can see them. Once
we exhaust the subject of the weather ("Two more days of it";
"Really, two?") our conversation tats its way through a host of sub-
jects, mostly work-related, gossip, really, but right down through
the dregs of the first beer we both skirt the elephant in the room
(Dawn, of course), before he comes around to the purpose of this
little visit, which is to chat and kick back with one of his crewmates, one of his very favorite crewmates, but also to gradually

and very subtly induce that crewmate to feel a certain burden of guilt over the way she's been ignoring the Mission Two MDA lately, her putative best friend.

"Why?" I say. "Has she said anything?"

He doesn't sprawl, Gavin, but he's feeling comfortable enough to sink way back into the couch and prop one leg up on the edge of it, careful not to allow any contact between his shoe and the material—an ugly tartan-plaid cotton polyester I got from Goodwill that could have been cleaner to begin with. "Well, yeah," he says. "She really misses you—your talks, you know. She thinks you're mad at her—"

"Me? For what?"

"Don't ask me—that's just what she says, is all. I mean, I really don't know. But she's got a lot on her plate right now, we can all appreciate that, and I was thinking, if you're not doing anything tonight—"

"No, no, not all," I say, my mind racing through the options of what to wear because everything's dirty and how long it's going to take me to get ready because at best we're going to have the space of his—our—second beer before he gets impatient, and if he wants to go to El Caballero for a change I'm willing to compromise, though I hate the place and he knows it . . .

"—I thought both of us could go over and see her. I know it would mean a lot to her."

Another flash, another rumble. I almost say "To who?," but then I get it and try to cover myself by standing up and crossing the room to the counter, pretending there's something there I need. Over my shoulder, I say, "In this weather?"

"I already told her we were coming."

"It's raining. There's lightning. We could be killed."

"The lightning's all off in the distance. And it's not much more than a drizzle, really—and I do have an umbrella."

And so he does, a minimalist fold-up thing two people would have to snuggle under to keep dry. He produces it now from behind his back, where he must have been sitting on it, and waves it in evidence. "I said eight—eight okay?"

"What time is it now?"

He flips his wrist to check his watch. "Like quarter of?"

* * *

He's right—the rain's beginning to taper off, though there's that wonderful smell on the air, which improves my mood right away and if I'm already thinking of what we'll do after we see Dawn, that helps my mood too. And he does unfurl the umbrella when we leave the apartment and we do both try to fit under it, which necessitates his putting one arm around me, but the rain stops dead about three minutes later and he drops his arm and shakes out the umbrella and that's that.

Dawn's waiting for us, as if she's starved for company. Her hair seems longer, fuller, and the way it frames her face makes her look prettier than ever, makes her look just like her pictures, like the cover girl she's become. She's thin, the flesh drawn down to muscle on her arms and legs and her cheeks sucked in, but she's wearing her belly as if she's proud of it and she looks healthy, whereas the others—Diane and Stevie, especially—are beyond skinny at this point, and I can only wonder where that's going to go when winter comes on.

There's a moment of confusion as Gavin and I both reach for the phone at the same time, but he defers to me—he's a gentleman, as I say, and I am really rooting for him to make the cut for Mission Three—and then I'm saying hi to Dawn and she's saying hi back and I hand the phone to Gavin and he says hi and asks how she's doing and her voice chokes up and she gets teary and says, "Not so great."

The thing is, our heads are together, mine and Gavin's, both of us leaning in to share the phone in the most natural way, and Dawn's emotional state isn't really the first thing on my mind at that moment—as far as I'm concerned, her teariness is just par for the course. But Gavin. He practically drools sympathy into the phone, her special friend, her confessor. If I thought he was drawing away from her, I see now how wrong I was. They have a bond, they're *intimate* in a way that makes me feel jealous all over again, and each little phrase they toss at one another, each little catch-word and euphemism cuts me out to the point where I'm ready to snatch the phone away from him.

That's when she says, "Everybody despises me," her voice drawn thin, so thin I can barely hear her.

"They're just jealous," Gavin says.

Thinner still: "Doesn't it amount to the same thing?"

Just when I think I'm about to explode, he says (to Dawn, not me), "Well, look, I've got to be going—I'm sure you two have a lot to catch up on." Then he steps back from the window and hands me the phone. "Sorry, Linda," he tells me, "but I promised Rita I'd help her with that grant thing Judy's got her working on—"

Before I can ask "What grant thing?," he's already turning to go. Both Dawn and I watch him, the squared-up shoulders, the long-legged strides, but then he stops suddenly, as if he's forgotten something, and swings round, proffering the folded-up umbrella. "You want this, Linda?" he offers.

I shake my head.

"You sure?"

"Uh-uh," I say, "it's not going to rain anymore," and he shrugs and starts off again and I'm left there watching Dawn watch him.

The first thing she says to me when he passes out of sight around the corner of the building is, "I hope you're not talking to any of these reporters. They're just looking for some way to tear me down. Johnny says—"

"No," I say, "no way. I mean, give me some credit, at least."

"Okay," she says, caressing the beach ball of her belly with both hands as if it's not her own flesh drawn tight over the placenta and the fetus inside that has its own fingernails and hair on its head and can open and close its eyes, but the baby itself, born and wriggling in her lap. "Just so you understand. I really want to make all this positive, you know? And they're sniffing around, looking for any-thing they can use to poke holes in E2, I know they are. Johnny says they've even been after him, if you can believe it—"

Am I feeling defensive? Yes. Sure. What does she think I am? "How do *you* know what Johnny says?"

Her eyes snap wide. I can hear her breathing, heavily, wetly, the baby squeezing her lungs like a constrictor so she has trouble catching her breath. What she says, wheezily, is, "He still drops by." A pause. "Unlike some people."

"I've been busy."

"More than busy," she says. "It's like you're ignoring me. But tell me, really—have I done anything to offend you? Because if I have, I swear I didn't mean it. You're my best friend. Still. And I need you more than ever, because"—and here she breaks down, more tears, instant tears—"everybody's being so shitty to me, and I didn't sign up for this, I really didn't . . . I thought we were a *team*."

Despite what people may think, I am not the Dragon Lady, I am not heartless, I am not a false friend. And in that moment at the glass, with a light rain beginning to fall and Dawn sobbing into the phone, I feel the world shift around me. All this time my jealousy has been blinding me to what we had between us, our special bond that was super-durable, a shield that made us impervious to the infighting and maneuvering of the others, just the two of us, together. It's not just about me. And what she's going through—the pressure on her, Judy, G.C., Ramsay, the reporters, the baby—is staggering. I feel ashamed of myself.

"Hush," I say. "It's okay. You know what I'd do if I was in there with you?"

"What?" She lifts her face, which is like some tragic mask, glistening with tears.

"I'd give you a hug. You want a hug? Come here, come to the glass."

And she stands up and we press ourselves to the window, body to body, till I can feel the weight of her through that transparent three-eighths-inch shell and the rain picks up to flatten my hair and for once I don't even care.

* * *

I'd like to say the feeling lasts, but that would be a lie. I do make a point of going to the glass more often, every three or four days now, but it isn't Dawn I'm soothing so much as myself—my own guilty conscience—and there's no percentage in that. She's weepy. Getting weepier. Terrified that something's going to go wrong with the delivery and sensitive to every slight, real or imagined, on the part of her fellow crewmembers, who really do begin to show their true colors as Dawn's due date looms nearer and nearer and the calories recycle in a closed loop and everybody tightens their belts and tiptoes around in dread of what the winter's going to bring, what with dwindling resources and another mouth to feed, little Adam Roothoorp, poster child for E2, whose very existence will make all the rest of them even more irrelevant than they already are.

That's when the food thefts begin in earnest.

Jeff Weston's the first to notice. He's on the cameras a lot now, along with Ellen and Malcolm—more than ever, actually, because I'm hardly monitoring at all since Judy anointed me her personal assistant/gofer/whipping girl, and though he's bored and yawning and taking longer and longer breaks each day, he just happens to glance at the monitor for the ag basement one morning, right where the food-storage closet is, and sees not Diane coming out the door but Stevie and Troy, and they've got something in their hands, something they're trying to hide behind their backs. He watches till they're off-camera, then rewinds and zooms in for positive identification, enlarging the image till the banana peels reveal themselves. The storeroom, by the way, is mainly for the bananas, which is what people want most, for the calories and sweetness both, and whenever a bunch on one of the trees begins to show the first sign of ripening, Diane cuts it down and removes it to the basement, where ostensibly people won't be tempted (out of sight, out of mind), as opposed to leaving it in the rain forest or the orchard where it would be so much harder to resist. Everybody's into the mission a hundred percent, and that means share and share alike, but when you're starving and the food's right there hanging over your head, it may not be so easy to think of your fellow crewmembers first. So the bananas are in the storeroom. Which doesn't—yet—have a lock on the door. And Stevie and T.T. are helping themselves.

That's the issue, and Jeff doesn't go straight to Judy with it out of some misguided but totally relatable notion of team loyalty, so he comes to me as the next best thing. My first reaction is *Gotcha!* but that's no good, that's wrong, because the crew inside has to self-regulate or the whole notion of E2 and all the missions to come is bankrupt. It's late morning and Jeff and I are sitting there looking at the tape with an eye out for Judas and Little Jesus, trying to figure out what we should do. Jeff—not homely, not exactly, but so ordinary-looking you couldn't pick him out of a lineup of one—says we're going to have to report this to somebody and I say, "Why?" and he says, "Because it's not right," and he has his finger right on the pulse of it. No, it's not right, and it's not right that Dawn and Ramsay have put them in this position either, so I say, "Maybe Diane. Maybe quietly, like in her room, and see what she wants to do?"

But then something else happens, another theft, not as blatant as raiding the banana room and yet symptomatic of what's going on inside now. It's Gyro. I'm sitting there with Jeff in the wake of catching T.T. and Stevie in the act, when one of the savanna monitors shows Gyro casually stuffing passion fruit into his mouth as he ambles by, spitting seeds and disappearing camera-right only to come back again and linger in the thorn trees there where the passion fruit vines have made a thatch of the branches. And then, later, much later, I'm in my cubicle doing paperwork when Ellen, who's on the night shift and has been tipped off by Jeff, calls me to look at *her* feed and there's Richard, just before dinner when everyone else is already gathering in the dining room, emerging from the banana closet and looking guilty. Richard. Who you'd think would be above it. But there's the lesson: nobody's above it.

Especially Dawn. All right, she's got an excuse, but still, you've got to consider she's already getting extra portions and I'm sure sneaking an egg here and there and skimming what she can off the top of the goat's milk. I don't confront her or anything and to this point Jeff, Ellen and I have kept quiet about what's going on, but the next time I see her she's the one who brings it up. "I feel terrible," she says. "I really do. I know it's not right. I know

I'm violating a trust here"—and she pauses, going from weepy to steely in a heartbeat—"but I will not put my baby at risk, no matter what it takes."

What it takes is Diane putting a padlock on the door to the storage room—without comment, is the way I hear it—while everybody, including Richard, runs around strenuously denying any involvement in the case of the missing bananas, which aren't the only things going missing. Avocados too. And avocados are like gold inside because of their fat content, oleic acid, the same thing you find in olive oil, which, of course, the crew doesn't have and won't have, not now or ever. There are only three avocado trees to begin with, all located right below the Habitat in the orchard, where any thief would be conspicuous, so you'd think nobody would dare go near them. Nonetheless, they all wake up one morning to find the lower branches considerably lighter and Diane orders all three trees stripped of their still-undersized rock-hard fruit and puts *that* in the storage room too. Ditto the few oranges and even lemons still ripening on the trees, and if this is a sad commentary on team unanimity, at least it doesn't get out to the press because the press is besotted with Dawn and only Dawn (mid-August and the baby drops, turning head-down for the big plunge, and you'd think nobody in the history of humankind has ever given birth before, reporters swarming the glass, paparazzi everywhere, the turnstiles spinning with tourists braving the heat in the hope of catching a glimpse of the expectant mother herself—and there she is, with her dirty feet and jam-packed T-shirt, milking the goats, pulling weeds, harvesting tomatoes!).

Still? I wouldn't want to be Dawn and I don't mean that in a catty way—I really do feel sorry for her. As she gets closer to her due date—it's in September, the twentieth or so, or that's Richard's best guess—the pressure just keeps mounting. Ramsay's no help. He's busy spinning the press about ninety percent of the time, and when he's not—or even when he is—you can see the boredom piling up in his eyes like the sand in an hourglass. Gretchen hates her. Stevie never much liked her to begin with, or that's my take on it, and now there's open antipathy between them. As for the rest, it's all about calories. And Mission Control never lets up, of course, playing this for all its worth. So she's got nowhere to turn—and she's afraid too, in the way I suppose any first-time mother must be, but any first-time mother, at least in this country, has an obstetrician on call and a hospital bed waiting for her. What does she tell me, at the glass, late, and I'm just back from the bar, where I've limited myself to three drinks and defied any son of a bitch (or plain straight-up bitch) from any newspaper to come within five feet of me? She says, "I'm scared."

And I say, "Scared of what? Everything's going to be fine."

"Of Richard," she says.

I'm in best-friend mode here, feeling her pain, and I don't know what to say, aside from reversing every desperate argument I made when suffering under the delusion that I could talk her into breaking closure. "Don't be," I say. "Delivering babies isn't brain surgery. And he *is* a doctor—and you trust him, right?"

She's exhausted. She can hardly keep her head up. "It's not that. I just wish, I don't know, it was more anonymous somehow. I mean, I know him *too* well."

"What, you're talking about that time he came on to you? That's like—he photographs you nude, right? Photographs every-body? It's a doctor/patient thing, Dawn, I'm sure it is. I'm sure he'll be able to—"

"I don't want his hands on me."

"Whoa, where's that coming from? If he doesn't do it, who will—Ramsay? Diane? Come on, Dawn, you're just being crazy now."

She lifts her head then and her eyes dig into me in a way that changes things all over again, a way that makes me think she knows everything I've done and thought through all these putrid months, about Johnny, about Gavin, about her. "Easy for you to say, but really, Linda, I think you're missing something here—"

"What?" I say.

"I'm the one that's pregnant." Long pause. "Not you."

Dawn Chapman

The ninth month was probably the worst, and not just because of the media circus and the guilt I felt every time I snuck a handful of monkey chow or took more than my share of milk, but because of sheer exhaustion, just that. Everything I did, from getting out of bed in the morning to bending over to pull weeds or trim plants, felt as if I were doing it underwater, as if I were one of Cousteau's Aquanauts burdened with a breathing device and dive weights and barely able to stroke my way through this atmosphere that seemed to be growing denser by the day. I was determined not to let my crewmates down, though, and no matter how hard it was I forced myself to keep on working right up until my water broke. I even waded into the fish ponds to do my share in the rice harvest, leeches or no, and took my turn at cooking as long as I could. As for the rest, Mission Control didn't miss a beat. They arranged for a Lamaze instructor to drive up from the birthing center in Tucson, along with eight other pregnant couples, who unfurled their foam mats outside the visitors' window so Vodge and I could have the full group experience, which was a huge comfort for me, just to see there were other women going through the same thing I was. (Or almost the same thing—they had obstetrics clinics to go to. And restaurants, supermarkets, fast-food outlets. All that, and nobody was photographing their every move.)

The instructor was a comfort too—a sweet-faced, fiftyish woman in sweats who was able to walk us through the stages of labor, massage techniques, use of the birth ball, squat bar and strategically placed pillows, and, of course, the breathing exercises, without getting either too clinical or too saccharine either. If it was hard on her, having to communicate through the phone at the visitors' window and deal with the press of photographers our security guards tried to keep at a respectful distance, she never showed it. As for Richard, despite my case of nerves and the fact that as we got closer to term I kept pushing him away, give him credit here—he was totally conscientious, poring over the literature on breech births and other nightmares, consulting regularly with the expert from Johns Hopkins, doing everything he could to try and put me at ease. And when we were two weeks out, he sat me and Vodge down to watch a video relayed over from Mission Control that painted the whole process of natural birth in what was meant to be a reassuring way.

The thing is, it didn't really seem to have the desired effect—if I was scared before the film, I was terrified after it. Not so much with the process itself, which I felt I had a pretty good grip on at that point, but with the whole series of decisions that had led up to my sitting there in the command center watching it in the first place. With my *husband*. I'd never dreamed I'd have a husband before reentry—just the term itself and all it conveyed was enough to make me feel as if I were taking a leap every time I pronounced it aloud (mainly to the press)—and if I'd imagined a husband somewhere down the road, it certainly wasn't Vodge. Or Johnny. Somebody like Gavin, maybe, but he was too young and really hadn't come aboard in time to make a difference.

So here was this film playing on the computer monitor, normal mothers, normal pregnancies, hospitals, nurses, dietary charts, and all I could think was I'd made the biggest mistake of my life. And no, I wasn't going to go back and blame myself for falling in love with Vodge or being careless that first night—that was done, that was over, and I'd already tortured myself enough on that account—but I kept asking myself how I could ever have defied Vodge and Mission Control and everybody else to insist on going through with this. Was I out of my mind? These were normal mothers smiling at me from the depths of the screen, but I wasn't a normal mother, I was starved, scrawny, fighting each day to make sure I got enough protein to keep my baby healthy, and I have to say, more and more, it had begun to feel like a losing battle.

If I was dying inside, Vodge was a mess. He had to excuse

himself and get up in the middle of the film and he didn't return till the end, when the baby, cleaned and swaddled, was blinking its eyes in its mother's arms—which was all right, I suppose, since he still hadn't committed to being there in the delivery room when the time came and I really wasn't going to press him on that score. (Typical Vodge: he tried to turn everything into a joke to cover the fact that he was as scared as I was, maybe even more so. "This New Age consciousness thing where the father's expected to be there gets it all wrong—it ought to be the way it was in the old movies, a bunch of guys in big-shouldered suits and hats sitting in the waiting room, passing a bottle around until the nurse pops her head in and chirps, 'It's a boy!' I mean, *that's* civilized.")

There came a morning in late August when I couldn't seem to get out of bed. I opened my eyes and couldn't think where I was, still lost in the dream I'd been having over and over lately, of me, unpregnant, wearing nothing but my two-piece and lying stretched out on the deck of The *Imago* under the real sun, the actual sun, and then slipping stealthily overboard and stroking my way across the flat belly of the sea toward the horizon that just seemed to open up forever. But there I was, staring up at the familiar ceiling, tentative in my own body, as if I'd borrowed it from somebody else. Vodge wasn't there. He'd taken to sleeping in his own room most nights, claiming I was keeping him awake with my tossing and turning ("It's like sleeping with a beached whale," he told me, and if it was meant as a joke, I have to say I really didn't find it all that funny). We hadn't had sex since maybe the seventh month, though certainly I wanted to—and wanted him to hold me, if nothing else—but he kept saying it was bad for the baby, when of course that was just nonsense. Both Richard and Dr. Reston—I asked them—said sex is fine right up until your water breaks. Vodge never said as much, but I think he was turned off by the way I looked and just decided to go back to being celibate (and yes, it did occur to me that he might be sneaking back to Gretchen, who did seem, I don't know, *softer* toward him all of a sudden, but that was probably just my own paranoia).

Anyway, I woke up from my dream and immediately felt

myself clench as if there was a punch-press stamping away inside me and realized I must be having—had just had—a contraction. I waited for another one, counting one-a-thousand, two-a-thousand, but it didn't come, and then it did. Which scared me. It was too early yet, nearly a month before my due date, and here was what we'd all been afraid of from the beginning: a premature baby. Underweight. Underdeveloped. A damaged baby, even— one that wouldn't represent E2 and its lifestyle the way Mission Control expected it to. A baby that had come prematurely because E2 couldn't provide enough calories for its mother to sustain it. Another contraction, then nothing. I pushed myself up, though my body felt like a sack of bowling balls, listened for Richard next door, then used the toilet, brushed my teeth and hair and sat heavily on the couch in the living room, waiting.

What was happening to me, though I didn't realize it yet, was what's called false labor (or Braxton Hicks contractions—named after a man, if you can believe it). I had another contraction while I was pulling on my shorts, then another two minutes later, then nothing. This went on, erratically, through the morning milking, breakfast and team meeting, and by that point I was in a state. The pain kept coming in waves. Somebody asked me something and I didn't respond. I couldn't. All I could do was clench my teeth and hold on. Still, I didn't want to go to Richard, not yet, not until it was absolutely necessary, so I pulled Vodge aside in the hallway just after the meeting and told him I thought it was time.

It took him a minute to process what I was saying, his face gone slack and his shoulders collapsed, one hand snatching at the air as if he were on a crowded bus and fumbling for a strap to hang on to. He looked lost. Looked as if *he* were the one having the contractions. "What are you saying?"

"I don't know. I think"—and here came another contraction, sharp and sudden, the punch-press stamping away so that he could see it in my face—"I think the baby's coming."

He just stood there, looking hopeless, and then his lips were moving, silently counting off the months and days. "But that can't be. It's not due for like a month yet—"

"Three and a half weeks."

"But still . . . You're telling me you're having contractions?"

I nodded. The pain made me want to sit down, collapse, grovel, but we were in the hall and there was nowhere to sit. "I think so. I mean, it hurts—it really hurts."

"Think so? What the hell are you talking about? Either you're having them or not—"

We were alone in the hallway. The morning light gilded the plants, clung to the spaceframe till it shone like something out of a sci-fi movie, which, in a way, I suppose it was. I felt . . . not sick, not exactly—more as if I were having my period and cramping, but cramping really badly. Was this what it was going to be like? Was this it? I didn't have a clue. What I said was, "Actually? I'm not sure."

He let out a curse. "What are you doing *here* then? And why the hell are you telling *me*—isn't it Richard you ought to be talking to? I mean, do I look like a doctor to you? *Jesus!*"

So I went to Richard—or actually, Vodge just about frog-marched me into his office, startling Richard, who'd been bent over one of the petri dishes in which he was cultivating a sample of the fungal matter he'd scraped off the glass in a back corner of the rain forest.

"You've got to do something!" Vodge shouted, his frame rigid now and his face drained of color but for its residue of carotene orange—Vodge, my Vodge, all in a panic.

Richard barely gave him a glance. It was me he looked to, swiping the little black-framed glasses from his face so he could focus on what mattered here, and if he looked as alarmed as Vodge, it was only in that moment. "Are you having contractions?" Richard asked.

"Yes," I told him.

"Regular?"

"No. Or I don't think so—I'm just, it *hurts*."

That was when Vodge said, "Okay, okay," then repeated it twice more before stepping back out into the hall and pulling the door shut behind him.

We both watched him go. Then Richard, totally composed now—all business—said, "Let's have a look."

* * *

As just about anybody with access to a TV, radio or newspaper will know, our daughter, Eve, was born full-term, on September 20, 1995, and despite all our fears and the hand-wringing in the press, weighed in at a respectable six pounds, fourteen ounces. I don't remember much of the birth itself, except that the pain was at a level I thought I could bear (and no, there would be no epidural, no drugs of any kind, not even oxytocin, which we wouldn't have had in any case, because to my mind natural means natural, period), but by the third hour of labor I felt as if somebody was tearing me open and then cauterizing everything inside me, over and over again. I didn't cry out, not that I can remember, but I was right there, right on the cusp of it the whole time, thinking I was going to die, thinking the baby was going to die—or worse, come out all twisted and deformed like the little monster in *Eraserhead.*

I tried to be strong, tried to push all that negativity out of my mind, but I couldn't, I just couldn't, and by the end all I wanted to do was die. Say what you will about Vodge, but he was there for me, right there beside me through the better part of my eight hours of labor, trying his best to comfort me and coach me through the breathing exercises, though that sort of thing—patience, loving care, the conventional reaction to a conventional situation—didn't come naturally to him. He was like Johnny in that regard, more concerned about keeping his cool or *being* cool to worry over-much about other people and their feelings. Again, I was pretty far gone by the time the baby came, but I do know it was Diane there assisting the physician and not Vodge. Vodge didn't have the strength for it. I'm not saying he wasn't capable in so many other ways or that he was less a man for being—what, squeamish?—but that this was a kind of intimacy he just couldn't seem to handle.

Richard could, though. And so could Diane. Richard did put his hands on me, of course he did, and I was glad of it. In fact, for a while there, after the baby came out, the whole issue was in doubt because the placenta wouldn't drop and I was bleeding heavily, big gouts of material, blood clots, and Richard finally had to go inside me and manually remove it, which opened up a whole new avenue of pain, pain that was far worse than the childbirth itself. That was no fun. And I didn't realize how close I'd come to passing out from blood loss until well after the fact. But the point is, I didn't bleed to death and the baby—our daughter, Eve—was healthy, normal, perfect, and the only people who knew Vodge wasn't present in the delivery room weren't about to say anything about it. And did it really matter all that much? My parents' generation certainly didn't think so. The men were strictly excluded—forcibly, if necessary—and the women had their epidurals and went under and woke up with a clean pink squalling baby in their arms.

So no, it didn't bother me, even when it came out that Vodge had got cold feet at the end and shirked his duty, because we were pioneers of a new world and a new way of thinking and people can't expect a kind of rigid mind-control over everything and everybody, whether it's laid down by society at large or Mission Control in microcosm—we were Terranauts, yes, but we were individuals too, now more than ever. We never did discover who'd ratted him out, incidentally—not that it mattered. What mattered was what we presented at the glass not two hours after Eve was born (and she'd not only come right on her due date but at four-forty-seven in the afternoon, as if she was already geared to the prime-time viewing schedule).

G.C. presided, as usual, while Vodge and I posed for pictures at the visitors' window, Eve cuddled in my arms with her little monkey face in repose, looking like nobody yet, not Vodge or me or my mother or any of my aunts either. Richard, calm and collected and with a celebratory dose of E2 arak running through his veins, took a bow and posed for photos with Vodge, Eve and me, then responded to questions from the press, both at the glass and later in the command center, via PicTel. He was clearly beat (and, if you knew what to look for, showing signs of the early stages of inebriation, his voice slowing to a crawl and his eyes focusing high over the heads of the crowd gathered there in the courtyard). Vodge was beat too—and under the influence of his own commemorative dose. I was the one who'd done all the work and yet the funny thing was I didn't feel tired at all—just the opposite: I was exhilarated, feeling higher than I'd ever felt in my life, and I hadn't needed any arak to get me there either.

After ten minutes or so, Little Jesus herded everybody away from the glass so we could do the network TV interviews he and Judy had set up, and Vodge and I sat there at the phone, alternately answering the queries they put to us, which were purely ritualistic and soft as baby powder. No one asked about diet or how we expected to feed our daughter or whether we'd be tempted to import food or anything like that. They wanted the good news only, the positive news, and that was just what we were there to give them.

Q: You've been through a lot, Dawn—how do you feel? And congratulations, by the way.

ME (hair snarled dramatically, lipstick and eye shadow freshly applied): Thank you so much—everybody. I feel great, I feel blessed, as we all do, the whole E2 family, both inside the Ecosphere and out there in Mission Control.

Q: You've got a beautiful daughter—have you given her a name yet?

ME (I've seen this tape probably twenty times): Eve.

Q: Eve?

RAMSAY (leaning in to share the phone): If it'd been a boy, we would have called him Adam.

Q: How about the reaction of your crewmates? I'll bet they're happy for you.

ME: Never happier.

Q: Were you at all concerned about not having the kind of care you'd get at a hospital?

ME: No. I had complete confidence in Dr. Lack. He's our medical officer. He's our crewmate. Anything happens, he's there for us. And, as you can see (angling the baby toward the camera) he's shown himself to be more than capable. Wouldn't you say?

And I stopped right there, letting Eve—whose eyes blinked open at that very moment—do the rest.

* * *

So we had an extra Terranaut—where once we were eight, now we were nine. It didn't happen right away, but most of my crewmates, I think, eventually came to see Eve's value to the mission. In a sense, she *was* the human experiment, or the result of it anyway, and nothing anyone had done through the course of Mission One and now Mission Two could even begin to touch the tsunami of publicity she generated. There were photography sessions every day, interviews, thousands upon thousands of people worldwide tracking each ounce and inch she put on and every hair that sprouted on her head, and forget the galagos—half the schoolchildren in the country were now drawing, coloring and painting pictures of little Princess Eve in her towering glass castle. Mission Control rushed an Eve doll into production for sale in the gift shop alongside the galago toys and went into negotiations to generate a line of coloring books for the younger kids. Vodge—and he was as charged up as I'd ever seen him—called it marketing the brand, and if that tended to distract people from the real science, Mission Control was on top of that too, bringing in a team of sociologists, anthropologists and early-childhood psychologists to weigh in on Eve and document her first five and a half months under glass. I'm sure every mother must feel her baby is unique, the apex of life on earth and the apple of everybody's eye, but in this case it was true.

What I didn't want was for people to defer to me in any way—my crewmates, I mean. There was already enough resentment, and for the first week or so after Eve was born people did have to cover for me, because, as I've said, it took eight of us working full-time, working to exhaustion, just to keep E2 up and running, and there was no provision for downtime. I wasn't really up to strength those first couple of days, which even the pettiest amongst us (I won't name names) had to appreciate, but still I didn't feel right about it. Richard insisted I take it easy—and Dr. Reston and G.C. backed him up—but even so there were all those interviews and, of course, adjusting to the new baby, what with breast-feeding, changing diapers (which we fashioned from a couple of old towels and things in the discarded clothes bin, mainly worn T-shirts doubled up, sewed into shape and washed and rewashed) and worrying about the baby sleeping through the night. (If you're curious, Vodge was no help there at all—he slept in his own room exclusively now, claiming he couldn't be expected to take up the slack for me in the IAB and animal pens, not to mention shoulder the ever-expanding PR burden he had to carry, if he couldn't get a full night's rest. Do I sound peeved? Maybe I am. At least a bit. It was all on me, always on me.)

Still, within a week I was back to my normal duties. Diane had helped me make a kind of papoose from an old pair of jeans fitted out with wooden ribs so I could work with Eve strapped to my back, and if it wasn't exactly the archetypal scenario of the peasant woman biting off the umbilical cord and going right back out to work in the fields, it was close enough. Eve was a good baby—a bit colicky, maybe, and furnished with an operatic pair of lungs—and I really think her easy adjustment to life in E2 had a lot to do with the fact that she was there with me, pressed close to my body, all day every day, instead of left in a cradle in an apartment somewhere like the vast majority of her contemporaries. Think of it: I was the ultimate stay-at-home mom. And when she woke and was hungry and her gurgles and grunts and teakettle shrieks rose to echo off the glass and blend with the exotic calls of all the other creatures sharing the enclosure with us, I was right there for her.

One night, after I was done feeding the animals, I took Eve up to the room to feed her and lost track of the time, with the result that I wound up being a few minutes late for dinner. (This was just after Eve had passed the five-week mark, which meant we would have been closing in on Halloween, and all anybody could seem to talk about was the party we were going to throw, Halloween commencing the holiday countdown to Thanksgiving, Christmas, New Year's and, finally, the shining nirvana of reentry, and all our spirits were up because the end was in sight now.) Everyone else was already seated at the table and they hardly glanced up when I came into the room, carrying Eve in a tummy sling so I could more easily prop her up in my lap and offer her the odd spoonful of solid food. My plate, with the biggest portion, was waiting for me on the counter, and I took it without hesitation—starving, as always—and slid in next to Vodge, who leaned over to make a silly face for the baby, though she wasn't yet able to acknowledge it with a smile of her own. She was drowsy. Her eyes fluttered. She was asleep.

By this time, I was neither shy nor apologetic about taking the biggest portion at each meal—or having it mandated for me by Mission Control. A nursing mother needs an extra five hundred calories a day and I was determined to get all I could. Again, we were a team, and a team had to bend before it would break. Plus, Eve was the best thing that had happened to E2 since it rose up off the desert floor and everybody had to know that. She was worth it. I was worth it. And if it had been any of the others who needed *my* support I would have given it gladly. What if one of us had sprained an ankle or broken a leg? Wouldn't we all have rallied around him? Or her? Of course we would, because that was what this was all about, that was the very definition of team solidarity. So I sat down, took up my fork and didn't think twice about it.

The fight, as ridiculous as it was, started over the question of costumes, of all things. I wasn't ready for it, for the level of sheer nastiness that just put everybody at odds all over again, and maybe I was too self-absorbed to see it coming, I'll admit it—I was eating, working at the process of absorbing nutrients so that I could keep on eating and breathing and redirecting calories to my baby, just like any other mother, like Lola, and I wasn't paying much attention to the conversation. Vodge was saying something to me, a joke about the way I was shoveling it in, I think. T.T. was holding forth at the other end of the table and somebody laughed and somebody said *Pass the salt* and whether the meal tasted as bland as paste or right up there with a four-star restaurant, I couldn't have said, I was that disconnected. But Gretchen—Snowflake—was calling my name, or had called it, and I looked up at the sound of the single long syllable—*E.*—and she repeated herself.

"I was just saying, E., I'm curious—have you decided what you're going to be yet?"

I was thick, I was eating, and to this point the conversation had breezed right by me. My daughter, still asleep, shifted in my lap. "What do you mean?"

"For Halloween. If you're not going to make it a surprise, I mean—?"

I set down my fork, looked round the table. Everyone was watching me. "Well," I said, feeling a little charge of satisfaction because Vodge and I had already talked it over, and I glanced at him first—the shag of his hair, a two-day growth of beard, his pale gray eyes fixed lovingly on mine—before I came back to her. "Vodge and I thought we'd go as Jimbo and Lola, and Eve could be Lolly." (Lolly, as most people will know, was Lola's surviving twin—Juniper, the male, had disappeared and was presumed dead, perhaps killed by his father as he came into sexual maturity, but maddeningly, we'd found no trace of his corpse.)

Gretchen—she was on the opposite side of the table, seated next to Stevie, who was, as always, beside Troy—took in a sharp breath. She let her mouth fall open. Her hair was no longer the pretty threaded gold it had been at closure, but more a kind of dull tarnished copper going to white. It was dirty. Her face was dirty. Her hands. Her nails. She said, "I'm just flabbergasted. You had to know I was going to be Lola. I mean, I've been working on my costume for a week now—" She shot her eyes up and down both sides of the table, as if looking for confirmation.

Richard, always quick on his feet, said, "Why don't we all go as galagos? Personally, I think I'd look pretty good with a long black-tipped tail, what do you think, Diane? Galagos all the way around?"

Gretchen wouldn't be swayed. "It's not funny. *She* knew—or she ought to know. Who's in charge of them? Who puts in twelve hours a week recording their behavior in her notebook—and takes pictures? Like a thousand pictures?"

Vodge said, "Hey, it's not set in stone—she's just saying what we were thinking about, is all. By the way, Gretch, what were you last year, I forget?"

She was like a big sulky pouch-faced child. She sucked in her cheeks, glared at him, at both of us. *"Lola."*

I don't know why I said what I did next but maybe it was because it had been my idea in the first place and I'd set my heart on it—it would be a way to include Eve, and the kids out there in the world were going to love it. I said—and regretted it the moment the words left my mouth—"You don't own the patent on them."

"Yeah, well I suppose you do? What, because you go around stealing from the feeding stations? That makes you an expert? That gives you dibs?"

This was the moment Eve chose to wake up, and that was probably my fault too, since I'd tensed when Gretchen started in on me and the baby must have felt it. Eve snapped open her eyes, and as if the lids were synchronized with her vocal cords, began to cry. But this wasn't just a normal cry—it was one of those startled reflexive tumbling-out-the-window shrieks that stopped the conversation dead in its tracks and started my milk (another hormonal reaction) so the front of my tee was wet, instantly. You'd think she'd give me a break—Diane and Stevie too. They were women, just like me. And yet none of them seemed to have the slightest bit of sympathy for me or my baby, no maternal instinct at all, and never once did any of them offer to hold the baby or play with her or anything else.

"Why don't you shut her up?" Troy said, nastily, in the interval before I could get up from the table, lift my shirt and put her to the nipple, and that just made me angry, I'm sorry. So I glared at him. And just sat there an extra minute and let her scream.

"Christ, I can't believe this!" Troy shot furiously to his feet, slamming the napkin down on his plate.

Vodge was on his feet now too—and I was about to get up and go down the hall to my room and calm both my daughter and myself, but something froze me there. Maybe it was stubbornness, maybe it was a release of all the pent-up pressure and resentment of the way everybody patronized me, talked behind my back, let the jealousy show in their selfish hateful faces, but I wasn't budging. Vodge said, "Give her a break."

Troy said—shouted—"Look who's talking! You want to know something? You're the bad seed here, you're the shitwad, you with the microphone up your ass—"

Vodge cursed him, Troy cursed back, and before Richard or Gyro could intervene, they were at each other, down on the wine-colored natural-weave wool carpet that was free of any trace of manufacturer's chemicals, trading blows, and Vodge getting the worst of it. It didn't go on for long, but while it did everybody was screaming, not just Eve, not just my daughter, but the whole unraveling Terranaut crew.

Ramsay Roothoorp

I didn't ask for it, but I should have seen it coming, and I tell you, I wound up bruised in more ways than one. The worst thing about a fight—what makes a coward of anybody who has more than a nanosecond to think about the outcome—is the possibility of losing. It's not about physical pain, not about cuts and bruises or even broken bones, but dominance and humiliation. And Troy certainly dominated me—and humiliated me too. I'd never been in the navy, never had any kind of combat training, never learned to box or anything like that—I'd always relied on my wits and sometimes my wits failed me. Like this time. I was on the floor before I could think, flailing away ineffectually while he jabbed a knee into my sternum and kept whacking me in the face with both fists till Richard and Gyro pulled him off, and who knew he was ambidextrous? I could taste blood in my mouth. There was a buzzing in my ears. Everybody kept shouting, especially Troy, who went on cursing me even as I pushed myself shakily up and went to E., who helped me limp down the hall to her room and clucked and cooed over me as if I were the baby and not Eve. It wasn't what I needed. And it only put me in a fouler mood. Everything she said about Troy, every animadversion and belittling remark, was true, but it just made me hurt all the more. I'll tell you, I was *writhing*.

I let her minister to the abrasions on both cheeks—rug burns, fist burns—and put an ice pack over my right eye, which by morning would look as if the butt of an eggplant had been grafted to the orbit there, and then without a word I got up from the couch and went out to the fish ponds, in the dark, to brood over the whole business. What I concluded, after maybe thirty minutes of letting my emotions even out, was that Troy Turner—T.T.—was an asshole, had always been and would always be an asshole, and that I'd gone too far out of my way in making allowances for him to this point, deluding myself into thinking he was a human being. If we weren't locked in, if we weren't crewmates? I wouldn't have given him a second glance. Yes, he was an asshole. Worse still, he was a bore. Of the first magnitude.

People reading this might remember the time around Halloween of the second year when a branch came crashing down out of the big ceiba in the rain forest and struck me smack in the face, which accounted for my black eye that lasted, incredibly, for something like two weeks. Well, know that there was no branch, only T.T.'s fists, and the truth is out now. Not that it matters, because I was all about cover-up, all about the mission, and if I'm not giving myself too much credit here, one of the champion *eliders* of my generation.

Elide though you might, life has a way of biting back, even life in as controlled an environment as E2. I'm talking about cosmic irony here, the kind of thing that makes you believe there must be a God after all, or at least his opposite number, a malicious turner of events who could make even the Astrophysical Society question whether the universe is truly indifferent. Three weeks after our little altercation, which Troy and I hadn't really got over, though we made a show of it for the sake of the crew and put on a face for Mission Control and the press (that hurtling branch), one of my molars on the lower left side began to throb. But not just throb—it manifested itself as a continuously rising blister of pain that started at breakfast that morning and never let up. By lunch, I could barely chew. I worked all the same, hoping it would pass, but by dinner it was so bad it felt as if my lower jaw were trying to detach itself from my skull. I needed help. I needed lidocaine, the drill, the amalgam—and needed it now. And who was our emergency dentist? That's right: Troy.

I don't have to tell you how much I had on my plate at this juncture, working the press, filling in for E. where I could, clawing away at the notion of fatherhood and trying my best to please everybody concerned, not the least of whom was Eve, this squalling wrinkled red-faced alien that had come out of nowhere to dominate our lives—or at least mine and E.'s. E. lectured me on the biochemistry involved in mother/child bonding, and I understood that, I appreciated it, but where was the biochemistry for the *father*? Everybody assumed I was the prototypical proud papa, just thrilled and delighted over this miraculous avatar of reproductive biology in our midst, but it wasn't like that at all—not at first anyway. The baby was an excrescence, an irritation, screeching when she wasn't asleep, excreting whether she was or not (which put an additional burden, however small, on the water retrieval system), and not yet capable even of smiling her gratitude when you picked her up and whispered nonsense in her ear or let her grab hold of your index finger in her rudimentary grasp.

Her gums were pink, her uvula a pink flag flapping on the wind her lungs generated, and she kicked her legs and waved her arms like a beetle turned over on its back. She was a prodigy at the tit and by the fifth or sixth week had begun to put away an alarming quantity of the porridge E. had begun to feed her, spoon to mouth, in a gagging ecstasy of flailing limbs and gustatory lip-smacking. Which was endearing, I suppose. Or meant to be, on a subliminal level. Talk about bonding, I had an easier time bonding with the leeches in the fish ponds (pun intended), because at least their needs were immediate and immediately consummated—and terminated. But babies? Babies just went on and on.

So there was all that, and I was doing my best to adjust. We all were, not only to the new presence in our midst but to the slow disintegration of the interrelationships that had sustained us to this juncture, the fistfight with Troy emblematic of the larger problem. It had been a long time brewing, I could see that now, but I'd been oblivious to it, or if not oblivious, certainly in denial. I wanted all this to work, the human experiment, brothers and sisters all, wanted it desperately, wanted E2 to stand as an exception to the kind of assured destruction you saw in the literature of closed systems. We were better than the Bios researchers or the crews in Antarctica, or that was what I'd wanted to believe. That was all over now. We were on the downward slope, the light declining, food supplies falling off, three and a half long months yet to go, and I had a toothache.

I couldn't bring myself to go directly to Troy, so after dinner that night I took Richard aside and explained the problem to him in the hope he would be my bridge here and maybe even agree to oversee Troy's efforts with the drill and dental pick—or at least be there as a presence in the room with us. People will tell you they don't like hospitals or they don't like going to the dentist, as if that singles them out from the vast majority who relish the gurney and the dental chair, but for me it wasn't so much about pain or the cessation of it as it was about loss of control. You put yourself in somebody else's hands because you have no other choice, unless you're going to drill your own teeth or sew up your own abdominal cavity, and that's difficult for me. I want to be the one in control, always.

Richard eyed me over the remains of the meal—the scraped and licked plates, that is—and asked me where it hurt. I opened my mouth and pointed to the tooth in question. "Close for a minute?" he said, then gingerly felt along the ridge of my jawbone, his fingers spread like the legs of an oversized spider, a tarantula, something poised to bite, and applied pressure to the spot I'd indicated. The pain was right there at the surface, searing and immediate, and it brought tears to my eyes.

"I was going to ask 'how's that feel?,' but I can see from your reaction it's bad. Tell me, on a scale of ten, ten being worst?"

"Ten."

"Can you wait till morning? We'll need to set up, and I can't imagine T.T.'s at his best right now, can you?"

I shook my head, not knowing which question I was answering, but I shouldn't have shaken my head because that just provoked the pain response. E. had gone back to the room with Eve. Diane—chef du jour—was cleaning up, and the others had already scattered (those who'd showed up, that is; both Troy and Stevie had taken to eating privately lately, carrying their plates off to their rooms or sometimes spreading a blanket down on the beach, which more and more seemed Stevie's private domain, for a secluded picnic).

Richard said, "Okay, how about this—what if I give you something for the pain and first thing in the morning, pre-breakfast, we'll see if we can't fix you up. Should I give you something?"

"Give me something. Definitely give me something."

What he gave me—codeine, 30 mg—got me through the night, or at least the first five hours of it, after which I woke in the dark with a crushing headache and a distant repetitive stab of pain that promised worse to come, and I got up, reached for the paper packet he'd given me and swallowed another pill, dry. I was sleeping in E.'s room that night, by the way, and I hadn't been with her overnight since sometime before the baby came, but I needed her presence, her comfort, her solidity, and I'd crept in beside her after she'd gone to sleep. When I sat up, she sat up too, and she whispered, "Vodge, are you all right?"

"I'm fine," I said. "Go back to sleep." But then the baby stirred in her cradle (a lopsided thing E. and I had managed to piece together from scrap wood we found in the shop in the basement) and began to fuss and we both held our breath. But then she fell off again and E. wrapped an arm around me and I put my head down till the sun came up to stripe the walls with light.

* * *

Richard was there at seven a.m., lightly knocking at E.'s door. "Vodge," he called, poking his head in the door and projecting his voice up the spiral stairs and into the bedroom. "Ramsay, you there?"

Next thing I knew (and yes, I was groggy from the opioids, my system flushed clean at this point of everything that wasn't E2-produced, and they hit me harder, I think, than they would have when I wasn't much more than a stew of intoxicants out there in the real world), I was in the med lab and settling into a makeshift dental chair, which was actually Richard's recliner, and Troy was snapping on a pair of rubber gloves and giving me a look I couldn't quite pin down. Was he reluctant? Put upon? Or—and here he inserted the hypodermic into the vial of lidocaine, then removed it for a trial squirt—was he enjoying this? "Open up," he said, and I wanted to delay him, stop him, and I guess I was actually reaching for his wrist when Richard, in a warning growl, said, "Don't even think about it."

What I *was* thinking about as Troy clumsily stuffed cotton wads inside my cheek and probed at the infected tooth with his dental pick in a way that might have been exploratory or sadistic or both, was a Browning poem I hadn't thought of in years. The poem was "Soliloquy of the Spanish Cloister," and all I could remember of it was two lines—"If hate killed men, Brother Lawrence,/ God's blood, would not mine kill you!"—but those two lines were enough, pounding inside my head as Troy propped himself up on my numbed lip and made the drill sing its song of vengeance, because that was what we'd come to in the depths of this grim November of Year Two when nobody was getting enough to eat and everybody was getting on everybody's nerves. It came to me that we were like Browning's monk, exactly like, all of us, even if we'd come into this with the best of intentions, and we had, I'm sure we had. But we'd been locked up too long, we were too familiar, every tic and gesture, every phrase and routine and story we'd heard a hundred times grating on our psyches till the notion of camaraderie was just a sick joke. In that moment, with my vanquisher standing above me plying his drill and Richard pinning me down with his voice alone, I'd never felt more trapped. All I wanted—with all my being—was to count down the days till I could walk through that airlock and go free and never have to see any of these people ever again.

* * *

Right then, right in the middle of all this chaos and bitterness and the declining food stocks and underwhelming harvests, G.C. devised a final theatrical exercise as a way of binding us together again. If we'd been hard-pressed to find the relevance in *The Skin of Our Teeth* and *The Bald Soprano*, we were entirely clueless this time around. What he wanted was for us to give two performances, with an alternating cast, of Sartre's *No Exit,* a play in which a man and two women are locked in a hellish afterlife in a single room, during which their only amusement is tearing each other to pieces. I'd say he was out of his mind—that's what I did say, privately, to E. and E. only, once the word came down—except the more I thought about it, the more it began to make sense. G.C. was a visionary, a genius of realization, probably the single most gifted individual I'd ever met, and if he wanted a *No Exit* input at this point, he must have had a purpose—and what was it? To defuse things. To make us act out our aggressions, even our hopelessness, and let us wallow in Aristotelean catharsis until we saw our way to freedom, because we *did* have an exit and that exit was going to hiss open in a matter of months—not an eternity, but just months now.

If it didn't exactly work out that way, it likely had more to do with extenuating circumstances than the play itself—but let me set the scene here. Deep dark November, cloud cover socking us in for a full week and a half because of an El Niño event off the West Coast of Mexico and O_2 levels plunging accordingly. It was unusual, that kind of weather at this time of year, but it was our bad luck that on top of all the other stresses on our systems, we were having a harder and harder time just catching our breath. Some of the frenzy surrounding Eve's birth had begun to subside—for me, at any rate, and that was a relief—but E. was spending an hour or two at the glass or on PicTel almost every day, and that, along with the stingy air and the demands Eve was making on her already deprived body, had her dragging through her days.

For my part, I'm happy to report that Troy's amateur dentistry efforts were successful, and I had to credit him there for draining the abscess, removing as much of the decayed dentin as he dared and sealing the chasm with a temporary filling, though I'd be heading straight for the endodontist the first week of reentry. And I still didn't like him. Nor would I—*ever*—forget the way he went at me with both fists when I was already down, and whether that had fractured the tooth or not I couldn't say, but the problems started in not long after, so you tell me.

Around that time there was a morning meeting that was more or less typical for the period, except, as I remember it, the tension was riding even higher than normal that day, on a number of counts. The first was G.C.'s announcement of the play, which had come via PicTel conference the preceding evening and which gave everybody a chance to vent (twice round the table and the ceremonial banana getting tireder and tireder as it passed from hand to hand). What was he thinking? was the general line of complaint. Didn't he realize we were starving? That we couldn't breathe? That we could barely summon the energy to keep E2 afloat, let alone waste calories (everything, ultimately, came down to calories) on some depressing play (which no one, to this point, had even read)?

After that had been batted around for a while, Diane brought up the question of the oxygen levels, which allowed Troy to give us the bad news we'd all suspected from the moment the first clouds had started rolling in and Linda Ryu, over at Mission Control, had given us the extended weather report for southeastern Arizona: we were in deep shit. The O_2 level had dropped below fifteen percent for the first time in Mission Two closure, which meant we were living and working in an atmosphere comparable to what you'd find at nine thousand feet, but we weren't at nine thousand feet, where the CO_2 would have thinned out along with the oxygen. Instead, it was trapped inside with us. Correspondingly, the ocean had become increasingly acidic in absorbing the higher concentrations of CO_2, which had Stevie and Troy buffering it almost daily with bags of calcium carbonate retrieved from the basement, and still the corals were stressed.

"I'm telling you," Stevie said, "the ocean pH is all over the board. Plus, I've got like a constant headache from the low oxygen. I can't sleep at night either. I mean, this is killing me."

"It's a nightmare," Gretchen chimed in, not bothering with the banana, just venting. I hadn't really given her a good look in I didn't know how long, but I saw her now, in the clarity of the morning light, as if she'd been away for months and come back transfigured. She was wearing a discolored smock, her legs and feet bare (none of us seemed to bother with shoes anymore), and it hung on her like a tent propped up on the poles of her shoulder-blades. That was shock enough, but her face was where the real transformation had occurred. Her face had been almost perfectly symmetrical, a round face, not beautiful by any stretch, but at least marginally attractive (I ought to know). Now she looked ten years older, her eyes staring out of their sockets, her double chin erased, her cheeks sucked in, every line and gouge and wrinkle on full display, riotous, like tracers shot out over a barren desert floor. Gretchen. And I'd been there, been in her bed, been inside her. "Really, I don't know how much longer I can take it. At this point, it's a matter of our health and well-being, I mean long-term damage—"

"What are you talking about? That's just crazy." Gyro was hunkered over his folded arms, his head dipping between his shoulders. His voice was lazy, but it was accusatory too and there was maybe a hint of alarm in it, as if he didn't know the dangers as well as the rest of us.

"I'm talking hypoxia and neural damage—loss of brain cells. Read some of the literature on mountain climbers if you want an eye-opener."

"We're not mountain climbers."

I was about to contradict him, about to say, *Yes we are,* when Diane slapped her hand down on the table and called for order. "You're out of turn, people," she said (and there it was again: *people*). "You want to be heard, you know the protocol. Thank you for the internal weather report, T.T."—nodding benevolently in his direction before raking her eyes across our collective faces— "and I know we're all suffering, but there's not much we can do about it, is there? Or not until the sun cooperates anyway. Which, I'm told, is tomorrow—tomorrow's supposed to be clear."

Gretchen, still ignoring the banana: "So big deal—what's that going to do, rocket us all the way up to fifteen percent again?"

"I'm sorry, but I am not going to recognize that—or your negativity either. Again, you want to be part of this meeting, of this *mission,* then you follow protocol. Understood?"

I saw Gretchen tense and for a moment I thought she was going to defy her, disrupt the meeting and drive yet another nail into the mission's coffin, but that didn't happen. She tensed, but she clamped her mouth shut and just glared, point made.

"I can't sleep either," Gyro said, out of turn. Diane gave him a sharp look and slid the banana across the table to him. "It's getting really bad. I keep dreaming I'm underwater or buried alive or something and then I wake up gasping. Like twenty times a night—"

"Sounds like sleep apnea." Richard, who was sitting on my left, delivered this as if it were the setup for a joke, which it was. "You ought to see a doctor about that."

"Very funny, Richard," Gyro said. "But, really, I'm with Gretchen on this—"

"*Banana*," Diane warned, but I'd already snaked out my hand and snatched it up. "On *what*?" I said, throwing it back at Gyro. "That we're all suffering, that the air is too thin and our diet even thinner? Okay, I agree. But it's what we signed on for and we're just going to have to live with it, *n'est-ce pas*? Tough it out? Show the world what we're made of? You know, 'Teammates in prosperity and adversity both'?"

Stevie, whining, out of turn: "Mission One brought in oxygen. They had no choice. And they weren't as low as we are now—"

"Yes, they were," I said, "lower, actually. They were at fourteen point seven—plus, they were wimps. Right? And we're not. Are we? Didn't we take a vow?"

"Fuck the vow," Troy said, and it would be pointless to say he was out of turn too because from that moment on we were all more or less out of turn. "I say we seriously consider bringing in oxygen because Snowflake's right—I mean is it worth risking brain damage?"

"You've already got it," I said, but E. had taken the banana from me and what she said, her eyes hard and Eve softly snoring in her lap, was, "I am not breaking closure. Not for anything, not even for my baby. This isn't Everest. We'll be fine, we will. The sun'll come out and levels will rise, just as they always have—I say no. No oxygen, no nothing. Please, just think a minute—we are so close to the finish line—"

"'No nothing'?" Gretchen cut in. "What about food, then? You're fine. You're getting *your* share, but what about the rest of us? The way I'm going I won't even have a stomach left when we get out of here—and maybe some of you don't value your neurons, maybe you're not planning on going back to the university or teaching or writing scientific papers, but I am, and I can use all the brain power God gave me—"

"God who?" I said because I couldn't help myself.

Gretchen tried to freeze me with a look, but I wasn't having it. "You might think this is all a big joke," she said, "and maybe you don't believe in anything except your own crappy little self, but I do"—and here she seemed on the verge of tears, exasperated, hopeless, a big dreary ongoing complaint given human form. "I believe in *science!*"

* * *

It came down to a vote, the headache contingent, led by Stevie and Gretchen and backed up by Gyro and Troy, pushing for the importation of oxygen, a one-time thing, one time only, on the grounds of crew liability, citing the precedent of Mission One as the benchmark here, while the rest of us (Richard, Diane, E. and myself) held firm. The Mission One crew, as I've pointed out, was completely bankrupt, a joke, throwing away their credibility and any chance at manning a successful mission because they didn't have the discipline to do what it took, because they were hungry, because they couldn't breathe, because they had *headaches*. Christ. What cowards, what shits! Three of them even had breathing tubes installed in their rooms like octogenarians laid out in a nursing home, and when Mission Control released pure oxygen in the south lung to bring ambient levels almost instantaneously up to nineteen percent, the whole crew snapped to life, racing madly around the enclosure, dancing in each other's arms, shouting and hallooing over the air that had made them drunk, and then finally taking the party down to the ocean, where they splashed and frolicked and dove deep, as if they were reborn instead of newly dead. Dead, at least, in the eyes of the world. And can anybody name any of them today? Was it any surprise that Mission Control brought only one of them back for our closure ceremony? That Mission Control was embarrassed by them? That failure merits nothing? Give me a break.

So the vote was a stalemate, 4–4, Gretchen in her desperation even going so far as to accuse E. of being a bad mother—"If you don't give a damn about yourself or any of us either, what about your *baby,* because how can you do this to *her?*"—but E. never wavered. Nor did I. And this time Diane and Richard were on our side, on the right side, the only side, so that I had to scramble to do my accounts all over again because they'd both been for breaking closure during the power outage—and we all know how that turned out. But this was different, this wasn't about the immediate threat of heatstroke but of something more subtle and, I agree, insidious, and while it affected each of us differently, I did actually have sympathy for my crewmates' concerns—but the sympathy ended at the airlock. Troy might have knocked me down and overpowered me, but I was stronger than he could ever even dream of being.

I'll admit that I wasn't affected by the low levels as much as they seemed to be—nor E. either—and I might have felt differently if I had to lie there gasping for breath every night or if the baby was affected, which thank god, as far as we could tell she wasn't because she'd been born inside and these were the conditions she'd inherited. Like a Sherpa. (And that's what I began calling her, our little Sherpa baby.) Still, I'd like to think I wouldn't have given in regardless. I felt sapped just like the others, capable of maybe a third less of what I would have been able to do on the outside—and, of course, this was complicated by being chronically undernourished, but to give up now? It was unthinkable.

We had a pared-down Thanksgiving feast that year, heavy on greens, sweet potatoes and beets, light on protein, if you discount the lablab bean/rice casserole with a sprinkle of goat cheese E. whipped up. We didn't want a feast, didn't have the provisions for it or the energy it would take to prepare it when we could barely summon the willpower to scrape together the morning's porridge, and it was almost an insult to expect us to celebrate the great annual glutting of America when we were starving ourselves. But that was exactly what Mission Control insisted we do. We had Eve to show off, we had our comradeship and self-sufficiency to trumpet to the world, all the more important now that we were counting down to the time when we would emerge triumphant and pass the baton to the Mission Three crew while the bands played and the banners flew. All right. Fine. We did what we were told, and if we didn't film the proceedings for outside transmission as we'd done the previous year, Mission Control glossed it over and brought their own celebration to the glass, where we posed deferentially for the cameras and hoisted glasses of arak and piss-yellow banana wine for the photographers gathered there in the courtyard.

About that arak, by the way—Richard was distilling more of it than ever, making use of the hulls and stalks that formerly would have gone to the pigs, who were with us no longer. I'm sure you remember the press accounts that fall when we sacrificed the last of them—Penelope herself, her piglets long since butchered and devoured—because we no longer could find enough to feed her and desperately needed the meat. We were accused of burning our bridges, and though the reporters attached to that story certainly lost no love for us, they were right—the dream of a seamless transition to Mission Three went right down our gullets. New pigs would have to be imported when they opened the airlock to admit the Mission Three crew, but that could be done in a matter of an hour or two, and even an off-earth colony would have had periodic relief. Mission Three would need new chickens and ducks too, though our goats would wind up surviving the mission simply because we couldn't do without their milk (and E., I think, would have sacrificed herself before she'd let anyone get within ten feet of them with a butcher's knife).

I don't want to give the impression that I wasn't concerned. Of course I was, worrying about E. and the baby every time I came huffing up the stairs to the Habitat, and when Richard gave us our last pre-reentry physicals just before Christmas, I took the opportunity to draw him out on the situation. Just to ease my mind, you understand. He'd just got done with the prostate exam, which always marks the moment of truth between a male patient and his physician (a few years earlier, on first joining SEE, I'd had a complete physical with a doctor who was new to me, and after the exam he'd asked me a series of questions, including if I'd ever had sex with a man, to which I replied, *Not till now*), and he was getting his camera ready to take the latest set of photographs documenting the physical transformation E2 had wrought in me, when I asked, "You think the baby's going to be all right? Considering what Gretchen has to say about it—and some of the shouters in the press too. Diet-wise, I mean?"

Richard—he was my ally now, soul of the mission (or one of its souls, along with E. and me)—took a moment to position me in front of the screen for the first of his series of four shots, front, back, right profile, left profile, before answering. "Gretchen's all right," he said, "and her concerns are legitimate, of course they are. We could all use more protein, more food—and more air. But she's an alarmist and under a ton of strain, just like all the rest of us." He paused, watching me closely. "And maybe a bit high-strung too, something the psychological profile really didn't properly address—or catch, I guess. So go easy on her." He let that hang a moment. "In answer to your question, Eve's fine."

"Even with—?" I waved a hand to take in everything around us, the glass panels, the space frame, the dwindling IAB, the riot of vegetation only the goats could process.

"Look," he said, "as long as Eve's getting her nutrition from E.—there, stand there, right profile first—she'll be as healthy as any baby, and yes, the vitamin D's coming through Dawn's milk, so no worries of rickets there. Or marasmus or kwashiorkor or whatever else you have on your mind."

I was about to tell him how much of a relief it was to hear it when he said, "Hold that," and the flash snapped. "Okay, frontal now," he said.

I moved into position, the flash went off and my wiry—scrawny?—frame was recorded for history, stomach evaporated, balls adangle. "But that's just it," I said. "I'm worried about E. getting enough calories—I mean even with a reduced workload, she still needs, what, like five hundred extra calories a day because she's nursing. That sound right?"

"Left profile. Okay, good. Hold that." I was the one standing there naked, and if I'd looked into the mirror lately it was only to brush my teeth or hair and not, ever, to assess the way my physique had been remade by E2, but glancing at Richard now I saw how reduced he was himself, almost like a child, the lab coat looking as if he'd borrowed it from a giant. How tall was he? Or had he been? He was the shortest among us—the men anyway. The oldest too.

"Turn around, rear view." One more flash. "Okay," Richard said, "you can put your clothes on now."

"What about my question?"

"Oh, about E.? She'll be all right—as long as we keep making sure she gets that extra portion each meal. Would I like to see her doing another five hundred calories on top of that? Sure. Of course I would. As her friend and physician both. But that's just not going to happen, not yet. Soon enough she can gorge all she wants—we all can."

I was stepping into my undershorts, which were pretty well tattered at this point, as were the jeans I pulled over them. "Food porn," I said.

"What?"

"You know, thinking about banana splits—"

"Don't even mention bananas. If I never see another banana once I get out of here—"

"Right," I said, "right," and we were both laughing. "I mean it's all I dream about—not sex, not the applause or the fame or G.C. striking up the band, but just McDonald's, just a Big Mac. Give me a Big Mac, fries and a Coke—man, a Coke!—and I'm in heaven. What are you going to get? I mean, first thing?" I was grinning at him now and he was grinning back, two men in an examining room in an enclosed airtight structure, fetishizing food.

"Two-pound lobster with drawn butter, scalloped potatoes and French bread—real French bread, with the crust that gives way with the faintest crackle and then you've got something to chew. Really, for me, there's nothing like good bread. *Really* good bread."

"What, no frogs' legs?" This was a reference to the meal I'd made last time I was up, something I'd put a lot of effort and ingenuity into. I called it *Grenouille Suprême,* and I'd spent a couple hours (and way more calories than I got back) splashing through the marsh and the fish ponds to catch two dozen frogs, which I patiently skinned, gutted and fried, with mixed results. The meat was pulpy and though the frogs had gone pretty much straight from the biomes to the frying pan, they somehow wound up tasting like week-old fish—we all ate them, but nobody was particularly happy about it, and for the remaining time left to us, even after the last of the tilapia had been exhausted and protein was at more of premium than ever, no one really encouraged me to go back for a second batch.

What Richard said now—and here we were, both of us, almost merry in our misery—was, "It's a tempting offer, Vodge, but I think I'll stick with the lobster."

* * *

Christmas—you've already heard my notions on that charade— was more muted than the previous year, no choruses or speeches or Girl Scout troops stringing lights and laying out wreaths for us in the courtyard. Mission Control, wisely, had foreseen that presenting a contingent of ragged, half-starved, out-of-breath Terranauts to the public wasn't going to do much for the brand and focused on Eve instead, the magical child tricked out in little red booties and clenching a homemade rattle in one tiny fist, gurgling over the first Christmas of her life. The rest of us were there, of course, having spruced ourselves up as best we could and waving good cheer to the cameras, but basically consigned to the background. Except for E. E. was front and center, holding the baby up to the glass, and I was poised behind her for the first assault of the flashbulbs, but then I stepped back into the shadows and left my wife and daughter to take center stage. Which was something of a relief, really—it wasn't my mission anymore, nor Gyro's or Diane's or Gretchen's or Richard's or Troy's or Stevie's. It was E.'s now. And Eve's.

If Christmas was subdued, New Year's would have been practically non-existent if it wasn't for the Sartre play, the two performances of which G.C. had ordained for New Year's Eve and New Year's Day, respectively. Why he'd chosen those two days was a mystery to me—just as it had initially been a mystery as to why, out of all the plays extant, he'd picked *No Exit* in the first place—but then I came to see the wisdom of that too. Feast days were huge for us—they'd given us something to look forward to (some silliness, some extra calories, some rest from the endless round of duties we all bore)—but this one, our last holiday before reentry, was going to be nothing but grim. We were into the seed stocks now, further dooming the program of a seamless transition and the fundamental concept of self-sufficiency on into the future, and while we were able to come up with a ceremonial cheesecake and a sweet potato pie crowned with a dollop of yogurt each, the meal itself wasn't much above the ordinary. Hardly worthy of a celebration—especially the penultimate celebration—and G.C. knew how spirit-crushing this whole scenario was bound to be, so he was determined to distract us as best he could. Enter Sartre.

By the way, an interesting side note: Richard's arak had become not just an escape mechanism, like all drugs, but a far-from-negligible source of calories too. You don't really think of calories when you belly up to the bar and order a beer (153 calories) or a vodka soda (200), but that's what you're getting, and calories equal energy, unless, of course, like most Americans, you're not getting enough exercise—then they equal fat. We could have given E. her extra five hundred calories a day by ordering her up a single piña colada, amazing as that might seem. And the grog the Royal Navy traditionally gave its sailors was not, as I'd always thought, to let them get a buzz on, but to deliver calories in a diet reduced to salt beef, hardtack and sauerkraut. There was no quick sugar fix, no Snickers bars or Coca-Cola in the twelve-ounce can, and rum was the way to make up for it. It was compact, portable, and it didn't spoil. So Richard. And his arak. Dinner wouldn't be dinner without it.

Nor would New Year's. And if some of us were maybe a bit tanked for the performances, something that really didn't come home to me till I saw the tapes two days later, then I think we can all be forgiven. It was strictly in-house anyway—and this time G.C. had decided to dispense with having the outside crew give their own performance, so there was nothing to measure us against except ourselves. The first night—six p.m., New Year's Eve—I was cast (by G.C.) as Garcin, the serial sexual adventurer who'd cheated on and devastated his wife, while Stevie played Inez, the young lesbian who'd seduced her cousin's wife, and Gretchen—Gretchen!—was Estelle, who'd had a liaison outside her marriage, and after giving birth to the child that resulted, tossed it in a lake to drown. Troy would take my role for the second performance, Diane would step in for Stevie and E. for Gretchen. It was strange, to say the least. All three characters reveal their secrets, thinking to defuse the situation, but it only makes it worse, since each now knows how to lacerate the other's wounds, and Estelle, trying to reclaim herself in the only way she knows how—sexually—tries to seduce Garcin while Inez, younger and more attractive, attempts to seduce him first, just to get at her. (And here I said to E., "Too bad Linda Ryu's not here to play the role." "What role?" "The dyke." "What are you talking about?" "I'm talking about the way she looks at you." "Don't be ridiculous—she's as hetero as you are. I mean, I, of all people, ought to know.")

Anyway, we slogged through our performances, essentially reading the text from the prompter since none of us could muster the energy to memorize our lines, or not thoroughly enough, and yet still the zingers the characters threw at each other resonated inside us like bomb blasts, as if we were suicide bombers pulling the detonator cord over and over. It was excruciating—especially acting against Gretchen after what had passed between us, but I suppose that was G.C.'s point. Make it hurt, make it work. I don't remember much of it now, but toward the end (in which nobody goes anywhere, and, as with the Ionesco, the scene is intended to keep going, ad infinitum, after the curtain drops) there's this exchange:

> ESTELLE (Gretchen): Kiss me, darling—then you'll hear her squeal.
>
> GARCIN (Me): That's true, Inez, I'm at your mercy, but you're at mine as well.
>
> [*He bends over* ESTELLE. INEZ *gives a little cry.*]
>
> INEZ (Stevie): Oh, you coward, you weakling, running to women to console you!
>
> ESTELLE: That's right, Inez. Squeal away.

If you think that was painful—the Mission *über alles*—then the second performance, with Troy putting his hands all over E., kissing her, or pretending to, was enough to make me get up and leave the room. That was when I really appreciated my daughter for maybe the first time, this proof of what we had going for us, E. and I. I went straight to where the baby lay sleeping in her cradle just off the very spare set we'd constructed—arranged—in the command center, and if I woke her up to see her smile (yes, there was that now) and hear her cry out for the milk E. had expressed in a ceramic coffee mug, that was just what I wanted. You can still hear the baby crying on the tape of the New Year's Day performance, not that anybody except maybe a masochist would want to see or hear any of it, but it's there. My daughter, protesting. At the top of her lungs.

* * *

The final month. Countdown to reentry. I would have begun crossing off the days on the calendar, except I didn't have a calendar—I hadn't thought that far ahead. If I recall correctly, I'd brought in a calendar for the first year, 1994, but that didn't do me much good now. 1994 was gone. So was 1995, which had to have been the slowest, most dragged-out year of my life. Of course, the timelessness of E2 was part of the mystique, each day unlike any other lived anywhere else on earth, and the schedules and appointments and helter-skelter life of all the billions of non-Terranauts out there meant nothing to us. Or almost nothing. I did have to arrange for interviews, of course, but after a while I found myself simply jotting down a name and a time and, increasingly, as the days wore on, relying on Mission Control to see to the logistics. Personally, I saw myself more as an idea man, a talker, a performer—not a secretary, definitely not a secretary, and wasn't that Josie Muller's job?—so that after the first few months I tended to just let myself go with the flow and focus on what mattered, which was generating the interviews in the first place.

So I didn't have a calendar, or not an official one, but like a prisoner in solitary—or a *New Yorker* cartoon—I started marking off the days on whatever surface came to hand, in my case the back cover of my notebook, beginning with a single slash on the first of February. On the second, Groundhog Day (though G.C. in his wisdom had chosen not to include groundhogs or gophers or even moles in the E2 bestiary, so the occasion really didn't have all that much resonance for us), I made a second slash—II—and so forth. Simple pleasures. Those uni-ball slashes on the glossy cardboard cover of my notebook represented a series of keys to me, each one unlocking another door in a long succession. When I got to the end of them I would find myself standing before the airlock, ready to step out into the oxygen-crazed air of that other, older world, and cash in all my chips.

But what chips were they, exactly? I was a celebrity now, a kind of eco-saint, spokesman for the crew and father of Eve, who was the true and undeniable fruit of the mission, but how did any of that add up to a salable skillset? I could stay on at E2 as support staff for Mission Three, I supposed—and here I saw Judy's face rise before me, not to mention her other parts too—but that would be complicated on a whole range of levels. Plus, I couldn't expect to bring home much more than minimum wage—cultists really didn't get paid; they did what they did for the good of the cause, for the good of people like G.C. and G.F. and projects like E2. I hadn't earned a nickel in two years—inside, money was unknown. And now I had a wife and child to support, didn't I?

That question—the way I've just phrased it—was part of the difficulty. Even to ask it of myself made me feel inadequate. I loved E., or at least I thought I did, and our marriage was not, as some people will have you believe, a marriage of convenience or necessity or whatever you want to call it. We were sleeping together again—having sex, that is, and occasionally I did stay through the night, especially if Eve was conked out—but it wasn't the same as it'd been before the baby. E. seemed distracted, more interested in Eve than me, even in the midst of sexual play, even when we were both naked and aroused, because if the baby made a sound, any sound, E. was up and out of bed, murmuring over her, and if the baby was quiet there was always the fear that she'd died in her sleep, SIDS, Sudden Infant Death Syndrome or whatever the flavor of the month was.

Ultimately, there came a day—somewhere around Groundhog Day, just after I'd started counting down—when I broached the subject of post-reentry to her. Of course, we'd talked about this before, but it had always seemed so distant we really didn't get much beyond the fantasy of that first day, where we were going to go and what we were going to eat, that sort of thing. We kept it on the surface because it was easier that way.

Now she said, wistfully, I thought, "A month to go."

"Yeah," I said. "I can't wait."

We were down at the beach, just E., the baby and me, eight-thirty at night, the panels dark overhead, the coquis rattling away, the waves washing in and the seascape before us half-lit with the influence of the stars and moon and the electric lights filtering down through the vegetation from the Habitat above. Behind us was the black void of the rain forest; across the sea was the equally black void of the marsh, savanna and desert. The wave machine belched and grunted, but we were so used to the sound by now we hardly noticed it—or we would have noticed it only if it ceased, because then the world we knew would have been thrown out of balance. I lived near a freeway once, for eighteen months, when I was in my early twenties. At first the noise of it—white noise, a hiss, a distant rush—kept me awake; toward the end I don't think I could have slept without it. That was the way it was with the wave machine, the air handlers, the crickets, frogs and galagos, the way it is with anything, I suppose—it becomes part of your auditory spectrum.

E., shadowy, her bare legs silvered on one side by the moonlight and painted gold on the other with what came to us from the electric lights, said, "I don't know. I think it's kind of sad."

"I know," I said, and I felt her sadness, felt it inside myself like a cold draft, everything we'd known and dedicated ourselves to about to dissolve into uncertainty, but for me, any regret, any *nostalgia,* was momentary, nothing compared to the thrill of getting out of here and back to the kind of world that was stocked with books and CDs and noisy bars—music!—and an apartment where you could shut and lock the door and be alone with yourself.

"It's scary."

"I know." And here was where I began to feel a whole new level of uneasiness, and it wasn't just about the change we were facing, but about us, about E. and the way she moved to her own rhythm, the way she'd defied me and the crew and Mission Control and gone ahead and had the baby when common sense—the *mission,* for Christ's sake—dictated against it. "But don't worry, I'll get a job—and I'm sure Mission Control's going to make provisions for us, I mean, what I hear is they're going to let us move back into the Residences—in the apartments vacated by the Mission Three crew. There'll be plenty of room. That's not a worry."

"What do you mean, you'll get a job? Aren't you going to stay here—with Mission Control, I mean?"

I shrugged, though I doubted she could see it. I felt her eyes on me. Her face was a pool of shadow, her hair a dark featureless shroud. She was all locked up. There, but not there. I said, "We're the stars now, aren't we? Can you even imagine going back to being what, a functionary, a tool of G.C. and Judas and all the rest?

I've been thinking about it a lot lately and I can't see it. I really can't."

Finally, her voice a whisper of breath caught somewhere between the racketing of the tree frogs and the doleful boom of the wave machine: "I can't either."

"So what are we going to do?"

"I don't know about you, but my mind's made up," she said, and left me hanging there, the distance between us—mere inches, hip to hip—jumping suddenly to hyperspace, miles, a million miles, a hundred million, the roaring updraft of the infinite.

"What do you mean?" I asked, though I already knew the answer.

"You want to know? You really want to know? I'm not going anywhere."

Linda Ryu

've got a calendar on my wall and I'm counting off the days. It's
nothing elaborate, no glossy Sierra Club thing with full-color
close-ups of mountain goats or whatever, but a freebie I picked up
at the local Jiffy Lube when I took the car in to get the oil changed,
thinking of Dawn, who'll be wanting it back no matter what she
says. She's a mother now and she's going to need transportation,
not to mention a baby seat and a new set of tires to carry her from
the Residences to the supermarket, the pediatrician's office, the
toy store and back. If that bothers me, if I have any attachment to
the car or my apartment or the second-string life I'm leading (and
really, why would I?), it all becomes moot—vanishes, *poof!*—on
February sixth, the most amazing day of my life. February sixth,
as many people will know, is the day Mission Control released the
roster of the Mission Three crew, with my name right there in the
middle, all but leaping off the page.

When the news comes, I'm sitting at my desk in the command center, typing up a document on the new IBM computer,
all but crucified with boredom and living only for the ten-forty-
five break. I look up and there's Dennis. He's got a grin on his face,
a grin for me, which really puzzles me, considering what went
down between us, which I've never forgotten and I don't think
he has either, and he hands me a little folded-up slip of paper with
the roster on it, moving on without a word to the next person—
Malcolm—before I can even begin to process what's happening.
At first I can't believe it. Everything feels like it's spinning—the
floor, the ceiling, the desks, people's heads—and I want to laugh
and cry at the same time but all I can do is just sit there in the
middle of the command center while people hoot and cheer and
rush up to congratulate me, but then suddenly it's like the chair's

an ejection seat and I'm on my feet and dancing around the room hooting along with them and shouting, *I made it, I finally made it!*

I can't say I wasn't nervous, especially since Mission Control never said boo about when—or even if—we'd be going through the final interviews, which, in retrospect must have meant their minds were already made up. The thing was, none of us knew that and it just cranked up the tension another notch as the days dropped dead and we all slashed them off on our calendars. As much as I'd prepared, putting in extra time in the test plots and animal pens and sucking up to Judy around the clock, I still thought there was a chance she'd screw me over because Tricia Berner and Rita Nord-quist (with her white-blond hair), were sucking up just as hard, and to put your faith in Judy Forester was like trusting a rattle-snake not to bite you the second time you swing open the door to toss a rat in its cage. Talking it over these past months with Dawn, Gretchen and Gavin—obsessing over it, really—I came to see that my best shot was as MDA because Francisco Viera (Ph.D., ocean-ography) was the obvious choice to replace Stevie, and Julie Ott, though she was younger, had her master's in rain forest ecology and that trumped me no matter what Gretchen might have done on my behalf. So I focused on MDA and it paid off.

It gets better. Gavin's in, as Technosphere Supervisor, and that sets all my bells ringing. I'm thinking moonlight swims, pinochle in his room or mine, slipping in beside him at the big granite table three meals a day. I'm thinking of real time together, crewmate time, celebrity time—because that's what we are, instant celebri-ties. Toss the turd-brown suits and get fitted for the crimson ones, because here we come! Of course, it's no surprise that Francisco's in, as I say, and let him hook up with Rita or Julie, I don't care. Matt—again, no surprise—is team physician. Malcolm—you could have taken this to Vegas—is Communications Officer, and Rita's Supervisor of Field Crops, which *is* something of a shock and means we'll be working together. Closely. And I don't know how I feel about that, but it's really a non-issue at this point. It'll work out. It'll work out fine.

To round out the crew, another shocker, is Tricia Berner, who

I really can't stand because she's petty and a nitwit and snaked her way into Gavin's inner circle before she blew that, but who knew she had a degree in chemistry? Or I guess I knew—everybody knows everybody's pluses and minuses because that's how you play the game—but to bring her in as Director of Analytic Systems? What are they thinking? I hope we're not all going to wind up asphyxiating in our sleep. Do I sound hypercritical? I am. But the point is, I'm in, and that's all that matters.

And who's not? Most of the newbies, and let them pay their dues, that's my attitude, but they're holding Jeff Weston back— and maybe that's because he's become too valuable to them on the cameras (spying, I mean). Ditto Ellen Shapiro. And I am nothing but glad she's been left out—make that ecstatic—though I'm not about to lord it over her or anybody else. I remember only too well the way it felt first time around and the humiliation Ramsay and the rest put me through that night at El Caballero. I am just not that sort of person. So, no, I am not going to gloat or hang around outside the also-rans' dinner or anything like that. I am going to be a model Terranaut. I am going to show them what it means to devote yourself to something—Dawn, Judy, G.C., *Ramsay,* all of them. And I'm going to call my mother. And I'm going to be the one with her picture on the cover of *Newsweek* or wherever.

And you know what else? I'm going to lose weight. Damn, I'd take bets on it.

* * *

So right away, before I can do the math and even begin to reca-librate all the hopes and expectations and crushing disasters I've ever entertained or been through or try to get hold of the euphoria that's surging through me like a whole bottle of *Bem Ju,* there's the fitting for our jumpsuits and then the annunciatory dinner at Alfano's. It's just like with Mission Two, tradition now, the official press conference to come the next day and everything from here on out pretty much set in stone. The fitting's nothing, a blip on my radar, because they already had my size, of course, Judy's deci-sion preceding me (and why couldn't she have dropped even the *slightest* hint?), and then I'm walking back across campus on a path as familiar as a cowpath must be to a cow, and I don't register a single moment of it, whether it's hot or cold, sunny, windy, nothing.

Back in my apartment, I'm in a daze, moving randomly from one thing to another as if my brain isn't sending the right signals to my limbs, and then I'm frantically trying to tame my hair and put on my makeup and cursing myself for not having gone into Tucson like a week ago for a new dress, and I can see it, see that dress just as clearly as if it's hanging in the closet, sapphire blue, not satiny but with maybe a subtle sheen and a high collar that would manage to be chic and businesslike at the same time because this is all about sending a message to the world—to my parents and grandparents and their circle of friends, to Sacramento and Sonoma State and everybody I went to high school with—and everything in my tired apartment that made it look like purgatory yesterday looks like the funky clothes-strewn gateway to heaven now.

The knock at my door isn't Gavin's, but Julie's, and that's all right because we take about half a second to look into each other's eyes and then we're dancing around the room, screaming all over again. Then Gavin shows—he's wearing a tie, which I've never seen him in before—and Rita, and we're all piling into the car and rolling on into town feeling unconquerable, more special than special, and if anybody in that car has ever been higher on life, I want to know about it. The air conditioner, the radio, all four of us talking at once. Buzz, buzz, buzz. Everything—the lizards scuttling across the road, the clouds like whipped cream on top of a root beer float, the friendly thoughtful double yellow line bisecting the blacktop—is like it's been manufactured just now, just for us. And here's Alfano's, even Alfano's, looking as if I've never seen it before, a kind of shining palace burning against the falling light of this day none of us ever wants to end.

Okay. We're inside now and G.C., Judas and Little Jesus are presiding, holding forth to the three lucky representatives of the print media who've been invited in advance of tomorrow's official press conference . . . and wait, who's that in the far corner, his face partially obscured by the totemic profile of some movie actor whose name escapes me but whose great shining donkey's jaw is seared into my consciousness? G.F. G.F. himself. I feel transported, as if I've stumbled out of my bedroom in the morning to see one of the princes of the earth bent over the sink, washing my dishes for me—or two princes, because this actor is definitely an A-lister, and his name is right on my lips, something with a *P*, two *P*'s . . .

"You see who's here?" It's Rita, leaning in with a drink in her hand, her face shining as if she's just had a facial peel, and maybe she has. Her hair's like the hair you see on ghosts in Norse mythology. And her nose—it's one of those fashion-model noses, pinched so high you can see right up her nostrils, which, because it's the featured nose on all the models in the magazines and even the Victoria's Secret catalogue, is right there front and center, advertising society's (and Mission Control's) preferences in female rhinology. Whereas my own nose—forget mine. It's just there, stubby and splayed, but it's a Terranaut nose now, just as much as hers.

"No," I say. "Who?"

"Over there, with G.F.?"

"Oh yeah, yeah—it's that actor, right?"

She gives me an incredulous look. "*That actor?* That's Umberto Battaglia. *Umberto Battaglia!* I can hardly believe it."

"Me either," I say, and I don't mean to be dismissive because I'm thrilled and can't wait to call my mother and tell her I was in the same room with him, all that and G.F. too, but we're going to be expected to give a little speech when G.C. announces us and I'm trying to keep my feet on the ground and not screw up in any way. Which is why the vodka soda in my hand is the only one I'm going to have, strictly, at least till we can wave bye-bye and get on with the real party.

But here's Gavin and Julie and now G.C.'s tapping a spoon on the rim of his glass and the room falls silent. He begins by congratulating us all and then, for the sake of the press, praises the efforts of the Mission Two crew and how brilliantly they've handled the adversity thrown their way by uncooperative weather and the power fiasco that would have brought down a less-committed group and how proud he is of them. And of us, the Mission Three crew, whose devotion to the ecological principles and questing spirit of E2 is every bit the equal of their colleagues inside. It's a good speech, a great speech, the best he's ever given, because for once I am included instead of forever being shunted into the background, and when he finishes—or just pauses, the last chesty phrase hanging there over the rattle from the kitchen and the low-voltage hum of the general public in the dining room behind us— I'm the first to burst into applause.

"And now," he says, "it's time to introduce our Mission Three crew, whose names will go down not only in the history of closed-systems research but in the history of our country and the world as well. Tricia Berner, step forward—"

We've already been told that this will go alphabetically, mean-ing that I'll be introduced seventh, just after Julie Ott and before Francisco Viera, which is just fine with me. I'm happy to be here— ecstatic, really—and I wouldn't have wanted to go first anyway. There hasn't been a whole lot of time to prepare, of course, but I have managed to jot down a few key phrases (keep it short) to express my gratitude and devotion and work in a little Eco-sphere boilerplate too. So I'm standing there, the glass in my hand drained right down to the ice cubes, which I'm nervously crunch-ing between my teeth while Tricia, the *actress,* goes on about ful-filling her life's greatest ambition and singling each of us out as her best friend in the world and then, incredibly, breaking into song, and not just any song, but a full hundred and eighty excruciating seconds of "The Impossible Dream," which, somewhere in the back of my mind I realize is from *Man of La Mancha* and all about kissing G.C.'s ass.

Have I mentioned Judy? She's standing there at G.C.'s side with that movie poster smile, dressed in red, of course, with matching red pumps. I should be grateful to her, I suppose, but even now, in my moment of glory, she's gone out of her way to kick the stool out from under me. Not two minutes after I stepped through the door she took me aside and let her face run through its gamut of disgust over the dress I've got on, the same bronze knee-length I wore two years ago to the final interview and the losers' dinner because nobody gave me a heads-up, and what was I supposed to do, rent a helicopter and set it down in front of Contempo Casuals in the Tucson mall? Dawn said the dress made me look blocky, which is just a code word for fat, but I don't care. And Judy can go ahead and make me feel bad—she can still do that—but I'm in now, and she really can't touch me, not once G.C. calls my name and the photographers snap their pictures and I give my little speech of enduring gratitude and team spirit.

If you're expecting me to say that I wind up fumbling the speech or that the vodka goes to my head or I trip or vomit or get all stalker-mode over Umberto Battaglia, I'm sorry to disappoint you. Everything goes great. My speech is short, to the point and heartfelt—so heartfelt I'm within a hair of collapsing in tears at the end of it, when I name each of my teammates in succession and raise my empty glass to cry out, "Let's go make history!" And if you look at the pictures from that day, both the official ones and the grainy newspaper shots, that's me right in the center, my bronze dress catching the light and my hands raised in triumph, locked in the tight grip of Gavin on my right and Malcolm on my left.

* * *

For some reason that's fathomable to exactly nobody, Mission Control decides to conflate the pre-press-conference announcement with the crew-only party Mission Two had held the following night, so once G.C. and Judy bail, it's off to El Caballero to let our hair down and do a little serious celebration without having to worry about what Mission Control might or might not think. The funny thing is, it's as if I have no memory of what went down here two years ago, all that erased in the outward-spiraling thrill of what's happened to me in the course of the last few intoxicating hours. And speaking of intoxication, I'm not holding back now, no way, and before I can even put in an order for the least fattening item on the menu (the tostada, oil and vinegar dressing, don't even look at the shell), I've lost count of my vodka sodas. Which doesn't matter, since the whole point of this is to get shit-faced and bond, bond, bond, all the prying eyes and snooping noses put to rest for this one night out of all the two-plus years to come. It's a party, a chance to let your hair down (though Malcolm and Matt barely have any to speak of, which, it occurs to me, is something of an evolutionary advantage when you're thinking of shampoo and H_2O usage in a closed system). So good. So I'm drunk, or almost drunk, and I make a beeline for Gavin the second time he comes out of the men's after draining off some of the beer he's been chain-drinking out of the longneck bottle since we walked in the door.

"Hi," I say, giving him a huge grin that somebody might describe as sloppy, but what does that even mean? Unsteady? Wavering? Too much lip, gum, teeth? Fuck it. "Hi," I repeat. "You, like, as ecstatic as me?"

Maybe his grin's a little sloppy too. But it's a beautiful grin on a beautiful face. He's like a boy who's not a boy anymore, tall and not muscular but—what, lithe—and you just want to hug him, which is what I do. And he hugs back. Drunkenly. When we unclench, and I am not seeing the looks on Julie's face or Rita's and especially not Tricia's, he tells me he just got off the phone with his parents in New York. "They were like 'we were praying for you,'" he says, "which is pretty funny because they're both atheists."

"Right," I say, "right—what's the use of praying in a Darwinian universe?"

He's nodding. "Do you even know anybody who's religious in the slightest bit?—I'm talking biologists here, ecologists. And it's not as if we're bringing a priest, rabbi and mullah in with us, is it?"

"Uh-uh. No way. And even if we did, we'd have to find some way to wash their beards without polluting the water supply—"

Gavin gives a sharp laugh, his eyes drawn down to bright comical slits. I love him. I think I love him. Really love him. "But priests don't have beards, do they?"

"No, but rabbis do. And mullahs. And"—for a moment I feel a wave of dizziness rise in me like high tide in my cerebral cortex and a nagging little thought that I'm going to pass out pops into my head—but it dissolves and he gives me a puzzled look, like what were you saying? To cover myself, not that I really need to, not anymore, I flick my eyes at the end of the table where Matt and Malcolm are waving beer bottles at Rita and say, "And at least two of our crew aren't going to run out of shampoo, I mean, like they're in no danger . . ."

Gavin doesn't seem to get it.

"Their hair, I mean." Still nothing. But it doesn't matter because we'll have all the time in the world to just chat away like this anytime we want—plus, I am feeling a real urge to find the ladies' and maybe use the telephone in the hall to call my parents, whose flat stunned faces suddenly rise in my mind like sunken logs bobbing up out of the depths on a current of swamp gas, *What, you couldn't even think to call and we had to learn about it on the news?*

"Okay," I say, "great, everything's great, but you'll have to excuse me—the ladies'—I mean, for a minute. But you'll wait for me, won't you?"

The question, I can see now, is pretty much idiotic. We're crewmates, this is our party, we live in the same Residences and I'm the one with the car. He's a little drunk, I'm a little drunk (more than a little, because I wind up in the third stall down puking up the tostada and the chips and too-spicy salsa I couldn't resist till my throat feels like it's been dredged with a steam shovel) and all he says is, "You going to be all right to drive?"

* * *

If you think this is building up to a confession of how I wrecked Dawn's car or wound up with a DUI or worse, you're wrong, because that's not me, that's not Linda Ryu. I might have overdone it in the spirit of the evening, but I am never incapable of handling myself. Though, finally, once the party winds down and we're all standing around in the dark parking lot, Gavin does insist on taking the wheel and here come Malcolm, Tricia and Rita squeezing into the backseat and we wind up singing along with the radio to a Beatles medley with a lot of *love* in it, both universal

and individual, and then we're back at the Residences and collapsing into our separate beds (or at least I collapse into my separate
bed), trying to get some rest (beauty sleep) for tomorrow's press
conference.

My parents? What can I say, they're both M.D.s and if I cured
cancer, made cold fusion work and healed all the orphans of Africa
of their multiple afflictions, I'd still fall a little short by their reck-
oning, but when I gave them the news—drunkenly, on the phone
in the hallway at El Caballero, scene of my greatest humiliation
and now my greatest triumph—they seemed to see the light. You
can't blame them for their confusion over just exactly what my
profession was, but now that I was about to don the red jumpsuit,
I think they got it, they finally got it. They both—my mother on
the kitchen phone, my father on the one in the den—told me how
proud they were of me, then my mother paused and said, "You
sound funny. You're not drinking, are you?"

The next hurdle, of course, as everyone will know, is the press
conference announcing the Mission Three Terranauts, with all the
fanfare that attended the Mission Two closure, and maybe more.
Definitely more. Like any sequel, it has to touch all the bases the
first two ceremonies did and go that extra mile too. So there are
the bands, the celebrities, speeches by G.C. and G.F. and some
German geneticist they roped into backing us by dangling the
carrot of grant money in front of his face, and then our crew
speeches, delivered by Malcolm, as Communications Officer, and
Matt, as Crew Chief. In the footage of the proceedings, which we
saw after the event that night, I'm looking good, I think, my hair
behaving, my makeup really kind of flawless and everything I'm
feeling radiating out of my big lightly hungover sincerest smile of
my life, and if the jumpsuit is a tad unflattering (Ramsay, I hear,
said that I looked like an overripe tomato), so what? As I say, in
twenty-seven short days I'll be living, breathing and eating in the
biggest weight-loss clinic in the history of the world.

So, fine. The days are flipping by, everything in a rush now,
and I'm x-ing away at my calendar, filling up cardboard boxes for
storage and getting out there ahead of the loop on what I'm going

to need inside, using Dawn's example as a guidepost (and yes, she did run out of shampoo, but miracle of miracles Richard of all people had squirreled away an extra 500 ml bottle of scentless Paul Mitchell Original to save her bacon, or her hair, actually). As for Dawn, by the way, we're still friends, of course, or more than ever, I suppose, since now that I'm in, my hurts and jealousies just vanish like hot breath on a cold day, but still it takes me a while to actually go to the glass and sit there with her and let her be happy for me the way she would have been and should have been the first time around.

I will never forget that day. People say that, *I will never forget that day,* and it's false and self-reflexive and not much more than a cliché, like pretty much everything that comes out of Dawn's mouth, but I say it now and there's nothing that can ever happen to me in this lifetime that will ever be truer. But if you know anything about Mission Three at all, you know exactly what I'm talking about. The date is February twelfth, five days after the press conference and the great dissemination of our names, faces and bios to all the news agencies in existence, and I've arranged to go to the glass to see Dawn and just bask in the whole thing, because we're rivals no more, but equals again, just like we were at the beginning when she picked me out of the crowd and I picked her.

The weather sucks. It's supposed to be dry, but it's drizzling, a fine feathery mist glistening on everything, including my hair. In my excitement—*Dawn, I'm going to celebrate with Dawn, finally, finally, finally*—I've forgotten my umbrella or even a hat, and where's my sombrero when I really need it? The moisture isn't kind to my hair—I need less body, not more—and when I peer into the glass I can see the ghost of my reflection there and the way my hair's swelled up on one side and flattened on the other, as if I've just got done balancing a great towering basket on that side of my head, like some of the women we'd seen humping themselves around the streets of Belize City.

The baby's there, of course, and when I come up to the window she's feeding it—*her*—with one breast exposed and the baby's mouth going like a sump pump (and if I don't sound sympathetic to this whole reproductive thing, believe me, I'm not—and I'm certainly not going to pretend to be. Like all the rest of the Mission Three crew, *and* the Mission Two crew, I can't help being resentful of Little Miss Eve Chapman-Roothoorp, cynosure of the heavens and the earths and half the cameras in operation in the state of Arizona. *What about me,* I'm thinking, what about us? Time for new blood, that's what I'm thinking). What I say is, "The baby's really growing."

Dawn's watching me out of her cat's eyes, blue cat's eyes, as if she's a big Siamese curled up on the sofa, and her smile is utterly complacent: she's a mother, *the* mother, and here's what she's produced. I don't blame her for that. Or maybe I do, just a little. For just an instant I feel empathy, feel what it must be like to go through what she's gone through and to hold the result of it in your arms, press it to your milk-swollen breast, the purpose of life fulfilled and the genes passed down to the next generation, satisfaction guaranteed. Funny thing is, she looks away, as if she's avoiding my eyes, and she doesn't say anything but "Yeah" in response to my comment, and what was I expecting—a little congratulations maybe? A little sisterly celebration? *Bravo,* that's all I want to hear. *It's your turn now. Well done.*

"So really, I can't wait," I say, the misting rain settling on the glass and accumulating till one streak after another melts down the face of the panel and segments Dawn and her baby as if they're pieces in a gigantic jigsaw puzzle. "It's like every day is a thousand days now. The sad thing is, we're not going to get to party because it'll be like a hug for the cameras and then I'm going in—but you've heard about Tricia, of course? I can't stand her. And really, I don't know how you were able to put up with Stevie for what, *two years*? Amazing. Just amazing."

"Linda," she says, and maybe she switches the baby to the other side, I don't really remember, the glass all streaky and her face so joyless and tragic she's like a mummy laid out in her tomb, "I've got something to tell you."

Part IV

REENTRY

Dawn Chapman

There are times in life when you have to do what your heart tells you, no matter who it hurts or what the consequences are. It would be hard for me to explain to anybody who hasn't lived inside just what it means to meld wholly with your environment, body and soul, to be so much a part of something you can't imagine it existing without you. When I was a girl I used to think of what would happen if I died, whether the world would go on as before—my parents, my brother, the kids at school—or just vanish as if it was my solitary dream and everything in creation belonged to me alone. That was how I felt about E2, whether it was justified or not. People called it a delusion, and that might have been the way it looked, I suppose, if you were viewing it from one perspective only—from *outside,* that is. Really, I heard it all. After word got out that I was hoping to stay on, I was accused of everything from child abuse to desertion. I was selfish. I was stubborn. I was engaging in risky behavior. I was a bad crewmate. I was jeopardizing my own future and my child's and E2's as well. I was a slut. A criminal. I had no right. There must have been some gas, people said, some spore, that had affected my brain chemistry. As I say, I heard it all.

Can I tell you that once I made my decision none of it touched me in the slightest bit? That all those voices might as well have been as far away from me as if I really was on Mars?

It wasn't a spur-of-the-moment thing, not at all—there was nothing rash about it. It may be true that when I told Vodge that night on the beach, when the words were actually out of my mouth, I wound up taking myself by surprise as much as him, but looking back on it, I can see that the idea had been building in me as we got closer and closer to reentry—a prospect I'd begun to dread even as my crewmates reached a point where they could talk about nothing else except what they would do, where they would go, what they would eat, once Gyro shot the bolts and flipped the lever on the airlock. *I'm going to have steak, steak and nothing but steak for a whole week; Me, I'm going to a concert, any concert, I don't care— just to hear music, you know?; I just want to see the sky; Or drive, just to drive with the wind in your face, a convertible, of course, red, like maybe a Corvette, and the stars overhead, the real stars, the ones you don't have to squint to see.*

I heard all this, heard it repeatedly, and it tugged at me, it did, the tempting pictures my crewmates painted—and Vodge, Vodge was most eloquent of all, spinning out elaborate fantasies of our first day back, our second, our third, the whole first week—but nobody seemed to notice I wasn't joining in. In fact, if anything shocked me about Mission Two, beyond what I've already laid out here, it was how everybody could just turn around and put everything we'd accomplished—and suffered for—behind them as if there was a button marked "Commitment" you could just turn on and off at will. I'm not going to criticize anybody, but if you want to talk about true colors, here's where they really showed. I mean, just Stevie alone, willing to turn her back on the ocean as if it were a fish tank in a pet store somewhere she'd got tired of? Or Gretchen, leaving Lola and Lolly behind without a second thought?

Vodge said, "You're joking, right?"

It was dark, the air its steady self, the ocean like a bath, my feet stirring there, the baby in my lap, the unearthly beauty of E2 all around us as if it were a cathedral built to sustain us, our little family, in just this moment. I didn't know how to say what I had to because it was just coming to me then and I'd had no time to work it through or soften it either. I said, "No, I'm not."

There was a long pause. I could just make out Vodge's features in the light filtering through the trees from the Habitat. I thought he looked angry, but I couldn't be sure—he was fixed there, then he blurred, then he was fixed again. "So let me get this straight," he said, and yes, he was angry, I could hear it in his tone. "You're actually saying you're going to give up everything—the world, grants, publicity, *money*—for another two years of *this*? Are you out of your mind? And G.C. G.C.'ll drag you out of here if he has to—"

"Just let him try."

"E., I can't believe you—just listen to yourself. You can't do this. Nobody can. There are hundreds of people involved here, thousands upon thousands if you think of everybody out there watching every move we make. And me, what about me? You really expect me to, what, go to G.C. and beg him to let us stay inside, which he won't do. You think I could take two more years of this, that I would even want to? Shit, E., I wouldn't stay two more days, two more *hours,* for Christ's sake."

"So what am I supposed to say—do you love me?"

That was the question, straightforward, risky, skirting the edges of heartbreak and going straight for what was real and not playacting, simple, binary, yes or no. He didn't answer right away, didn't answer at all. "That's not the point—" he said.

And I said, "Then what is?"

* * *

The vote, because we did take a vote, was 7–1 against me. Can you believe it? Really, what was it to them? I wasn't asking anybody to do anything, beyond being charitable and sympathetic and true to our ideals, and I have to say their reaction was maybe the unkindest cut of all. We were so close to reentry at that point I couldn't fathom why anybody would object to my staying on, which was only logical and made absolute sense to me—if the galagos and goats and even the crazy ants and the volunteer scorpions and sparrows and leeches could pass down their genes through the generations of E2 to come, then why couldn't we, why couldn't *I*? Of course, my crewmates didn't see it that way—*Ramsay* didn't see it that way.

I was prepared for at least some degree of contention—everything was contention inside—and even jealousy. My eyes were open. Who was I to take this on myself, who was I to stand apart from the team yet again, blah-blah-blah? I got that. I did. But the antipathy, the depth of what I can only call rancor, really took me by surprise. Even Richard opposed me, even Diane. Things had been on an uneasy footing ever since my marriage and Eve's birth, of course, and there were times I'd come to feel increasingly isolated from my crewmates, right down to having to take the occasional meal in my room because I couldn't abide the hissing and backstabbing and the way everybody looked at me as if I'd intentionally gone out and sharpened a stake to drive through the heart of the mission. I'd learned to live with that, as much as it hurt me, but I have to say I wasn't at all prepared for the kind of reaction I got the morning I made my announcement. Or plea, call it a plea.

It was at breakfast meeting, the day after I'd had my more or less shattering talk on the beach with Vodge, with my husband, and I'd asked Diane beforehand to let me have the banana after she was done with the day's announcements. The breakfast was typical—porridge sweetened with mango and banana and featuring a squirt of goat's milk each—though by this juncture we were depleting the seed stocks, a catalogue of which Diane and I had been meticulously keeping against Mission Three's importation. (And we'd decided, along with Mission Control's input, to reduce to two the number of pigs for Mission Three, while bringing in four extra she-goats for milk production, which would make up for the lost protein, as well as doubling our stock of ducks, chickens and tilapia.) The previous night's meal had been particularly grim, Vodge having netted maybe a hundred inch-long mosquito fish for what he called a *Friture des fruits du lac* and Richard immediately labeled "a guppy fry," and nobody was particularly happy. Even the porridge had begun to taste like nothing, like emptiness, because when you think about seven hundred–plus mornings with the same pale mucousy mess appearing in your bowl, you can't help but revolt no matter how much your body cries out for it. Anyway, Eve had had her share and was gurgling and cooing in my lap, Vodge was beside me, scraping the bottom of his bowl, Diane was giving out the day's assignments and I was feeling a bit tentative about what I had to say, expecting some objections maybe, but nothing like what was to come.

"All right," Diane said, "everybody clear on everything?" And then, though Stevie was already holding out her hand for the banana, Diane slid it across the table to me and said, "E. has an announcement for us," giving me a puzzled look because I hadn't confided in her or anybody else yet. Except Vodge.

"I just want you to know," I said, gazing at each of my crew-mates in succession, "how much of an honor it's been to serve with all of you and how it's been the high point of my life—and I hope you feel the same." I paused a moment to gather myself, even as everybody got that "What the—?" look on their faces. "So now we're counting down and I know you're all looking forward to reentry, but maybe some of you are saddened too by the thought that what we've had here is coming to an end—"

"All things come to an end," Richard cut in. "Sic transit gloria mundi."

"Right," I said. "Which is why I want to tell you—to ask you—to think about continuing what we've accomplished here into Mission Three,"

Their faces were blank. Some of them were still eating, the rhythmic chime of spoon on porcelain as much a part of the E2 soundtrack as the chirring of the crickets and the hoots of the galagos. They weren't getting it. I was just reiterating what our overriding team goal had been from the start, but I had to get at this somehow and I couldn't help myself from wandering a bit, from talking in generalizations, in Ecosphere-speak. "So it's an honor," I reiterated, "and I love each and every one of you and I'll miss you all terribly . . . but what I want to do, with your approval, of course—all your approval—is to stay on."

Now their faces showed something. The spoons stopped scraping.

Troy, though he didn't have the banana—I did—set down his bowl and said, "Stay on? Stay where? You're not making any sense—"

Richard interpreted for me. "She means stay on at Mission

Control, which I know several of us are planning to do—Troy, right? And Stevie? And you too, Diane." He looked to me now, his features soft and forgiving. "There'll be a place for you, E., I'm sure. I mean, we really haven't discussed it as a group, but Judy and Dennis say they're going to want us all to stay on, at least for the transition—six months, is what I hear."

"No," I said. "That's not what I mean. I want to stay here, inside, for Mission Three—that's what I'm saying."

Suddenly everybody was talking at once, the banana snatched out of my hand, as if it mattered at this point. What I heard was, "Jesus, you've got to be kidding" and "You are the Queen Bitch, you know that?"

My husband—and it still feels strange to me to call him that—defended me as best he could, but even I could see his heart wasn't in it. He started to reiterate my argument about genetic continuity as the cornerstone of the human experiment—Mars, what about Mars?—when Gretchen cut him off.

She leveled on me, so angry she actually rose from her chair, and when Richard tried to hand her the banana she swatted it away. "What is it with you," she demanded. "Do you have a God complex or something? Maybe all the cover girl stuff went to your head, but this isn't about you, it's about *us,* about the team." She gritted her teeth as if she was trying to chew something tough, chew me, then threw a wild look around the table. "Bottom line: we went in as a team and we're going to go out as a team."

Everybody seemed to swell up then till they were twice their size, blow-up dolls, puppets, monsters of ego. Gyro applauded. Troy said, "Shit yeah!" What followed, aside from Eve's punctuating the dialogue—or harangue, or whatever you want to call it—by snatching at my water glass and sending it crashing to the floor, was a shouting session that ended only after Diane fetched the breadboard from the counter and slammed it down on the table so hard the whole foundation seemed to shake. "Enough," she said. "You're all out of order." She had a glare for everybody, but me especially, as if I was the one who'd abandoned the rules and spoken out of turn.

"We're still a team," she said, her shoulders rigid, the bread-board lying there flat on the table like something she'd choked to death with her own two hands. "And what does a team do?" I reached for Vodge's hand and gave it a squeeze, but he wouldn't look at me. "A team treats everybody with respect. Dawn says she wants to stay inside, as incredible as that may seem, and I say we put it to a vote. Show of hands, people—how many say 'aye'?"

Not a single hand went up but mine, not even Vodge's.

* * *

After the meeting we all went our separate ways, except Gretchen, who followed me down the hall haranguing me till I ducked into my room and slammed the door in her face. Eve wasn't hungry—she'd just been fed—but to calm myself I put her to my breast anyway, at which point she promptly fell off to sleep, and I was left alone to sort things out on my own. All I could think about was them overpowering me, main strength, six against two (that is, assuming Vodge would stand up for me), but it wouldn't be just six—there'd be eight new Terranauts coming through that airlock too, none of whom would be all that thrilled to see me staying on. They were a team, same as we were, and all I had to do was summon the look of disbelief shading into outrage on Linda's face to get that straight. But then this was going to hit Linda hardest, of course—if I stayed inside, Linda was the odd one out. And even if we converted some of the savanna to food production, as planned, there was no way E2 could support nine—ten, if you included Eve. There was the oxygen question too. While the O_2 levels had miraculously risen to stabilize at around sixteen percent (percep-tibly shorter nights, a run of three weeks of sun-drenched days), getting enough air to breathe was going to be a continuing prob-lem no matter how many Terranauts there were. Believe me, I wasn't entering into this lightly—for one thing, it would mean the end of my friendship with Linda, and for another, it would involve my convincing Vodge too, and that wasn't going to be easy.

I was late that day getting back out into the IAB, where Diane, Vodge, Gyro, Gretchen and I were putting in the spring crops as diligently as we could, given the declining seed stocks, determined to leave things in the best possible condition for the incoming crew. After setting Eve down in her basket, I took my place beside Vodge, helping him plant our barley crop in the way of the ages—the stick, the hole, the seed—while the others turned over the soil in the vegetable beds. Nobody had much to say, even Vodge, who was clearly angry with me, and that would have hurt me even beyond what the morning had already wrought, except that while I'd been sitting there in my room with Eve, I'd seen a way clear of all this. I was determined to stay; they were just as determined that it wasn't going to happen. That was the reality I was up against, but what they weren't taking into account, atheists all, was that there *was* a God in our universe and He had the final say.

At lunch break, though Vodge was being sweet to me by way of making up (and, I knew, trying to maneuver me into doing what he wanted me to do) and Richard plunked himself down next to me to try and reason with me, I took my plate—and Eve—up the flight of stairs to the command center and sat down at the desk where the phone was. Now, as I've already stated here, the phone was tightly regulated, as was the computer, which had no outside access beyond Mission Control, but we could pick up the receiver, dial "0" and get through to Josie Muller instantaneously. Which was what I did now.

Josie, in her official tones, said, "Mission Control," as if she were broadcasting to the nation, though, of course, there was no need since it could only have been one of us eight calling.

"Hi, Josie. It's me, Dawn. I just wondered if Jeremiah's around?"

"Jeremiah?" she echoed, as if she'd never heard of him.

"Yeah, I need to talk to him. It's urgent. Or no, it's an emergency, really—is he there?"

He wasn't. He'd been in earlier but he'd gone home for lunch. She could try him at home, but he really didn't like to be disturbed once he left the office . . .

I could feel my heart going. It was as if my life depended on this (and from where I sat that morning, I really felt it did). "Please,

Josie, I'm telling you, this is an emergency—I have to speak with him, I have to."

"Could I have him call you back?"

"Yes, *please*—"

"You'll be there?"

"I'm not going to move a muscle. But please, *hurry*."

The phone rang five minutes later and G.C. was on the line, sounding not peeved (we just didn't call him directly; no one did), but friendly, cheerful, as if he'd been waiting for the past twenty-three months for me to interrupt his lunch and invade his privacy at home. "What's up, E.?" he asked. "Everything okay in there?"

"Yes," I said, too quickly. "Or, actually, no. There's something I want to ask you—or propose, really. It's something I've been thinking about for a long time now—"

Would any of the others have gotten away with this? Vodge, maybe. Maybe Diane. But I had special status now, and if the others wouldn't let me forget it, I wasn't about to forget it either. I don't remember what I said to him, not exactly, though I suppose I should have at least jotted down some notes, just for the record, but you already know my argument, which had all to do with practicality, continuity and, most of all, publicity. G.C., give him credit, heard me out (and of course, like the others he'd have to have assumed that the seven-to-one vote had put the matter to rest, if not buried it altogether). I waited, all tensed up, and listened to his breathing on the far end of the line. And then, as if musing to himself, he murmured, "Linda Ryu's not going to like it—it's really not fair to her, not at all, or Malcolm either—"

"No," I said, "no—and she's my best friend. I hate to do it, but just think of what this'll mean for E2, for the mission—and the mission after that. Think of it, Eve growing up inside, the first child born off-planet in the history of—"

"What about Vodge," he said, cutting me off. "He on board with this?"

So I had to go and get Vodge and we had to share the phone

while G.C. thought out loud and it was just like the time at the glass when he'd dictated the terms of our marriage to us, only this time his voice alone had to carry all the freight of what he was saying, and it changed during the course of it, changed radically, from the open cheerfulness he'd begun with to the kind of hectoring tone you'd expect from Judy, but that was all right because it meant he was taking me seriously, and, as it turned out, had been anticipating some version of this ever since Eve had been born. But he was afraid too, afraid of things going wrong with the other crewmembers, with Linda, but most of all with Vodge.

"You behind her?" he demanded.

Vodge mumbled something neither of us caught.

"Speak up—I'm asking if you're on board with this, because the complications here . . . I don't have to tell you. But the way I read you is you're as hot to get out of there as anybody, or am I wrong?"

Vodge looked straight at me. Eve would have been snatching at the cord, making her little noises, smiling maybe—she was a serial smiler at this juncture—and I must have looked scared, because there was no going back from this. "Truthfully? I can't really say. I mean this is taking me by surprise as much as you—"

"Don't presume, my friend, because I could see this coming a mile off, and it's something I didn't dare hope for, but just think of it, think what this is going to do for revenues—it's a sensation, it really is, and I've got to give you the credit, E. E.? You there?"

I whispered into the phone, two little words—"I'm here"—but there were marching bands parading inside of me, flags waving, the sun bursting over hills. Could it really be this easy?

Vodge, staring at me still, never wavering, his eyes locked on mine, murmured, "Can I at least have some time to think it through?"

"Yeah," G.C. said, "sure, think all you want. But I don't have to remind you the time's getting short, and, of course, we're going to have to make a few adjustments since we've already named the Mission Three crew, but it can be done, anything can be done . . . So what I'm saying? Think fast."

* * *

If anything, the day of reentry—March 6, 1996—was an even bigger production than all the hoopla of the closure ceremony two years before. G.C. trotted out his celebrities, the TV cameras, the Girl Scouts and the bands, and he, Judy, Dennis and Vodge had been busy priming the pumps of public awareness, but this time there was to be a black-tie event too, as well as a speech by Martin Rodbell, the biochemist who'd co-won the Nobel two years earlier for his discovery of G-proteins and their role in signal transduction in cells. And, of course, there was the irresistible draw of watching the Terranauts dig into their first outside meal in 730 days, and we'd each already submitted our first choices to Mission Control, which ranged from Richard's lobster tail to Troy's pepperoni pizza and Gretchen's butterscotch sundae to my shrimp scampi with angel hair pasta, though what no one knew— yet—was that I wasn't coming out, so the Girl Scouts or reporters or Judy herself would have to polish it off in my stead.

What we'd decided, privately, quietly, just G.C., Vodge and I, was to time the announcement to coincide with reentry—to make it a surprise, a shock, the sort of thing that would galvanize the public and all but assure us of being the lead story of the day on all three major networks. Vodge and I would don our red jumpsuits along with the others, looking for all the world as if we were about to parade through the airlock and wave and whistle and sink our teeth into our favorites for the cameras (he was going for the calories, Big Mac, fries, large Coke), but there was the kicker, there was the hook, as he called it: we weren't going back out into the world. Or, actually, he was, but just for the two hours of the ceremony while staff members positioned the Mission Three supplies and livestock just outside the airlock so that when the new crew came in they could bring it all with them in a matter of minutes, minimizing any transference of gases between E2 and the outside world. I was to stay inside. That was my choice.

In the aftermath, people said I was too hard-core, that I was really overdoing it, but as far as I'm concerned you just don't bend your principles or what's the worth of them anyway? I didn't want to have to take a single breath of E1 air, which would defeat the whole purpose of continuous closure. If I was going to stay inside, to break the record for the most consecutive days anyone had ever spent in an enclosed self-sustaining system—and keep on breaking it with every minute of every day of the next two years—then it would be beyond ridiculous to throw it all away for a plate of shrimp scampi, wouldn't it? I was famous, yes, but famous for what? For this. Only this. And now I truly was going where no woman—or man—had ever gone before.

Vodge wasn't so scrupulous. He wanted the outside world, needed it in a way I didn't and didn't think I ever would again. He might have been the most committed among us in terms of keeping the purity of the mission intact through our various crises, fighting with everything he had to keep that airlock inviolate, but now the mission was over and he wanted out. I didn't blame him. Who could? It took a full three days of badgering from me and G.C. before he finally caved into the pressure, before he said, "Yes, okay, for the sake of E2 and for both of you, for you E., and Eve too, I'll sign on or re-up or whatever you want to call it, but you've got to give me this. No joke, but I really think I'll go out of my mind if I can't at least walk through that airlock with the others."

All right. I understood that, I gave him that. And I understood what a sacrifice he was making, and so did G.C., who kept insisting he had to stay on if I did because he was the father of Eve and we were a family and it would have been awkward in the extreme to explain to the public just why he was turning his back not only on the project but his own wife and daughter into the bargain. So Vodge was going to go out and raise his arms in triumph, give his speech and eat his Big Mac and reap his portion of the glory, which to his mind, and I'm sorry to have to say this, was spelled m-o-n-e-y down the road, and then he was going to come back inside. With me. And Eve.

That was the plan. And as a hint to the press and the larger world they served, a delicious little clue to our intentions, only six of the Mission Three crew showed up that day in red—the other two, Linda and Malcolm, were right there, front and center, but they were in brown, turd-brown, as Linda put it. Why? everyone wondered. Had they run out of red cloth? Or . . . was this a signal that something was up? Something outrageous, something that was going to turn the whole world of E2 on its head? The cameras zeroed in. Every face in the audience turned to G.C. This was the moment.

Inside, as the minutes counted down to reentry and we lined up at the airlock, boy/girl, boy/girl, everybody was so excited they could barely stand in place. Gyro, especially. He was always squirrely, the gangling hyperactive nerd with the too-big nose and too-small head, but he was our nerd, my nerd, the one who'd plied me with M&M's and worn his heart on his sleeve, and I was going to miss him. Richard too, Richard who'd coached me through my crisis and tucked my daughter into my arms. A sadness so vast came over me I thought it was going to engulf me like a shroud, like an eight-foot-deep hole and all the dirt it would take to fill it back up again. I was going to miss them, miss them all (except maybe Troy and Stevie, and, I'm sorry to have to say it, Gretchen, sour Gretchen), because despite our differences and the feuds and hostilities that inevitably emerged, we'd been through something together no one else but the Mission One crew and a handful of astronauts ever had. That was bonding, true bonding, the kind you could never get from all the exercises and research voyages there ever were.

I was in tears as G.C. stood poised outside the airlock, microphone in hand, counting down the final sixty seconds—all the pictures from that day captured me with a crumpled face, my eyes glistening, my nose red and my cheeks wet, looking for all the world like a mourner at a funeral. I couldn't help myself. The fact that this was the end of something just seemed to overwhelm me, even though it was the beginning of something too, something unprecedented and joyful to the highest degree and no matter the sacrifice I was getting exactly what I wanted. I was inside now, inside for good.

What else? My crewmates were in the dark, totally, as to what was to come. They assumed, to a man and woman, that the vote had settled everything, thought that G.C. was on their side, that team order took precedence over everything. If I had to fight Diane over my place in line—"Last? Why would you want to be last?"—she wound up accommodating me (just to make sure, I'd gone behind her back to G.C. so he could weigh in if need be). It only made sense that the stars of this enterprise—Vodge, Eve and me—would be the last ones out of the airlock, just like any other stage act. I hate to put it this way, but really, we *were* the headliners. The rest of them didn't like it, but they didn't suspect a thing either—the truth of it is they were too concentrated on themselves, their lives outside, escaping, to really focus on what was going on here.

So we lined up. And G.C. counted down, "Five, four, three, two, one," and the airlock was breached and for the first time in two years the atmosphere of E1 comingled with the atmosphere of E2. And seven Terranauts, in their bold bright designer uniforms, marched through the open door and into the arms of the crowd, and one stayed behind.

Ramsay Roothoorp

Hello, world! *Wow!* I stepped through the wide-open mouth of that airlock and all the smells of the planet hit me in the face as if I were a bloodhound hanging my head out the window of a pickup truck doing ninety-five down a country road. It was a rush. And the oxygen! Jesus! It was like crack cocaine—three breaths and I was delirious, four and I was as high as I've ever been in my life. Add to this the roar of the crowd, the crush of the cameras, the real and actual sun on my face and women everywhere, women in skimpy tops and short skirts, stockings, *heels,* and you can begin to imagine what it was like in those first few skyrocketing moments. The Christians say they've been born again, but that's a metaphor—this was literal. All right, not technically, not exactly, but you know what I mean. You want a metaphor? E2 was my womb and the airlock the birth canal itself. There was nothing of the old me left behind, *nothing.*

I wasn't actually prancing as I marched out the door with my fellow Terranauts and up onto the dais, as one report had it, but I might as well have been—that was what it felt like anyway. The point is, there was no time to adjust. Out we came, the sun blinded us, the air injected us, and before we could think we were mounting the dais to sustained applause, an avalanche of applause, my fellow Terranauts preceding me into G.C.'s congratulatory grasp, one by one, and then we were raising our arms high over our heads and making the victory sign with both exultant hands. Did I see Judy first thing? Yes, Judy, with her greedy eyes and perfect legs, in red, of course, seated right there on the dais beside Little Jesus and the Nobel winner, but it was only a snapshot because I was blinking still, still trying to figure out how to breathe without turning my lungs inside out, and the crowd was going wild.

I remember how the cameras seemed to snatch at our faces. How the sun just exploded in the sky. How I knew exactly where I was but at the same time felt as lost as I'd ever been in my life.

The moment—the initial moment, there on the dais—seemed to go on forever. I was grinning so hard my gums ached, light-headed, heavy of foot and ankle and haunch, *planted* there and yet soaring too. But then the applause faltered, the cheers died, and I realized what was happening: they were waiting for Dawn and Eve, every head turned to the airlock even as my crewmates began to cast glances over their shoulders. My crewmates were frowning now, their six identical grimaces so familiar to me, so alike, so predictable they might have been sextuplets. Everything was madness, but it was calculated too, and I had no trouble at all reading their minds—*Not again, not now, the bitch, the unforgiveable bitch, how could she?* They weren't grinning anymore, nobody was, because this wasn't funny, this joke that was all on them, and they weren't high on the moment or relieved or perplexed or anything else—they were seething now and it showed in their faces.

But then suddenly E. was there, Eve clasped to one shoulder— not at the entrance, but the window, the visitors' window, inside still, and what did it mean, what was going on? A low murmur rolled through the crowd. There were gasps, cries of shock, con- sternation, surprise, the reality beginning to dawn on them in a long slow reveal. We were out here and E. was in there. Which meant—?

G.C. put the microphone to his lips. "Ladies and gentlemen, friends of the Ecosphere and distinguished guests, I give you the Mission Two crew!" he roared out over the crowd in a voice made fuller, richer, deeper by the massive sub-woofers pummeling the thin startled Arizona air and echoing off the glass panels of E2 till it was like the clapping of a pair of god-sized hands. The applause rose halfheartedly, confusedly, and he went on, ignoring the response—or no, drawing the crowd in, ever deeper, to the very lip of the pit we'd dug for them: "And"—pause—"the Mis- sion Three crew!" A broad gesture now for the replacement crew seated beneath us in the first row, only six of whom were dressed in red and only six of whom stood to acknowledge the tentative wavelet of applause that seemed to break and slosh in confusion.

He was a showman, G.C., one of the best I've ever seen in action, and he took his time now, standing there silently and staring out over the massed heads and shoulders of the seated audience to where the University of Arizona Wildcats marching band stood at the ready, their instruments molten under the sun. "We speak of miracles," he said finally, his voice booming and clapping till it felt like it was inside each and every one of us, "as if they were everyday occurrences. It's a miracle that it's raining or not raining, a miracle that the dry cleaner didn't ruin our best suit or skirt, a miracle that the traffic jam on Route 77 cleared and we could all be here today." He paused to shift his gaze to us, the Mission Two crew arrayed beside him. "All that's just a figure of speech. You want the true miracle? It's what these dedicated young people have endured—and celebrated—in the name of the science of closed systems. And I'm here to tell you there's another miracle in the making . . . But, Ramsay, why don't you step up to the mike and tell these good people all about it?"

So I did. I took the microphone from G.C.'s hand and told everybody that the human legacy of E2 was its single greatest accomplishment and that just as with the life of the ponds and the ocean and the rain forest, we were going to have generational continuity between the missions. I looked over my shoulder to where E. and our daughter stood poised at the window, ready to wave at my signal. "I want to announce that my wife, Dawn Chapman, and my daughter, Eve Chapman-Roothoorp, will not be walking out into this glorious sunshine to join you all today, or any other day, for that matter—not till the Mission Three Terranauts emerge two full years from now!"

I shouted this last bit, expecting an answering roar from the crowd, but it didn't come, people shifting uneasily, their parched white faces uplifted and straining to comprehend, and what was wrong, hadn't I been speaking clearly? And in English? In my excitement—my intoxication, my O_2 drunkenness—I'd forgotten the key element here, the role of the husband and father, of me, Ramsay Roothoorp, first among equals. And what did they think—I was abandoning my responsibilities? Deserting my wife and child? That I was some blowhard hypocrite standing up here before them in the red jumpsuit I really didn't measure up to?

"And I myself," I blurted, my super-amplified voice looping back to startle them all over again, "will be making the same commitment to my little family gathered there behind the window— and to my greater one too." Here I gazed down on the baffled faces of the Mission Three crew, who were standing erect just below the podium. "If you, Gavin, and you, Matt, and Francisco, Rita, Tricia and Julie will have me—have us—as your companions and crewmates, we will be honored to join you."

I tried not to look at Linda or Malcolm, though I had no use for them at all and if they both dried up and blew away on a good stiff wind it wouldn't have affected me one iota. I was going to say more—this was my moment, this was my stage—but thank god I had the sense to shut up and let Dawn and Eve take over for me, the two of them waving tirelessly from behind the glass while the crowd whistled and cheered till they ran out of breath and the University of Arizona Wildcats marching band came in right on cue to take up the slack.

* * *

I don't think I'd be inflating my sense of myself or my significance to that little moment of regional, national and even international history if I say there probably aren't many people reading this who don't know what came next, what fell out, that is—or at least some version of it. Which, in a way, I suppose, is why I've written this account in the first place. What began as a record of Mission Two has incrementally morphed into a kind of apologia pro vita sua, a way of finding some peace for myself in all the confusion of conflicting ideals and desires, and not least, of deflecting a portion of the criticism. But if I'm strong, if I'm iron-willed—and I've emphasized this throughout—I'm also weak, I'm also *human*. So understand me.

There I was, up on the dais, the microphone in my hand, G.C.,

G.F., Judy and Little Jesus paying public homage and my fellow Terranauts soaking up the adulation of the crowd and never mind the little surprise that had thrown them off balance, they were all right with it now, all right with everything, because this was the single defining moment of all of our lives. The Mission Three crew joined us onstage for G.C.'s introductions and blessings and still I stood there, stood right there with them and not my former crew, and how special was that? It was a heady moment. We'd managed what no one else ever had, making it through 730 days without breaking closure, and now one of us (two of us, that is— three, if you count Eve) was going to do it all over again. Heady, yes, but why was I simultaneously feeling this emptiness at the core of me, down deep, where my emotions went to hide? A gut feeling. *I have a gut feeling,* that's what people say, but what does that mean, really? That there's an imperative that lies outside the control of the brain, the personality, the will? For just an instant, the crowd cheering and applauding and everything right with the world, it hit me, but then I dismissed it. I told myself it was just hunger, that was all.

Cue up the food. Not simply the Big Mac I ceremonially tore into for the cameras while Richard lashed at his lobster tail and Gretchen smeared her face with butterscotch syrup, but the spread Mission Control had laid out in the command center for the hundred or so of the inner circle. I stood there in the middle of it all in my red jumpsuit, glutting myself on caviar, chorizo-and-prawn skewers and slice after slice of thin-cut filet mignon, a flute of champagne—*champagne!*—clutched in one hand while people swarmed round me with their worshipful faces and my ego swelled till I could have floated off on it and never touched ground again. Did I give even a glancing thought to my wife and daughter? No, I didn't.

But Judy was there now, right there, right at my elbow, and I did give her a whole lot more than just a glancing thought (and what would be the opposite of that—a fixed thought? A bull's-eye of a thought that locks on the flight of the arrow till it sticks there quivering in the very center of all those concentric circles?). Can I even begin to tell you how magnetic Judy was—*is*—and how she looked and smelled and *felt* to a man marooned as long as I'd been? I've already told you what her heels and stockings did to me from behind the inert glass walls of the little prison cell we called the visitors' window, not to mention the frisson of her bared crotch that propelled me in what was nothing short of sexual panic right up the stairs to my heavy sleeping pregnant wife. Well, all right: here she was.

"Congratulations," she said, pulling me aside even as I began to experience the first gaseous rumble in my stomach from the too-rich food served up in an equally rich environment.

"Thanks," I said, watching her smooth down her skirt and shift her weight beneath the ironic smirk she was wearing. "That means a lot, Judy. Coming from you. Especially."

"Yeah, I'll bet," she said, in a voice of pure smoke. And here she raised her wrist to glance at the thin ribbon of her watch. "But you've got I guess just over an hour and a half now before Jeremiah strikes up the band and you go marching back in with Rita and Julie and the rest of them. I don't mean to keep you—you're probably anxious to get back to your wife. And the kid, right?"

I was thinking about the last time, the time we were interrupted in the executive washroom by the sound of G.C.'s key in the lock, and beating myself up over why I hadn't thought to maybe jam a paper clip in the aperture there (and I'm not trying to summon Freudian images of lock and key or rod and receptacle, just giving you a sense of my thought processes in the moment—remember, I was drunk on the air, the occasion, the food, and most of all, Judy). She was toying with me. Waiting for me to drop my voice and whisper, *Do you want to maybe see what it's like in the washroom— remember the washroom?*, so she could say, *No*, so she could say, *Oh, come on, Vodge, I'm surprised at you, I really am.* But that didn't happen. I just shrugged. "You know how it is," I said.

"No, actually, I don't." Her lips were glistening, a sheen of Louis Roederer Cristal Brut there, champagne, the fine French champagne that had been denied us inside, just like everything else.

I took a gulp from my own glass, drained it, set it down on a passing tray and snatched up another. I was feeling no pain. I was way up there now, my hands right on the controls of the shuttle taking us to Mars. "Why don't we cut the crap," I said.

She was balancing on one leg, leaning back into one of the high cocktail tables the caterers had brought in for the occasion, her ankles crossed, the glass at her lips. "You've got your duty," she said.

"Yeah," I said, bitter now, the shuttle dropping so fast I felt dizzy, thrusters jammed, clogged, dead in the sky, "and so do you."

Of course, that wasn't the end of it. If that was the end of it I wouldn't be telling you this because it wouldn't be germane to the mission, wouldn't be seared into the record or even faintly relevant. What happened, right at that moment, right as the words passed my lips, was that somebody wanted a photo, the guy from *Time,* I think it was. Not a group shot, but just a portrait of me alone—the famous shot, or infamous, I guess, where I'm posed against the glow of the new command center computers—because I was the story at that juncture, I was the one outside the glass and intimately connected to the two inside. (And yes, for the full two hours the press and the public had my wife and daughter posing for them at the visitors' window, though E. wouldn't go near the airlock, not even for ten seconds, which was what everybody wanted, of course. Why do I say that? Because while people might admire purity, or give lip service to it, they all secretly want to see it compromised, ideals crushed and sullied and dragged down into the mud they inhabit. We might need our heroes and mad saints to live for us, but we certainly don't want to exchange places with them and all the while we're yearning for the sick thrill of their temptation and fall. Read Genesis. They got that right, at least.)

So I sat for the portrait and Judy wandered off and somebody else was there, everybody else, more and more of them. I saw Stevie and Troy across the room in a swarm of people, Stevie's hair as dull as one of the goat's till she could get her hands on a box of Clairol Natural Instincts for the next day's official photo session. Was I eating too much? Drinking too much? Had I lost control, totally? Yes, yes and yes. But before you criticize me, put yourself in my place. I'd just been freed from prison—or no, not freed: I was out on parole. For two hours. Two dwindling pinched little hours of ego-stroking and sensory overload, of reward for all the deprivation I'd put myself through, the aperture growing narrower and narrower as I shifted from foot to foot and smiled and nodded and drained one glass after another, until all at once it hit me as if I'd seized hold of a three-thousand-volt electrified fence: I didn't want to go back inside. No: I *wasn't* going to go back inside.

Maybe you *can* blame me—everybody else did. I did go to the restroom, not the executive washroom, for which I didn't have a key in any case, but the one at the other end of the hall, which was there to accommodate employees and guests alike. While I was in there—and the place was a miracle, make no mistake about it, with water that just ran and ran on infinitely from some vast reservoir out there in the greater world that made it all possible, E2, Eve, E. and me, and everything else under the sun too—I unzipped and began to drain off some of the residue of the champagne, feeling woozy, as I've said, and sick to my stomach on top of it (too much, too soon). I was still ringing with the shock of that electrified fence and before I knew what I was doing I was shucking off the red jumpsuit till I was standing there in my best battered pair of Terranaut high-top sneakers, shorts and a T-shirt that was just a T-shirt, sans slogan or corporate logo. Oh, that water flowed like in some magic show, the toilets flushing over and over, the sinks running, hand dryers roaring, but then there came an interval—seconds, that was all—when the sounds fell off and the outer door wheezed shut and all at once I was out in the middle of the floor, catching a quick glimpse of myself in the mirror over the sink. I looked—reduced. Looked guilty. Looked like somebody who had no principles, who had never had any principles, who was driven by the raw impulses of the id, by cowardice and fear and the glorification of the moment, who didn't think, didn't stop to think, who just . . . ran.

* * *

To say I was unprepared for life on the outside was to speak truth, in spades. Perhaps the greatest technological transformation in human history had exploded on the scene while I was locked away—the computer revolution, dial-up, the worldwide Web, p.c.'s in something like thirty-six percent of the households in the country—and I didn't know a thing about it. I didn't know about world events either, didn't know about Rwanda or the Serbs or Nancy Kerrigan, Aldrich Ames or O.J. Simpson. And money. I didn't know about money, the feel of it between thumb and fore-finger, or its value, and when I slipped down the back stairway at Mission Control and ducked into the head-high scrub that fringed the back courtyard and ran on unbroken all the way to the slopes of the Santa Catalinas, I didn't have any either. Not a cent. I didn't have a hat. Or a jacket. Or water. I wasn't in the rain forest any-more, wasn't in a controlled atmosphere: I was out in the Sonoran Desert, and I was drunk and sick to my stomach and caught up in the greatest crisis of my adult life.

I didn't go far, maybe half a mile, a mile. Far enough, in any case, so that I could no longer distinguish the celebratory strains of the party Mission Control was throwing. By the time I stopped running—or sidling or creeping or just shoving through one unforgiving bush after another—both my legs and both arms were striped with thin horizontal cuts, but I didn't feel a thing. The air was a banquet for the alveoli of my lungs, for my blood-stream, for my brain, and it made me feel unconquerable, made me feel I could keep on going, all the way up the mountains and over the other side, down through Tucson and on into Mexico—Nogales, Guaymas, Culiacán—and who needed water? Not me. I'd made my break for it and now here I was, crouched under a creosote bush that was all but identical to ten thousand others, listening for sounds of pursuit like a child playing at hide-and-seek. Nothing was irretrievable yet. I could have gone back, could have re-donned the jumpsuit and marched in through the airlock to extend my sentence for another two years and no time off for good behavior—there was time still, at least an hour, maybe more. I sat, stretched my legs, tried to think things through. A period of time slid by, how long I couldn't say—I had no watch either. Very slowly my heartbeat began to decelerate, and though I wasn't tired (just the opposite: I was riding a wave of exhilaration that had yet to crest), I laid myself down on my side in the prickling dirt, buffered my head with two folded hands (like a child) and fell off to sleep.

If that seems incredible—that anybody could fall asleep under those conditions—I can only say it was beyond my conscious control, my body dealing with the burden of what I'd just done and what I was facing, not just now but on into the future. A brownout. Systems overload. If I hadn't been drunk, hadn't been out of my mind on oxygen and the mad caloric rush of all that sugary, salty, fat-drenched *food,* things might have been different. But that's just making excuses, isn't it? The truth is, even if I was stone-cold sober and fasting like a true believer and hadn't been pushed into a corner by E. and G.C. and the exigencies of the unending mission, I still don't think I would have been able to go back inside—not then, not ever. Once I breached the airlock, once I felt the sun on my face—and it wasn't Judy, or not yet, wasn't the cheers of the crowd or the food or drink or anything more than the world itself, E1 in all its glory—it would have been easier to shoot myself in the head than submit to *that.* I'd done my two years' time and that was enough. *Please.*

When dusk fell, birds ricocheting through the branches, things buzzing and chittering and humming against the coming night (wild things, things that weren't necessarily innocuous, that weren't imprisoned under glass in the world's biggest terrarium, things that could—and would—bite), I was wide awake. My head had begun to clear. The exotic food lay heavy on my stomach and the various nicks and scratches I'd suffered began to sting. I wasn't cold, but when the desert floor gave up its heat I would be. And I was thirsty, me, the water-meister of E2, where even in our own artificial desert it was insufferably humid and a drink was never more than fifty feet away. Irony? Sure, irony enough for another chapter altogether. Turn the page. Here it is, staring you in the face.

Any prisoner thinks of escape. I'd broken out of one jail and now I was in another. They would be looking for me, *G.C.* would be looking for me, and what were we going to tell the public? That I'd had a medical emergency. Not a breakdown, and especially not a nervous breakdown—Terranauts didn't have breakdowns—but something sudden and unavoidable, a burst appendix, a seizure of some sort. Of course, Terranauts didn't have burst appendixes or seizures either. Maybe an allergic reaction—to the world, the dirty, fucked-up, irretrievably polluted world the Ecosphere was meant to put in perspective . . .

I had no illusions. I was done. Period. Mission Control would have sent in Malcolm in my place, and the press would have been fed some elaborate lie about how I'd been suddenly stricken and was under a doctor's care in our private on-site facility and as soon as they knew anything, they'd issue a press release. And they were deeply concerned, of course, as they were concerned for all our team members, the whole intertwined family of E2 and all it stood for, but they were hoping for a full recovery. Patience, please, they would have told the clamoring, shouting, red-faced horde of reporters. *We'll know more in the morning* . . .

It grew dark. The temperature kept dropping—the high for the day was in the upper seventies, but by the hour of the wolf, I knew, it would hover in the forties. I let out a laugh, I couldn't help myself. Inside, we'd faced heatstroke; out here I could die of hypothermia. I pushed myself up then and scanned the horizon, looking for the lights of E2 or even the highway beyond, but saw nothing but the darkness of the world.

At one point, blundering, lost, I was startled by the sudden fierce warning rattle of an invisible serpent—a diamondback or ridge-nose or rock rattler that could kill with its bite but probably wouldn't, that would likely just leave its human victim with a leg that swelled and blackened and a whole lot of necrotic tissue— and again, I had to laugh. This was the world, the real world, and nobody was in control. In any case, as luck would have it— *luck!*—nothing lashed out of the blackness to put a pair of puncture wounds in me. Warned off, I made a wide circuit of whatever lurked there in the dark, shivering now from the cold, my nicks and cuts freshened and freshened again, various thistles, stickers and thorns penetrating my socks and shoes so that each step was a little crucifixion, a penance for abandoning my God and Creator, whose concern by now would have mutated into fury.

He wouldn't have slept, I knew that, wouldn't have done anything but storm and fume and rage. No doubt he would have enlisted the state troopers, sent out the bloodhounds and helicopters with their heat-seeking cameras and all the rest, except that he couldn't because that would only make matters worse, that would be an admission of the inadmissible, that a Terranaut had broken ranks. Beyond that, he couldn't have known I was blundering around in the dark within a mile or so of the campus—for all he knew I was in a car somewhere, hurtling through the night. It must have killed him. And here, though I was shivering, quaking head to foot with the cold, actually, I had to laugh once more, a delirious laugh that caught like a plug of unchewed gristle in the clenched pit of my throat—to think of it, G.C., the omnipotent, at a loss for once. But it wasn't funny, not really. Nothing was funny now. And when I realized that the faint glow in the distance wasn't the first hint of dawn or the lingering visual memory of headlights along the highway but E2 itself rising above the nullity of the bush with all its lights burning against the night, I made straight for it.

* * *

They found me just before dawn huddled outside the airlock, where I'd wrapped myself in the pair of flags that had flown over the proceedings the previous day (the green Ecosphere II banner, with the white crosshatchings etched in the center of it to represent the spaceframe, and the Arizona state flag, with its red-and-yellow evocation of the sun's rays crowning its field). When I say "they," incidentally, I do not mean the reporters or the E2 cabbalists or whatever incarnation of Dad, Mom, Junior and Sis, but the staff members G.C. had kept up all night searching the grounds for me. In fact, it was two of the newbies and, of all people, Linda Ryu, who found me pinned there in a collision of flashlight beams and escorted me up the hill to the command center, the three of them struck silent (except for Linda Ryu, who said, pithily, "You royally fucked up this time, *Vodge*") while I limped and hung my head, feeling as if the night had transformed me into an octogenarian.

Know that G.C., Judy and Little Jesus were waiting for me in the command center, Judy looking nothing like she had the previous afternoon, but rumpled and tired and worn down around the residual glow of her flammable eyes, and Dennis, with his ludicrous greased-back hair and spit curl, could have been on his way back from a tryout for a revival of *Grease,* but for the look he was wearing. Of umbrage. Of the dog that's just pissed on the wet patch left by the lesser dog—by me, that is. And G.C.—he was leaning all the way back in his recliner, long and knobby, his feet propped up on his desk and his hair and beard inundating the pinched visible portion of his face, as if he was surviving his own personal blizzard. Nobody said anything till Linda Ryu and the two newbies (I didn't even know their names, don't even remember if one was male and the other female or if they were both the same gender) had bowed their way out the door to make their way down the hallway, out the front door and across campus to their waiting beds in the Residences. I was guilty of a whole array of crimes here, not the least of which was keeping everybody up all night.

Judy was the first to open her mouth. "You look like crap," she informed me.

Then G.C., and his voice was pained, broken: "You couldn't have told me? Couldn't have taken me aside and let me know what you were feeling? Couldn't, at least, have given me that?"

As exhausted as I was, as dehydrated and disoriented and humiliated, I still couldn't do what was expected of me because this was no different from one of Stalin's show trials except it was in camera, and the result, I was sure, would be the same: confess and then squeeze yourself onto the next train for Siberia. "No," I said, "I couldn't. Not after E. made her decision—and it's her who's to blame here, her pigheadedness, from the baby right on down to this."

"I'm not blaming anybody," G.C. said, and that surprised me. I hadn't expected him to take that tone, to be *reasonable*. In a way, I suppose, I wanted the rebuke, wanted the lashing, tongue- or otherwise, wanted to be absolved and cleansed and welcomed back into the fold, even if I'd never been very good at confession. Or humility.

"But once she got it in her head," I fumbled on, "I mean, it's a brilliant PR coup, the whole thing, of course it is, but I felt squeezed, as if I had no way out, because you"—and here I raised my sleep-deprived eyes to him—"you pushed so hard for it I just didn't want to disappoint you. I mean, what could I do?" I wasn't talking to the room now, but G.C. alone. By that point I wasn't even aware of Judy and Dennis except as patches of color that might as well have been framed and nailed up on the wall.

G.C. tented his long fingers, snatched his knees up and dropped his feet to the floor in a jerky, almost spastic motion. He was tired, I saw that. And old. Older than anyone I knew. "You realize we had to cover you, right? Malcolm went in in your place and we told the press you'd had an accident—"

"Good," I said, surprised at myself, at how glad I was all of a sudden to see a way of putting this behind me—and maybe, if I was very, very lucky—of making something positive of it. "That's what I thought, what I assumed—"

My brain spun. I was a free agent here. They needed me, I realized, now more than ever—or all of Mission Three was compromised. I was the father, I was key, and though I'd taken a tragic spill on the back stairs and strained some tendons in my ankle, suffered a concussion, or so the story went, I was as much in the picture as ever. And that picture was now one of pathos, a heart-rending scenario of a young family separated by circumstance, by tragedy, a family that would henceforth meet at the visitors' window and touch hands through the thin transparent wall of glass while the daughter grew and gained weight and held up her finger paintings for praise and the wife pined and the otherworldly life of E2 counted down to reentry once again. It was beautiful, it was inevitable, and no matter how I'd fucked up, I was right there dead center in the middle of it.

Dennis spoke up now. "You're going to have to wear a boot. And one of those gauze bandages around your head. And you won't be able to leave here, the medical facility here in the command center, for, let's say"—a look for G.C.—"a week?"

I was confused. So much had changed, so much was rushing at me. Twenty-four hours ago I'd been inside, now I wasn't. "But we don't have a medical facility here—?"

G.C., collapsing the tent of his fingers and giving me a look that, under the circumstances, wasn't entirely hostile, got to his feet. "We do now," he said.

* * *

I don't want to give you the impression that it was easy, that I was let off lightly and got what I wanted into the bargain (a salary, for one thing, because as I made G.C. understand as clearly as I was able under the circumstances, E2 simply could not do without me, not given my new status and what I might have to say to the press if I were terminated), because in fact everything in those first few weeks was painful in the extreme. I'd never have G.C.'s trust again, and that hurt, but if it meant anything to him, he had mine. My loyalty too. And there was E., what I'd done to her, the guilt of it that tore me awake in the morning and wouldn't let me sleep at night. After the prescribed week had passed, I hobbled out the door with one of those black orthopedic walking boots encasing my left leg from ankle to knee and bullshitted my way through a news conference, G.C. on one side of me, Judy on the other, after which, with the aid of a pair of gleaming silver crutches, I dragged my foot across the courtyard to the visitors' window, where E. and the baby were waiting for me and E. hid her outrage long enough to break down in tears, which got Eve wailing along with her and made for some heartrending photos and a video clip that pretty much dominated the evening news that night.

But wait. I don't think I'm getting this right. I'm giving you the facts, the sequence of events, but what went on beneath the surface is a different story altogether. I admit I wasn't a natural father and, as I've said, I hadn't had enough time with my daughter to really bond with her—she was only five and a half months at reentry, for Christ's sake, and anybody, even Dr. Spock himself, would have needed more time than that, but by this point I'd begun to feel stirrings of paternal instinct, at least. This is a phenomenon that goes deep into our species memory, hardwired, the way it is with the chimp or gorilla—or no, a better example would be certain bird species, the emperor penguin, for instance, in which the cooperation of both parents is necessary to ensure the survival of their offspring, and, by extension, the species. I loved Eve, no matter what people say. I love her now. And E., I think I've loved E. since the first moment she came into my life, though it might have taken me a while to fully appreciate it, I'll admit that.

So I presented myself at the glass and posed there, G.C.'s creature, and I went through the imposture of the boot and the gauze wrapped round my skull as if I were a member of the Abraham Lincoln Brigade returned from the Spanish Civil War, and I watched E. cry and stood there while she and the baby solemnly pressed their hands to the glass and I pressed back. Then I limped over to Mission Control and right on out the back door to the Residences, where they'd put me up in Malcolm's hastily vacated apartment.

About that apartment, incidentally: Malcolm was a slob and crumb-bum of the first order, dirty clothes and traces of just about everything he'd had to eat in the past week scattered over every horizontal surface, unwashed dishes in the sink, newspapers and magazines spilling over onto the floor like scree—which wasn't necessarily a bad thing. I needed something to occupy me in those first few days, and here it was—making order out of chaos. He had a TV, an oracular portal to another world I'd forgotten all about, and I left it on pretty much permanently, whether I was scrubbing stains off the counter, washing dishes or reading through the periodical literature he'd inadvertently left me, *Time*, *Newsweek*, *Sports Illustrated* and *Penthouse* included. The latter, of course, made me think of Judy, but I didn't do anything about it for a whole host of reasons, not the least of which was that I was a married man, albeit married to a woman who was all but incorporeal now, and that I was still recuperating, readjusting, getting used to planet earth in my soft boot and headgear that was like a nun's wimple and made me laugh every time I caught a glimpse of myself in the mirror.

The strangest thing? Living with Malcolm's leavings, his drawers stuffed with graying Joe Boxer undershorts and bunched-up shirts that invariably featured horizontal stripes in either black-and-white or orange-and-white, as if he'd been apprenticing for prison (which, in a way, I suppose he had). He had a collection of dusty conch shells, ten or twelve of them, each with an inch-long hole tapped in the base of it where the meat had been extracted, recruited no doubt on one of the voyages of The *Imago*. And baseball cards. Boxes and boxes of baseball cards, some still wrapped in the original cellophane, and what could be more useless? I fought the impulse to toss them, along with the rest of his crap, but restrained myself: he'd had all of what, fifteen minutes, to throw some things together and hustle himself through the airlock, and who was to blame for that? So I wound up stuffing everything into a dozen or so white cardboard boxes I got from Mission Control and stacking the boxes up to the ceiling in the bedroom. I did use his bike, though, once I was officially healed. And his skateboard. And for the first couple of weeks, before I came to an arrangement with Mission Control and began to draw a salary, I have to admit I wound up wearing his Joe Boxers too, because, as you can no doubt appreciate, I had nothing—zero, zilch—till I could manage to get myself together and extract my own stuff from the public storage facility in Tucson.

Of course, telling you all this is just a way of avoiding the issue here—Dawn, I mean. My wife. She was behind the glass and I wasn't. If I hadn't exactly lied to her, I'd deceived her, even if I'd deceived myself too. No matter the official story, I'd had what amounted to a nervous breakdown there in that restroom on the third floor of Mission Control and it had driven me out into the scrub where the pain and confusion of it took my will away. I'm not asking for sympathy. If there was a victim here, it wasn't me, it was Dawn.

I waited till the second week had gone by and the medical props were no longer necessary before I saw her alone for the first time. I'd tried to explain myself over the phone, of course, and there was that initial meeting when we were just acting out our roles for the press, but I'd been reluctant to see her face-to-face, for obvious reasons. Is it hard to be married to an icon? Is there a point at which duty and determination become just another kind of fanaticism? I don't know. I'm not making accusations and I'm not trying to defend myself either—I'm just saying that I avoided her for the full term of my so-called recuperation, holed up in Malcolm Burts' shitpit of an apartment, letting the determined idiocy of the TV penetrate my every waking moment till it became my solace and my balm.

The day was cloudless and bright, the sun arching high overhead and the crew inside getting the full benefit of it, the days stretching longer now and every leafy thing pumping out the oxygen and soaking up CO_2. I'd had breakfast in the cafeteria—an omelet, toast, butter, jam, a side of bacon, home fries and coffee, all the coffee I could want (free refills, what a concept!)—and I had a to-go cup of heavily sugared java to sustain me on the trip down the slope to the visitors' window. It was eight a.m., so Dawn would already have put in an hour or so in the IAB, which was pretty much her exclusive province now, and never mind the installment of Rita Nordquist as Supervisor of Field Crops because she was and would always be a newbie and E. was more now than simply a veteran—she *was* the IAB, its presiding spirit and its regulator too, just as she was the doyenne of the domestic animals and the shining star of the whole enterprise.

We'd arranged the time on the phone the night before, but the window was empty when I came round the corner in my naturalist's trance to see the Ecosphere all aglow with the morning sun, the struts shining and the glass so invested with it the structure seemed to be generating its own light from within. I hadn't fully acclimated yet and it was strange and disorienting to see the place as independent, as a material presence slapped down there in the middle of the desert when for so long I'd known it only from the inside, in the way the blood knows the body that contains it. I sat myself down on the stool outside the window, picked up the phone and waited. I don't know how much time went by—I still didn't have a watch—but each dragged-down minute began to seem unendurable. I'd been rehearsing what to say to her, though I felt guilty and depressed and knew what little we'd worked out over the phone wouldn't hold water once she was staring me in the face. One part of me dreaded seeing her, and the other? The other was hopeful, because we were still man and wife and we still had a daughter as proof of it and we'd both got what we wanted, at least temporarily. But then she hadn't gotten what she wanted at all if what she wanted was me, and I hoped that was the case—that she still wanted me—but as you can imagine I was anxious about it. Anxious about Judy too, whom I hadn't called, and wasn't going to call—or not right then, not for a while, not till I could get a grip and things began to sort themselves out.

I was about to leave, angry suddenly to think that she was standing me up and wondering just what that meant, when there was a movement of the curtains and she was there, her shoulders slumped and eyes downcast, making for the stool set just inside the glass, where the phone was. She glanced up as she lifted one leg to settle herself on the stool, but she didn't smile. I was trying to gauge her mood, but I was coming up with nothing. I'd already told her half a dozen times the truth of what had happened—I'd got cold feet, had a nervous breakdown, freaked out, whatever you want to call it—because I had too much respect for her to try to put the official story over on her, which she wouldn't have believed anyhow. I have to admit I'd thought about it, though. It would have made everything a whole lot easier, but I just couldn't do it. Talk about ethics, talk about *trust:* it just wasn't right.

How did she look? Her fingernails were dirty, ten black half-moons of E2's earth defining the fingertips she ran through her hair, which looked as if it hadn't seen a comb for a week, and she was wearing the oversized MDA shirt I'd seen on her maybe a thousand times and which just emphasized the thinness of her limbs. It wasn't flattering. Her feet were bare. And dirty. She wasn't wearing any makeup, not even lipstick, and that told me something I didn't want to know, because (from her point of view now) whether she made herself attractive for me or not didn't seem to matter. Still, she was Dawn, my E., and she couldn't hide her beauty, not if she'd shaved off her hair and plastered herself in mud.

"Where's Eve?" I asked.

"Rita's watching her." Her voice was faraway, a dull voice, uninflected—uninterested.

"I'd like to see her. What's she up to, I mean, is she, what—teething yet?"

A weary look. "Not yet."

I'd read up a bit on this because I wanted to do my share, do what I could, make it up to her if only in the small ways. "But soon, right? Aren't babies supposed to have their teeth come in at six months?"

"I guess."

"You guess? Come on, E., help me out here."

She just stared at me, and that was unnerving because we were so close and yet so far, no touching, no scents, no sounds but for what the phone line gave up. In Frankfurt, at the zoo there, the zoologists have achieved an extraordinary success rate in breeding lowland gorillas because, for one thing, the gorillas are kept behind glass instead of the more conventional arrangement of moats or steel bars, and that relaxes them—they can see us, but we're not a threat or even a presence because all the intimacy is in the touch, the taste, the smell, the noise. In the words, the ceaseless repetitive *rat-tat-tat* of the words. We're a noisy species, a gabbling species. We explain. Endlessly.

"Are you okay with this?" I asked, giving her a quick glance, then looking past her because I didn't like what I saw in her eyes.

She didn't answer. She said, "Is that coffee you're drinking?"

"Yeah," I said, "I guess."

"That's just cruel."

"You want me to pour it out? I'll pour it out—"

Again no reaction. A long moment had time to spin its wheels. "So what now?" she said. "We fake sex at the glass? You want to see my breasts? Johnny wanted to see my breasts way back when."

I wasn't going to play this game. I was guilty, yes, I was a shit, I was everything my enemies accused me of and worse, but we had to get a grip here. "He probably still does," I said.

I watched her lip curl, a little tic of hers, the slightest adjustment of the muscles there, as if she'd taken a bite of something too hot to swallow. What she said was, "How's Judy?"

"I don't know," I said. "How's Gavin, or who, *Malcolm*?"

"Are we really going to do this? Don't you think you've already done enough to me—and Eve? What about Eve?"

I had, there was no denying it. I was in the wrong—now, then, always. I'm a talker, I'm a conciliator, it's my profession to smooth things over. But not this time. Not yet. I swung my leg off the stool, straightened up and started picking my way back across the courtyard, around the corner of the white-boned pyramid that housed the rain forest and on up the hill to the Residences. Maybe it wasn't the smartest thing to do, but there wasn't any use sitting there arguing. Really, what can I say? She was there, I was here, two years is a very long time, and when you came right down to it, there was this wall between us.

Linda Ryu

I don't even want to address the Dawn situation. I wouldn't give her the satisfaction—if she could even begin to know how I feel, and why should she? My question is, why does my story always have to be her story? She didn't say word one to me, never even gave me a hint so I could prepare myself, let alone apologize, and yes, while she might have broached the subject that day at the glass, she was voted down seven to one, and all I could think was she'd gone completely out of her mind till her crewmates put an end to it. But they hadn't put an end to it and they wound up being fooled just as much as me. Dawn stayed in, I stayed out, and I waited three full days before the call finally came—Dawn, Queen and Empress of E2, deigning to call me, the peasant, the serf, the nobody, trying to explain herself in what was really all about her and her guilty conscience and had nothing to do with me because by that point I must have been all but anonymous to her. I wasn't inside. I wasn't a member of Team Two or Team Three either. I didn't have a microphone and I wasn't from CBS News, so really, who was I?

She told me she felt bad. Told me how she just couldn't help herself, as if some sort of spell had come over her—"Really, Linda, E2 has that kind of power, it's almost mystical"— before she broke down and started mewling over how Ramsay had stabbed her in the back (without mentioning the cold steel blade she'd stuck in mine), which is when I hung up on her. And refused to pick up the phone when it rang five seconds later and kept on ringing on my desk till somebody said, "Will you pick up, already?" and I said, "No, I won't."

By the way, in case you're wondering how I could swallow all the shit they threw at me and keep on swallowing it, let me just say that I am determined, no matter what I'm up against or how two-faced and scheming people really show themselves to be. Mission Control—and Dawn—couldn't have made it any worse if their intention was to annihilate me, as if all of E2 and its ambitions and pronouncements and funding schemes existed only as an elaborate joke on me, because there's no advance warning, nothing, and I don't actually find out what's going on till the day of the reentry/closure ceremony. And why is that? Because they want to make it a surprise. Because they want to churn the TV ratings and don't really care who or what they stomp in their wake. Can you even imagine it? My parents are there. Two of my best friends from college. The *Sacramento Bee* ran my picture on the front page and I've been through the press conference and my fitting and I've cleaned out my apartment and put everything in storage, and even, irony of irony, polished Dawn's car for her.

And then, the very morning of Mission Three closure, Judy and Dennis show up at my stripped-to-the-basics apartment in the Residences and tell me what? That there's been a change of plan. That's how Judy puts it, after sprinkling cinnamon and sugar on it for a full ten minutes while Little Jesus nods along and licks his lips and tugs at his ears. *There's been a change of plan.* But I've asked a rhetorical question here and I haven't really answered it: how could I even think of staying on for another second, let alone don the turd-brown uniform and sit there dutifully in the front row, my lips sealed, while the worst humiliation of my life plays out in public? Answer: it isn't easy.

What happens is this: after I throw my fit, a true tear-up-the-cushions and pound-the-walls-with-both-fists display and run out of breath cursing the two of them in English and Korean both (and before I can say, *Fuck you all, I'm out of here*), Judy calmly props her briefcase up on the coffee table, flips the twin latches and extracts two items. The first is a check drawn on SEE in the amount of $50,000. "For your services over the course of three years, and I know it should be more," she says, "but we're hoping you'll accept it as a peace offering, at least," and, of course, in my rage and hurt and disappointment I won't even look at it, let alone touch it. The second is a contract, fully executed and witnessed, but for my signature, appointing me, Linda Darlene Ryu, Executive Vice President of SEE, Tillman, and—in a clause set off with five blue asterisks from the pen Judy hands me across the table—guaranteeing me a place as MDA for Mission Four. And what do I have to do in return? Shut up and smile.

* * *

Think what you will, but everybody has their price, and what was I supposed to do, take an axe to the airlock and force my way in? I could have, easily, could have called every newspaper in the country and spilled the kind of dirt that would bring down the whole shitty lot of them, from G.C. to Dawn and Ramsay and even poor innocent gung-ho Gavin (who's inside now, with *Dawn,* as if I don't have enough to fume over), but what I do instead is put on my Dragon Lady face and start plotting my revenge. It's Dawn I want, more than anybody, Dawn and Ramsay, and if I just walk away I'll never sleep another night in my life.

As soon as the door closes behind Judy and Dennis, the silence just screams through the apartment. I want to turn on the radio, the TV, the vacuum cleaner and the blender, all at once—anything to fill the void—but I can't summon the energy. I just sit there, the check in one hand, the contract in the other, and stare at the wall as if I can see through it, all the way across the campus and deep into E2, where the Mission Two crew must be helping each other zip up their jumpsuits and Dawn's busy pulling her imposture. Along with Ramsay, the King Shit of all time. I am weary, so very, very weary. But still, as numb as I am, as numb to everything as one of the living dead with a stake driven right through one side of her head and out the other, I force myself to pull on the turd-brown jumpsuit Judy handed me after she saw I was going to take the check. What I need to do, above all else, is go out there into the rising glare of Arizona sunshine and find my parents, where I know they'll be sitting patiently in the special section reserved for relatives of the Mission Three crew. It's two hours before the ceremony, the tech staff up on the dais fiddling with things, the odd guests beginning to arrive. My parents, who always like to be early, rigidly and anal-retentively early, are already there, my mother poised beneath a red-and-black checkered parasol and fanning herself though the temperature can't be much more than seventy-five or so, and my father, one knee crossed over the other, sitting beside her bent over a copy of the *New England Journal of Medicine,* his bifocals radiant in the sun.

Both my parents speak with an accent, a soft charming purr of an accent people would have a hard time placing if they were talking to them over the telephone, nothing at all like the exaggerated consonant-challenged gibberish you hear from the stereotypical mild-mannered Asian characters on TV and in the movies, characters who always seem to play for comic effect. My parents are not stereotypical. They are definitely not mild-mannered. And they do not play for comic effect, not in my life anyway. They are kind and loving and they want the very best for me, even if they do tend to set their expectations in concrete and have never really understood my devotion to E2. They're my parents. I love them. And going to them now is maybe the hardest thing I've ever had to do.

My father glances up first, instant smile, and then he's rising nimbly from the white folding chair to take hold of me, murmuring, "Hi, Angel, we missed you," and I'm rocking in his arms before bending down to kiss my mother's cheek under the stiff straw-smelling brim of her hat. That moment, embracing my parents there amid the rigid geometry of waiting chairs, brings back all the concerts and graduation ceremonies of my life, from elementary school to junior high to my first (and last) viola recital in ninth grade to high school commencement and college too, and I'm so heartbroken, so defeated, it's all I can do to keep from breaking down in front of them.

My mother's right on it. She tilts her head to get a better look at me, the sun slicing in under the brim of her hat to cut a bright crescent out of her face. I watch her photochromic lenses darken till her eyes shade into invisibility. She says, "What's wrong, honey? You're getting your dream, aren't you? Why the long face?"

"She's nervous, that's all," my father says. And then to me: "It's only natural—the jitters, I mean. They'll go away, you'll see—"

"It's not that," I say.

My mother, her inflection rising hopefully, makes her best guess, her radar for misery all but infallible. "You're having second thoughts, is that it?" She's never been happy about this *(I can't see it, I really can't see you locking yourself away from the world like some sort of nun, because where's the future in that?)*, and since the Mission Three roster was released she's become more and more protective, ringing me up two or three times a day to take my emotional temperature and coincidentally to mention job openings she's read about in the paper or a new grad course in environmental studies one of the UC schools just announced.

I look away for a moment, as if I'm distracted by what the tech staff are doing up on the dais, and when I turn back to her, the lie is right there on my lips. "Mom," I say, "Mom, you're amazing, you really are. How did you guess?"

My father's about to say something, but my mother shushes him. "So what does that mean?"

Again I have to look away, but I brave it out and tell her they've decided I'm too valuable to waste inside, at least for this mission. "Mom, can you believe it? They made me Executive Vice President of Space Ecosphere Enterprises"—and now a look for my father—"and they gave me a bonus. Are you ready for this?"

They're both locked in now, not even breathing, and why do I feel like I'm in the fifth grade, flagging a report with a gold star on it? Why, actually, is my heart turning to ash while my voice spikes with all the false enthusiasm I can muster? "Are you?" I repeat, even as somebody up on the dais—Chad Streeter, one of the Mission Four newbies—blows into the microphone and says, *"Testing, one, two, three."*

They *are* ready, more than ready, the relief on my mother's face as palpable as if this is the end of a movie and she the heroine who's survived the most harrowing ordeal the scriptwriters could devise. She's relieved I'm not going inside. Glad I'm not getting what I've so desperately wanted through every waking moment of the last three years. At least somebody's happy, I tell myself, at least there's that.

I take a deep breath, as if I'm getting ready to blow the candles out on a birthday cake. "It's for *fifty thousand dollars!*" I say, fighting to keep my voice under control. "Can you believe it?"

* * *

If I've got my new status and Ellen Shapiro does too (she's officially Executive Officer of Acquisitions for Space Ecosphere Enterprises, Tillman, a title as meaningless as mine but better, of course, than nothing), what really gets me is Ramsay. Ramsay, who's the ultimate cheat and who all but pissed in G.C.'s face with that whole closure fiasco, is, of course, getting rewarded for it, with a salary twice mine (and the title of Senior Director of Public Relations). Whether he got a bonus or not, I don't know, though I've done my best to find out, snooping through the files when I stay after hours because I am "so fiercely dedicated to my work," as Judy puts it without a trace of irony. Of course, I *am* fiercely dedicated—only it's to getting my own back against the trio, or make that a quartet, that sucked the blood right out of my body. Dawn, number one, then Ramsay, then Judy, then Dennis, in that order. My aim, my objective, my *obsession,* is to bring them all down, one by one, and climb right on up the ladder to occupy the space they vacate. I am going to rise and they are going to fall.

I can't get at Dawn directly, of course. She's become the jewel of E2 and more to G.C. at this point I think even than Judy herself, though Judy's still with him, or at least nominally anyway. Whether they actually screw anymore or not, I can't say, but I can picture her down on her knees in his office taking him in her mouth or slipping into her teddy for him after one of the dinner parties they're forever throwing at their Oro Valley condo. But that's not the point. The point is Judy and Ramsay. I know they're going at it—or will be—and what I want is to be there to catch them at it, what I want is evidence I can *use.*

So what I do, even before I see my first paycheck, is reserve four hundred and seventy-two dollars of the SEE funds Judy handed me and buy a used Canon SLR EOS-A2 camera, with telephoto lens, at Monument Camera in downtown Tucson. I'm no expert, and the array of cameras is pretty bewildering, but as soon as I see the name EOS I know it's for me, and how appropriate is that, a camera with Dawn's crew moniker stamped right on the face of it? I'd say it's karma, but karma is just the kind of imaginative construct I don't believe in and never will, along the lines of the ultimate banal question, *What sign are you?* Let's just say it's a happy coincidence, and leave it at that.

At first, just to get used to it, I take my camera out into the scrub that all but engulfs the campus and shoot a couple rolls of typical nature shots, whatever catches my eye through the squint of the lens: a fence lizard fifty feet away, a stand of saguaro that looks like a troop of people getting held up by a gunman, a bird with a red underbelly and speckled back I never do manage to identify. I'm an amateur and I take amateur photos, but I'm not thinking of an exhibit in a gallery somewhere or of art or plaudits or anything else, but only of getting comfortable enough to hang out the window of my car from let's say a block or so away and get a nice close-up of two people going into a motel room. Together.

It's not like it was before closure, by the way. If Judy and Ramsay are up to anything, there's no evidence of it, not a shred, though I'm watching every move they make, especially when they're out in the hall or down in the cafeteria where they think there's less scrutiny, but as far as I can see they're just going about their business like any two colleagues of any going concern that just might or might not happen to be a cult. Ramsay's been installed in a glorified carrel across the command center from mine (which is just a particleboard enclosure three feet higher than my desk, hastily erected in honor of my new status but still located right outside Judy's office, where I remain her gofer, attack dog and all-purpose snoop). His carrel's as slapdash as mine, only it's shoved up against the side wall of G.C.'s inner sanctum, making him readily available to serve our God and Creator's needs throughout the day, every day. What's obvious, no matter the penance being exacted here, is that Ramsay's using the same sort of not-so-subtle blackmail I am and that not only is G.C. leaning toward easing him into Dennis' position, leaving Dennis the odd executive out (and one less target for me), but that forgiveness in the name of advancing E2's agenda isn't exactly the hardest thing in the world to come by. At least for Ramsay, that is, no matter how much it might sting for the rest of us.

Anyway, I'm watching. And there comes a night a month or so into Mission Three closure when I'm working late (or pretending to), and a bit of urgent business—a report that actually could wait till morning—propels me into Judy's office, with its glass walls that are frosted waist high and a door that locks with a key, which, of course, as Judy's intimate, I have my own clone of. If anybody on the night shift should see me there leafing through Judy's files or even accessing her computer—Jeff Weston, for instance, who's still on the cameras and still has no guarantee for Mission Four, and I do feel sorry for him, or Crystal Waters, a Mission Four candidate with honey-blond hair and a résumé that includes stints at Woods Hole *and* Scripps, if that tells you anything about her chances—they would just assume I'm carrying out Judy's orders. So really, there's zero risk in sitting down at Judy's desk and bringing up her e-mail account, which has no password or encryption or any security measures whatever, and seeing what she's up to, both professionally and privately too. For all her hardheadedness and attention to detail, Judy's pretty casual about this new technology, and I'm sure it's never entered her head that her e-mails might not be strictly private—lucky for me. Because as soon as I sit down and start scrolling through her mail, this one—from Ramsay—leaps out at me:

6:30, then? Same place?

And her reply: *Don't be late.*

Then he types a single word: *Roses?*

And she types back: *Stuff the roses. Champagne.*

It's 6:05, a Thursday night, early April. Sundown in Tillman this time of year is in just over half an hour, forty minutes actually, and I am already in motion because, as you can appreciate, it's a whole lot harder to get a clear shot after dark than before, and I'm already at the door, Jeff calling out something behind me—a joke, no doubt, about the hours I'm keeping, because, sadly, he's got to suck up to me now along with all the others—but I've got no time to acknowledge him or even be civil. I'm gone. But where, you might ask? What does "the same place" mean? It means the Saguaro Motel on Route 77, or that's my best guess after having noticed a charge from that very location on Judy's credit card account the previous week. Besides, I don't have time to think, just act. I've got to get there, get parked in a place where I'll be hidden but still have a clear field of view, catch my breath and stop my hands from trembling, and why are my hands trembling?

I'm in the car, out of the lot and tearing down the winding blacktop road that connects the campus with Route 77, where I'll have to swing north and go flat out for something like nine or ten miles before the motel appears on my right, if it's even the right motel, if that's what *same place* means and maybe there's more than one place where they have their little trysts, who knows, but here I am rocketing past some doddering hunched-over old lady in a Honda doing fifty—*fifty,* for God's sake—and I don't care who's coming the opposite way in a crazy dopplering blare of horns as I dodge back in at the last possible second with about a coat of paint's width between us and I just don't care. The clock on the dashboard reads 6:15 and I'm still only maybe halfway there, but then the clock's fast, isn't it? Or no—the thought hits me like a brick—it's ten minutes slow! But that can't be, it can't. Now there's a truck in the way, one of those big double-trailer things with wheels as high as the roof of my car and a shimmering silver back end that blots out the world, and what am I doing? I'm passing it too—on a curve—and it's nothing short of a miracle there's nobody coming the other way or I wouldn't be here to tell you this.

Okay. All right. I'm there now, sailing on past and stealing a furtive glance at the neon-framed front window of the motel office and the twenty or so rooms facing the road, scanning for Judy's car—or Ramsay's, which I don't even know the make of, just that it's some Japanese thing the color of those marshmallow candies you get at Easter, the yellow ones shaped to look like newly hatched chicks . . . Judy's car is a Mercedes, black, but it's really G.C.'s car, as is the other one she drives, a red sportscar of some kind or other, but now I've already passed by and I don't see his car or either of hers and suddenly all the energy seems to hiss right out of me as if I'm a balloon with a fast leak. *Swing a U-turn,* I tell myself. *Find a place to park. Get the camera out.* Right. Because you never know.

The motel, incidentally, is on the outskirts of Tillman— walking distance, actually, from Alfano's or El Caballero, and I walked to it myself one night, hand in hand with John, of the three gold bicuspids and stringy white ponytail. There's a gas station right next to it and beyond that a side street with various suburban landscape features that would provide cover but make a shot of the front office dicey at best. Directly across from the motel is a fast-food place with maybe a half dozen cars parked in front of it and various bodies going in and out the twin side doors. Golden arches. McDonald's. Death on a bun.

When I wheel into the lot and squeeze in between two massive big-dick pickups that have seen better days, one black, one white, the clock on the dashboard reads 6:33, and whatever's about to unfold is in the hands of fate. What I'm thinking, even as my unsteady hands adjust the camera, find the angle, the distance, is that they'd be too smart to just park out front where anybody could see their cars, and for a moment the terrible thought hits me that they've parked around back, booked one of the rooms you can't see from the road, because that's what they'd do—it's what I would do if I was them. *But why,* I'm asking myself, *why didn't I think of this earlier? Why am I just sitting here? Why don't I put the car in reverse, back out and go see—I've got to do something, don't I?*

And I'm about to—I actually set the camera down on the seat beside me, 6:35 now and the sky getting denser, grayer, the shadows beginning to blur in the trees beyond the gas station and all trace of the sun gone—when a movement out front of the motel snaps me back to attention. It's Ramsay, Ramsay himself, dressed in a baseball cap, a pair of blue jeans and a paisley shirt with the collar turned up, coming across the macadam lot in a quick easy athletic stride, Ramsay—*click, click*—disappearing into the motel's office, where I can just make out the shadow of him hovering there over the desk. Can I believe my luck? I don't know and I'm not ready to revise my opinion as to signs and God and all the other idiotic superstitious claptrap people live by, not until I see Judy making her way across the lot from the opposite direction— and it's unmistakably Judy, though she's wearing a hat too and a long belted raincoat that erases her entirely, from the tops of her shoes to her throat. Judy. Does she think she can hide—*click, click*—from me? They're fools. Careless, petty, banal people, and I'll never dance to their tune again—they won't even have a tune. *Wait till G.C. sees this,* that's the thought racing through my head. *Wait till Dawn sees it.*

What about the money shot? I don't mean in the sense of a porno film, which I personally find disgusting, not to mention degrading to women, but just a shot of the two of them together, colluding, backstabbing, whatever you want to call it—there's nobody alive who's going to believe they're here at the Saguaro Motel at 6:41 in the evening to discuss wastewater treatment options and the intricacies of the O_2/CO_2 cycle. I mean, really. Just then, just as she reaches the door of the office, out comes Ramsay, jerking his head to look both ways up and down the street and then communicating something to her—the room number?—before bouncing down the steps and moving fluidly along the row of parked cars till he reaches the last room down on the right-hand side—in front!—and slips the key in the door . . . and holds it open. And flicks on the interior light as if he's a photographer's assistant. Too perfect. She's there, no embrace, just there for a split second—*click, click*—and then she's inside and the door's shut and the night closes in.

I could end it here, but this is about me, this is about settling scores and seeing my way to the future the way I want it designed for a change. So what happens next, just as I'm unscrewing the lens and reverentially packing my equipment away, is Johnny. Johnny's there, on the other side of my car, standing at the door of the black pickup clutching a white grease-stained McDonald's bag in one hand and patting down his front pocket for his keys with the other. Actually? I didn't even know he had a pickup, not that it matters one way or the other to me, just that I failed to recognize it as his, and now he's standing there, digging his hand into the tight unyielding pocket of his jeans, and for just an instant my blood pressure jumps. Did he see me hanging out the window of my car all of sixty seconds ago? Did he see me spying? Gathering evidence? Betraying—or getting ready to betray—two of my coworkers who're probably already deep into it, Ramsay stripping her and Judy stripping him, *his cock, her cunt?*

No, I decide. No, he didn't. And in the next moment, without thinking twice, I lean over the passenger's seat, roll down the window and call Johnny's name. I watch him start, then recognize me with a cool clean look that admits no surprise because surprise would take him out of himself, and that's a place he never wants to leave. He bends down to poke his head in the window, a strand of his hair falling loose to dangle over one eyebrow, and maybe there's a breeze blowing, maybe not. "Hi," he says.

"Hi," I say, and I'm feeling better than I have in a long, long time. I give him a smile, fiddle with the top button of my blouse just to draw his eyes. "So," I say, as if I'm summing up a discussion that's gone on for hours, "you doing anything special tonight?"

* * *

In case you're wondering, the pictures turn out fine. I take them back to Monument Camera to have them developed and blown up, though it costs a small fortune, and even with the bonus and the fact that I'm finally drawing a regular salary, it still makes me nervous laying out that kind of cash. But it's an investment, really, look at it that way. What I'm going to do, when the time is right, and I haven't decided yet just when that's going to be, except of course that I'll be looking for optimum impact, is I'm going to take maybe four of the best shots—solo of Ramsay going into the office, solo of Judy waiting outside for him, the backlit shot of them together at the door of room 23 and a final shot of the door slammed tight—seal them in a manila envelope and slip the envelope anonymously under the door of G.C.'s office. And then I'm going to take one, just one—the two of them backlit—and press it to the visitors' window for Dawn's enjoyment or edification or whatever you'd like to call it.

If I sound bitter, if I sound like a bitch, well, forgive me—bull's-eye on both counts. I don't think anybody who understands the facts as I've tried to present them would blame me, because it couldn't be any clearer at this juncture. I'm the one who's been hurt. I'm the one who went into this with her heart wide open and the very highest of ideals and what did I get for it? I got humiliation, I got pain and more pain, and I got to discover the dirty truth of just how far you can rely on your crewmates—or your best friend, for that matter.

There's a day a week or so after I get the photos back when it all comes home to me in a way that's so dead-on it's almost frightening. I'm sitting there in my carrel listening to the phones ring and Ramsay's voice carrying across the room and I'm watching Judy sit perched on the chair in her office with her posture that's beyond perfect and I'm thinking I could be in any office anywhere, I could be bond trading or selling insurance or basketball memorabilia, because, really, what does it matter? I'm a functionary in an office, not an ecologist, not a *Terranaut,* just a drudge with a contract and yet another promise. I decide the time has come. I've got a bomb. And I'm going to drop it.

It takes a while to get Dawn on the phone over in the command center at E2, and she's breathless when she picks up and I can tell from her tone she was hoping maybe it was somebody else calling, like Ramsay or maybe even Johnny or one of the newspapers, the *New York Times* or the *Wall Street Journal.* "Oh, Linda," she says, her voice dropping off a ledge, "so what's up?"

"I don't know," I say, "I just wanted to see you. Could we meet at the glass, maybe after dinner?"

"Tonight?"

"Yeah, tonight."

"Really, I'd love to—we need to catch up—but tonight's Rita's birthday? And we're going to do a feast down on the beach and then a group swim . . . ?"

"Come on," I say, coaxing now, needy, or doing my best impression of needy and all it implies about who owes who here. "You can't spare like fifteen minutes? There's something I've got for you, something I really wanted to show you—"

So we arrange to meet at eight for fifteen minutes only, because this is such a big deal for Rita, her first birthday inside and all the rest of it, so Dawn really can't spare the time, today of all days, so she's really sorry and will ten minutes be okay? Will that work? It's dark when I leave the apartment, temperature in the seventies, a moon, an owl sailing out of the blackness with a soft determined swish of her wings, and I get there fifteen minutes early, the photo in hand, with every intention of inflicting damage. The thing is, once I get there, once I plant myself on that hard stool outside the visitors' window while the moths bat at the light and all the interwoven sounds of E2 come to me in a muted symphony—a snatch of somebody's voice, the coquis rattling away, the distant pulse of the wave machine—all the air seems to go out of me. *Before you set out for revenge, be sure to dig two graves.* That was what my grandfather used to say, and whether it was a Korean proverb or a Chinese one or just something he made up, I never knew, but it comes to me now, and without thinking I get up from the stool—Dawn isn't here yet; no one's seen me—and back off into the darkness till I'm halfway across the courtyard, where I settle myself down on the grass, pull my knees up to my chest and wait.

E2 is right here, all around me, riding the night like a mystery ship. Lights glow from deep inside, the black burgeoning leaves of banana and fern and palm press up against the glass as if they're trying to break free, the spaceframe goes gray, goes dark, hides. Overhead, even deeper inside, a soft rollicking light keeps playing high off the panels, then vanishing and coming back again, and it takes me a while to realize it's the reflection off the surface of the ocean, the big pool where the Terranauts, wearing suits or not, are even now bobbing gently in the water that's warm as a bath and stirred and stirred again by the power of hidden machines no one can begin to visualize, not now, not at this hour.

I don't know how long I sit there, just dreaming—a long time, a very long time. I hear the echo of voices, watch the play of lights. The night deepens, deepens again, and Dawn never comes.

Acknowledgments

A portion of this book appeared previously in *Narrative,* under the title "Dawn Chapman."

Author's Note

I would like to acknowledge my debt to the accounts of the original Biospherians, especially Abigail Ailing and Mark Nelson's *Life Under Glass* and Jane Poynter's *The Human Experiment,* as well as to Rebecca Reider's thorough history of the project, *Dreaming the Biosphere,* and John Allen's foundational *Biosphere 2: The Human Experiment.*

ALSO AVAILABLE BY T. C. BOYLE

THE HARDER THEY COME

'So gloriously, cheekily, full of colour that you can only sit back and applaud a master at work'
THE TIMES

Sten Stenson, Vietnam veteran and retired principal, is on a cruise in Costa Rica when his coach excursion is hijacked. Sten's military training kicks in and within moments one of the attackers lies dead. Sten finds himself hailed a hero. Back home in San Francisco, anti-government protestor Sara Jennings is arrested for resisting police at a routine stop. A chance meeting with Sten's unstable son Adam sparks a strange but passionate relationship fuelled by a mutual hatred of the law. But as Adam's views and behaviour become steadily more extreme, he descends into a spiral of fanatical violence that is impossible for his family or Sara to halt.

'Wonderful ... Utterly believable'
LOUISE DOUGHTY

'A sort of Frank Zappa of American letters ... Like the Beat writers before him, Boyle documents American life in the underbelly'
FINANCIAL TIMES

'Boyle is a craftsman who chooses a large canvas and fills it to the edges'
BARBARA KINGSOLVER

SAN MIGUEL

'Compelling, beautifully written, and imaginative'
LIONEL SHRIVER, FINANCIAL TIMES BOOKS OF THE YEAR

The schooner from Santa Barbara arrives at the island of San Miguel on New Year's Day, 1888. Marantha looks at the cliffs falling into the churning sea. This is the first day of her new life. Before long, the constant wind and sheep-ravaged wasteland shatter her illusions; her husband promised paradise. As he obsessively resolves to stay – and becomes increasingly distant from her and their adopted daughter, Edith – Marantha's blighted lungs grow weaker in the dampness. Forty-two years later another family – and another bride – will arrive on San Miguel. But the unyielding island is haunted by its history; by stories of isolation, the desires of stubborn men, and the unbearable burden of love.

'Boyle tells an extraordinary story of human weakness and survival, with high intelligence and a terrific eye for detail'
THE TIMES

'Permeated with an elegiac tone ... Atmospherically it is resonant of *The Piano*, Jane Campion's passionate novel of pioneering tenacity'
INDEPENDENT

'A novel of almost heroic restraint ... A touching, even gripping allegory of the doomed nature of human striving'
SPECTATOR

ORDER YOUR COPY:

BY PHONE: +44 (0) 1256 302 699; **BY EMAIL:** DIRECT@MACMILLAN.CO.UK
DELIVERY IS USUALLY 3–5 WORKING DAYS. FREE POSTAGE AND PACKAGING FOR ORDERS OVER £20.
ONLINE: WWW.BLOOMSBURY.COM/BOOKSHOP
PRICES AND AVAILABILITY SUBJECT TO CHANGE WITHOUT NOTICE.

WWW.BLOOMSBURY.COM/AUTHOR/TC-BOYLE

BLOOMSBURY

WHEN THE KILLING'S DONE

'Boyle's devotees will find everything they expect in the way of manic plotlines, flamboyant obsessions and cool comeuppances outlandlishly delivered'
BARBARA KINGSOLVER, NEW YORK TIMES

The island of Anacapa, off the coast of California, is overrun with black rats which are threatening the ancient population of ground-nesting birds. Alma Boyd Takesue of the National Park Service is campaigning to exterminate them once and for all, but her systematic plan is in danger of sabotage by two notorious environmental activists, Anise Reed and Dave LaJoy. But when Alma's sights turn to the infestation of non-native pigs on the island of Santa Cruz – where Anise was brought up by her rancher mother – the stakes are raised and the debate threatens to boil over into something much more real...

'An often brilliant and always thoroughly entertaining satirical eco-thriller which poses questions at the heart of the ecological debate'
DAILY MAIL

'An absorbing novel, full of plausible and involving human drama'
DAILY TELEGRAPH

'Boyle writes with a conversational ease and fluidity that is enviable, and often breathtaking'
FINANCIAL TIMES

BLOOMSBURY

THE WOMEN

'Frank Lloyd Wright's three dramatic love affairs, abandoned children, scandalized headlines and cruel conflagrations ... Gripping'
THE TIMES

Welcome to the troubled, tempestuous world of Frank Lloyd Wright. Scandalous affairs rage behind closed doors, broken hearts are tossed aside, fires rip through the wings of the house and paparazzi lie in wait outside the front door for the latest tragedy in this never-ending saga. This is the home of the great architect of the twentieth century, a man of extremes in both his work and his private life: at once a force of nature and an avalanche of need and emotion that sweeps aside everything in its path. Sharp, savage and subtle in equal measure, *The Women* plumbs the chaos, horrors and uncontainable passions of a formidable American icon.

'Boyle ratchets up every ounce of tension from the story. A stunning achievement'
DAILY MAIL

'[A] rollicking, entertaining story of a great man's failings'
GUARDIAN

'A mesmerizing story of women who invest everything, at great risk, in that mysterious "bank of feeling" named Frank Lloyd Wright'
NEW YORK TIMES

ORDER YOUR COPY:

BY PHONE: +44 (0) 1256 302 699; **BY EMAIL:** DIRECT@MACMILLAN.CO.UK
DELIVERY IS USUALLY 3–5 WORKING DAYS. FREE POSTAGE AND PACKAGING FOR ORDERS OVER £20.
ONLINE: WWW.BLOOMSBURY.COM/BOOKSHOP
PRICES AND AVAILABILITY SUBJECT TO CHANGE WITHOUT NOTICE.

WWW.BLOOMSBURY.COM/AUTHOR/TC-BOYLE

BLOOMSBURY